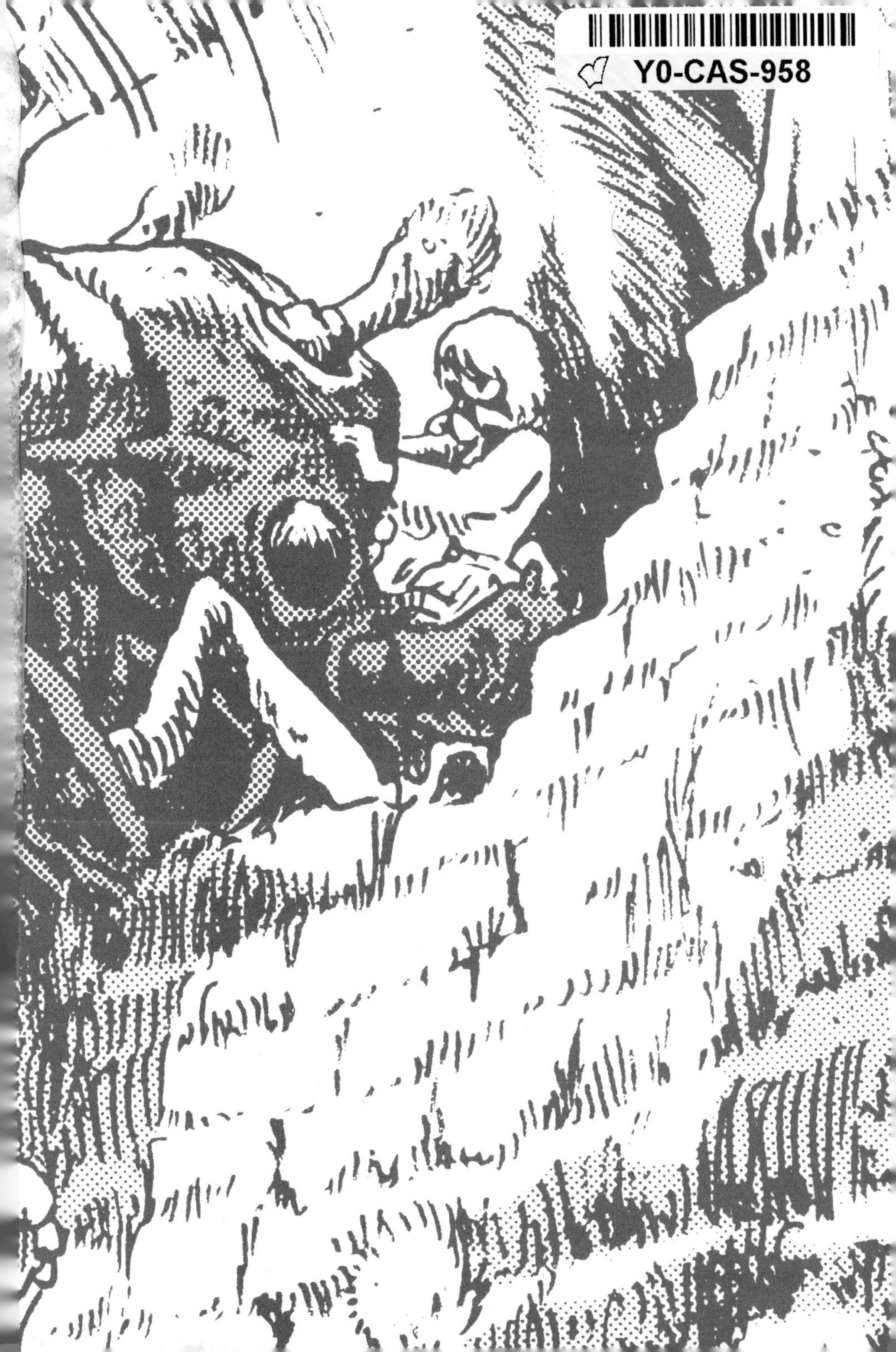

The Last Great Epic of the Human Race...
In a Dying Future, One Girl is the World's Last Hope...

NAUSICAÄ OF THE VALLEY OF WIND

From the Creator of "Kiki's Delivery Service" and "Princess Mononoke"

"**Hayao Miyazaki** is modest about his comic skills, being better known in Japan for his animation, but this is quite frankly a masterpiece that deserves to be read by anyone with an interest in the medium. His humane scripting, sense of action, deftness of characterization and story-telling and his control of the emotional highs and lows are all first-rate."

The Slings and Arrows Comic Guide

"**Nausicaä of the Valley of Wind** is a gorgeously epic fable... it succeeds in fully realizing a different, other world... It is a meditation on faith, pacifism, and deep ecology disguised as a thrilling quest. **Miyazaki** isn't afraid to point out that any meaningful solution to our ecological crises may very well require the end of humanity, and does so with melancholic grace."

Anodyne Magazine

""**Hayao Miyazaki** is acknowledged as an inspiration among his American counterparts who have reinvented animated storytelling...""

The New York Times

"...He also crafts some fairly serious works which communicate his own thoughts about man and his place in the universe. Being **Miyazaki**, he also makes them highly entertaining."

Wizard Magazine

"Hyperbole cheapens criticism, or at least flattens it, but in this case I'll risk it: **Nausicaä** is the finest example of high fantasy I've encountered in the comics -- and one of the greatest comics stories I've ever read, period."

Comics Journal

NAUSICAÄ OF THE VALLEY OF WIND™

PERFECT COLLECTION

2

STORY AND ART BY
HAYAO MIYAZAKI

This volume contains NAUSICAÄ OF THE
VALLEY OF WIND, volume 3 and volume 4
in their entirety.

Story & Art by Hayao Miyazaki

Translation/David Lewis and Toren Smith
(Studio Proteus)
Lettering and Retouch/Tom Orzechowski (Studio Proteus)
Cover Design/Viz Graphics
Editor/Annette Roman

Senior Editor/Trish Ledoux
Managing Editor/Satoru Fujii
Director of Sales & Marketing/Oliver Chin
Executive Editor/Seiji Horibuchi
Publisher/Keizo Inoue

Printed in Canada

Published by Viz Communications, Inc.
P.O. Box 77010, San Francisco, CA 94107

10 9 8 7 6 5 4
First printing, August 1995
Fourth printing, December 1999

Get your Free Viz Shop-By-Mail Catalog!
(800) 394-3042
or Fax (415) 348-8936

www.viz.com   www.j-pop.com   www.animerica-mag.com   www.pulp-mag.com

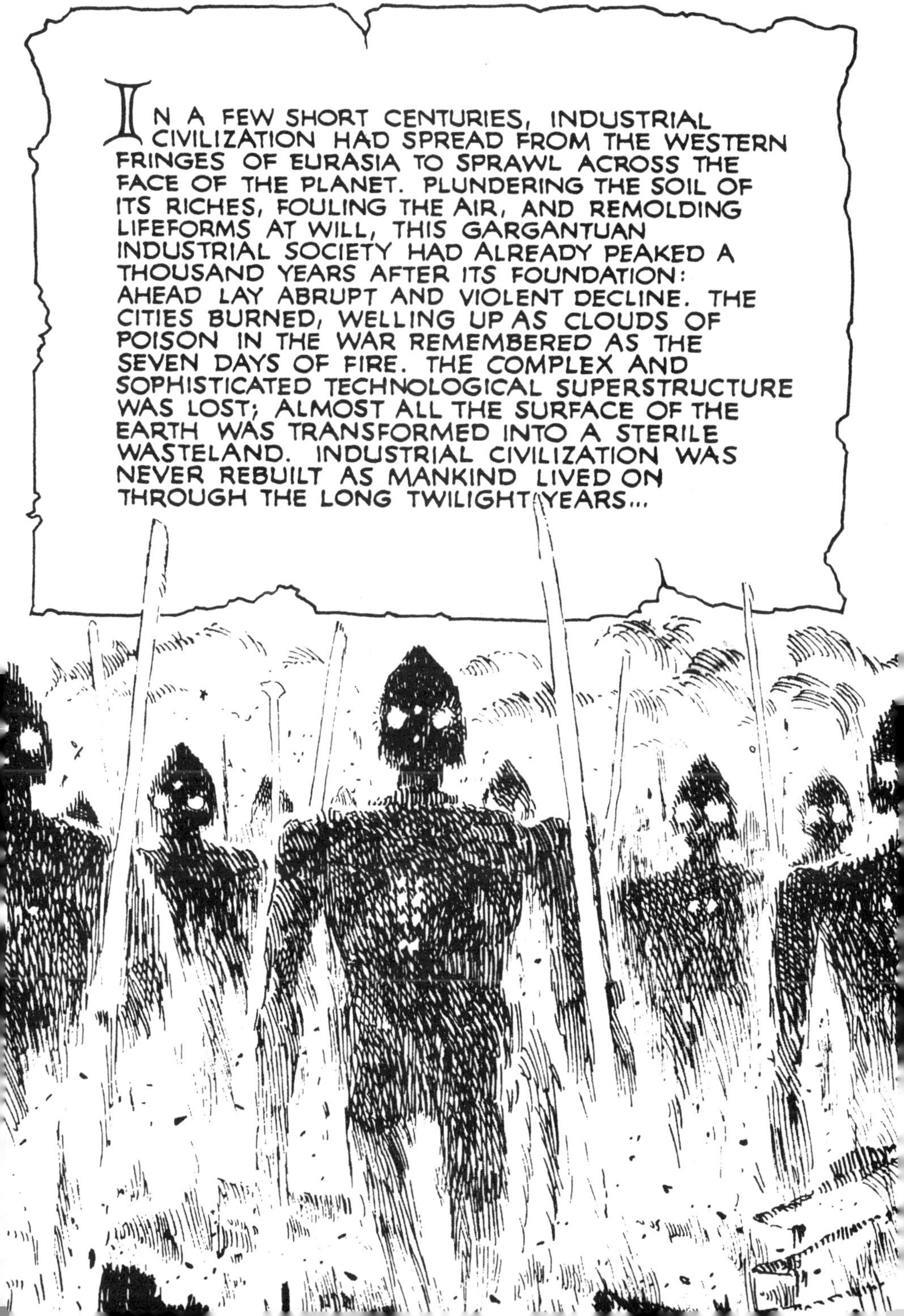
IN A FEW SHORT CENTURIES, INDUSTRIAL CIVILIZATION HAD SPREAD FROM THE WESTERN FRINGES OF EURASIA TO SPRAWL ACROSS THE FACE OF THE PLANET. PLUNDERING THE SOIL OF ITS RICHES, FOULING THE AIR, AND REMOLDING LIFEFORMS AT WILL, THIS GARGANTUAN INDUSTRIAL SOCIETY HAD ALREADY PEAKED A THOUSAND YEARS AFTER ITS FOUNDATION: AHEAD LAY ABRUPT AND VIOLENT DECLINE. THE CITIES BURNED, WELLING UP AS CLOUDS OF POISON IN THE WAR REMEMBERED AS THE SEVEN DAYS OF FIRE. THE COMPLEX AND SOPHISTICATED TECHNOLOGICAL SUPERSTRUCTURE WAS LOST; ALMOST ALL THE SURFACE OF THE EARTH WAS TRANSFORMED INTO A STERILE WASTELAND. INDUSTRIAL CIVILIZATION WAS NEVER REBUILT AS MANKIND LIVED ON THROUGH THE LONG TWILIGHT YEARS...

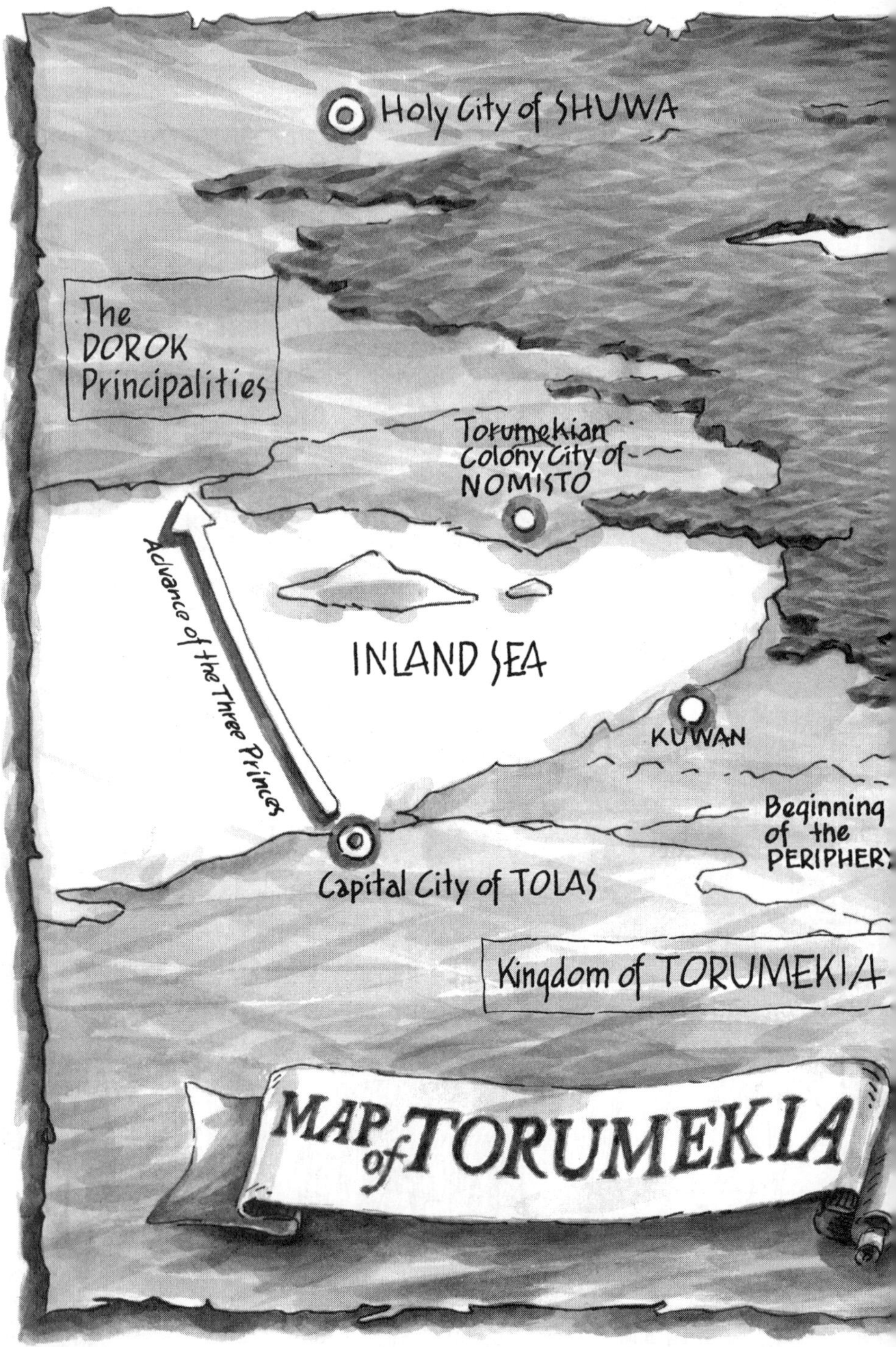

Holy City of SHUWA
The DOROK Principalities
Torumekian Colony City of NOMISTO
Advance of the Three Princes
INLAND SEA
KUWAN
Beginning of the PERIPHERY
Capital City of TOLAS
Kingdom of TORUMEKIA
MAP of TORUMEKIA

LAKES
S
E
W
N
Advance of Kushana
PAGASE
Aerial Rendezvous Site
EA OF
CORRUPTION
PEJITEI
Autonomous
States of the
PERIPHERY
EFTAL DESERT
VALLEY of SAND
WAJI VALLEY
VALLEY of WIND
SEMO
EPO,
The Westernmost
City of
Torumekia
OCEAN of SALT

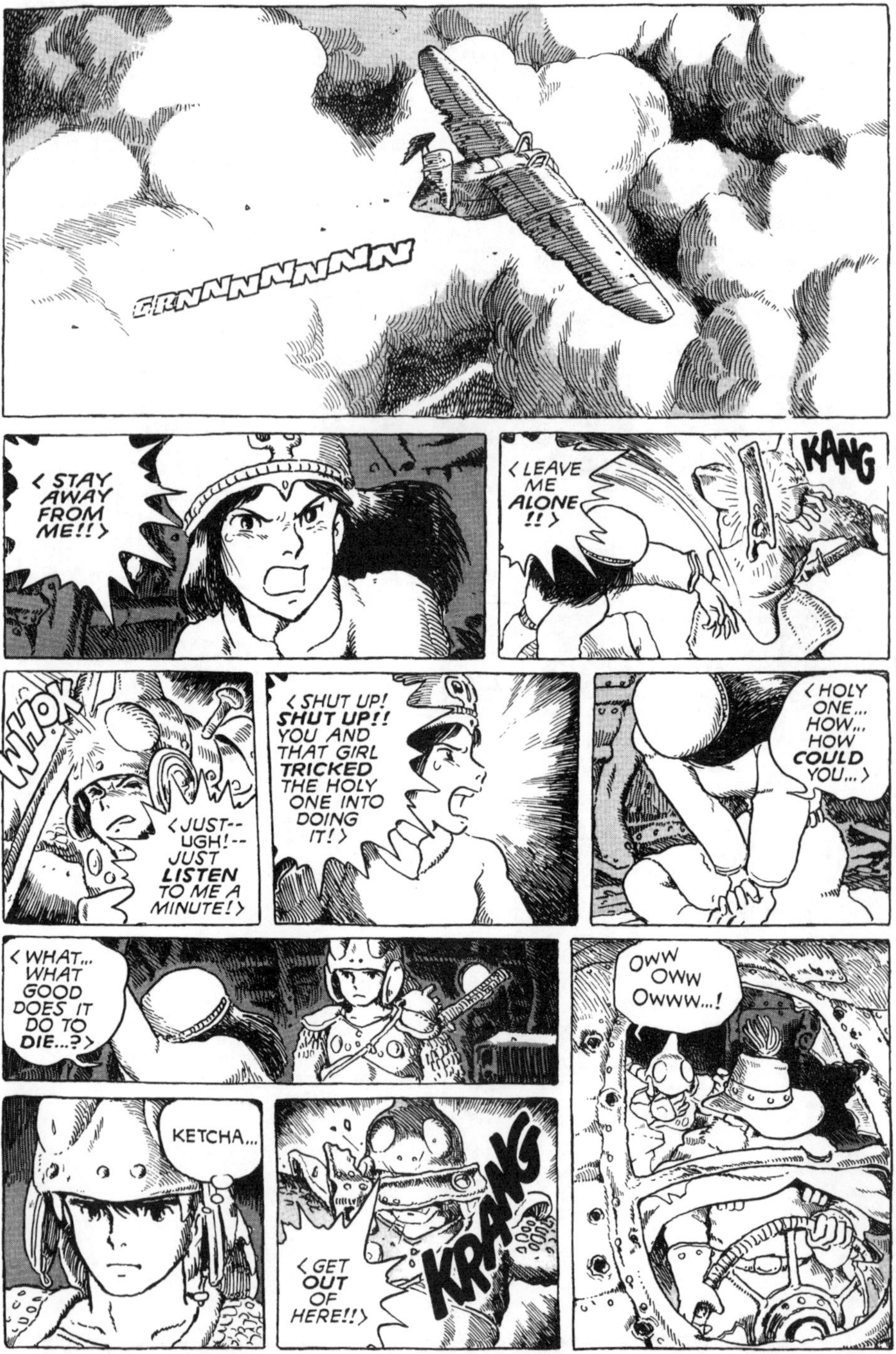
GRNNNNNNNN
< STAY AWAY FROM ME!! >
< LEAVE ME ALONE!! >
KANG
WHOK
< JUST-- UGH!-- JUST LISTEN TO ME A MINUTE! >
< SHUT UP! SHUT UP!! YOU AND THAT GIRL TRICKED THE HOLY ONE INTO DOING IT! >
< HOLY ONE... HOW... HOW COULD YOU... >
< WHAT... WHAT GOOD DOES IT DO TO DIE...? >
KETCHA...
KRANG
< GET OUT OF HERE!! >
OWW OWW OWWW...!

MAYBE IT'S BEST TO LEAVE HER ALONE FOR A WHILE.

GUESS SO...

SH ANG!

BUT I KNOW EXACTLY HOW SHE FEELS...

I LOST MY COUNTRY, TOO...

I'M WORRIED ABOUT WHAT WILL HAPPEN TO THE MANI FOLK.

WAS IT THE DECISION OF THE WHOLE TRIBE TO DESTROY THAT TANK?

THE HOLY ONE TOLD ONLY ME AND *KETCHA*--THAT'S HER NAME--WHAT HE WANTED TO DO.

GRRNNNN

I SEE... HE MUST HAVE KNOWN MIRALUPA WAS COMING. HE WAS TAKING PRECAUTIONS IN CASE HE FAILED.

"MIRALUPA"?! YOU MEAN *THAT* WAS THE HOLY EMPEROR'S YOUNGER BROTHER?

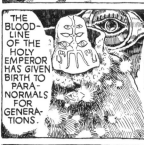

THE BLOOD-LINE OF THE HOLY EMPEROR HAS GIVEN BIRTH TO PARA-NORMALS FOR GENERA-TIONS.

THAT FAMILY HAS BROUGHT INTO THE WORLD POSSESSORS OF MANY STRANGE POWERS, LIKE MIRALUPA HIM-SELF. HE'S THE REAL LEADER OF THE DOROKS, AND THE POWER BEHIND THE THRONE.

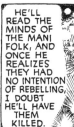

HE'LL READ THE MINDS OF THE MANI FOLK, AND ONCE HE REALIZES THEY HAD NO INTENTION OF REBELLING, I DOUBT HE'LL HAVE THEM KILLED.

I DON'T LIKE THE LOOKS OF THIS-- THE CLOUDS ARE BUILDING.

THEY STILL HAVEN'T SHOWN UP... I WONDER IF WE REALLY *DID* SHAKE THEM...

COULD YOU TELL ME ABOUT THE DESTRUCTION OF KUSHANA'S ARMY?

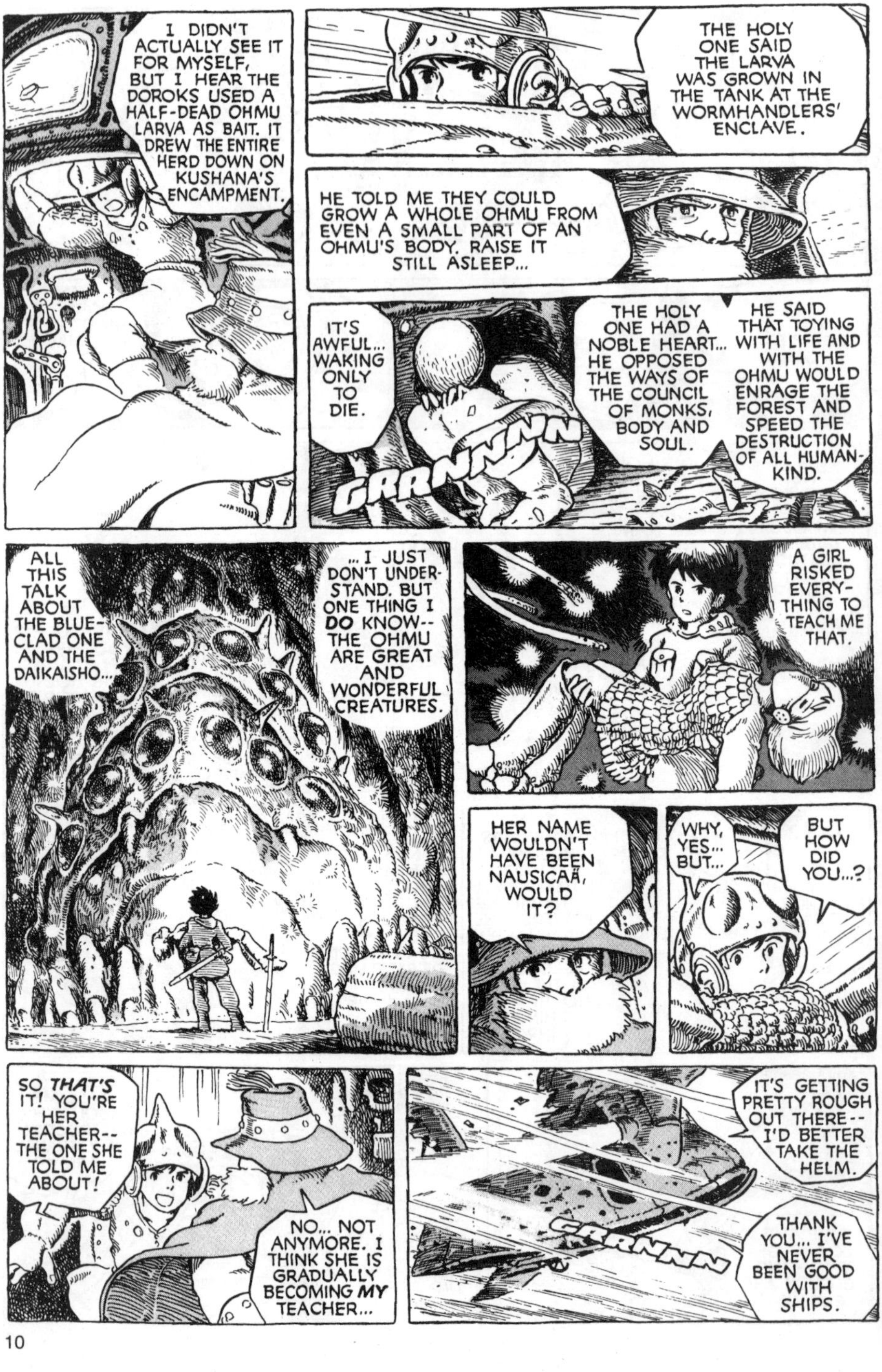
I DIDN'T ACTUALLY SEE IT FOR MYSELF, BUT I HEAR THE DOROKS USED A HALF-DEAD OHMU LARVA AS BAIT. IT DREW THE ENTIRE HERD DOWN ON KUSHANA'S ENCAMPMENT.
THE HOLY ONE SAID THE LARVA WAS GROWN IN THE TANK AT THE WORMHANDLERS' ENCLAVE.
HE TOLD ME THEY COULD GROW A WHOLE OHMU FROM EVEN A SMALL PART OF AN OHMU'S BODY. RAISE IT STILL ASLEEP...
IT'S AWFUL... WAKING ONLY TO DIE.
GRRNNNN
THE HOLY ONE HAD A NOBLE HEART... HE OPPOSED THE WAYS OF THE COUNCIL OF MONKS, BODY AND SOUL.
HE SAID THAT TOYING WITH LIFE AND WITH THE OHMU WOULD ENRAGE THE FOREST AND SPEED THE DESTRUCTION OF ALL HUMANKIND.
ALL THIS TALK ABOUT THE BLUE-CLAD ONE AND THE DAIKAISHO...
...I JUST DON'T UNDERSTAND. BUT ONE THING I *DO* KNOW-- THE OHMU ARE GREAT AND WONDERFUL CREATURES.
A GIRL RISKED EVERYTHING TO TEACH ME THAT.
HER NAME WOULDN'T HAVE BEEN NAUSICAÄ, WOULD IT?
WHY, YES... BUT...
BUT HOW DID YOU...?
SO *THAT'S* IT! YOU'RE HER TEACHER-- THE ONE SHE TOLD ME ABOUT!
NO... NOT ANYMORE. I THINK SHE IS GRADUALLY BECOMING *MY* TEACHER...
IT'S GETTING PRETTY ROUGH OUT THERE-- I'D BETTER TAKE THE HELM.
GRRNNNN
THANK YOU... I'VE NEVER BEEN GOOD WITH SHIPS.

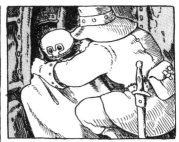

THE POOR CHILD... SHE CRIED HERSELF TO SLEEP.

Ah! THANK YOU!

IT'S DRAFTY UP HERE, TOO, BUT A LOT SAFER THAN BACK THERE.

kreek

THE CLOUDS ARE GETTING HIGHER... WE'RE REALLY GOING TO HAVE A BLOW.

THE WORM-HANDLERS COULD GET A PIECE OF AN OHMU'S SHELL EASILY ENOUGH -- THAT MUST BE WHY THE DOROKS LOCATED THEIR CULTURE VAT IN THAT ENCLAVE. THE QUESTION IS, ARE THERE MORE VATS ELSEWHERE?

THE HOLY ONE WAS WORRIED ABOUT THAT, TOO.

BETTER PUT YOUR MASK ON... WE SHOULD BE PREPARED FOR THE WORST.

COULD YOU TAKE OVER THE THROTTLE? I CAN'T LET GO OF THE RUDDER.

AYE, AYE.

HE'S A GOOD SAILOR... CALM AND CONFIDENT.

I WOULD NEVER HAVE BELIEVED THEY COULD GROW AN OHMU IF I HADN'T SEEN IT WITH MY OWN EYES.

11

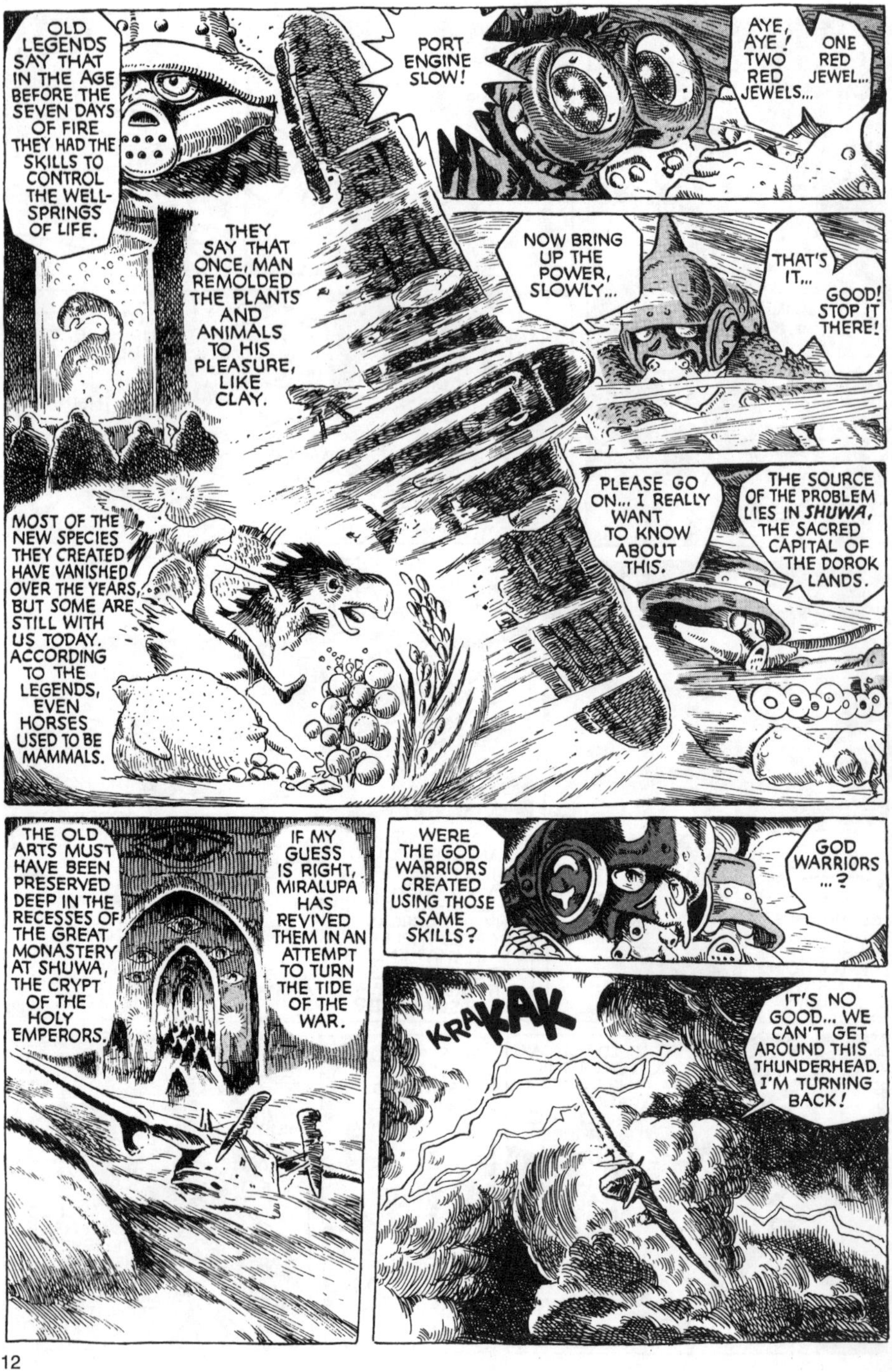
OLD LEGENDS SAY THAT IN THE AGE BEFORE THE SEVEN DAYS OF FIRE THEY HAD THE SKILLS TO CONTROL THE WELL-SPRINGS OF LIFE.
PORT ENGINE SLOW!
AYE, AYE! TWO RED JEWELS...
ONE RED JEWEL...
THEY SAY THAT ONCE, MAN REMOLDED THE PLANTS AND ANIMALS TO HIS PLEASURE, LIKE CLAY.
NOW BRING UP THE POWER, SLOWLY...
THAT'S IT...
GOOD! STOP IT THERE!
MOST OF THE NEW SPECIES THEY CREATED HAVE VANISHED OVER THE YEARS, BUT SOME ARE STILL WITH US TODAY. ACCORDING TO THE LEGENDS, EVEN HORSES USED TO BE MAMMALS.
PLEASE GO ON... I REALLY WANT TO KNOW ABOUT THIS.
THE SOURCE OF THE PROBLEM LIES IN SHUWA, THE SACRED CAPITAL OF THE DOROK LANDS.
THE OLD ARTS MUST HAVE BEEN PRESERVED DEEP IN THE RECESSES OF THE GREAT MONASTERY AT SHUWA, THE CRYPT OF THE HOLY EMPERORS.
IF MY GUESS IS RIGHT, MIRALUPA HAS REVIVED THEM IN AN ATTEMPT TO TURN THE TIDE OF THE WAR.
WERE THE GOD WARRIORS CREATED USING THOSE SAME SKILLS?
GOD WARRIORS ...?
KRAKAK
IT'S NO GOOD... WE CAN'T GET AROUND THIS THUNDERHEAD. I'M TURNING BACK!

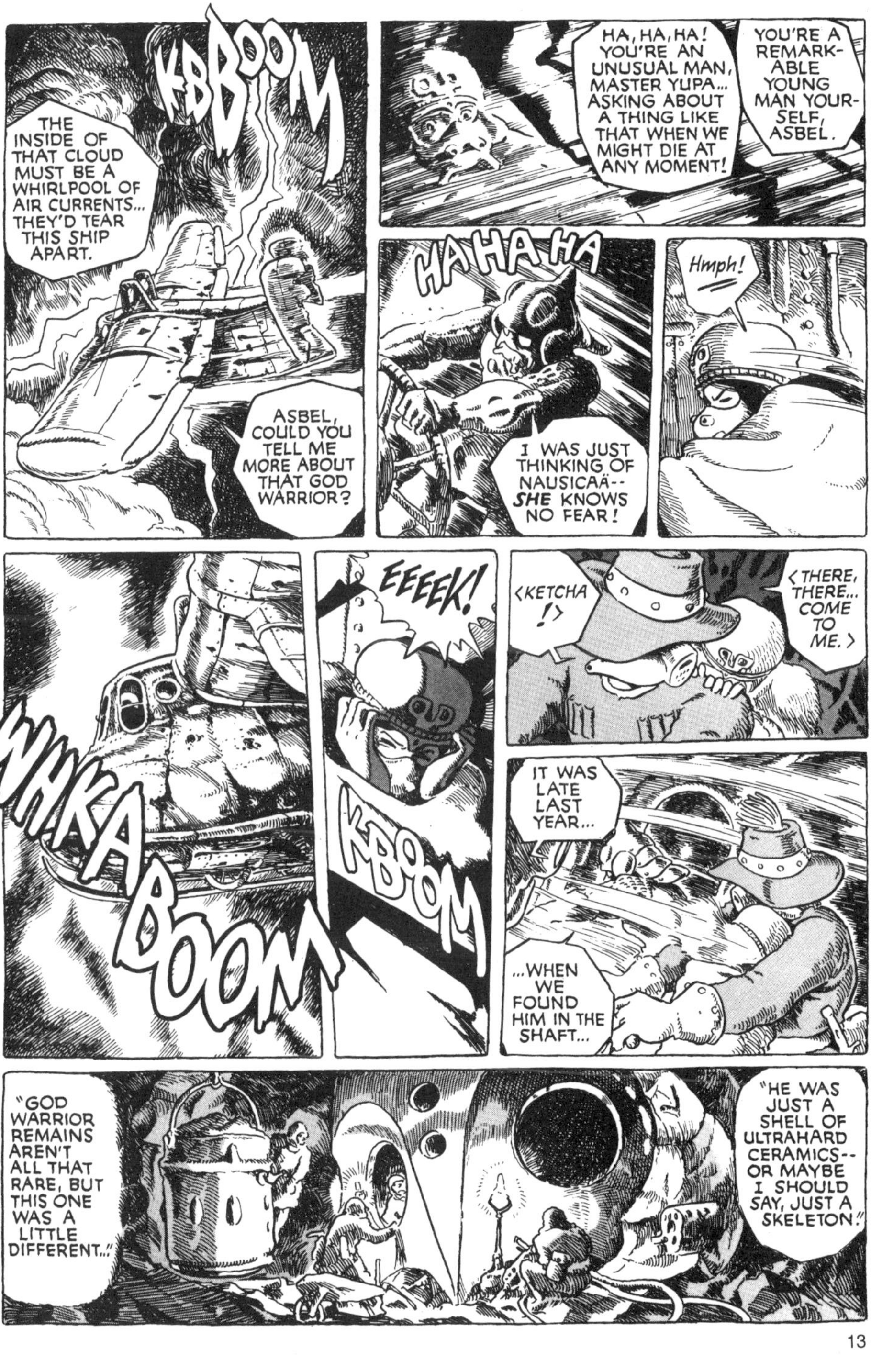
KBOOM
THE INSIDE OF THAT CLOUD MUST BE A WHIRLPOOL OF AIR CURRENTS... THEY'D TEAR THIS SHIP APART.
ASBEL, COULD YOU TELL ME MORE ABOUT THAT GOD WARRIOR?
HA, HA, HA! YOU'RE AN UNUSUAL MAN, MASTER YUPA... ASKING ABOUT A THING LIKE THAT WHEN WE MIGHT DIE AT ANY MOMENT!
YOU'RE A REMARKABLE YOUNG MAN YOURSELF, ASBEL.
HAHAHAHA
I WAS JUST THINKING OF NAUSICAÄ-- *SHE* KNOWS NO FEAR!
Hmph!
WHKABOOM
EEEEK!
KBOOM
<KETCHA!>
<THERE, THERE... COME TO ME.>
IT WAS LATE LAST YEAR...
...WHEN WE FOUND HIM IN THE SHAFT...
"GOD WARRIOR REMAINS AREN'T ALL THAT RARE, BUT THIS ONE WAS A LITTLE DIFFERENT..."
"HE WAS JUST A SHELL OF ULTRAHARD CERAMICS-- OR MAYBE I SHOULD SAY, JUST A SKELETON."

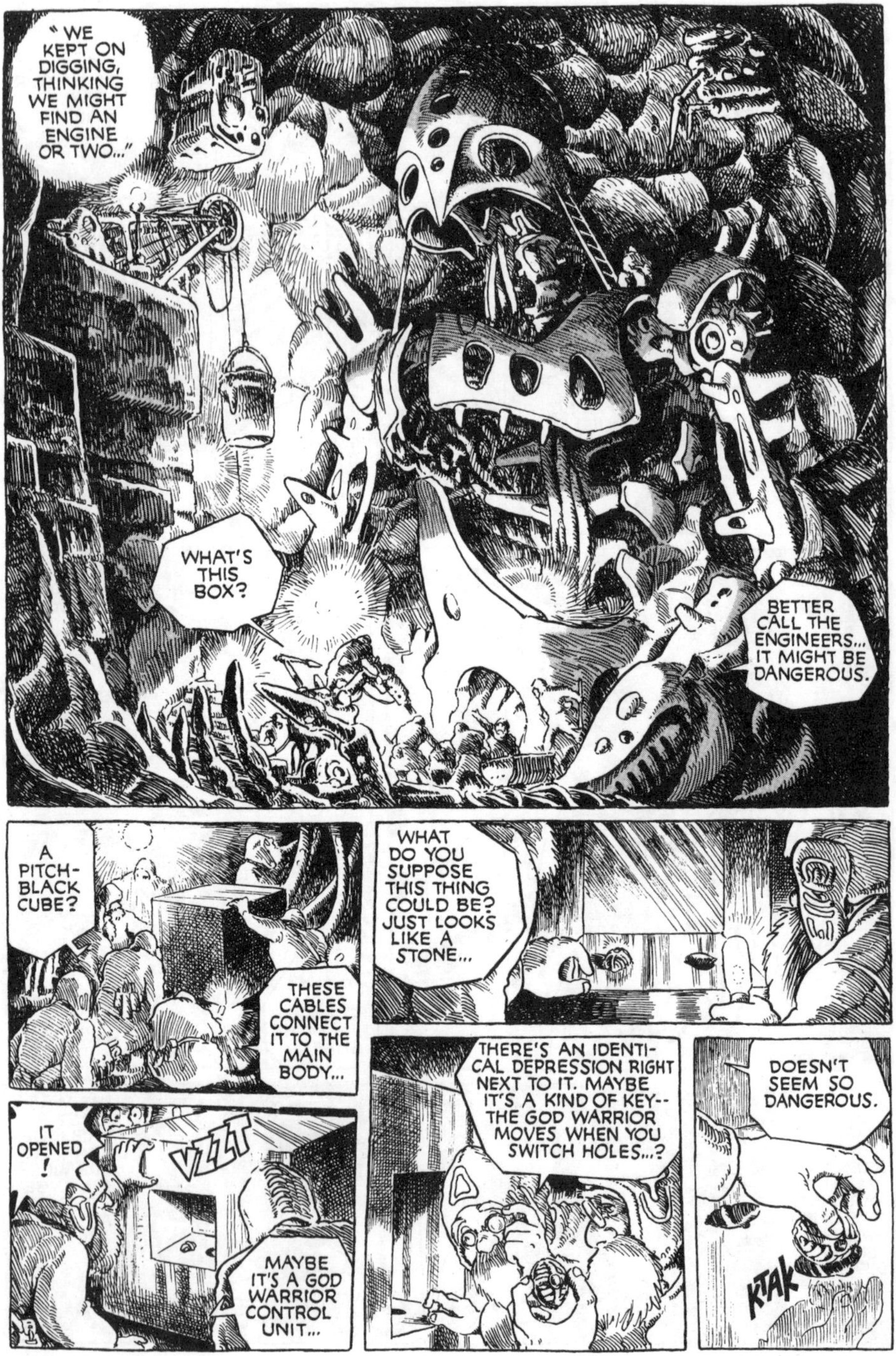
"WE KEPT ON DIGGING, THINKING WE MIGHT FIND AN ENGINE OR TWO..."
WHAT'S THIS BOX?
BETTER CALL THE ENGINEERS... IT MIGHT BE DANGEROUS.
A PITCH-BLACK CUBE?
THESE CABLES CONNECT IT TO THE MAIN BODY...
WHAT DO YOU SUPPOSE THIS THING COULD BE? JUST LOOKS LIKE A STONE...
IT OPENED!
VZZZT
MAYBE IT'S A GOD WARRIOR CONTROL UNIT...
THERE'S AN IDENTICAL DEPRESSION RIGHT NEXT TO IT. MAYBE IT'S A KIND OF KEY-- THE GOD WARRIOR MOVES WHEN YOU SWITCH HOLES...?
DOESN'T SEEM SO DANGEROUS.
KTAK

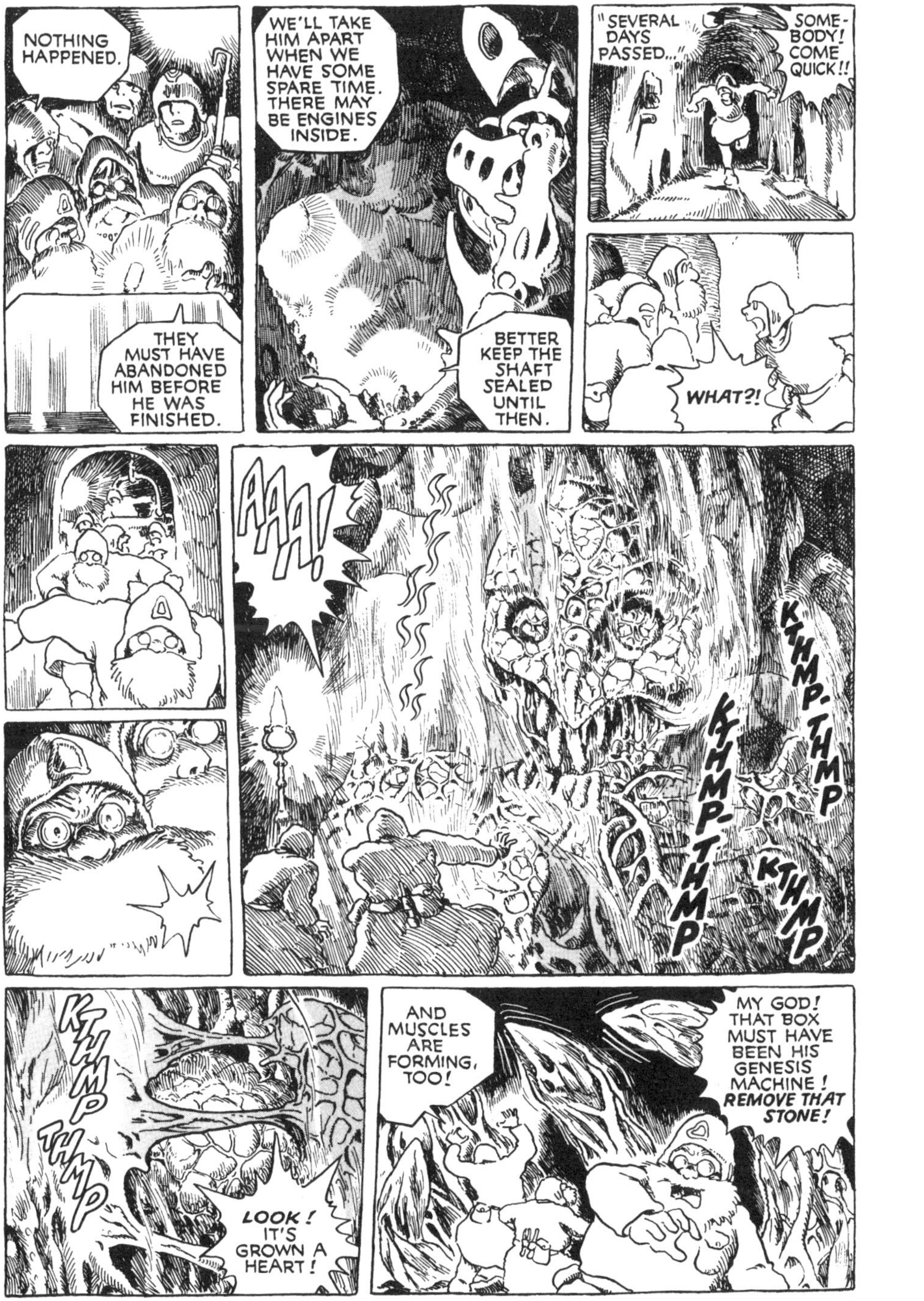
NOTHING HAPPENED.
THEY MUST HAVE ABANDONED HIM BEFORE HE WAS FINISHED.
WE'LL TAKE HIM APART WHEN WE HAVE SOME SPARE TIME. THERE MAY BE ENGINES INSIDE.
BETTER KEEP THE SHAFT SEALED UNTIL THEN.
"SEVERAL DAYS PASSED..."
SOMEBODY! COME QUICK!!
WHAT?!
AAAA!
KTHMP-THMP
KTHMP-THMP
KTHMP
KTHMP THMP
LOOK! IT'S GROWN A HEART!
AND MUSCLES ARE FORMING, TOO!
MY GOD! THAT BOX MUST HAVE BEEN HIS GENESIS MACHINE! REMOVE THAT STONE!

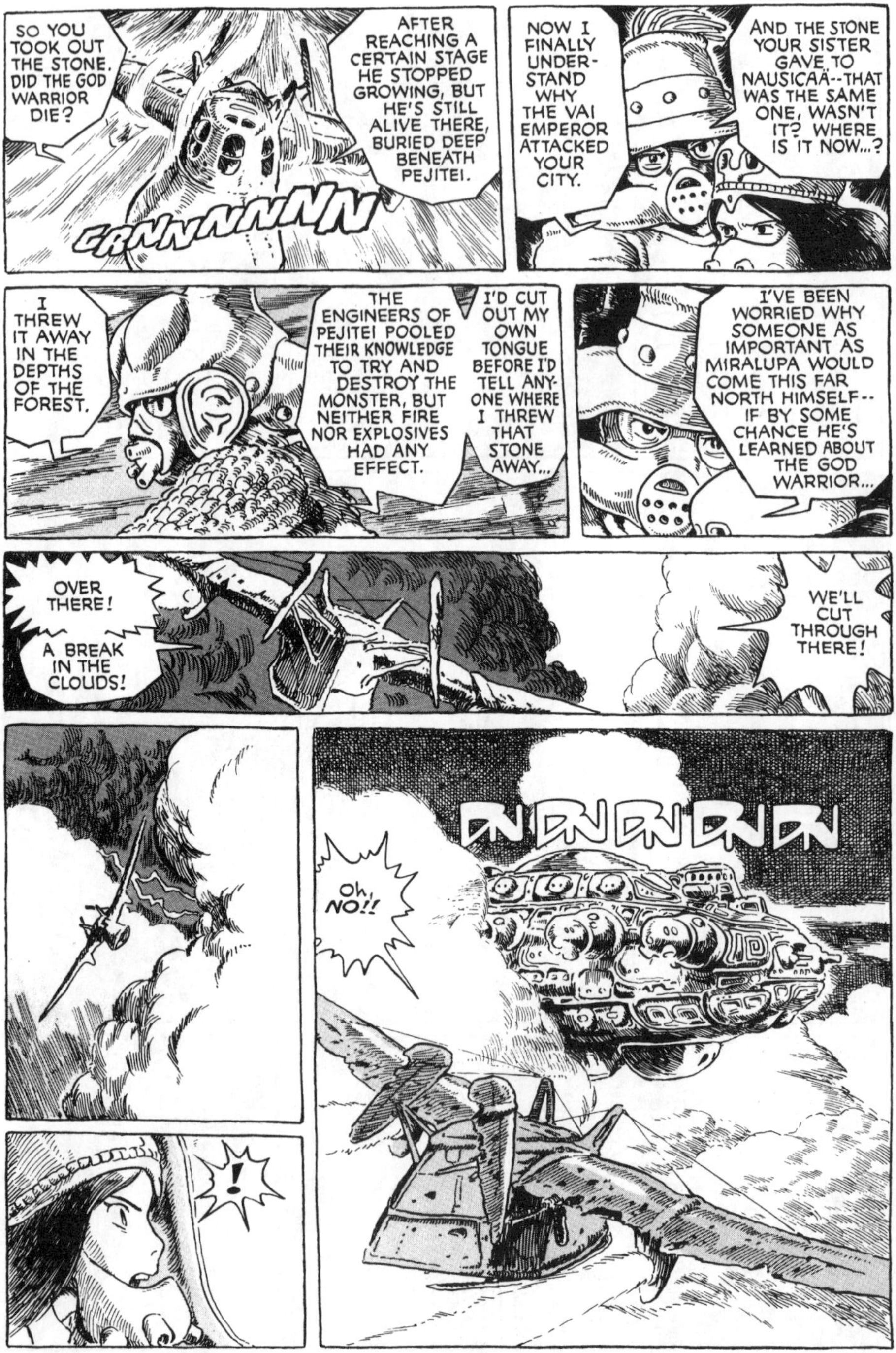
SO YOU TOOK OUT THE STONE. DID THE GOD WARRIOR DIE?
AFTER REACHING A CERTAIN STAGE HE STOPPED GROWING, BUT HE'S STILL ALIVE THERE, BURIED DEEP BENEATH PEJITEI.
GRNNNNNNN
NOW I FINALLY UNDERSTAND WHY THE VAI EMPEROR ATTACKED YOUR CITY.
AND THE STONE YOUR SISTER GAVE TO NAUSICAÄ--THAT WAS THE SAME ONE, WASN'T IT? WHERE IS IT NOW...?
I THREW IT AWAY IN THE DEPTHS OF THE FOREST.
THE ENGINEERS OF PEJITEI POOLED THEIR KNOWLEDGE TO TRY AND DESTROY THE MONSTER, BUT NEITHER FIRE NOR EXPLOSIVES HAD ANY EFFECT.
I'D CUT OUT MY OWN TONGUE BEFORE I'D TELL ANYONE WHERE I THREW THAT STONE AWAY...
I'VE BEEN WORRIED WHY SOMEONE AS IMPORTANT AS MIRALUPA WOULD COME THIS FAR NORTH HIMSELF-- IF BY SOME CHANCE HE'S LEARNED ABOUT THE GOD WARRIOR...
OVER THERE!
A BREAK IN THE CLOUDS!
WE'LL CUT THROUGH THERE!
DN DN DN DN DN DN
Oh, NO!!
!

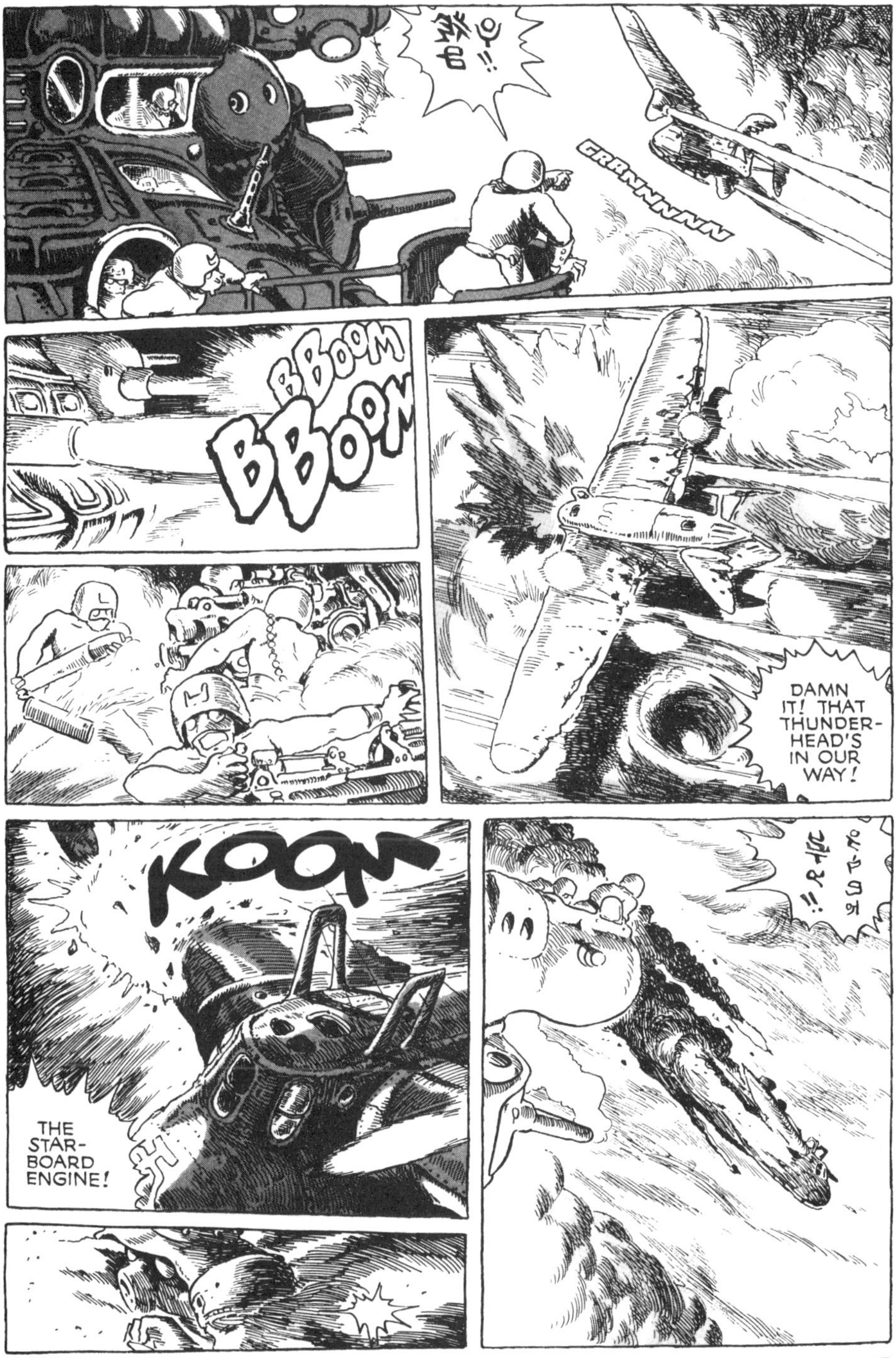
GRANNNNNN
BBOOM
BBOOM
DAMN IT! THAT THUNDER-HEAD'S IN OUR WAY!
KOOM
THE STAR-BOARD ENGINE!

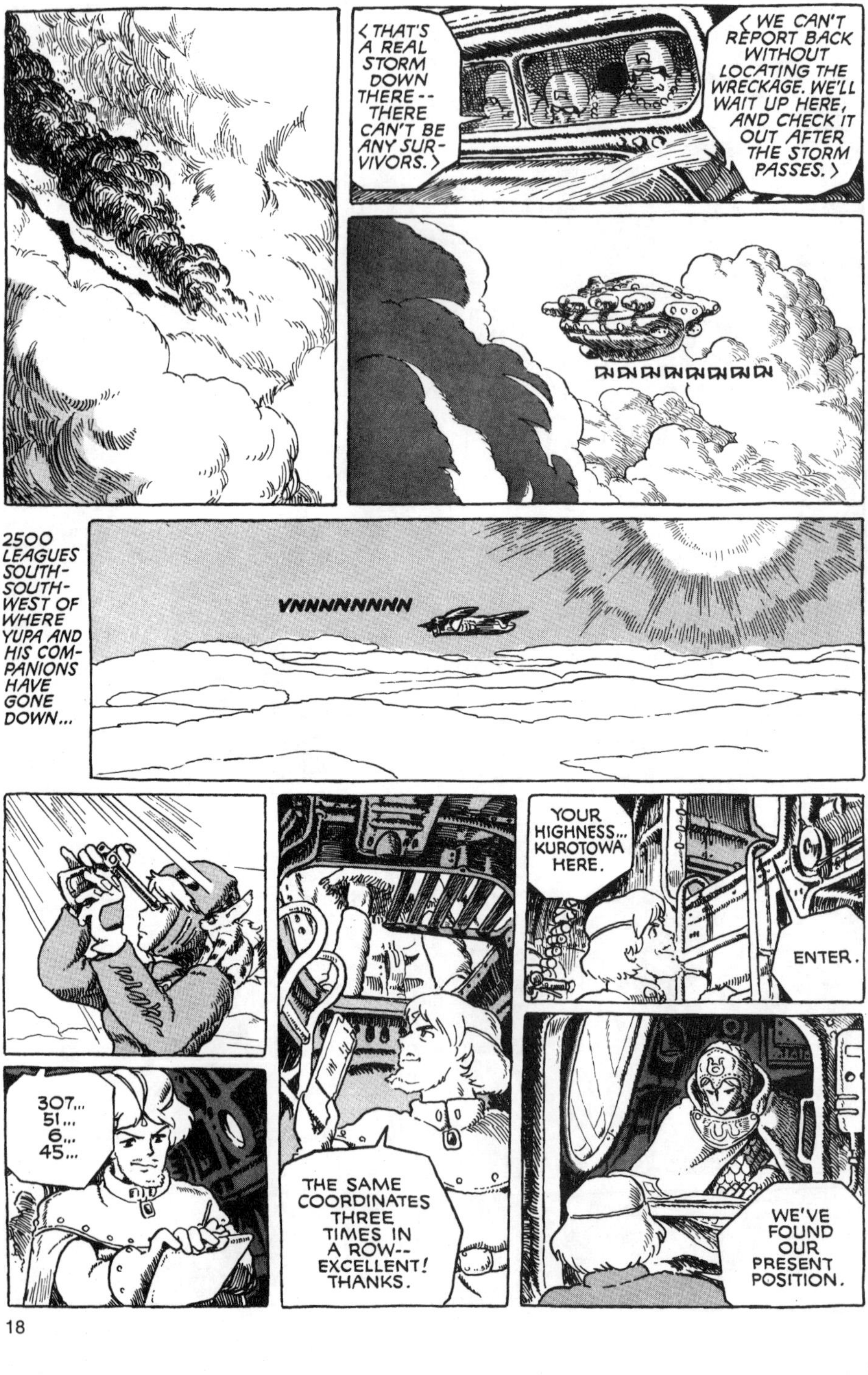

<THAT'S A REAL STORM DOWN THERE--THERE CAN'T BE ANY SURVIVORS.>
<WE CAN'T REPORT BACK WITHOUT LOCATING THE WRECKAGE. WE'LL WAIT UP HERE, AND CHECK IT OUT AFTER THE STORM PASSES.>
2500 LEAGUES SOUTH-SOUTHWEST OF WHERE YUPA AND HIS COMPANIONS HAVE GONE DOWN...
VNNNNNNNN
YOUR HIGHNESS... KUROTOWA HERE.
ENTER.
307... 51... 6... 45...
THE SAME COORDINATES THREE TIMES IN A ROW--EXCELLENT! THANKS.
WE'VE FOUND OUR PRESENT POSITION.

ALTHOUGH WE CAN'T SEE IT BECAUSE OF THE CLOUD COVER, WE'VE CLEARED THE SEA OF CORRUPTION. WE SHOULD BE OVER THE DOROK PRINCIPALITY OF SAPATA.

SHOW ME ON THE MAP.

Mmm... SHE SMELLS NICE...

YES, YOUR HIGHNESS.

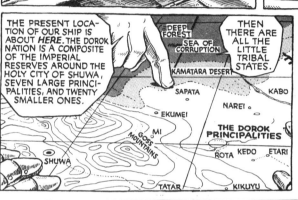
THE PRESENT LOCATION OF OUR SHIP IS ABOUT *HERE.* THE DOROK NATION IS A COMPOSITE OF THE IMPERIAL RESERVES AROUND THE HOLY CITY OF SHUWA, SEVEN LARGE PRINCIPALITIES, AND TWENTY SMALLER ONES.

THEN THERE ARE ALL THE LITTLE TRIBAL STATES.

DEEP FOREST

SEA OF CORRUPTION

KAMATARA DESERT

SAPATA

KABO

NAREI

EKUMEI

THE DOROK PRINCIPALITIES

MI

GOSS MOUNTAINS

SHUWA

ROTA KEDO ETARI

TATAR

KIKUYU

AND THESE ARE THE FRONT LINES OF OUR FORCES.

MITOS

KINGDOM OF TORUMEKIA

SEMI

NII

AP

MANI AD GOH

MIRI

TEKYU

BIDA

MODO

RATTE

NANAKI

INLAND SEA

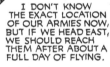
I DON'T KNOW THE EXACT LOCATION OF OUR ARMIES NOW, BUT IF WE HEAD EAST, WE SHOULD REACH THEM AFTER ABOUT A FULL DAY OF FLYING.

WHICH ARMY IS ON THE FRONT LINES?

Hmm... NOW, *THAT* I DON'T KNOW...

WE'RE NOT GOING EAST. WE'LL LAND HERE. FIND A GOOD SPOT.

P-PARDON? BUT... BUT WE'RE JUST *ONE* SHIP! FOR THE MOMENT, AT LEAST, SHOULDN'T WE--

YOU SEEM RATHER EAGER TO REJOIN THE MAIN ARMY GROUP, KUROTOWA.

THE FRONT IS HELD BY MY ELDER BROTHER, ISN'T IT?

WHAT? AH, I, I REALLY DON'T...

W-WHAT ARE YOU DOING?!

I'M WEARY OF YOUR BAD ACTING, KUROTOWA.

19

THIS WHOLE OPERATION HAS BEEN A TRAP TO GET RID OF ME, PLANNED BY MY OLDER BROTHERS.

AND I SUPPOSE *YOUR* MISSION IS TO GET THAT STONE AND TAKE IT BACK TO TORUMEKIA.

I KNOW YOU'VE BEEN TRYING TO WIN OVER THE CREW OF THIS SHIP...

BUT YOUR HIGHNESS! HAVEN'T I PROTECTED YOU? EVEN SAVED YOUR LIFE?

Heh... YOU COULD HARDLY KILL ME BEFORE YOU FOUND OUT WHERE THE STONE WAS, COULD YOU?

"BUT NOW, YOU CAN STAB ME IN THE BACK ANY TIME YOU PLEASE-- AFTER ALL, YOU'VE GOT A LITTLE GIRL WHO KNOWS WHERE THAT STONE WENT, TOO."

HA HA HA!

WELL, I THOUGHT YOU'D PROBABLY SEEN THROUGH ME!

"I SUPPOSE YOU MEANT TO TAKE HER BACK WITH YOU AND TORTURE IT OUT OF HER..."

TO TELL THE TRUTH, I FIGURED THE ORDERS TO GO SOUTH WOULD MAKE YOU SO ANGRY YOU'D GO STRAIGHT TO THE CAPITAL FROM PEJITEI. THAT'S WHAT THEY WANTED, BACK HOME.

DEFYING ORDERS, PLOTTING REBELLION... YOUR HIGHNESS WAS SUPPOSED TO BE EXECUTED, BUT INSTEAD YOU'VE FAITHFULLY FOLLOWED ORDERS TO THE LETTER, EVEN WITH YOUR ARMY SMASHED. WHY, I WONDER?

BECAUSE YOUR HIGHNESS NEVER MEANT TO FIGHT THE DOROKS IN THE FIRST PLACE. YOUR *REAL* PLAN WAS TO LINK UP WITH THE CORE OF THE 3rd ARMY...

...THE ARMY YOUR HIGHNESS TRAINED HERSELF, FORGING THEM INTO THE EMPIRE'S FINEST. THE ARMY STOLEN FROM YOU, WHOSE LOYAL TROOPS STILL PINE FOR YOUR RETURN.

YOU MEAN TO LEAD THEM BACK TO THE IMPERIAL CAPITAL, AND SEIZE THE CROWN FOR YOUR OWN...

Heh... NOW IT SEEMS I REALLY *WILL* HAVE TO KILL YOU...

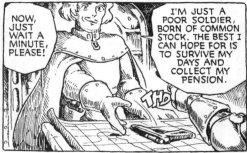

NOW, JUST WAIT A MINUTE, PLEASE!

I'M JUST A POOR SOLDIER, BORN OF COMMON STOCK. THE BEST I CAN HOPE FOR IS TO SURVIVE MY DAYS AND COLLECT MY PENSION.

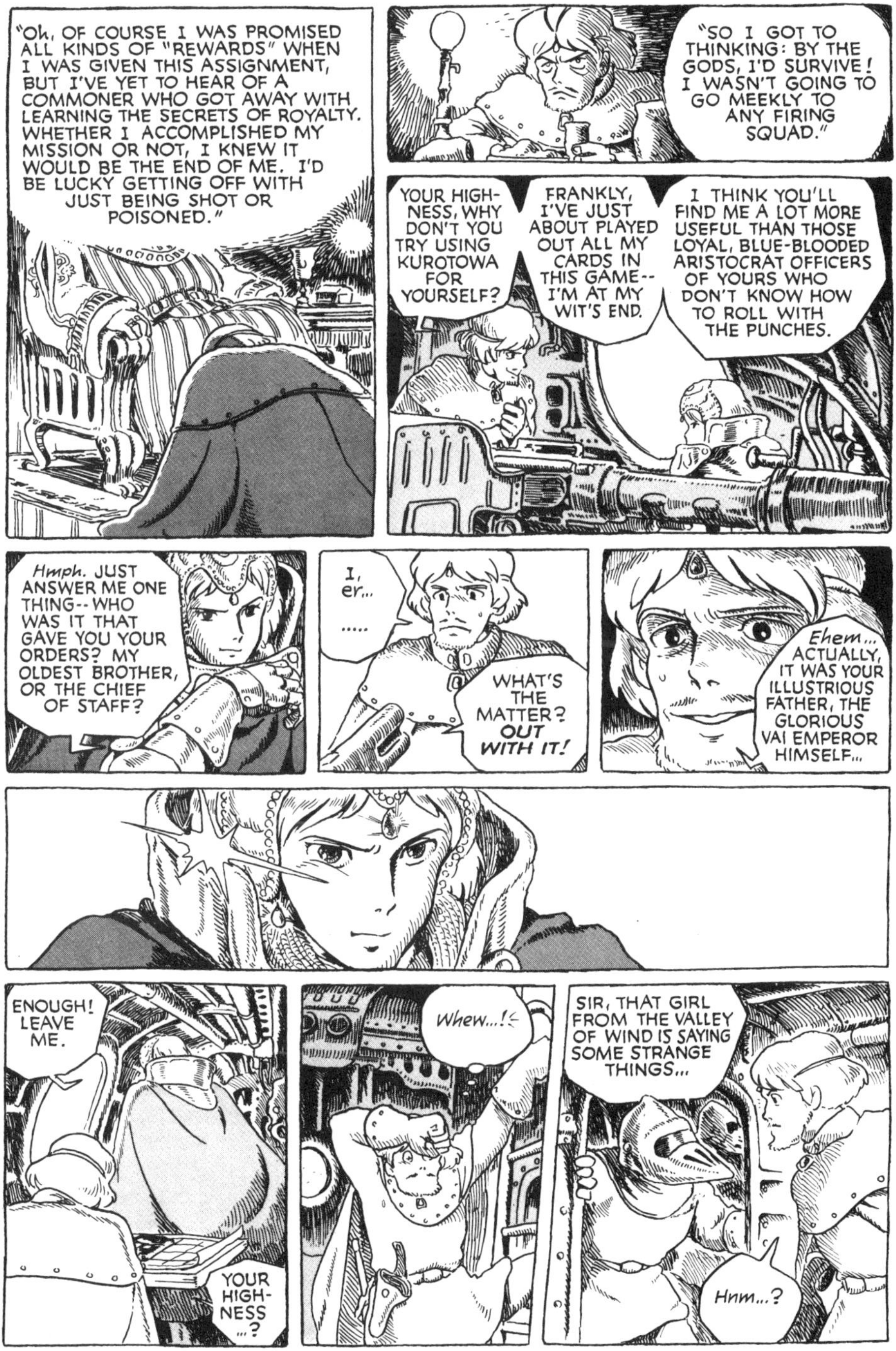
"Oh, OF COURSE I WAS PROMISED ALL KINDS OF "REWARDS" WHEN I WAS GIVEN THIS ASSIGNMENT, BUT I'VE YET TO HEAR OF A COMMONER WHO GOT AWAY WITH LEARNING THE SECRETS OF ROYALTY. WHETHER I ACCOMPLISHED MY MISSION OR NOT, I KNEW IT WOULD BE THE END OF ME. I'D BE LUCKY GETTING OFF WITH JUST BEING SHOT OR POISONED."
"SO I GOT TO THINKING: BY THE GODS, I'D SURVIVE! I WASN'T GOING TO GO MEEKLY TO ANY FIRING SQUAD."
YOUR HIGHNESS, WHY DON'T YOU TRY USING KUROTOWA FOR YOURSELF?
FRANKLY, I'VE JUST ABOUT PLAYED OUT ALL MY CARDS IN THIS GAME-- I'M AT MY WIT'S END.
I THINK YOU'LL FIND ME A LOT MORE USEFUL THAN THOSE LOYAL, BLUE-BLOODED ARISTOCRAT OFFICERS OF YOURS WHO DON'T KNOW HOW TO ROLL WITH THE PUNCHES.
Hmph. JUST ANSWER ME ONE THING-- WHO WAS IT THAT GAVE YOU YOUR ORDERS? MY OLDEST BROTHER, OR THE CHIEF OF STAFF?
I, er...
.....
WHAT'S THE MATTER? OUT WITH IT!
Ehem... ACTUALLY, IT WAS YOUR ILLUSTRIOUS FATHER, THE GLORIOUS VAI EMPEROR HIMSELF...
ENOUGH! LEAVE ME.
YOUR HIGHNESS ...?
Whew...!
SIR, THAT GIRL FROM THE VALLEY OF WIND IS SAYING SOME STRANGE THINGS...
Hnm...?

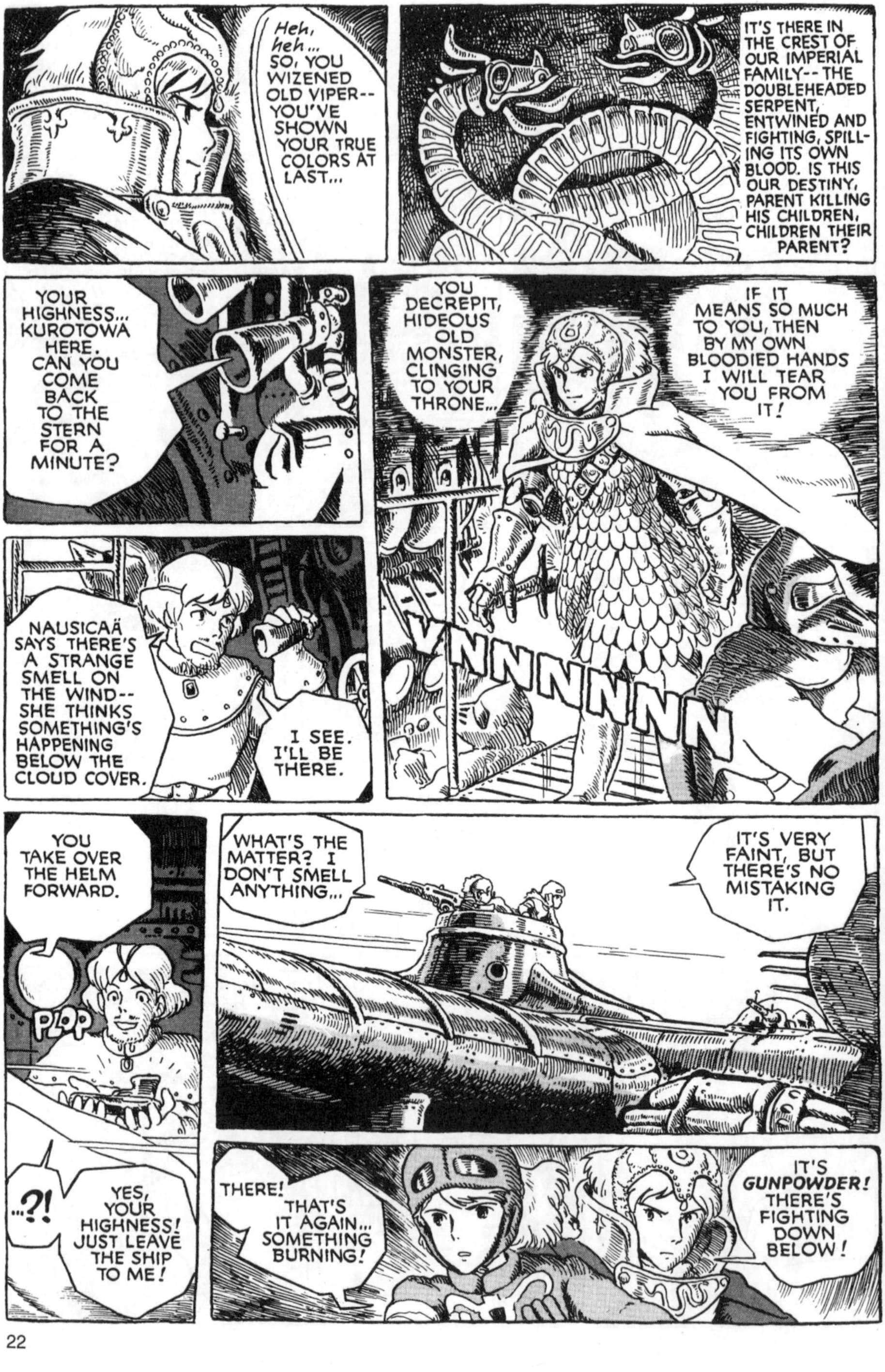
Heh, heh... SO, YOU WIZENED OLD VIPER-- YOU'VE SHOWN YOUR TRUE COLORS AT LAST...
IT'S THERE IN THE CREST OF OUR IMPERIAL FAMILY-- THE DOUBLEHEADED SERPENT, ENTWINED AND FIGHTING, SPILLING ITS OWN BLOOD. IS THIS OUR DESTINY, PARENT KILLING HIS CHILDREN, CHILDREN THEIR PARENT?
YOUR HIGHNESS... KUROTOWA HERE. CAN YOU COME BACK TO THE STERN FOR A MINUTE?
NAUSICAÄ SAYS THERE'S A STRANGE SMELL ON THE WIND-- SHE THINKS SOMETHING'S HAPPENING BELOW THE CLOUD COVER.
I SEE. I'LL BE THERE.
YOU DECREPIT, HIDEOUS OLD MONSTER, CLINGING TO YOUR THRONE...
IF IT MEANS SO MUCH TO YOU, THEN BY MY OWN BLOODIED HANDS I WILL TEAR YOU FROM IT!
VNNNNNNNN
YOU TAKE OVER THE HELM FORWARD.
PLOP
...?!
YES, YOUR HIGHNESS! JUST LEAVE THE SHIP TO ME!
WHAT'S THE MATTER? I DON'T SMELL ANYTHING...
IT'S VERY FAINT, BUT THERE'S NO MISTAKING IT.
THERE! THAT'S IT AGAIN... SOMETHING BURNING!
IT'S GUNPOWDER! THERE'S FIGHTING DOWN BELOW!

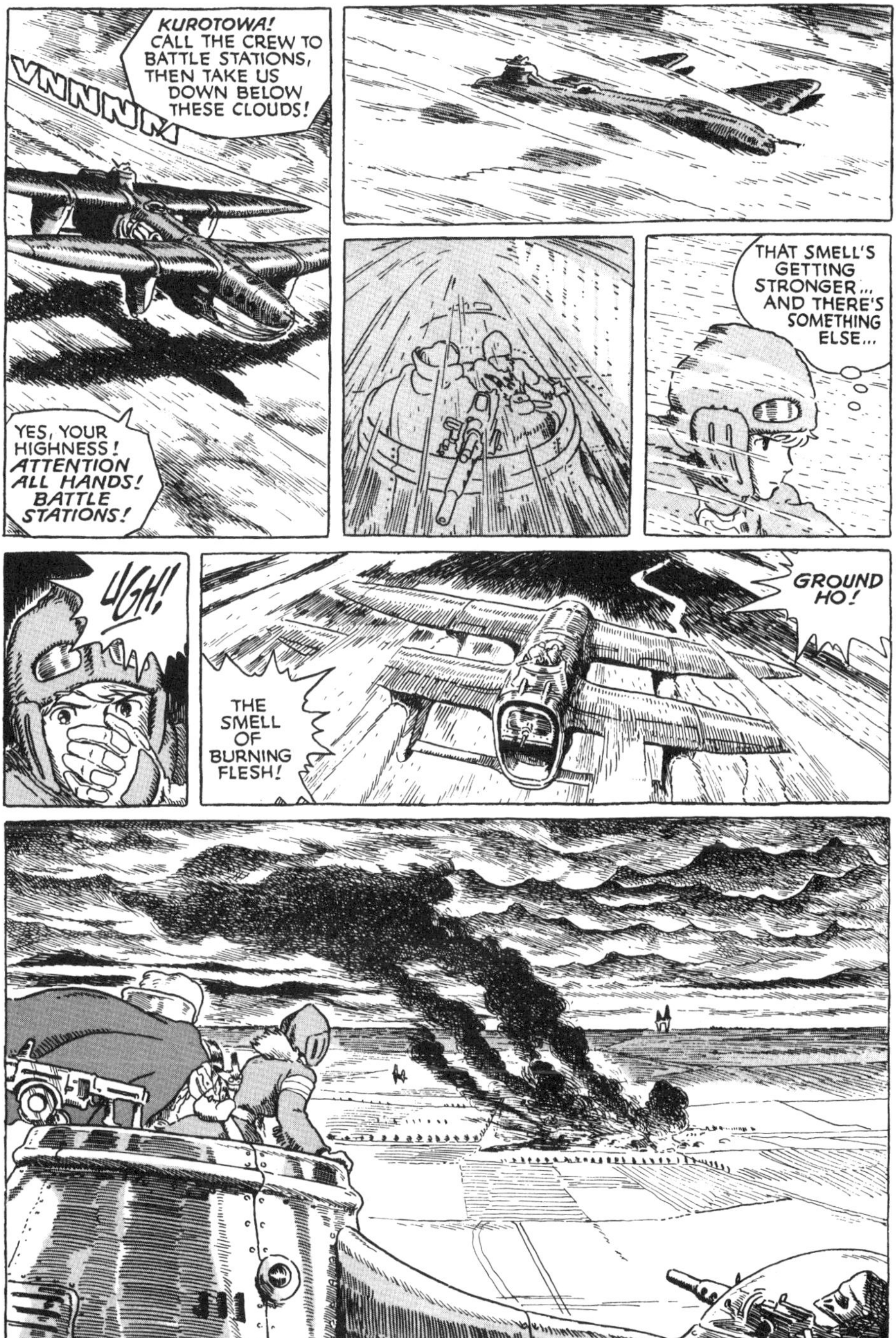
VNNNN
KUROTOWA! CALL THE CREW TO BATTLE STATIONS, THEN TAKE US DOWN BELOW THESE CLOUDS!
YES, YOUR HIGHNESS! ATTENTION ALL HANDS! BATTLE STATIONS!
THAT SMELL'S GETTING STRONGER... AND THERE'S SOMETHING ELSE...
UGH!
GROUND HO!
THE SMELL OF BURNING FLESH!

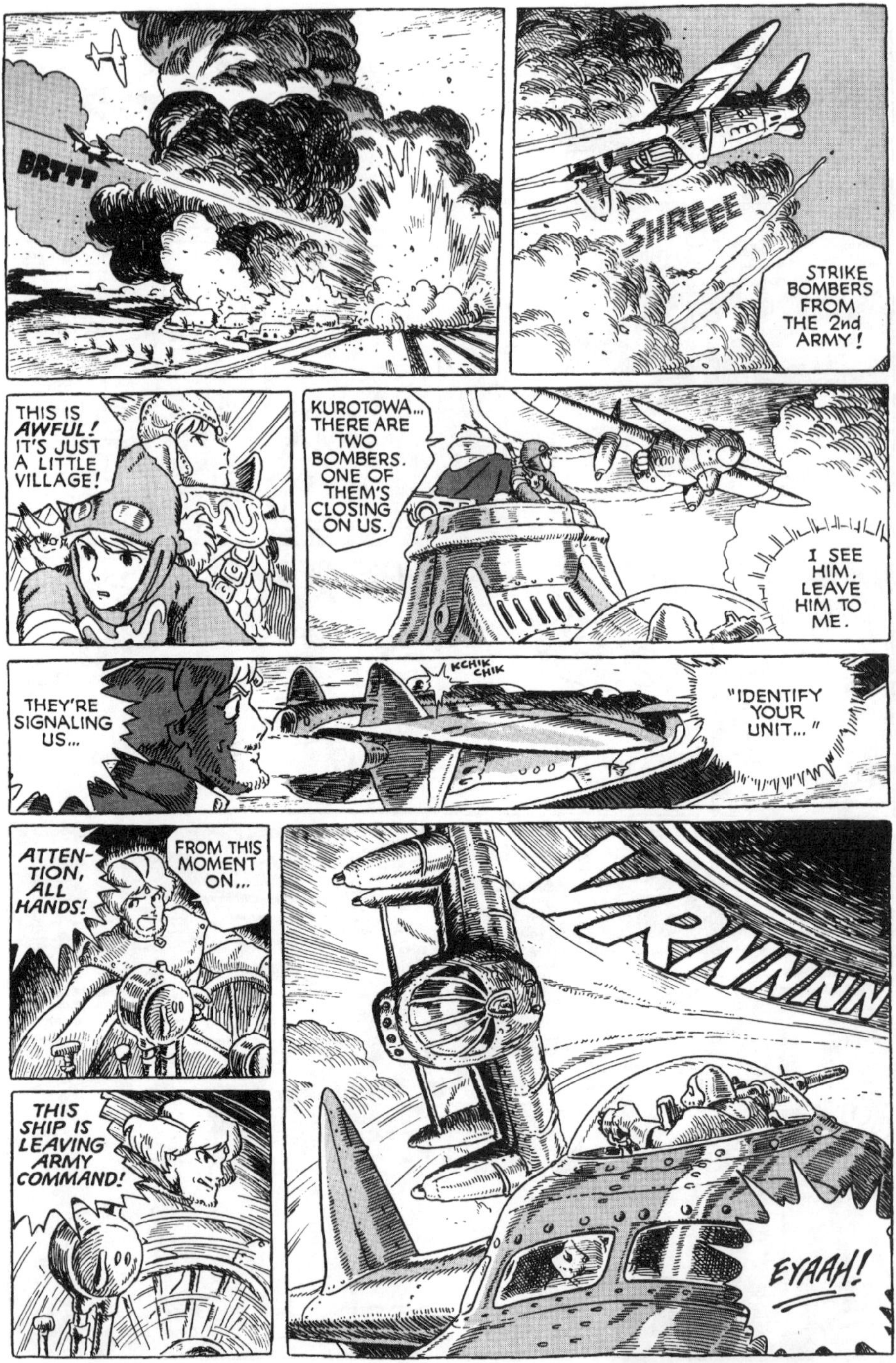
BRTTT
SHREEE
STRIKE BOMBERS FROM THE 2nd ARMY!
THIS IS AWFUL! IT'S JUST A LITTLE VILLAGE!
KUROTOWA... THERE ARE TWO BOMBERS. ONE OF THEM'S CLOSING ON US.
I SEE HIM. LEAVE HIM TO ME.
THEY'RE SIGNALING US...
KCHIK CHIK
"IDENTIFY YOUR UNIT..."
ATTENTION, ALL HANDS!
FROM THIS MOMENT ON...
THIS SHIP IS LEAVING ARMY COMMAND!
VRNNNNN
EYAAH!

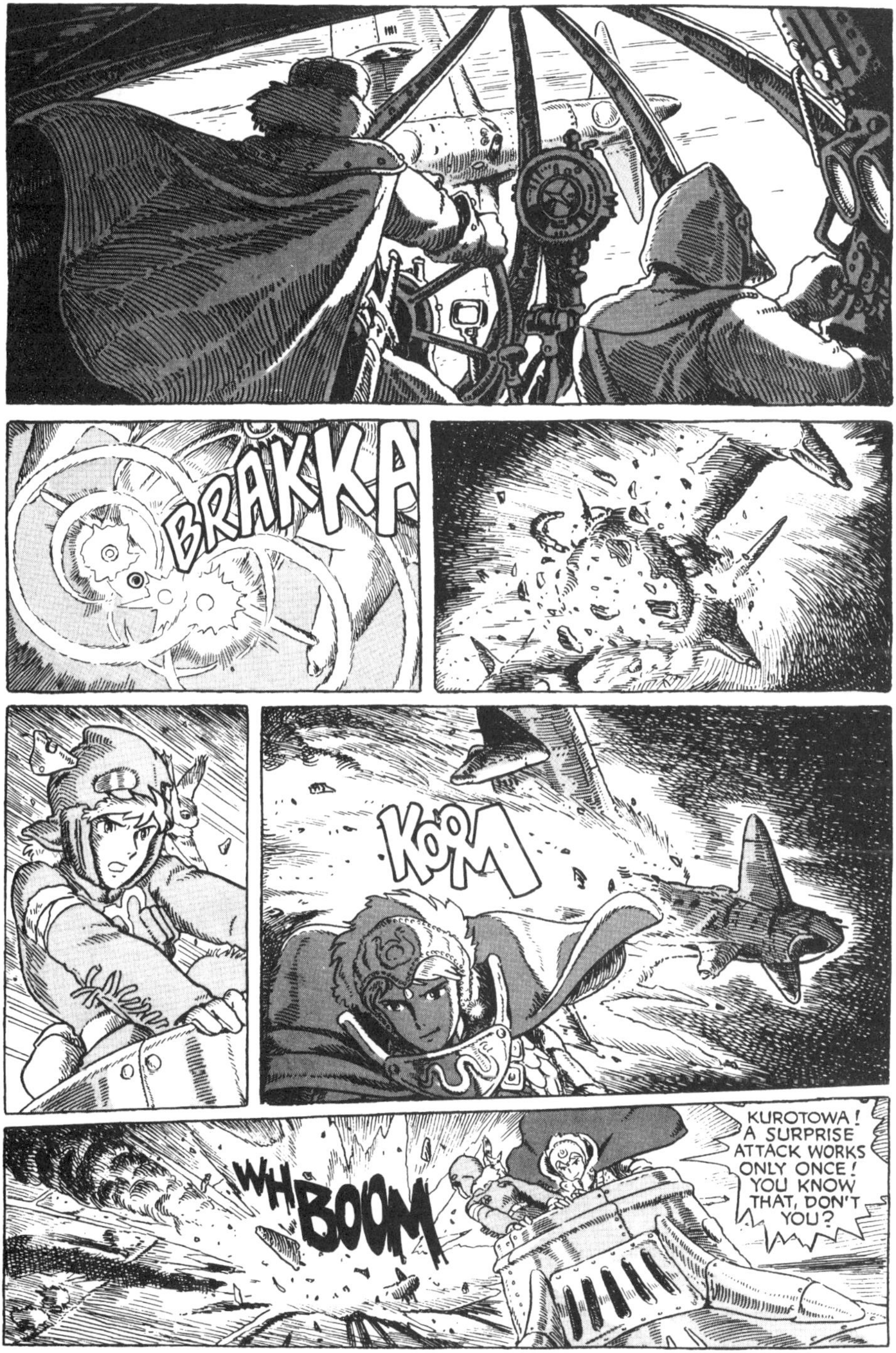
BRAKKA
KOOM
WHBOOM
KUROTOWA! A SURPRISE ATTACK WORKS ONLY ONCE! YOU KNOW THAT, DON'T YOU?

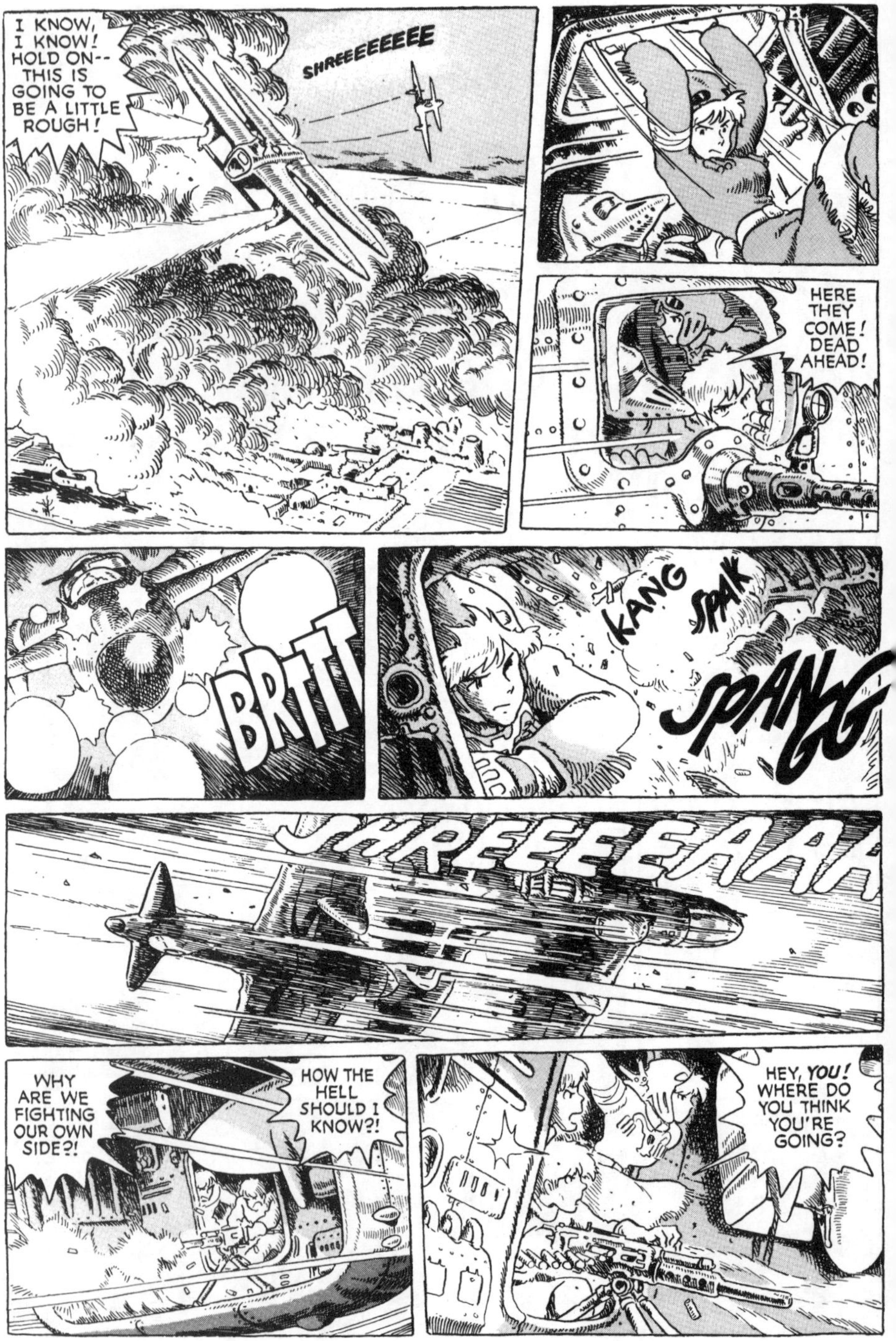
I KNOW, I KNOW! HOLD ON-- THIS IS GOING TO BE A LITTLE ROUGH!
SHREEEEEEEE
HERE THEY COME! DEAD AHEAD!
BRTTT
KANG
SPAK
SPANGG
SHREEEEEAAA
WHY ARE WE FIGHTING OUR OWN SIDE?!
HOW THE HELL SHOULD I KNOW?!
HEY, ***YOU!*** WHERE DO YOU THINK YOU'RE GOING?

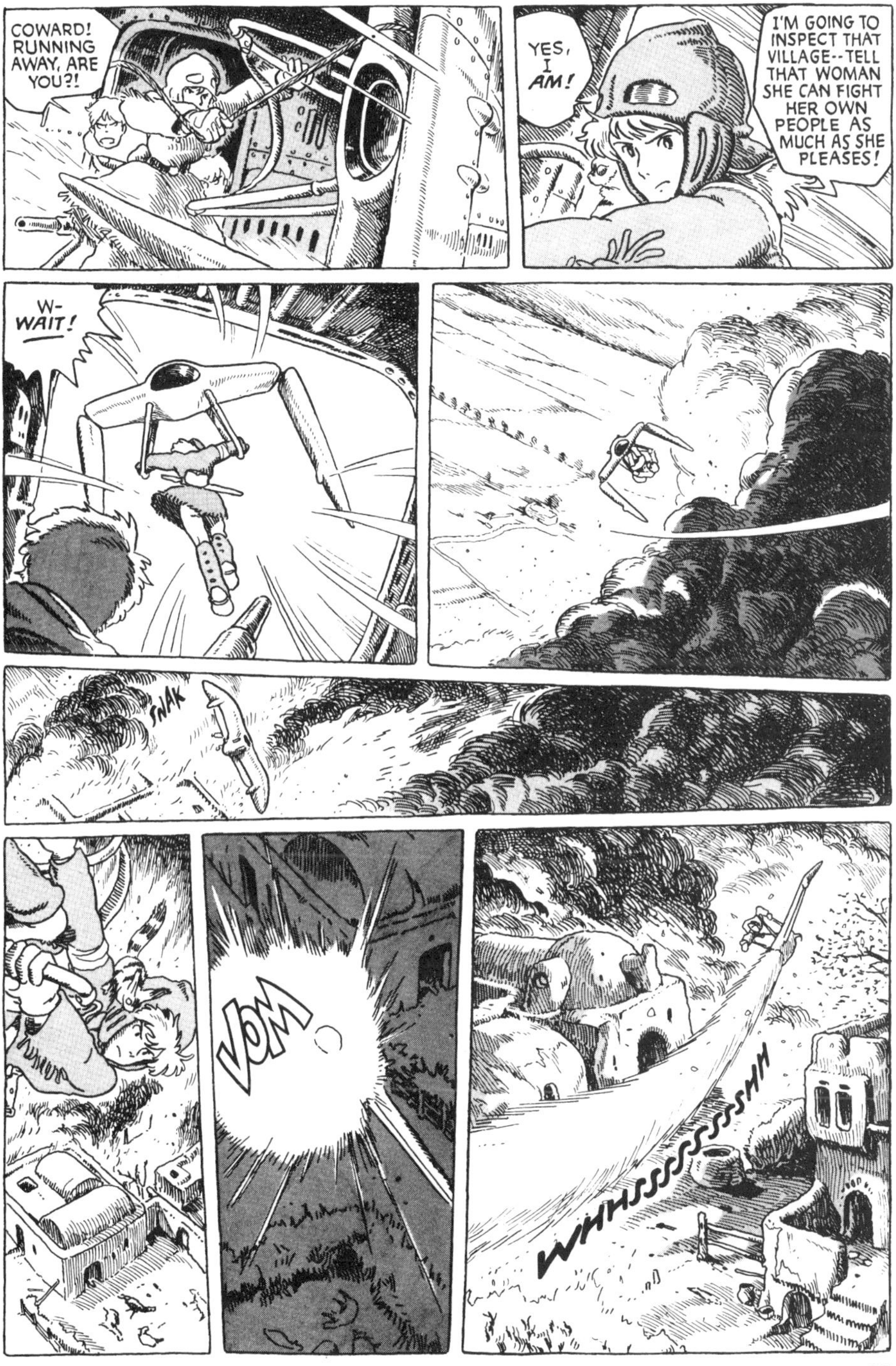
COWARD! RUNNING AWAY, ARE YOU?!
YES, I AM!
I'M GOING TO INSPECT THAT VILLAGE--TELL THAT WOMAN SHE CAN FIGHT HER OWN PEOPLE AS MUCH AS SHE PLEASES!
W- WAIT!
SNAK
VOM
WHHSSSSSSSSHH

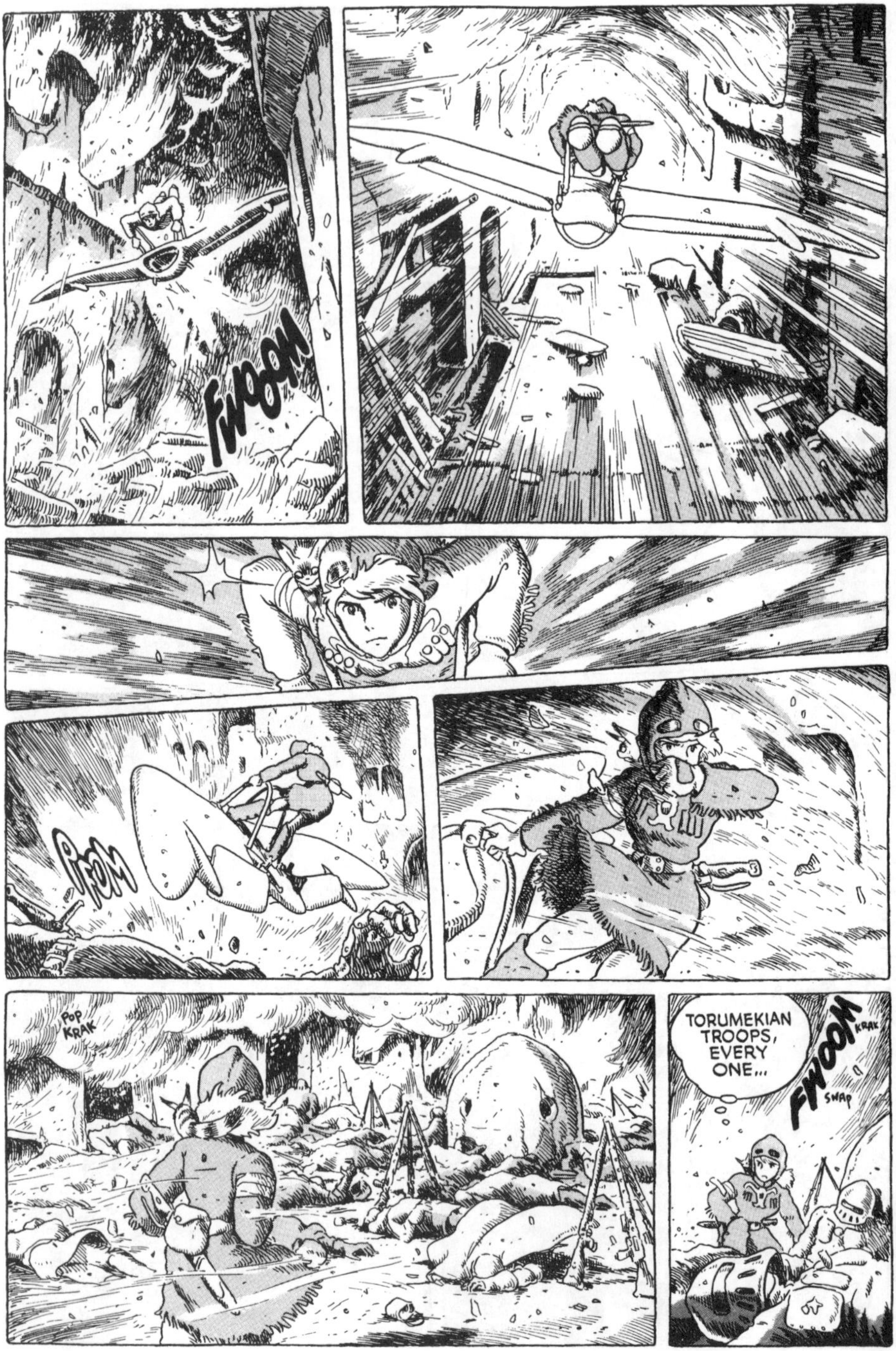
FWOOOM
PFOOM
POP KRAK
TORUMEKIAN TROOPS, EVERY ONE...
FWOOOM
KRAK
SNAP

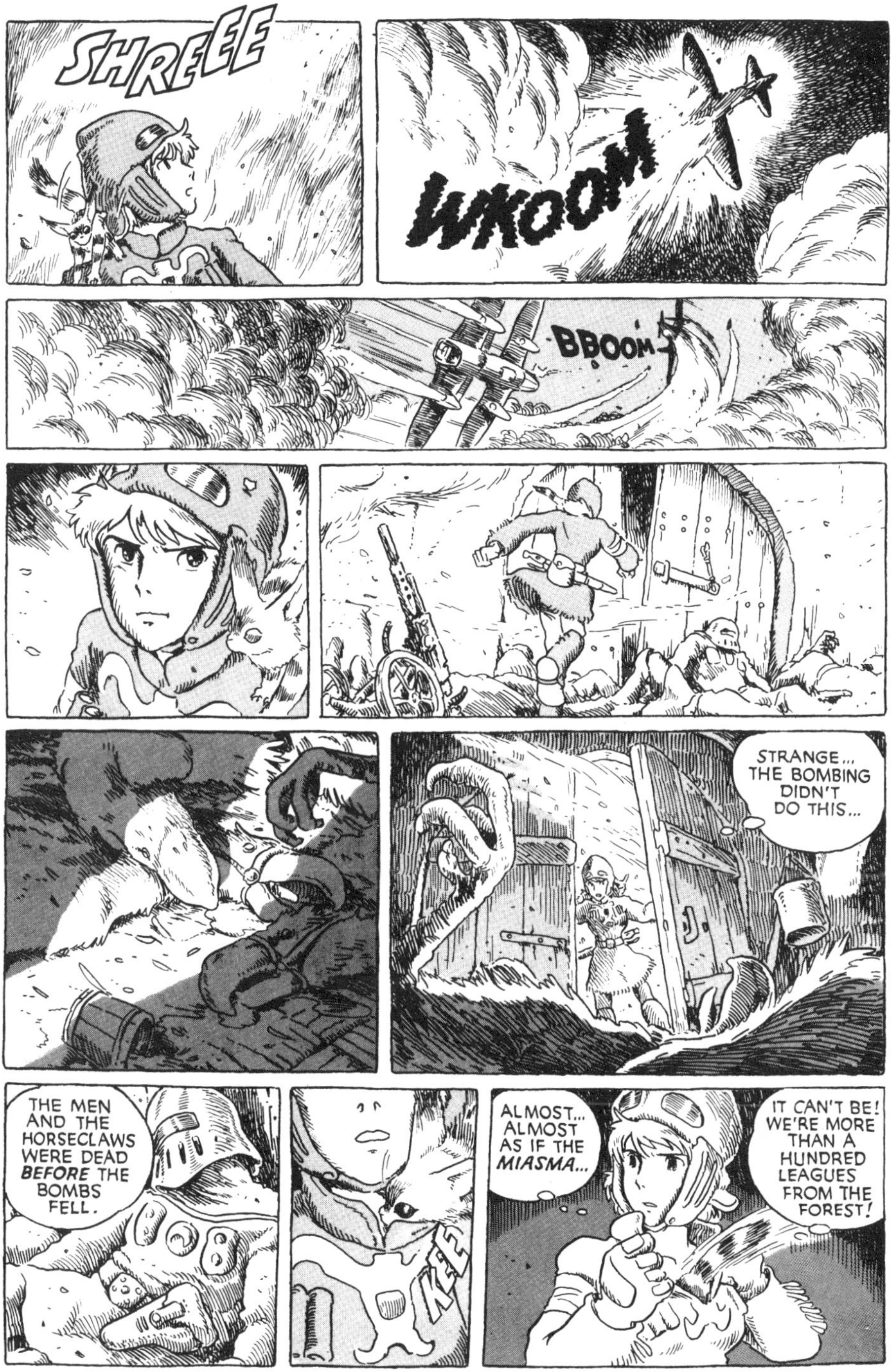
SHREEE
WKOOM
BBOOM
STRANGE... THE BOMBING DIDN'T DO THIS...
THE MEN AND THE HORSECLAWS WERE DEAD *BEFORE* THE BOMBS FELL.
KEE
ALMOST... ALMOST AS IF THE *MIASMA*...
IT CAN'T BE! WE'RE MORE THAN A HUNDRED LEAGUES FROM THE FOREST!

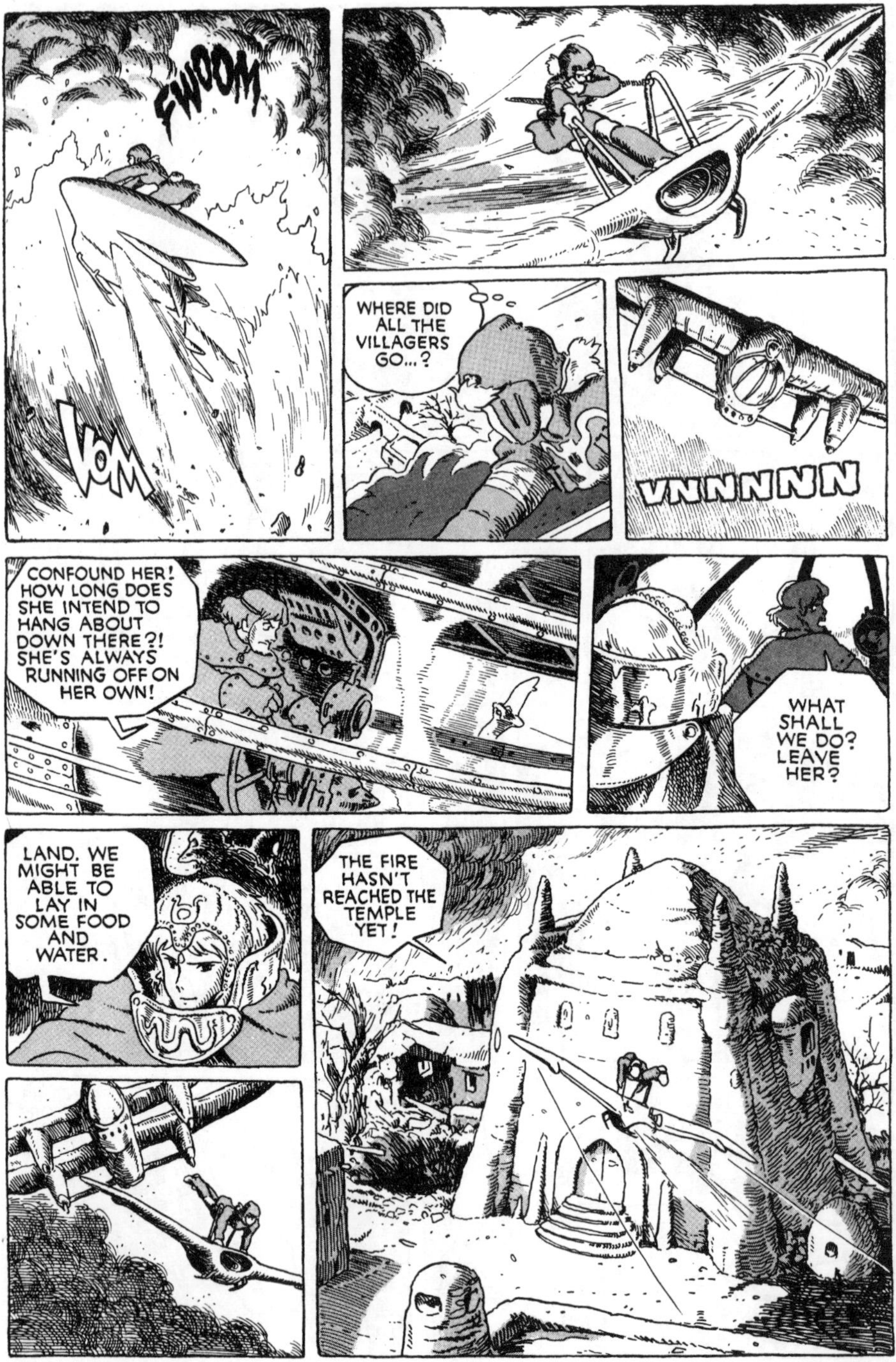
FWOOM
VOM
WHERE DID ALL THE VILLAGERS GO...?
VNNNNN
CONFOUND HER! HOW LONG DOES SHE INTEND TO HANG ABOUT DOWN THERE?! SHE'S ALWAYS RUNNING OFF ON HER OWN!
WHAT SHALL WE DO? LEAVE HER?
LAND. WE MIGHT BE ABLE TO LAY IN SOME FOOD AND WATER.
THE FIRE HASN'T REACHED THE TEMPLE YET!

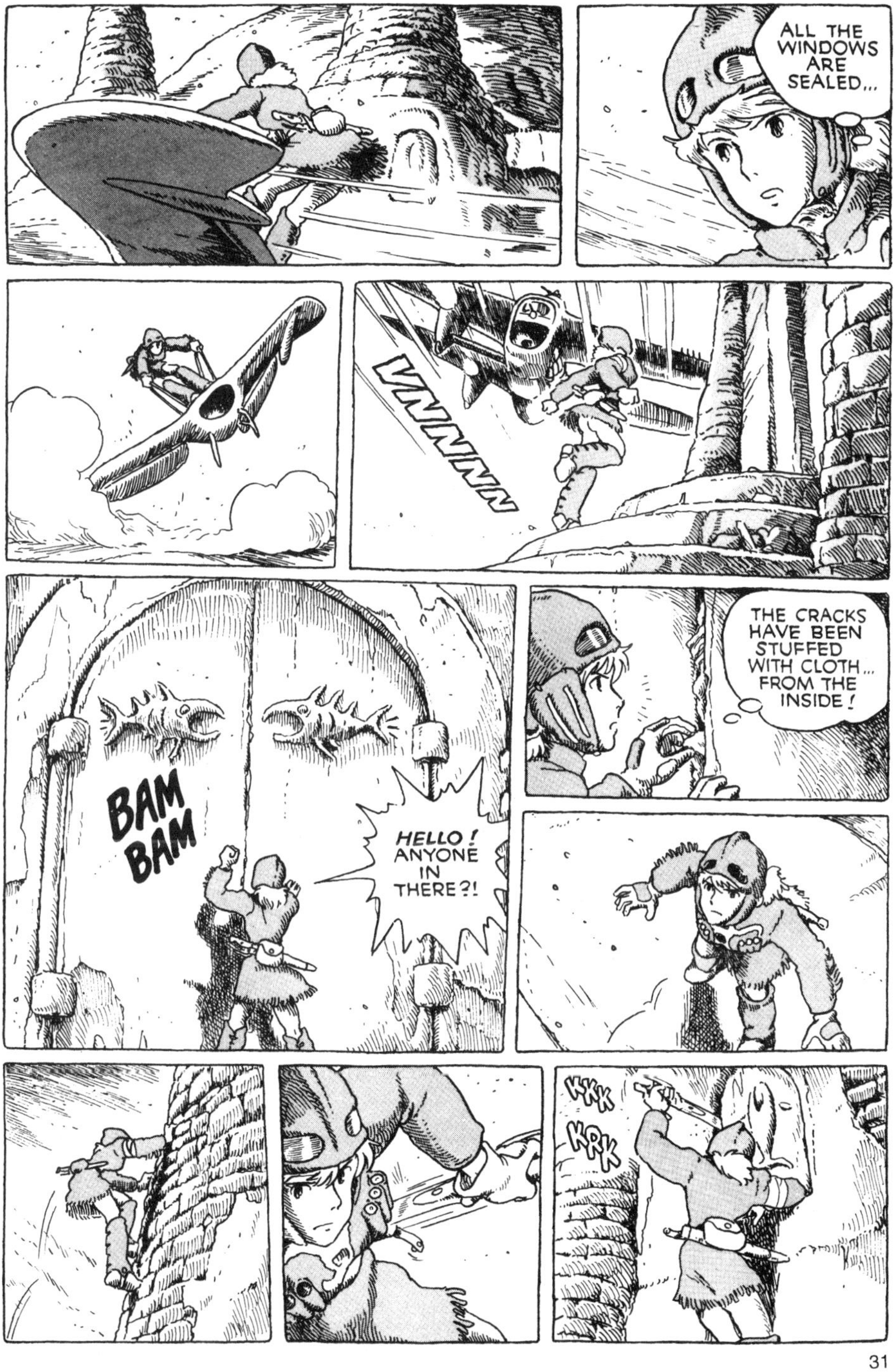

ALL THE WINDOWS ARE SEALED...
VNNNNN
BAM BAM
HELLO! ANYONE IN THERE?!
THE CRACKS HAVE BEEN STUFFED WITH CLOTH... FROM THE INSIDE!
KKK
KRK

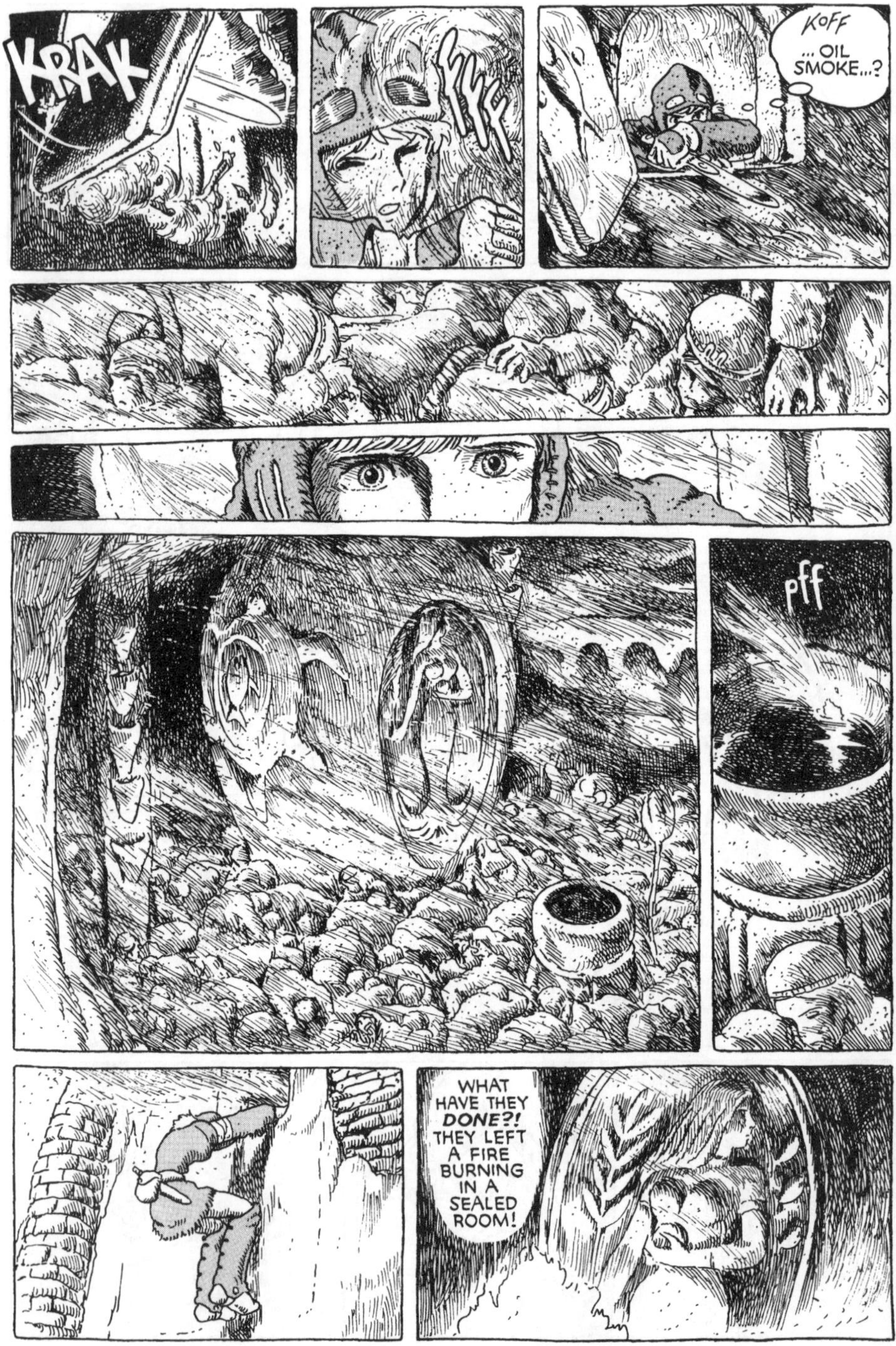
KRAK
KOFF
... OIL SMOKE...?
pff
WHAT HAVE THEY DONE?! THEY LEFT A FIRE BURNING IN A SEALED ROOM!

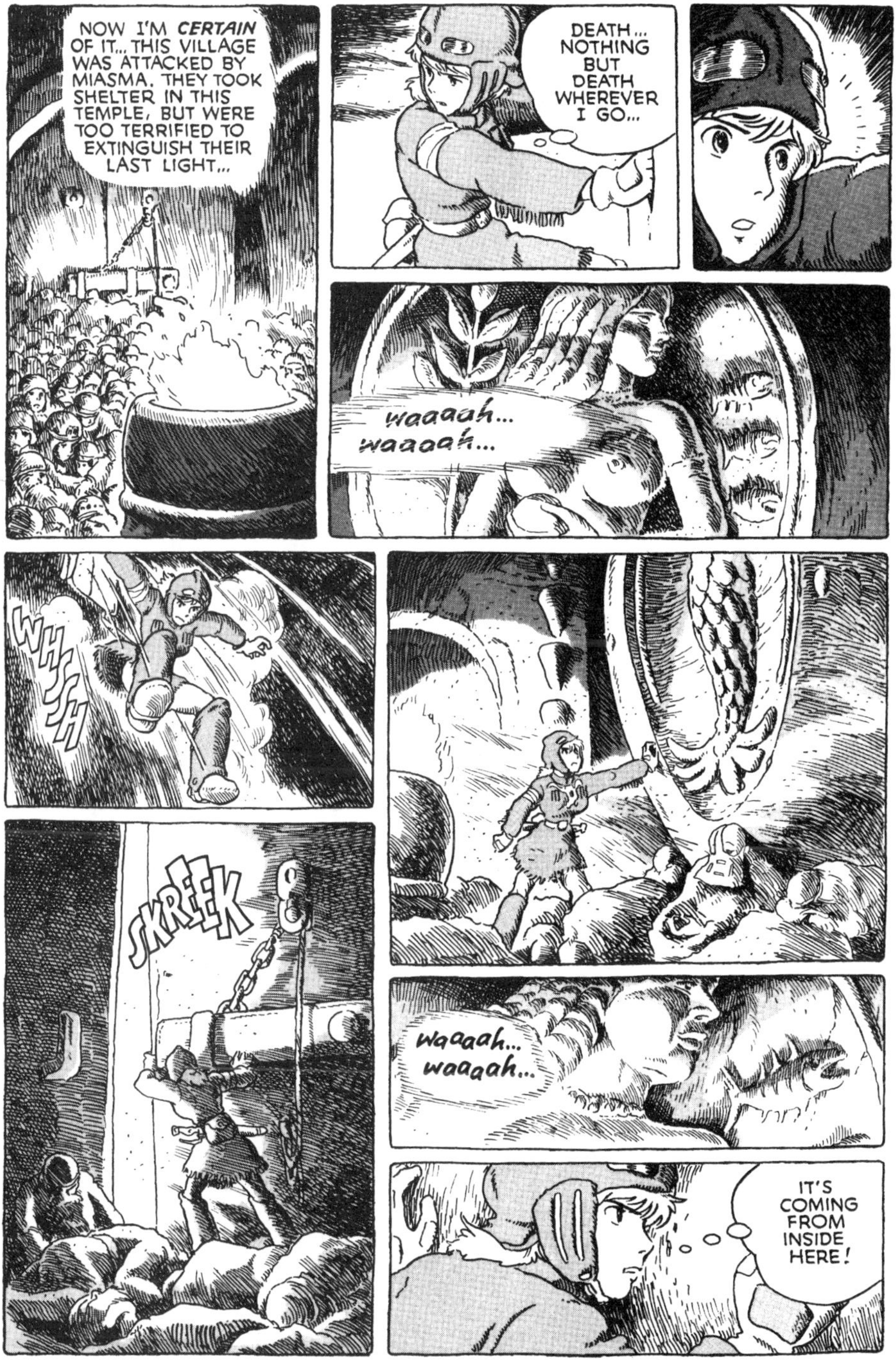
NOW I'M *CERTAIN* OF IT... THIS VILLAGE WAS ATTACKED BY MIASMA. THEY TOOK SHELTER IN THIS TEMPLE, BUT WERE TOO TERRIFIED TO EXTINGUISH THEIR LAST LIGHT...
DEATH... NOTHING BUT DEATH WHEREVER I GO...
waaaah... waaaah...
WHSSH
SKREEEK
waaaah... waaaah...
IT'S COMING FROM INSIDE HERE!

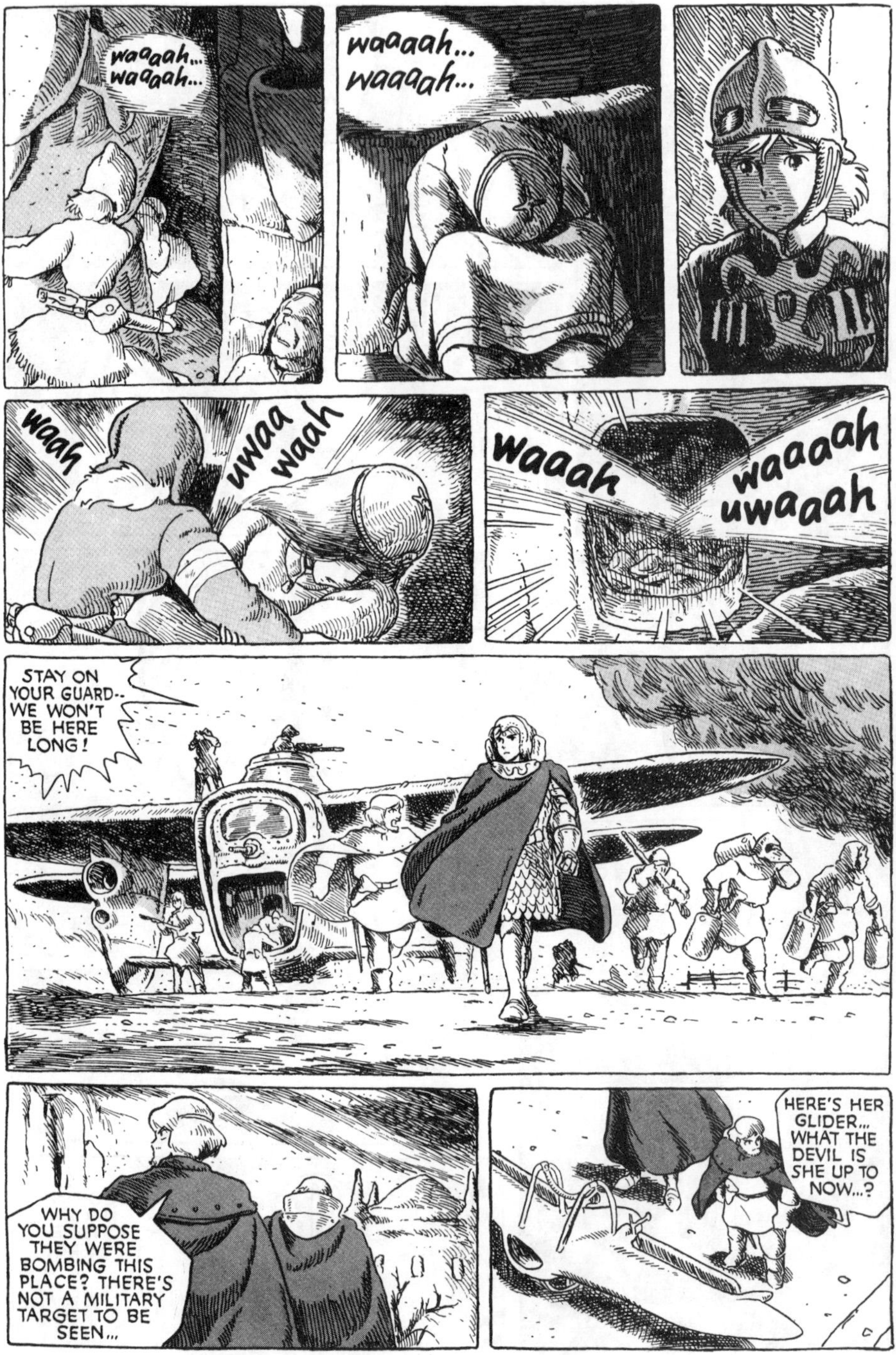
waaaah... waaaah...
waaaah... waaaah...
waah
uwaa waah
waaah
waaaah uwaaah
STAY ON YOUR GUARD-- WE WON'T BE HERE LONG!
WHY DO YOU SUPPOSE THEY WERE BOMBING THIS PLACE? THERE'S NOT A MILITARY TARGET TO BE SEEN...
HERE'S HER GLIDER... WHAT THE DEVIL IS SHE UP TO NOW...?

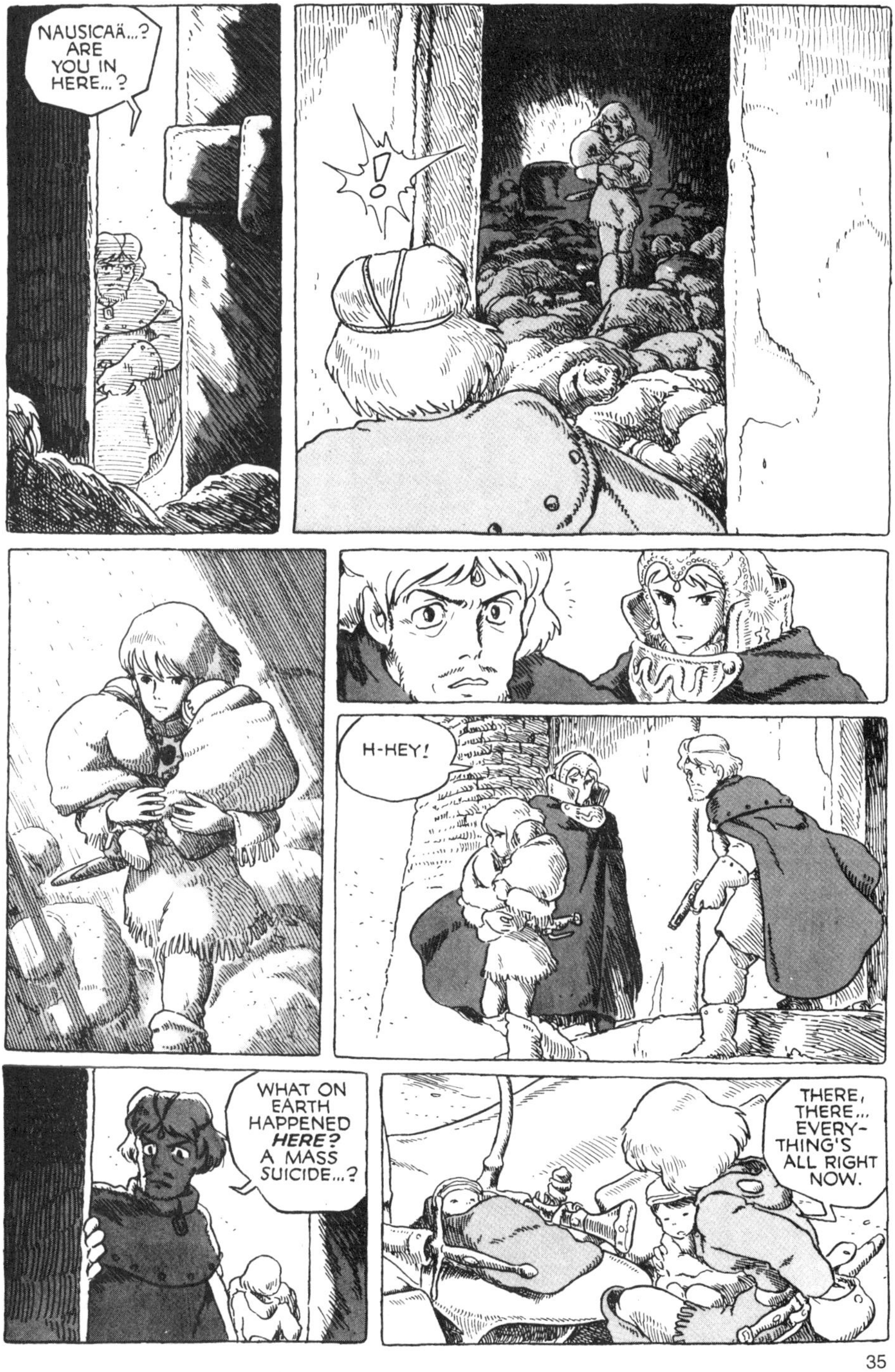
NAUSICAÄ...? ARE YOU IN HERE...?
!
H-HEY!
WHAT ON EARTH HAPPENED *HERE?* A MASS SUICIDE...?
THERE, THERE... EVERY-THING'S ALL RIGHT NOW.

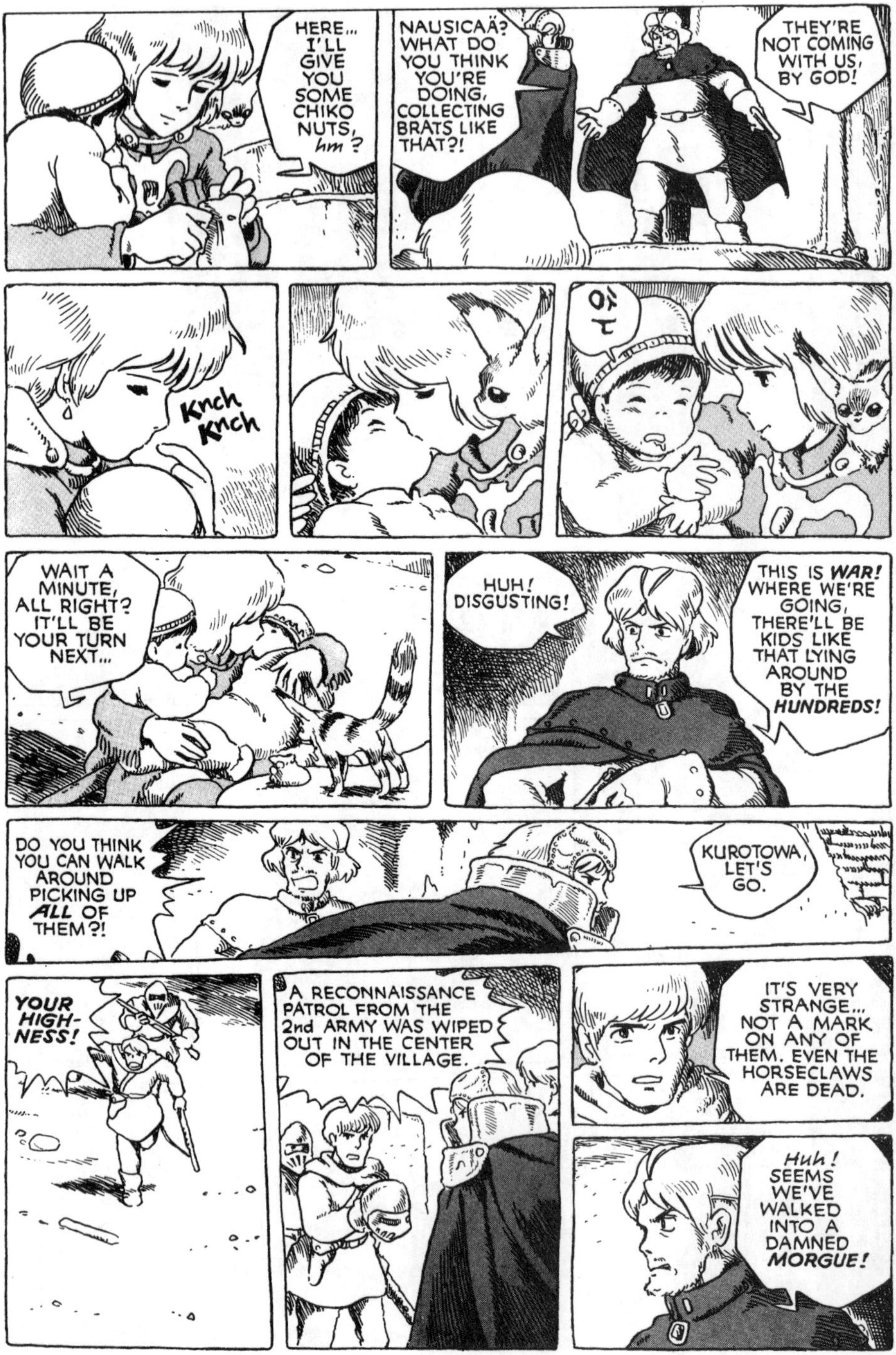
HERE... I'LL GIVE YOU SOME CHIKO NUTS, hm?
NAUSICAÄ? WHAT DO YOU THINK YOU'RE DOING, COLLECTING BRATS LIKE THAT?!
THEY'RE NOT COMING WITH US, BY GOD!
Knch Knch
WAIT A MINUTE, ALL RIGHT? IT'LL BE YOUR TURN NEXT...
HUH! DISGUSTING!
THIS IS WAR! WHERE WE'RE GOING, THERE'LL BE KIDS LIKE THAT LYING AROUND BY THE HUNDREDS!
DO YOU THINK YOU CAN WALK AROUND PICKING UP ALL OF THEM?!
KUROTOWA, LET'S GO.
YOUR HIGHNESS!
A RECONNAISSANCE PATROL FROM THE 2nd ARMY WAS WIPED OUT IN THE CENTER OF THE VILLAGE.
IT'S VERY STRANGE... NOT A MARK ON ANY OF THEM. EVEN THE HORSECLAWS ARE DEAD.
Huh! SEEMS WE'VE WALKED INTO A DAMNED MORGUE!

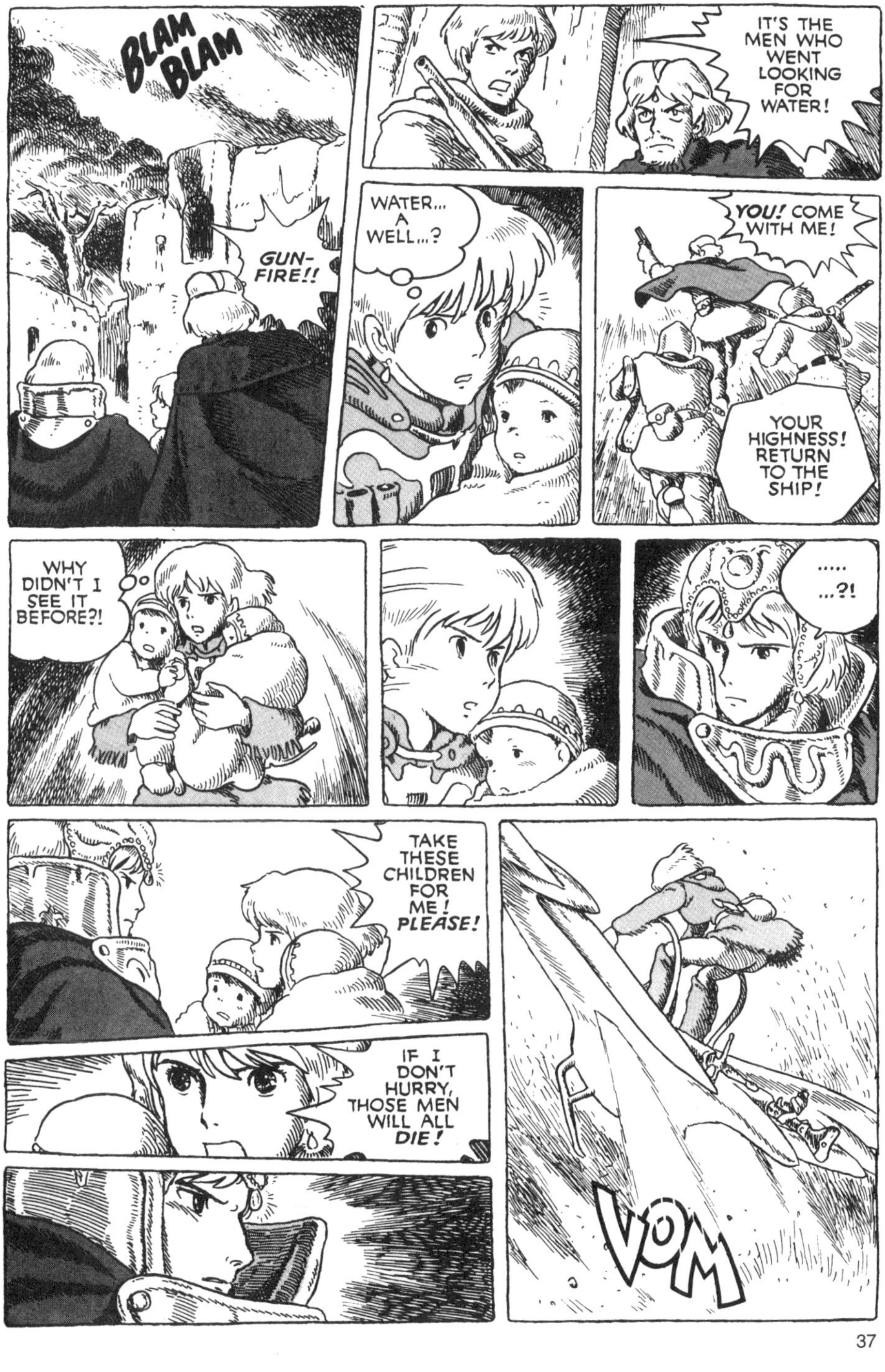
BLAM BLAM
GUN-FIRE!!
IT'S THE MEN WHO WENT LOOKING FOR WATER!
WATER... A WELL...?
YOU! COME WITH ME!
YOUR HIGHNESS! RETURN TO THE SHIP!
WHY DIDN'T I SEE IT BEFORE?!
....?!
TAKE THESE CHILDREN FOR ME! PLEASE!
IF I DON'T HURRY, THOSE MEN WILL ALL DIE!
VOM

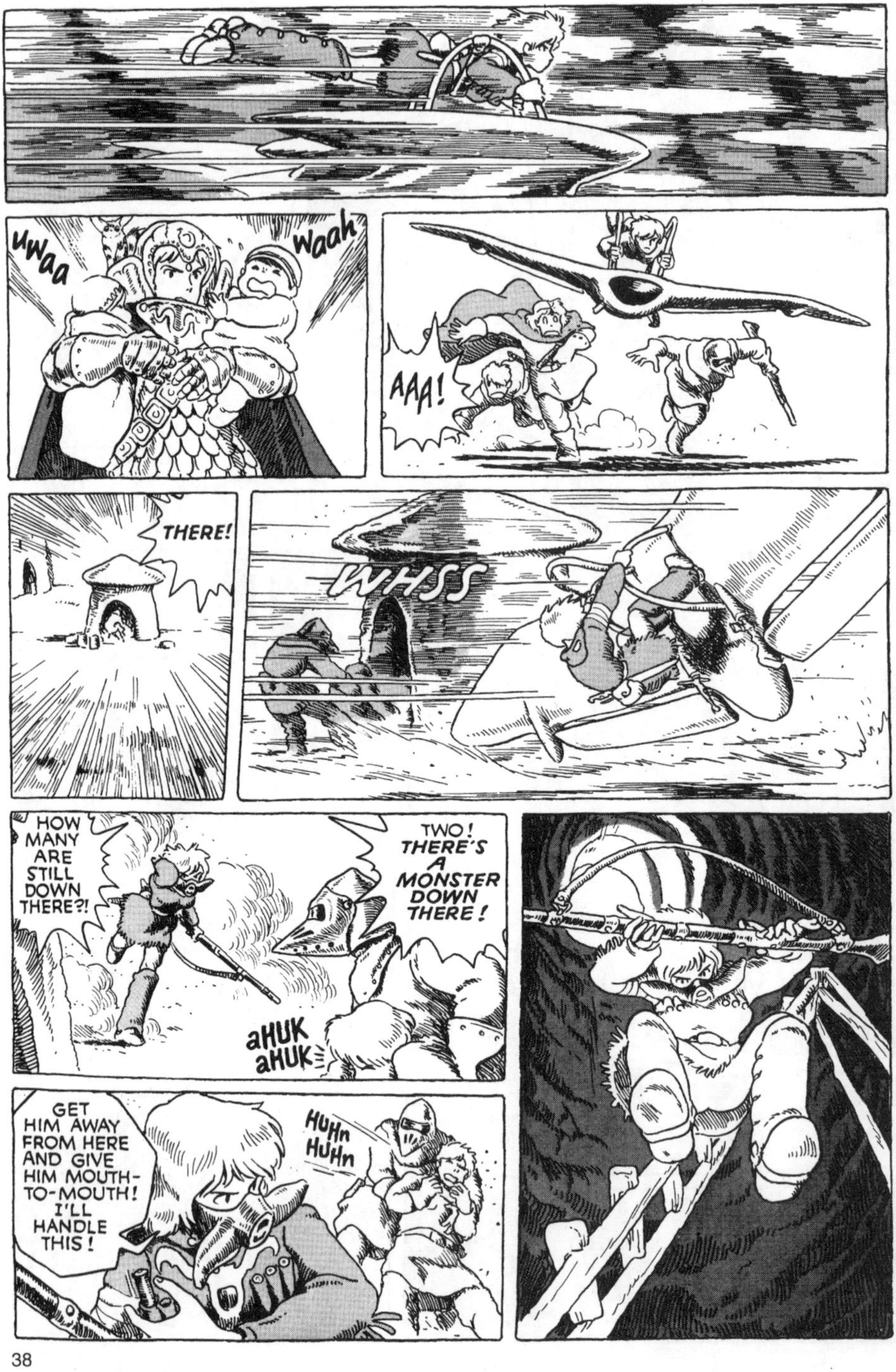

uWaa
Waah
AAA!
THERE!
WHSS
HOW MANY ARE STILL DOWN THERE?!
TWO! THERE'S A MONSTER DOWN THERE!
aHUK aHUK
GET HIM AWAY FROM HERE AND GIVE HIM MOUTH-TO-MOUTH! I'LL HANDLE THIS!
HUHn HUHn

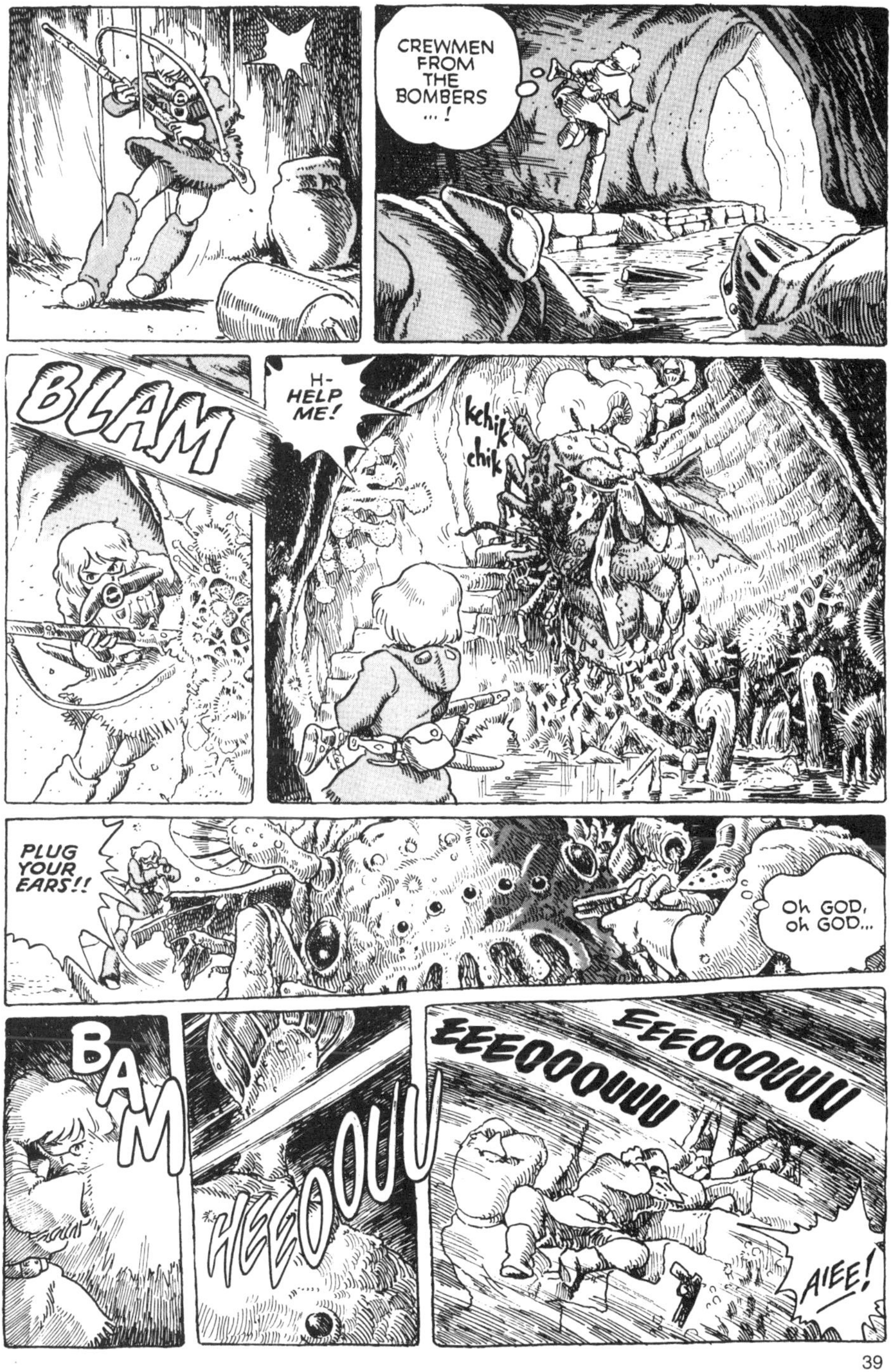
CREWMEN FROM THE BOMBERS ...!
BLAM
H- HELP ME!
kchik chik
PLUG YOUR EARS!!
Oh GOD, oh GOD...
BAM
HEEOOUU
EEEOOOUUU
EEEOOOUUU
AIEE!

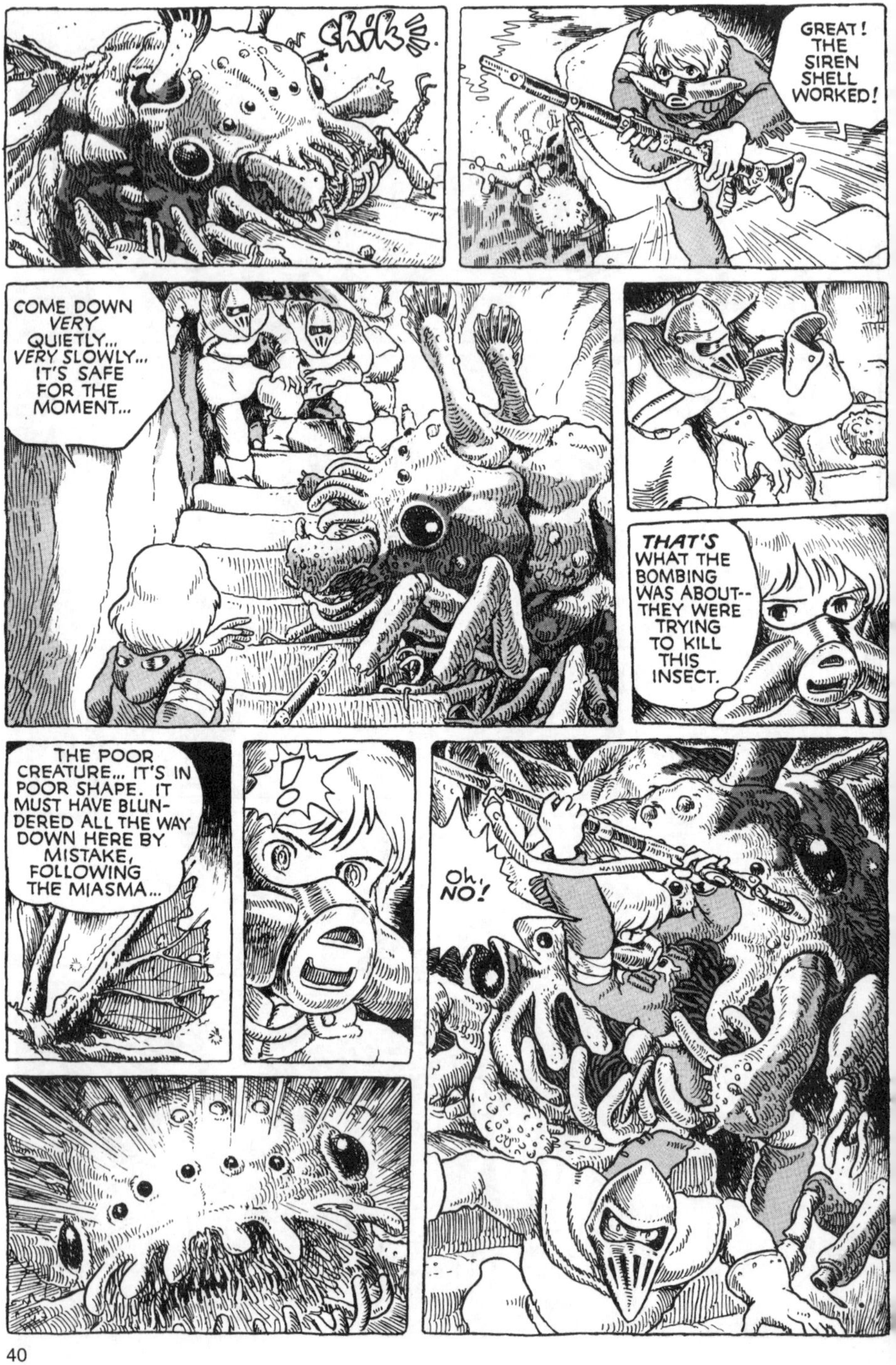
CHIK
GREAT! THE SIREN SHELL WORKED!
COME DOWN VERY QUIETLY... VERY SLOWLY... IT'S SAFE FOR THE MOMENT...
THAT'S WHAT THE BOMBING WAS ABOUT-- THEY WERE TRYING TO KILL THIS INSECT.
THE POOR CREATURE... IT'S IN POOR SHAPE. IT MUST HAVE BLUN-DERED ALL THE WAY DOWN HERE BY MISTAKE, FOLLOWING THE MIASMA...
!
OH, NO!

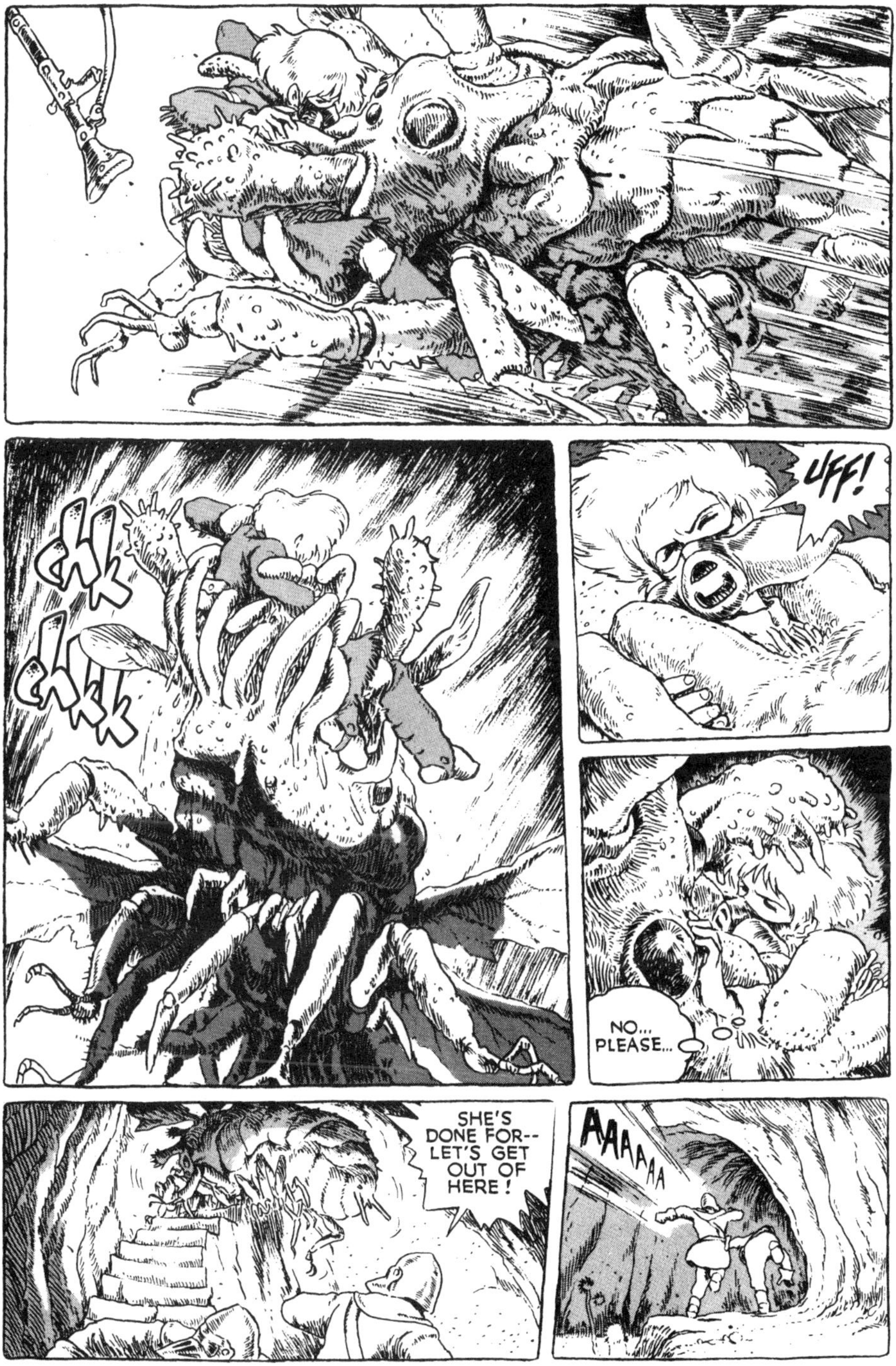
UFF!
CHK CHKK
NO... PLEASE...
SHE'S DONE FOR-- LET'S GET OUT OF HERE!
AAAAAAA

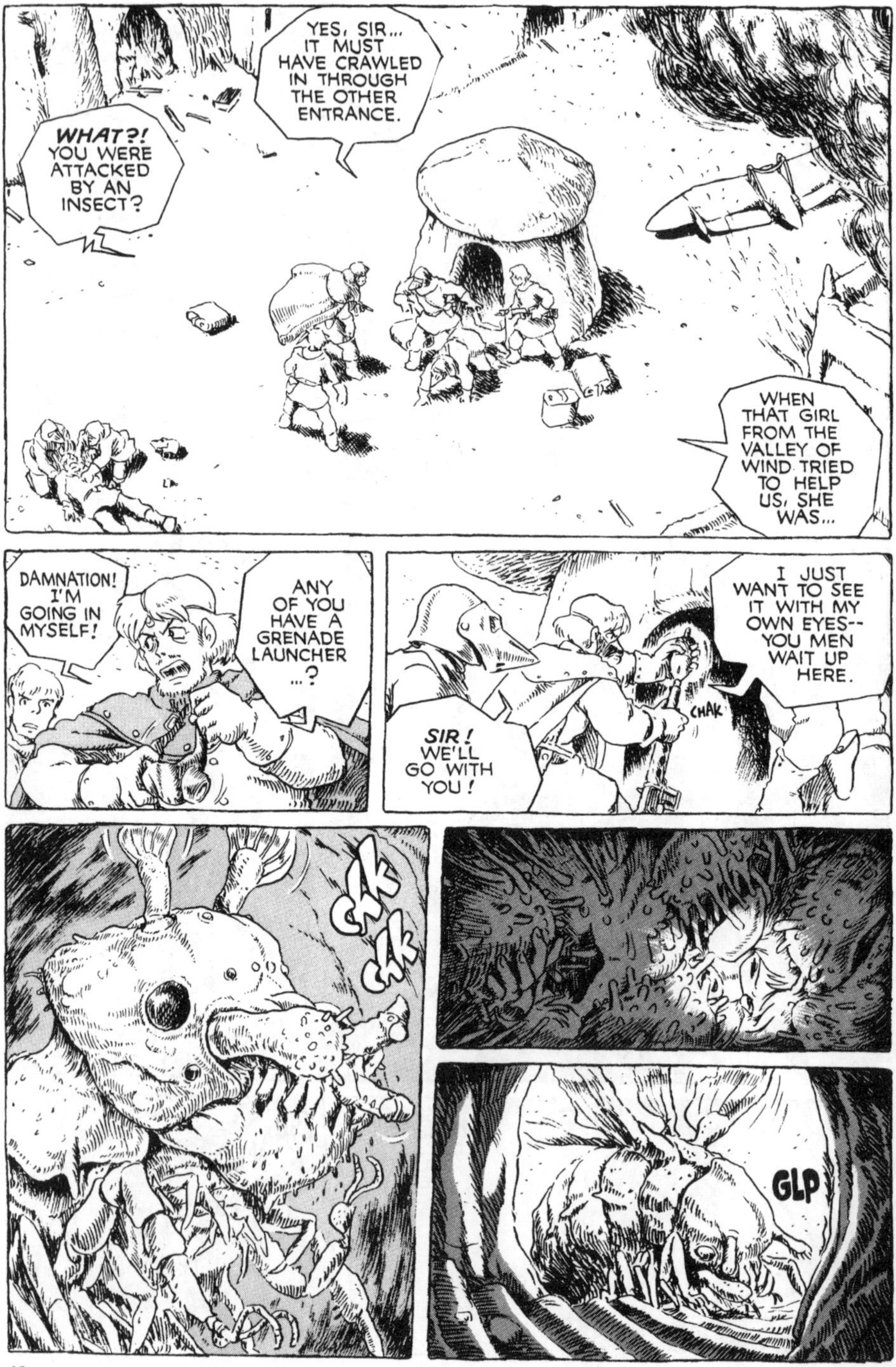
YES, SIR... IT MUST HAVE CRAWLED IN THROUGH THE OTHER ENTRANCE.
WHAT?! YOU WERE ATTACKED BY AN INSECT?
WHEN THAT GIRL FROM THE VALLEY OF WIND TRIED TO HELP US, SHE WAS...
ANY OF YOU HAVE A GRENADE LAUNCHER ...?
DAMNATION! I'M GOING IN MYSELF!
I JUST WANT TO SEE IT WITH MY OWN EYES-- YOU MEN WAIT UP HERE.
CHAK
SIR! WE'LL GO WITH YOU!
CHAK
CHAK
GLP

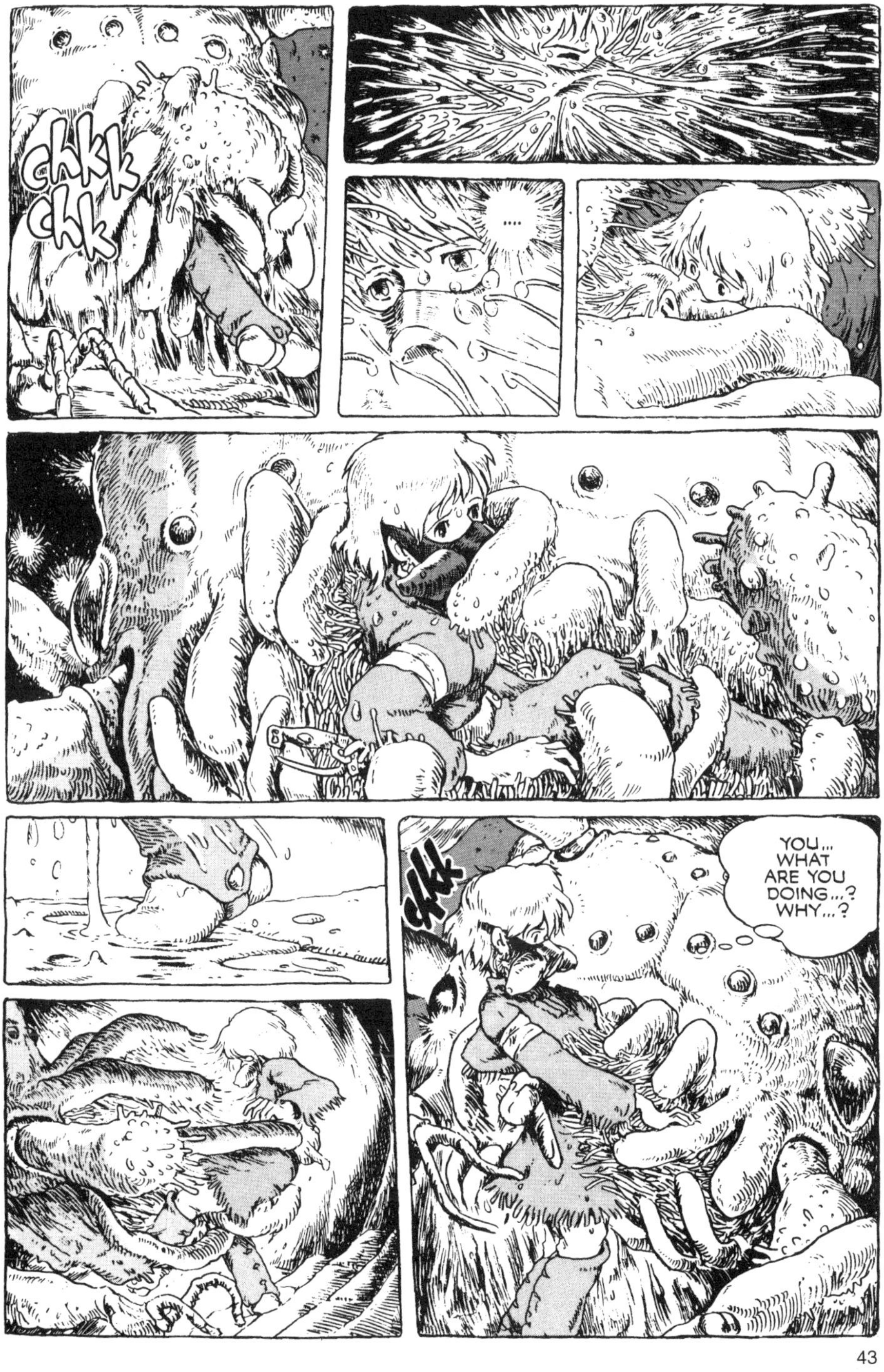
CHKK
CHK
....
CHKK
YOU... WHAT ARE YOU DOING...? WHY...?

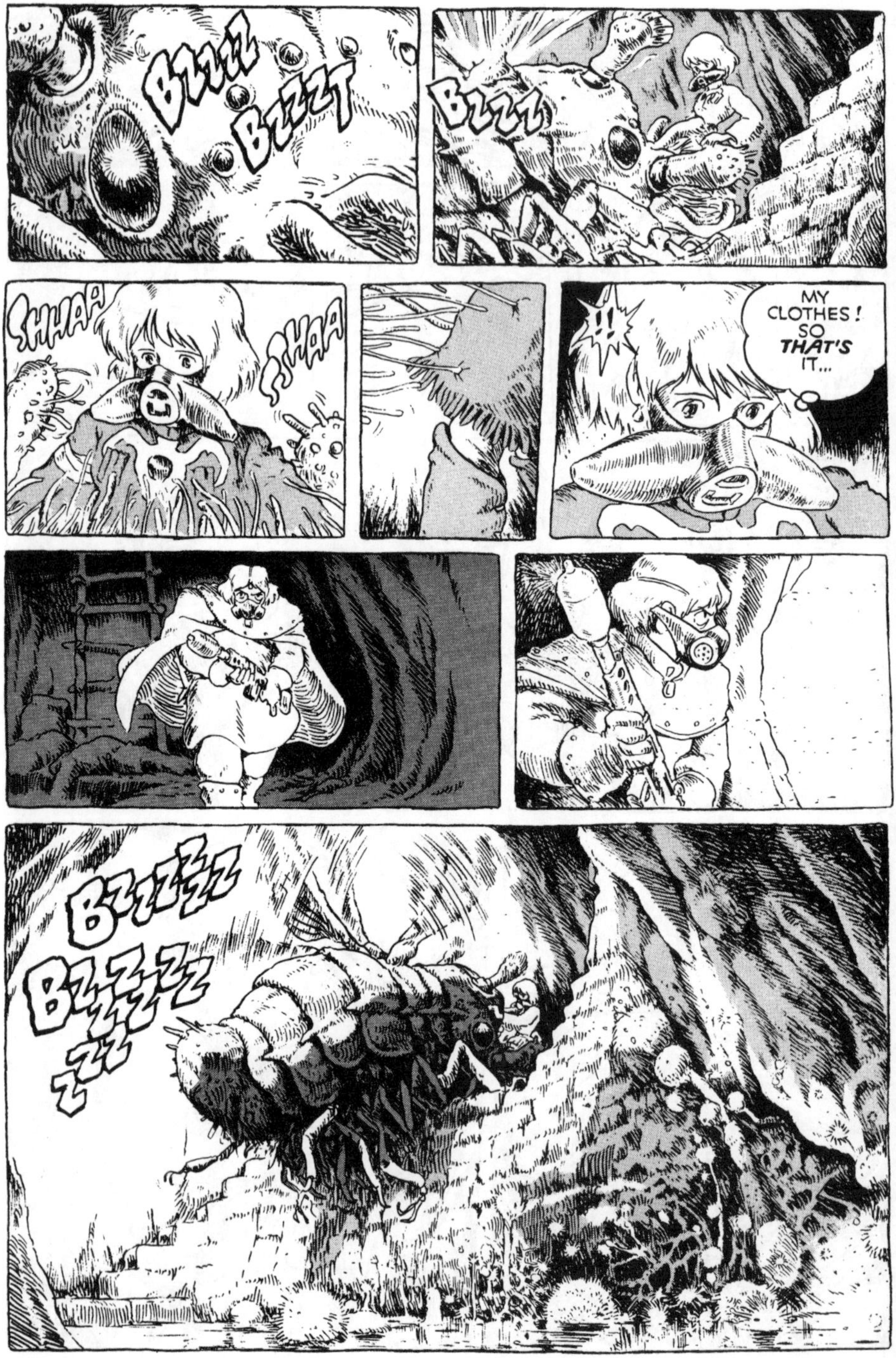
BZZZZ
BZZZZT
BZZZZ
SHHAA
SHHAA
!!
MY CLOTHES! SO *THAT'S* IT...
BZZZZZZZ
BZZZZZZZZZZ

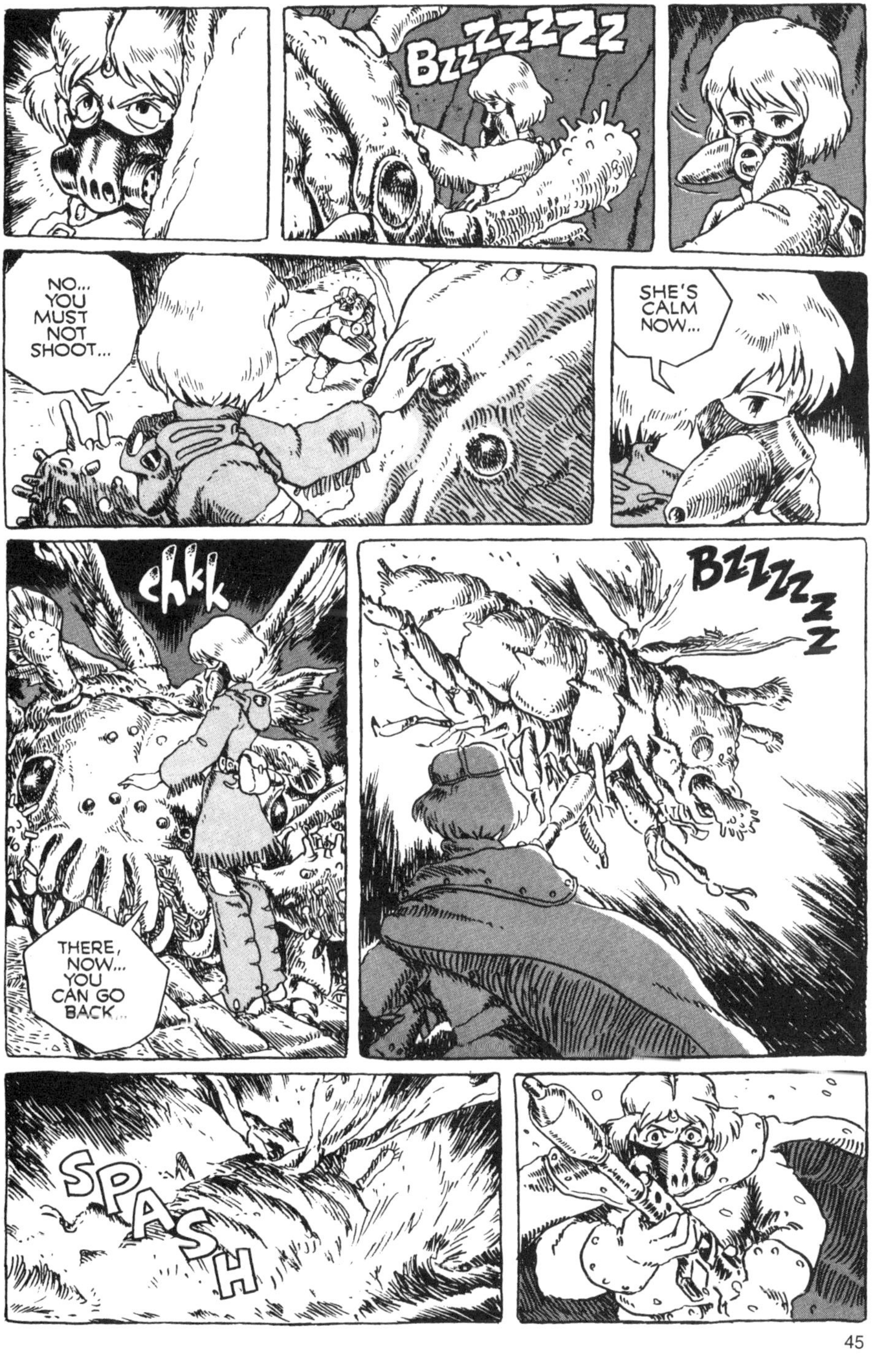
BZZZZZZZZ
NO... YOU MUST NOT SHOOT...
SHE'S CALM NOW...
chkk
THERE, NOW... YOU CAN GO BACK...
BZZZZZZZ
SPASH

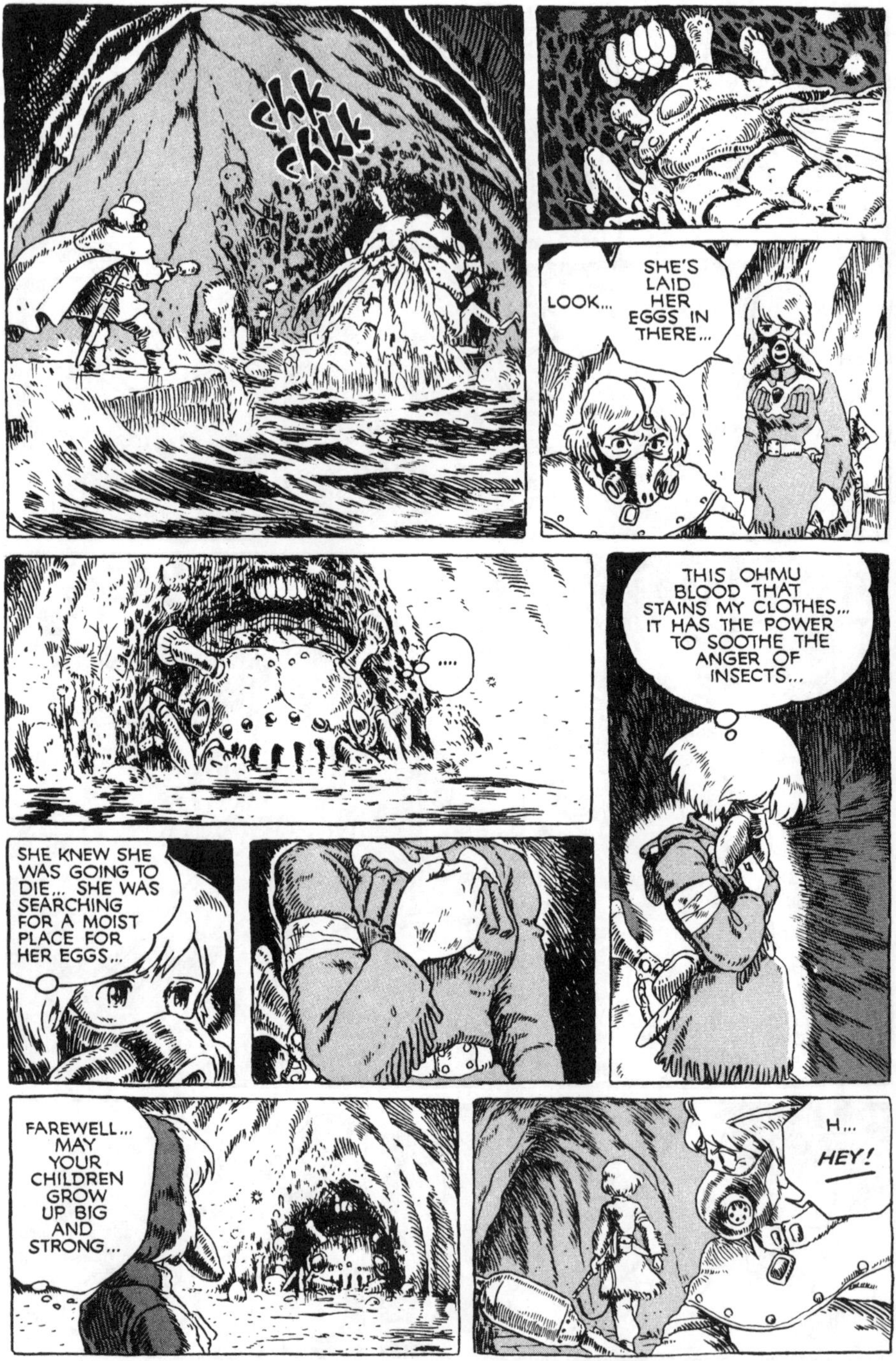

CHK CHKK
LOOK...
SHE'S LAID HER EGGS IN THERE...
....
THIS OHMU BLOOD THAT STAINS MY CLOTHES... IT HAS THE POWER TO SOOTHE THE ANGER OF INSECTS...
SHE KNEW SHE WAS GOING TO DIE... SHE WAS SEARCHING FOR A MOIST PLACE FOR HER EGGS...
FAREWELL... MAY YOUR CHILDREN GROW UP BIG AND STRONG...
H...
HEY!

YOU! IT'S *YOU*!

YOU GOT AWAY!!

ARE YOU OKAY? YOU'RE WHITE AS A GHOST...!

huhhh huhhh

FORGIVE US... WE RAN AWAY AND LEFT YOU ALONE. WE WERE ONLY THINKING OF OURSELVES...

IT'S ALL RIGHT.

WHAT'S MORE IMPORTANT IS TO GET THE BOY WHO BREATHED THE MIASMA BACK TO THE SHIP.

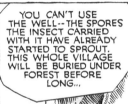

YOU CAN'T USE THE WELL-- THE SPORES THE INSECT CARRIED WITH IT HAVE ALREADY STARTED TO SPROUT. THIS WHOLE VILLAGE WILL BE BURIED UNDER FOREST BEFORE LONG...

hahh

GET SOME EXPLOSIVES! WE'LL BLAST THE ENTRANCES AND SEAL IT UNDER-GROUND!

WE'LL... .....?

SHOOM

WHSST

HEY... *HEY!!*

DAMMIT!! WAIT FOR *ME*!

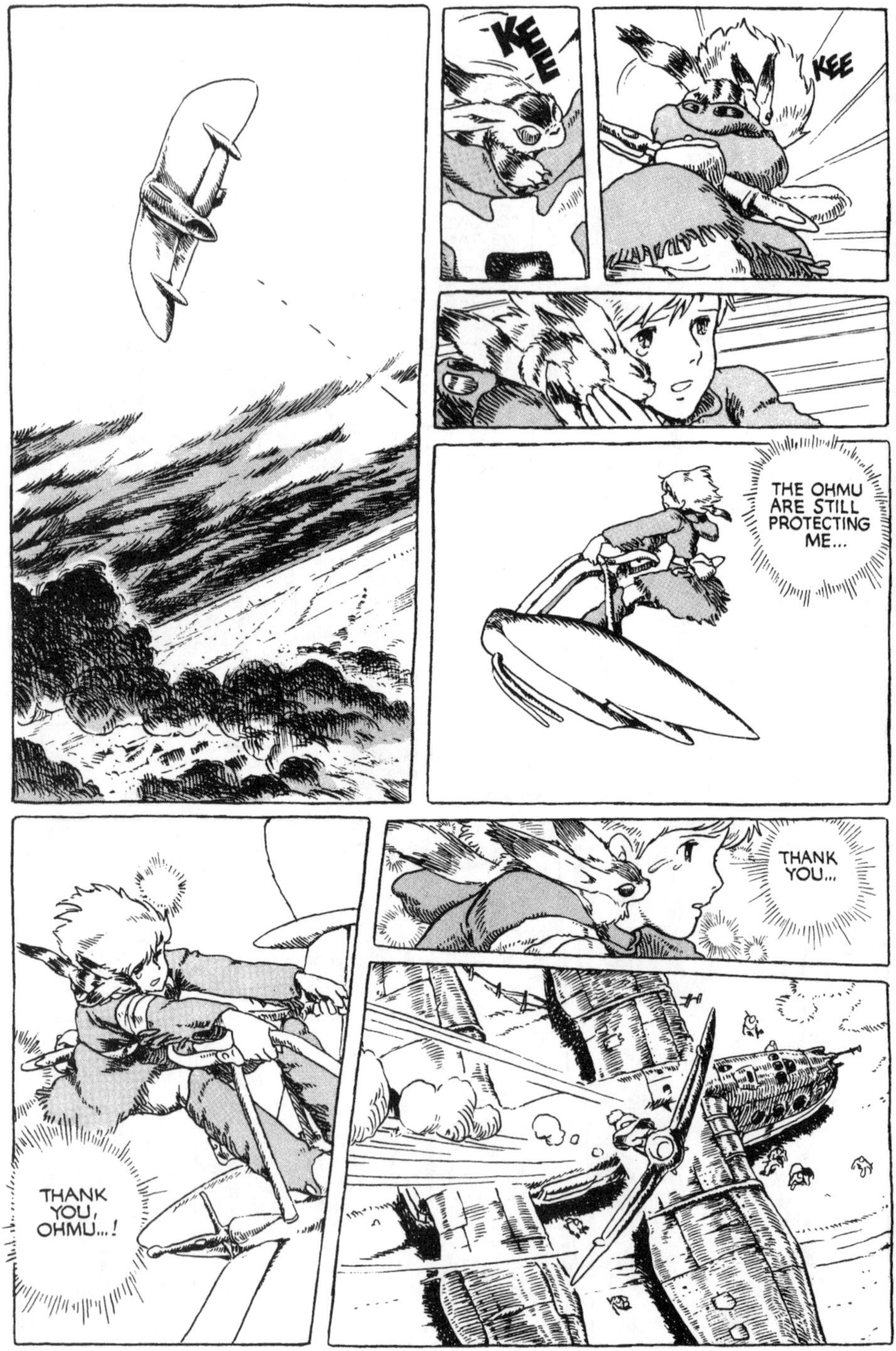
KEEE
KEE
THE OHMU ARE STILL PROTECTING ME...
THANK YOU...
THANK YOU, OHMU...!

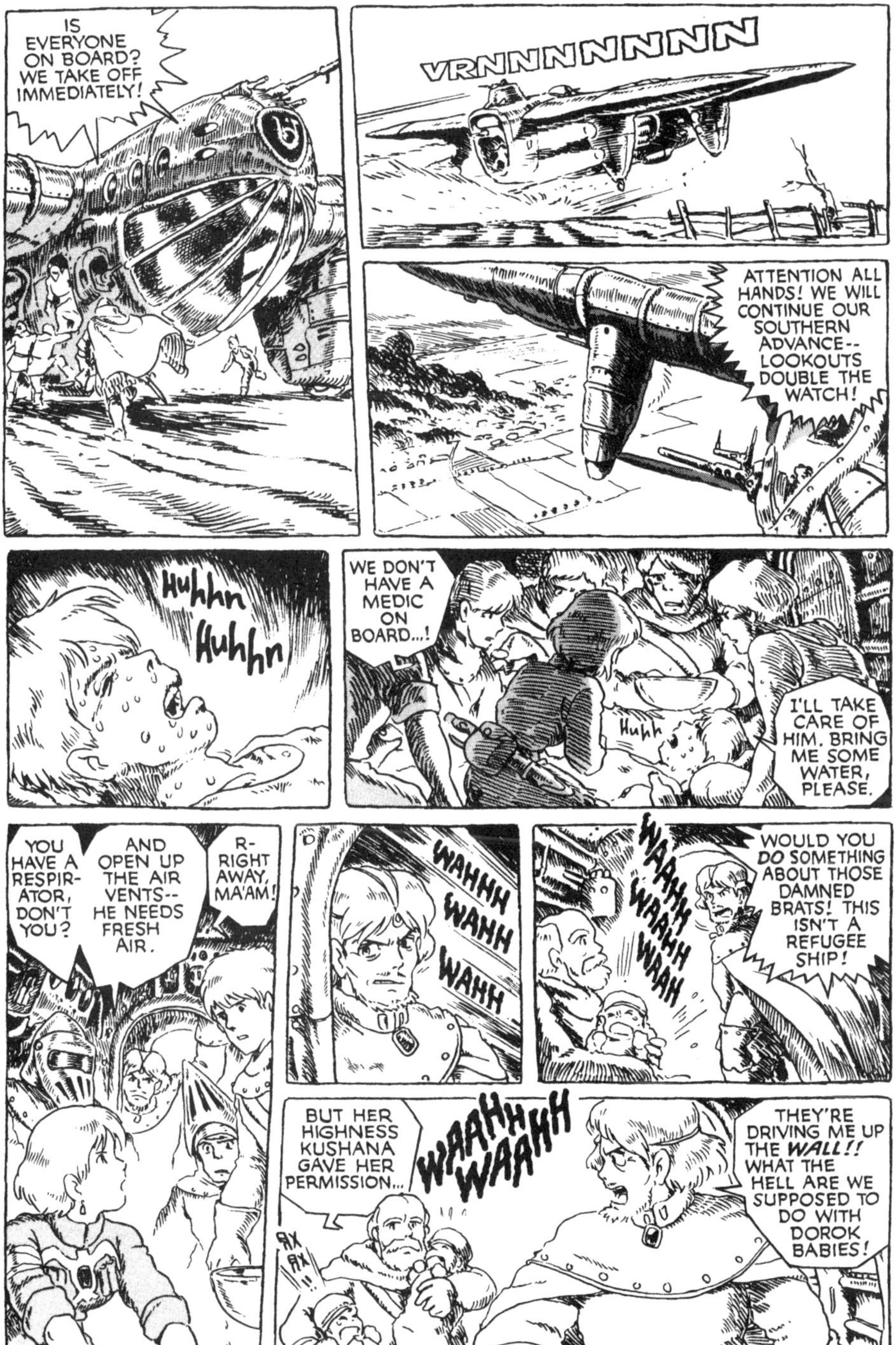
IS EVERYONE ON BOARD? WE TAKE OFF IMMEDIATELY!
VRNNNNNNNN
ATTENTION ALL HANDS! WE WILL CONTINUE OUR SOUTHERN ADVANCE-- LOOKOUTS DOUBLE THE WATCH!
Huhhn Huhhn
WE DON'T HAVE A MEDIC ON BOARD...!
I'LL TAKE CARE OF HIM. BRING ME SOME WATER, PLEASE.
Huhh
YOU HAVE A RESPIR-ATOR, DON'T YOU?
AND OPEN UP THE AIR VENTS-- HE NEEDS FRESH AIR.
R-RIGHT AWAY, MA'AM!
WAHHH WAHH WAHH
WOULD YOU *DO* SOMETHING ABOUT THOSE DAMNED BRATS! THIS ISN'T A REFUGEE SHIP!
WAAHH WAAHH WAAH
BUT HER HIGHNESS KUSHANA GAVE HER PERMISSION...
WAAHH WAAHH
THEY'RE DRIVING ME UP THE ***WALL!!*** WHAT THE HELL ARE WE SUPPOSED TO DO WITH DOROK BABIES!

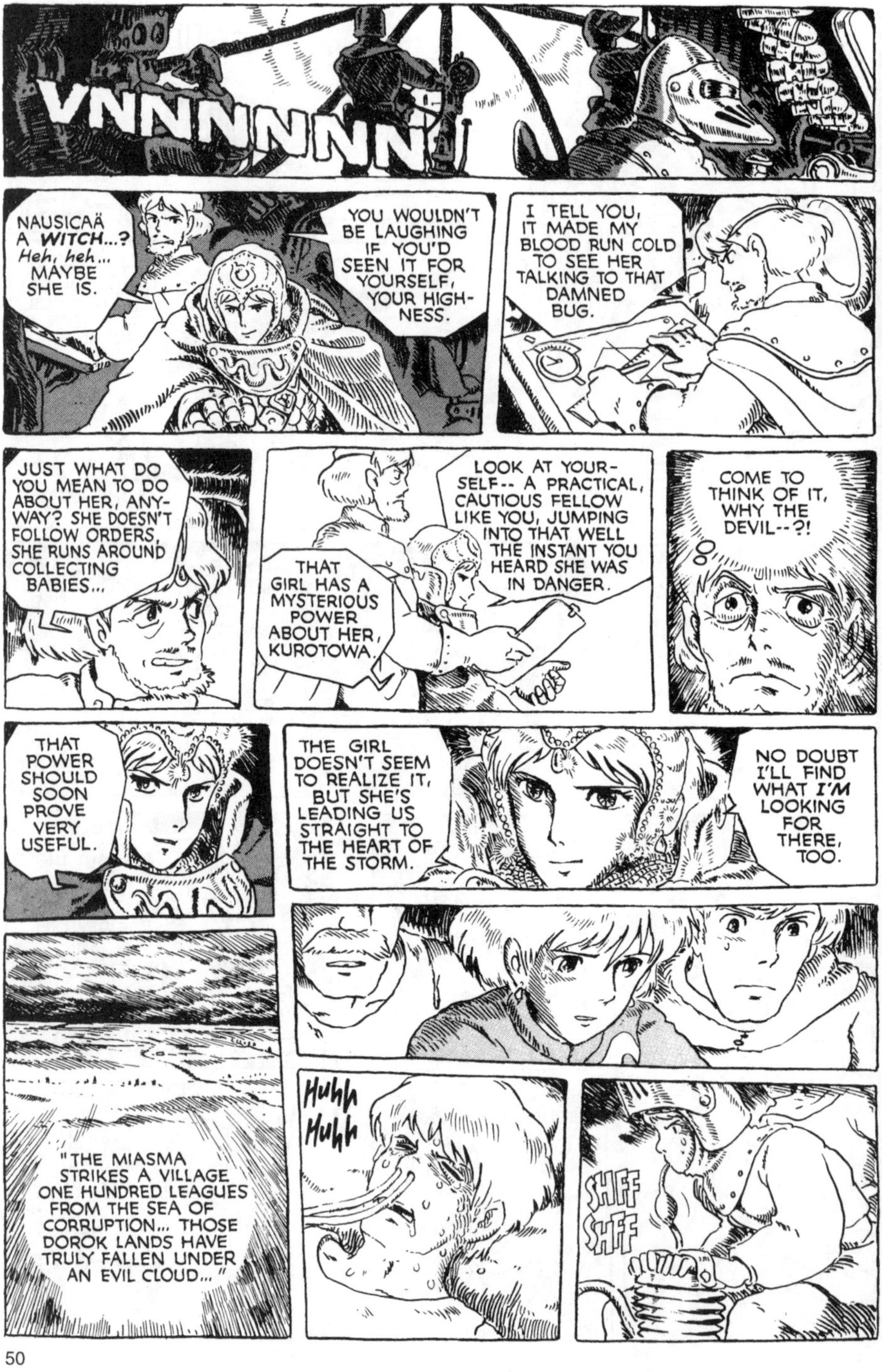
VNNNNNNN
NAUSICAÄ A *WITCH*...? *Heh, heh*... MAYBE SHE IS.
YOU WOULDN'T BE LAUGHING IF YOU'D SEEN IT FOR YOURSELF, YOUR HIGHNESS.
I TELL YOU, IT MADE MY BLOOD RUN COLD TO SEE HER TALKING TO THAT DAMNED BUG.
JUST WHAT DO YOU MEAN TO DO ABOUT HER, ANYWAY? SHE DOESN'T FOLLOW ORDERS, SHE RUNS AROUND COLLECTING BABIES...
LOOK AT YOURSELF-- A PRACTICAL, CAUTIOUS FELLOW LIKE YOU, JUMPING INTO THAT WELL THE INSTANT YOU HEARD SHE WAS IN DANGER.
THAT GIRL HAS A MYSTERIOUS POWER ABOUT HER, KUROTOWA.
COME TO THINK OF IT, WHY THE DEVIL--?!
THAT POWER SHOULD SOON PROVE VERY USEFUL.
THE GIRL DOESN'T SEEM TO REALIZE IT, BUT SHE'S LEADING US STRAIGHT TO THE HEART OF THE STORM.
NO DOUBT I'LL FIND WHAT *I'M* LOOKING FOR THERE, TOO.
"THE MIASMA STRIKES A VILLAGE ONE HUNDRED LEAGUES FROM THE SEA OF CORRUPTION... THOSE DOROK LANDS HAVE TRULY FALLEN UNDER AN EVIL CLOUD..."
HUHH HUHH
SHFF SHFF

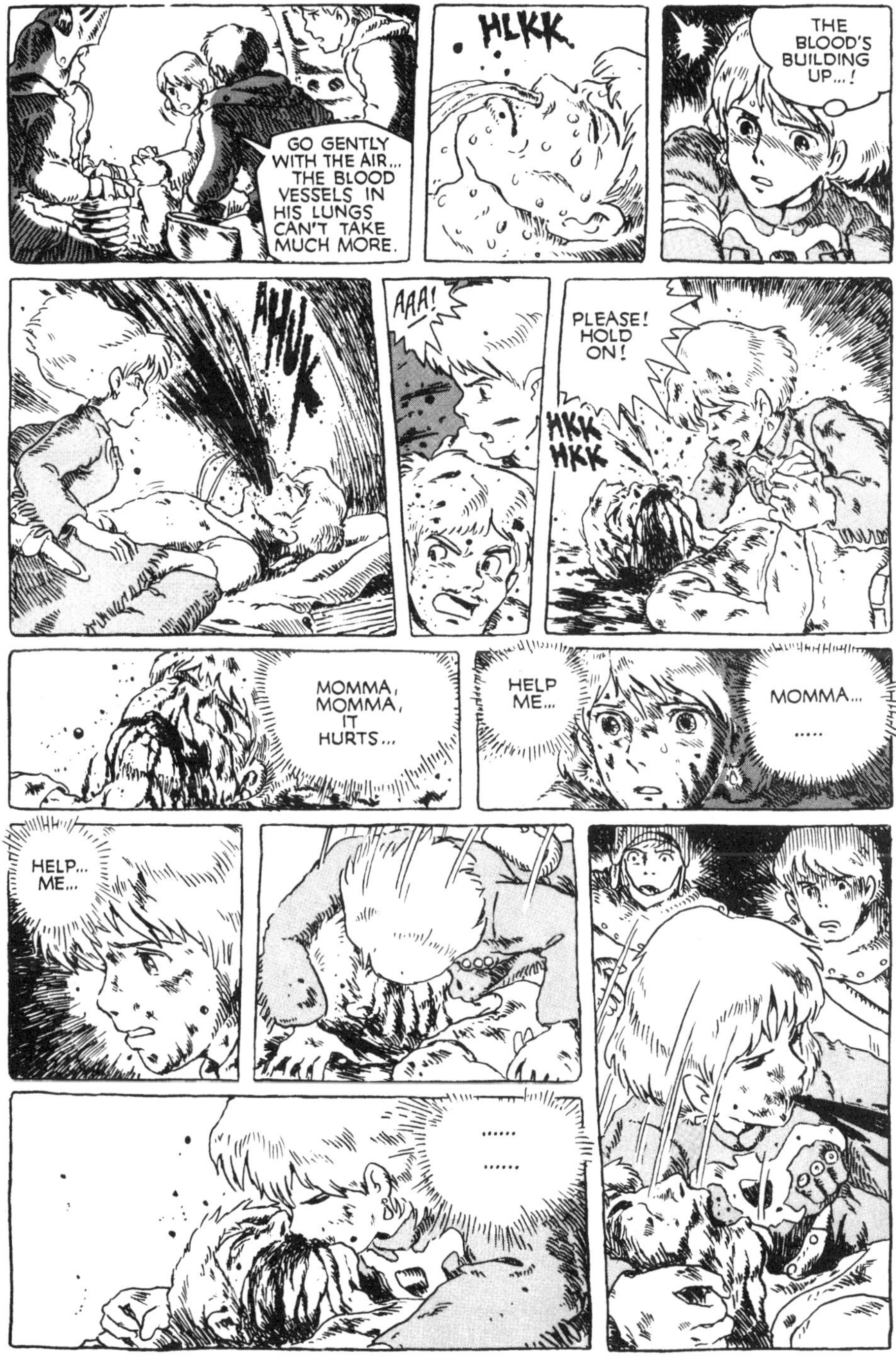
GO GENTLY WITH THE AIR... THE BLOOD VESSELS IN HIS LUNGS CAN'T TAKE MUCH MORE.
HLKK
THE BLOOD'S BUILDING UP...!
AHUK
AAA!
PLEASE! HOLD ON!
HKK HKK
MOMMA, MOMMA, IT HURTS...
HELP ME...
MOMMA... .....
HELP... ME...
....

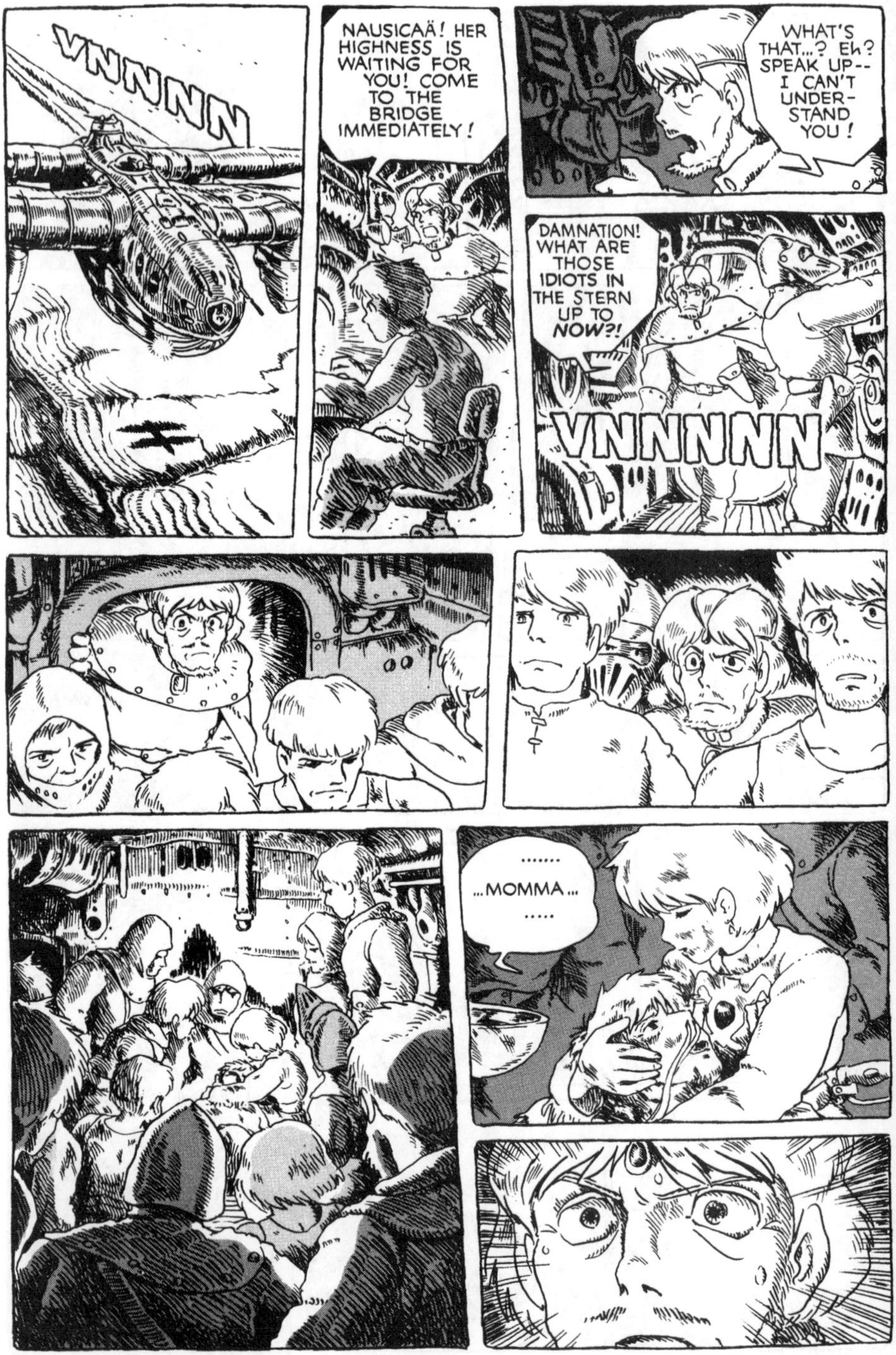
VNNNNN
NAUSICAÄ! HER HIGHNESS IS WAITING FOR YOU! COME TO THE BRIDGE IMMEDIATELY!
WHAT'S THAT...? Eh? SPEAK UP-- I CAN'T UNDER-STAND YOU!
DAMNATION! WHAT ARE THOSE IDIOTS IN THE STERN UP TO NOW?!
VNNNNNN
....
...MOMMA...
.....

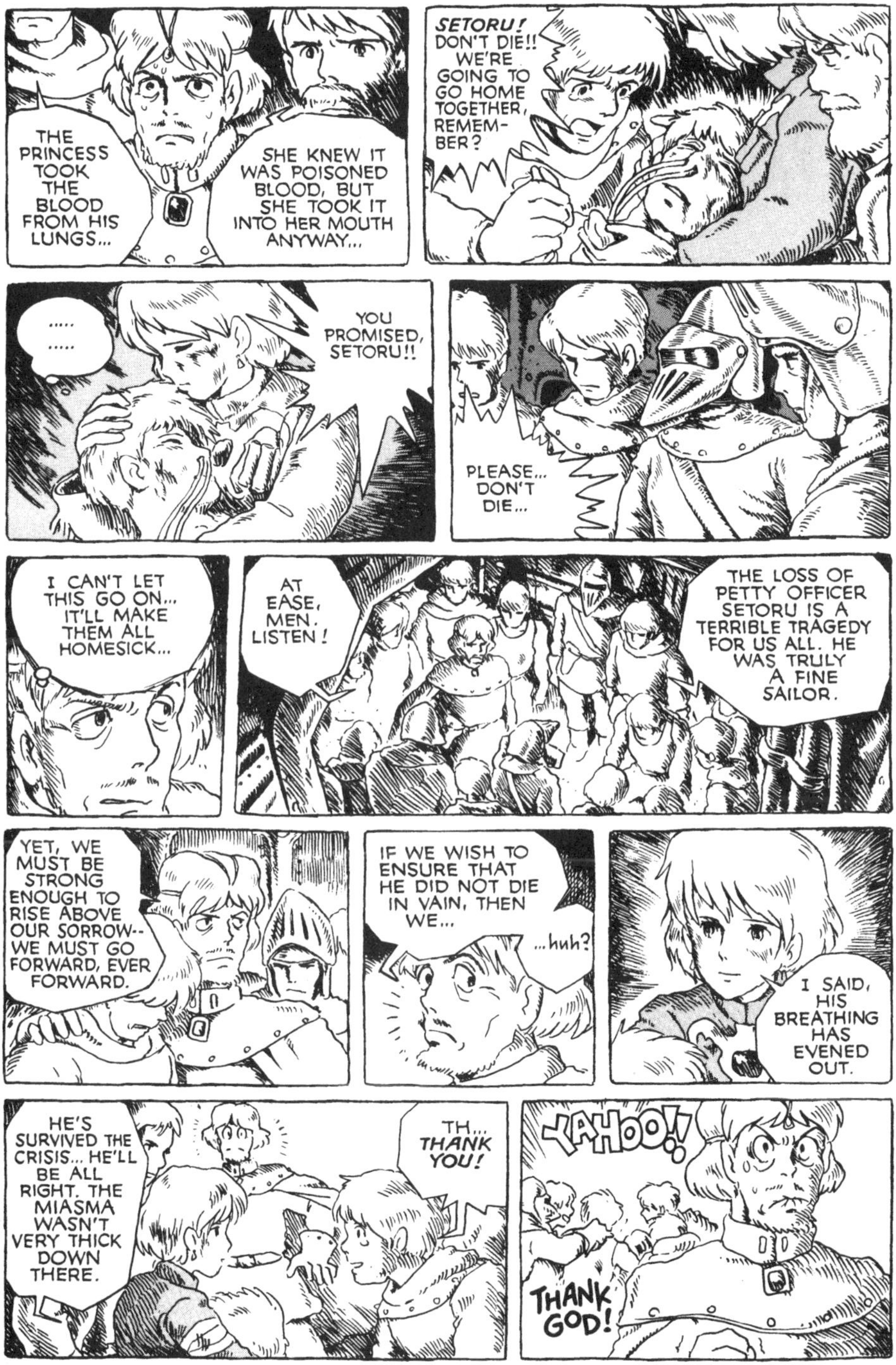

THE PRINCESS TOOK THE BLOOD FROM HIS LUNGS...
SHE KNEW IT WAS POISONED BLOOD, BUT SHE TOOK IT INTO HER MOUTH ANYWAY...
SETORU! DON'T DIE!! WE'RE GOING TO GO HOME TOGETHER, REMEMBER?
.....
.....
YOU PROMISED, SETORU!!
PLEASE... DON'T DIE...
I CAN'T LET THIS GO ON... IT'LL MAKE THEM ALL HOMESICK...
AT EASE, MEN. LISTEN!
THE LOSS OF PETTY OFFICER SETORU IS A TERRIBLE TRAGEDY FOR US ALL. HE WAS TRULY A FINE SAILOR.
YET, WE MUST BE STRONG ENOUGH TO RISE ABOVE OUR SORROW-- WE MUST GO FORWARD, EVER FORWARD.
IF WE WISH TO ENSURE THAT HE DID NOT DIE IN VAIN, THEN WE...
...huh?
I SAID, HIS BREATHING HAS EVENED OUT.
HE'S SURVIVED THE CRISIS... HE'LL BE ALL RIGHT. THE MIASMA WASN'T VERY THICK DOWN THERE.
TH... THANK YOU!
YAHOO!!
THANK GOD!

FORGIVE ME... I DIDN'T MEAN TO FORCE THEM ON YOU...

VNNNN

NO, NO...IT'S NOTH-ING.

NOTHING COMPARED TO ALL *YOU'VE* DONE, eh?

MY MOTHER DIED WHEN I WAS STILL A KID...

I HAD TO RAISE MY LITTLE SISTER, FEEDING HER THIS WAY...

DOROK OR NO, DOESN'T MAKE ANY DIFFERENCE ...BABIES ARE BABIES...

PRINCESS NAUSICAÄ...? THIS IS MY WATER RATION... PLEASE USE IT TO WASH THE BLOOD OFF YOUR FACE...

Oh, THANK YOU!

THAT DAMN GIRL...

KANG KANG KANG KANG

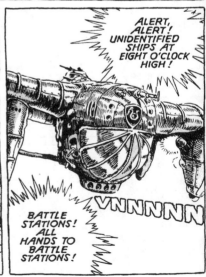

ALERT, ALERT! UNIDENTIFIED SHIPS AT EIGHT O'CLOCK HIGH!

VNNNNN

BATTLE STATIONS! ALL HANDS TO BATTLE STATIONS!

54

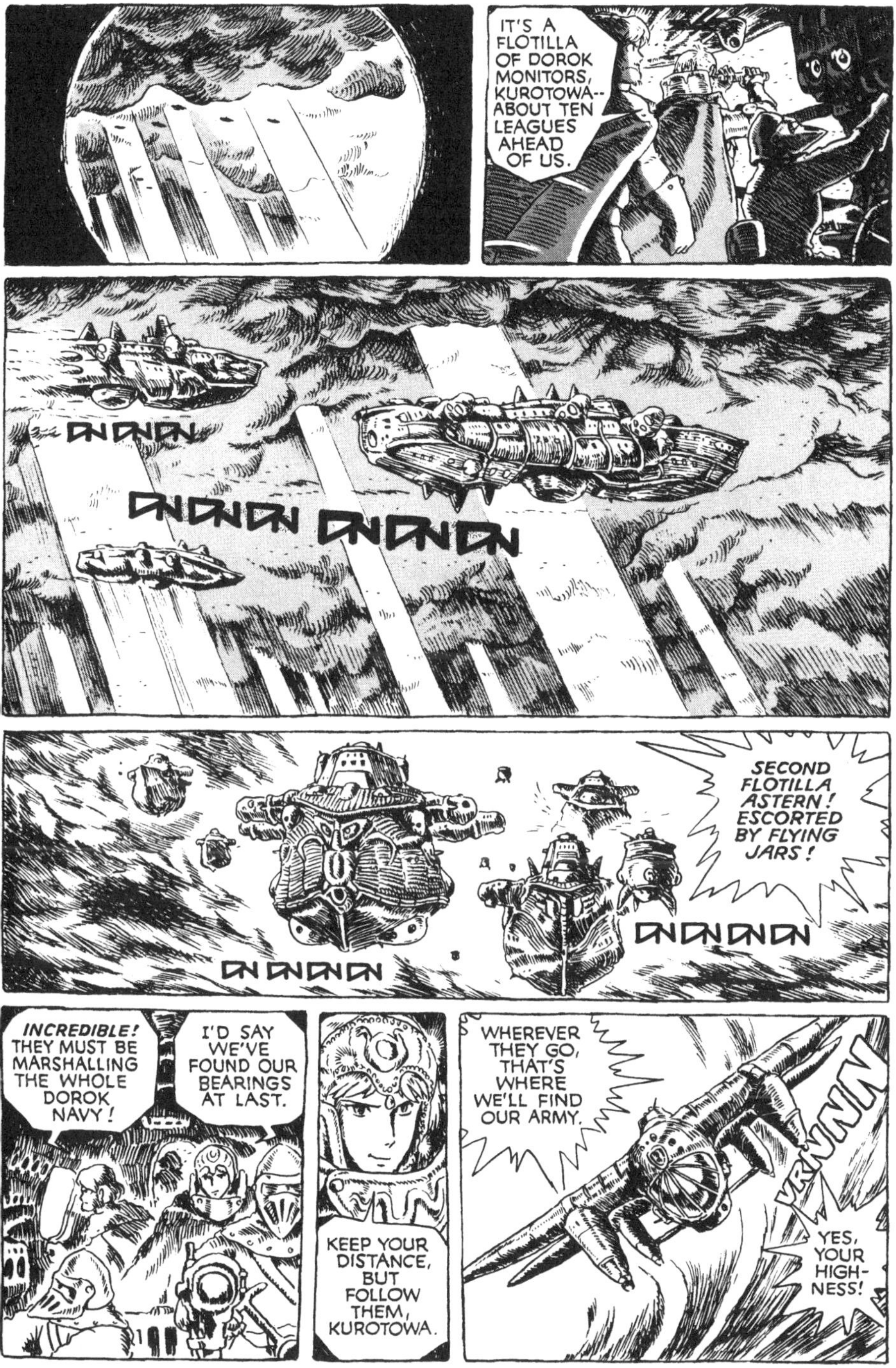
IT'S A FLOTILLA OF DOROK MONITORS, KUROTOWA-- ABOUT TEN LEAGUES AHEAD OF US.
DN DN DN
DN DN DN
DN DN DN DN
SECOND FLOTILLA ASTERN! ESCORTED BY FLYING JARS!
DN DN DN DN
DN DN DN DN
INCREDIBLE! THEY MUST BE MARSHALLING THE WHOLE DOROK NAVY!
I'D SAY WE'VE FOUND OUR BEARINGS AT LAST.
KEEP YOUR DISTANCE, BUT FOLLOW THEM, KUROTOWA.
WHEREVER THEY GO, THAT'S WHERE WE'LL FIND OUR ARMY.
VRNNNN
YES, YOUR HIGH-NESS!

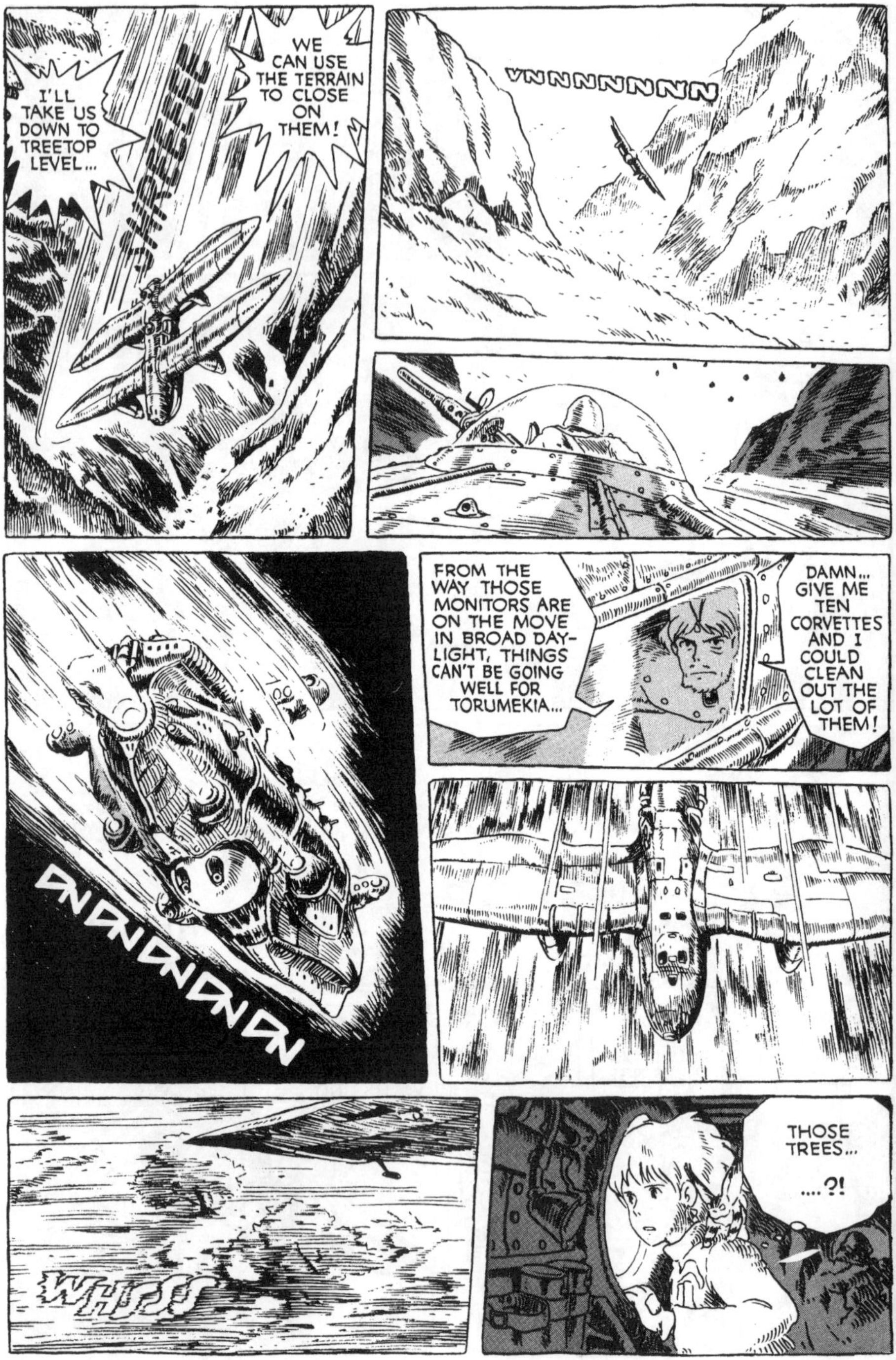
I'LL TAKE US DOWN TO TREETOP LEVEL...
WE CAN USE THE TERRAIN TO CLOSE ON THEM!
FROM THE WAY THOSE MONITORS ARE ON THE MOVE IN BROAD DAY-LIGHT, THINGS CAN'T BE GOING WELL FOR TORUMEKIA...
DAMN... GIVE ME TEN CORVETTES AND I COULD CLEAN OUT THE LOT OF THEM!
THOSE TREES...
....?!

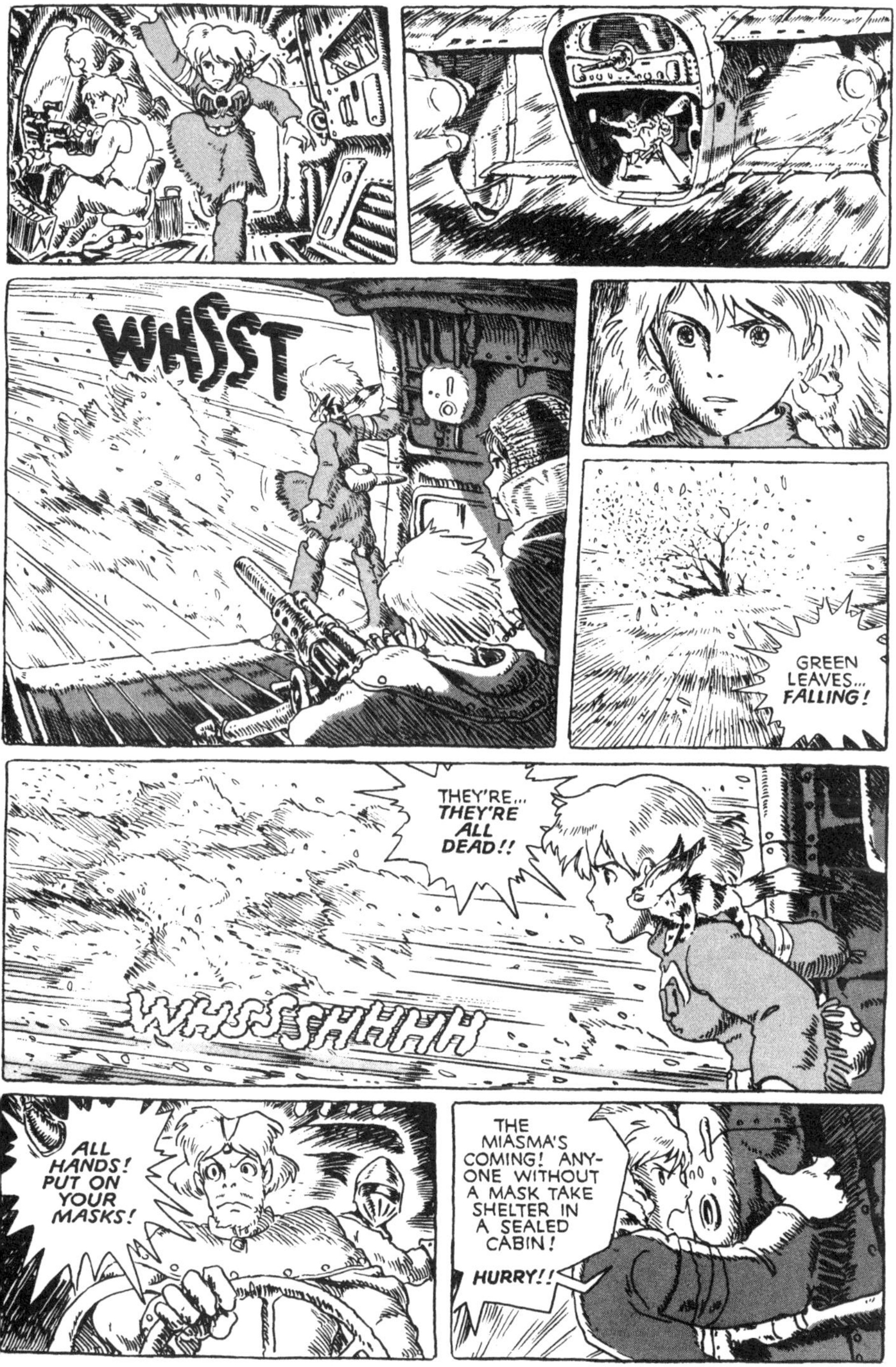
WHSST
GREEN LEAVES... FALLING!
THEY'RE... THEY'RE ALL DEAD!!
WHSSSHHHH
ALL HANDS! PUT ON YOUR MASKS!
THE MIASMA'S COMING! ANYONE WITHOUT A MASK TAKE SHELTER IN A SEALED CABIN!
HURRY!!

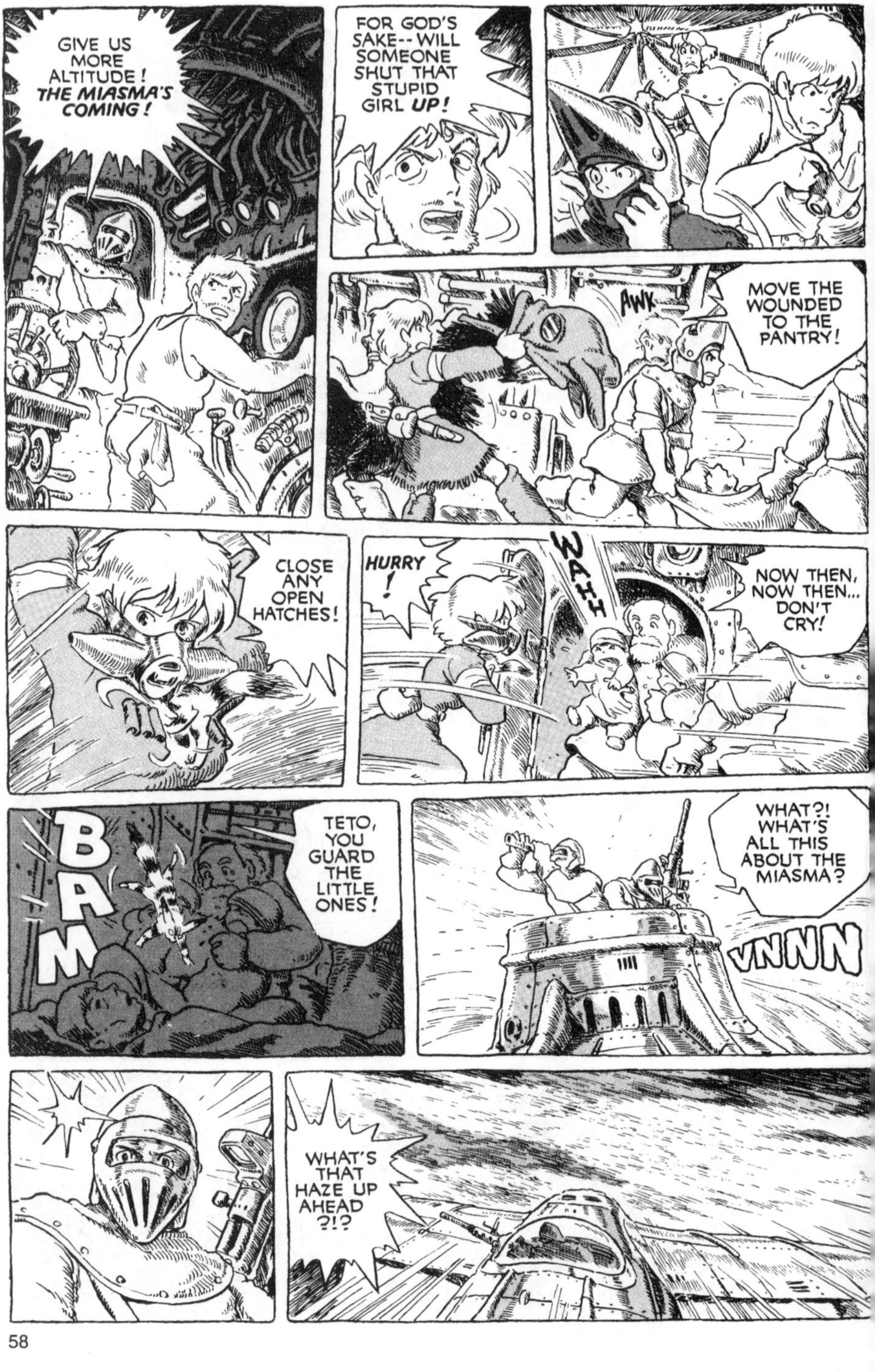
GIVE US MORE ALTITUDE! ***THE MIASMA'S COMING!***
FOR GOD'S SAKE--WILL SOMEONE SHUT THAT STUPID GIRL ***UP!***
AWK
MOVE THE WOUNDED TO THE PANTRY!
CLOSE ANY OPEN HATCHES!
HURRY!
WAHH
NOW THEN, NOW THEN... DON'T CRY!
BAM
TETO, YOU GUARD THE LITTLE ONES!
WHAT?! WHAT'S ALL THIS ABOUT THE MIASMA?
VNNN
WHAT'S THAT HAZE UP AHEAD?!?

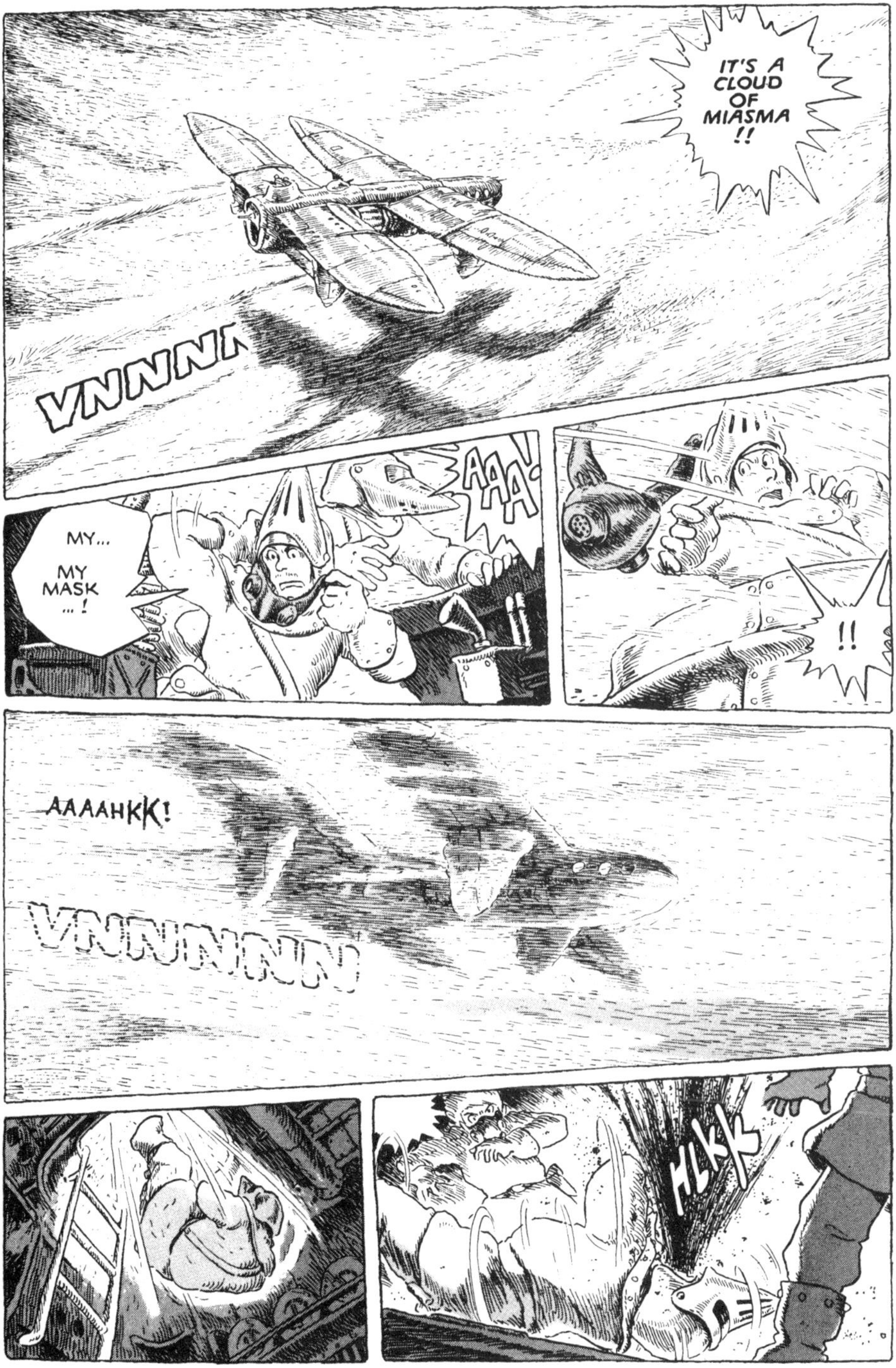
IT'S A CLOUD OF MIASMA !!
VNNNN
AAAA!
MY... MY MASK ...!
!!
AAAAHKK!
VNNNNNN
HLKK

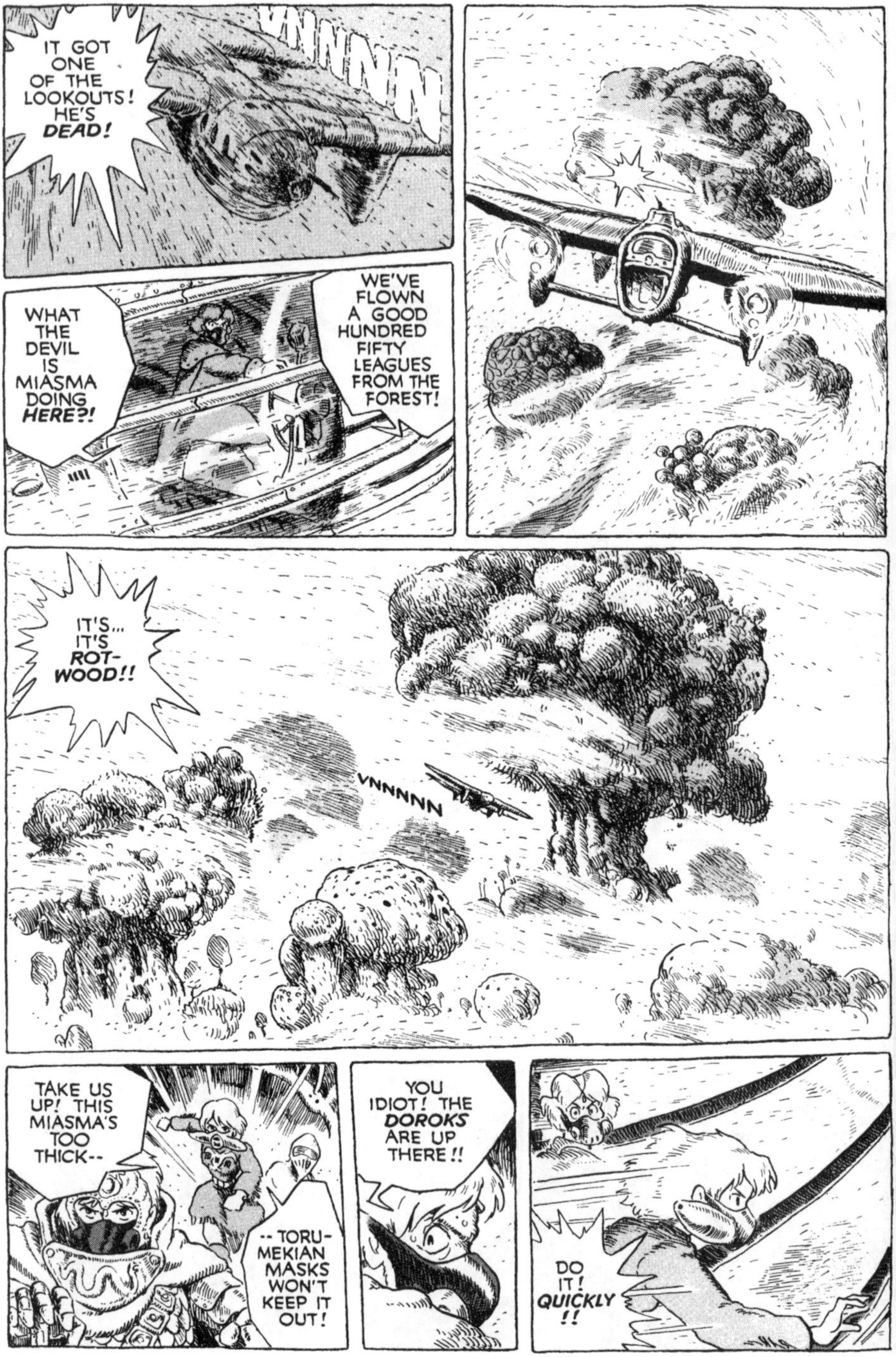
IT GOT ONE OF THE LOOKOUTS! HE'S DEAD!
VNNNNNN
WHAT THE DEVIL IS MIASMA DOING HERE?!
WE'VE FLOWN A GOOD HUNDRED FIFTY LEAGUES FROM THE FOREST!
IT'S... IT'S ROT-WOOD!!
VNNNNNN
TAKE US UP! THIS MIASMA'S TOO THICK--
--TORU-MEKIAN MASKS WON'T KEEP IT OUT!
YOU IDIOT! THE DOROKS ARE UP THERE!!
DO IT! QUICKLY!!

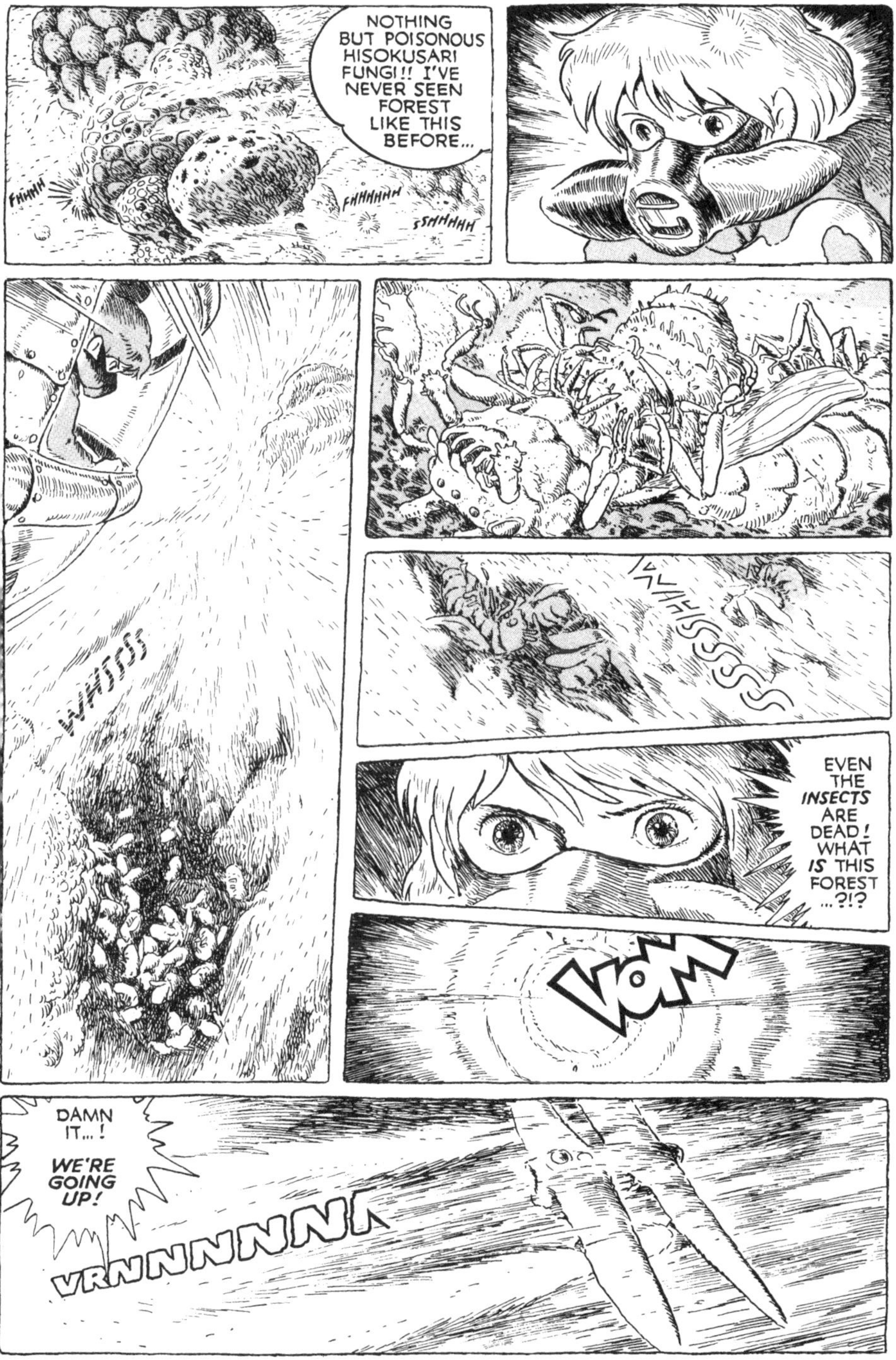
NOTHING BUT POISONOUS HISOKUSARI FUNGI!! I'VE NEVER SEEN FOREST LIKE THIS BEFORE...
FHHHH
FHHHHHH
SSHHHHHH
WHSSSS
WHISSSSSS
EVEN THE INSECTS ARE DEAD! WHAT IS THIS FOREST ...?!?
VOM
DAMN IT...!
WE'RE GOING UP!
VRNNNNNN

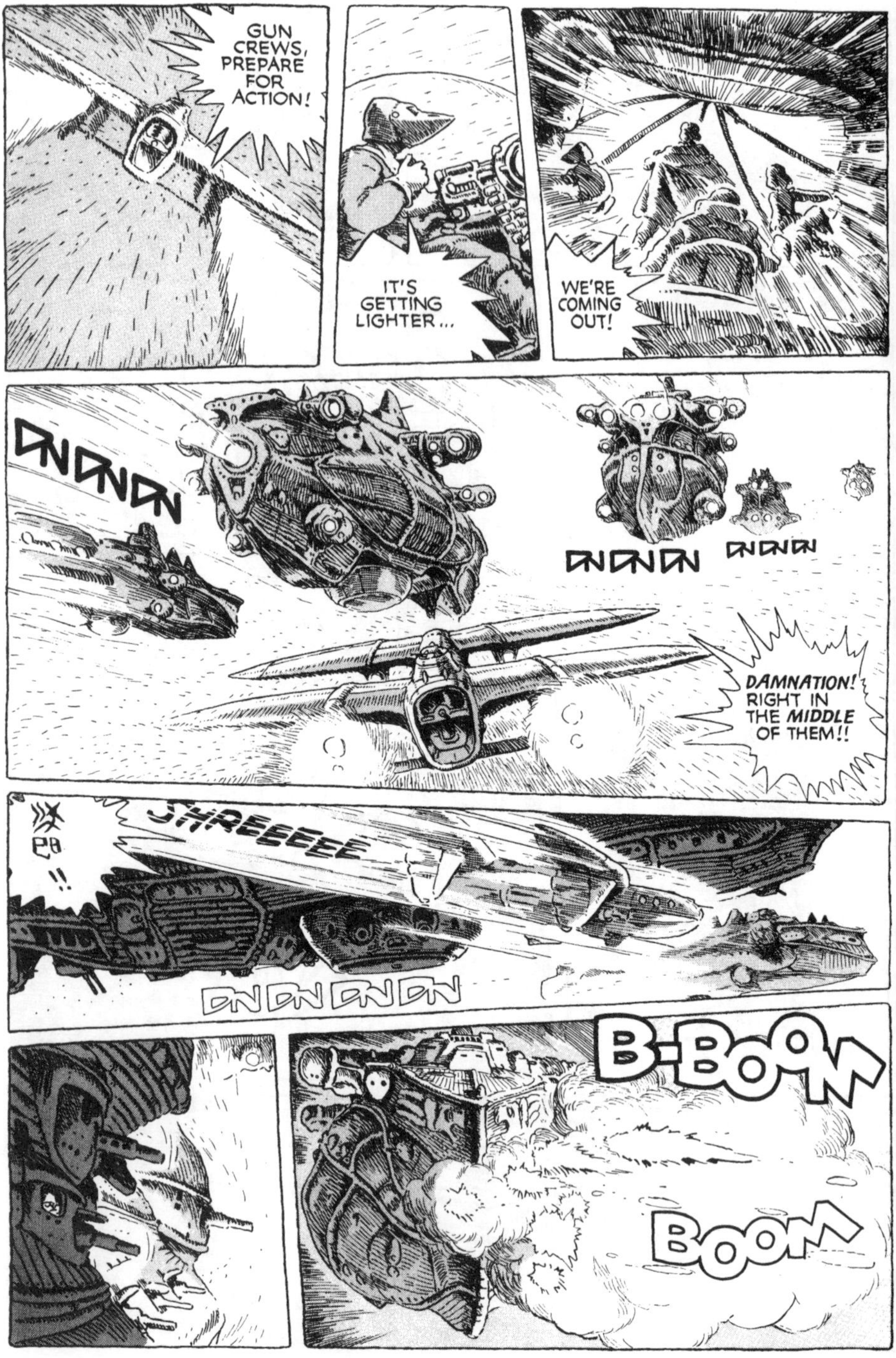
GUN CREWS, PREPARE FOR ACTION!
IT'S GETTING LIGHTER...
WE'RE COMING OUT!
DN DN DN
DN DN DN
DN DN DN
DAMNATION! RIGHT IN THE MIDDLE OF THEM!!
SHREEEEEE
DN DN DN DN DN
B-BOOM
BOOM

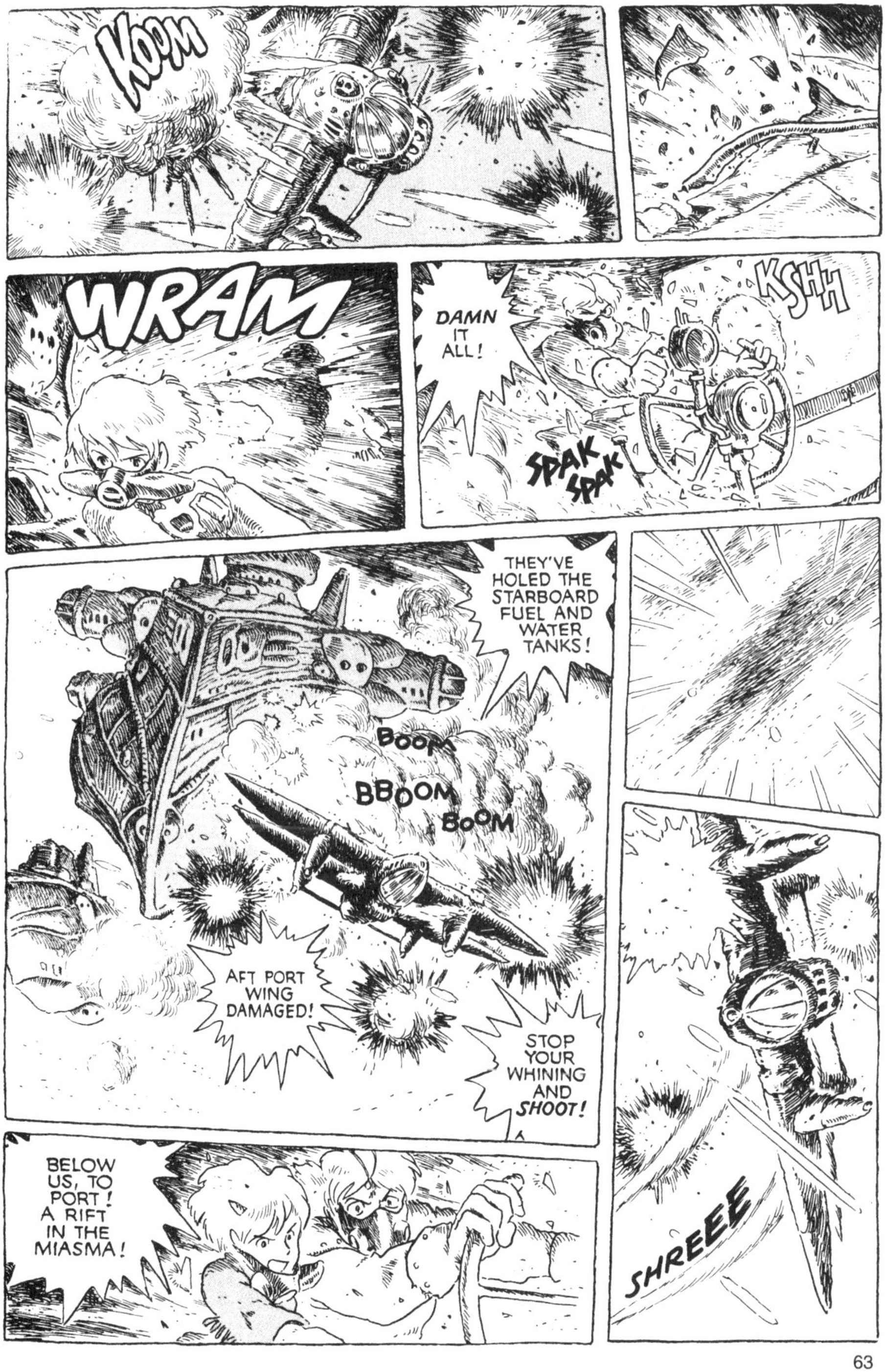
KOOM
WRAM
DAMN IT ALL!
KSHH
SPAK SPAK
THEY'VE HOLED THE STARBOARD FUEL AND WATER TANKS!
BOOM
BBOOM
BOOM
AFT PORT WING DAMAGED!
STOP YOUR WHINING AND SHOOT!
BELOW US, TO PORT! A RIFT IN THE MIASMA!
SHREEE

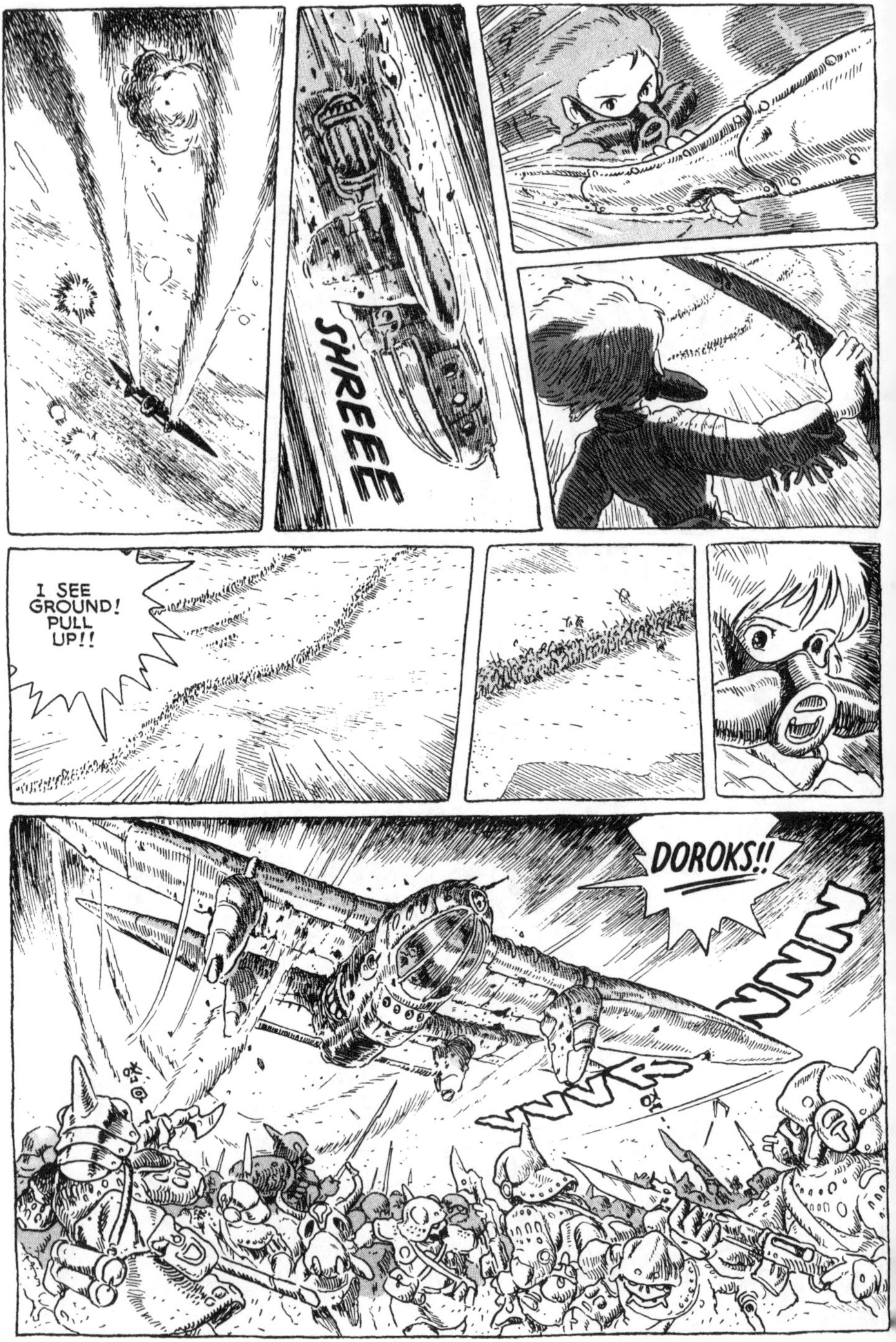
SHREEEE
I SEE GROUND! PULL UP!!
DOROKS!!
NNNN

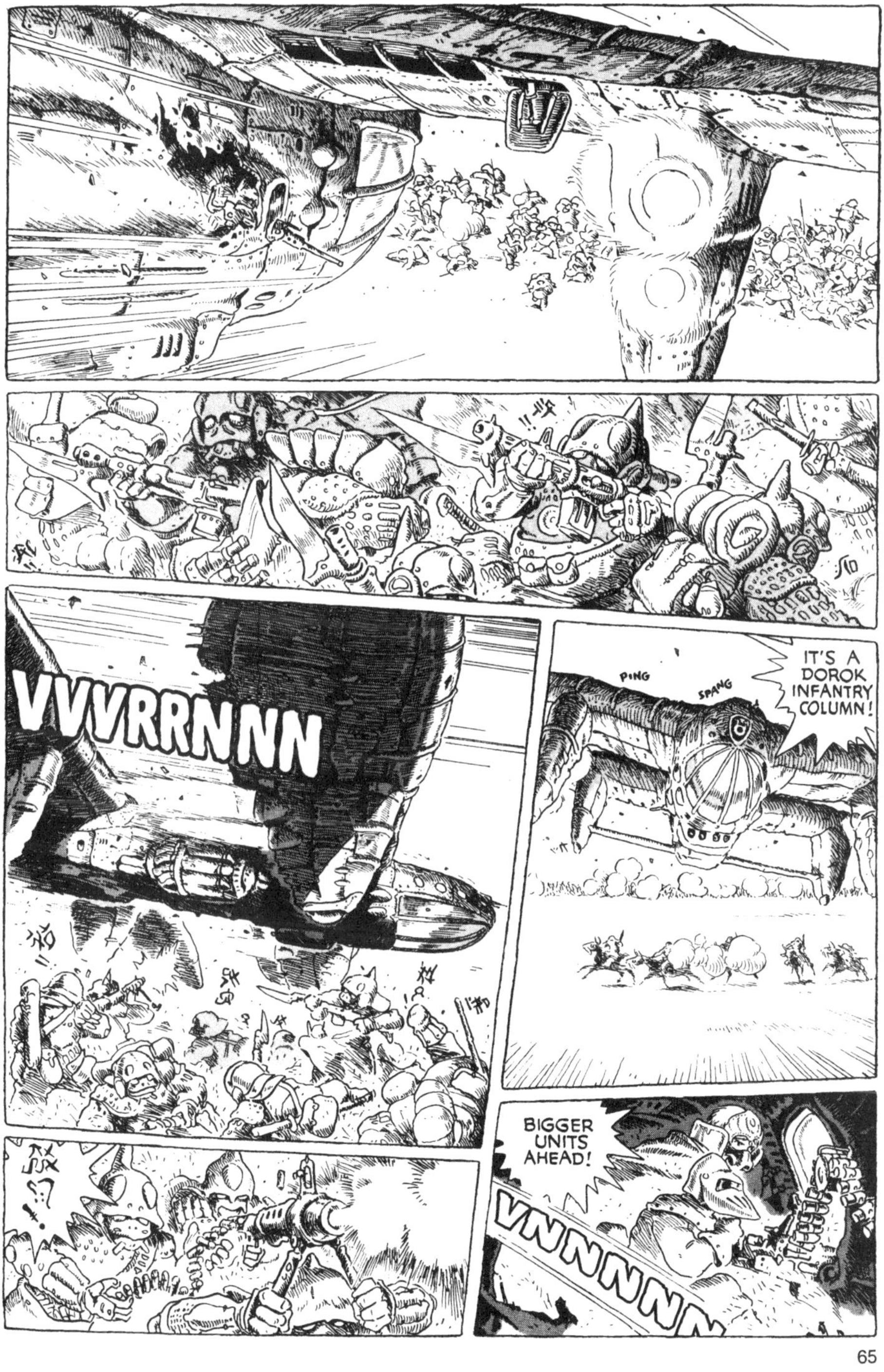
VVVRRNNN
PING
SPANG
IT'S A DOROK INFANTRY COLUMN!
BIGGER UNITS AHEAD!
VNNNNNN

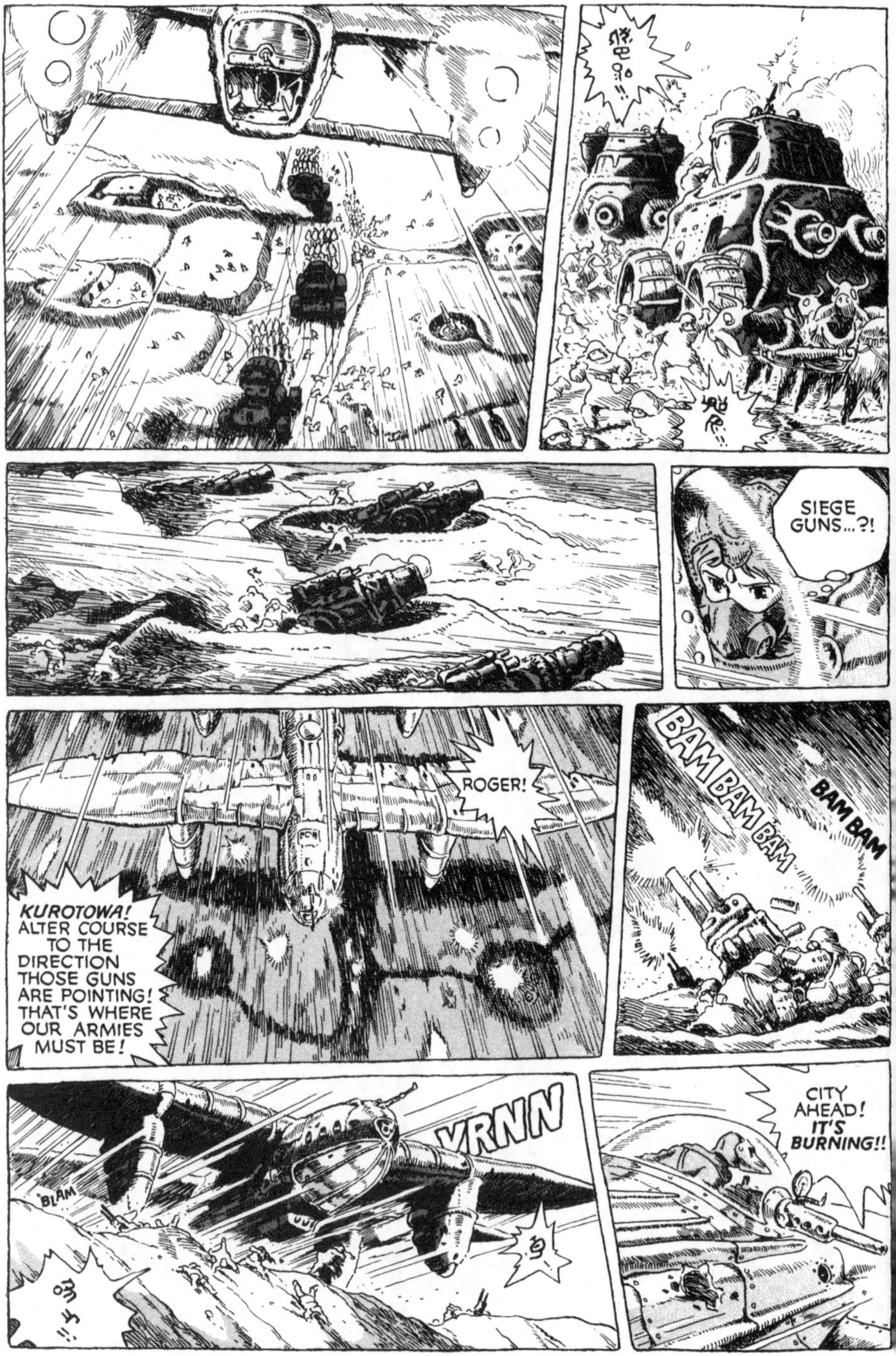
SIEGE GUNS...?!
ROGER!
BAM BAM BAM
BAM BAM
KUROTOWA! ALTER COURSE TO THE DIRECTION THOSE GUNS ARE POINTING! THAT'S WHERE OUR ARMIES MUST BE!
VRNN
BLAM
CITY AHEAD! IT'S BURNING!!

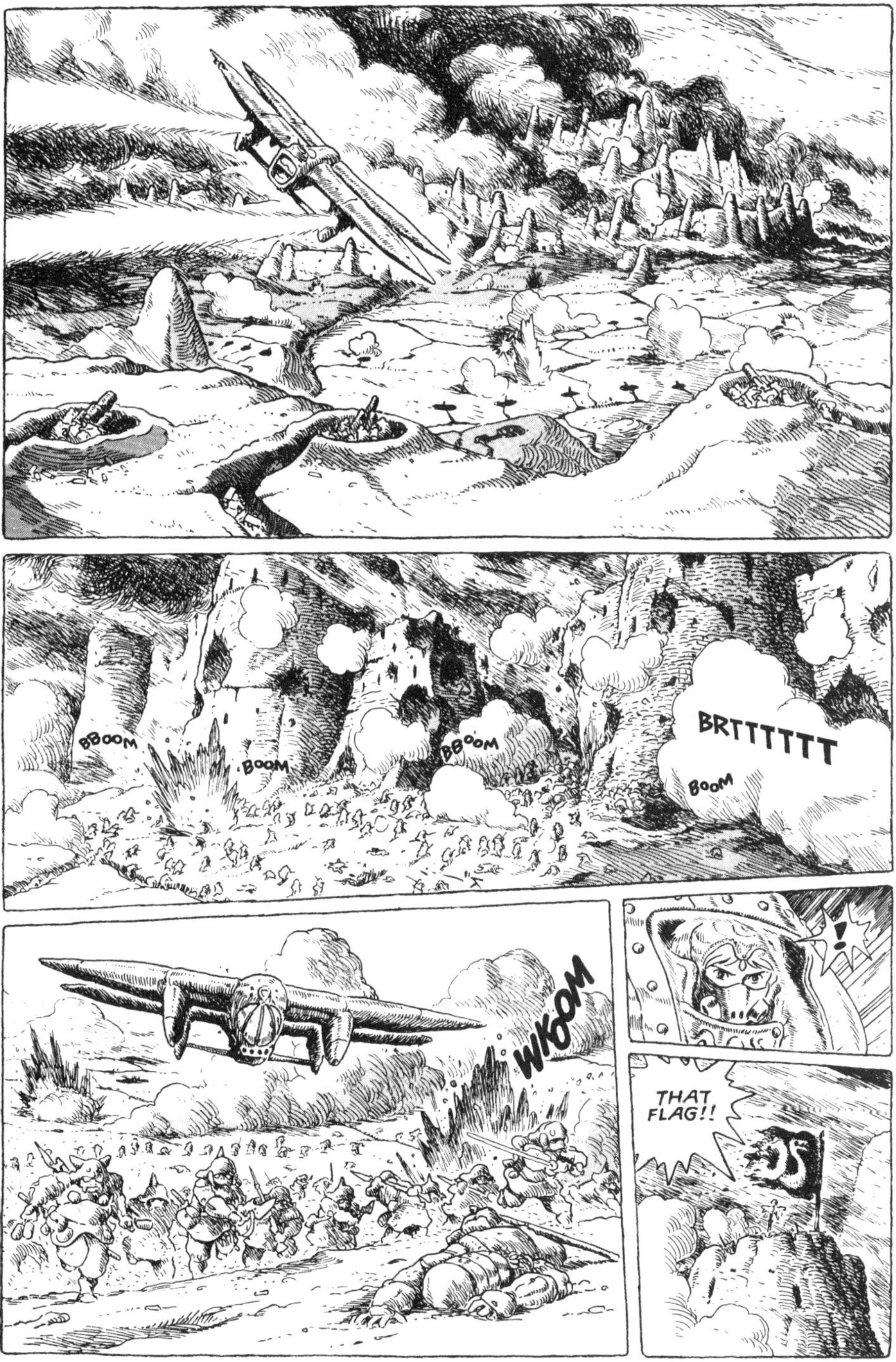
BBOOM
BOOM
BBOOM
BRTTTTTT
BOOM
WKOOM
!!
THAT FLAG!!

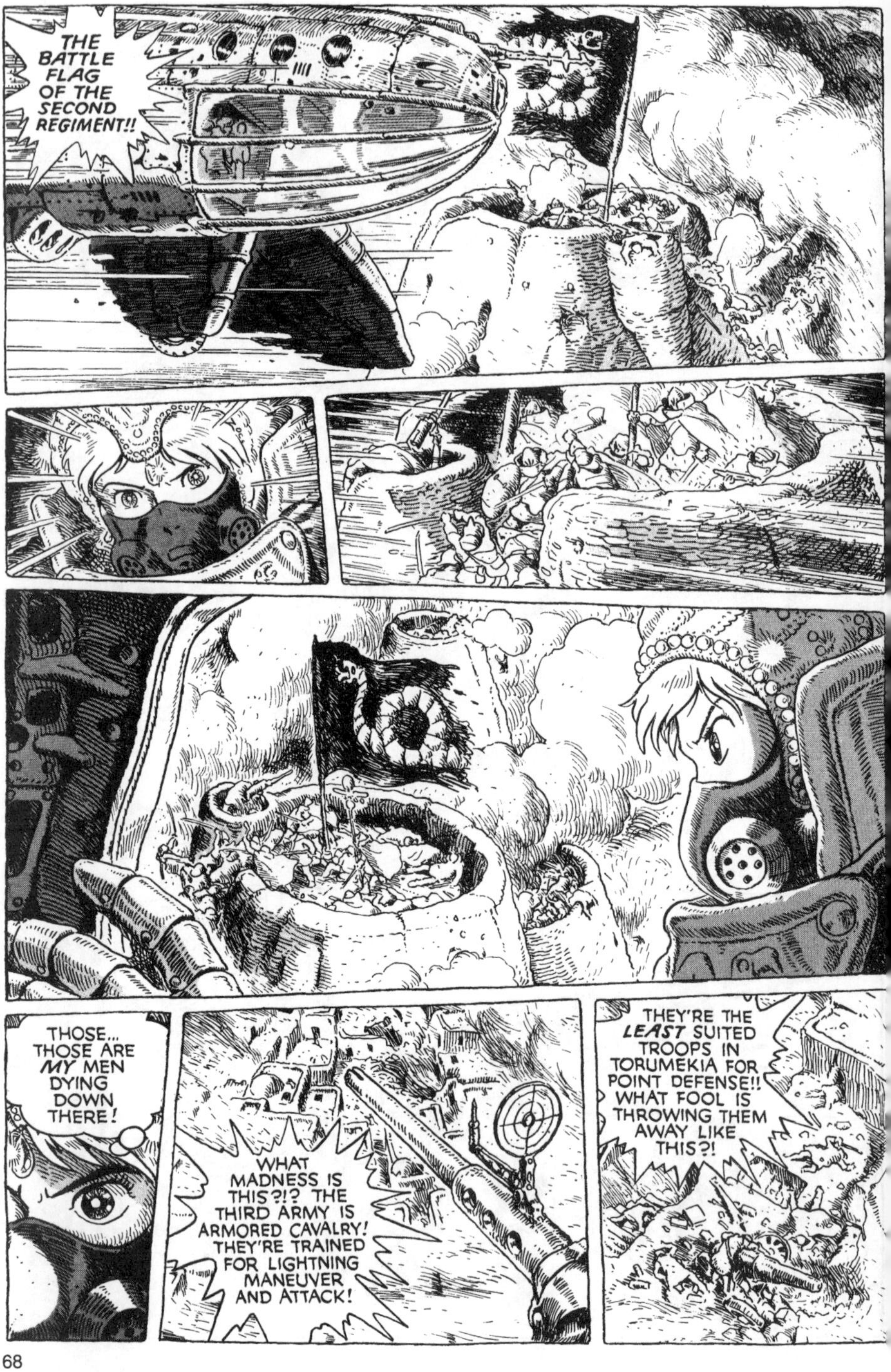
THE BATTLE FLAG OF THE SECOND REGIMENT!!
THOSE... THOSE ARE *MY* MEN DYING DOWN THERE!
WHAT MADNESS IS THIS?!? THE THIRD ARMY IS ARMORED CAVALRY! THEY'RE TRAINED FOR LIGHTNING MANEUVER AND ATTACK!
THEY'RE THE *LEAST* SUITED TROOPS IN TORUMEKIA FOR POINT DEFENSE!! WHAT FOOL IS THROWING THEM AWAY LIKE THIS?!

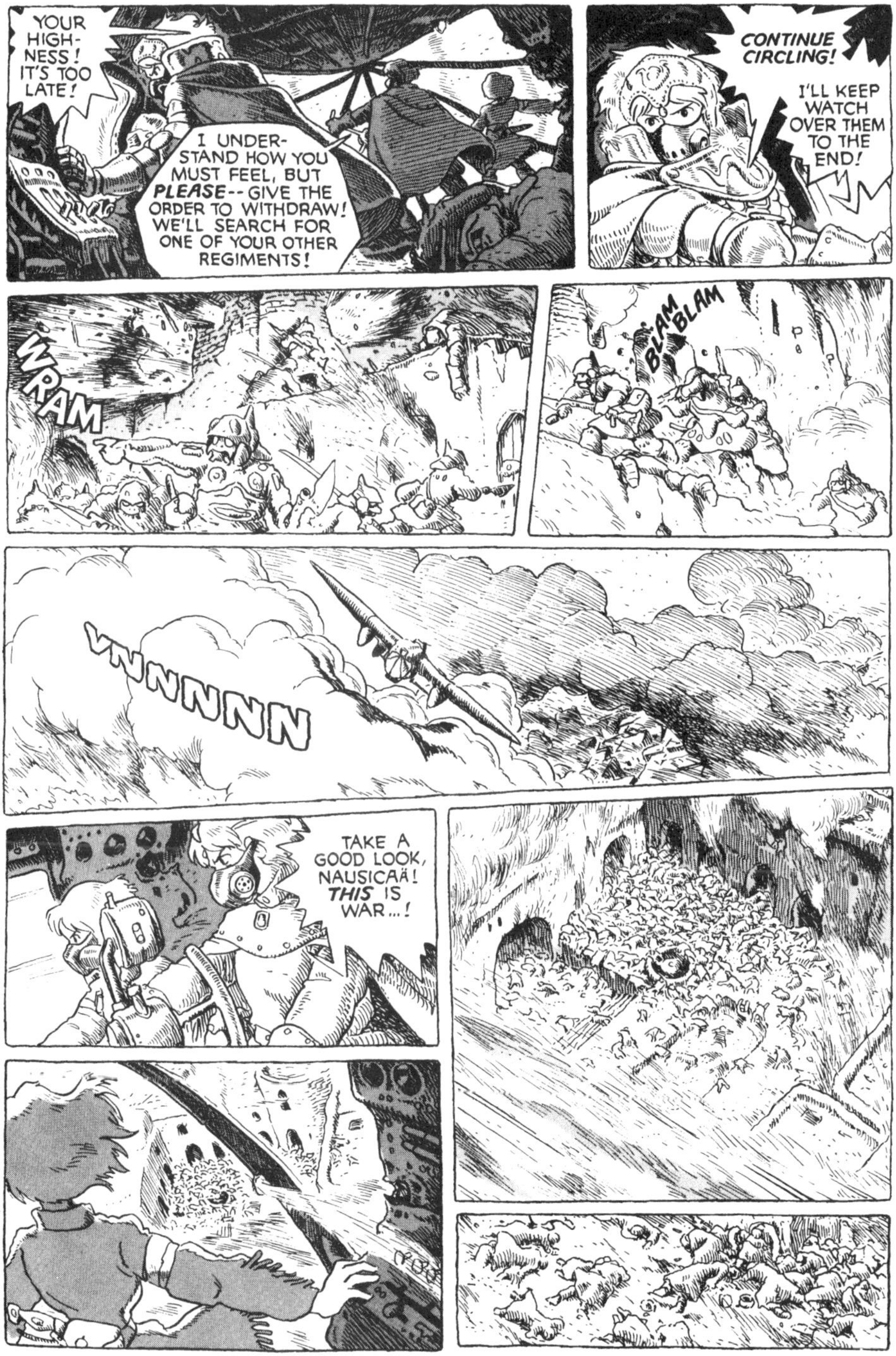
YOUR HIGHNESS! IT'S TOO LATE!
I UNDERSTAND HOW YOU MUST FEEL, BUT **PLEASE**-- GIVE THE ORDER TO WITHDRAW! WE'LL SEARCH FOR ONE OF YOUR OTHER REGIMENTS!
CONTINUE CIRCLING!
I'LL KEEP WATCH OVER THEM TO THE END!
WRAM
BLAM BLAM
VNNNNNN
TAKE A GOOD LOOK, NAUSICAÄ! ***THIS*** IS WAR...!

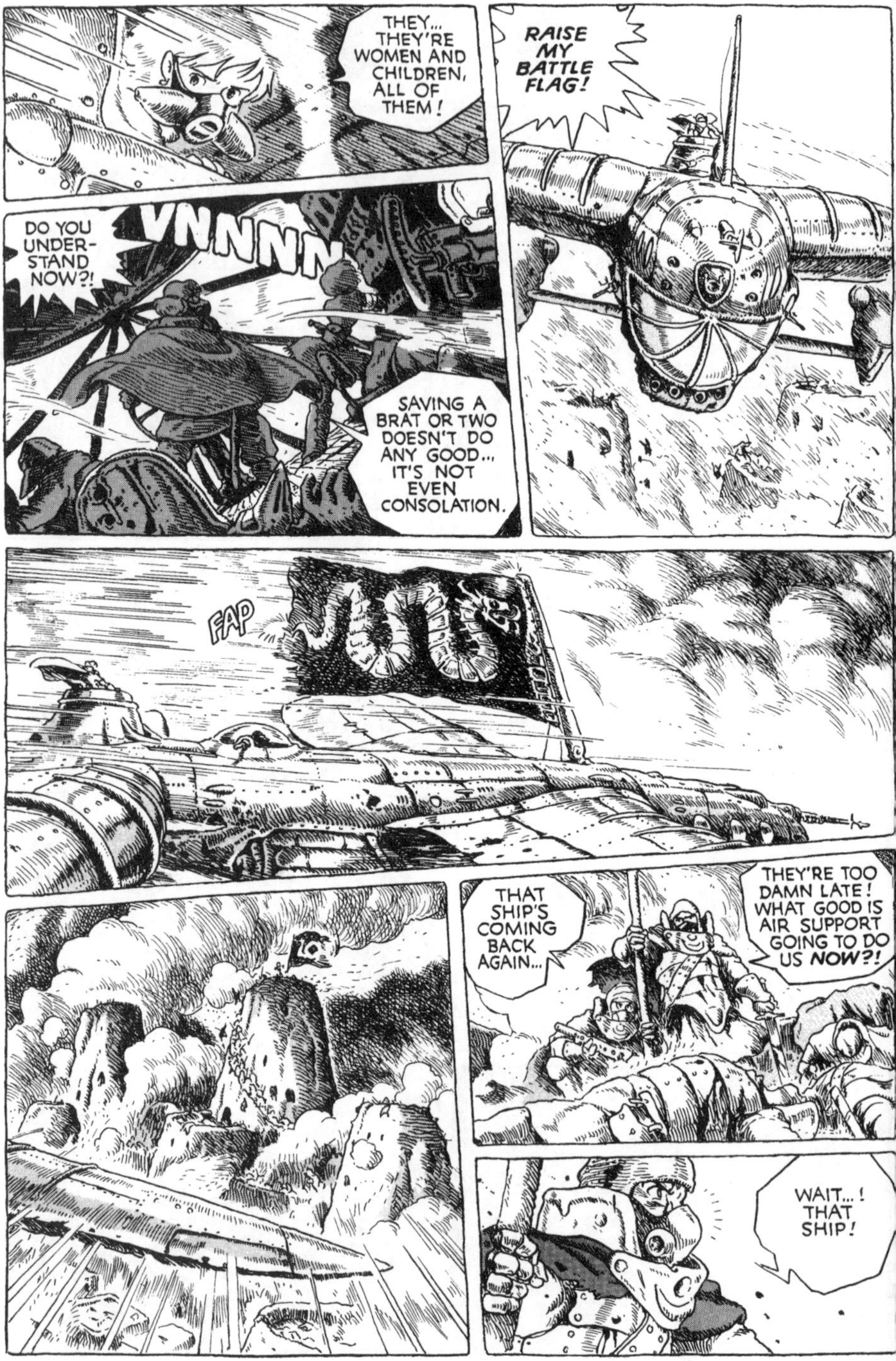
THEY... THEY'RE WOMEN AND CHILDREN, ALL OF THEM!
RAISE MY BATTLE FLAG!
VNNNN
DO YOU UNDER-STAND NOW?!
SAVING A BRAT OR TWO DOESN'T DO ANY GOOD... IT'S NOT EVEN CONSOLATION.
FAP
THAT SHIP'S COMING BACK AGAIN...
THEY'RE TOO DAMN LATE! WHAT GOOD IS AIR SUPPORT GOING TO DO US NOW?!
WAIT...! THAT SHIP!

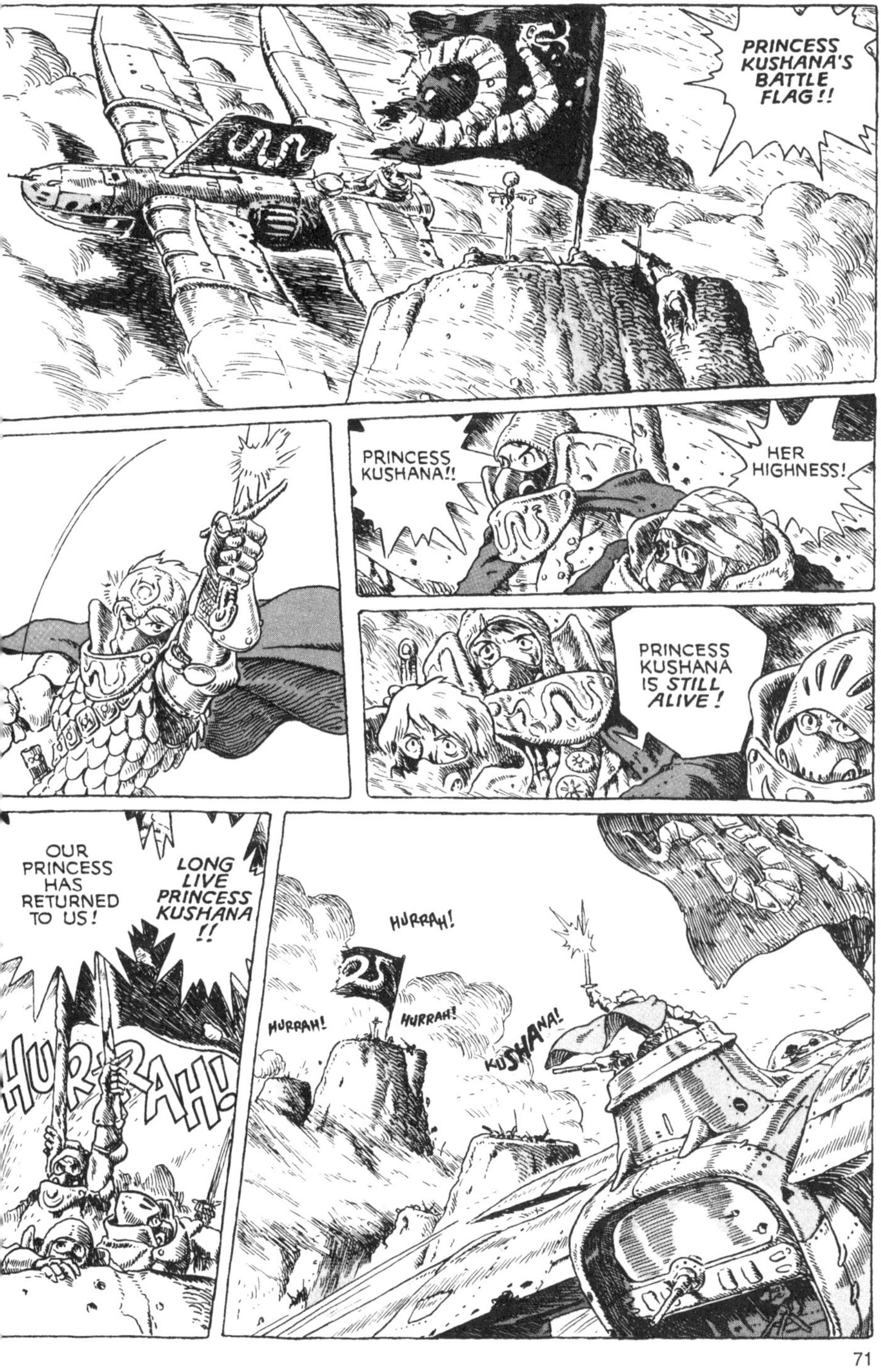
PRINCESS KUSHANA'S BATTLE FLAG!!
PRINCESS KUSHANA!!
HER HIGHNESS!
PRINCESS KUSHANA IS STILL ALIVE!
OUR PRINCESS HAS RETURNED TO US!
LONG LIVE PRINCESS KUSHANA!!
HURRAH!
HURRAH!
HURRAH!
HURRAH!
KUSHANA!

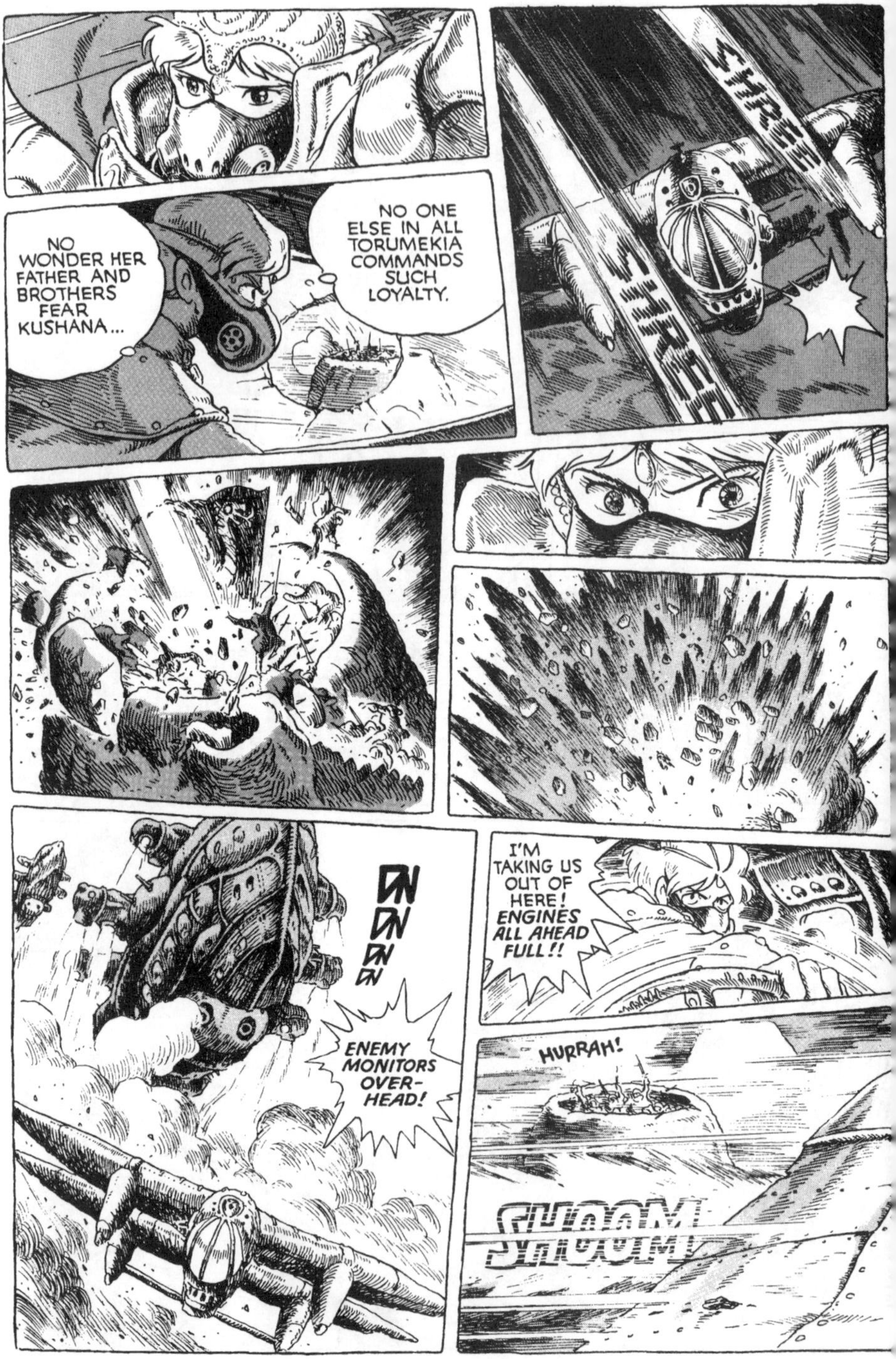
SHREEE
NO ONE ELSE IN ALL TORUMEKIA COMMANDS SUCH LOYALTY.
NO WONDER HER FATHER AND BROTHERS FEAR KUSHANA...
I'M TAKING US OUT OF HERE! ENGINES ALL AHEAD FULL!!
DN DN DN DN
ENEMY MONITORS OVER-HEAD!
HURRAH!
SHOOOM

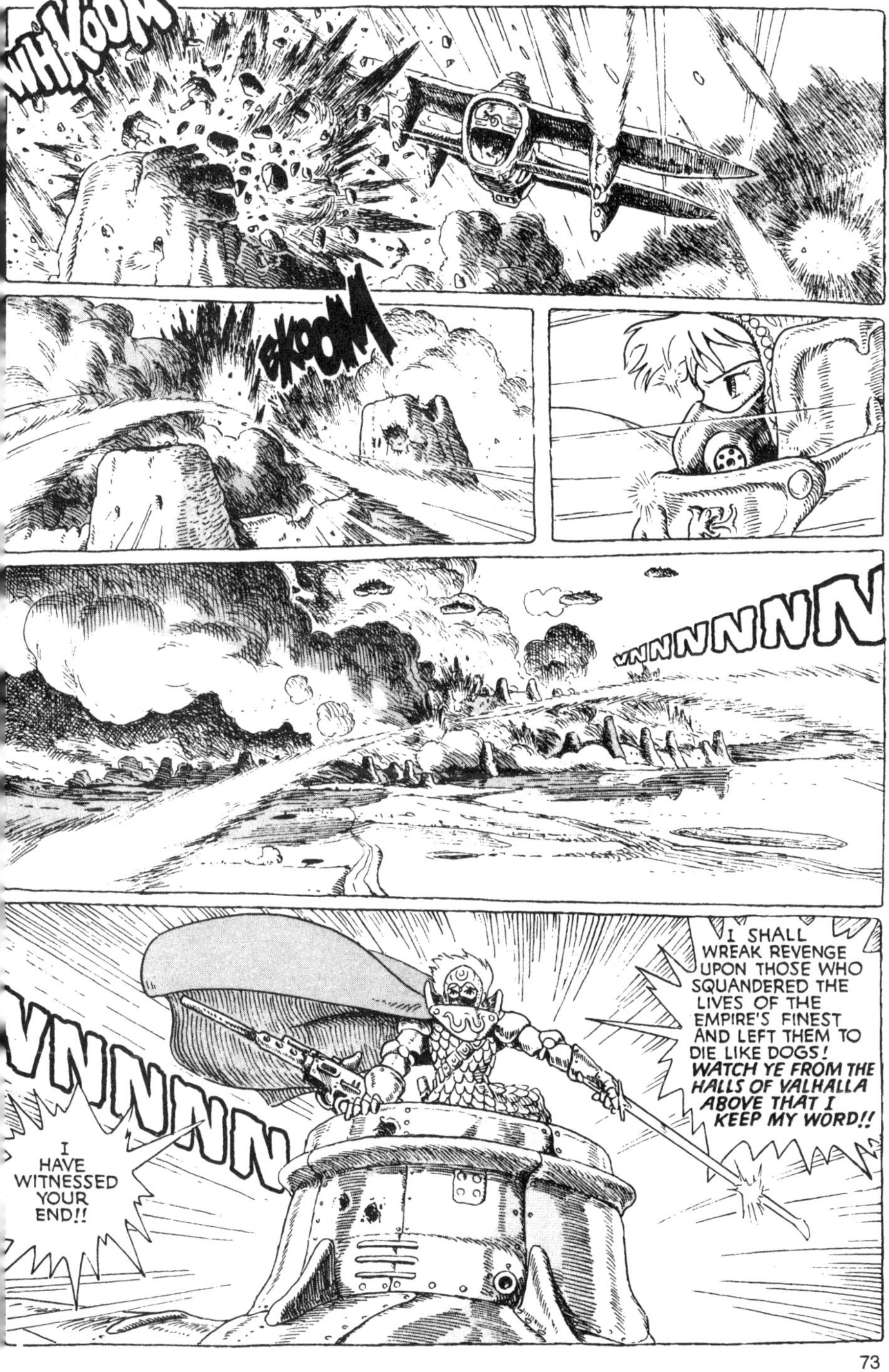
WHKOOM
BKOOM
VNNNNNNN
I SHALL WREAK REVENGE UPON THOSE WHO SQUANDERED THE LIVES OF THE EMPIRE'S FINEST AND LEFT THEM TO DIE LIKE DOGS! *WATCH YE FROM THE HALLS OF VALHALLA ABOVE THAT I KEEP MY WORD!!*
VNNNNN
I HAVE WITNESSED YOUR END!!

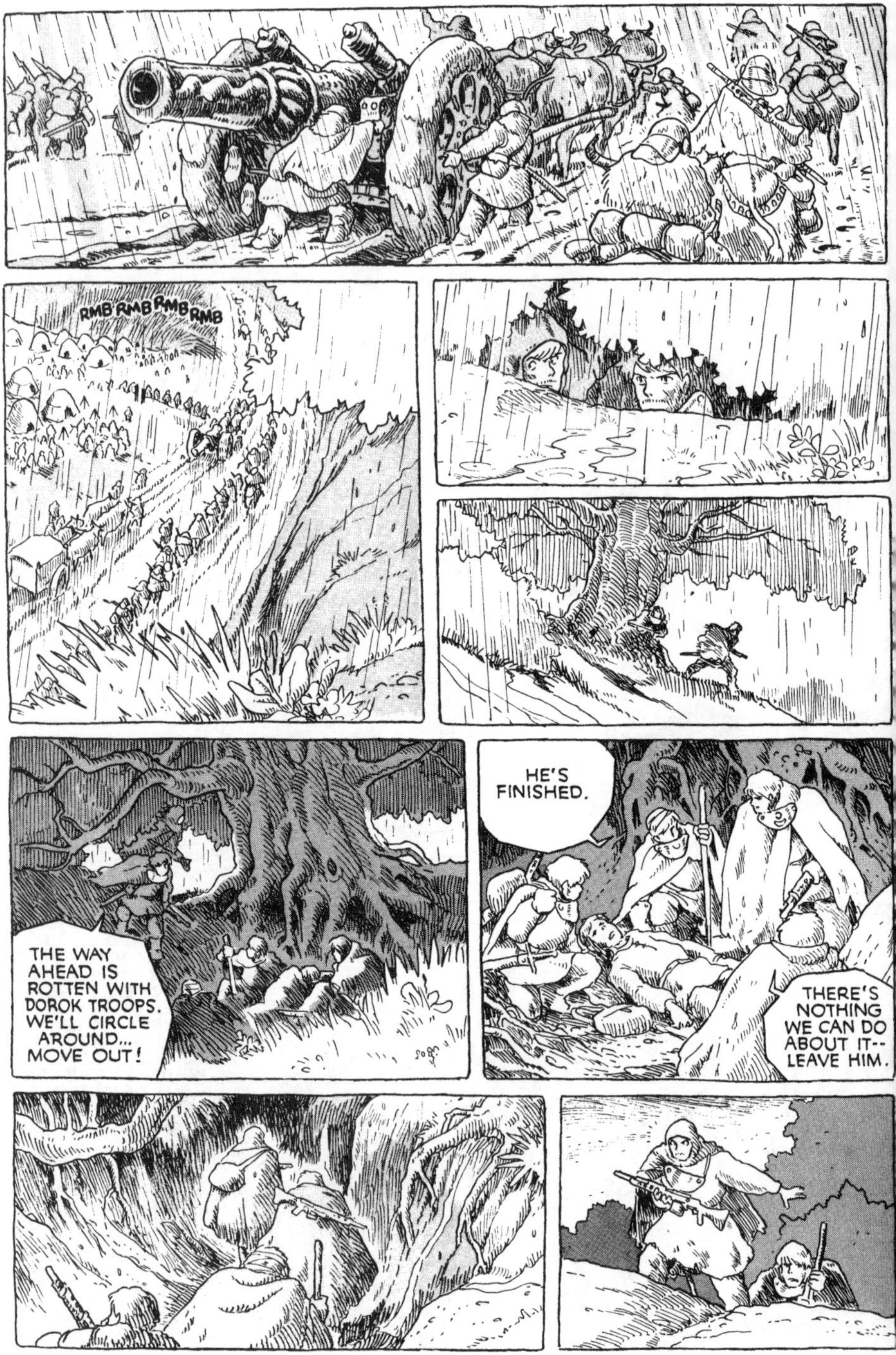
RMB RMB RMB RMB
THE WAY AHEAD IS ROTTEN WITH DOROK TROOPS. WE'LL CIRCLE AROUND... MOVE OUT!
HE'S FINISHED.
THERE'S NOTHING WE CAN DO ABOUT IT-- LEAVE HIM.

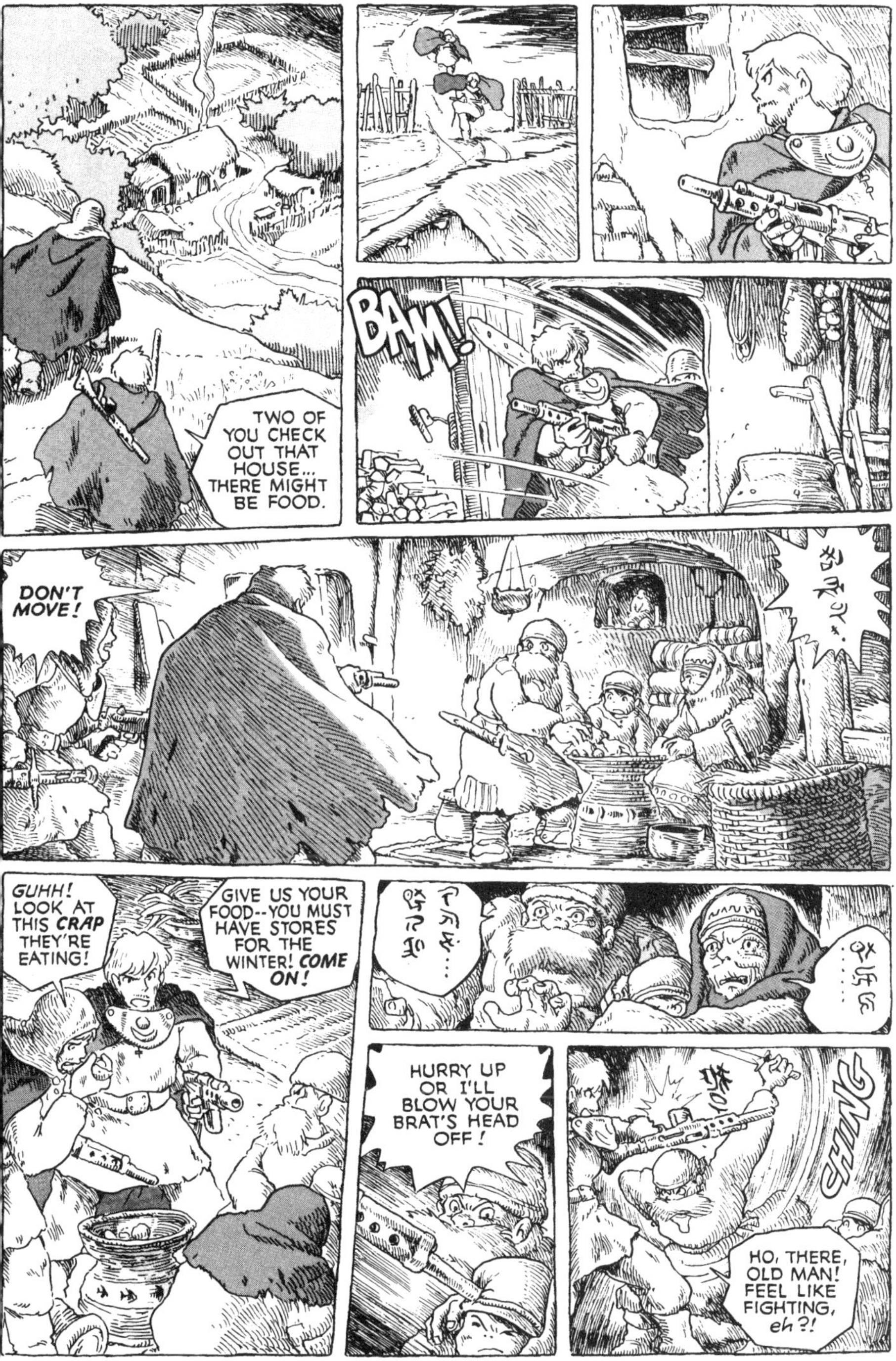

TWO OF YOU CHECK OUT THAT HOUSE... THERE MIGHT BE FOOD.
BAM!
DON'T MOVE!
GUHH! LOOK AT THIS CRAP THEY'RE EATING!
GIVE US YOUR FOOD--YOU MUST HAVE STORES FOR THE WINTER! COME ON!
HURRY UP OR I'LL BLOW YOUR BRAT'S HEAD OFF!
CHING
HO, THERE, OLD MAN! FEEL LIKE FIGHTING, eh?!

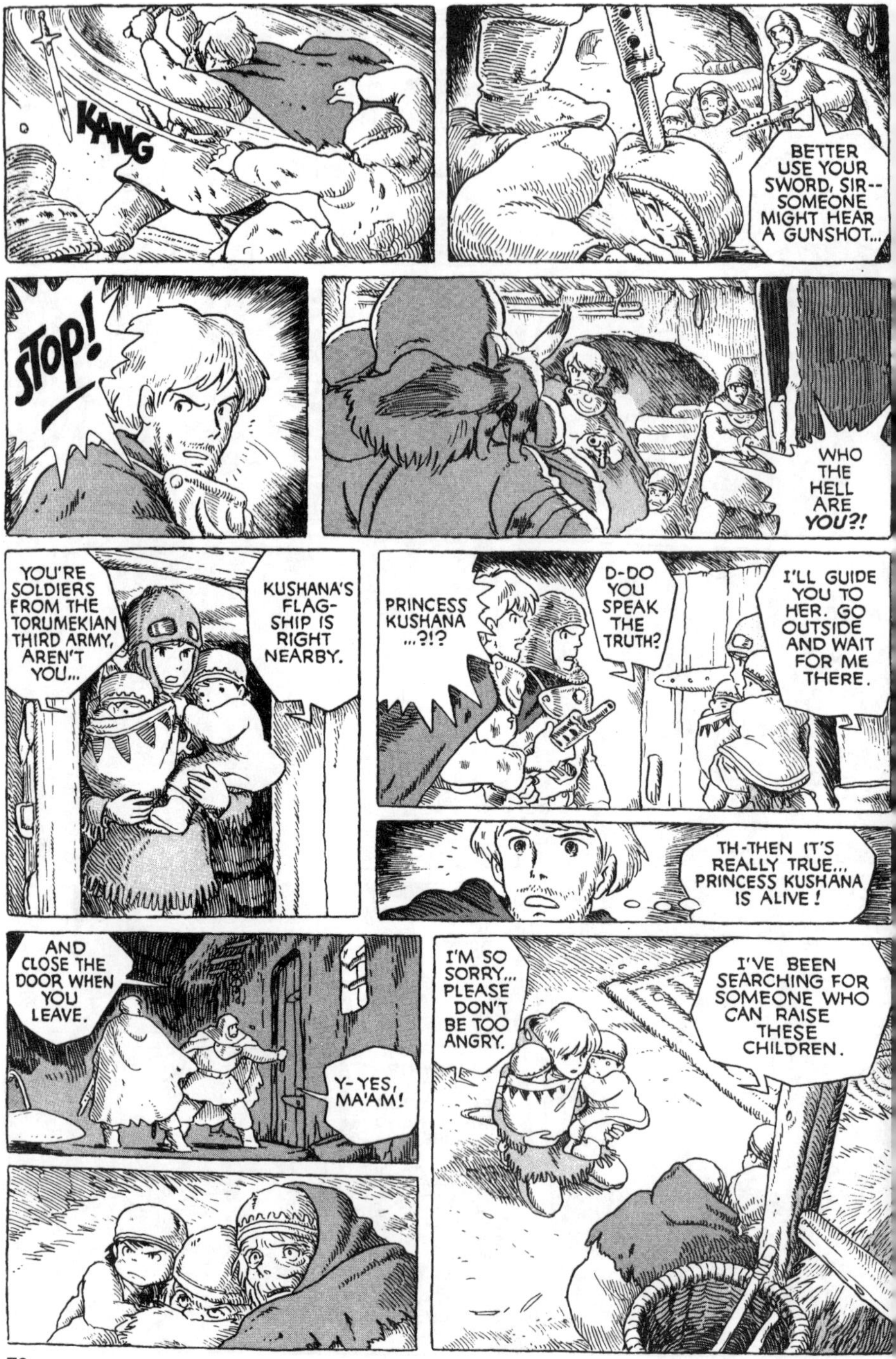
KANG
BETTER USE YOUR SWORD, SIR-- SOMEONE MIGHT HEAR A GUNSHOT...
STOP!
WHO THE HELL ARE *YOU?!*
YOU'RE SOLDIERS FROM THE TORUMEKIAN THIRD ARMY, AREN'T YOU...
KUSHANA'S FLAG-SHIP IS RIGHT NEARBY.
PRINCESS KUSHANA ...?!?
D-DO YOU SPEAK THE TRUTH?
I'LL GUIDE YOU TO HER. GO OUTSIDE AND WAIT FOR ME THERE.
TH-THEN IT'S REALLY TRUE... PRINCESS KUSHANA IS ALIVE!
AND CLOSE THE DOOR WHEN YOU LEAVE.
Y-YES, MA'AM!
I'M SO SORRY... PLEASE DON'T BE TOO ANGRY.
I'VE BEEN SEARCHING FOR SOMEONE WHO CAN RAISE THESE CHILDREN.

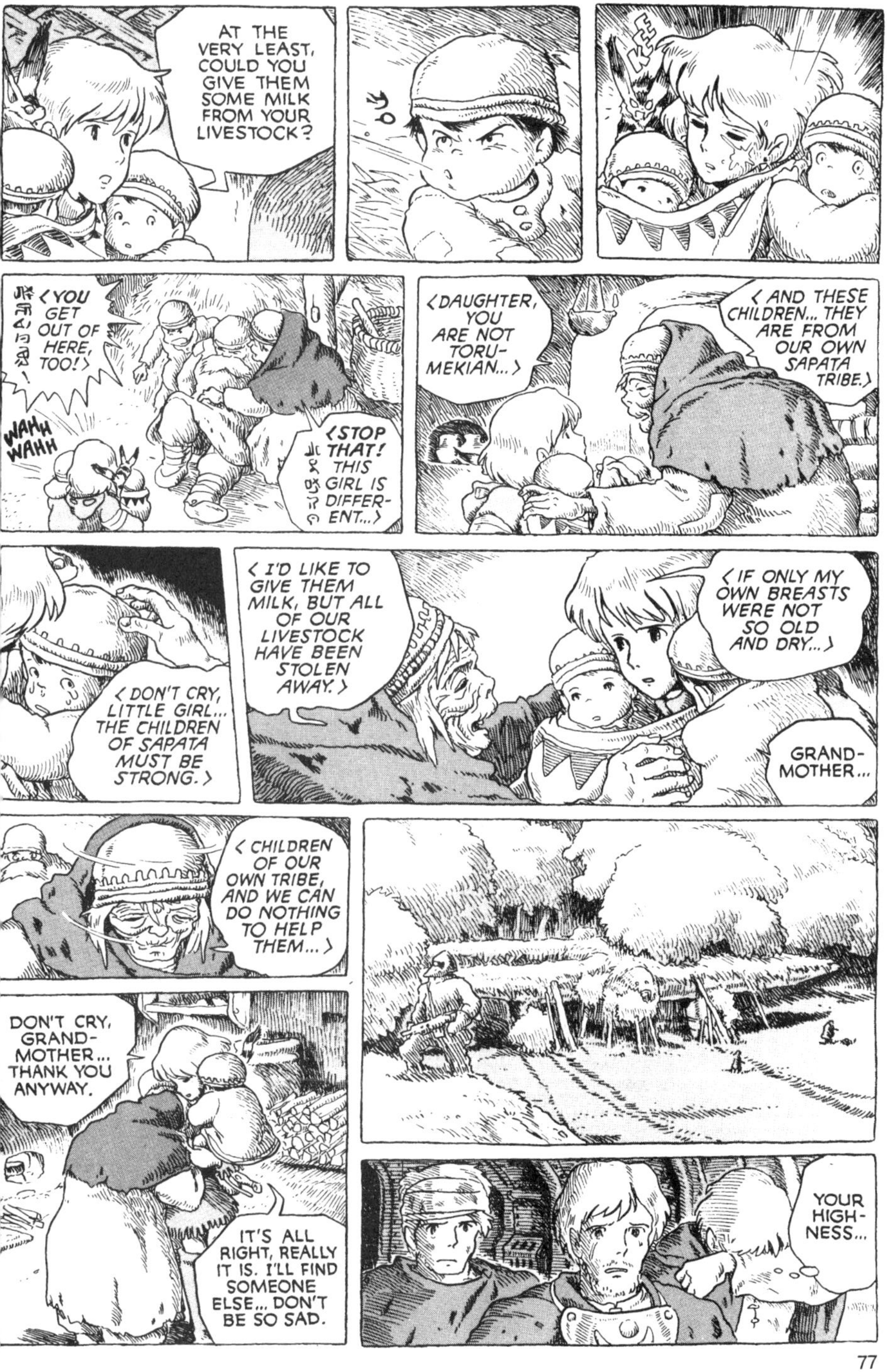
AT THE VERY LEAST, COULD YOU GIVE THEM SOME MILK FROM YOUR LIVESTOCK?
KEE
<YOU GET OUT OF HERE, TOO!>
WAHH WAHH
<STOP THAT! THIS GIRL IS DIFFERENT...>
<DAUGHTER, YOU ARE NOT TORUMEKIAN...>
<AND THESE CHILDREN... THEY ARE FROM OUR OWN SAPATA TRIBE.>
<DON'T CRY, LITTLE GIRL... THE CHILDREN OF SAPATA MUST BE STRONG.>
<I'D LIKE TO GIVE THEM MILK, BUT ALL OF OUR LIVESTOCK HAVE BEEN STOLEN AWAY.>
<IF ONLY MY OWN BREASTS WERE NOT SO OLD AND DRY...>
GRANDMOTHER...
<CHILDREN OF OUR OWN TRIBE, AND WE CAN DO NOTHING TO HELP THEM...>
DON'T CRY, GRANDMOTHER... THANK YOU ANYWAY.
IT'S ALL RIGHT, REALLY IT IS. I'LL FIND SOMEONE ELSE... DON'T BE SO SAD.
YOUR HIGHNESS...

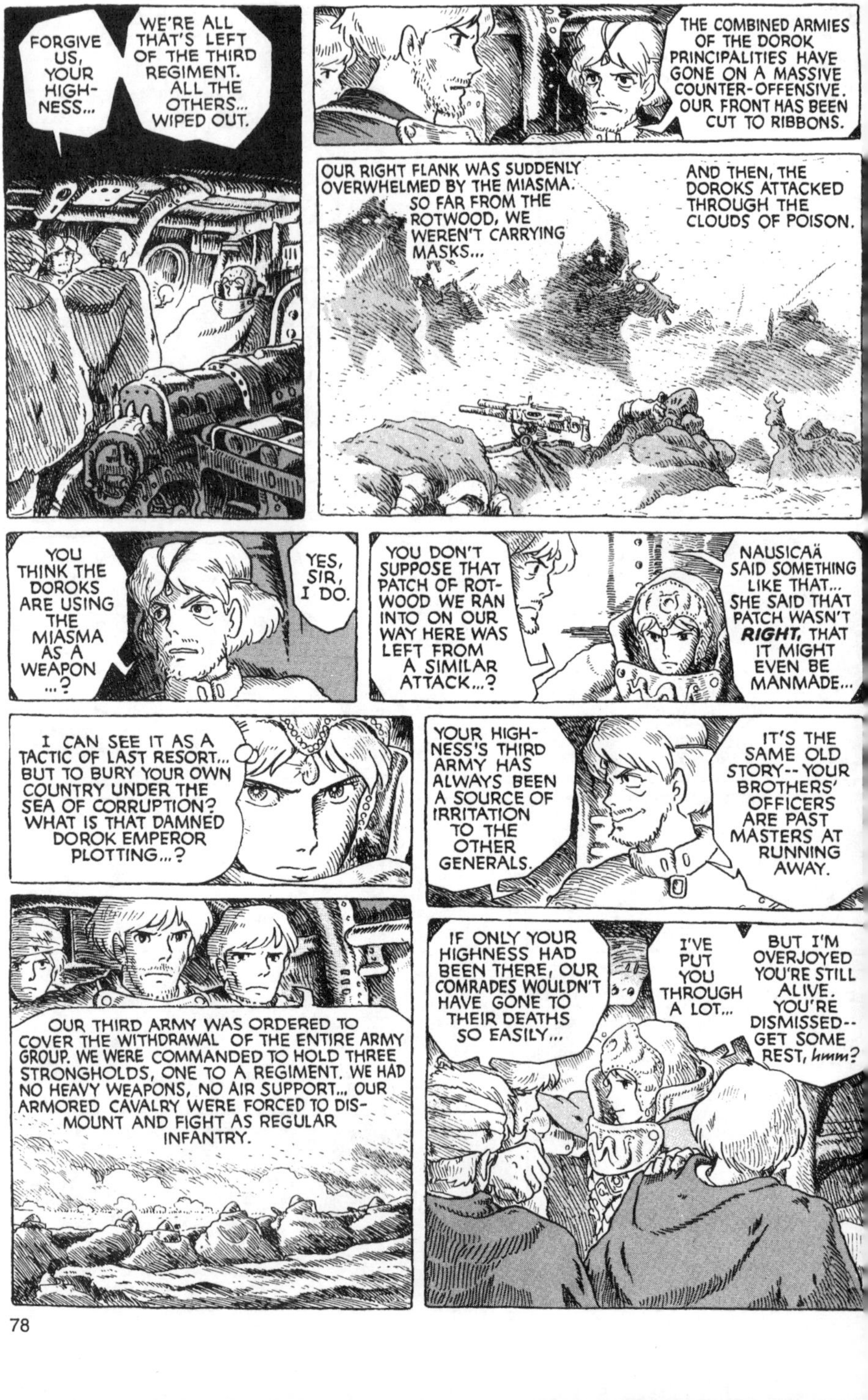
FORGIVE US, YOUR HIGH-NESS...
WE'RE ALL THAT'S LEFT OF THE THIRD REGIMENT. ALL THE OTHERS... WIPED OUT.
THE COMBINED ARMIES OF THE DOROK PRINCIPALITIES HAVE GONE ON A MASSIVE COUNTER-OFFENSIVE. OUR FRONT HAS BEEN CUT TO RIBBONS.
OUR RIGHT FLANK WAS SUDDENLY OVERWHELMED BY THE MIASMA.
SO FAR FROM THE ROTWOOD, WE WEREN'T CARRYING MASKS...
AND THEN, THE DOROKS ATTACKED THROUGH THE CLOUDS OF POISON.
YOU THINK THE DOROKS ARE USING THE MIASMA AS A WEAPON ...?
YES, SIR, I DO.
YOU DON'T SUPPOSE THAT PATCH OF ROT-WOOD WE RAN INTO ON OUR WAY HERE WAS LEFT FROM A SIMILAR ATTACK...?
NAUSICAÄ SAID SOMETHING LIKE THAT... SHE SAID THAT PATCH WASN'T ***RIGHT***, THAT IT MIGHT EVEN BE MANMADE...
I CAN SEE IT AS A TACTIC OF LAST RESORT... BUT TO BURY YOUR OWN COUNTRY UNDER THE SEA OF CORRUPTION? WHAT IS THAT DAMNED DOROK EMPEROR PLOTTING...?
YOUR HIGH-NESS'S THIRD ARMY HAS ALWAYS BEEN A SOURCE OF IRRITATION TO THE OTHER GENERALS.
IT'S THE SAME OLD STORY-- YOUR BROTHERS' OFFICERS ARE PAST MASTERS AT RUNNING AWAY.
OUR THIRD ARMY WAS ORDERED TO COVER THE WITHDRAWAL OF THE ENTIRE ARMY GROUP. WE WERE COMMANDED TO HOLD THREE STRONGHOLDS, ONE TO A REGIMENT. WE HAD NO HEAVY WEAPONS, NO AIR SUPPORT... OUR ARMORED CAVALRY WERE FORCED TO DIS-MOUNT AND FIGHT AS REGULAR INFANTRY.
IF ONLY YOUR HIGHNESS HAD BEEN THERE, OUR COMRADES WOULDN'T HAVE GONE TO THEIR DEATHS SO EASILY...
I'VE PUT YOU THROUGH A LOT...
BUT I'M OVERJOYED YOU'RE STILL ALIVE. YOU'RE DISMISSED-- GET SOME REST, *hmm*?

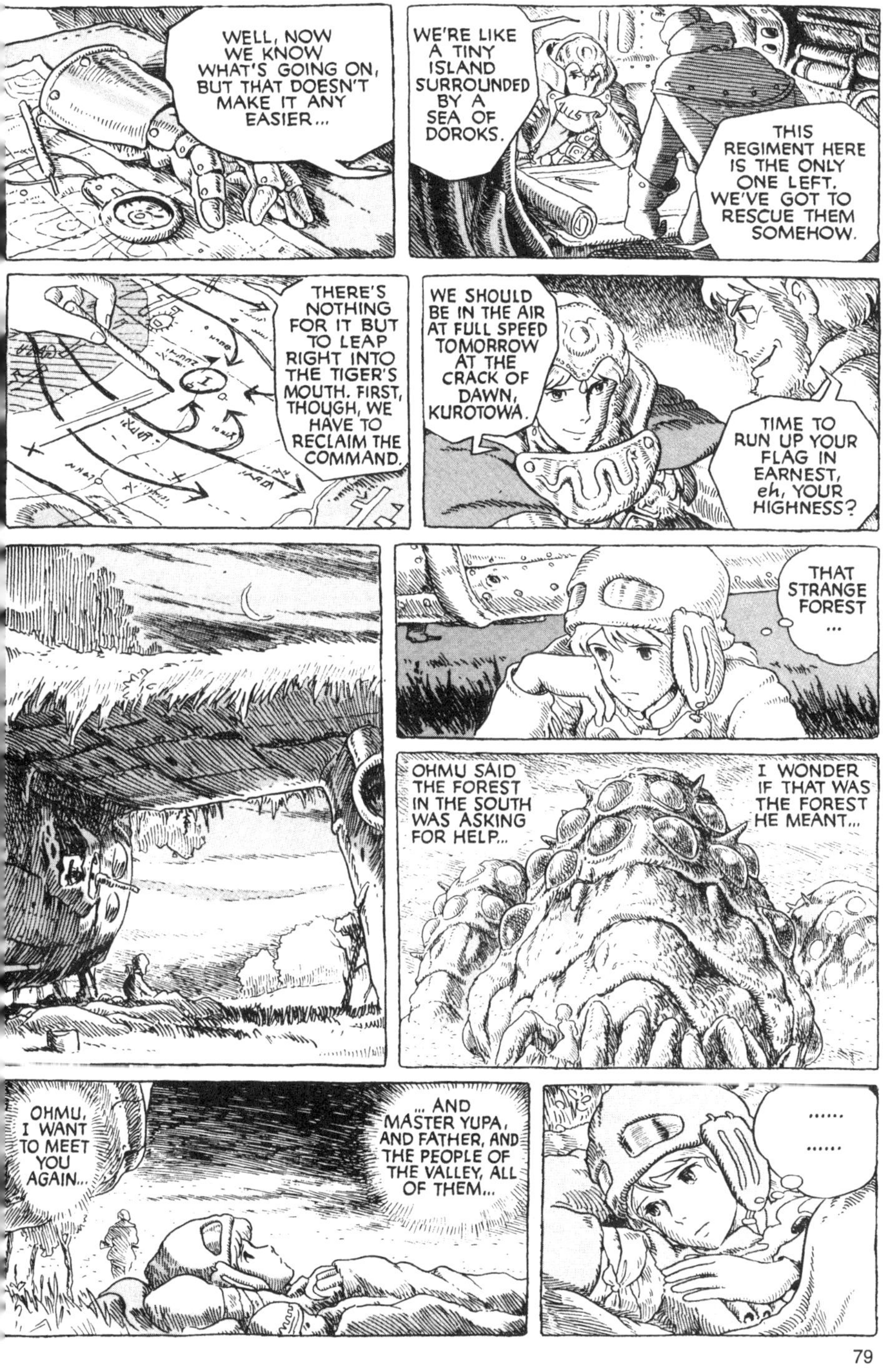
WELL, NOW WE KNOW WHAT'S GOING ON, BUT THAT DOESN'T MAKE IT ANY EASIER...
WE'RE LIKE A TINY ISLAND SURROUNDED BY A SEA OF DOROKS.
THIS REGIMENT HERE IS THE ONLY ONE LEFT. WE'VE GOT TO RESCUE THEM SOMEHOW.
THERE'S NOTHING FOR IT BUT TO LEAP RIGHT INTO THE TIGER'S MOUTH. FIRST, THOUGH, WE HAVE TO RECLAIM THE COMMAND.
WE SHOULD BE IN THE AIR AT FULL SPEED TOMORROW AT THE CRACK OF DAWN, KUROTOWA.
TIME TO RUN UP YOUR FLAG IN EARNEST, *eh*, YOUR HIGHNESS?
THAT STRANGE FOREST ...
OHMU SAID THE FOREST IN THE SOUTH WAS ASKING FOR HELP...
I WONDER IF THAT WAS THE FOREST HE MEANT...
OHMU, I WANT TO MEET YOU AGAIN...
... AND MASTER YUPA, AND FATHER, AND THE PEOPLE OF THE VALLEY, ALL OF THEM...
......
......

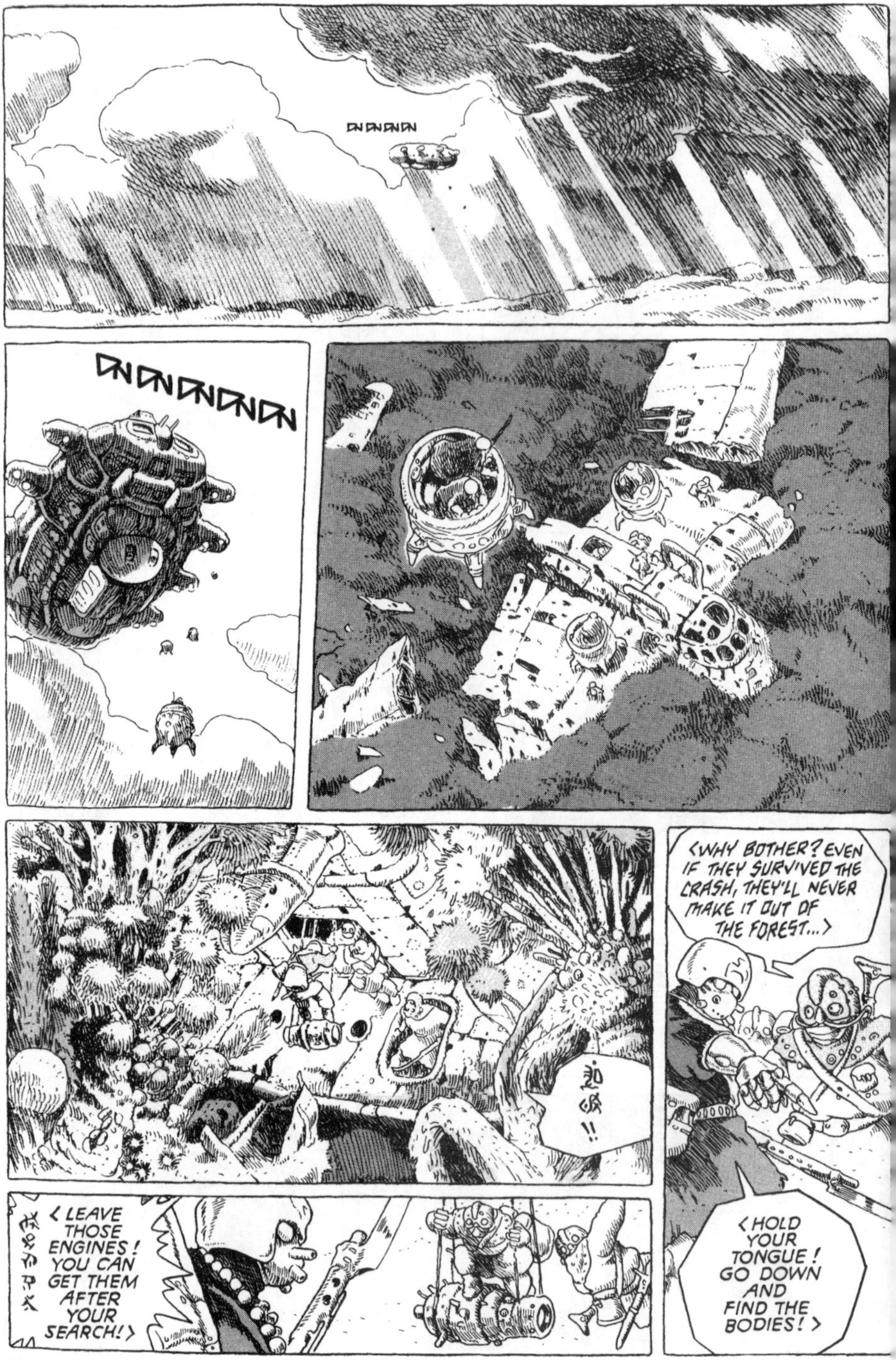
DN DN DN DN
DN DN DN DN DN DN
‹WHY BOTHER? EVEN IF THEY SURVIVED THE CRASH, THEY'LL NEVER MAKE IT OUT OF THE FOREST...›
‹LEAVE THOSE ENGINES! YOU CAN GET THEM AFTER YOUR SEARCH!›
‹HOLD YOUR TONGUE! GO DOWN AND FIND THE BODIES!›

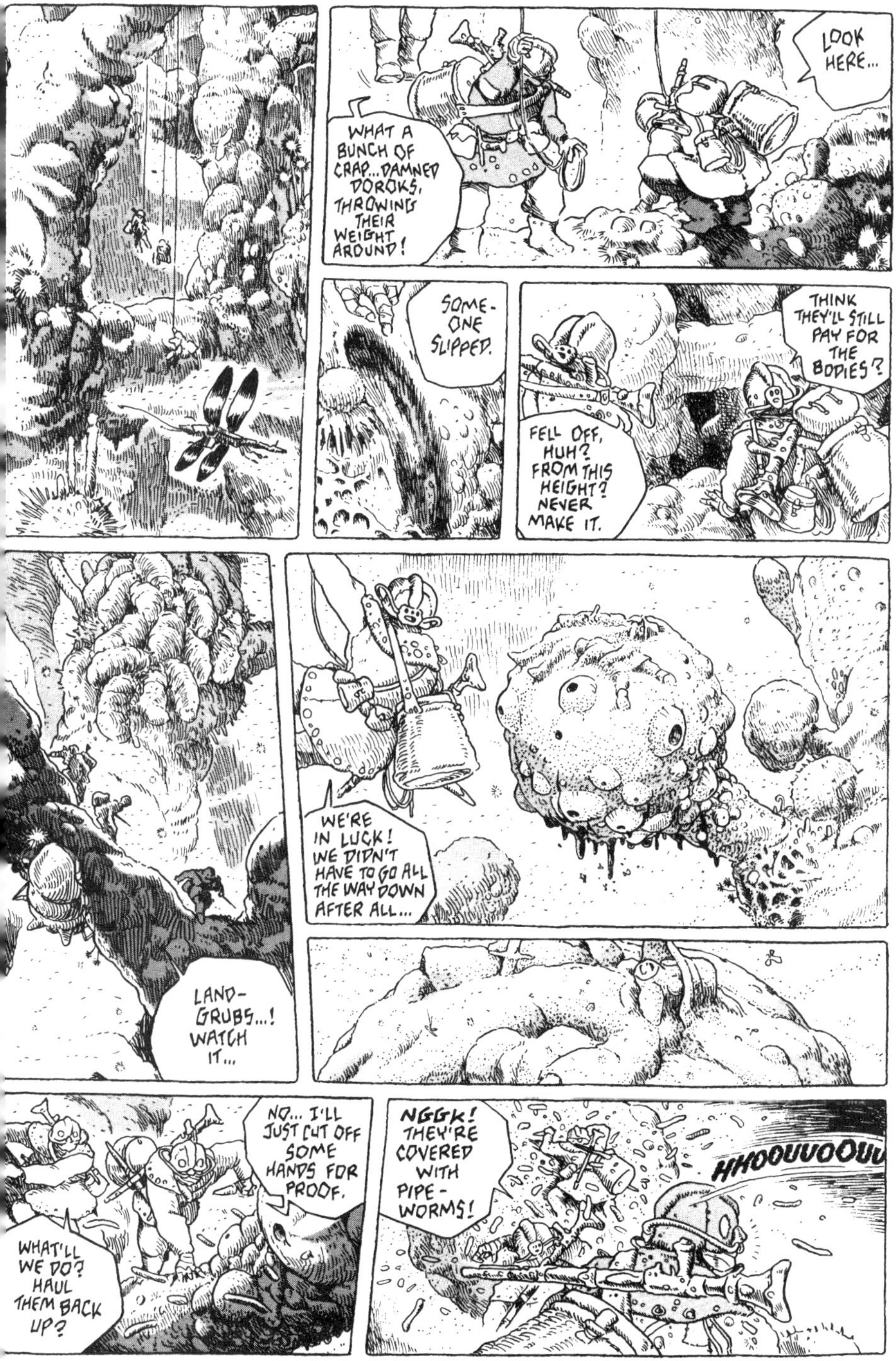
LOOK HERE...
WHAT A BUNCH OF CRAP...DAMNED DOROKS, THROWING THEIR WEIGHT AROUND!
SOME-ONE SLIPPED.
THINK THEY'LL STILL PAY FOR THE BODIES?
FELL OFF, HUH? FROM THIS HEIGHT? NEVER MAKE IT.
WE'RE IN LUCK! WE DIDN'T HAVE TO GO ALL THE WAY DOWN AFTER ALL...
LAND-GRUBS...! WATCH IT...
NO... I'LL JUST CUT OFF SOME HANDS FOR PROOF.
WHAT'LL WE DO? HAUL THEM BACK UP?
NGGK! THEY'RE COVERED WITH PIPE-WORMS!
HHOOUVOOUU

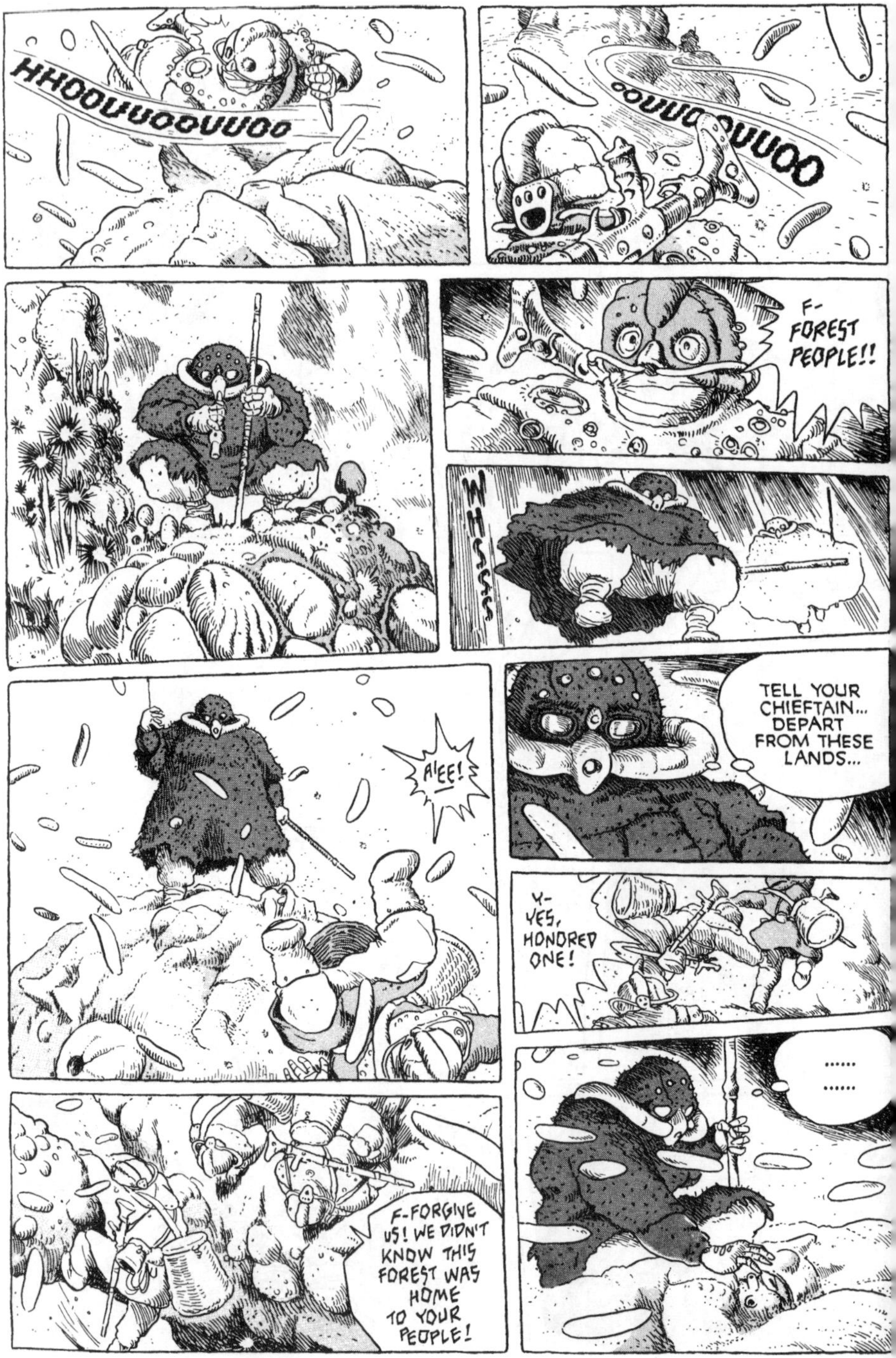
HHOOUUOOUUOO
OOUUOOUUOO
F-FOREST PEOPLE!!
WHSSSS
TELL YOUR CHIEFTAIN... DEPART FROM THESE LANDS...
AIEE!
Y-YES, HONORED ONE!
......
......
F-FORGIVE US! WE DIDN'T KNOW THIS FOREST WAS HOME TO YOUR PEOPLE!

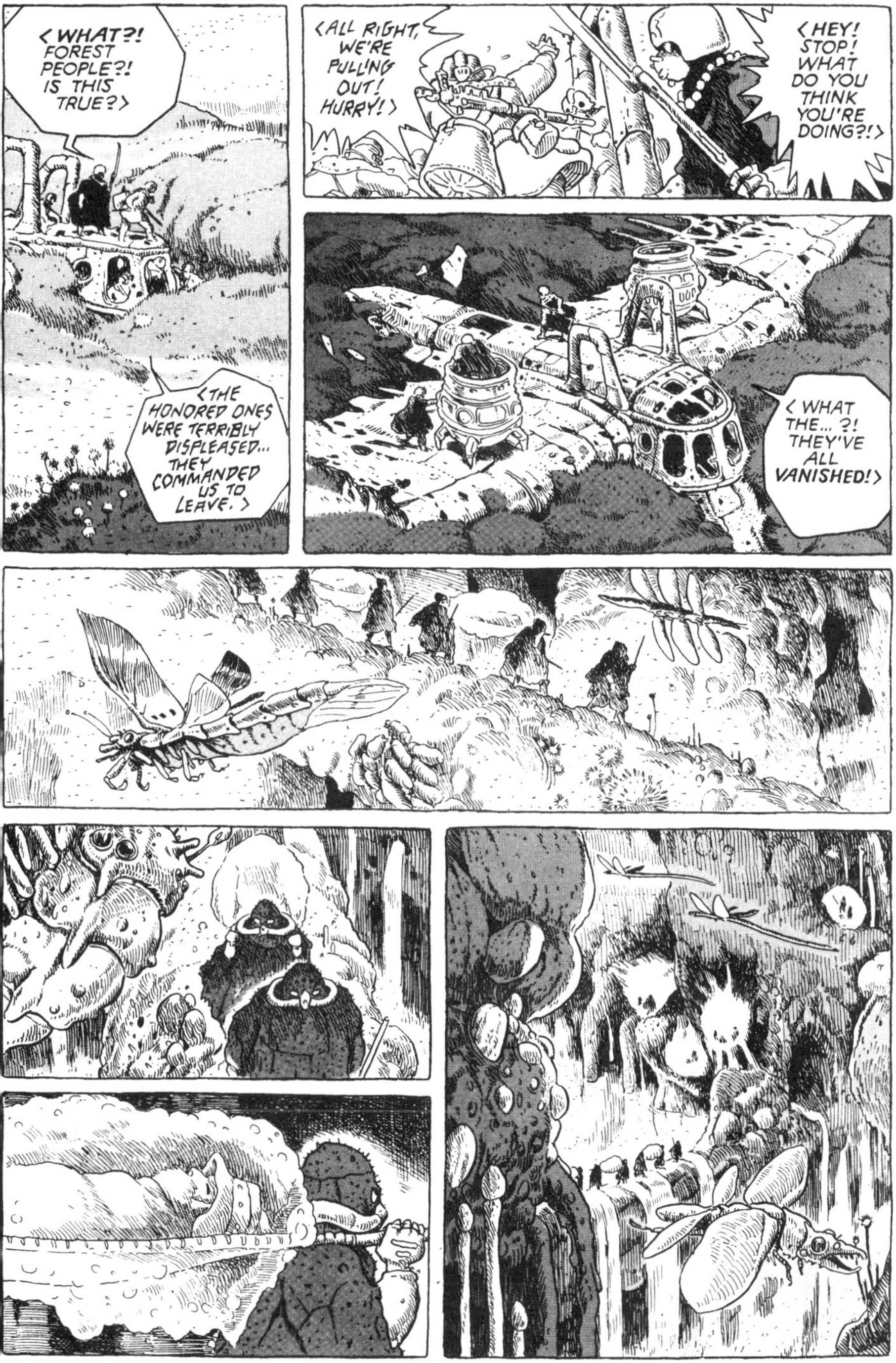

<WHAT?! FOREST PEOPLE?! IS THIS TRUE?>
<THE HONORED ONES WERE TERRIBLY DISPLEASED... THEY COMMANDED US TO LEAVE.>
<ALL RIGHT, WE'RE PULLING OUT! HURRY!>
<HEY! STOP! WHAT DO YOU THINK YOU'RE DOING?!>
< WHAT THE... ?! THEY'VE ALL VANISHED!>

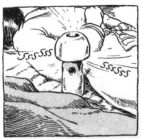

HOW ARE YOU? FEELING OKAY...?

......

ASBEL...?

WH- WHERE WE NOW? INSECT HOME?

TAKE A LOOK OVER THERE...

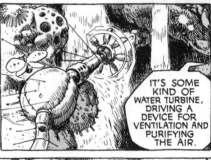
IT'S SOME KIND OF WATER TURBINE, DRIVING A DEVICE FOR VENTILATION AND PURIFYING THE AIR.

EEEEK! ???

THIS WALL JUST BUBBLES ...!

DON'T BE AFRAID, KETCHA. WE'RE IN ONE OF THE FOREST PEOPLE'S TENTS.

MASTER YUPA...

IF THEY PLANNED TO KILL US, THEY WOULDN'T HAVE LEFT US OUR WEAPONS.

I'VE HEARD TALES ABOUT THEM FROM THE WORMHANDLERS... BUT I NEVER REALLY BELIEVED THEY EXISTED.

I DON'T KNOW WHY, BUT THE WORMHANDLERS HOLD THE FOREST PEOPLE IN DREAD AND AWE.

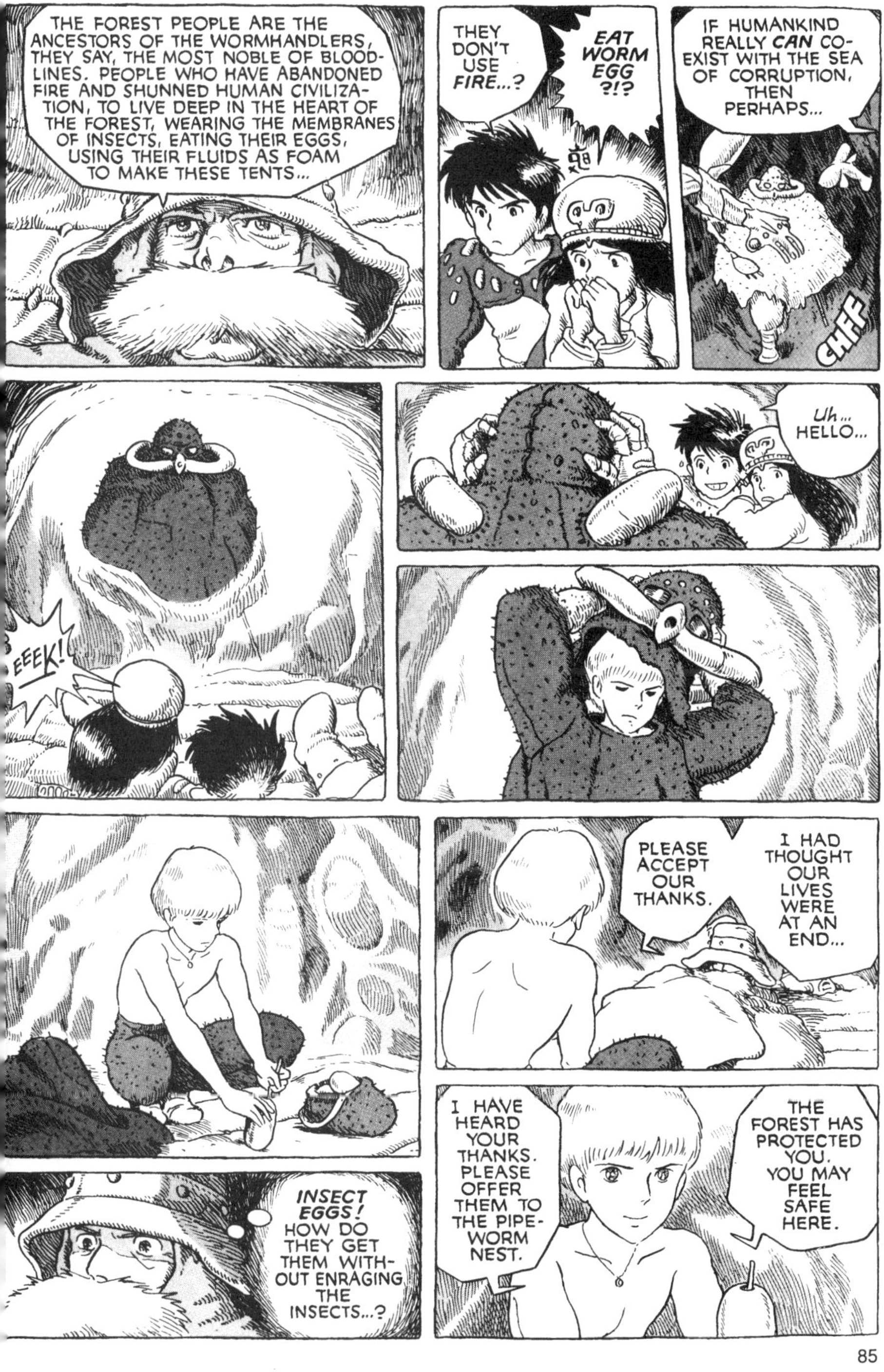

THE FOREST PEOPLE ARE THE ANCESTORS OF THE WORMHANDLERS, THEY SAY, THE MOST NOBLE OF BLOODLINES. PEOPLE WHO HAVE ABANDONED FIRE AND SHUNNED HUMAN CIVILIZATION, TO LIVE DEEP IN THE HEART OF THE FOREST, WEARING THE MEMBRANES OF INSECTS, EATING THEIR EGGS, USING THEIR FLUIDS AS FOAM TO MAKE THESE TENTS...
THEY DON'T USE *FIRE*...?
EAT WORM EGG ?!?
IF HUMANKIND REALLY *CAN* COEXIST WITH THE SEA OF CORRUPTION, THEN PERHAPS...
CHFF
EEEK!
Uh... HELLO...
PLEASE ACCEPT OUR THANKS.
I HAD THOUGHT OUR LIVES WERE AT AN END...
INSECT EGGS! HOW DO THEY GET THEM WITHOUT ENRAGING THE INSECTS...?
THE FOREST HAS PROTECTED YOU. YOU MAY FEEL SAFE HERE.
I HAVE HEARD YOUR THANKS. PLEASE OFFER THEM TO THE PIPEWORM NEST.

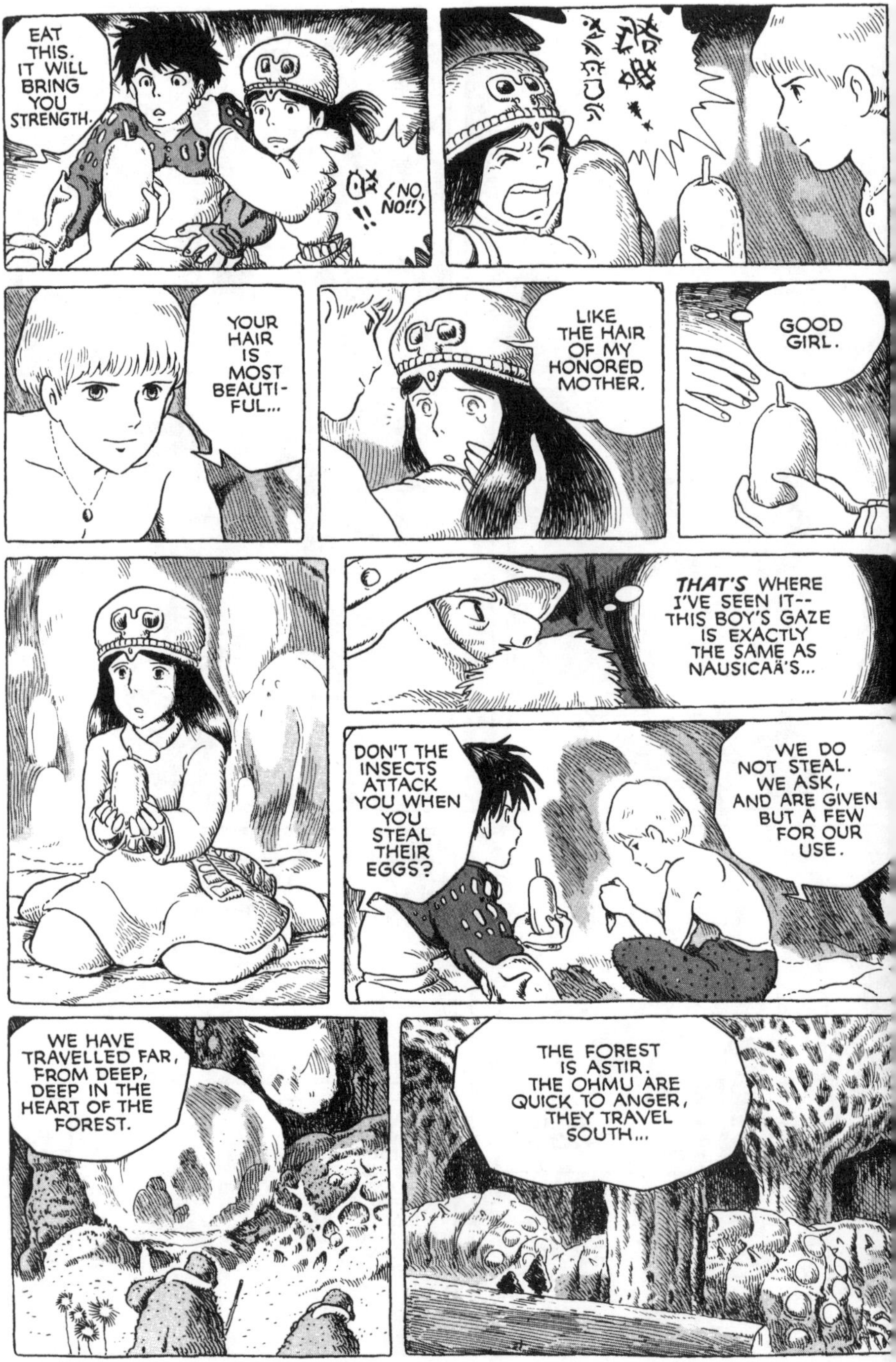

EAT THIS. IT WILL BRING YOU STRENGTH.
〈NO, NO!!〉
YOUR HAIR IS MOST BEAUTIFUL...
LIKE THE HAIR OF MY HONORED MOTHER.
GOOD GIRL.
THAT'S WHERE I'VE SEEN IT-- THIS BOY'S GAZE IS EXACTLY THE SAME AS NAUSICAÄ'S...
DON'T THE INSECTS ATTACK YOU WHEN YOU STEAL THEIR EGGS?
WE DO NOT STEAL. WE ASK, AND ARE GIVEN BUT A FEW FOR OUR USE.
WE HAVE TRAVELLED FAR, FROM DEEP, DEEP IN THE HEART OF THE FOREST.
THE FOREST IS ASTIR. THE OHMU ARE QUICK TO ANGER, THEY TRAVEL SOUTH...

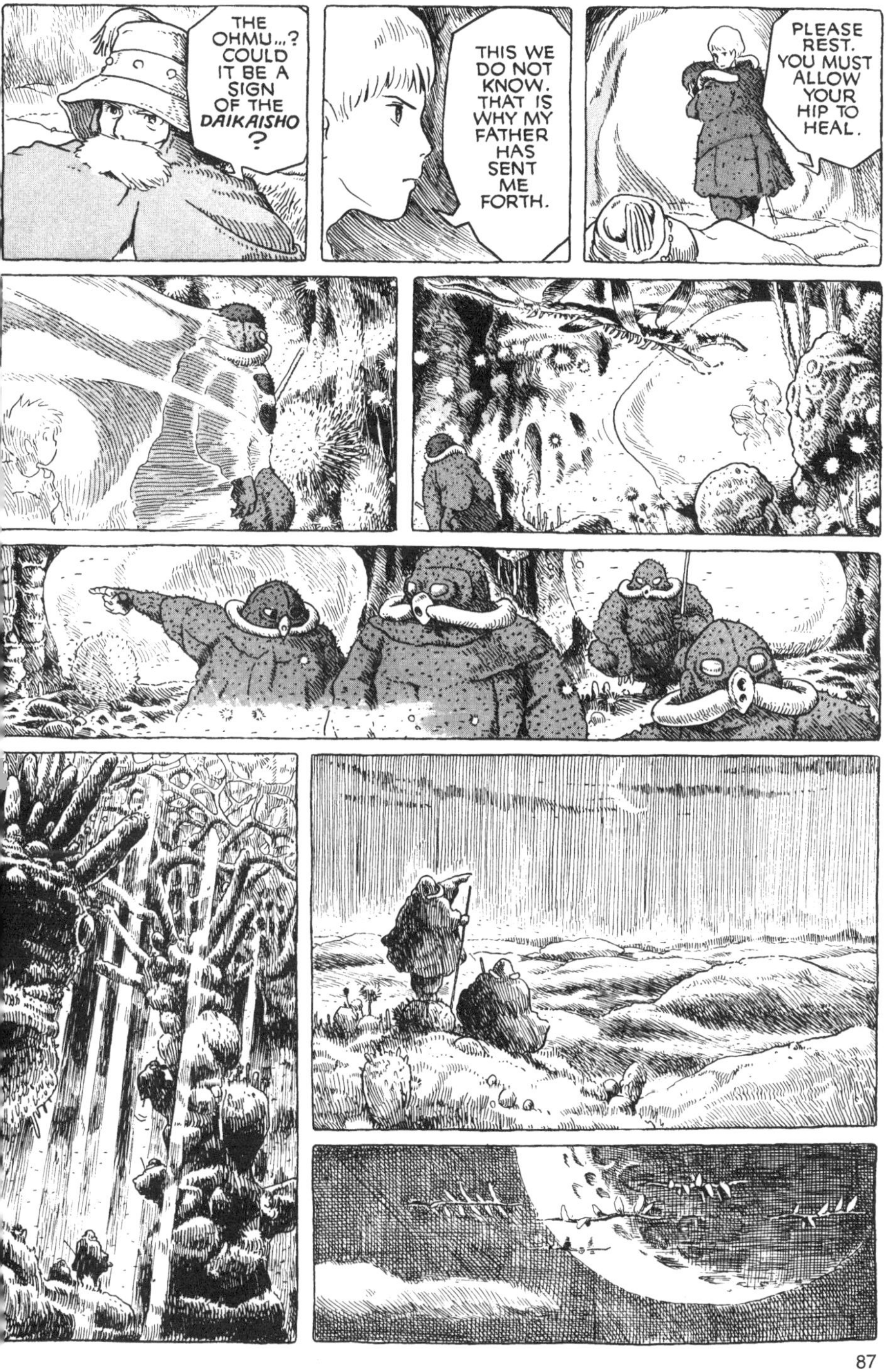
THE OHMU...? COULD IT BE A SIGN OF THE *DAIKAISHO* ?
THIS WE DO NOT KNOW. THAT IS WHY MY FATHER HAS SENT ME FORTH.
PLEASE REST. YOU MUST ALLOW YOUR HIP TO HEAL.

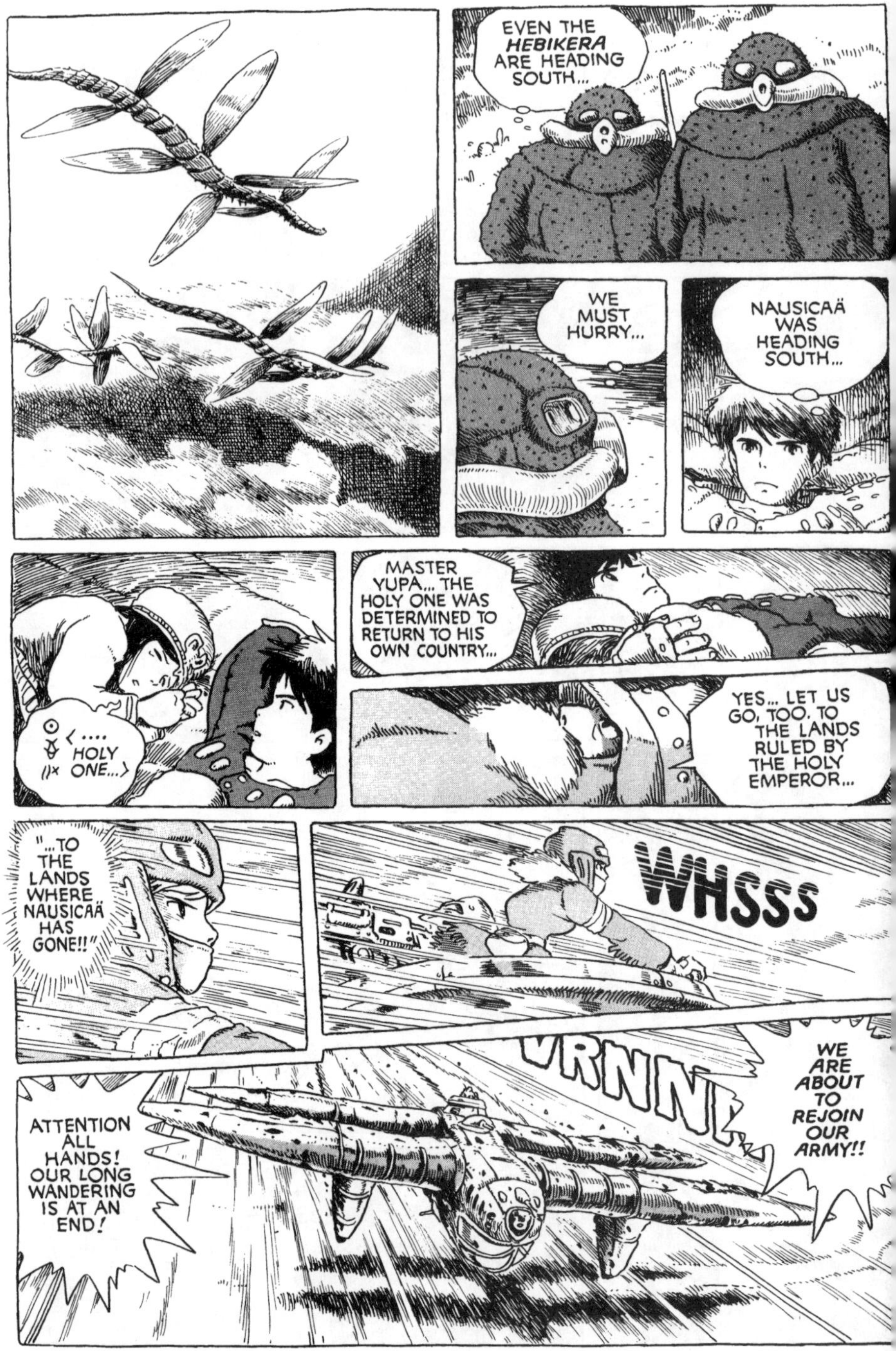
EVEN THE *HEBIKERA* ARE HEADING SOUTH...
WE MUST HURRY...
NAUSICAÄ WAS HEADING SOUTH...
⊙ <.... HOLY ONE...>
MASTER YUPA... THE HOLY ONE WAS DETERMINED TO RETURN TO HIS OWN COUNTRY...
YES... LET US GO, TOO, TO THE LANDS RULED BY THE HOLY EMPEROR...
"...TO THE LANDS WHERE NAUSICAÄ HAS GONE!!"
WHSSS
VRNNN
ATTENTION ALL HANDS! OUR LONG WANDERING IS AT AN END!
WE ARE ABOUT TO REJOIN OUR ARMY!!

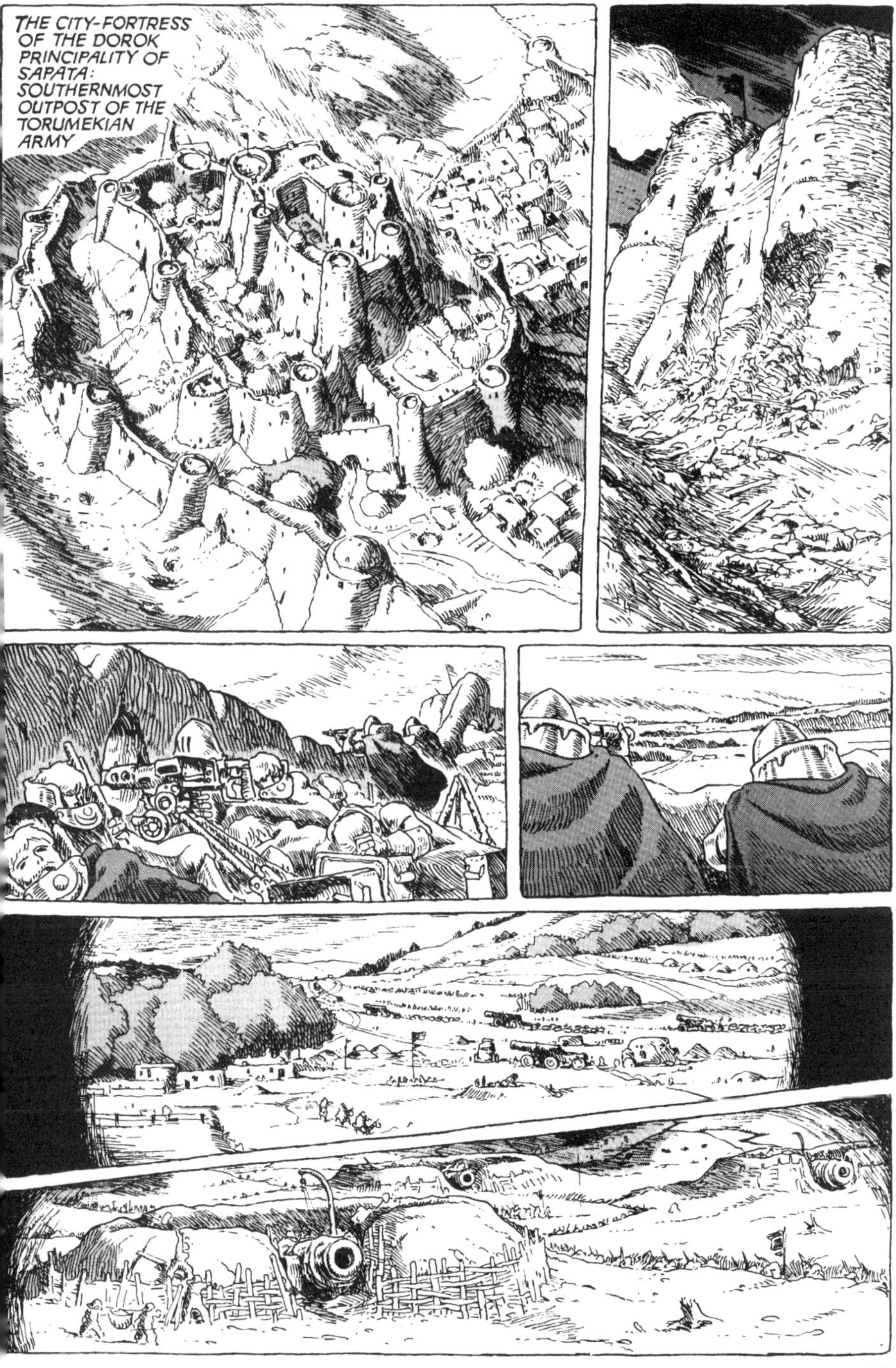
THE CITY-FORTRESS OF THE DOROK PRINCIPALITY OF SAPATA: SOUTHERNMOST OUTPOST OF THE TORUMEKIAN ARMY

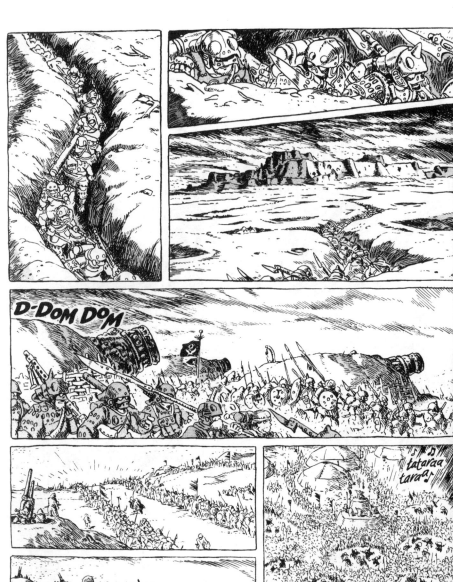

D-DOM DOM

tataraa tara

DOM DOM DOM

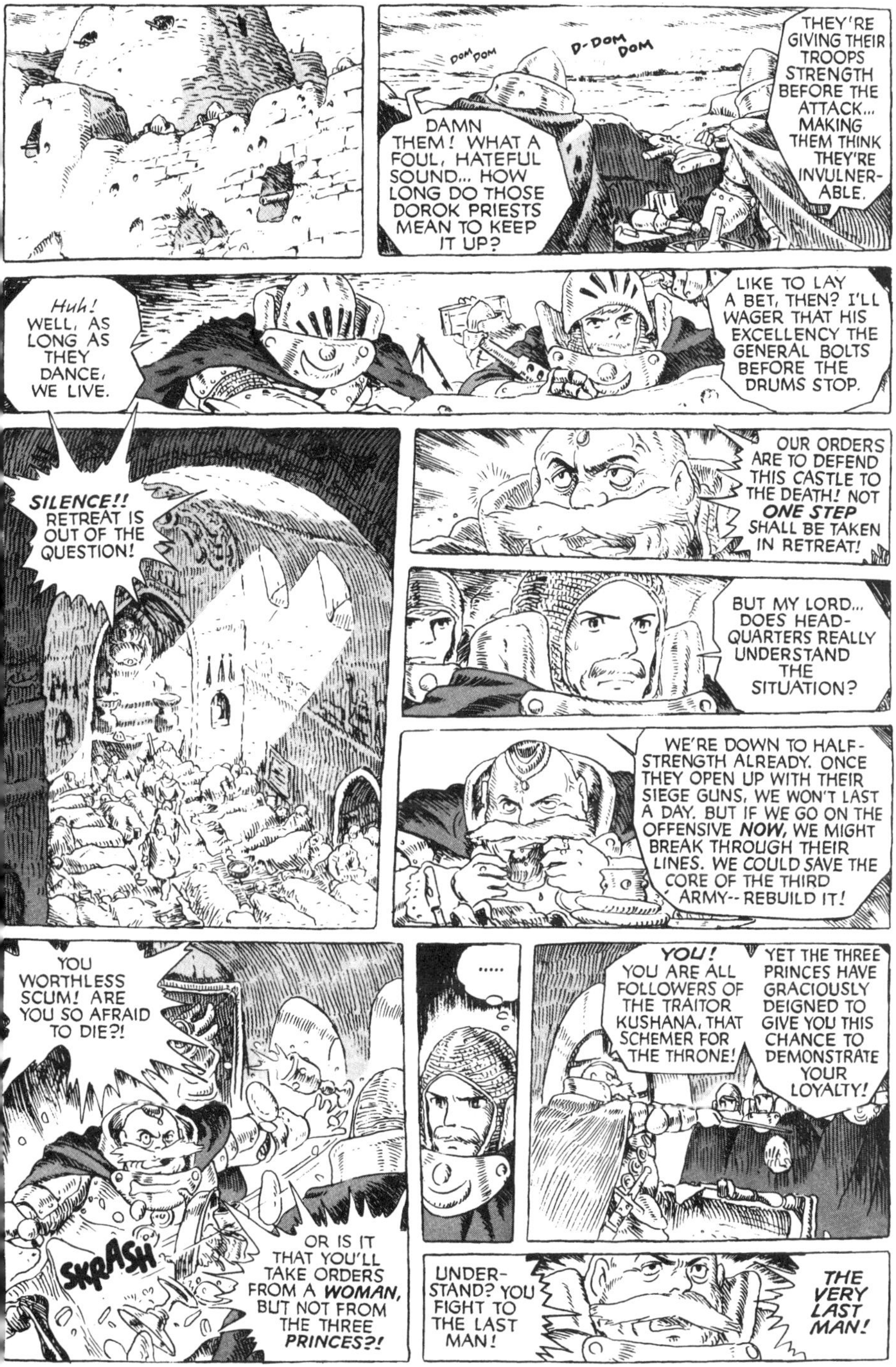
DOM DOM
D-DOM DOM
DAMN THEM! WHAT A FOUL, HATEFUL SOUND... HOW LONG DO THOSE DOROK PRIESTS MEAN TO KEEP IT UP?
THEY'RE GIVING THEIR TROOPS STRENGTH BEFORE THE ATTACK... MAKING THEM THINK THEY'RE INVULNERABLE.
Huh! WELL, AS LONG AS THEY DANCE, WE LIVE.
LIKE TO LAY A BET, THEN? I'LL WAGER THAT HIS EXCELLENCY THE GENERAL BOLTS BEFORE THE DRUMS STOP.
SILENCE!! RETREAT IS OUT OF THE QUESTION!
OUR ORDERS ARE TO DEFEND THIS CASTLE TO THE DEATH! NOT ONE STEP SHALL BE TAKEN IN RETREAT!
BUT MY LORD... DOES HEAD-QUARTERS REALLY UNDERSTAND THE SITUATION?
WE'RE DOWN TO HALF-STRENGTH ALREADY. ONCE THEY OPEN UP WITH THEIR SIEGE GUNS, WE WON'T LAST A DAY. BUT IF WE GO ON THE OFFENSIVE NOW, WE MIGHT BREAK THROUGH THEIR LINES. WE COULD SAVE THE CORE OF THE THIRD ARMY-- REBUILD IT!
YOU WORTHLESS SCUM! ARE YOU SO AFRAID TO DIE?!
SKRASH
OR IS IT THAT YOU'LL TAKE ORDERS FROM A WOMAN, BUT NOT FROM THE THREE PRINCES?!
.....
YOU! YOU ARE ALL FOLLOWERS OF THE TRAITOR KUSHANA, THAT SCHEMER FOR THE THRONE!
YET THE THREE PRINCES HAVE GRACIOUSLY DEIGNED TO GIVE YOU THIS CHANCE TO DEMONSTRATE YOUR LOYALTY!
UNDER-STAND? YOU FIGHT TO THE LAST MAN!
THE VERY LAST MAN!

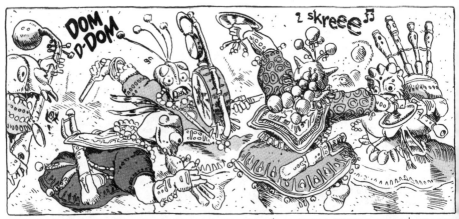

‹WARRIORS! THE HOUR OF REVERENCE IS NIGH! DESTROY THE HERETICS WHO HAVE VIOLATED OUR SACRED LAND!›

‹SLAY THEM! SLAY THE HERETICS! DEATH TO THE TORUMEKIAN DOGS!›

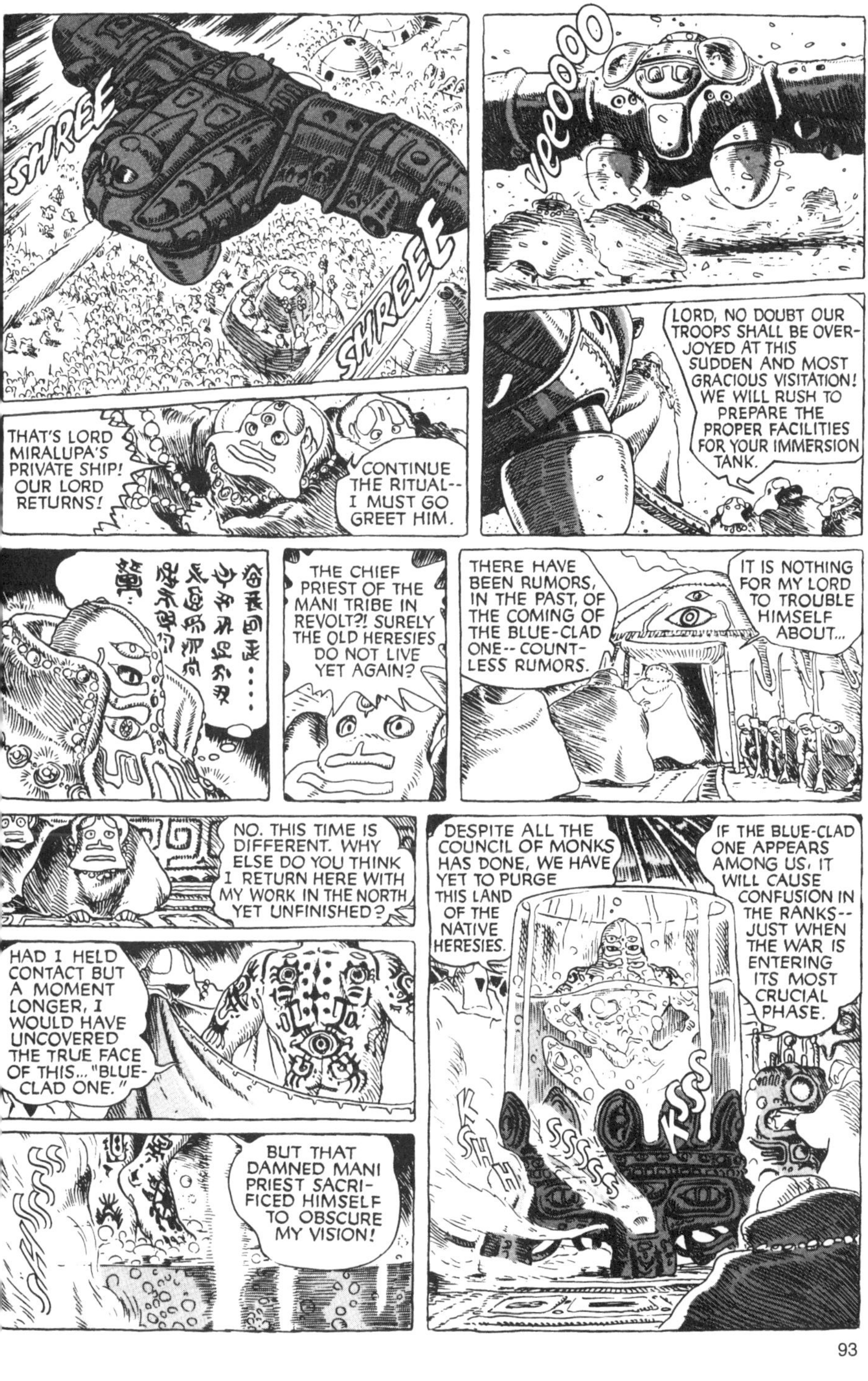
SHREE
SHREEE
SHREEE
THAT'S LORD MIRALUPA'S PRIVATE SHIP! OUR LORD RETURNS!
CONTINUE THE RITUAL-- I MUST GO GREET HIM.
VEEOOOO
LORD, NO DOUBT OUR TROOPS SHALL BE OVER-JOYED AT THIS SUDDEN AND MOST GRACIOUS VISITATION! WE WILL RUSH TO PREPARE THE PROPER FACILITIES FOR YOUR IMMERSION TANK.
THE CHIEF PRIEST OF THE MANI TRIBE IN REVOLT?! SURELY THE OLD HERESIES DO NOT LIVE YET AGAIN?
THERE HAVE BEEN RUMORS, IN THE PAST, OF THE COMING OF THE BLUE-CLAD ONE-- COUNT-LESS RUMORS.
IT IS NOTHING FOR MY LORD TO TROUBLE HIMSELF ABOUT...
NO. THIS TIME IS DIFFERENT. WHY ELSE DO YOU THINK I RETURN HERE WITH MY WORK IN THE NORTH YET UNFINISHED?
HAD I HELD CONTACT BUT A MOMENT LONGER, I WOULD HAVE UNCOVERED THE TRUE FACE OF THIS... "BLUE-CLAD ONE."
BUT THAT DAMNED MANI PRIEST SACRI-FICED HIMSELF TO OBSCURE MY VISION!
DESPITE ALL THE COUNCIL OF MONKS HAS DONE, WE HAVE YET TO PURGE THIS LAND OF THE NATIVE HERESIES.
IF THE BLUE-CLAD ONE APPEARS AMONG US, IT WILL CAUSE CONFUSION IN THE RANKS-- JUST WHEN THE WAR IS ENTERING ITS MOST CRUCIAL PHASE.
KSSS
SSSSS
KSHHH

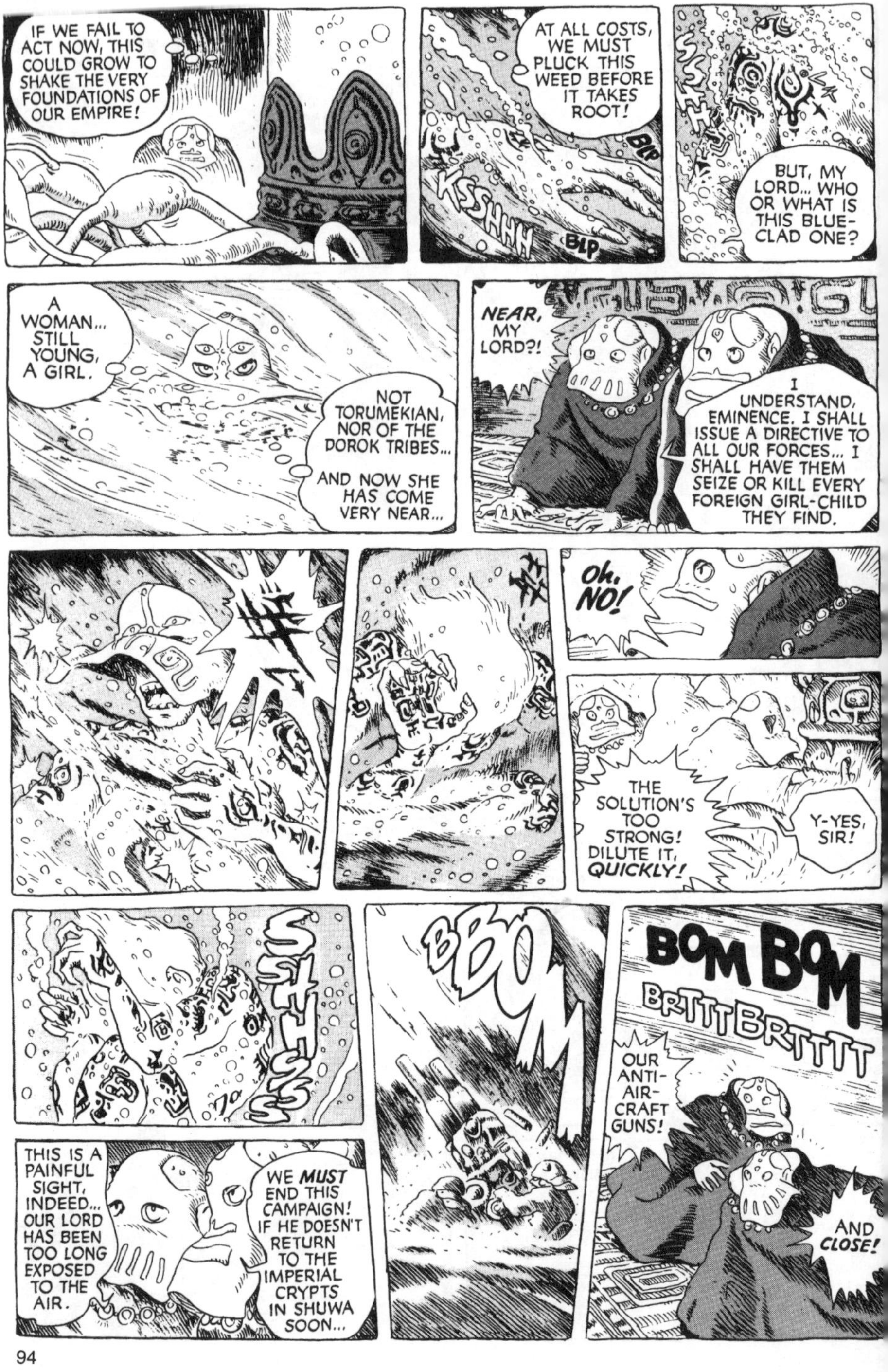

IF WE FAIL TO ACT NOW, THIS COULD GROW TO SHAKE THE VERY FOUNDATIONS OF OUR EMPIRE!
AT ALL COSTS, WE MUST PLUCK THIS WEED BEFORE IT TAKES ROOT!
BLP
KSSHHH
BLP
BUT, MY LORD... WHO OR WHAT IS THIS BLUE-CLAD ONE?
A WOMAN... STILL YOUNG, A GIRL.
NOT TORUMEKIAN, NOR OF THE DOROK TRIBES...
AND NOW SHE HAS COME VERY NEAR...
NEAR, MY LORD?!
I UNDERSTAND, EMINENCE. I SHALL ISSUE A DIRECTIVE TO ALL OUR FORCES... I SHALL HAVE THEM SEIZE OR KILL EVERY FOREIGN GIRL-CHILD THEY FIND.
Oh, NO!
THE SOLUTION'S TOO STRONG! DILUTE IT, QUICKLY!
Y-YES, SIR!
SSHHSSS
BBOM
BOM BOM
BRTTT BRTTTTT
OUR ANTI-AIR-CRAFT GUNS!
THIS IS A PAINFUL SIGHT, INDEED... OUR LORD HAS BEEN TOO LONG EXPOSED TO THE AIR.
WE MUST END THIS CAMPAIGN! IF HE DOESN'T RETURN TO THE IMPERIAL CRYPTS IN SHUWA SOON...
AND CLOSE!

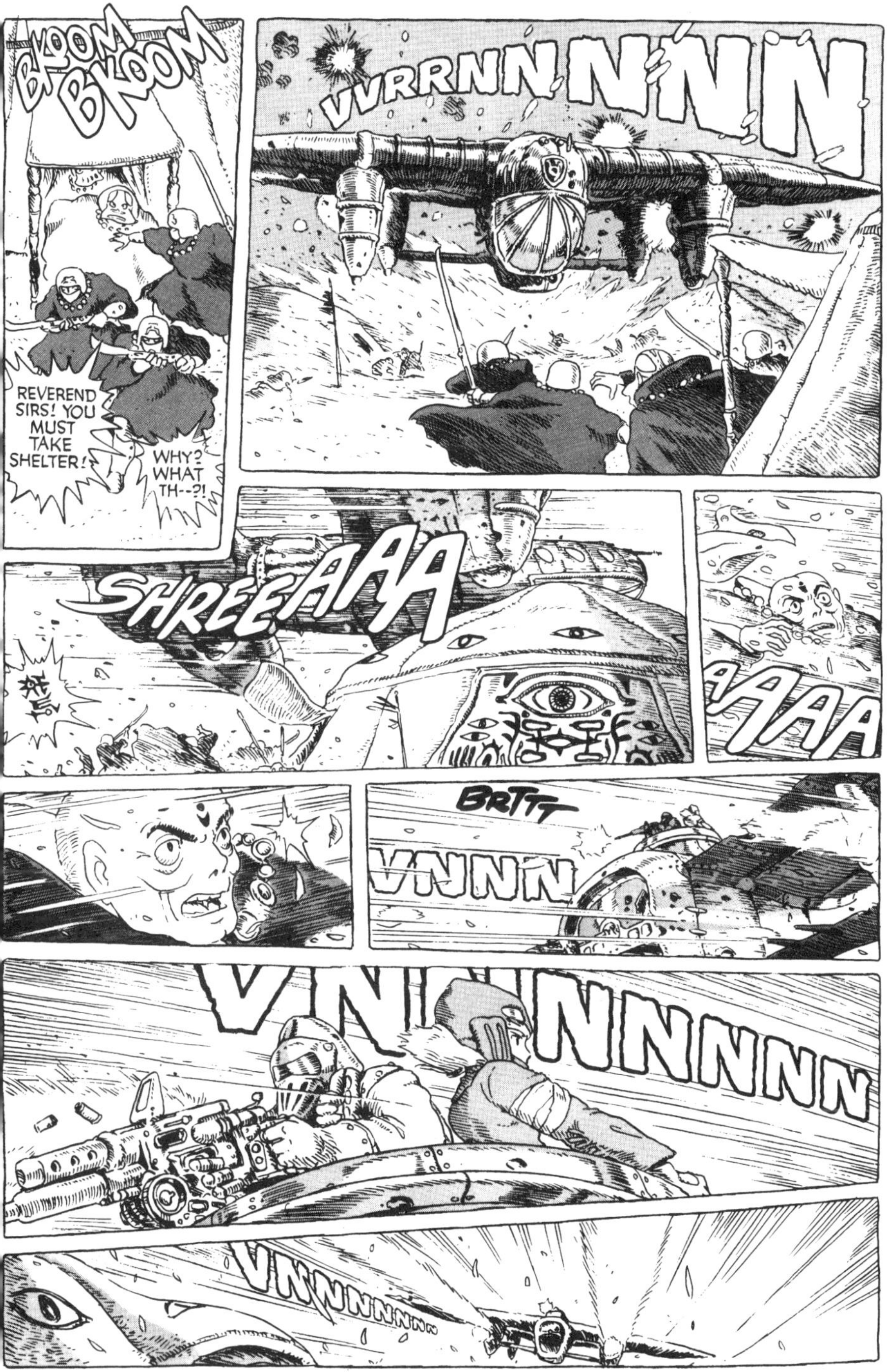
BKOOM BKOOM
REVEREND SIRS! YOU MUST TAKE SHELTER!
WHY? WHAT TH--?!
VVRRNNNNNN
SHREEAAAA
AAAA
BRTTT
VNNN
VNNNNNNNNN
VNNNNNNNNN

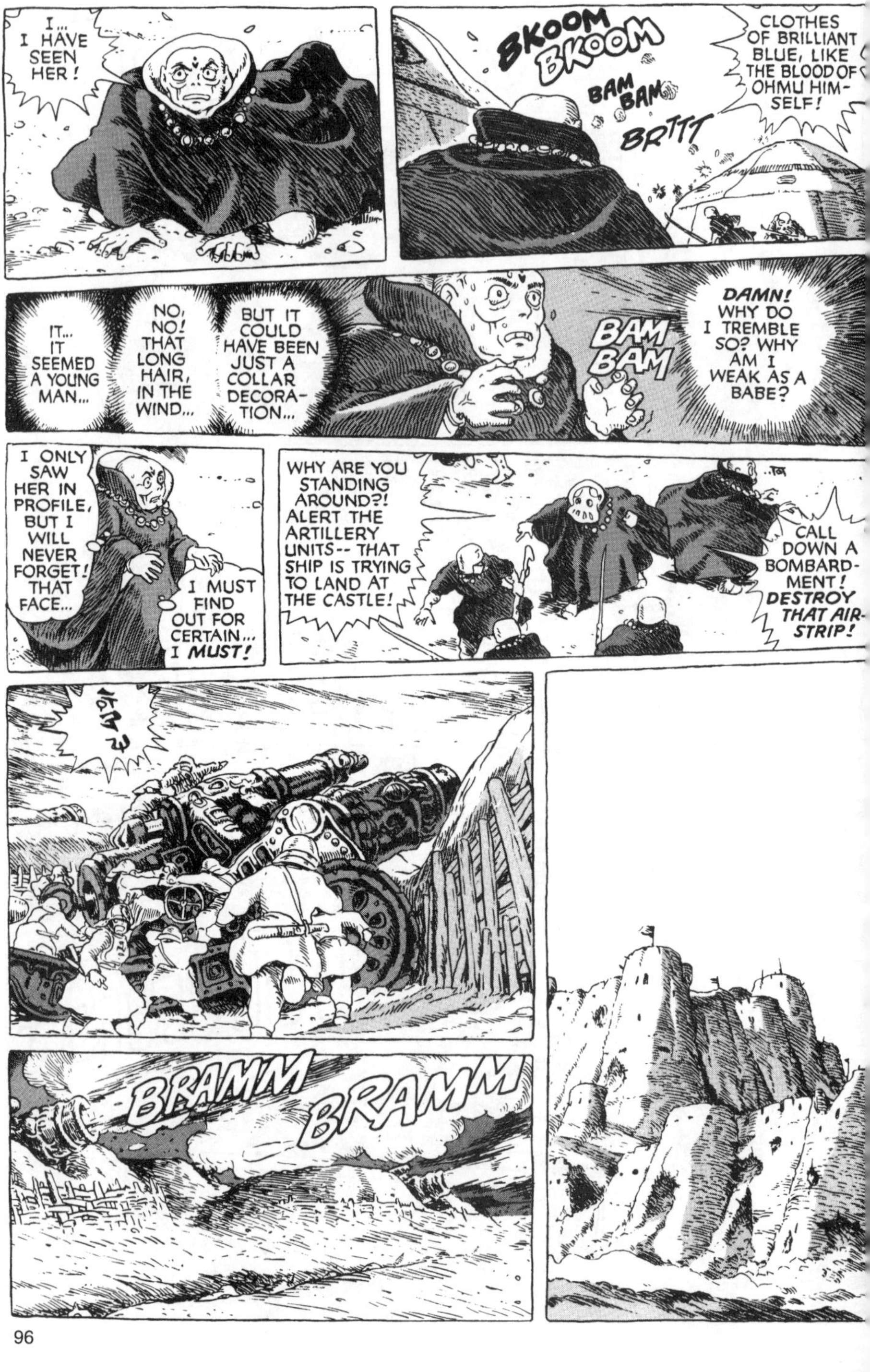
I... I HAVE SEEN HER!
BKOOM BKOOM
BAM BAM
BRTTT
CLOTHES OF BRILLIANT BLUE, LIKE THE BLOOD OF OHMU HIMSELF!
IT... IT SEEMED A YOUNG MAN...
NO, NO! THAT LONG HAIR, IN THE WIND...
BUT IT COULD HAVE BEEN JUST A COLLAR DECORATION...
BAM BAM
DAMN! WHY DO I TREMBLE SO? WHY AM I WEAK AS A BABE?
I ONLY SAW HER IN PROFILE, BUT I WILL NEVER FORGET! THAT FACE...
I MUST FIND OUT FOR CERTAIN... I MUST!
WHY ARE YOU STANDING AROUND?! ALERT THE ARTILLERY UNITS-- THAT SHIP IS TRYING TO LAND AT THE CASTLE!
CALL DOWN A BOMBARDMENT! DESTROY THAT AIRSTRIP!
BRAMM BRAMM

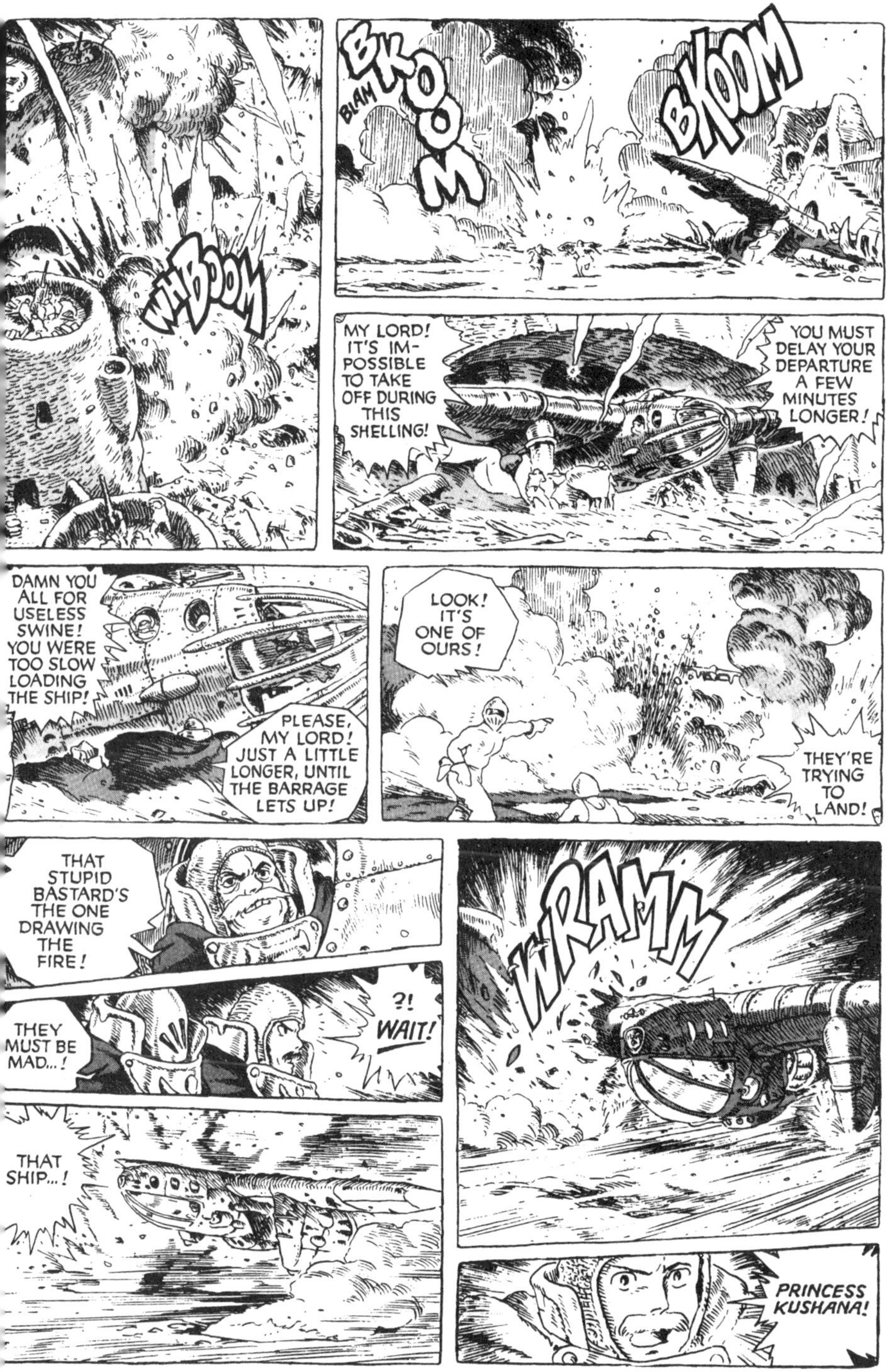
WHBOOM
BKOOM
BLAM
BKOOM
MY LORD! IT'S IMPOSSIBLE TO TAKE OFF DURING THIS SHELLING!
YOU MUST DELAY YOUR DEPARTURE A FEW MINUTES LONGER!
DAMN YOU ALL FOR USELESS SWINE! YOU WERE TOO SLOW LOADING THE SHIP!
PLEASE, MY LORD! JUST A LITTLE LONGER, UNTIL THE BARRAGE LETS UP!
LOOK! IT'S ONE OF OURS!
THEY'RE TRYING TO LAND!
THAT STUPID BASTARD'S THE ONE DRAWING THE FIRE!
THEY MUST BE MAD...!
?! WAIT!
THAT SHIP...!
WRAMM
PRINCESS KUSHANA!

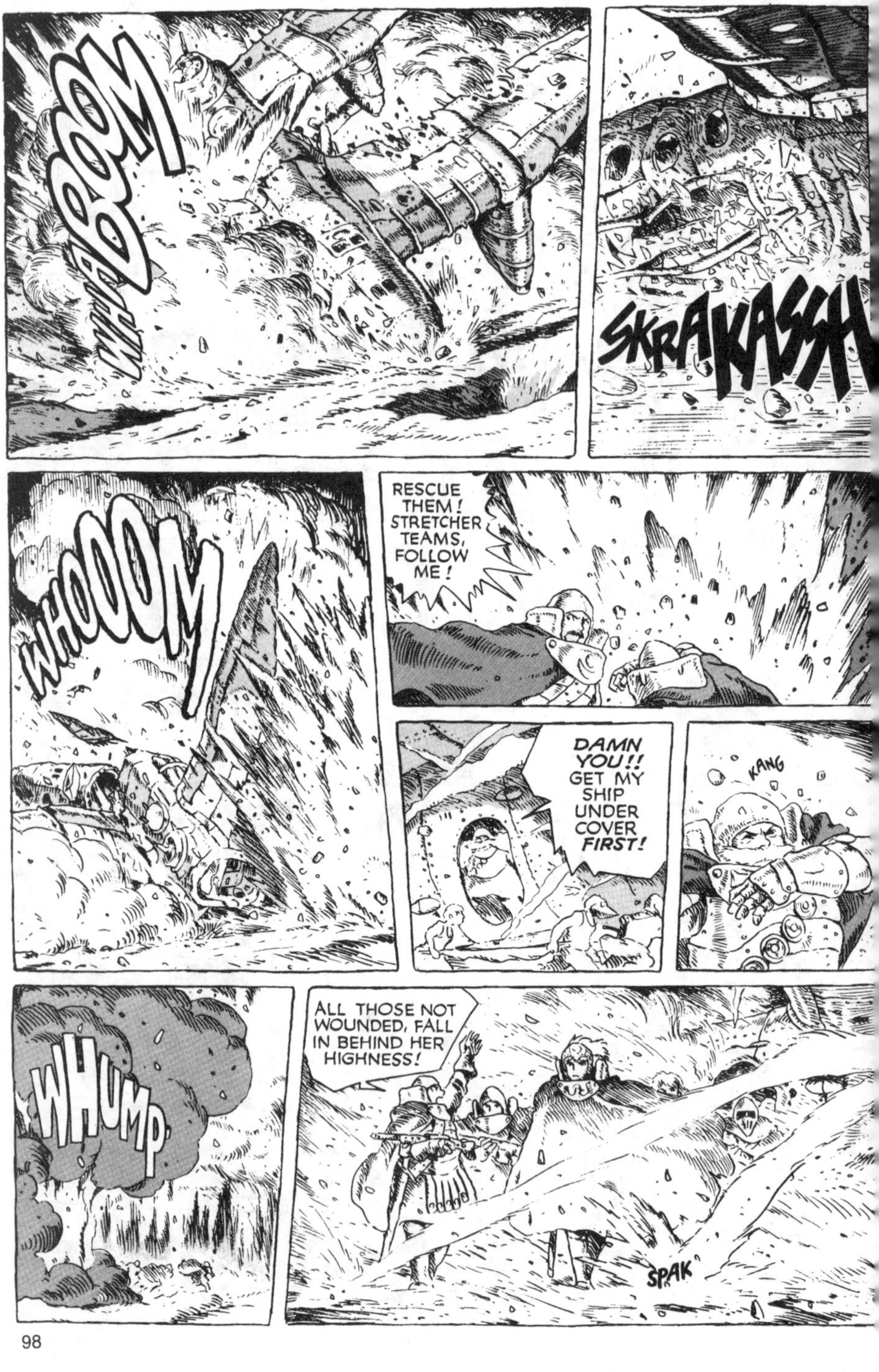
WHOOOOOMMM
SKRAKASSH
WHOOOOM
RESCUE THEM! STRETCHER TEAMS, FOLLOW ME!
DAMN YOU!! GET MY SHIP UNDER COVER FIRST!
KANG
WHUMP
ALL THOSE NOT WOUNDED, FALL IN BEHIND HER HIGHNESS!
SPAK

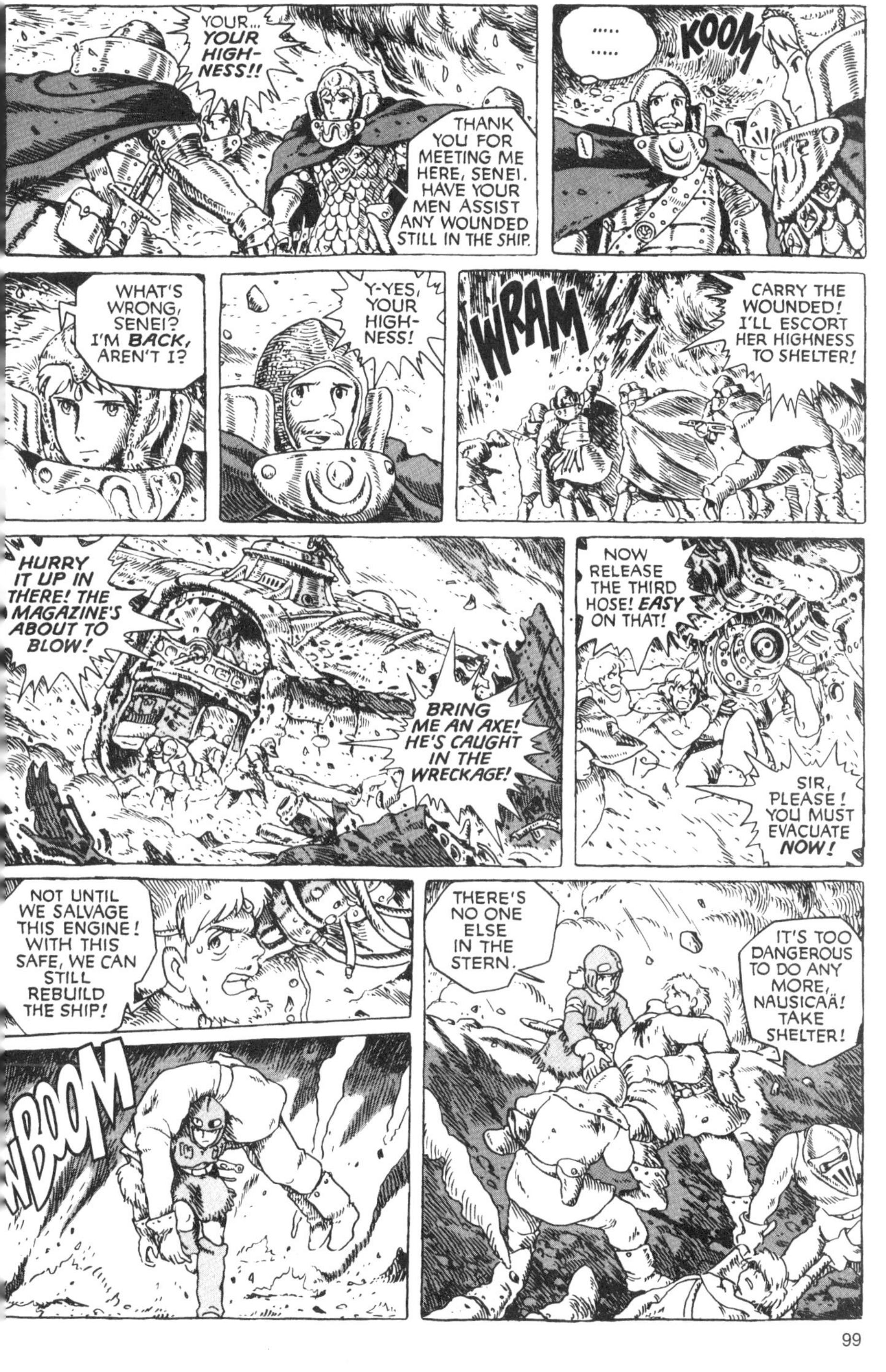
YOUR... YOUR HIGHNESS!!
THANK YOU FOR MEETING ME HERE, SENEI. HAVE YOUR MEN ASSIST ANY WOUNDED STILL IN THE SHIP.
.....
.....
KOOM
WHAT'S WRONG, SENEI? I'M BACK, AREN'T I?
Y-YES, YOUR HIGHNESS!
WRAM
CARRY THE WOUNDED! I'LL ESCORT HER HIGHNESS TO SHELTER!
HURRY IT UP IN THERE! THE MAGAZINE'S ABOUT TO BLOW!
BRING ME AN AXE! HE'S CAUGHT IN THE WRECKAGE!
NOW RELEASE THE THIRD HOSE! EASY ON THAT!
SIR, PLEASE! YOU MUST EVACUATE NOW!
NOT UNTIL WE SALVAGE THIS ENGINE! WITH THIS SAFE, WE CAN STILL REBUILD THE SHIP!
THERE'S NO ONE ELSE IN THE STERN.
IT'S TOO DANGEROUS TO DO ANY MORE, NAUSICAÄ! TAKE SHELTER!
WBOOM

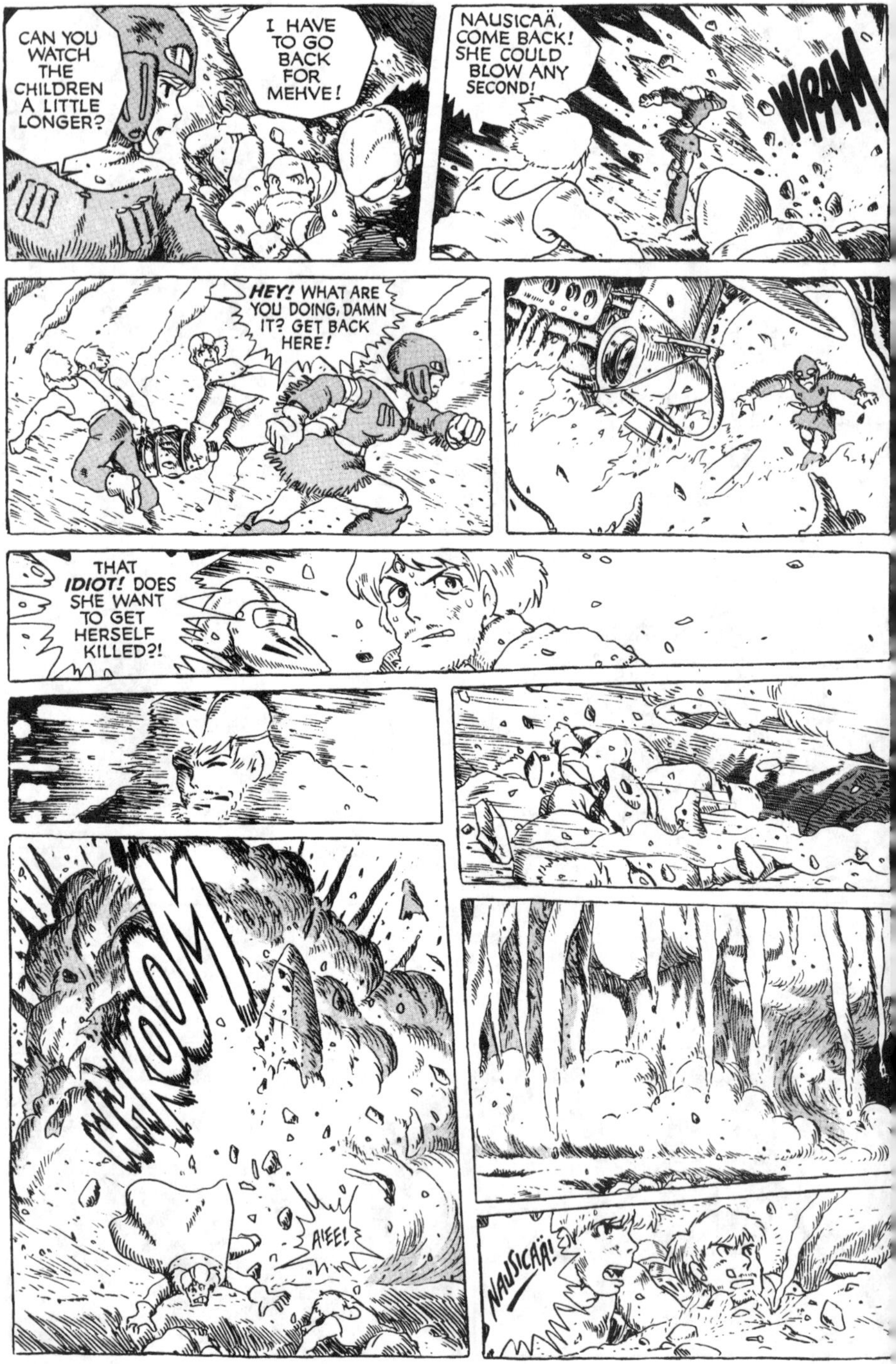
CAN YOU WATCH THE CHILDREN A LITTLE LONGER?
I HAVE TO GO BACK FOR MEHVE!
NAUSICAÄ, COME BACK! SHE COULD BLOW ANY SECOND!
WRAM
HEY! WHAT ARE YOU DOING, DAMN IT? GET BACK HERE!
THAT IDIOT! DOES SHE WANT TO GET HERSELF KILLED?!
WHOOM
AIEE!
NAUSICAÄ!

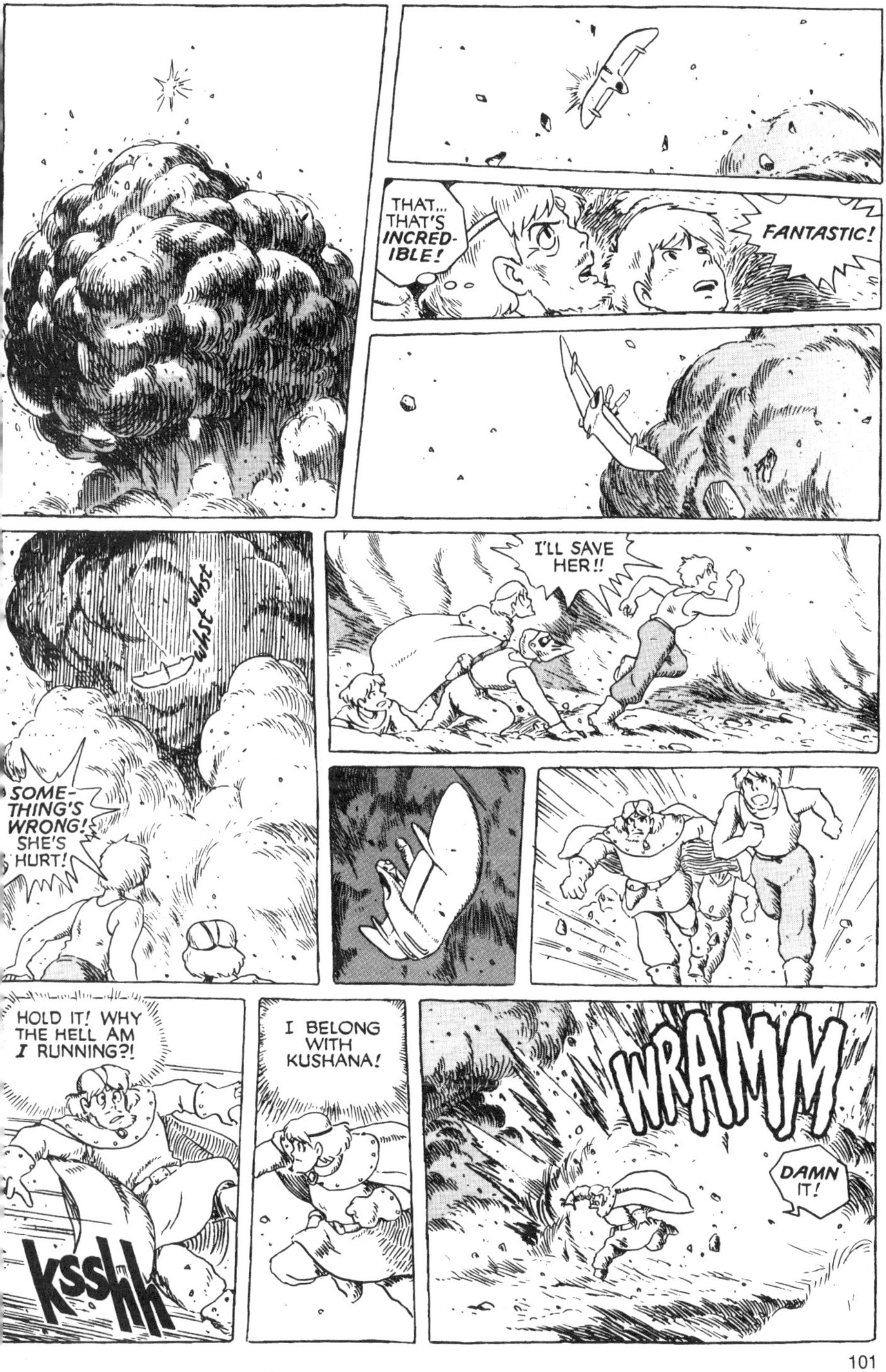
THAT... THAT'S INCREDIBLE!
FANTASTIC!
whst whst
I'LL SAVE HER!!
SOMETHING'S WRONG! SHE'S HURT!
HOLD IT! WHY THE HELL AM I RUNNING?!
ksshh
I BELONG WITH KUSHANA!
WRAMM
DAMN IT!

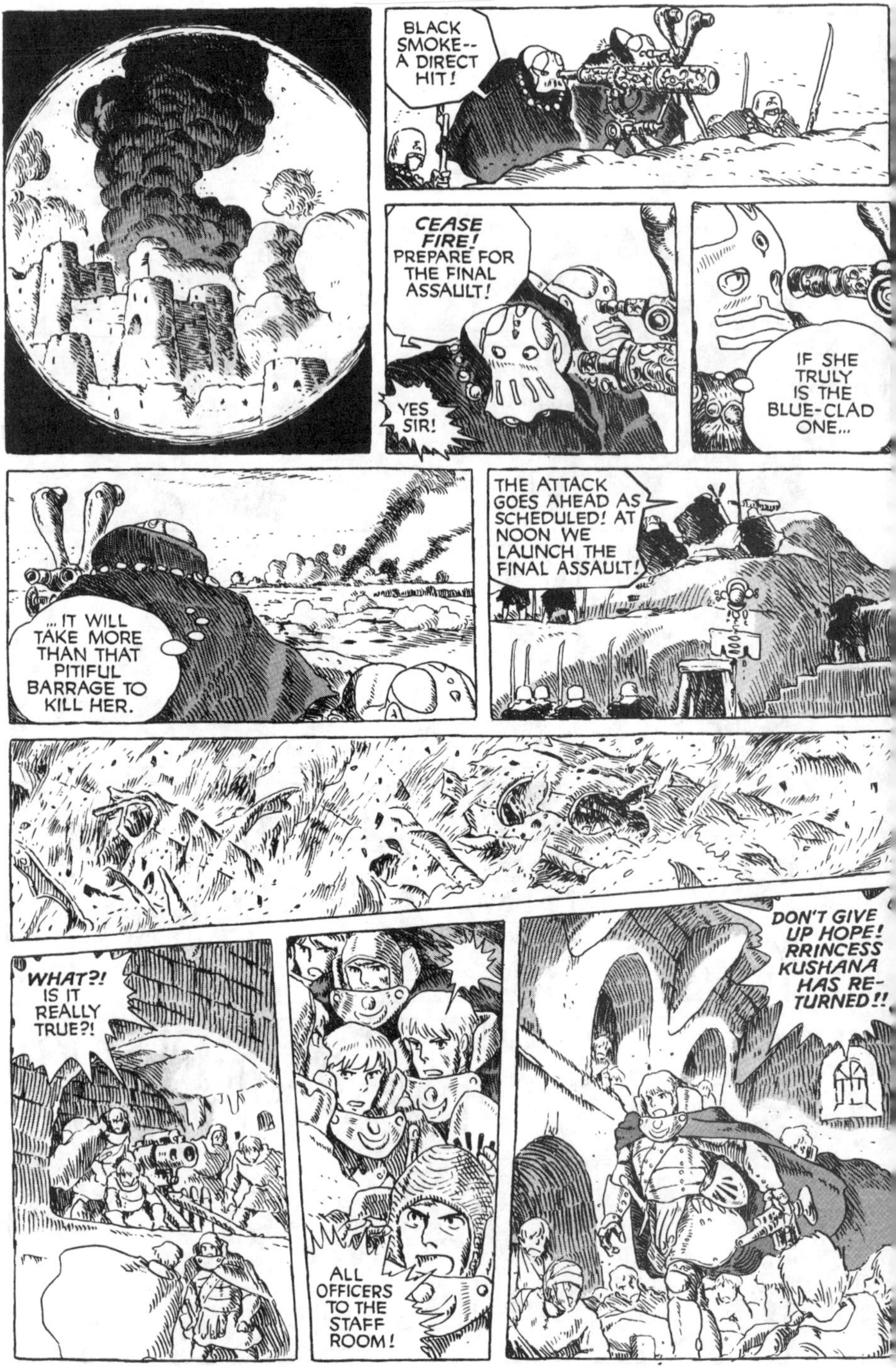
BLACK SMOKE-- A DIRECT HIT!
CEASE FIRE! PREPARE FOR THE FINAL ASSAULT!
YES SIR!
IF SHE TRULY IS THE BLUE-CLAD ONE...
...IT WILL TAKE MORE THAN THAT PITIFUL BARRAGE TO KILL HER.
THE ATTACK GOES AHEAD AS SCHEDULED! AT NOON WE LAUNCH THE FINAL ASSAULT!
DON'T GIVE UP HOPE! RRINCESS KUSHANA HAS RE-TURNED!!
ALL OFFICERS TO THE STAFF ROOM!
WHAT?! IS IT REALLY TRUE?!

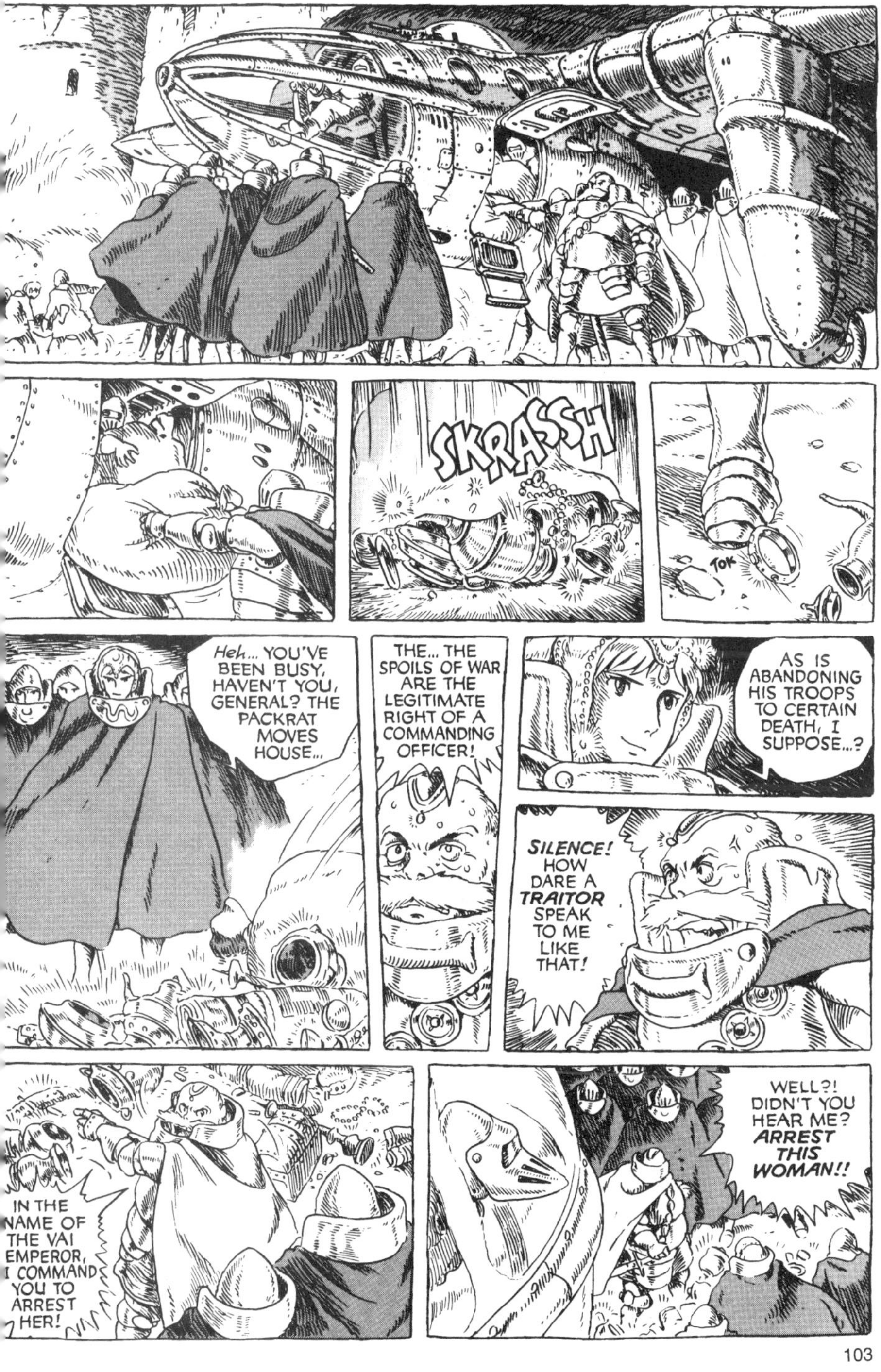
SKRASSH
TOK
Heh... YOU'VE BEEN BUSY, HAVEN'T YOU, GENERAL? THE PACKRAT MOVES HOUSE...
THE... THE SPOILS OF WAR ARE THE LEGITIMATE RIGHT OF A COMMANDING OFFICER!
AS IS ABANDONING HIS TROOPS TO CERTAIN DEATH, I SUPPOSE...?
SILENCE! HOW DARE A TRAITOR SPEAK TO ME LIKE THAT!
IN THE NAME OF THE VAI EMPEROR, I COMMAND YOU TO ARREST HER!
WELL?! DIDN'T YOU HEAR ME? ARREST THIS WOMAN!!

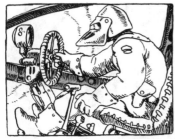

Uh, uh! NO, YOU DON'T!

THIS VESSEL HAS BEEN, *er*, "REQUISITIONED" BY THE THIRD ARMY.

GENERAL STAFF HEADQUARTERS REALLY KNOWS HOW TO EQUIP ITSELF, THOUGH... THIS SHIP'S A REAL BEAUTY.

I'VE NO INTENTION OF STRIPPING YOU OF YOUR RANK. I MERELY EXPECT YOU TO PERFORM YOUR DUTY AS A PROFESSIONAL SOLDIER.

DON'T MAKE ME LAUGH! YOU SERIOUSLY EXPECT ME TO HELP A *TRAITOR*?!

DON'T JUMP TO CONCLUSIONS, GENERAL. OUR GOALS MAY DIFFER SLIGHTLY, BUT SURELY YOU CAN STILL FIGHT THE DOROK?

THERE'S NOT MUCH TIME BEFORE THE SORTIE, SO REST NOW, WHILE YOU CAN.

THREE CHEERS FOR PRINCESS KUSHANA!

HURRAH! HURRAH!

HURRAH!

SENEI, I WANT TO SEE ALL THE COMPANY COMMANDERS.

THEY'RE ALREADY WAITING, YOUR HIGHNESS.

My body won't move... I feel so cold...

I wonder where I am...

This place... like a tomb...

...?

Something... in that corner...

Zhnnn

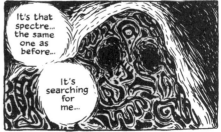

It's that spectre... the same one as before...

It's searching for me...

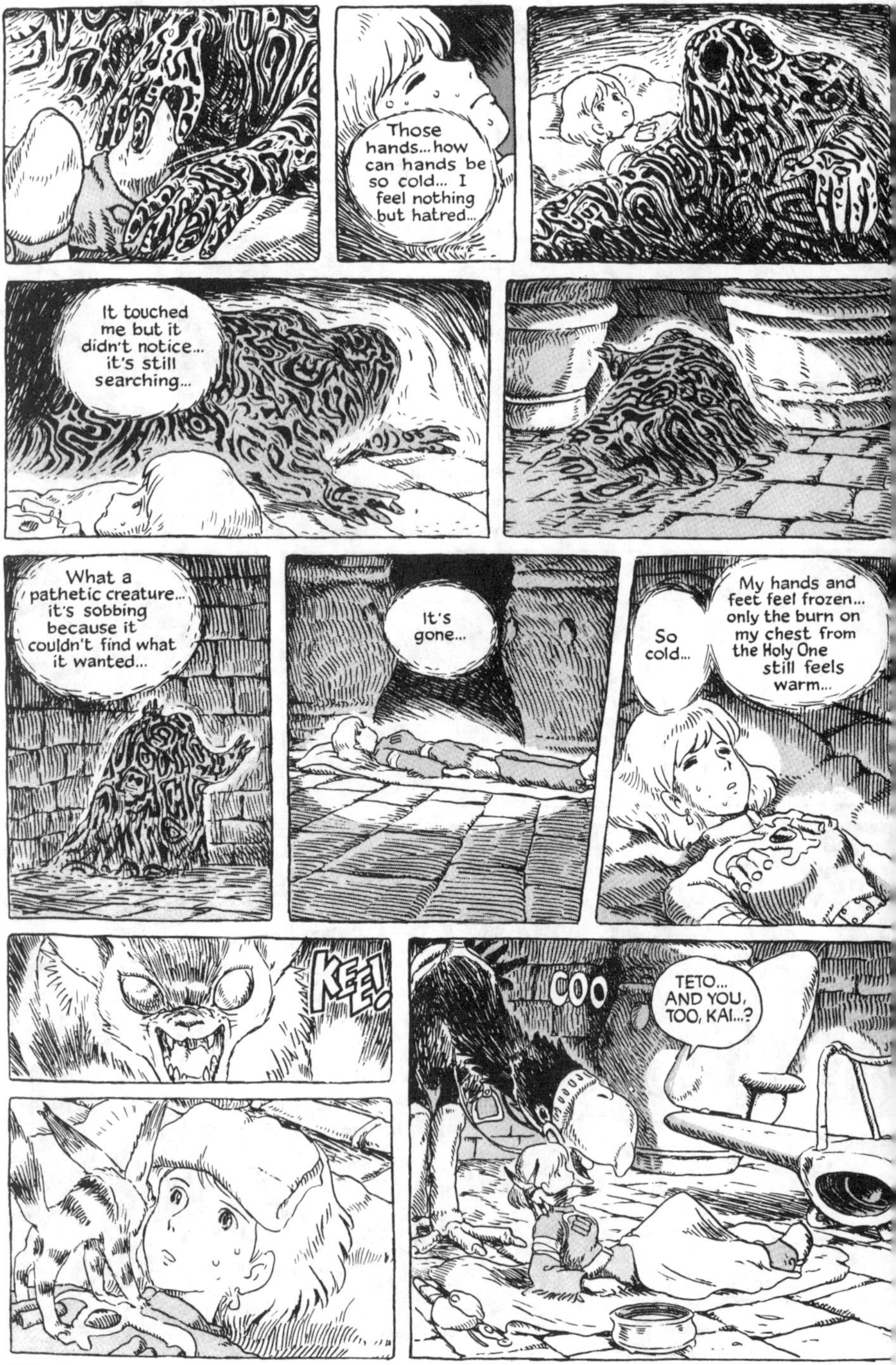
Those hands... how can hands be so cold... I feel nothing but hatred...
It touched me but it didn't notice... it's still searching...
What a pathetic creature... it's sobbing because it couldn't find what it wanted...
It's gone...
So cold...
My hands and feet feel frozen... only the burn on my chest from the Holy One still feels warm...
KEE!
COO
TETO... AND YOU, TOO, KAI...?

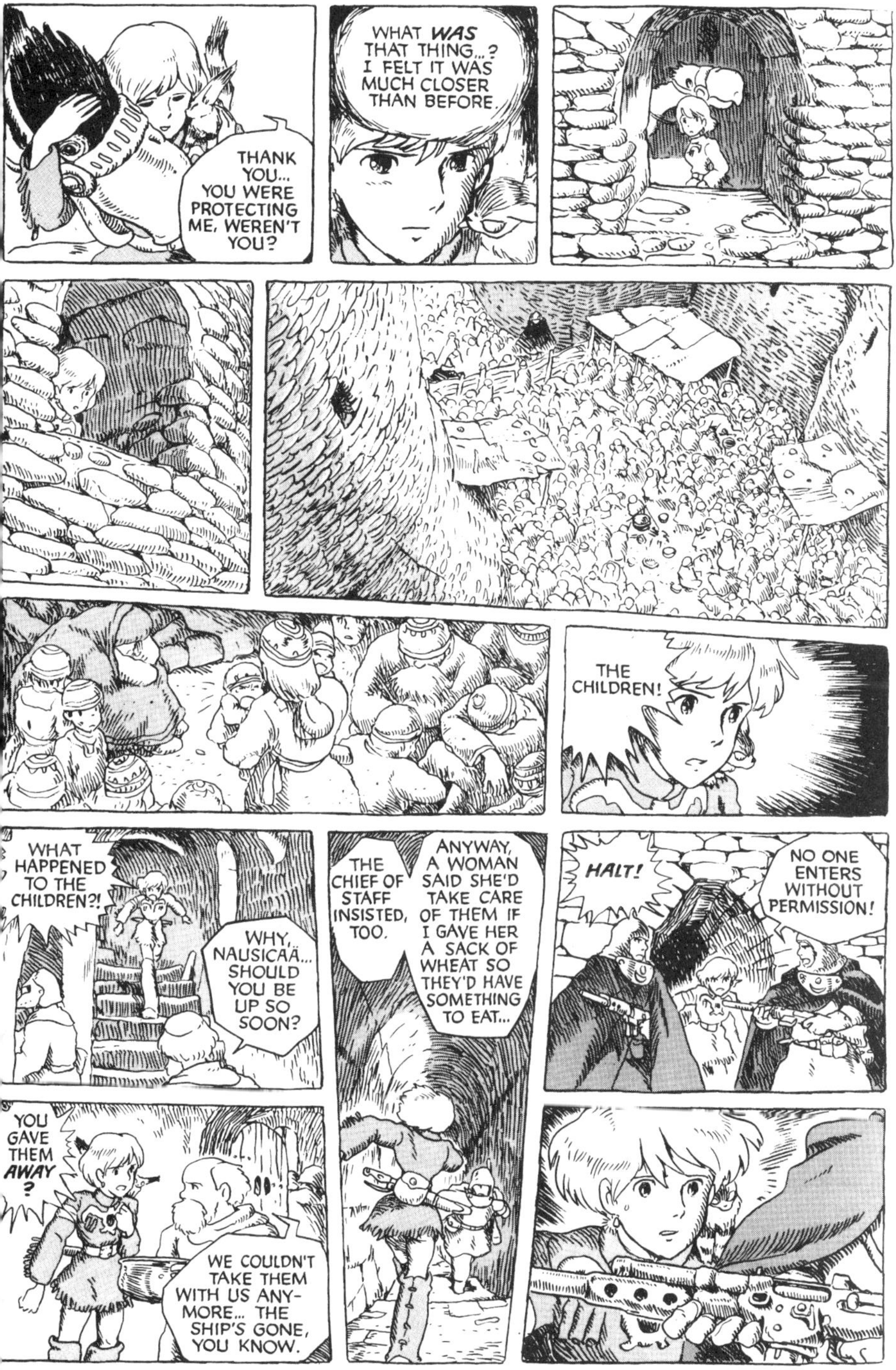
THANK YOU... YOU WERE PROTECTING ME, WEREN'T YOU?
WHAT *WAS* THAT THING...? I FELT IT WAS MUCH CLOSER THAN BEFORE.
THE CHILDREN!
WHAT HAPPENED TO THE CHILDREN?!
WHY, NAUSICAÄ... SHOULD YOU BE UP SO SOON?
ANYWAY, A WOMAN SAID SHE'D TAKE CARE OF THEM IF I GAVE HER A SACK OF WHEAT SO THEY'D HAVE SOMETHING TO EAT...
THE CHIEF OF STAFF INSISTED, TOO.
HALT!
NO ONE ENTERS WITHOUT PERMISSION!
YOU GAVE THEM *AWAY*?
WE COULDN'T TAKE THEM WITH US ANYMORE... THE SHIP'S GONE, YOU KNOW.

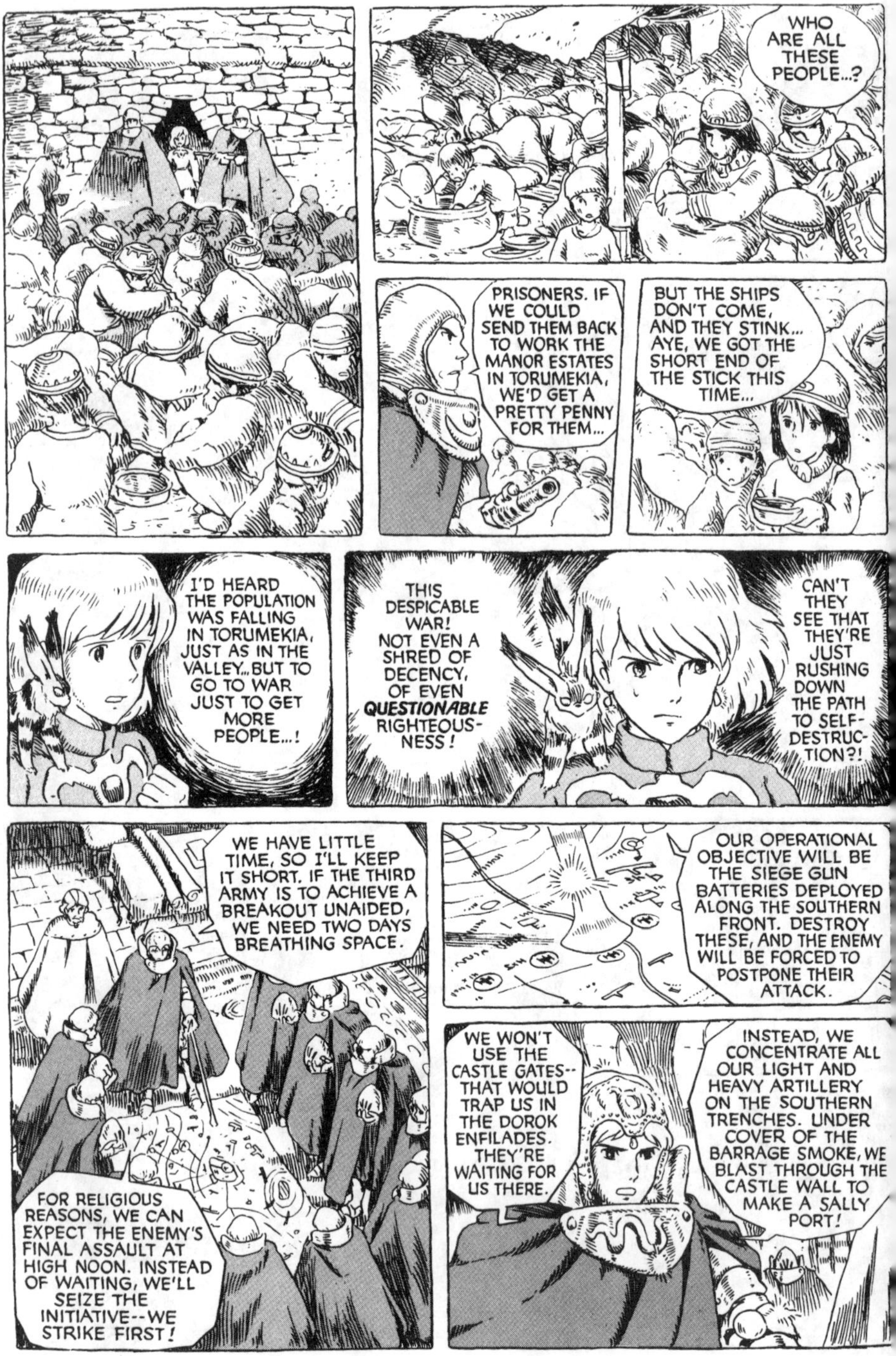
WHO ARE ALL THESE PEOPLE...?
PRISONERS. IF WE COULD SEND THEM BACK TO WORK THE MANOR ESTATES IN TORUMEKIA, WE'D GET A PRETTY PENNY FOR THEM...
BUT THE SHIPS DON'T COME, AND THEY STINK... AYE, WE GOT THE SHORT END OF THE STICK THIS TIME...
I'D HEARD THE POPULATION WAS FALLING IN TORUMEKIA, JUST AS IN THE VALLEY...BUT TO GO TO WAR JUST TO GET MORE PEOPLE...!
THIS DESPICABLE WAR! NOT EVEN A SHRED OF DECENCY, OF EVEN QUESTIONABLE RIGHTEOUSNESS!
CAN'T THEY SEE THAT THEY'RE JUST RUSHING DOWN THE PATH TO SELF-DESTRUCTION?!
WE HAVE LITTLE TIME, SO I'LL KEEP IT SHORT. IF THE THIRD ARMY IS TO ACHIEVE A BREAKOUT UNAIDED, WE NEED TWO DAYS BREATHING SPACE.
FOR RELIGIOUS REASONS, WE CAN EXPECT THE ENEMY'S FINAL ASSAULT AT HIGH NOON. INSTEAD OF WAITING, WE'LL SEIZE THE INITIATIVE--WE STRIKE FIRST!
OUR OPERATIONAL OBJECTIVE WILL BE THE SIEGE GUN BATTERIES DEPLOYED ALONG THE SOUTHERN FRONT. DESTROY THESE, AND THE ENEMY WILL BE FORCED TO POSTPONE THEIR ATTACK.
WE WON'T USE THE CASTLE GATES--THAT WOULD TRAP US IN THE DOROK ENFILADES. THEY'RE WAITING FOR US THERE.
INSTEAD, WE CONCENTRATE ALL OUR LIGHT AND HEAVY ARTILLERY ON THE SOUTHERN TRENCHES. UNDER COVER OF THE BARRAGE SMOKE, WE BLAST THROUGH THE CASTLE WALL TO MAKE A SALLY PORT!

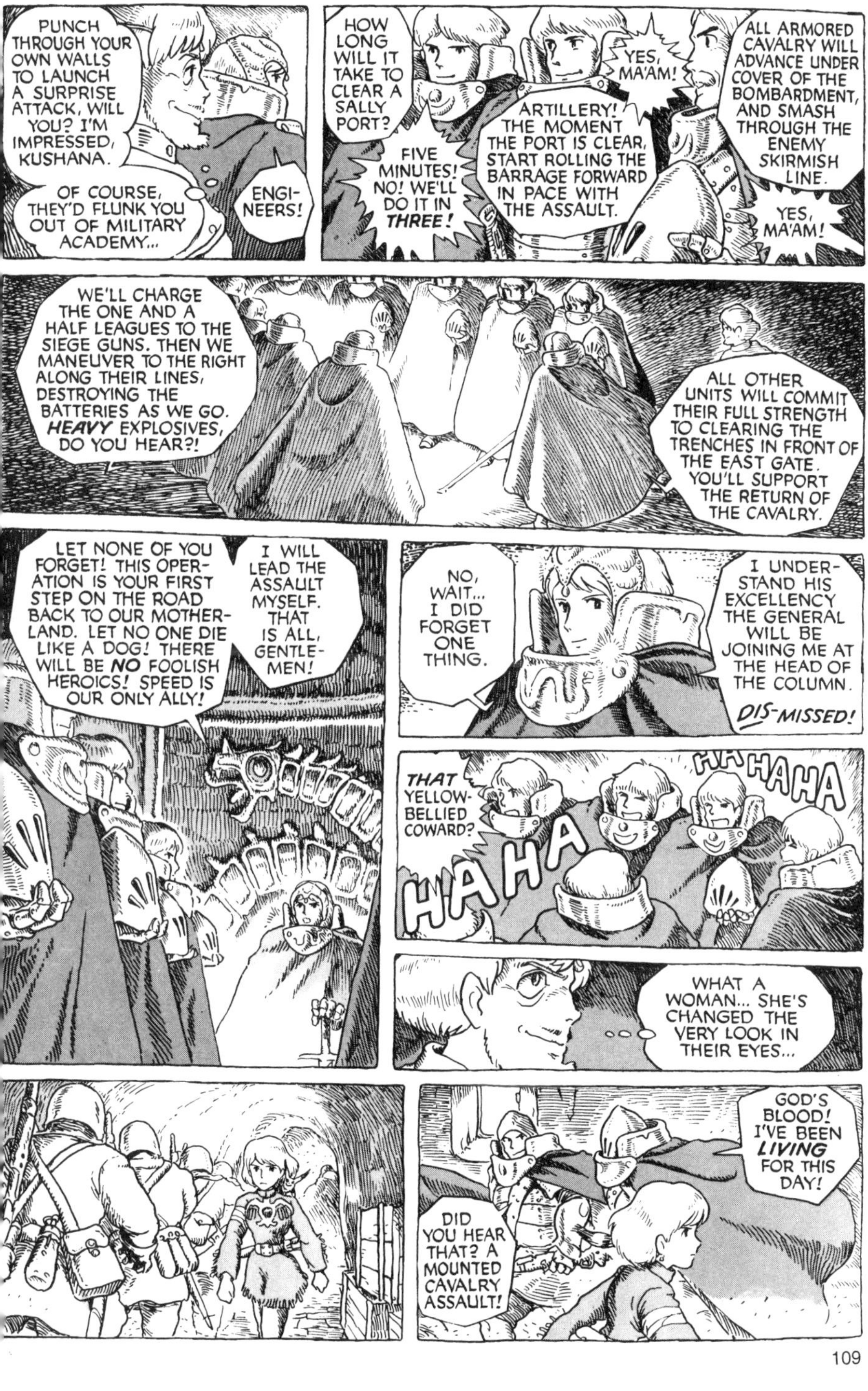
PUNCH THROUGH YOUR OWN WALLS TO LAUNCH A SURPRISE ATTACK, WILL YOU? I'M IMPRESSED, KUSHANA.
OF COURSE, THEY'D FLUNK YOU OUT OF MILITARY ACADEMY...
ENGI-NEERS!
HOW LONG WILL IT TAKE TO CLEAR A SALLY PORT?
FIVE MINUTES! NO! WE'LL DO IT IN THREE!
YES, MA'AM!
ARTILLERY! THE MOMENT THE PORT IS CLEAR, START ROLLING THE BARRAGE FORWARD IN PACE WITH THE ASSAULT.
ALL ARMORED CAVALRY WILL ADVANCE UNDER COVER OF THE BOMBARDMENT, AND SMASH THROUGH THE ENEMY SKIRMISH LINE.
YES, MA'AM!
WE'LL CHARGE THE ONE AND A HALF LEAGUES TO THE SIEGE GUNS. THEN WE MANEUVER TO THE RIGHT ALONG THEIR LINES, DESTROYING THE BATTERIES AS WE GO. HEAVY EXPLOSIVES, DO YOU HEAR?!
ALL OTHER UNITS WILL COMMIT THEIR FULL STRENGTH TO CLEARING THE TRENCHES IN FRONT OF THE EAST GATE. YOU'LL SUPPORT THE RETURN OF THE CAVALRY.
LET NONE OF YOU FORGET! THIS OPERATION IS YOUR FIRST STEP ON THE ROAD BACK TO OUR MOTHERLAND. LET NO ONE DIE LIKE A DOG! THERE WILL BE NO FOOLISH HEROICS! SPEED IS OUR ONLY ALLY!
I WILL LEAD THE ASSAULT MYSELF. THAT IS ALL, GENTLEMEN!
NO, WAIT... I DID FORGET ONE THING.
I UNDERSTAND HIS EXCELLENCY THE GENERAL WILL BE JOINING ME AT THE HEAD OF THE COLUMN.
DIS-MISSED!
THAT YELLOW-BELLIED COWARD?
HAHAHA
HAHA
WHAT A WOMAN... SHE'S CHANGED THE VERY LOOK IN THEIR EYES...
GOD'S BLOOD! I'VE BEEN LIVING FOR THIS DAY!
DID YOU HEAR THAT? A MOUNTED CAVALRY ASSAULT!

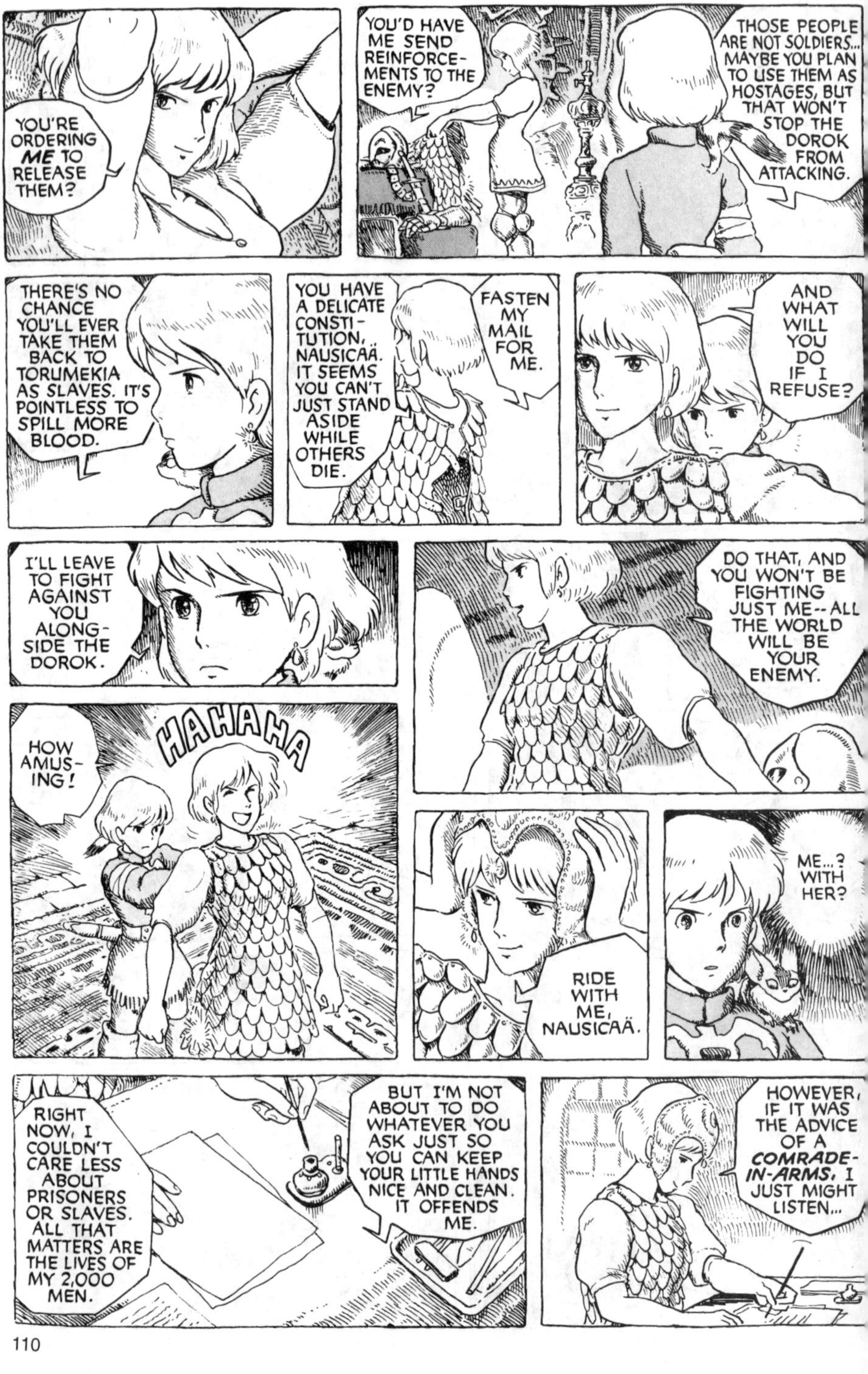
YOU'RE ORDERING ME TO RELEASE THEM?
YOU'D HAVE ME SEND REINFORCE-MENTS TO THE ENEMY?
THOSE PEOPLE ARE NOT SOLDIERS... MAYBE YOU PLAN TO USE THEM AS HOSTAGES, BUT THAT WON'T STOP THE DOROK FROM ATTACKING.
THERE'S NO CHANCE YOU'LL EVER TAKE THEM BACK TO TORUMEKIA AS SLAVES. IT'S POINTLESS TO SPILL MORE BLOOD.
YOU HAVE A DELICATE CONSTI-TUTION, NAUSICAÄ. IT SEEMS YOU CAN'T JUST STAND ASIDE WHILE OTHERS DIE.
FASTEN MY MAIL FOR ME.
AND WHAT WILL YOU DO IF I REFUSE?
I'LL LEAVE TO FIGHT AGAINST YOU ALONG-SIDE THE DOROK.
DO THAT, AND YOU WON'T BE FIGHTING JUST ME--ALL THE WORLD WILL BE YOUR ENEMY.
HOW AMUS-ING!
HAHAHA
RIDE WITH ME, NAUSICAÄ.
ME...? WITH HER?
RIGHT NOW, I COULDN'T CARE LESS ABOUT PRISONERS OR SLAVES. ALL THAT MATTERS ARE THE LIVES OF MY 2,000 MEN.
BUT I'M NOT ABOUT TO DO WHATEVER YOU ASK JUST SO YOU CAN KEEP YOUR LITTLE HANDS NICE AND CLEAN. IT OFFENDS ME.
HOWEVER, IF IT WAS THE ADVICE OF A COMRADE-IN-ARMS, I JUST MIGHT LISTEN...

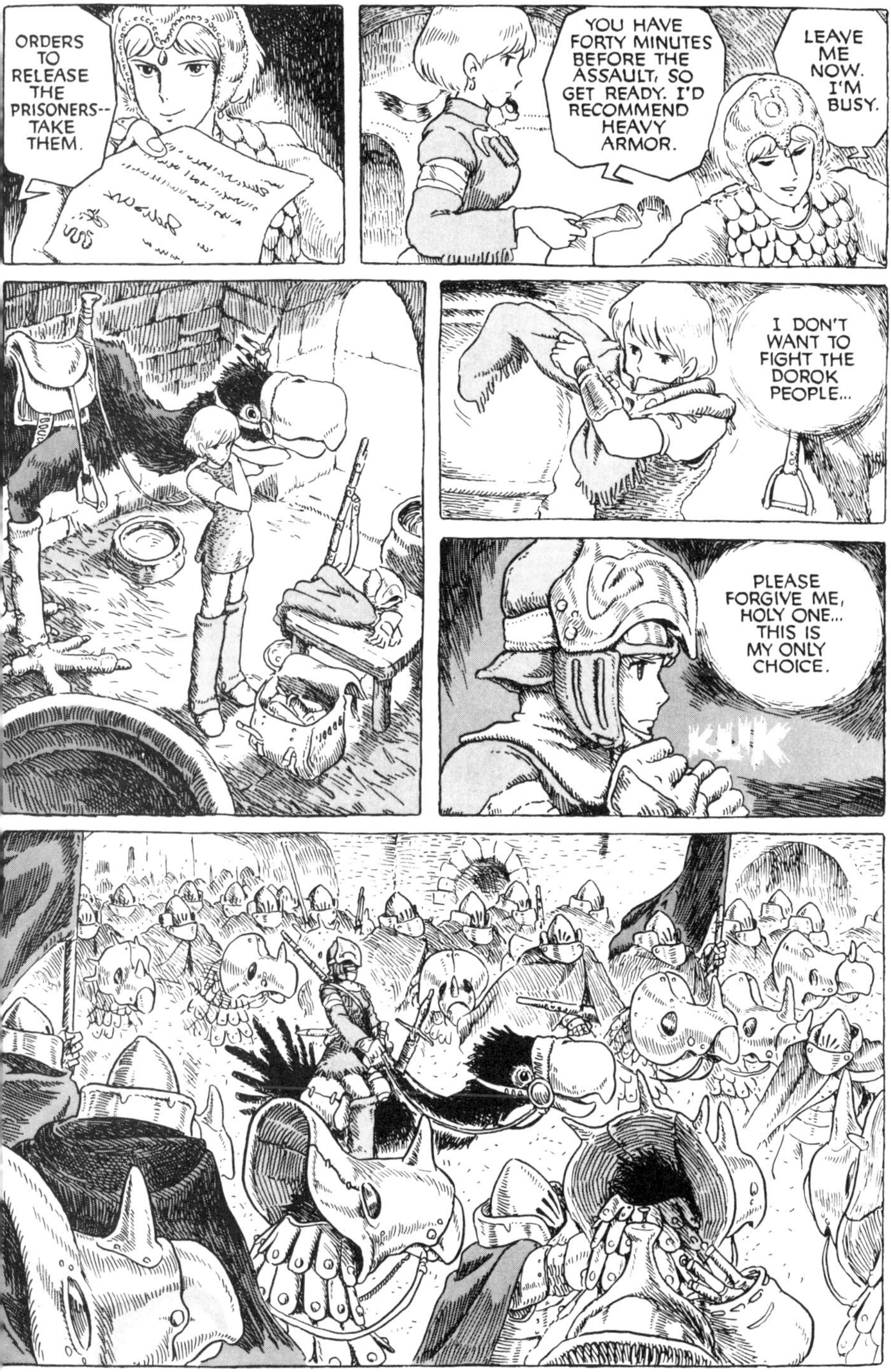
ORDERS TO RELEASE THE PRISONERS-- TAKE THEM.
YOU HAVE FORTY MINUTES BEFORE THE ASSAULT, SO GET READY. I'D RECOMMEND HEAVY ARMOR.
LEAVE ME NOW. I'M BUSY.
I DON'T WANT TO FIGHT THE DOROK PEOPLE...
PLEASE FORGIVE ME, HOLY ONE... THIS IS MY ONLY CHOICE.
KLIK

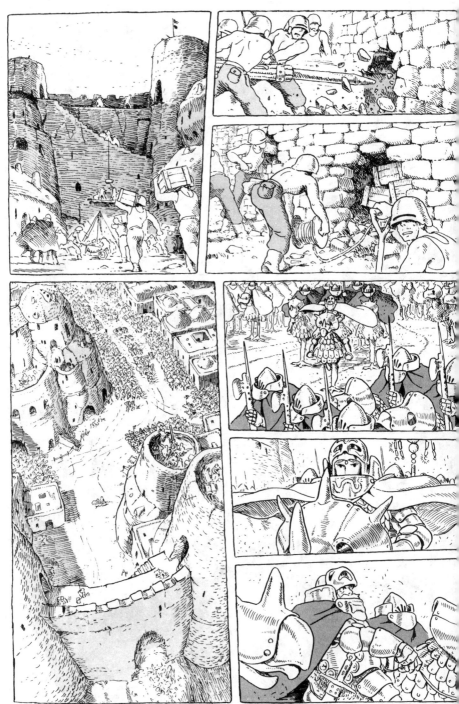

RIDE WITH ME.

YOU'RE LOOKING GALLANT, NAUSICAÄ.

LISTEN WELL! A SINGLE BRAVE WARRIOR FROM THE ALLIED NATIONS OF THE PERIPHERY RIDES WITH US IN OUR HOUR OF NEED!

LOOK UPON *NAUSICAÄ,* CHILD OF JHIL, CHIEFTAIN OF THE VALLEY OF WIND! LOOK UPON HER, AND HONOR HER!

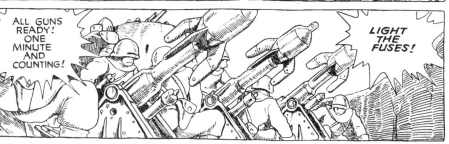

ALL GUNS READY! ONE MINUTE AND COUNTING!

LIGHT THE FUSES!

⟨LET ME OUT! FREE ME!⟩

MY LORD!

BLAM

BLAM

BLAM

BLAM

FIRE!!

THE ENEMY IS COMING! *SHE* IS COMING!

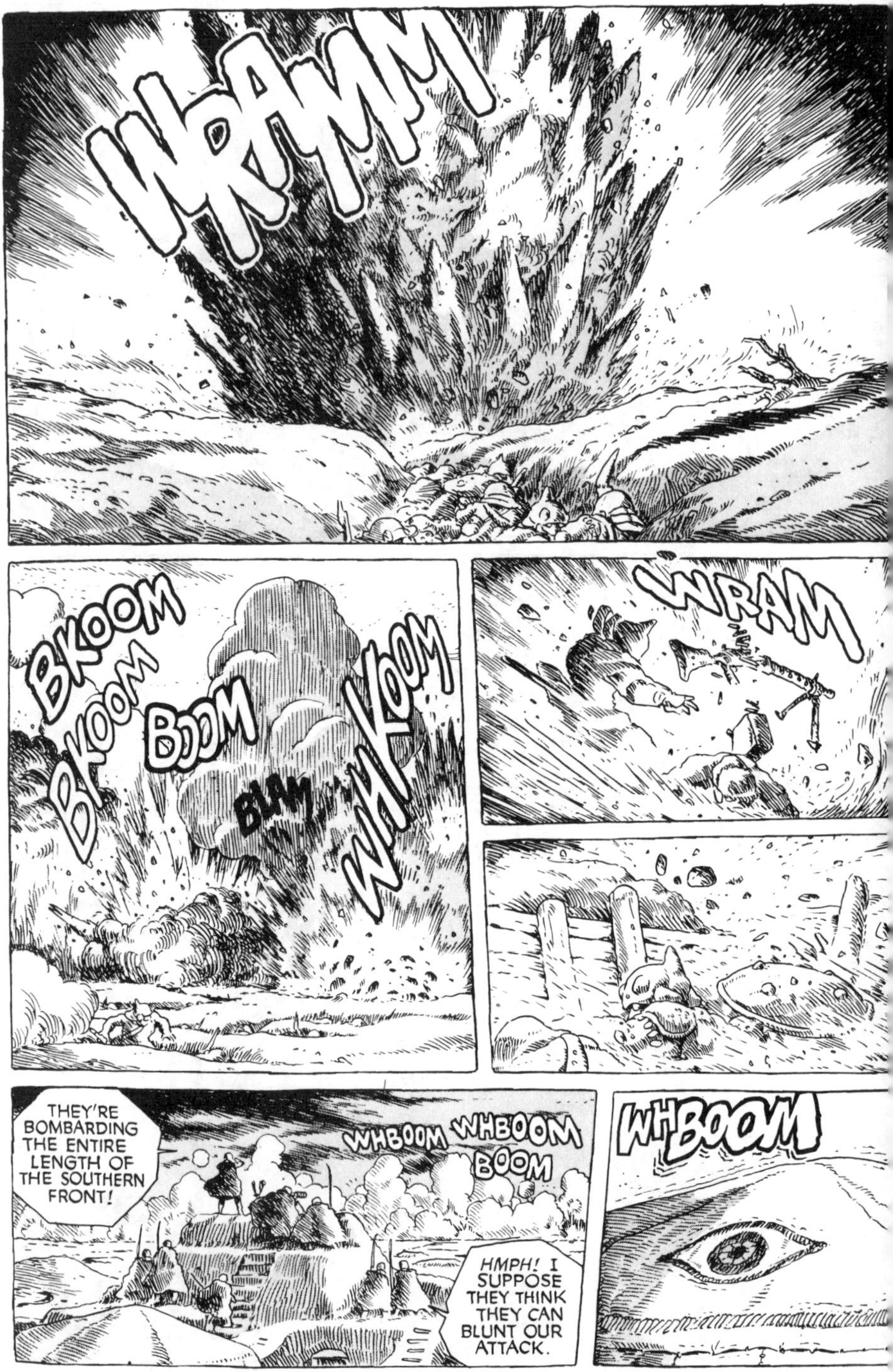
WHAMM
BKOOM
BKOOM
BOOM
BLAM
WHKOOM
WRAM
THEY'RE BOMBARDING THE ENTIRE LENGTH OF THE SOUTHERN FRONT!
WHBOOM WHBOOM
BOOM
HMPH! I SUPPOSE THEY THINK THEY CAN BLUNT OUR ATTACK.
WHBOOM

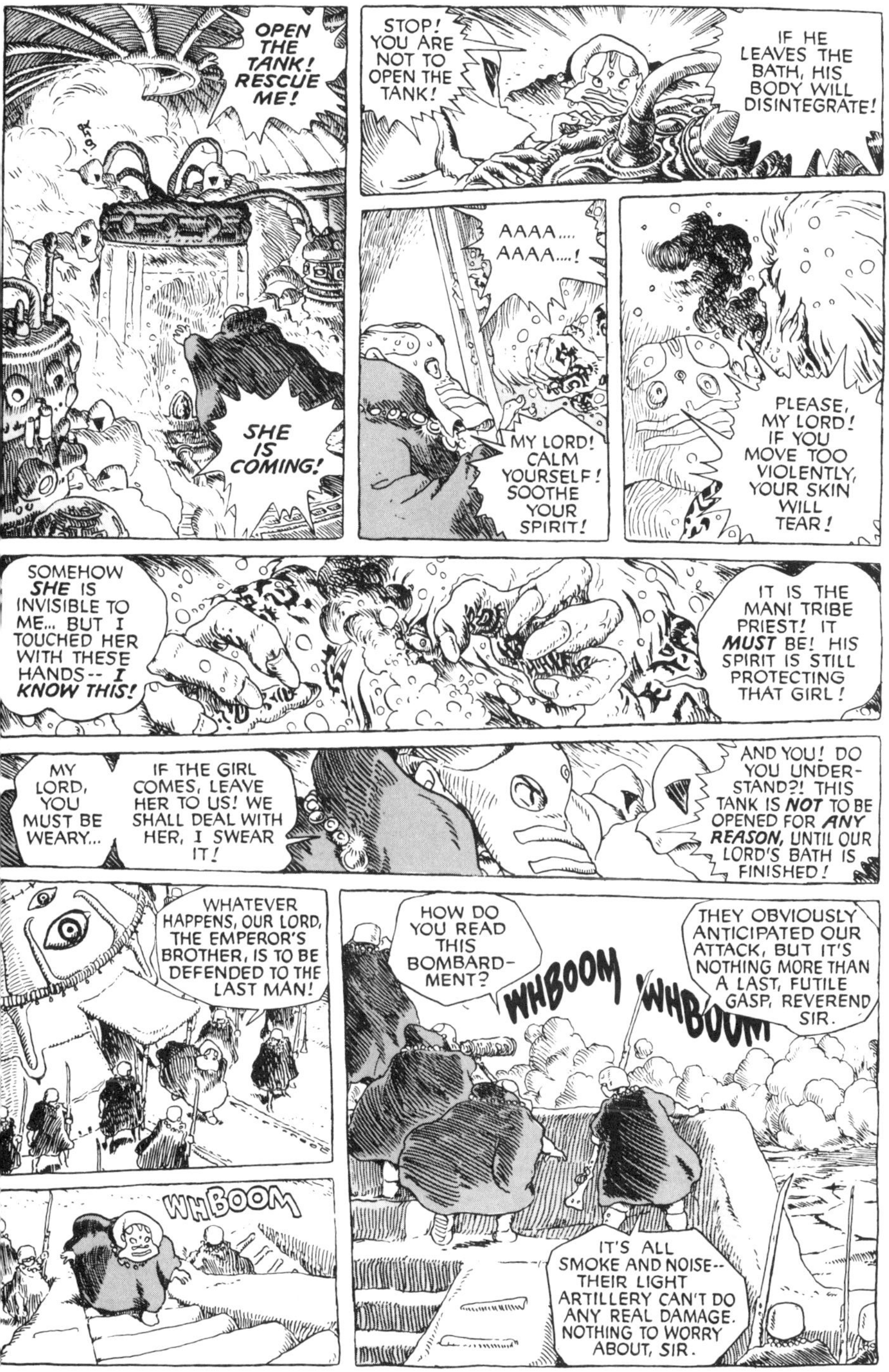
OPEN THE TANK! RESCUE ME!
SHE IS COMING!
STOP! YOU ARE NOT TO OPEN THE TANK!
IF HE LEAVES THE BATH, HIS BODY WILL DISINTEGRATE!
AAAA.... AAAA....!
MY LORD! CALM YOURSELF! SOOTHE YOUR SPIRIT!
PLEASE, MY LORD! IF YOU MOVE TOO VIOLENTLY, YOUR SKIN WILL TEAR!
SOMEHOW SHE IS INVISIBLE TO ME... BUT I TOUCHED HER WITH THESE HANDS-- I KNOW THIS!
IT IS THE MANI TRIBE PRIEST! IT MUST BE! HIS SPIRIT IS STILL PROTECTING THAT GIRL!
MY LORD, YOU MUST BE WEARY...
IF THE GIRL COMES, LEAVE HER TO US! WE SHALL DEAL WITH HER, I SWEAR IT!
AND YOU! DO YOU UNDERSTAND?! THIS TANK IS NOT TO BE OPENED FOR ANY REASON, UNTIL OUR LORD'S BATH IS FINISHED!
WHATEVER HAPPENS, OUR LORD, THE EMPEROR'S BROTHER, IS TO BE DEFENDED TO THE LAST MAN!
WHBOOM
HOW DO YOU READ THIS BOMBARDMENT?
WHBOOM
WHBOOM
THEY OBVIOUSLY ANTICIPATED OUR ATTACK, BUT IT'S NOTHING MORE THAN A LAST, FUTILE GASP, REVEREND SIR.
IT'S ALL SMOKE AND NOISE-- THEIR LIGHT ARTILLERY CAN'T DO ANY REAL DAMAGE. NOTHING TO WORRY ABOUT, SIR.

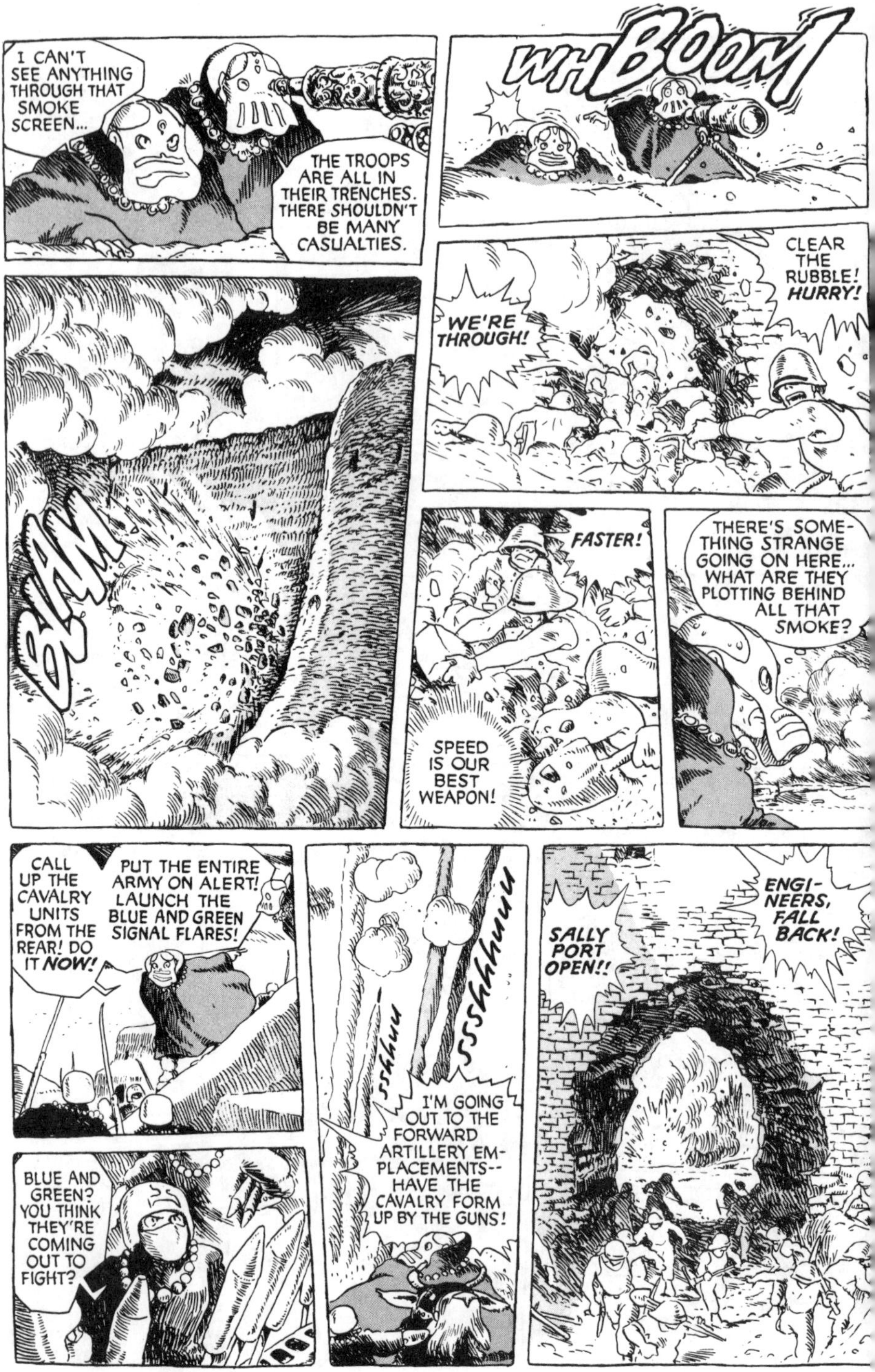
I CAN'T SEE ANYTHING THROUGH THAT SMOKE SCREEN...
THE TROOPS ARE ALL IN THEIR TRENCHES. THERE SHOULDN'T BE MANY CASUALTIES.
WHBOOM
BLAM
CLEAR THE RUBBLE! HURRY!
WE'RE THROUGH!
FASTER!
SPEED IS OUR BEST WEAPON!
THERE'S SOMETHING STRANGE GOING ON HERE... WHAT ARE THEY PLOTTING BEHIND ALL THAT SMOKE?
CALL UP THE CAVALRY UNITS FROM THE REAR! DO IT NOW!
PUT THE ENTIRE ARMY ON ALERT! LAUNCH THE BLUE AND GREEN SIGNAL FLARES!
BLUE AND GREEN? YOU THINK THEY'RE COMING OUT TO FIGHT?
SSSHHHUUU
SSHHUU
I'M GOING OUT TO THE FORWARD ARTILLERY EMPLACEMENTS-- HAVE THE CAVALRY FORM UP BY THE GUNS!
ENGINEERS, FALL BACK!
SALLY PORT OPEN!!

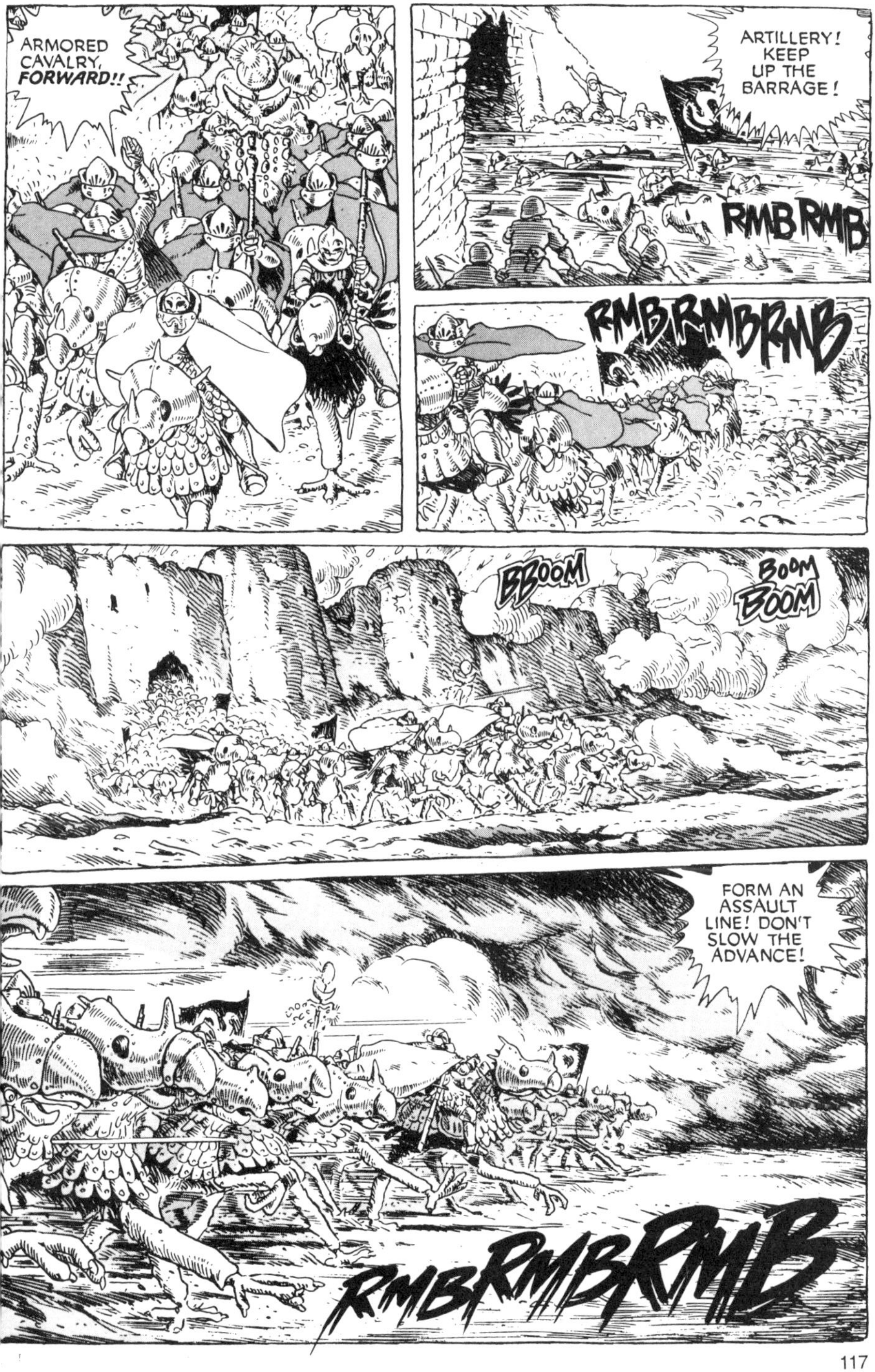
ARMORED CAVALRY, FORWARD!!
ARTILLERY! KEEP UP THE BARRAGE!
RMB RMB
RMBRMBRMB
BBOOM
BOOM BOOM
FORM AN ASSAULT LINE! DON'T SLOW THE ADVANCE!
RMBRMBRMB

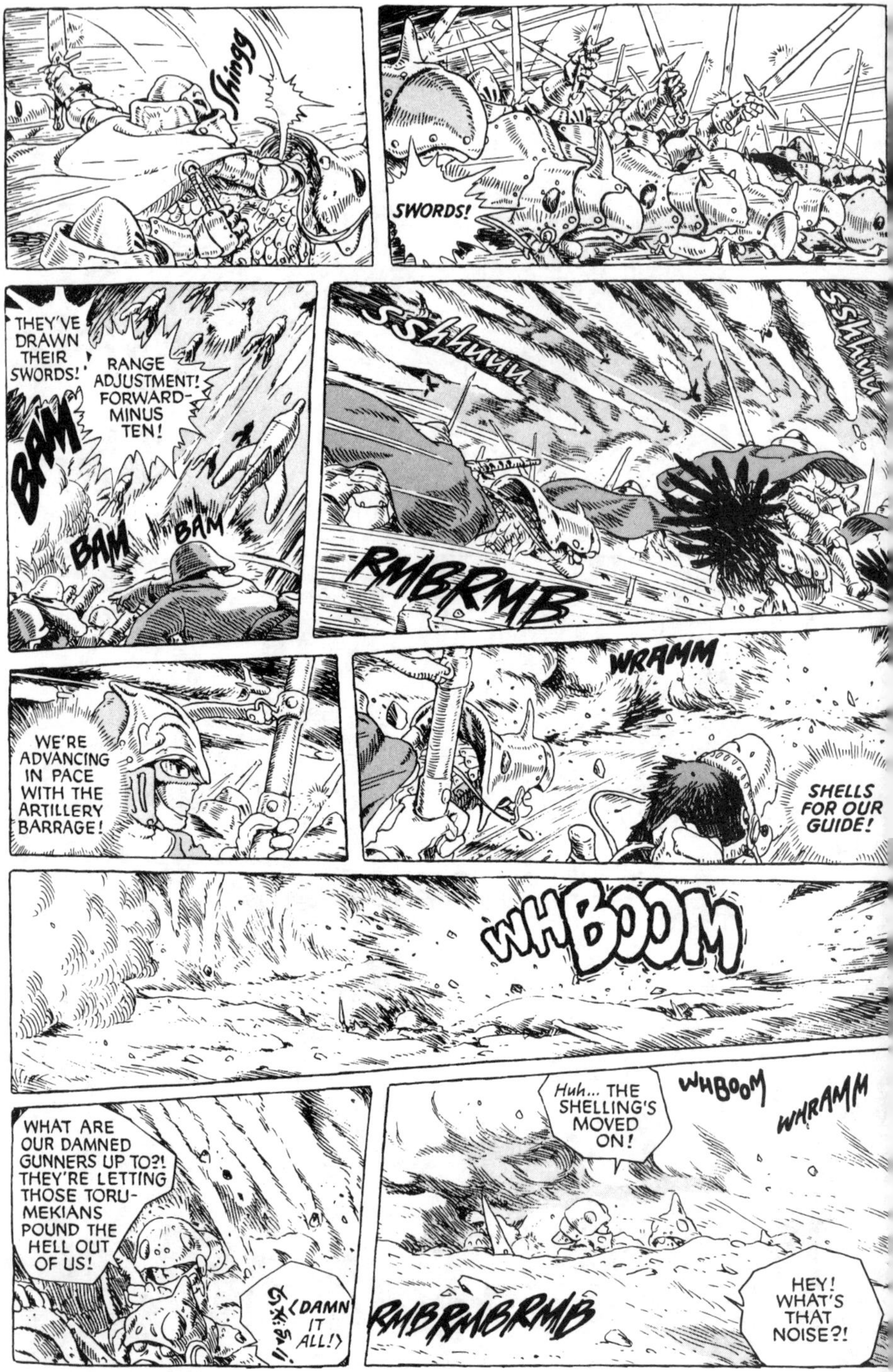
Shingg
SWORDS!
THEY'VE DRAWN THEIR SWORDS!
RANGE ADJUSTMENT! FORWARD-MINUS TEN!
BAM
BAM
BAM
sshhuuu
sshhuu
RMBRMB
WE'RE ADVANCING IN PACE WITH THE ARTILLERY BARRAGE!
WRAMM
SHELLS FOR OUR GUIDE!
WHBOOM
WHAT ARE OUR DAMNED GUNNERS UP TO?! THEY'RE LETTING THOSE TORU-MEKIANS POUND THE HELL OUT OF US!
〈DAMN IT ALL!〉
Huh... THE SHELLING'S MOVED ON!
WHBOOM
WHRAMM
RMBRMBRMB
HEY! WHAT'S THAT NOISE?!

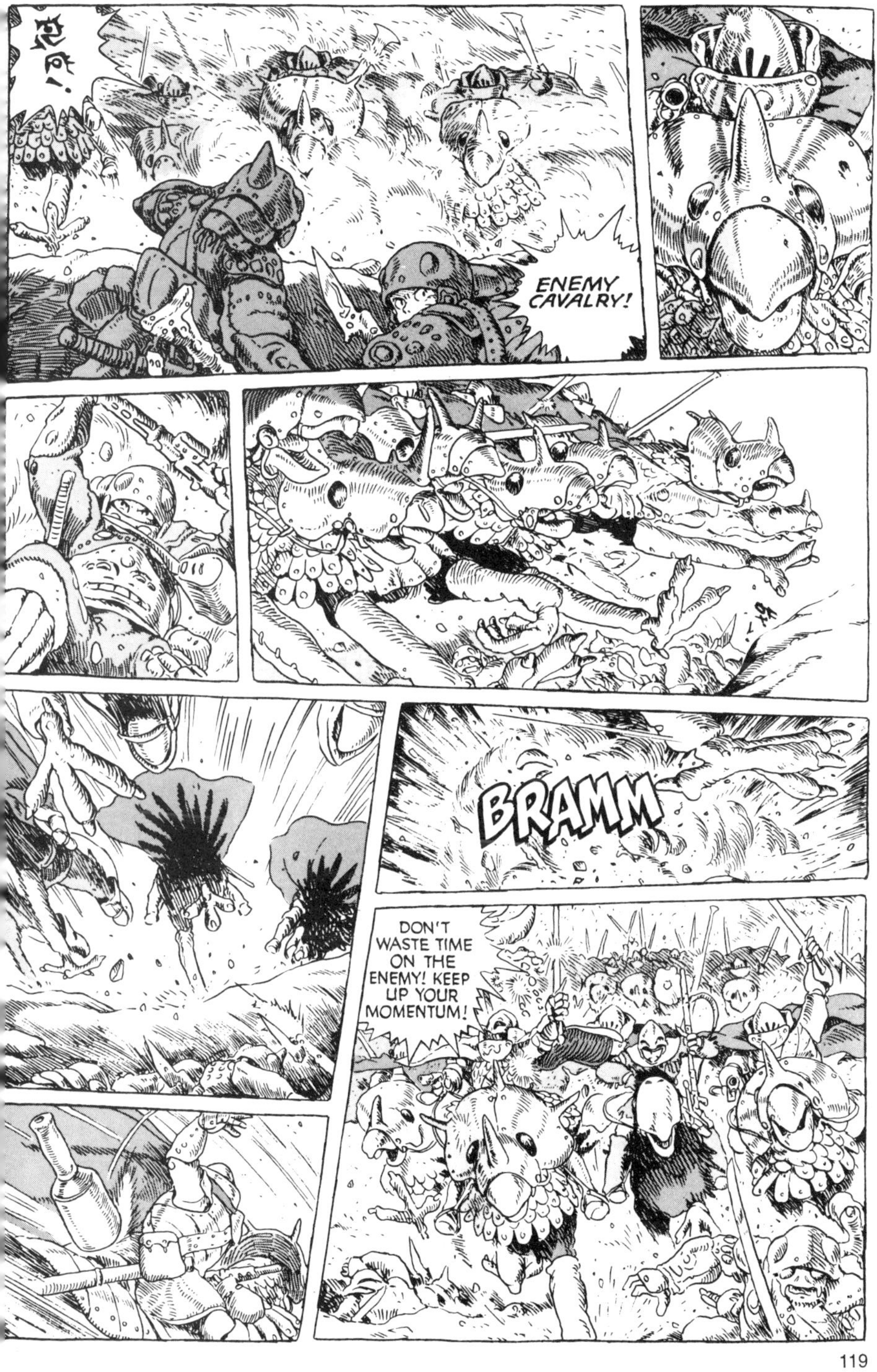
ENEMY CAVALRY!
BRAMM
DON'T WASTE TIME ON THE ENEMY! KEEP UP YOUR MOMENTUM!

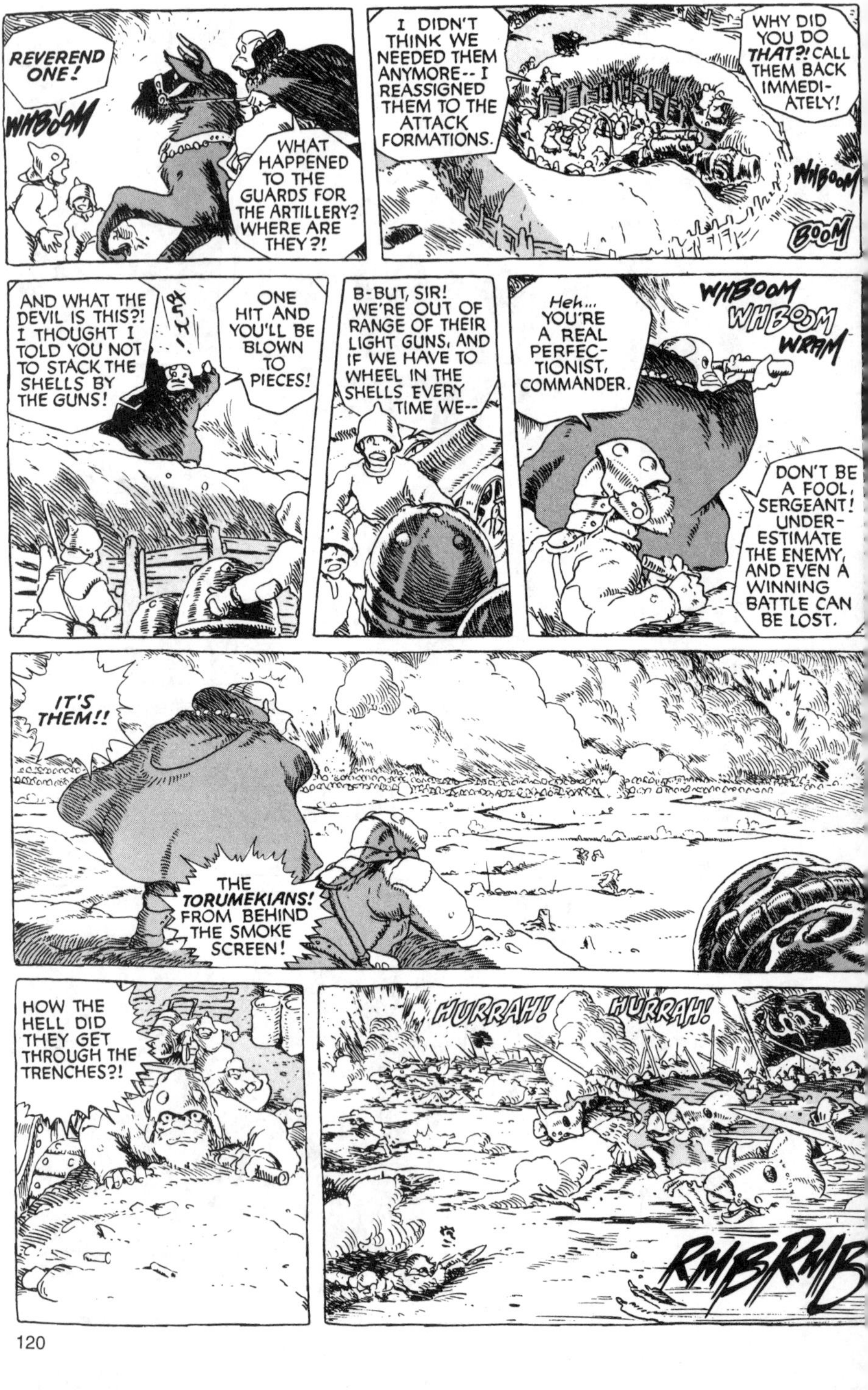

REVEREND ONE!
WHBOOM
WHAT HAPPENED TO THE GUARDS FOR THE ARTILLERY? WHERE ARE THEY?!
I DIDN'T THINK WE NEEDED THEM ANYMORE-- I REASSIGNED THEM TO THE ATTACK FORMATIONS.
WHY DID YOU DO THAT?! CALL THEM BACK IMMEDI-ATELY!
WHBOOM
BOOM
AND WHAT THE DEVIL IS THIS?! I THOUGHT I TOLD YOU NOT TO STACK THE SHELLS BY THE GUNS!
ONE HIT AND YOU'LL BE BLOWN TO PIECES!
B-BUT, SIR! WE'RE OUT OF RANGE OF THEIR LIGHT GUNS, AND IF WE HAVE TO WHEEL IN THE SHELLS EVERY TIME WE--
Heh... YOU'RE A REAL PERFEC-TIONIST, COMMANDER.
WHBOOM
WHBOOM
WRAM
DON'T BE A FOOL, SERGEANT! UNDER-ESTIMATE THE ENEMY, AND EVEN A WINNING BATTLE CAN BE LOST.
IT'S THEM!!
THE TORUMEKIANS! FROM BEHIND THE SMOKE SCREEN!
HOW THE HELL DID THEY GET THROUGH THE TRENCHES?!
HURRAH!
HURRAH!
RMBRMB

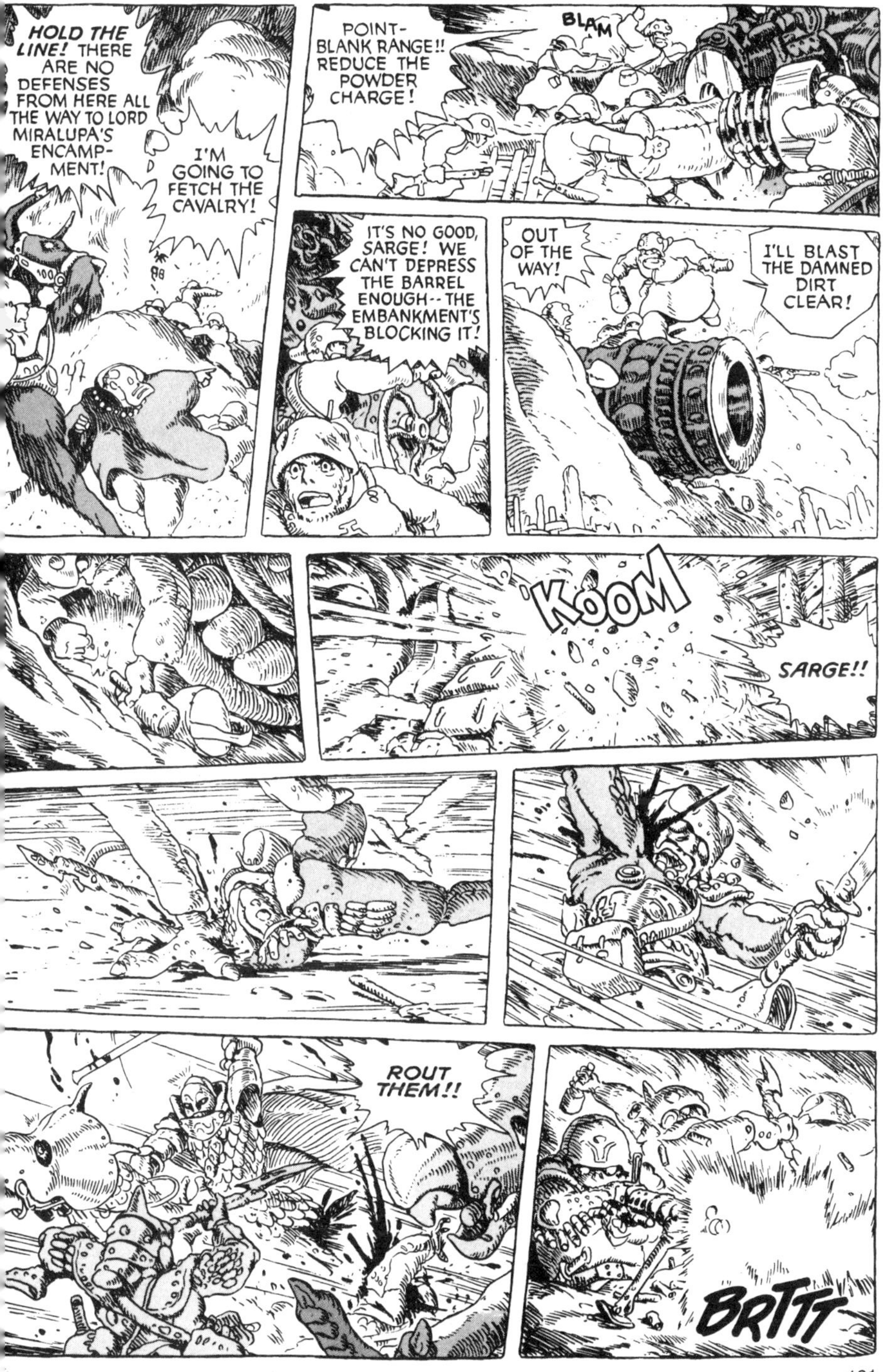
HOLD THE LINE! THERE ARE NO DEFENSES FROM HERE ALL THE WAY TO LORD MIRALUPA'S ENCAMPMENT!
I'M GOING TO FETCH THE CAVALRY!
POINT-BLANK RANGE!! REDUCE THE POWDER CHARGE!
BLAM
IT'S NO GOOD, SARGE! WE CAN'T DEPRESS THE BARREL ENOUGH--THE EMBANKMENT'S BLOCKING IT!
OUT OF THE WAY!
I'LL BLAST THE DAMNED DIRT CLEAR!
KOOM
SARGE!!
ROUT THEM!!
BRTTT

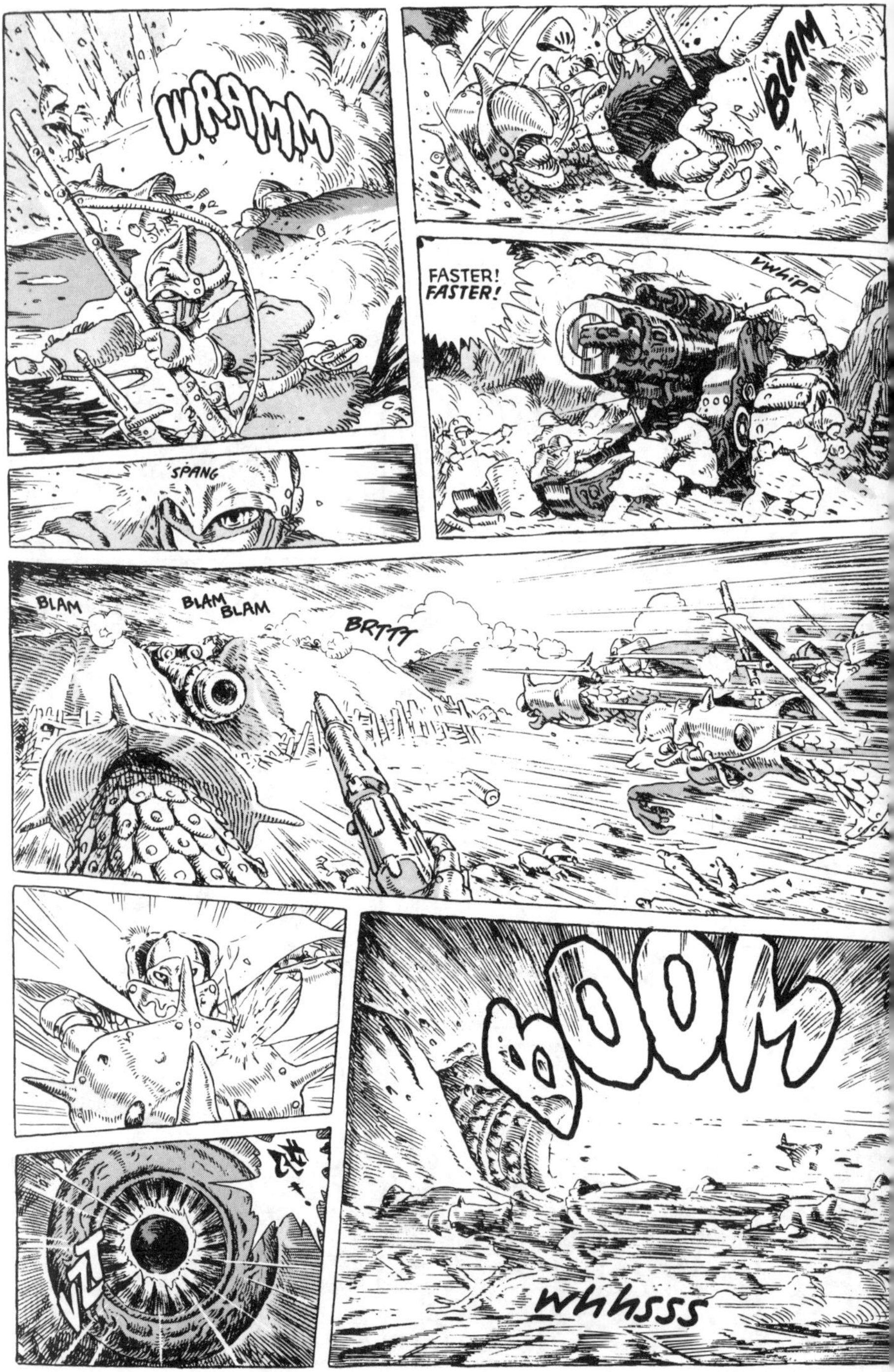

WRAMM
BLAM
SPANG
FASTER! FASTER!
vwhipp
BLAM
BLAM BLAM
BRTTT
VZT
BOOM
whhsss

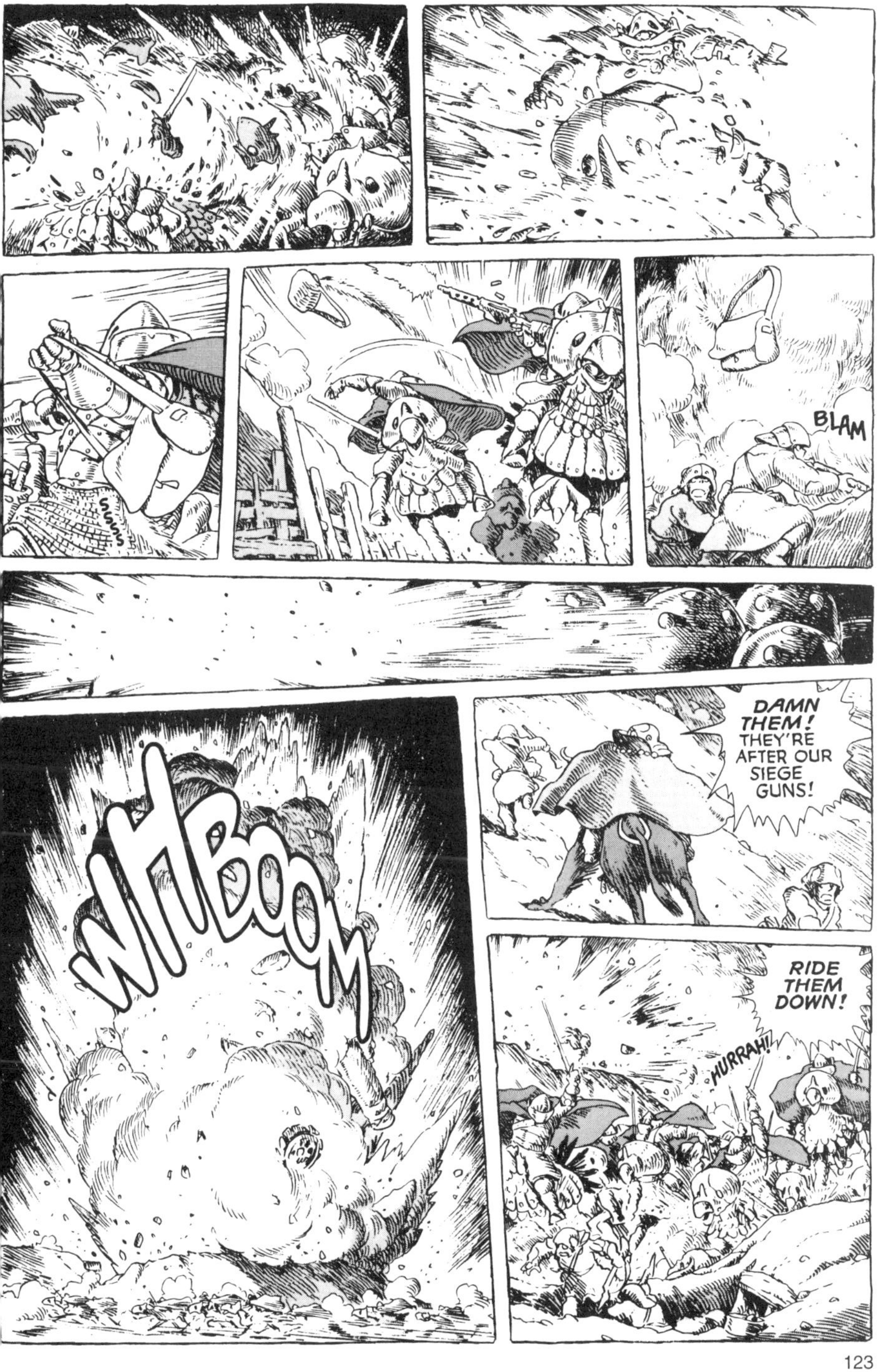
SSSS
BLAM
WHBOOM
DAMN THEM! THEY'RE AFTER OUR SIEGE GUNS!
RIDE THEM DOWN!
HURRAH!

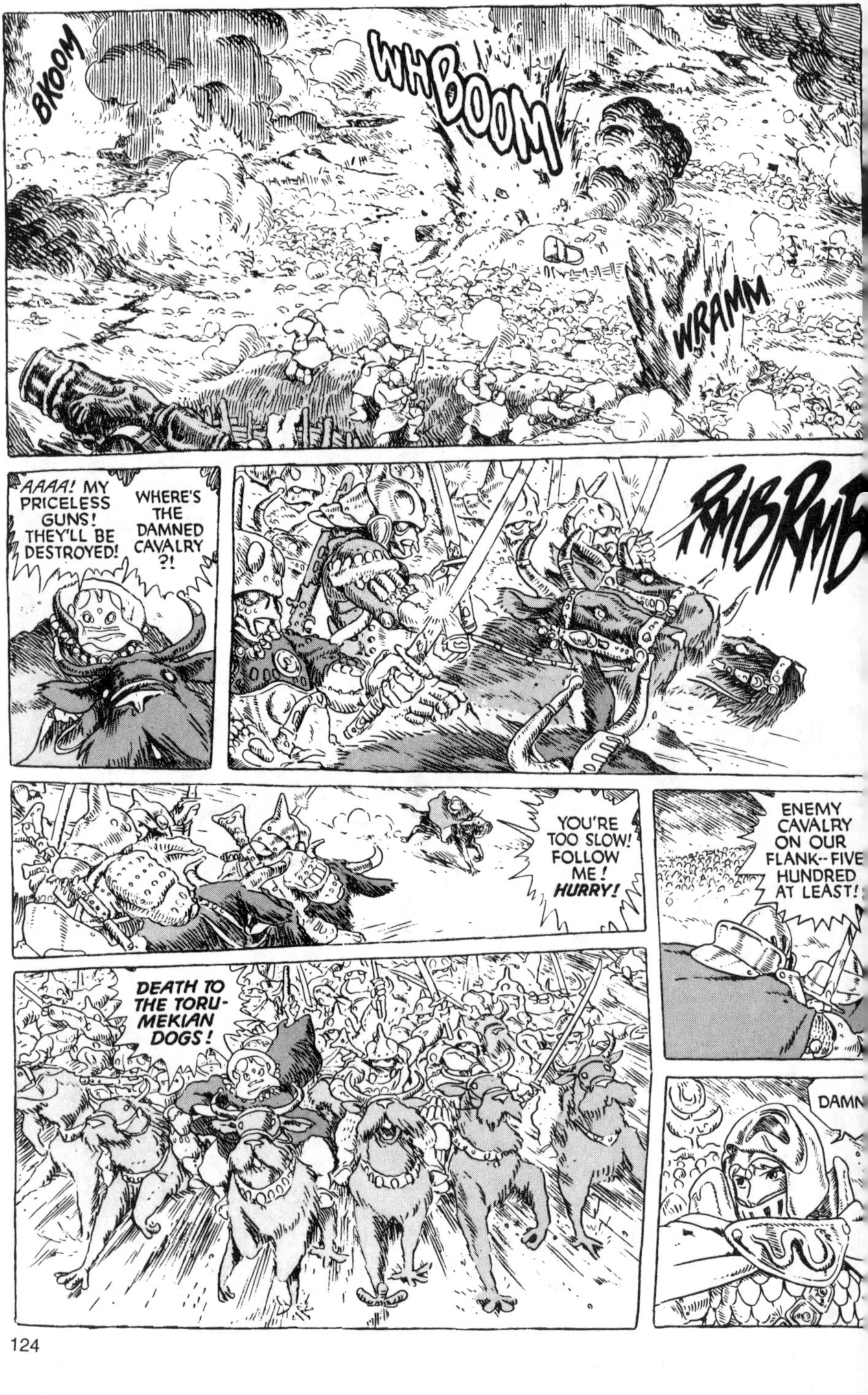

BKOOM
WHBOOM
WRAMM
AAAA! MY PRICELESS GUNS! THEY'LL BE DESTROYED!
WHERE'S THE DAMNED CAVALRY ?!
YOU'RE TOO SLOW! FOLLOW ME! HURRY!
ENEMY CAVALRY ON OUR FLANK--FIVE HUNDRED AT LEAST!
DEATH TO THE TORU-MEKIAN DOGS!
DAMN

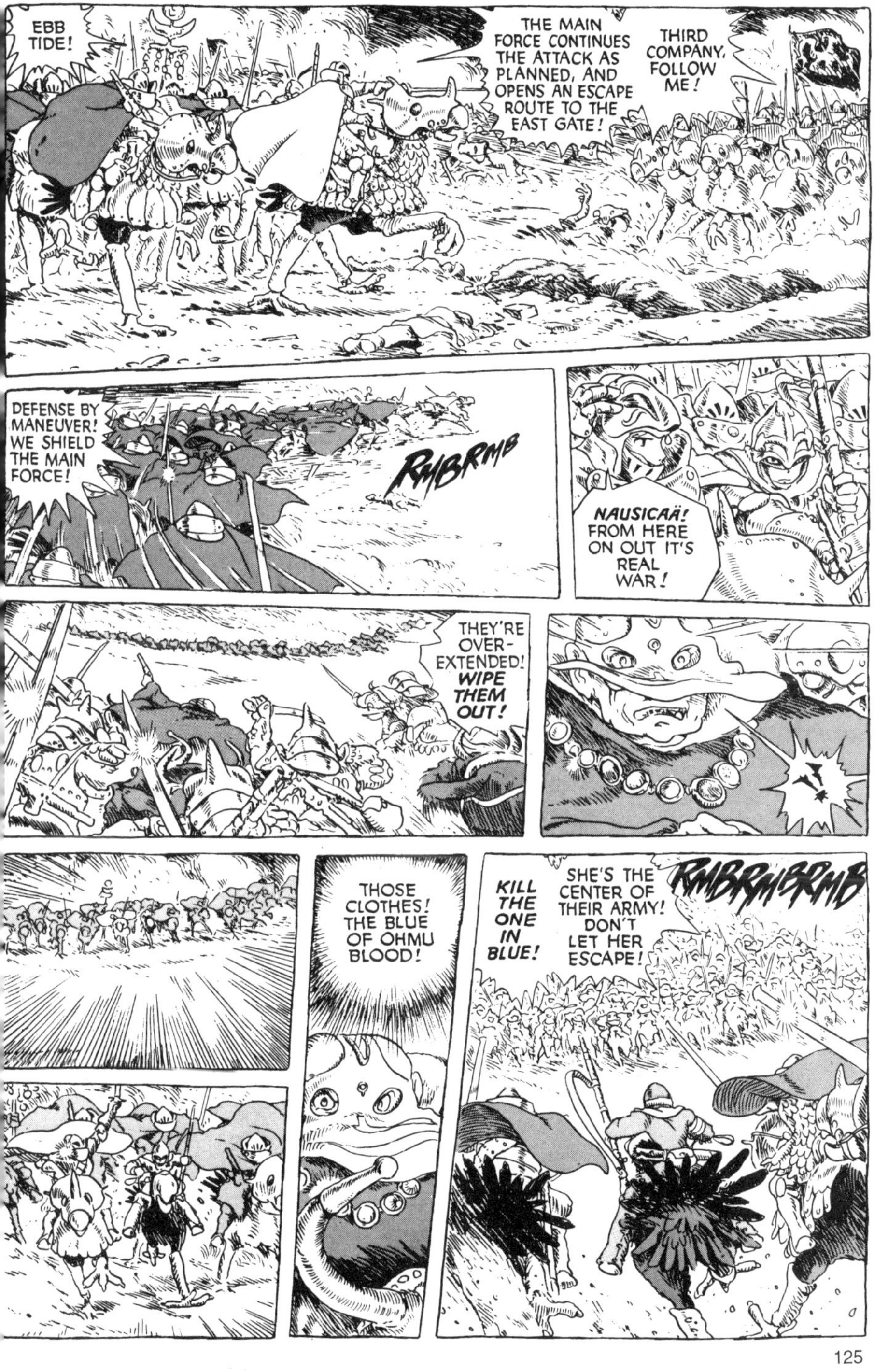
EBB TIDE!
THE MAIN FORCE CONTINUES THE ATTACK AS PLANNED, AND OPENS AN ESCAPE ROUTE TO THE EAST GATE!
THIRD COMPANY, FOLLOW ME!
DEFENSE BY MANEUVER! WE SHIELD THE MAIN FORCE!
RMBRMB
NAUSICAÄ! FROM HERE ON OUT IT'S REAL WAR!
THEY'RE OVER-EXTENDED! WIPE THEM OUT!
THOSE CLOTHES! THE BLUE OF OHMU BLOOD!
KILL THE ONE IN BLUE!
SHE'S THE CENTER OF THEIR ARMY! DON'T LET HER ESCAPE!
RMBRMBRMB

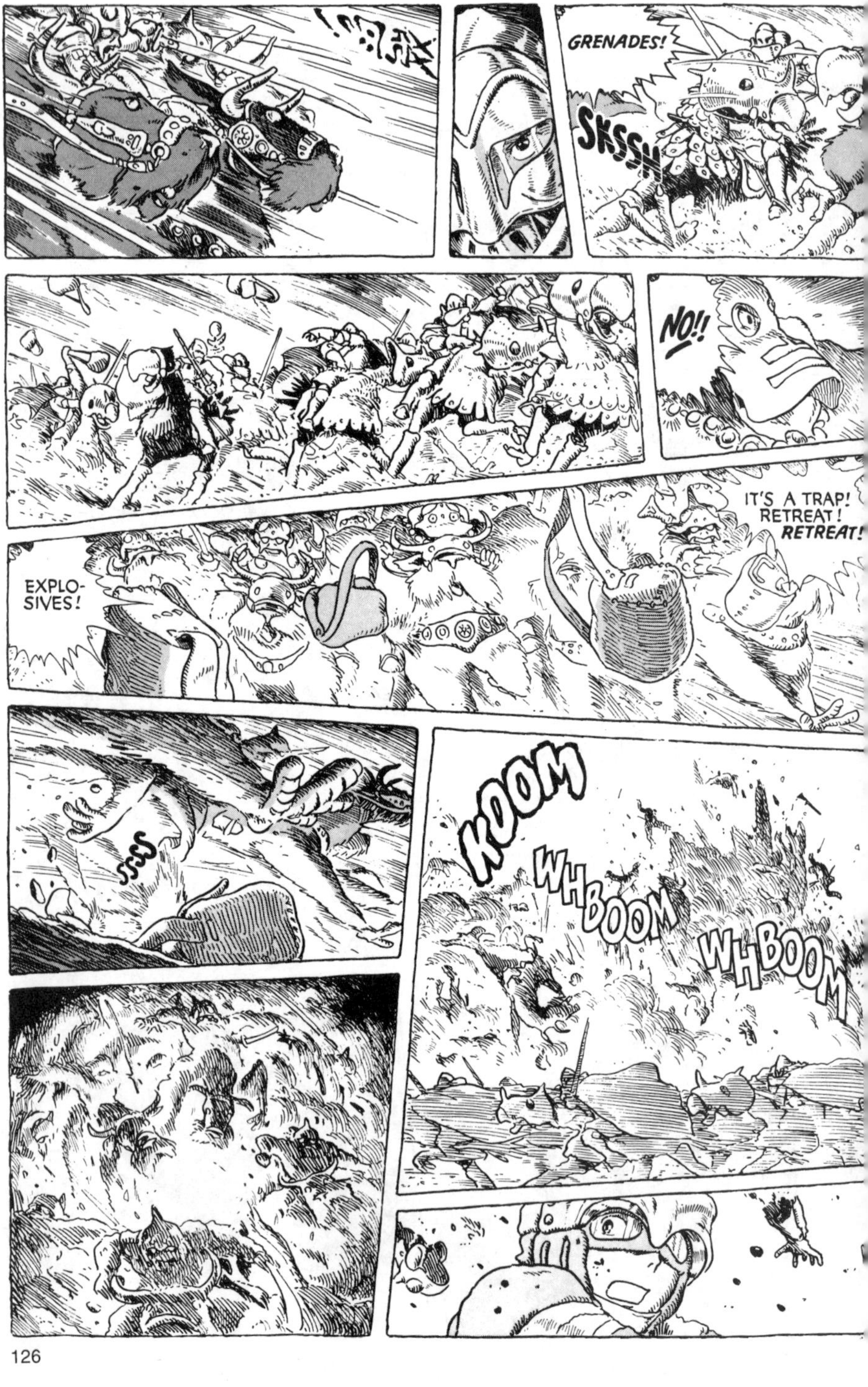
GRENADES!
SKSSH
NO!!
EXPLOSIVES!
IT'S A TRAP! RETREAT! RETREAT!
SSSS
KOOM
WHBOOM
WHBOOM

WHOOM

HOW COULD I HAVE BEEN SO CARELESS?! HOW COULD I HAVE *MISSED HER!*

HURRAH, HURRAH!

RMBRMBRMB

THE *WHITE WITCH* OF TORU-MEKIA!

KUSHANA, DAUGHTER OF THE VAI EMPEROR?! SHE STILL LIVES!

CHOK

KANGG

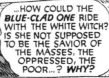

Aaahh...

...HOW COULD THE *BLUE-CLAD ONE* RIDE WITH THE WHITE WITCH? IS SHE NOT SUPPOSED TO BE THE SAVIOR OF THE MASSES, THE OPPRESSED, THE POOR...? *WHY?*

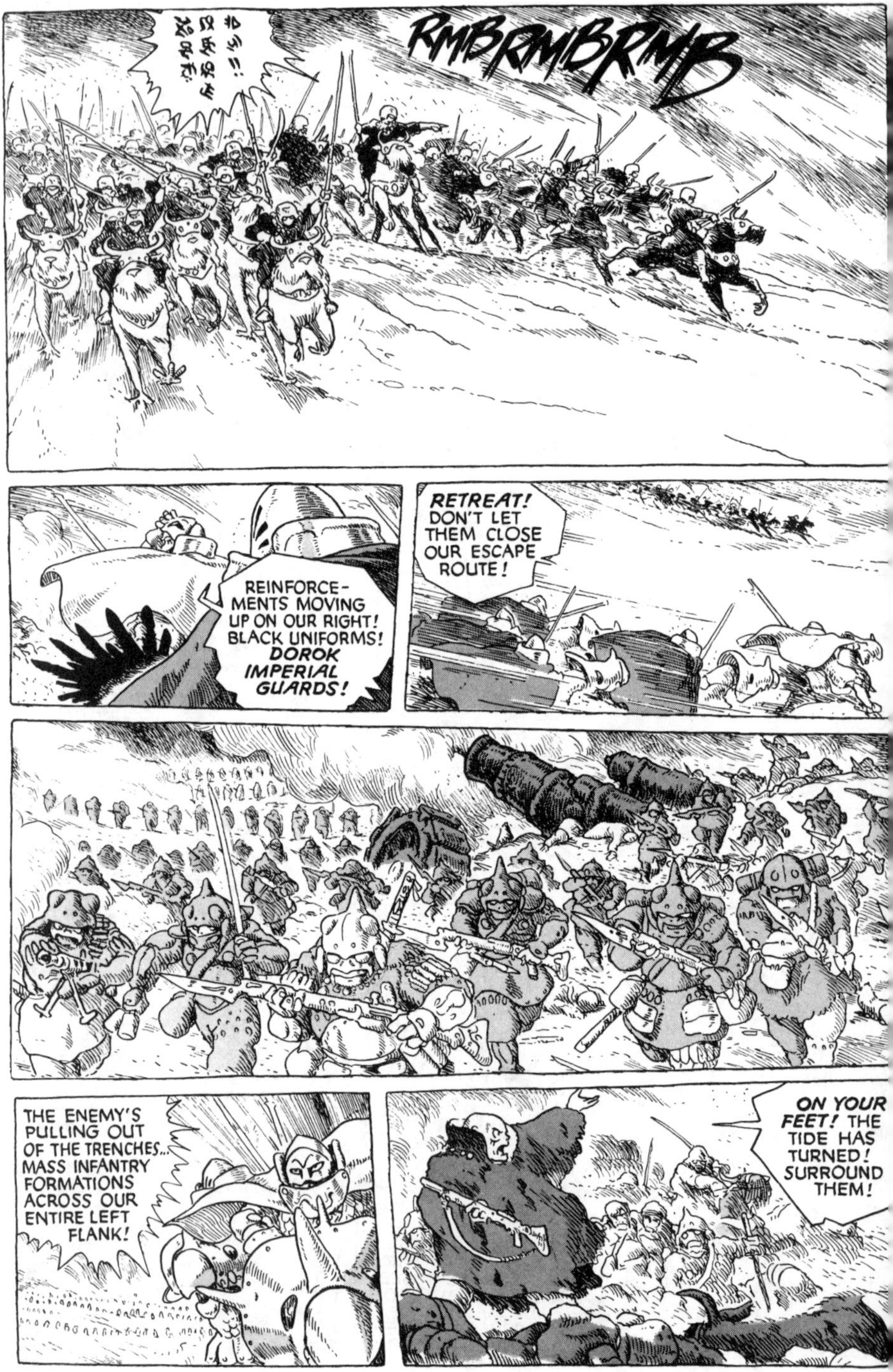
RMBRMBRMB
REINFORCEMENTS MOVING UP ON OUR RIGHT! BLACK UNIFORMS! DOROK IMPERIAL GUARDS!
RETREAT! DON'T LET THEM CLOSE OUR ESCAPE ROUTE!
THE ENEMY'S PULLING OUT OF THE TRENCHES... MASS INFANTRY FORMATIONS ACROSS OUR ENTIRE LEFT FLANK!
ON YOUR FEET! THE TIDE HAS TURNED! SURROUND THEM!

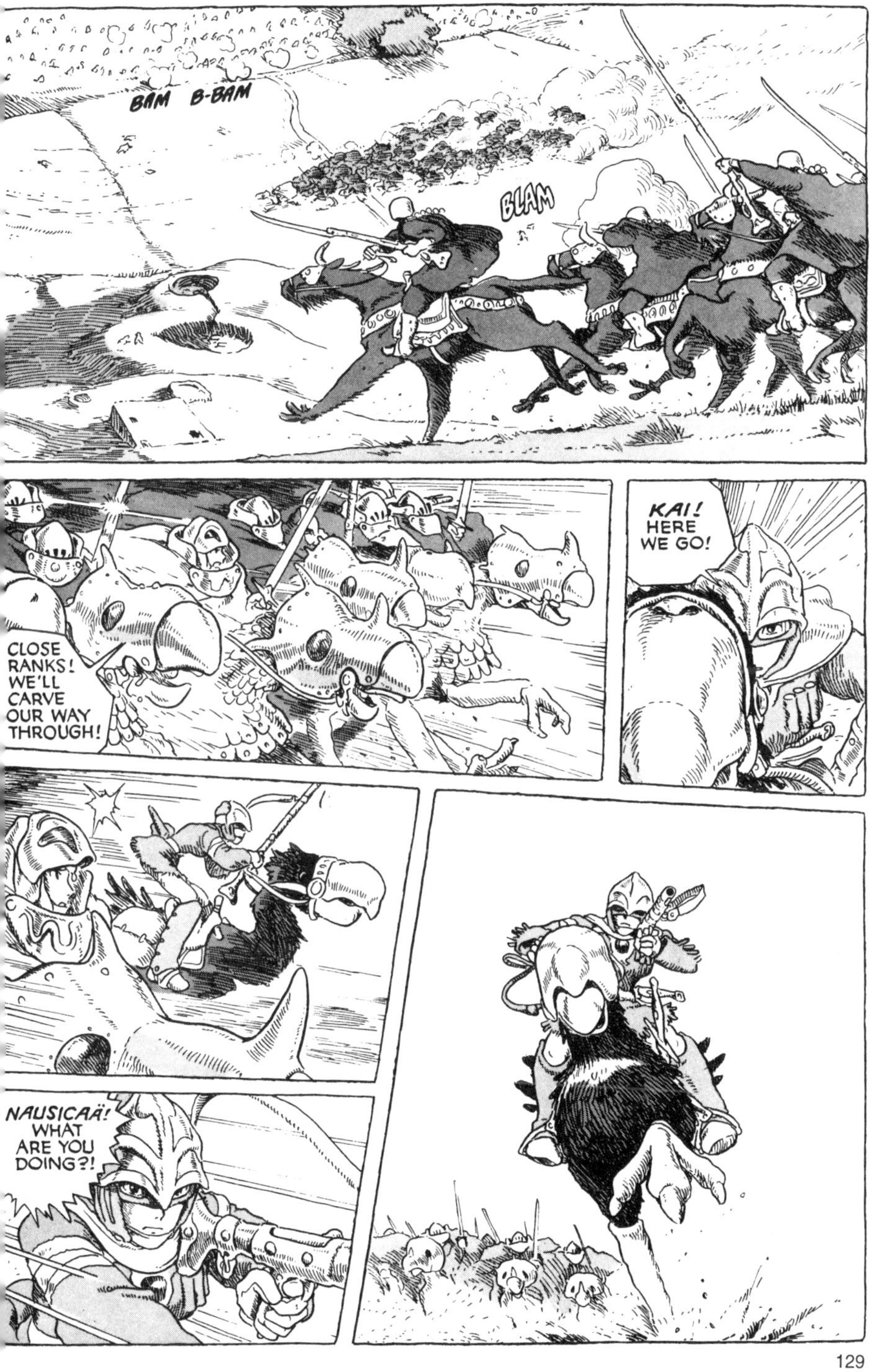
BAM B-BAM
BLAM
CLOSE RANKS! WE'LL CARVE OUR WAY THROUGH!
KAI! HERE WE GO!
NAUSICAÄ! WHAT ARE YOU DOING?!

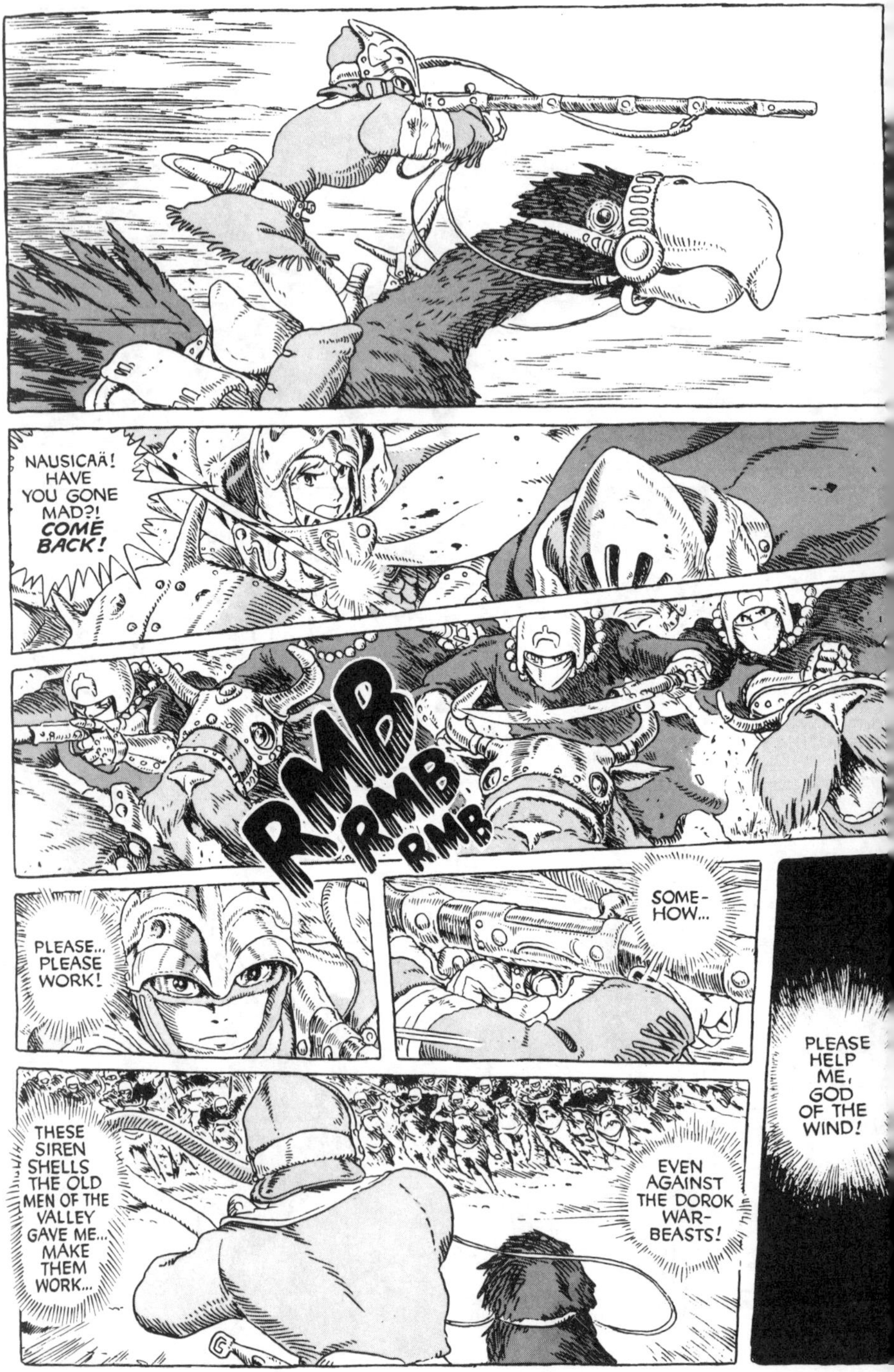
NAUSICAÄ! HAVE YOU GONE MAD?! COME BACK!
RMB RMB RMB
PLEASE... PLEASE WORK!
SOME-HOW...
PLEASE HELP ME, GOD OF THE WIND!
THESE SIREN SHELLS THE OLD MEN OF THE VALLEY GAVE ME... MAKE THEM WORK...
EVEN AGAINST THE DOROK WAR-BEASTS!

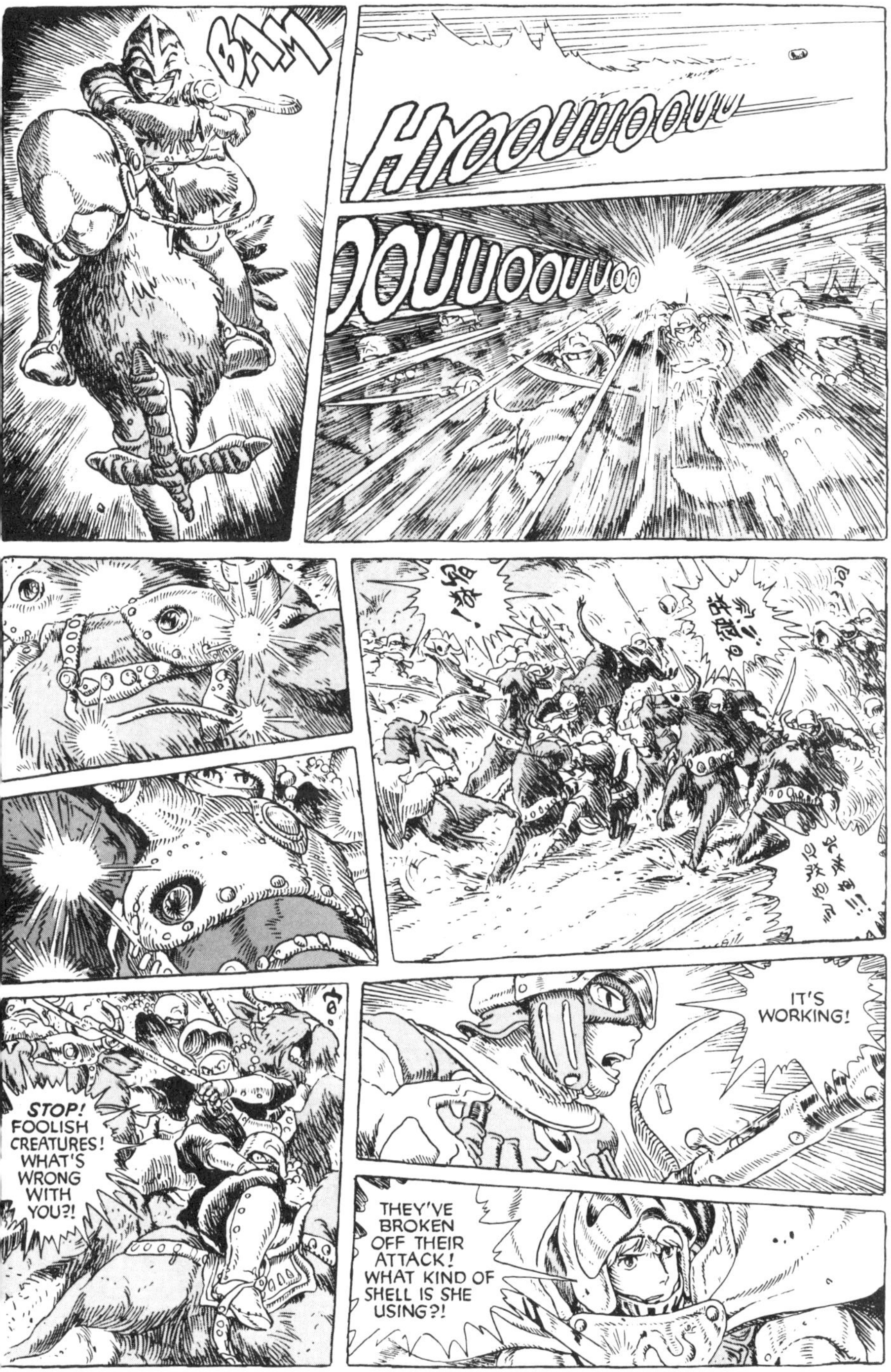
BAM
HYOOUUOOUU
OOUUOOUUOO
STOP! FOOLISH CREATURES! WHAT'S WRONG WITH YOU?!
IT'S WORKING!
THEY'VE BROKEN OFF THEIR ATTACK! WHAT KIND OF SHELL IS SHE USING?!

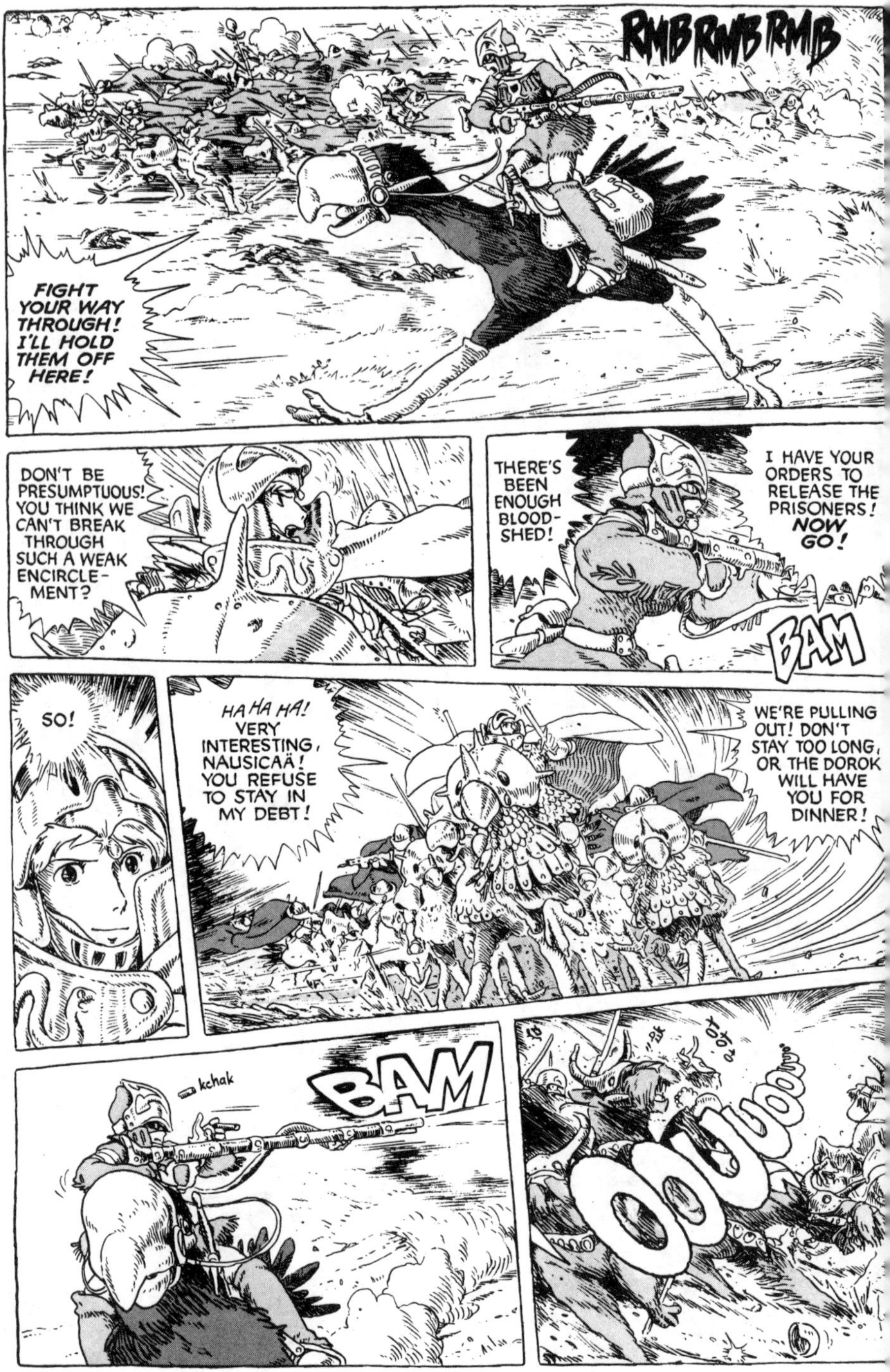
RMB RMB RMB
FIGHT YOUR WAY THROUGH! I'LL HOLD THEM OFF HERE!
DON'T BE PRESUMPTUOUS! YOU THINK WE CAN'T BREAK THROUGH SUCH A WEAK ENCIRCLEMENT?
THERE'S BEEN ENOUGH BLOODSHED!
I HAVE YOUR ORDERS TO RELEASE THE PRISONERS! NOW GO!
BAM
SO!
HA HA HA! VERY INTERESTING, NAUSICAÄ! YOU REFUSE TO STAY IN MY DEBT!
WE'RE PULLING OUT! DON'T STAY TOO LONG, OR THE DOROK WILL HAVE YOU FOR DINNER!
kchak
BAM
OOOUOOO

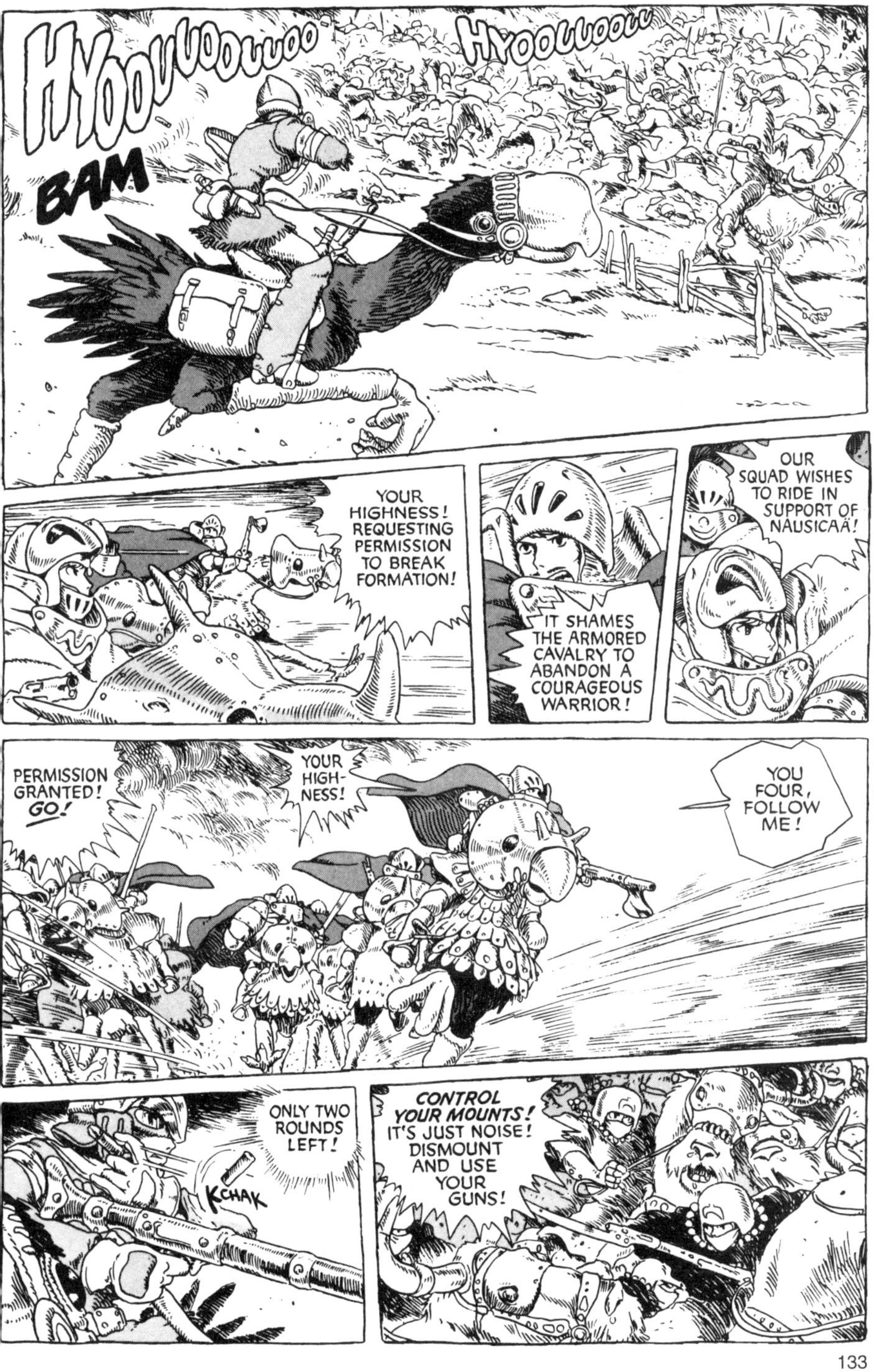
HYOOLLOOLLOO
HYOOLLOOLL
BAM
YOUR HIGHNESS! REQUESTING PERMISSION TO BREAK FORMATION!
IT SHAMES THE ARMORED CAVALRY TO ABANDON A COURAGEOUS WARRIOR!
OUR SQUAD WISHES TO RIDE IN SUPPORT OF NAUSICAÄ!
PERMISSION GRANTED! GO!
YOUR HIGHNESS!
YOU FOUR, FOLLOW ME!
ONLY TWO ROUNDS LEFT!
KCHAK
CONTROL YOUR MOUNTS! IT'S JUST NOISE! DISMOUNT AND USE YOUR GUNS!

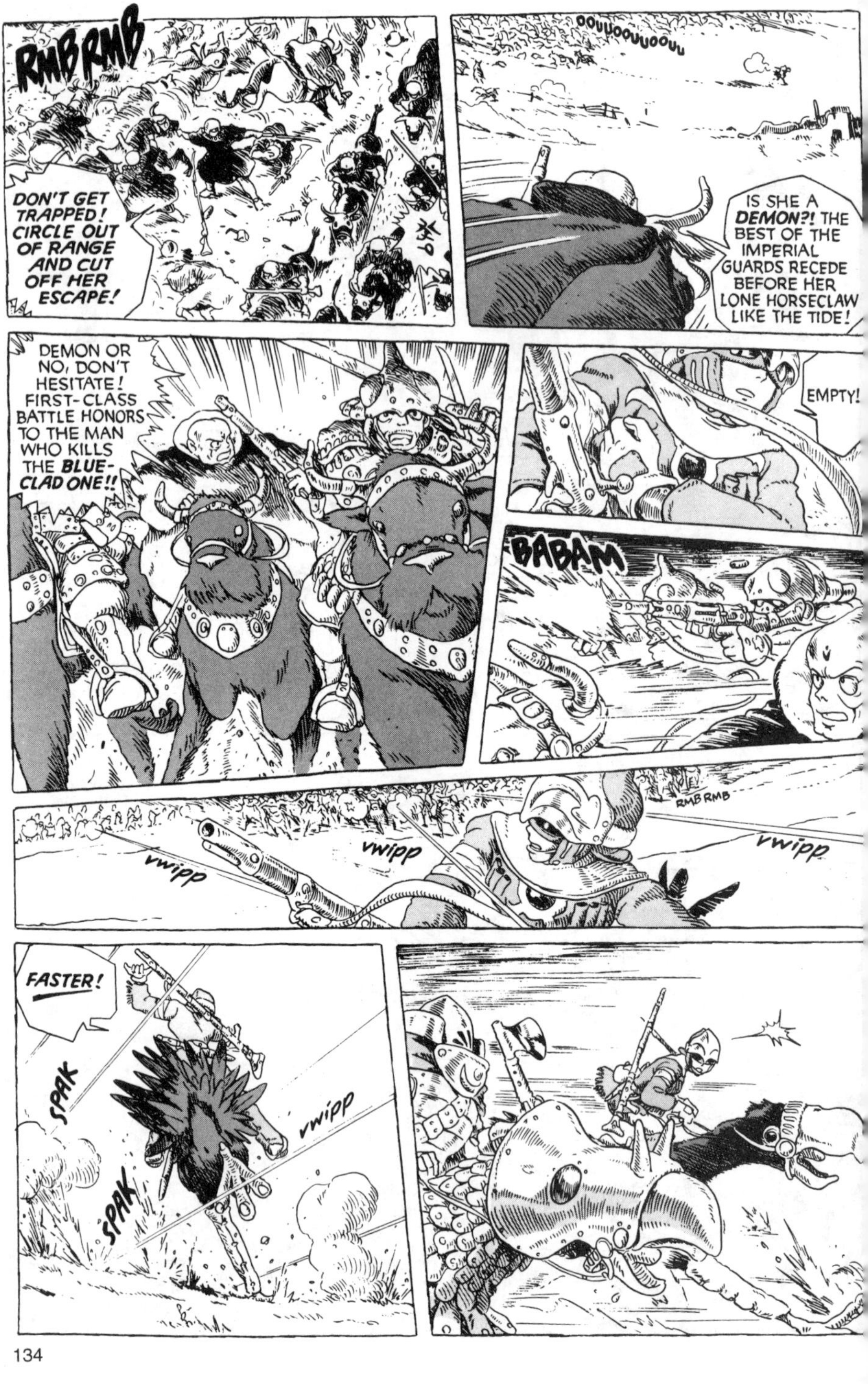
RMB RMB
DON'T GET TRAPPED! CIRCLE OUT OF RANGE AND CUT OFF HER ESCAPE!
OOUUOOUUOOUU
IS SHE A DEMON?! THE BEST OF THE IMPERIAL GUARDS RECEDE BEFORE HER LONE HORSECLAW LIKE THE TIDE!
DEMON OR NO, DON'T HESITATE! FIRST-CLASS BATTLE HONORS TO THE MAN WHO KILLS THE BLUE-CLAD ONE!!
EMPTY!
BABAM
RMB RMB
vwipp
vwipp
vwipp
FASTER!
SPAK
SPAK
vwipp

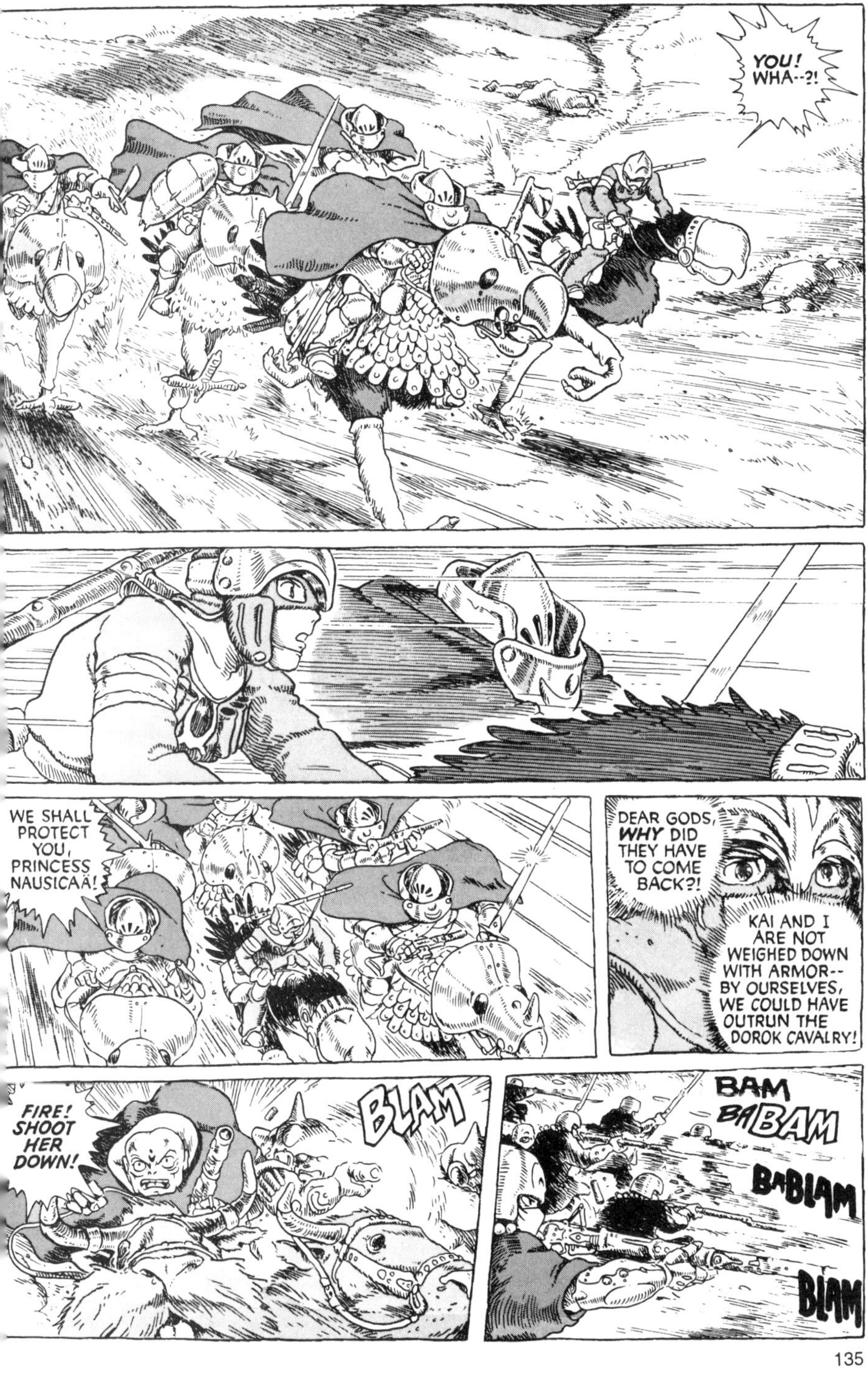
YOU! WHA--?!
WE SHALL PROTECT YOU, PRINCESS NAUSICAÄ!
DEAR GODS, WHY DID THEY HAVE TO COME BACK?!
KAI AND I ARE NOT WEIGHED DOWN WITH ARMOR-- BY OURSELVES, WE COULD HAVE OUTRUN THE DOROK CAVALRY!
FIRE! SHOOT HER DOWN!
BLAM
BAM BABAM
BABLAM
BLAM

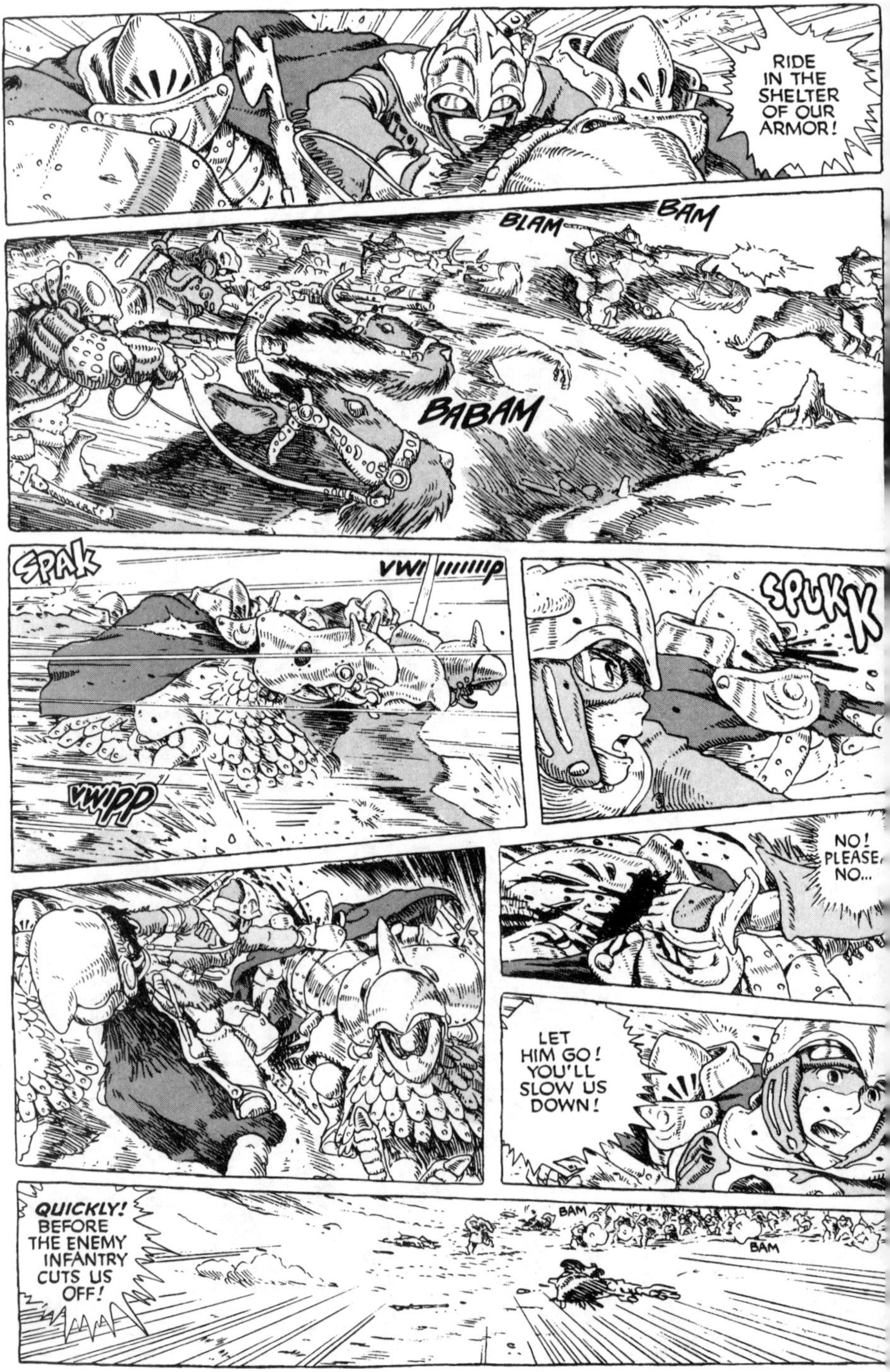
RIDE IN THE SHELTER OF OUR ARMOR!
BLAM
BAM
BABAM
SPAK
VWIIIIIIIP
VWIPP
SPUKK
NO! PLEASE, NO...
LET HIM GO! YOU'LL SLOW US DOWN!
QUICKLY! BEFORE THE ENEMY INFANTRY CUTS US OFF!
BAM
BAM

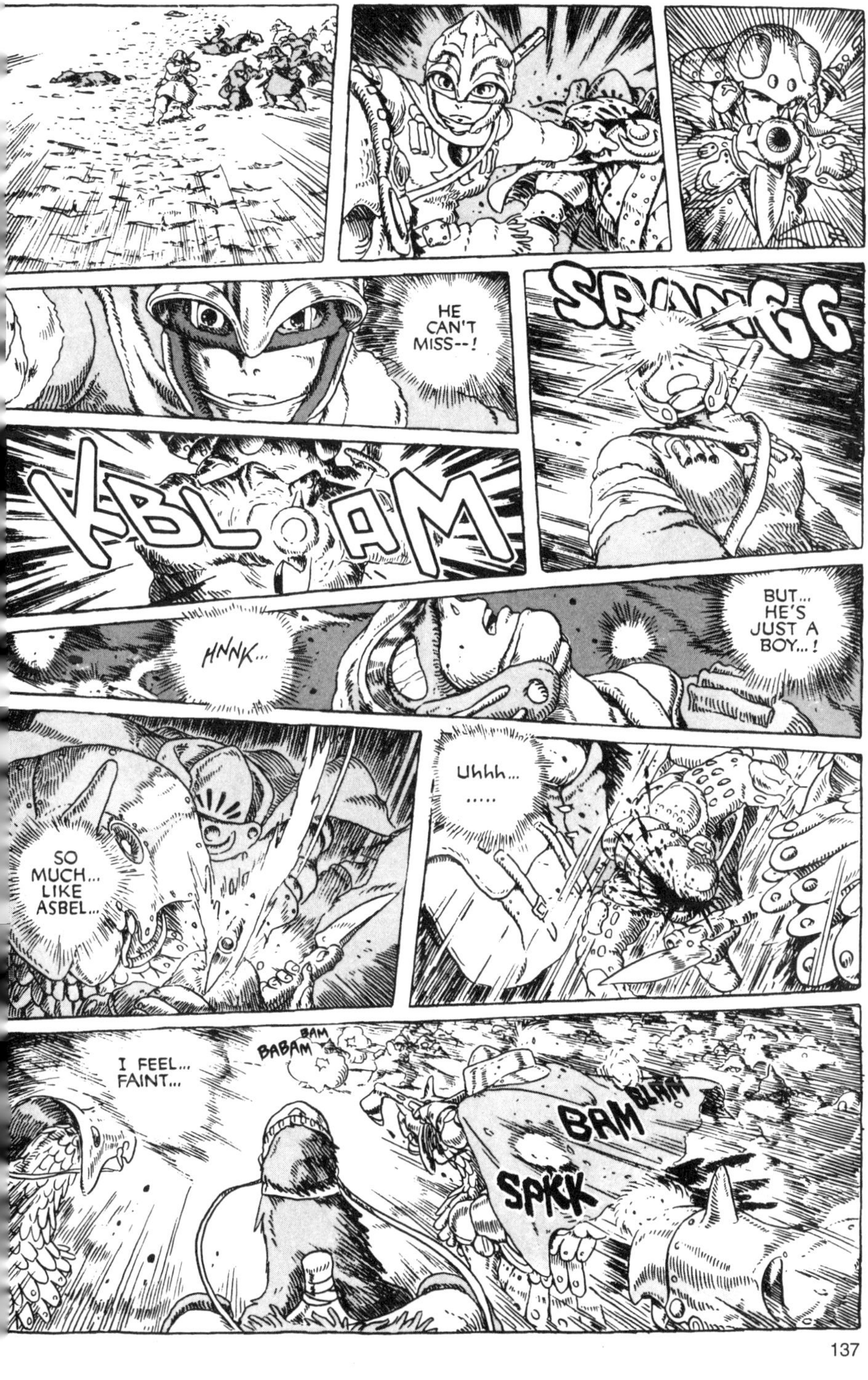
HE CAN'T MISS--!
SPANGG
KBLAM
HNNK...
BUT... HE'S JUST A BOY...!
SO MUCH... LIKE ASBEL...
Uhhh... .....
I FEEL... FAINT...
BABAM BAM
BAM BLAM
SPKK

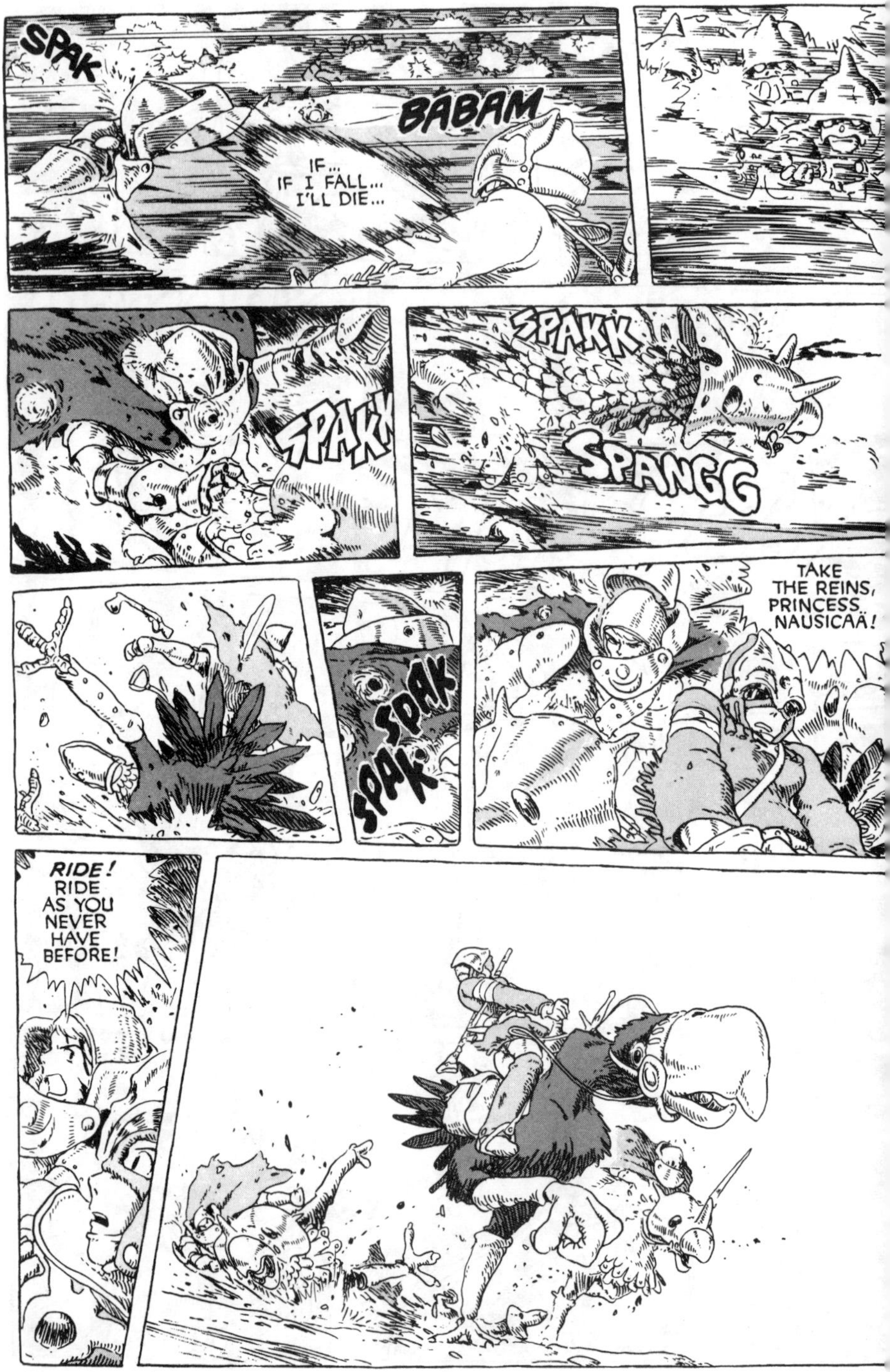
SPAK
BABAM
IF... IF I FALL... I'LL DIE...
SPAKK
SPAKK
SPANGG
SPAK SPAK
TAKE THE REINS, PRINCESS NAUSICAÄ!
RIDE! RIDE AS YOU NEVER HAVE BEFORE!

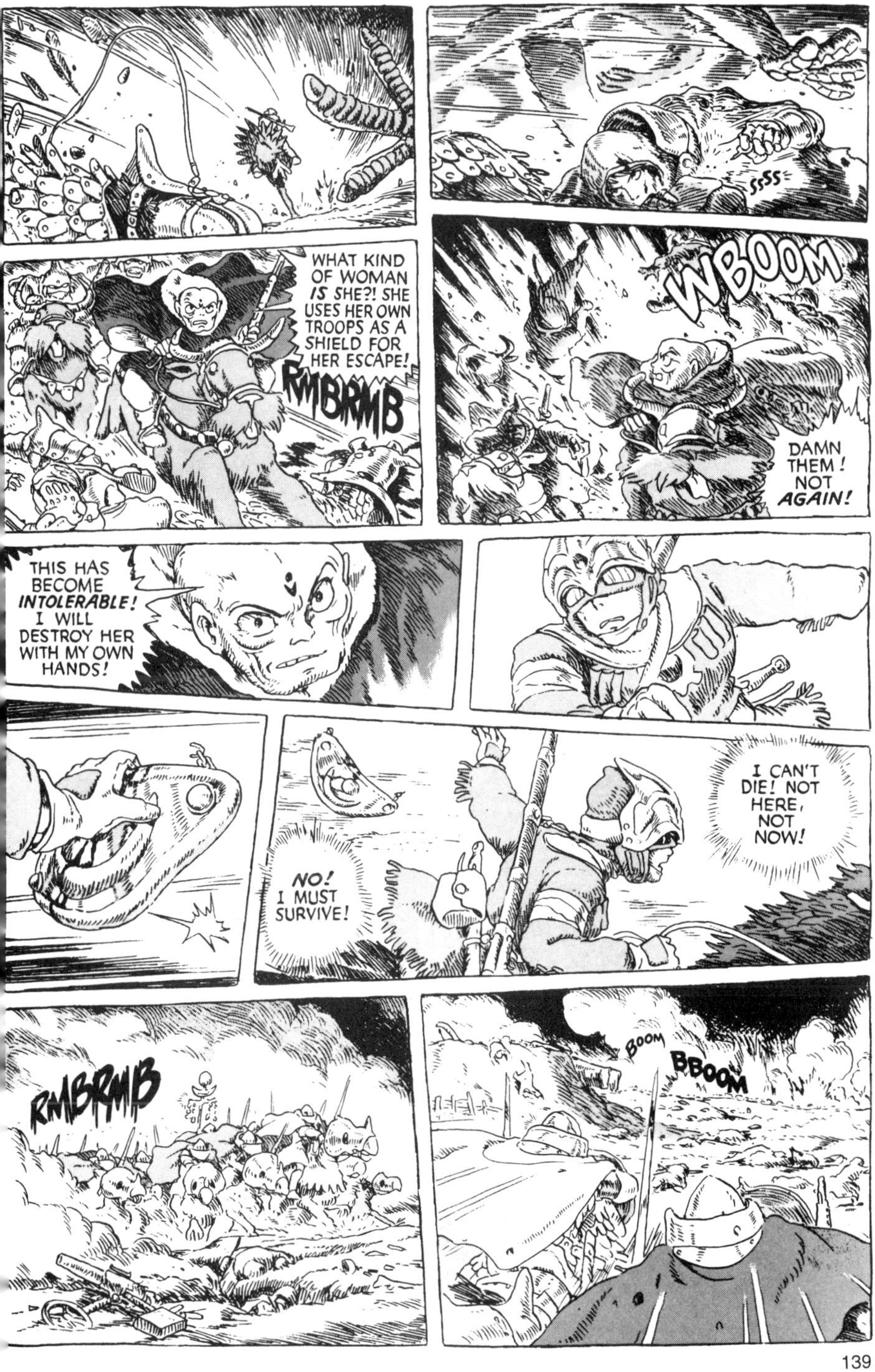
SSSS
WHAT KIND OF WOMAN IS SHE?! SHE USES HER OWN TROOPS AS A SHIELD FOR HER ESCAPE!
RMBRMB
WBOOM
DAMN THEM! NOT AGAIN!
THIS HAS BECOME INTOLERABLE! I WILL DESTROY HER WITH MY OWN HANDS!
I CAN'T DIE! NOT HERE, NOT NOW!
NO! I MUST SURVIVE!
RMBRMB
BOOM
BBOOM

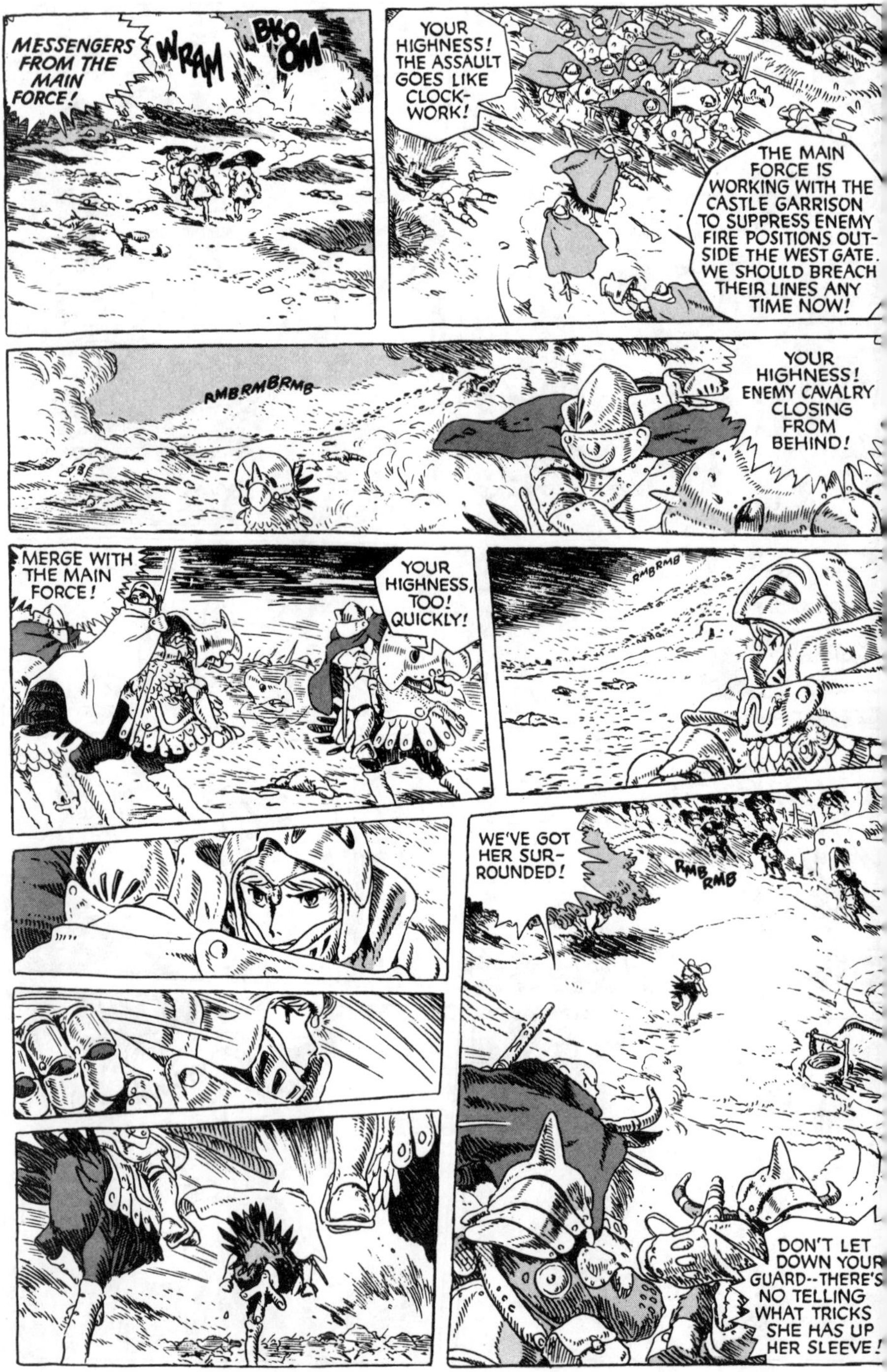
MESSENGERS FROM THE MAIN FORCE!
WRAM
BKOOM
YOUR HIGHNESS! THE ASSAULT GOES LIKE CLOCK-WORK!
THE MAIN FORCE IS WORKING WITH THE CASTLE GARRISON TO SUPPRESS ENEMY FIRE POSITIONS OUT-SIDE THE WEST GATE. WE SHOULD BREACH THEIR LINES ANY TIME NOW!
RMBRMBRMB
YOUR HIGHNESS! ENEMY CAVALRY CLOSING FROM BEHIND!
MERGE WITH THE MAIN FORCE!
YOUR HIGHNESS, TOO! QUICKLY!
RMBRMB
WE'VE GOT HER SUR-ROUNDED!
RMBRMB
DON'T LET DOWN YOUR GUARD--THERE'S NO TELLING WHAT TRICKS SHE HAS UP HER SLEEVE!

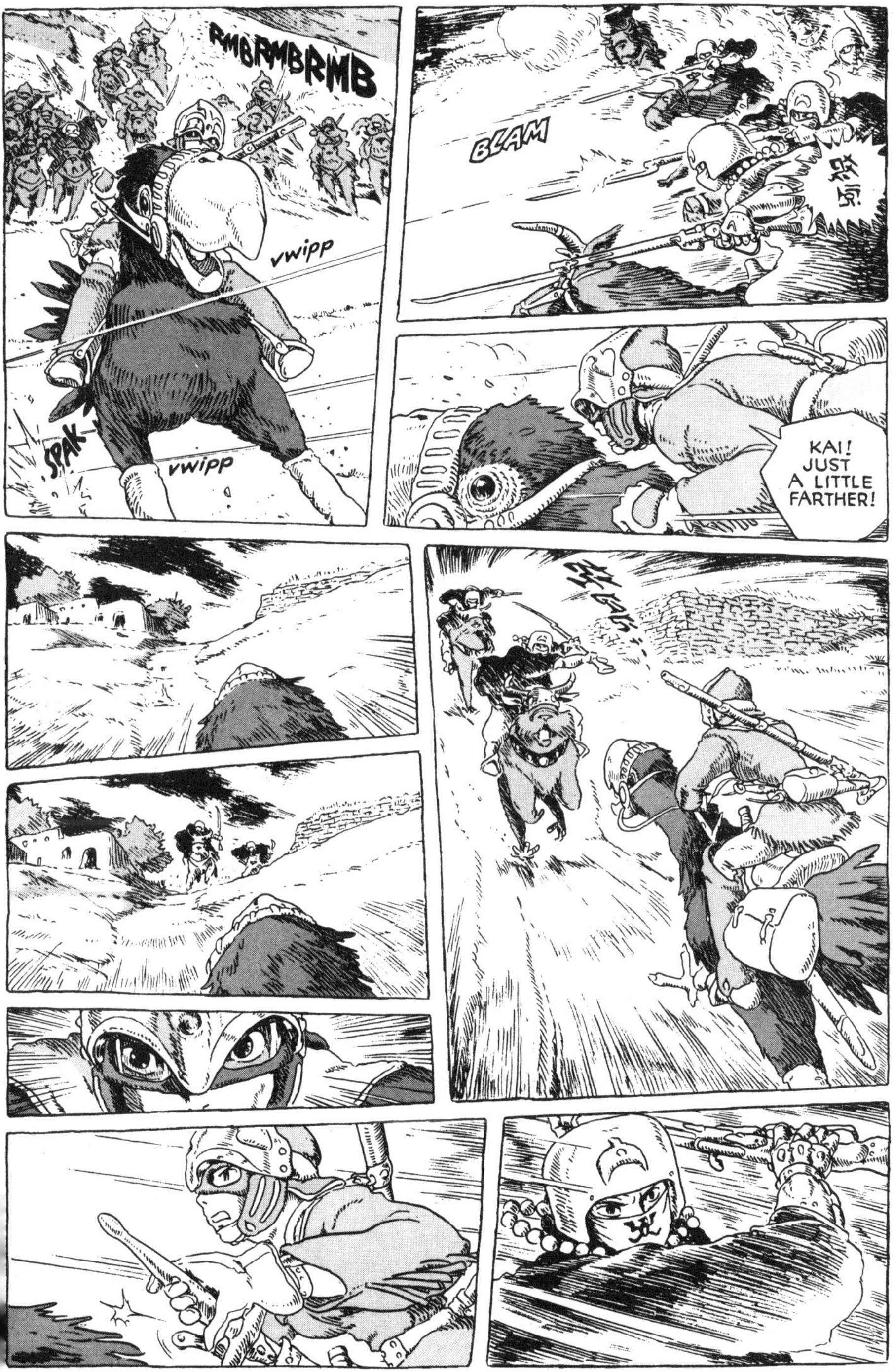
RMBRMBRMB
vwipp
SPAK
vwipp
BLAM
KAI! JUST A LITTLE FARTHER!

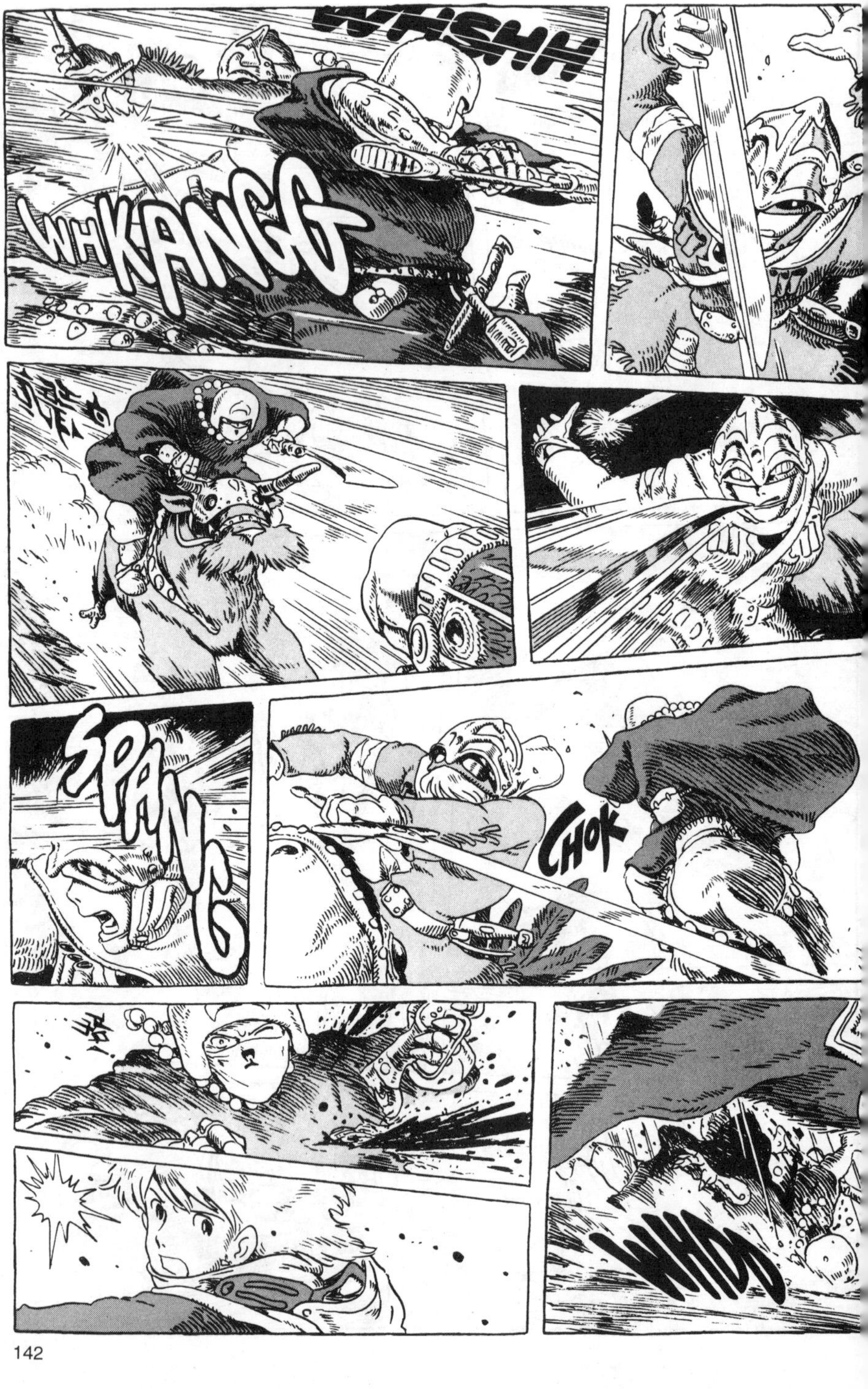
WASHH
WHKANGG
SPANG
CHOK
WHOS

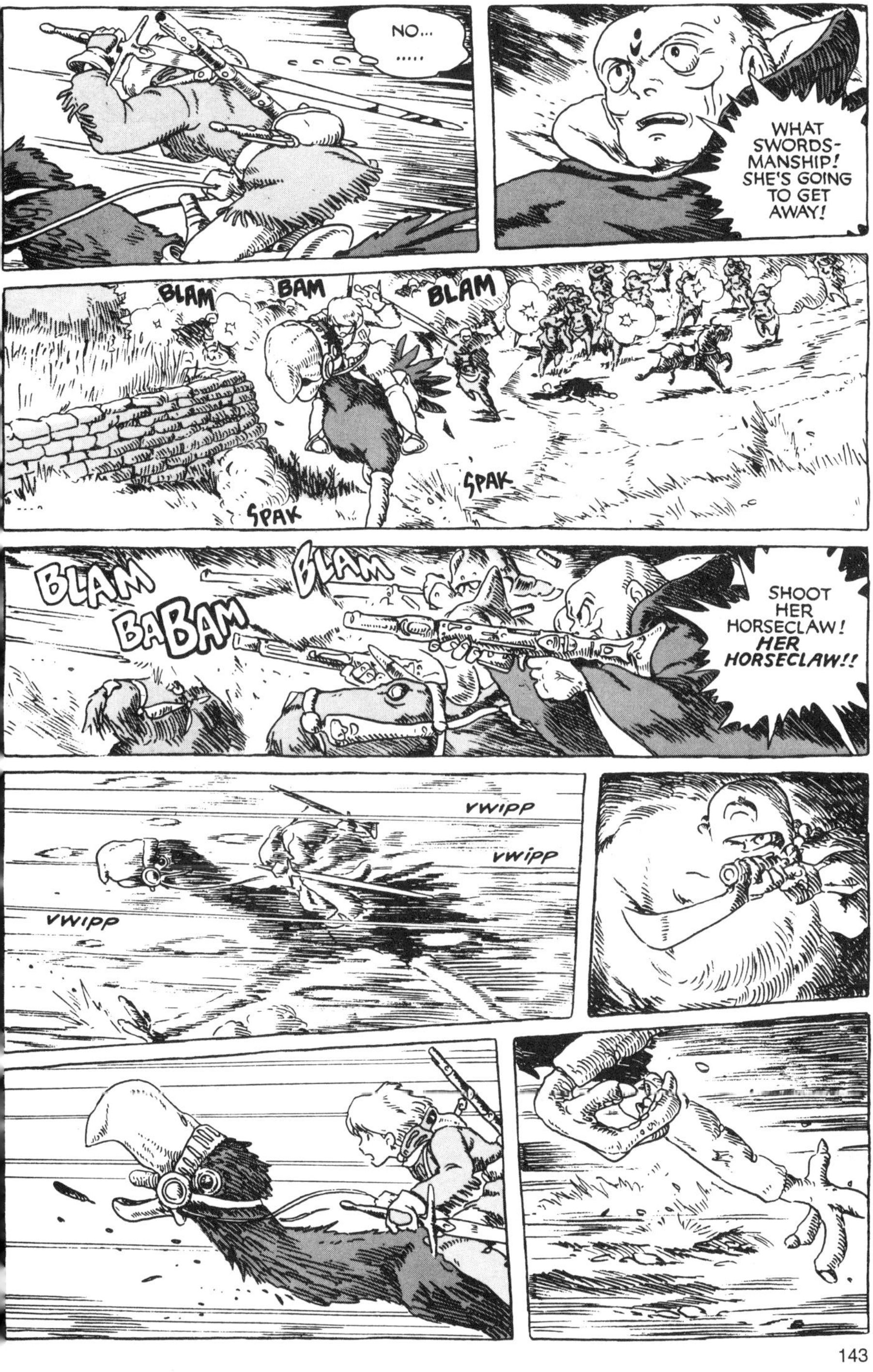
NO...
.....
WHAT SWORDS-MANSHIP! SHE'S GOING TO GET AWAY!
BLAM
BAM
BLAM
SPAK
SPAK
BLAM
BLAM
BABAM
SHOOT HER HORSECLAW! HER HORSECLAW!!
VWIPP
VWIPP
VWIPP

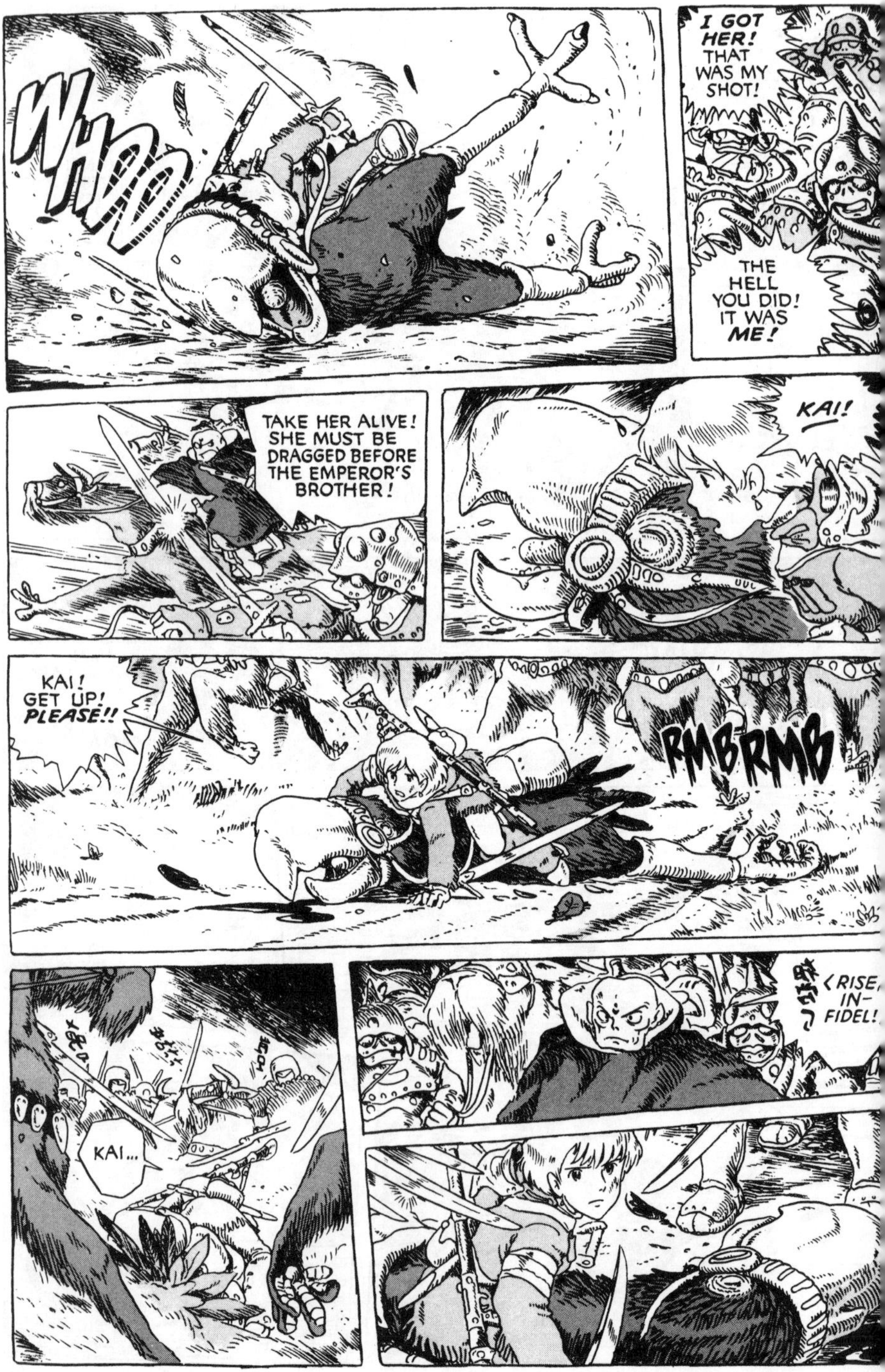
WHOO
I GOT HER! THAT WAS MY SHOT!
THE HELL YOU DID! IT WAS ME!
TAKE HER ALIVE! SHE MUST BE DRAGGED BEFORE THE EMPEROR'S BROTHER!
KAI!
KAI! GET UP! PLEASE!!
RMBRMB
KAI...
RISE, IN-FIDEL!

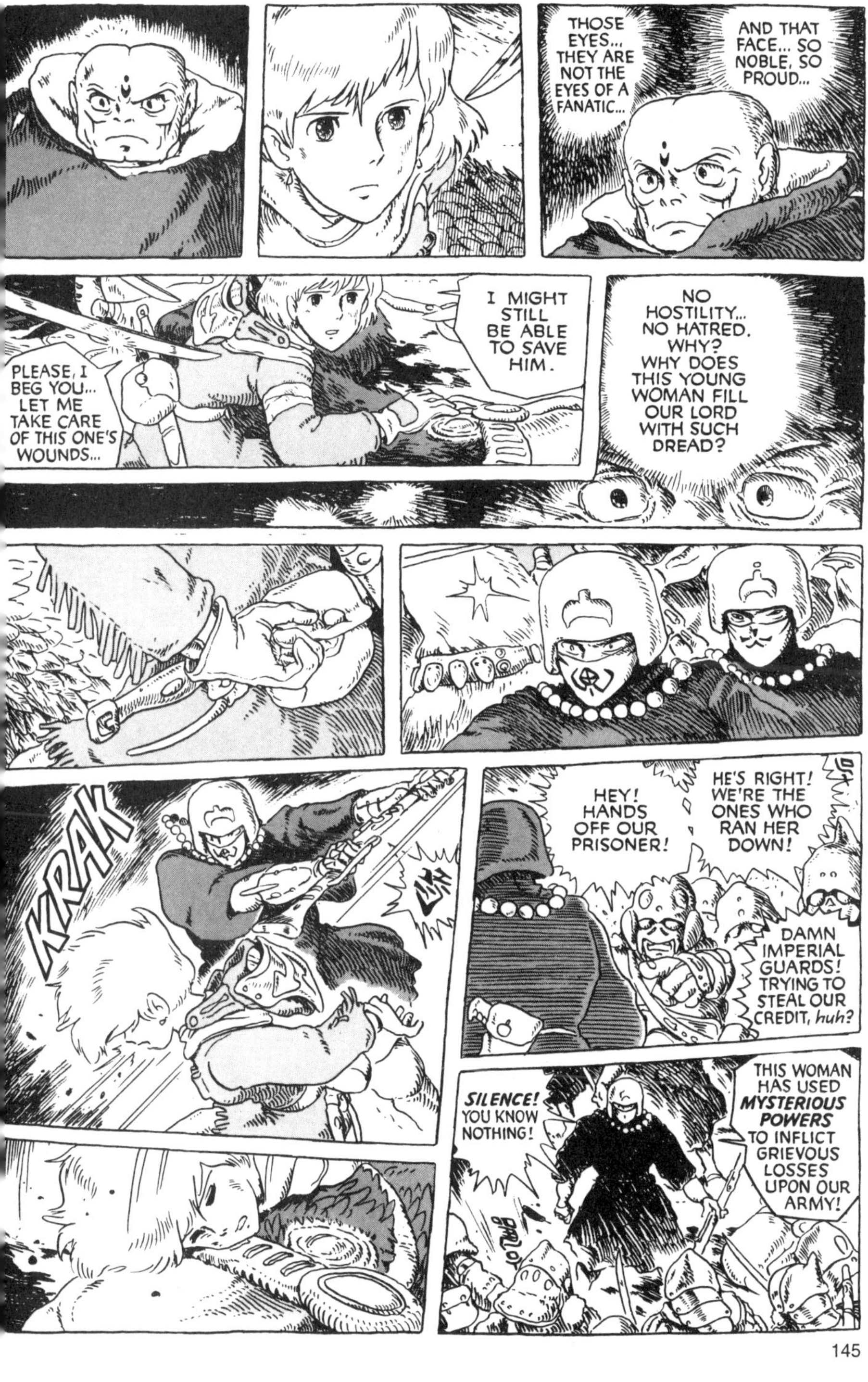
THOSE EYES... THEY ARE NOT THE EYES OF A FANATIC...
AND THAT FACE... SO NOBLE, SO PROUD...
PLEASE, I BEG YOU... LET ME TAKE CARE OF THIS ONE'S WOUNDS...
I MIGHT STILL BE ABLE TO SAVE HIM.
NO HOSTILITY... NO HATRED. WHY? WHY DOES THIS YOUNG WOMAN FILL OUR LORD WITH SUCH DREAD?
KRAK
HEY! HANDS OFF OUR PRISONER!
HE'S RIGHT! WE'RE THE ONES WHO RAN HER DOWN!
DAMN IMPERIAL GUARDS! TRYING TO STEAL OUR CREDIT, huh?
THIS WOMAN HAS USED MYSTERIOUS POWERS TO INFLICT GRIEVOUS LOSSES UPON OUR ARMY!
SILENCE! YOU KNOW NOTHING!

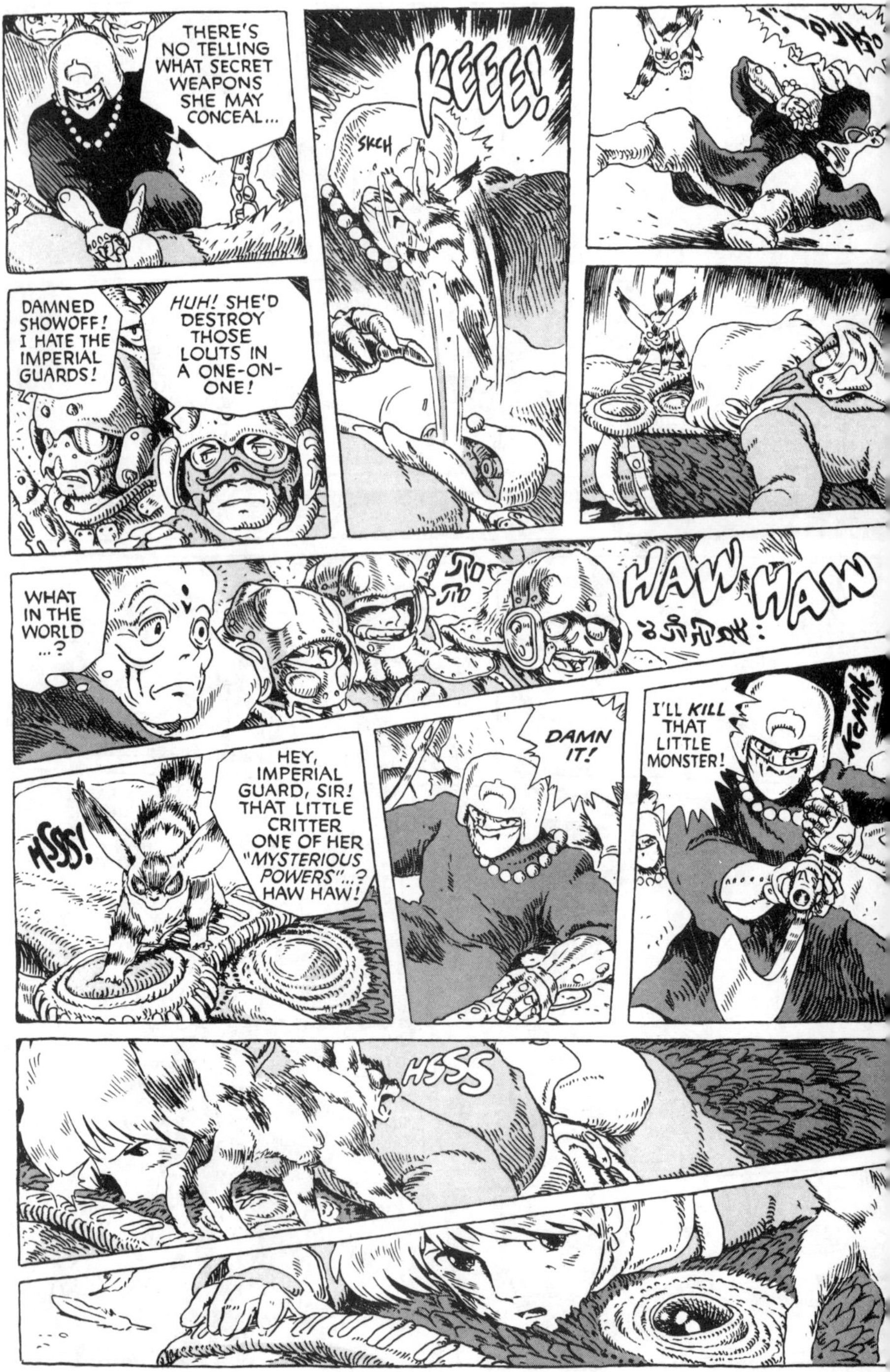
THERE'S NO TELLING WHAT SECRET WEAPONS SHE MAY CONCEAL...
KEEE!
SKCH
DAMNED SHOWOFF! I HATE THE IMPERIAL GUARDS!
HUH! SHE'D DESTROY THOSE LOUTS IN A ONE-ON-ONE!
WHAT IN THE WORLD ...?
HAW HAW
HEY, IMPERIAL GUARD, SIR! THAT LITTLE CRITTER ONE OF HER "MYSTERIOUS POWERS"...? HAW HAW!
HSSS!
DAMN IT!
I'LL KILL THAT LITTLE MONSTER!
KCHAK
HSSS

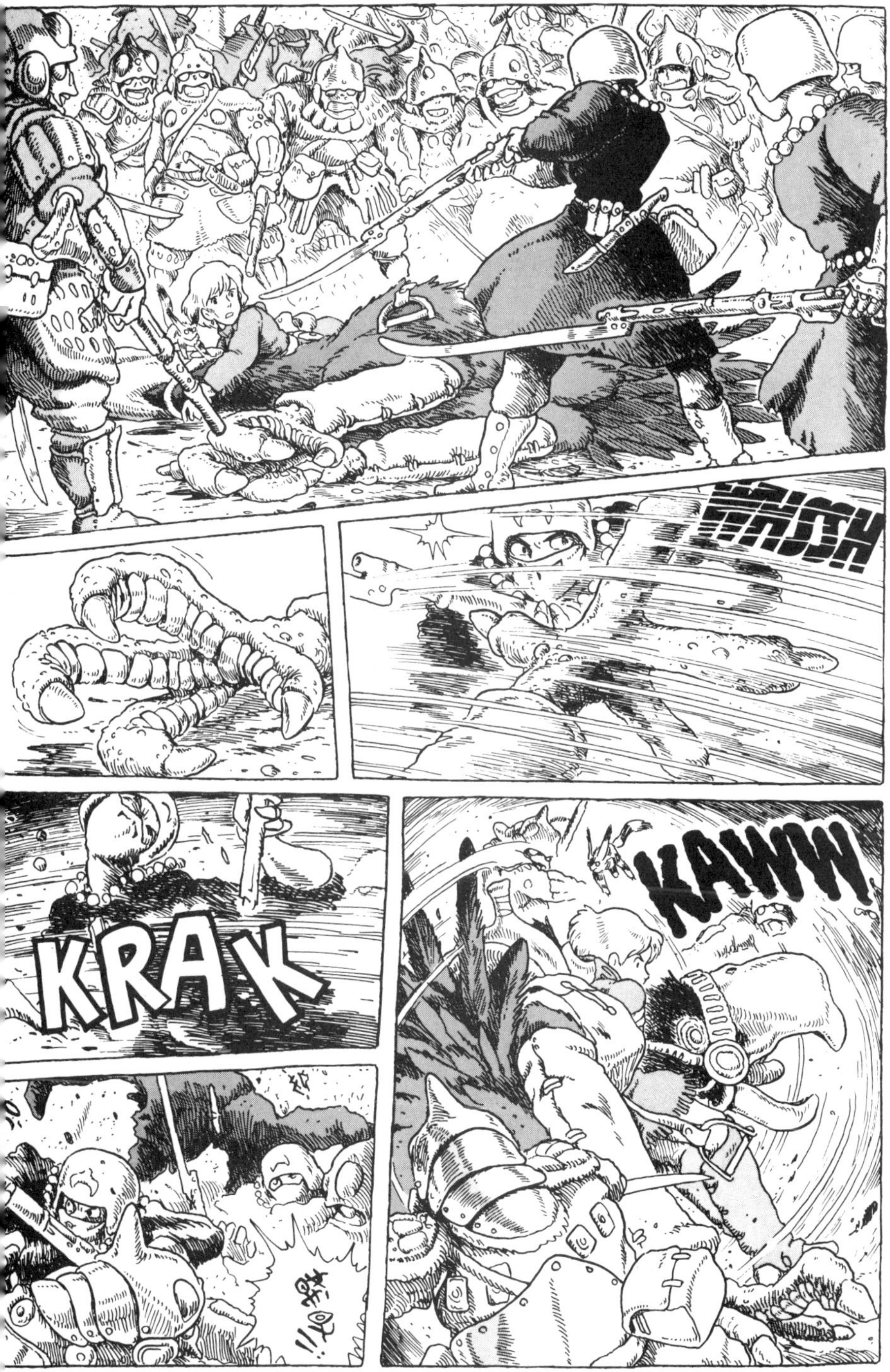
WHSH
KRAK
KAWW

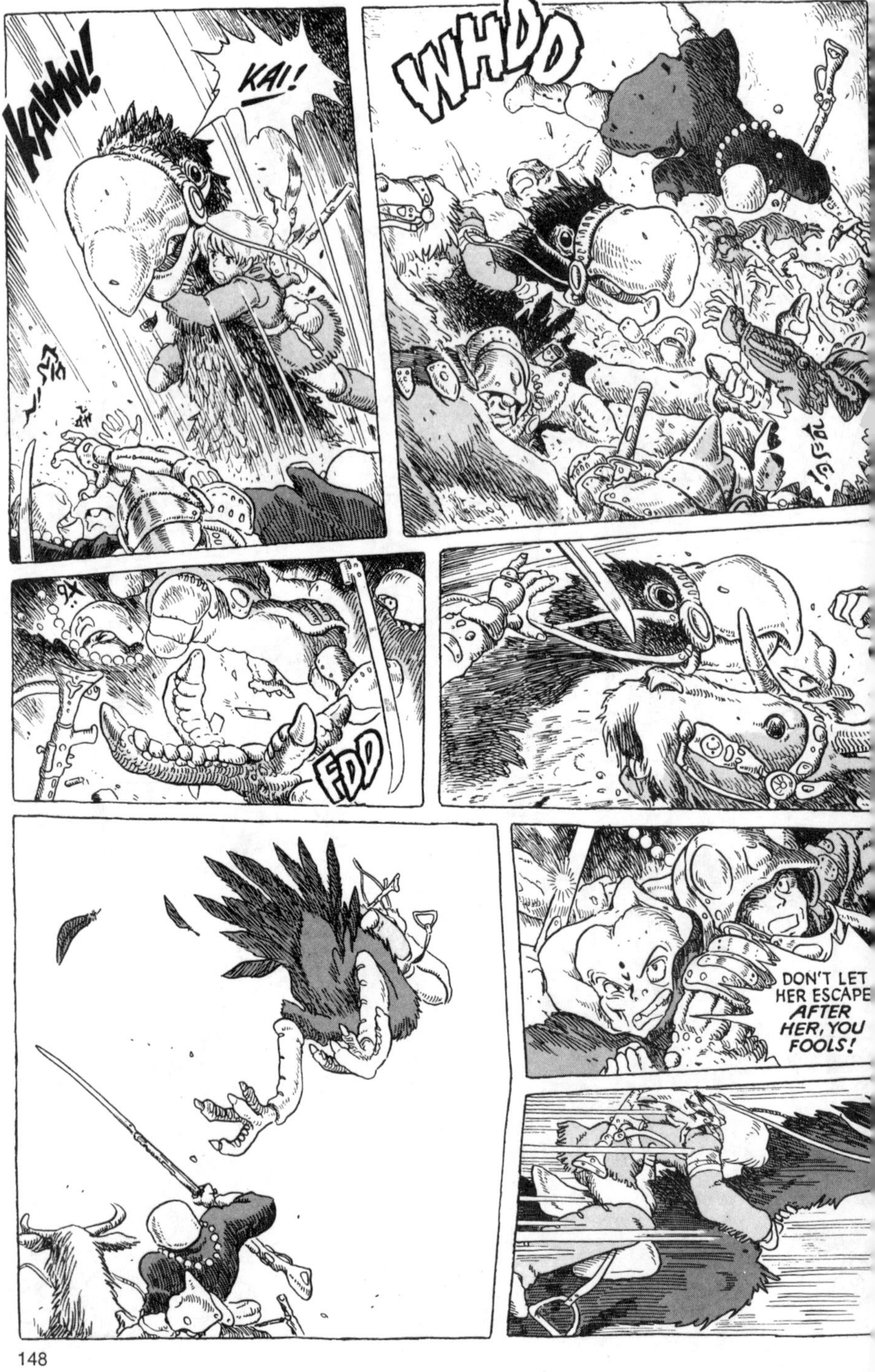
KAI!
KAWW!
WHDD
FDD
DON'T LET HER ESCAPE
AFTER HER, YOU FOOLS!

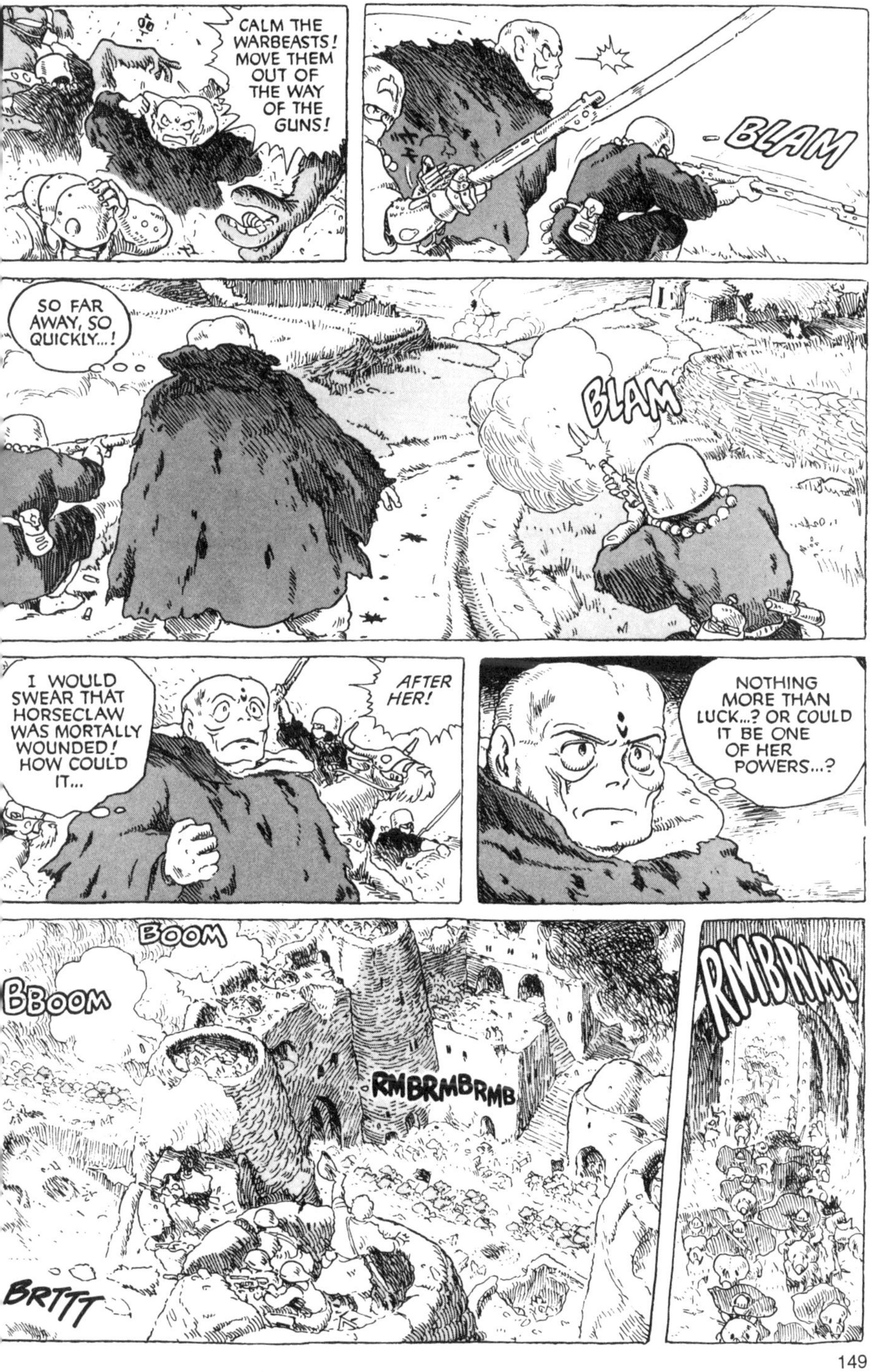
CALM THE WARBEASTS! MOVE THEM OUT OF THE WAY OF THE GUNS!
BLAM
SO FAR AWAY, SO QUICKLY...!
BLAM
I WOULD SWEAR THAT HORSECLAW WAS MORTALLY WOUNDED! HOW COULD IT...
AFTER HER!
NOTHING MORE THAN LUCK...? OR COULD IT BE ONE OF HER POWERS...?
BOOM
BBOOM
RMBRMBRMB
BRTTT
RMBRMB

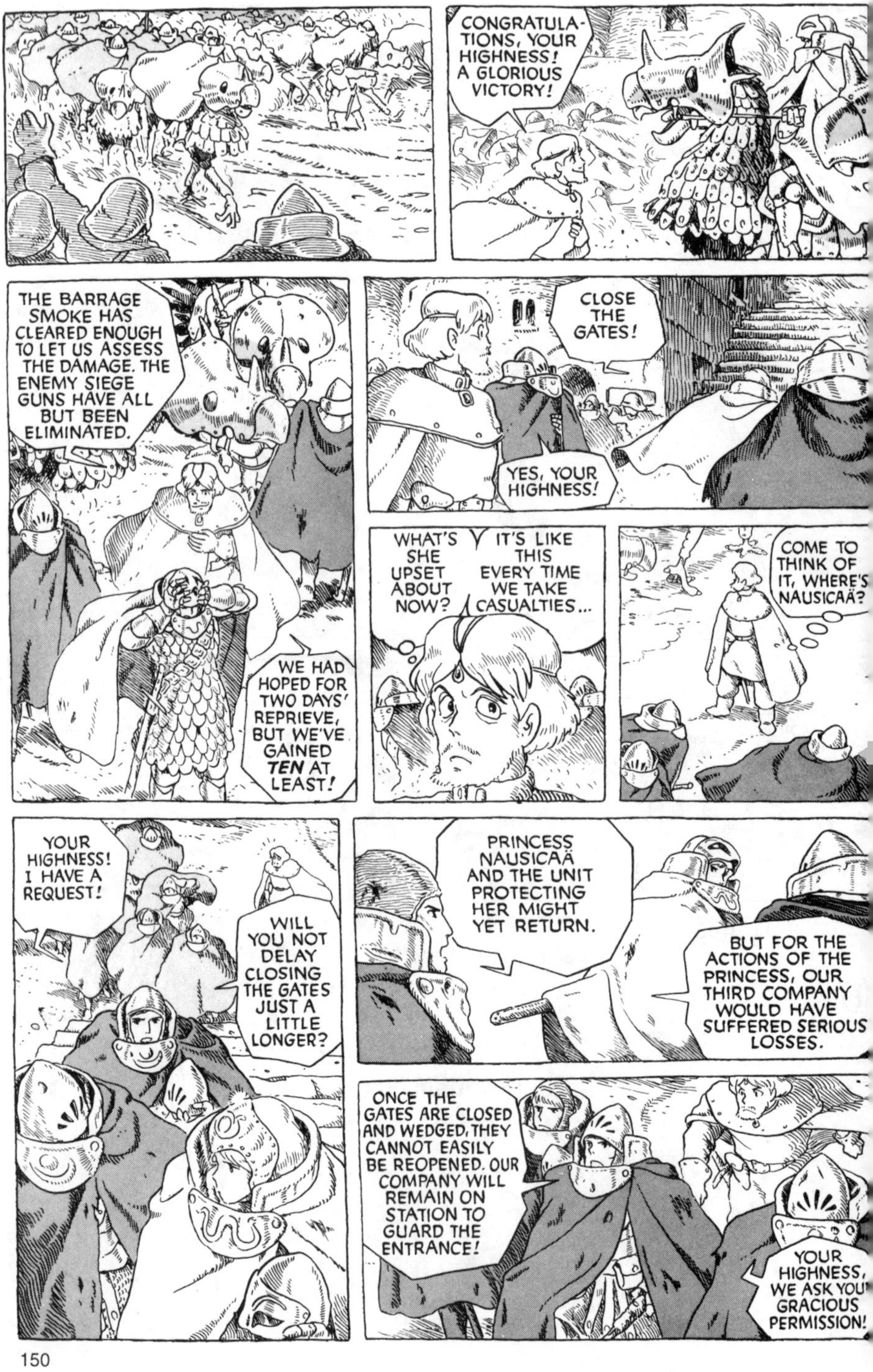
CONGRATULATIONS, YOUR HIGHNESS! A GLORIOUS VICTORY!
THE BARRAGE SMOKE HAS CLEARED ENOUGH TO LET US ASSESS THE DAMAGE. THE ENEMY SIEGE GUNS HAVE ALL BUT BEEN ELIMINATED.
WE HAD HOPED FOR TWO DAYS' REPRIEVE, BUT WE'VE GAINED TEN AT LEAST!
CLOSE THE GATES!
YES, YOUR HIGHNESS!
WHAT'S SHE UPSET ABOUT NOW?
IT'S LIKE THIS EVERY TIME WE TAKE CASUALTIES...
COME TO THINK OF IT, WHERE'S NAUSICAÄ?
YOUR HIGHNESS! I HAVE A REQUEST!
WILL YOU NOT DELAY CLOSING THE GATES JUST A LITTLE LONGER?
PRINCESS NAUSICAÄ AND THE UNIT PROTECTING HER MIGHT YET RETURN.
BUT FOR THE ACTIONS OF THE PRINCESS, OUR THIRD COMPANY WOULD HAVE SUFFERED SERIOUS LOSSES.
ONCE THE GATES ARE CLOSED AND WEDGED, THEY CANNOT EASILY BE REOPENED. OUR COMPANY WILL REMAIN ON STATION TO GUARD THE ENTRANCE!
YOUR HIGHNESS, WE ASK YOU GRACIOUS PERMISSION!

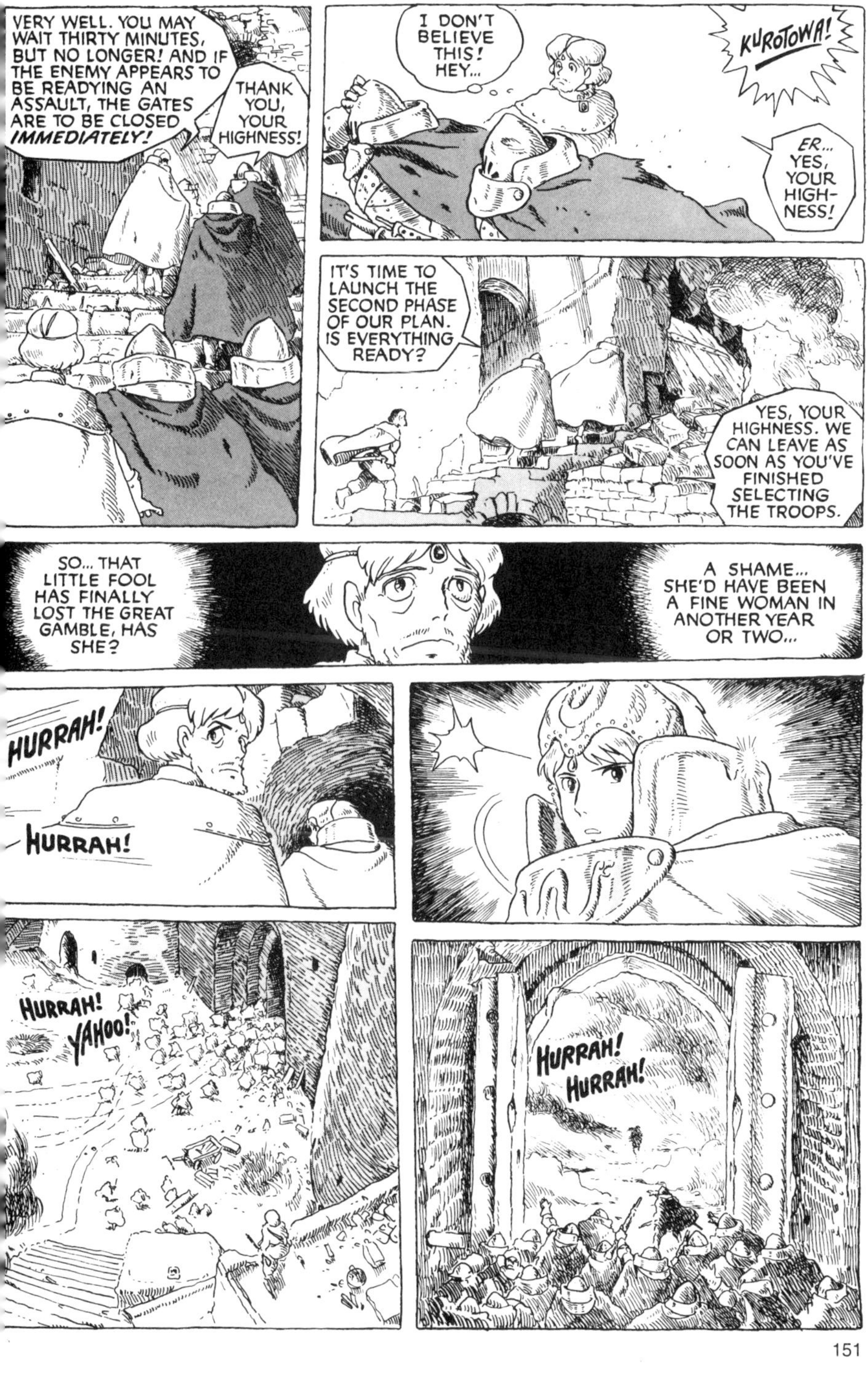

VERY WELL. YOU MAY WAIT THIRTY MINUTES, BUT NO LONGER! AND IF THE ENEMY APPEARS TO BE READYING AN ASSAULT, THE GATES ARE TO BE CLOSED IMMEDIATELY!
THANK YOU, YOUR HIGHNESS!
I DON'T BELIEVE THIS! HEY...
KUROTOWA!
ER... YES, YOUR HIGH-NESS!
IT'S TIME TO LAUNCH THE SECOND PHASE OF OUR PLAN. IS EVERYTHING READY?
YES, YOUR HIGHNESS. WE CAN LEAVE AS SOON AS YOU'VE FINISHED SELECTING THE TROOPS.
SO... THAT LITTLE FOOL HAS FINALLY LOST THE GREAT GAMBLE, HAS SHE?
A SHAME... SHE'D HAVE BEEN A FINE WOMAN IN ANOTHER YEAR OR TWO...
HURRAH!
HURRAH!
HURRAH! YAHOO!
HURRAH! HURRAH!

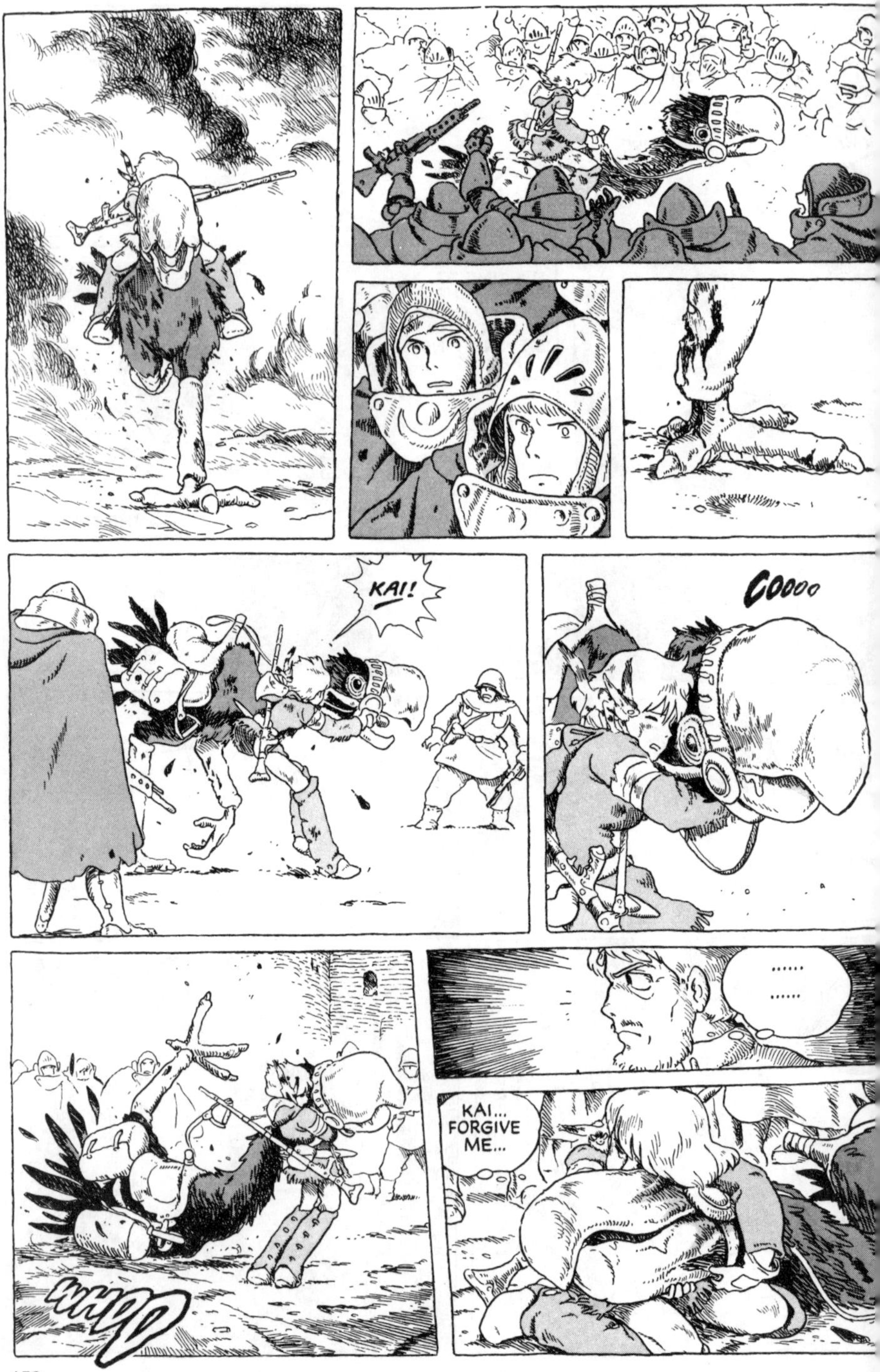
KAI!
COOOO
......
......
KAI... FORGIVE ME...
WHIP

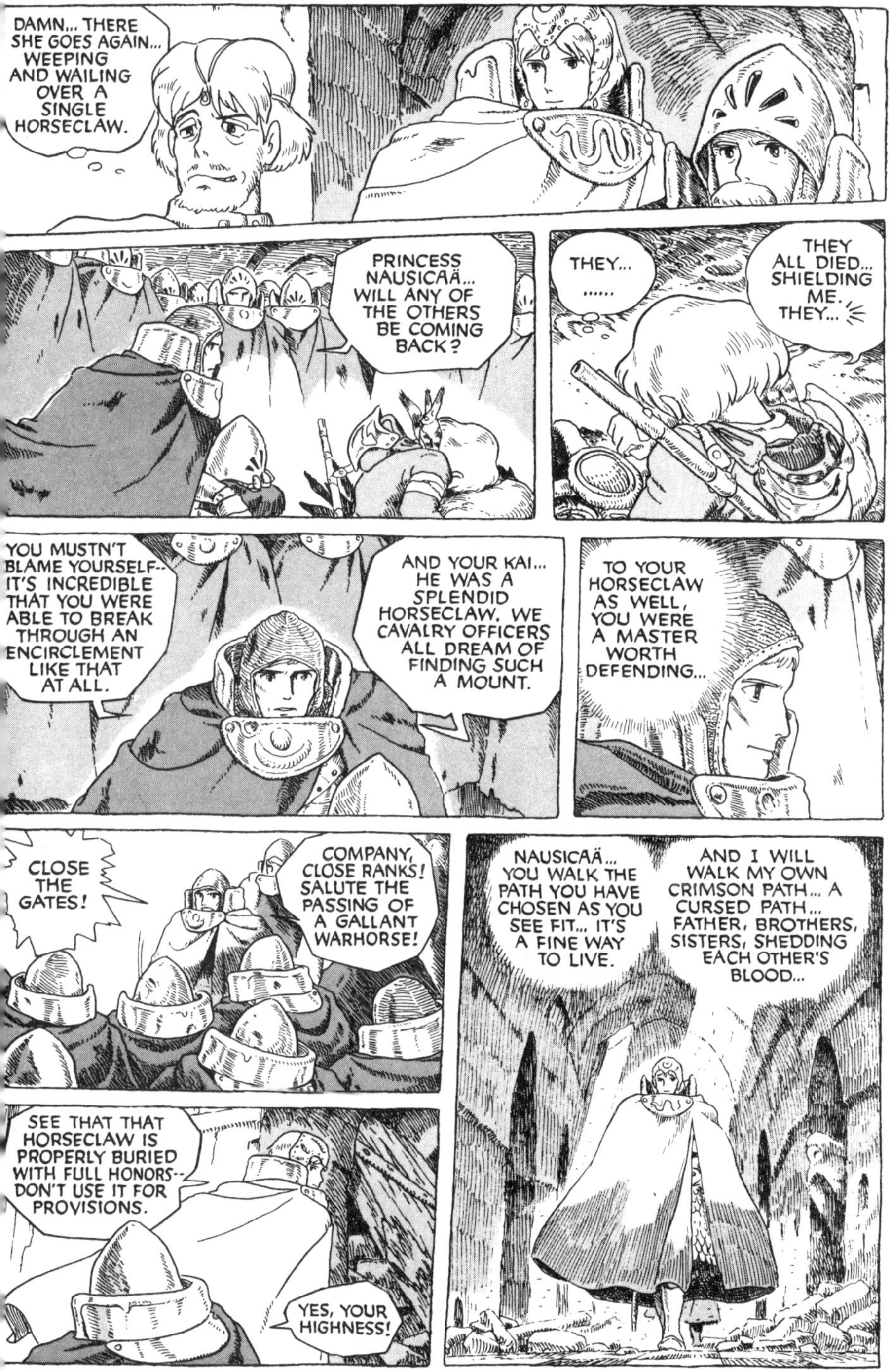
DAMN... THERE SHE GOES AGAIN... WEEPING AND WAILING OVER A SINGLE HORSECLAW.
PRINCESS NAUSICAÄ... WILL ANY OF THE OTHERS BE COMING BACK?
THEY... ......
THEY ALL DIED... SHIELDING ME. THEY...
YOU MUSTN'T BLAME YOURSELF-- IT'S INCREDIBLE THAT YOU WERE ABLE TO BREAK THROUGH AN ENCIRCLEMENT LIKE THAT AT ALL.
AND YOUR KAI... HE WAS A SPLENDID HORSECLAW. WE CAVALRY OFFICERS ALL DREAM OF FINDING SUCH A MOUNT.
TO YOUR HORSECLAW AS WELL, YOU WERE A MASTER WORTH DEFENDING...
CLOSE THE GATES!
COMPANY, CLOSE RANKS! SALUTE THE PASSING OF A GALLANT WARHORSE!
SEE THAT THAT HORSECLAW IS PROPERLY BURIED WITH FULL HONORS-- DON'T USE IT FOR PROVISIONS.
YES, YOUR HIGHNESS!
NAUSICAÄ... YOU WALK THE PATH YOU HAVE CHOSEN AS YOU SEE FIT... IT'S A FINE WAY TO LIVE.
AND I WILL WALK MY OWN CRIMSON PATH... A CURSED PATH... FATHER, BROTHERS, SISTERS, SHEDDING EACH OTHER'S BLOOD...

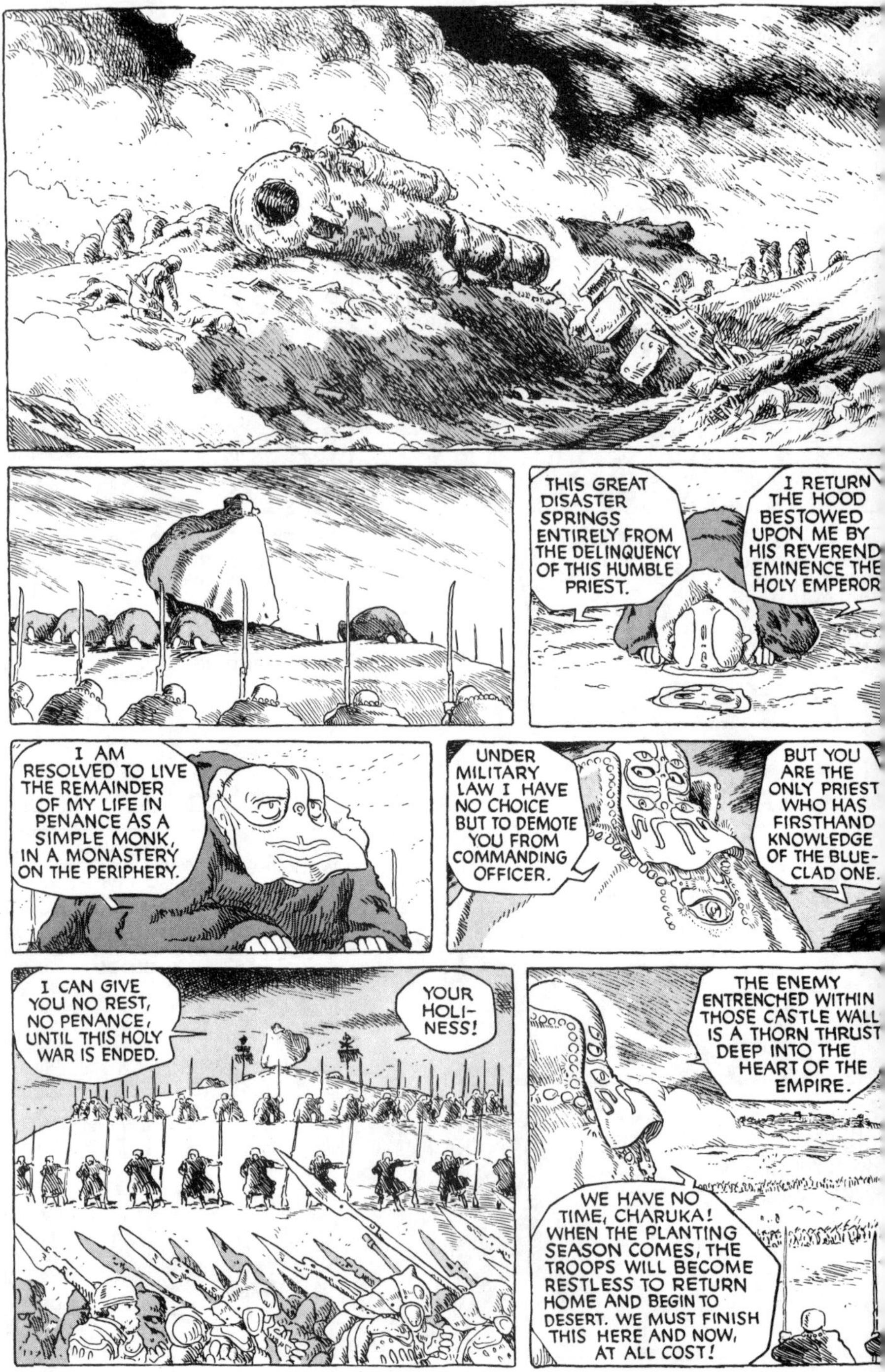
THIS GREAT DISASTER SPRINGS ENTIRELY FROM THE DELINQUENCY OF THIS HUMBLE PRIEST.
I RETURN THE HOOD BESTOWED UPON ME BY HIS REVEREND EMINENCE THE HOLY EMPEROR
I AM RESOLVED TO LIVE THE REMAINDER OF MY LIFE IN PENANCE AS A SIMPLE MONK, IN A MONASTERY ON THE PERIPHERY.
UNDER MILITARY LAW I HAVE NO CHOICE BUT TO DEMOTE YOU FROM COMMANDING OFFICER.
BUT YOU ARE THE ONLY PRIEST WHO HAS FIRSTHAND KNOWLEDGE OF THE BLUE-CLAD ONE.
I CAN GIVE YOU NO REST, NO PENANCE, UNTIL THIS HOLY WAR IS ENDED.
YOUR HOLI-NESS!
THE ENEMY ENTRENCHED WITHIN THOSE CASTLE WALL IS A THORN THRUST DEEP INTO THE HEART OF THE EMPIRE.
WE HAVE NO TIME, CHARUKA! WHEN THE PLANTING SEASON COMES, THE TROOPS WILL BECOME RESTLESS TO RETURN HOME AND BEGIN TO DESERT. WE MUST FINISH THIS HERE AND NOW, AT ALL COST!

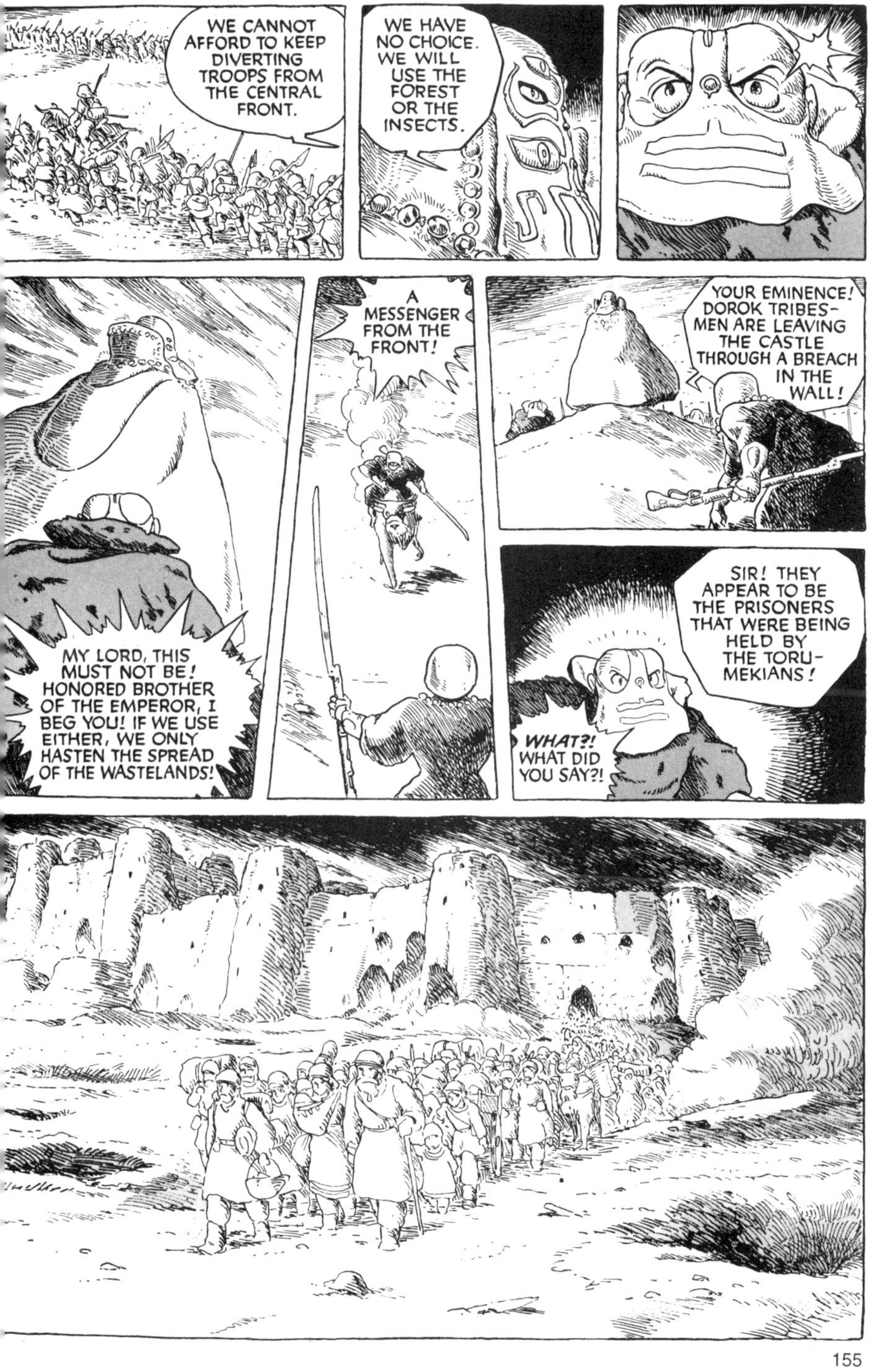
WE CANNOT AFFORD TO KEEP DIVERTING TROOPS FROM THE CENTRAL FRONT.
WE HAVE NO CHOICE. WE WILL USE THE FOREST OR THE INSECTS.
MY LORD, THIS MUST NOT BE! HONORED BROTHER OF THE EMPEROR, I BEG YOU! IF WE USE EITHER, WE ONLY HASTEN THE SPREAD OF THE WASTELANDS!
A MESSENGER FROM THE FRONT!
YOUR EMINENCE! DOROK TRIBES-MEN ARE LEAVING THE CASTLE THROUGH A BREACH IN THE WALL!
SIR! THEY APPEAR TO BE THE PRISONERS THAT WERE BEING HELD BY THE TORU-MEKIANS!
WHAT?! WHAT DID YOU SAY?!

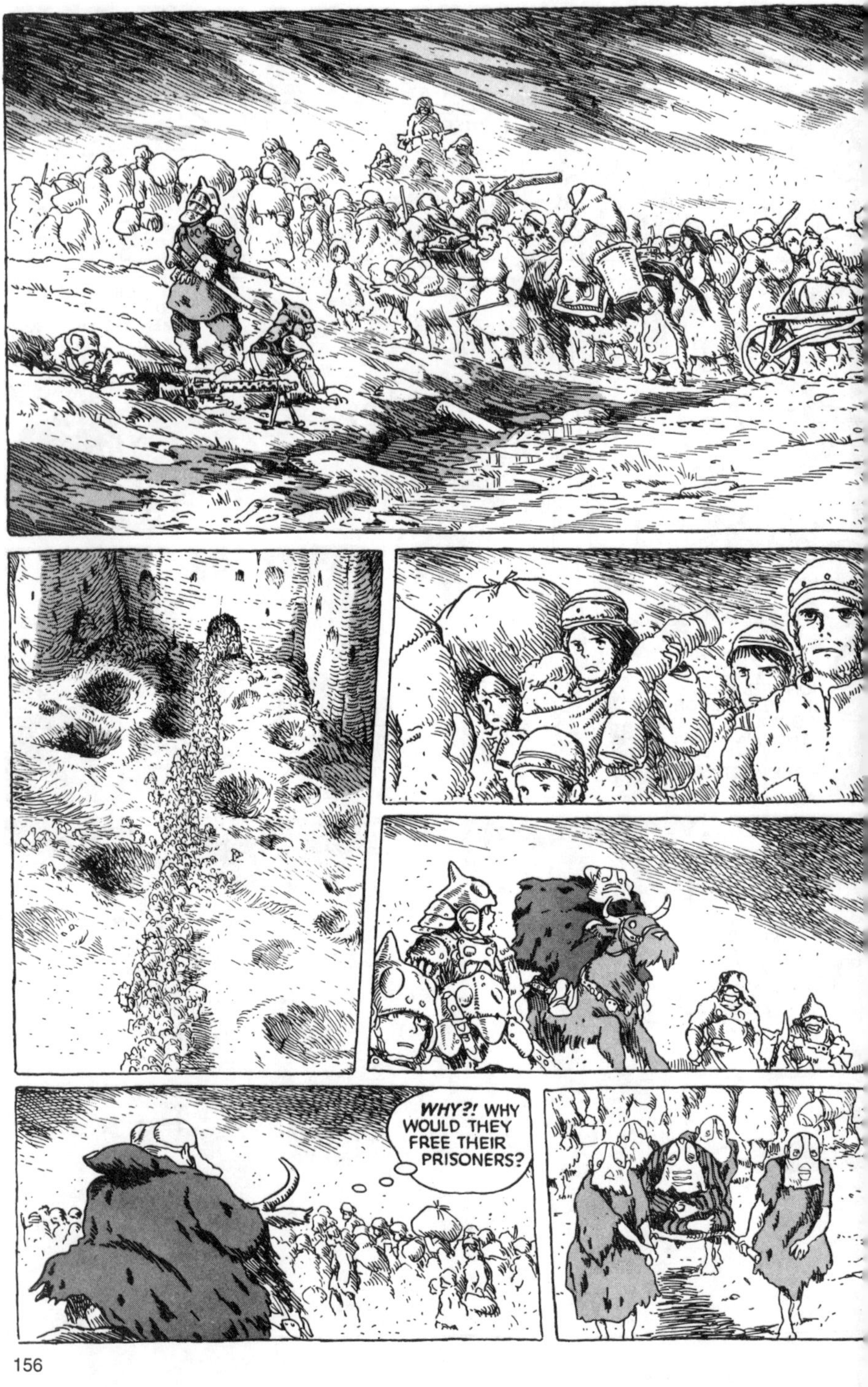
WHY?! WHY WOULD THEY FREE THEIR PRISONERS?

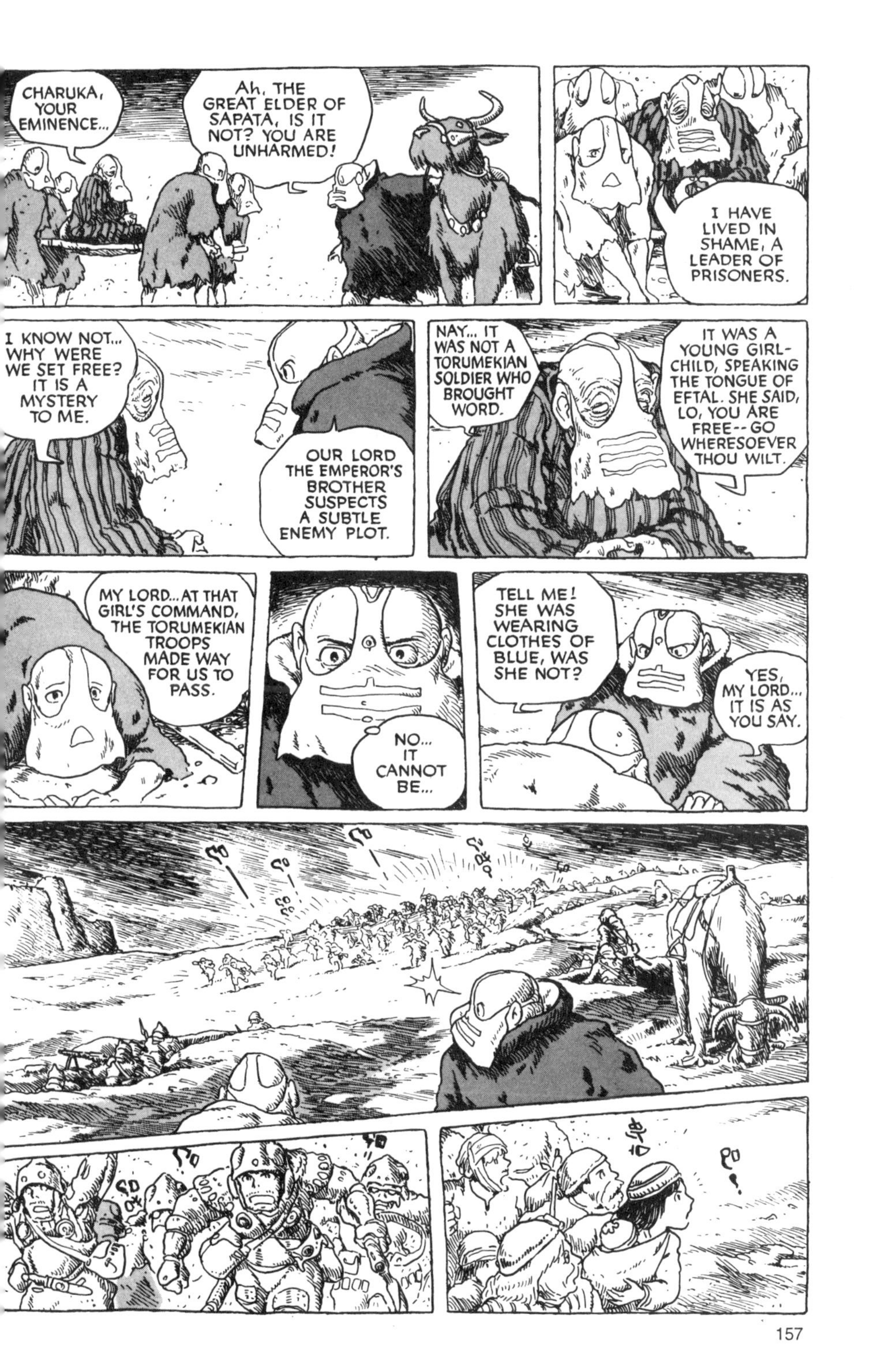
CHARUKA, YOUR EMINENCE...
Ah, THE GREAT ELDER OF SAPATA, IS IT NOT? YOU ARE UNHARMED!
I HAVE LIVED IN SHAME, A LEADER OF PRISONERS.
I KNOW NOT... WHY WERE WE SET FREE? IT IS A MYSTERY TO ME.
OUR LORD THE EMPEROR'S BROTHER SUSPECTS A SUBTLE ENEMY PLOT.
NAY... IT WAS NOT A TORUMEKIAN SOLDIER WHO BROUGHT WORD.
IT WAS A YOUNG GIRL-CHILD, SPEAKING THE TONGUE OF EFTAL. SHE SAID, LO, YOU ARE FREE--GO WHERESOEVER THOU WILT.
MY LORD...AT THAT GIRL'S COMMAND, THE TORUMEKIAN TROOPS MADE WAY FOR US TO PASS.
NO... IT CANNOT BE...
TELL ME! SHE WAS WEARING CLOTHES OF BLUE, WAS SHE NOT?
YES, MY LORD... IT IS AS YOU SAY.

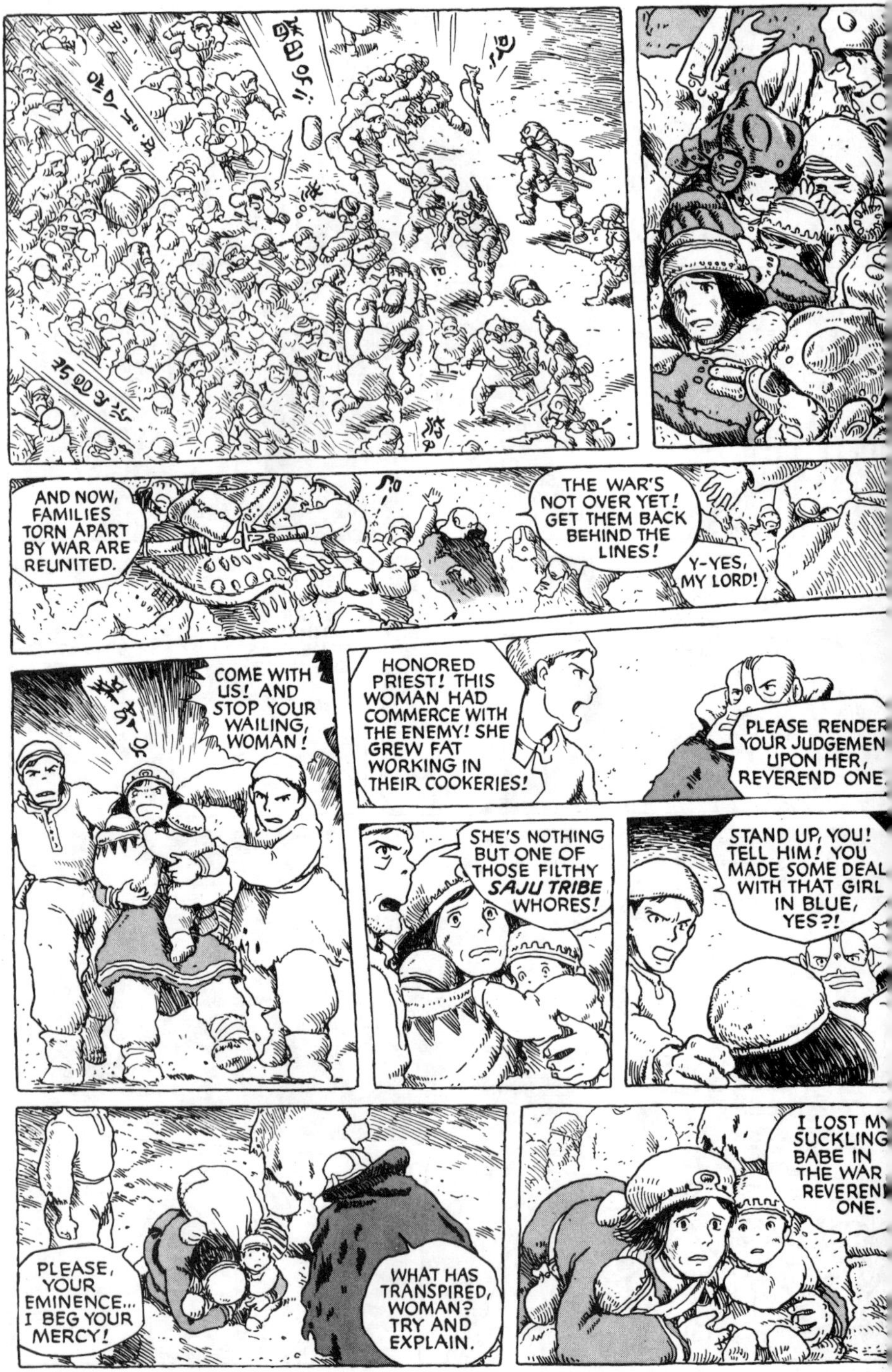
AND NOW, FAMILIES TORN APART BY WAR ARE REUNITED.
THE WAR'S NOT OVER YET! GET THEM BACK BEHIND THE LINES!
Y-YES, MY LORD!
COME WITH US! AND STOP YOUR WAILING, WOMAN!
HONORED PRIEST! THIS WOMAN HAD COMMERCE WITH THE ENEMY! SHE GREW FAT WORKING IN THEIR COOKERIES!
PLEASE RENDER YOUR JUDGEMEN UPON HER, REVEREND ONE.
SHE'S NOTHING BUT ONE OF THOSE FILTHY SAJU TRIBE WHORES!
STAND UP, YOU! TELL HIM! YOU MADE SOME DEAL WITH THAT GIRL IN BLUE, YES?!
PLEASE, YOUR EMINENCE... I BEG YOUR MERCY!
WHAT HAS TRANSPIRED, WOMAN? TRY AND EXPLAIN.
I LOST MY SUCKLING BABE IN THE WAR REVEREN ONE.

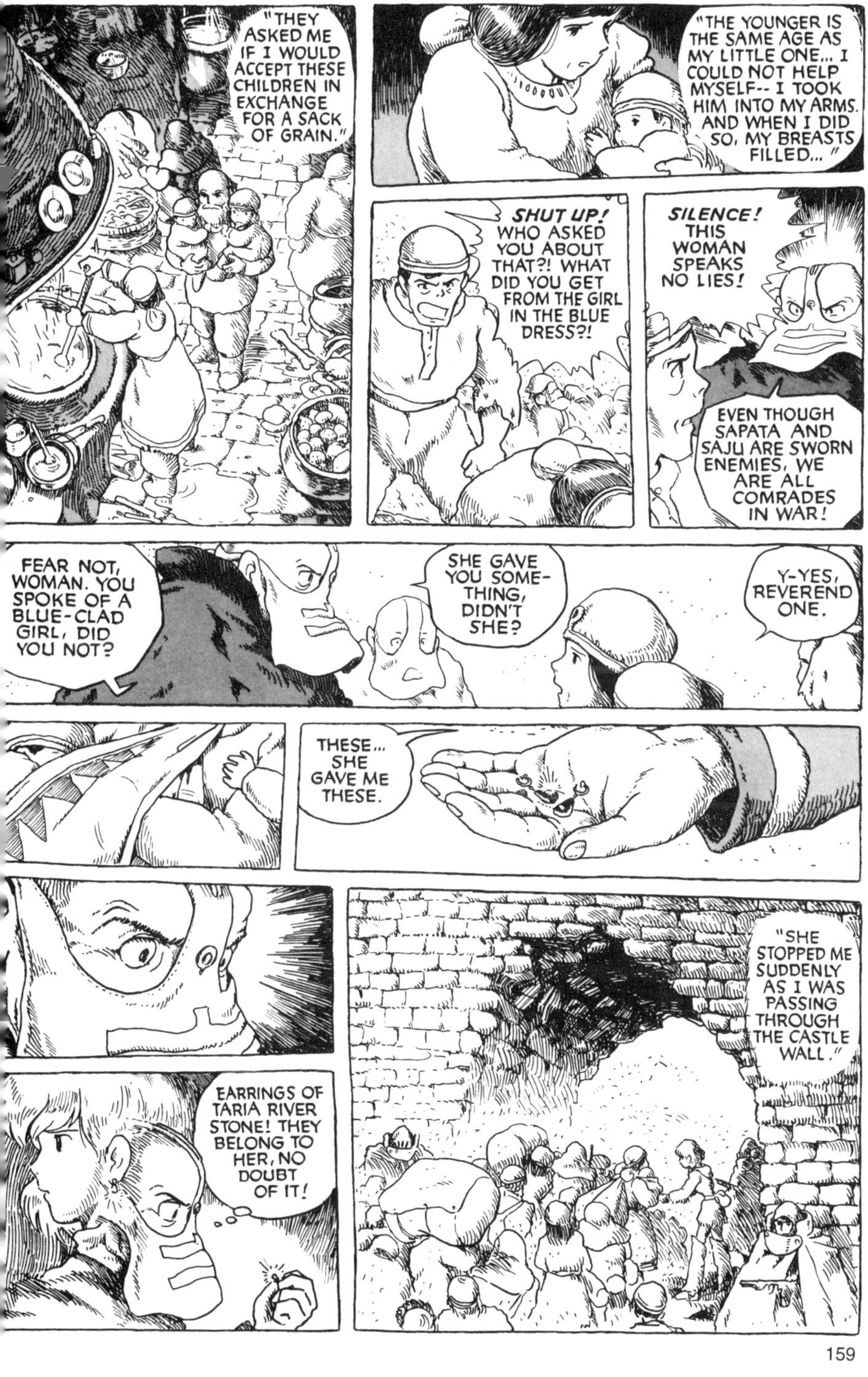
"THEY ASKED ME IF I WOULD ACCEPT THESE CHILDREN IN EXCHANGE FOR A SACK OF GRAIN."
"THE YOUNGER IS THE SAME AGE AS MY LITTLE ONE... I COULD NOT HELP MYSELF-- I TOOK HIM INTO MY ARMS. AND WHEN I DID SO, MY BREASTS FILLED..."
SHUT UP! WHO ASKED YOU ABOUT THAT?! WHAT DID YOU GET FROM THE GIRL IN THE BLUE DRESS?!
SILENCE! THIS WOMAN SPEAKS NO LIES!
EVEN THOUGH SAPATA AND SAJU ARE SWORN ENEMIES, WE ARE ALL COMRADES IN WAR!
FEAR NOT, WOMAN. YOU SPOKE OF A BLUE-CLAD GIRL, DID YOU NOT?
SHE GAVE YOU SOMETHING, DIDN'T SHE?
Y-YES, REVEREND ONE.
THESE... SHE GAVE ME THESE.
"SHE STOPPED ME SUDDENLY AS I WAS PASSING THROUGH THE CASTLE WALL."
EARRINGS OF TARIA RIVER STONE! THEY BELONG TO HER, NO DOUBT OF IT!

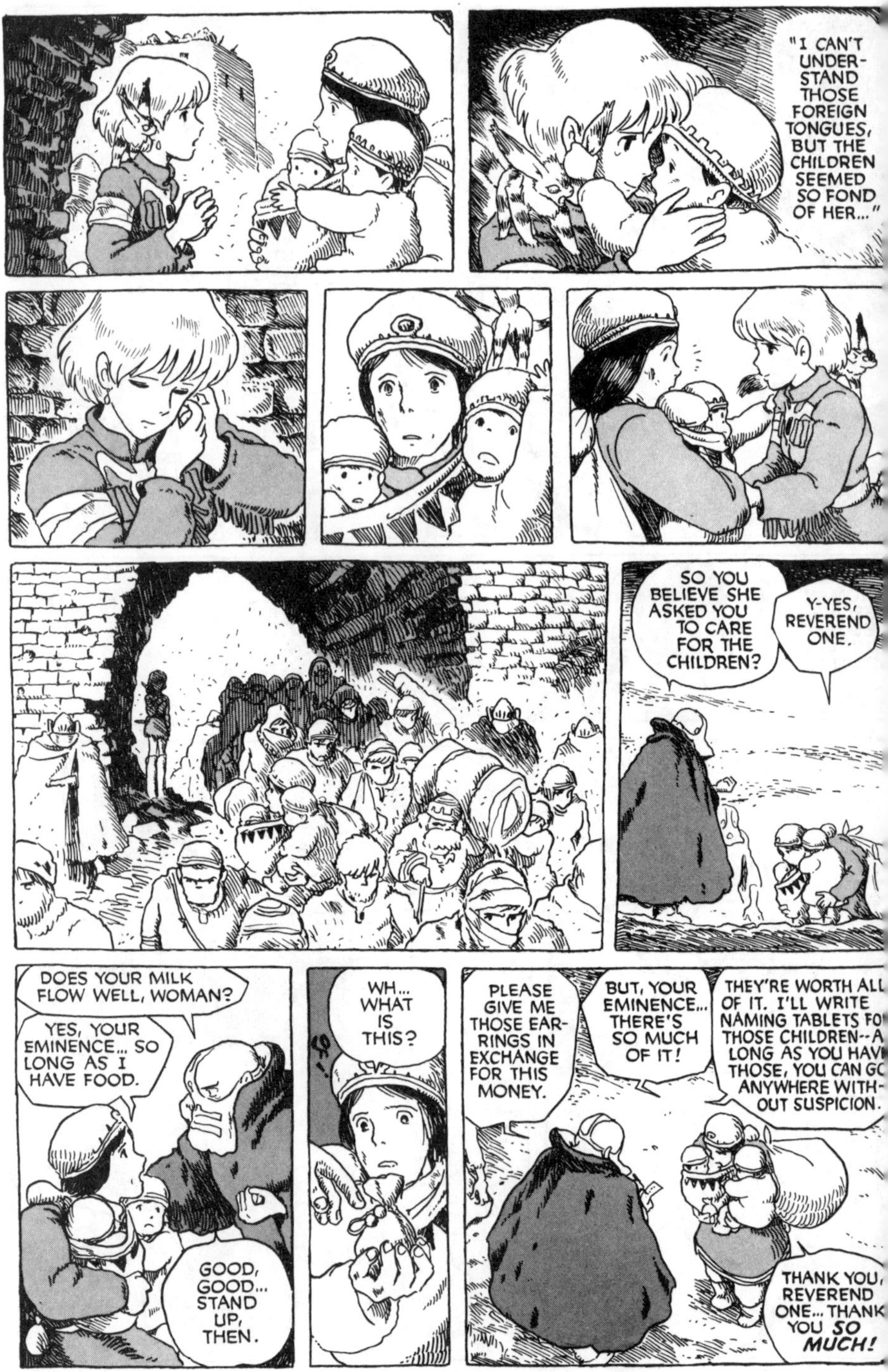
"I CAN'T UNDER-STAND THOSE FOREIGN TONGUES, BUT THE CHILDREN SEEMED SO FOND OF HER..."
SO YOU BELIEVE SHE ASKED YOU TO CARE FOR THE CHILDREN?
Y-YES, REVEREND ONE.
DOES YOUR MILK FLOW WELL, WOMAN?
YES, YOUR EMINENCE... SO LONG AS I HAVE FOOD.
GOOD, GOOD... STAND UP, THEN.
WH... WHAT IS THIS?
PLEASE GIVE ME THOSE EAR-RINGS IN EXCHANGE FOR THIS MONEY.
BUT, YOUR EMINENCE... THERE'S SO MUCH OF IT!
THEY'RE WORTH ALL OF IT. I'LL WRITE NAMING TABLETS FOR THOSE CHILDREN--AS LONG AS YOU HAVE THOSE, YOU CAN GO ANYWHERE WITH-OUT SUSPICION.
THANK YOU, REVEREND ONE... THANK YOU SO MUCH!

NOW LISTEN TO ME. YOU MUST NOT STAY IN THESE PARTS. TRAVEL TO THE LANDS IN THE EAST.

.....

...?!

BUT YOUR EMINENCE... MY COUNTRY LIES TO THE WEST. I WISH TO RETURN THERE, TO TILL MY FIELDS, TO PLANT GRAIN...

YOU MUST NOT! USE THAT MONEY TO BUY A MOUNT. YOU MUST GET UPWIND OF THESE LANDS AS QUICKLY AS POSSIBLE!

KEDO WOULD BE A GOOD PLACE FOR YOU. GO TO KEDO, AND SEARCH FOR WORK AS A WET NURSE.

I... I WILL, REVEREND ONE!

CHARUKA, EMINENCE, SURELY YOU DO NOT INTEND...

HIS HOLINESS MIRALUPA HAS MADE HIS DECISION.

YOU SHOULD THANK DIVINE PROVIDENCE THAT YOU WERE FREED AT THIS TIME.

GREAT ELDER, YOU TOO MUST LEAVE. TAKE ALL OF YOUR TRIBE BUT THE WARRIORS, AND PUT THESE LANDS BEHIND YOU AS SOON AS YOU CAN!

WE SHALL NOT! WE SHALL NOT ABANDON THIS SOIL! IF WE ABANDON THESE LANDS, OUR HOLY MOTHER SAPATA SHALL *PERISH!*

EVEN WERE IT THE COMMAND OF THE EMPEROR HIMSELF, WHAT WORD OF GOD PERMITS THE FOULING OF THE LAND?!

THERE CAN BE NO EMPEROR WITHOUT THE PEOPLE! CEASE THIS MADNESS! I BEG YOU!

LET US SAY THAT I DID NOT HEAR YOU.

SPEAK WITH CAUTION, GREAT ELDER. SHOULD THIS REACH THE EARS OF THE COUNCIL OF MONKS, WHAT THEN?

CHARUKA! *YOUR EMINENCE!*

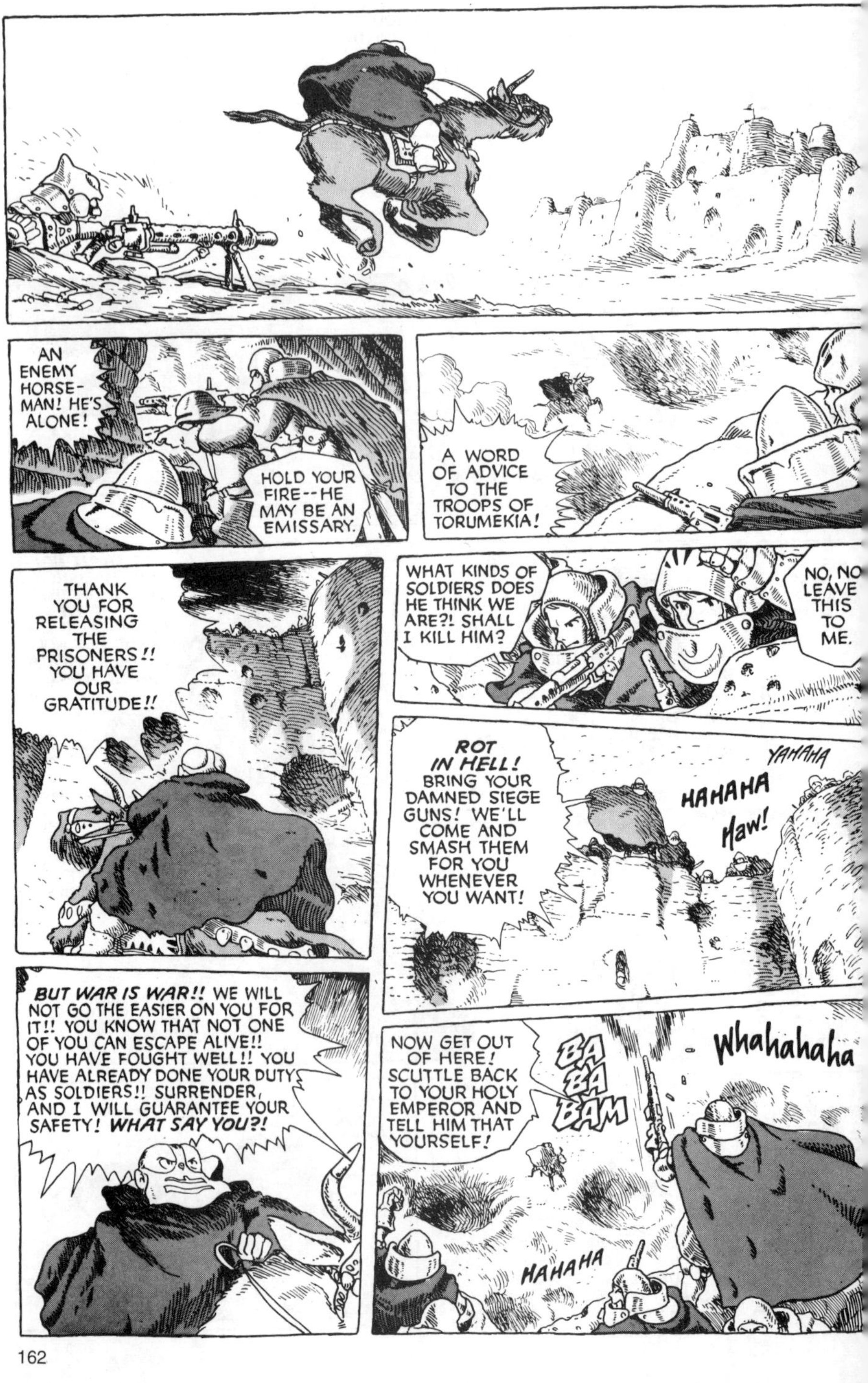
AN ENEMY HORSE-MAN! HE'S ALONE!
HOLD YOUR FIRE--HE MAY BE AN EMISSARY.
A WORD OF ADVICE TO THE TROOPS OF TORUMEKIA!
THANK YOU FOR RELEASING THE PRISONERS!! YOU HAVE OUR GRATITUDE!!
WHAT KINDS OF SOLDIERS DOES HE THINK WE ARE?! SHALL I KILL HIM?
NO, NO LEAVE THIS TO ME.
ROT IN HELL! BRING YOUR DAMNED SIEGE GUNS! WE'LL COME AND SMASH THEM FOR YOU WHENEVER YOU WANT!
YAHAHA
HAHAHA
Haw!
BUT WAR IS WAR!! WE WILL NOT GO THE EASIER ON YOU FOR IT!! YOU KNOW THAT NOT ONE OF YOU CAN ESCAPE ALIVE!! YOU HAVE FOUGHT WELL!! YOU HAVE ALREADY DONE YOUR DUTY AS SOLDIERS!! SURRENDER, AND I WILL GUARANTEE YOUR SAFETY! WHAT SAY YOU?!
NOW GET OUT OF HERE! SCUTTLE BACK TO YOUR HOLY EMPEROR AND TELL HIM THAT YOURSELF!
BA BA BAM
Whahahaha
HAHAHA

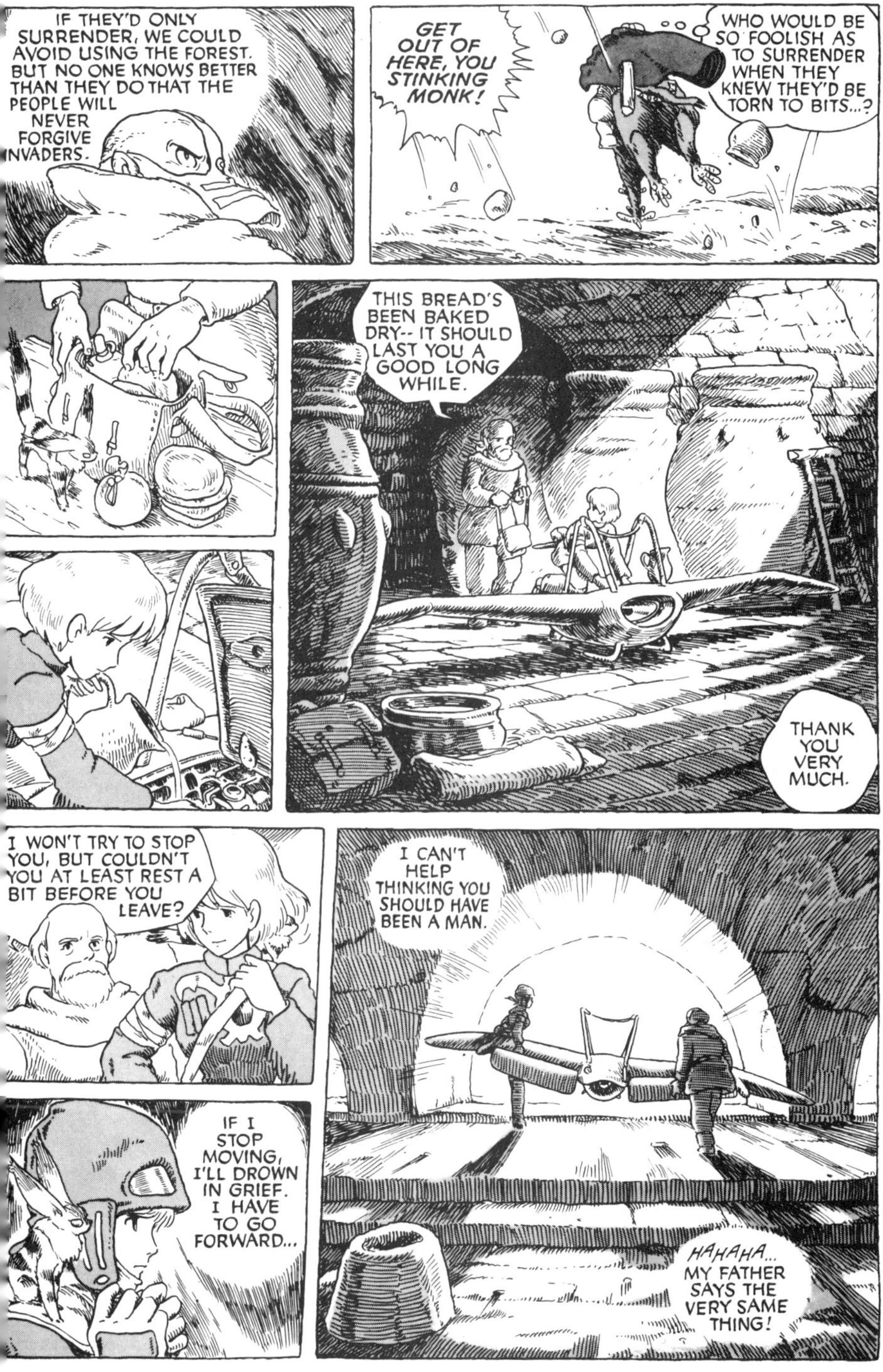
IF THEY'D ONLY SURRENDER, WE COULD AVOID USING THE FOREST. BUT NO ONE KNOWS BETTER THAN THEY DO THAT THE PEOPLE WILL NEVER FORGIVE INVADERS.
GET OUT OF HERE, YOU STINKING MONK!
WHO WOULD BE SO FOOLISH AS TO SURRENDER WHEN THEY KNEW THEY'D BE TORN TO BITS...?
THIS BREAD'S BEEN BAKED DRY-- IT SHOULD LAST YOU A GOOD LONG WHILE.
THANK YOU VERY MUCH.
I WON'T TRY TO STOP YOU, BUT COULDN'T YOU AT LEAST REST A BIT BEFORE YOU LEAVE?
IF I STOP MOVING, I'LL DROWN IN GRIEF. I HAVE TO GO FORWARD...
I CAN'T HELP THINKING YOU SHOULD HAVE BEEN A MAN.
HAHAHA... MY FATHER SAYS THE VERY SAME THING!

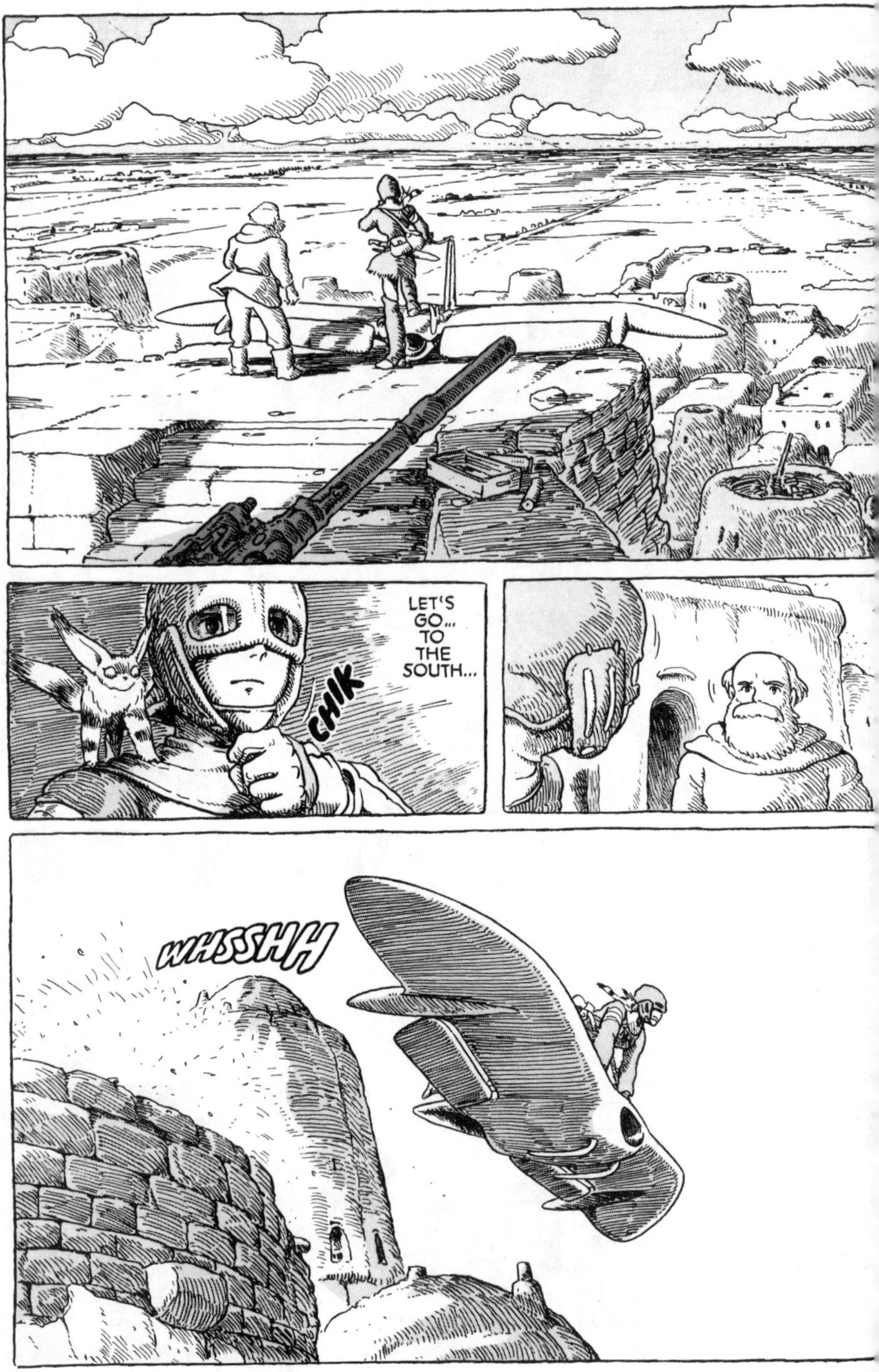
LET'S GO... TO THE SOUTH...
CHIK
WHSSHH

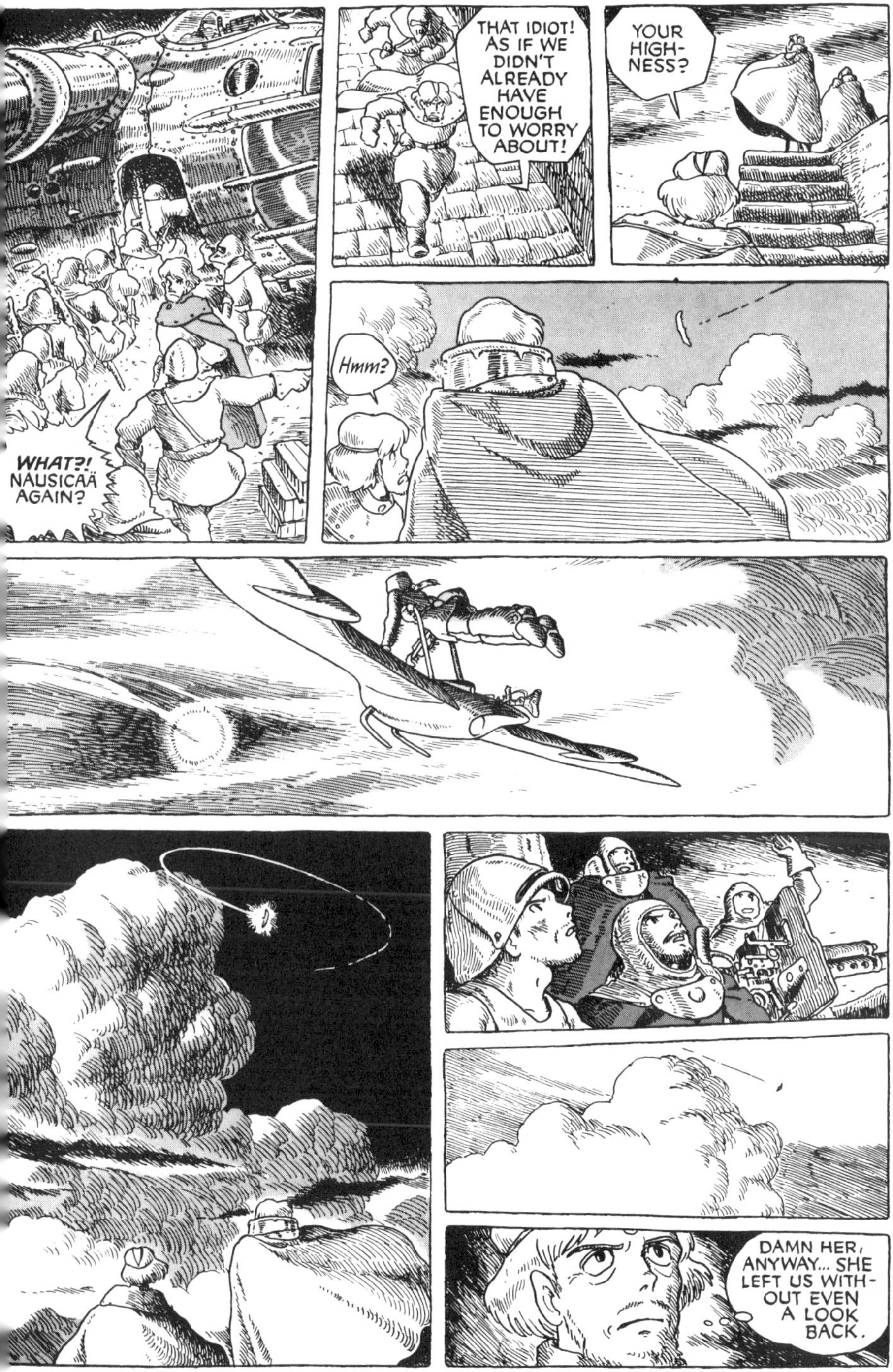
WHAT?! NAUSICAÄ AGAIN?
THAT IDIOT! AS IF WE DIDN'T ALREADY HAVE ENOUGH TO WORRY ABOUT!
YOUR HIGH-NESS?
Hmm?
DAMN HER, ANYWAY... SHE LEFT US WITH-OUT EVEN A LOOK BACK.

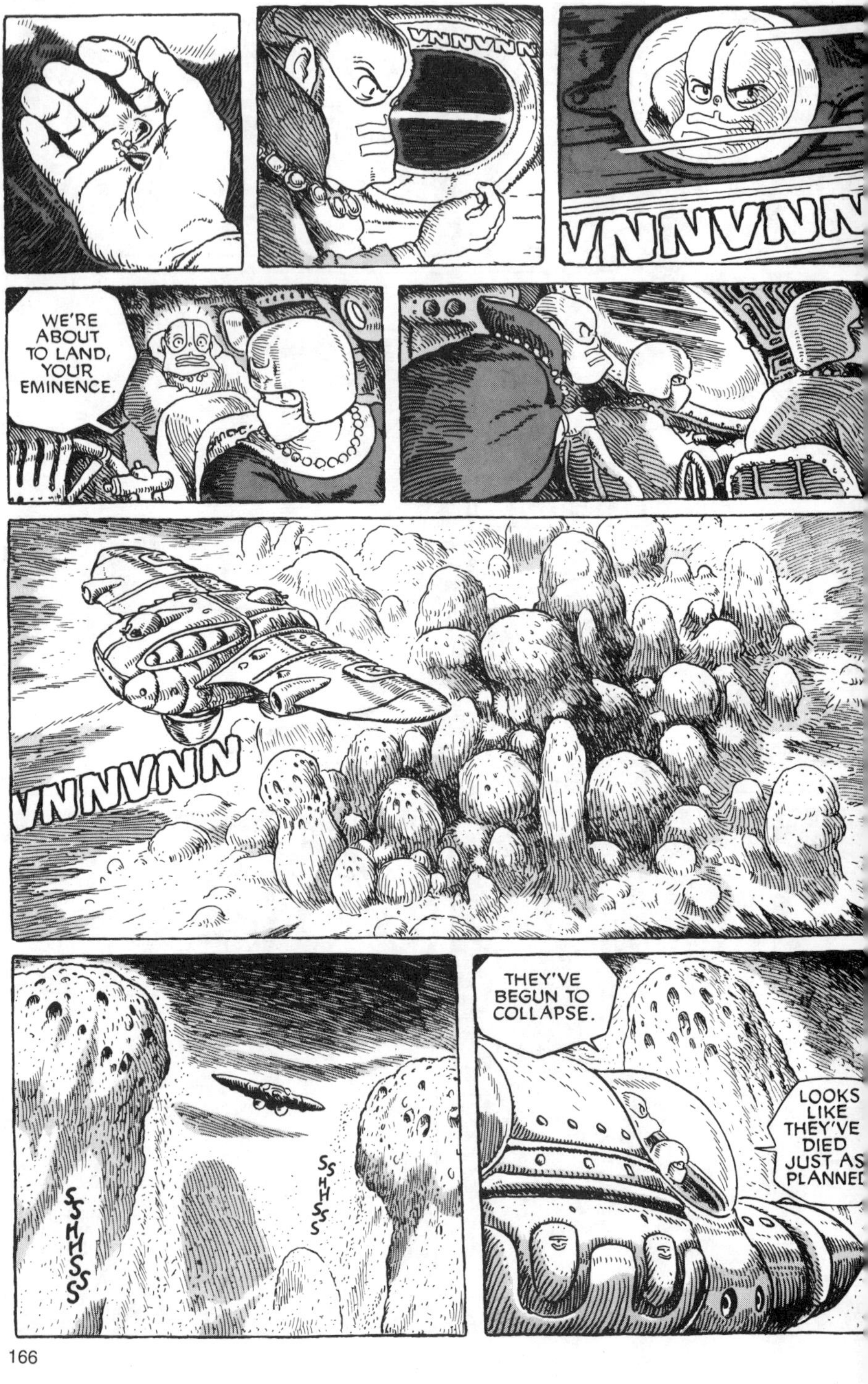
VNNVNN
VNNVNN
WE'RE ABOUT TO LAND, YOUR EMINENCE.
VNNVNN
SSHHSS
SSHHSS
THEY'VE BEGUN TO COLLAPSE.
LOOKS LIKE THEY'VE DIED JUST AS PLANNED

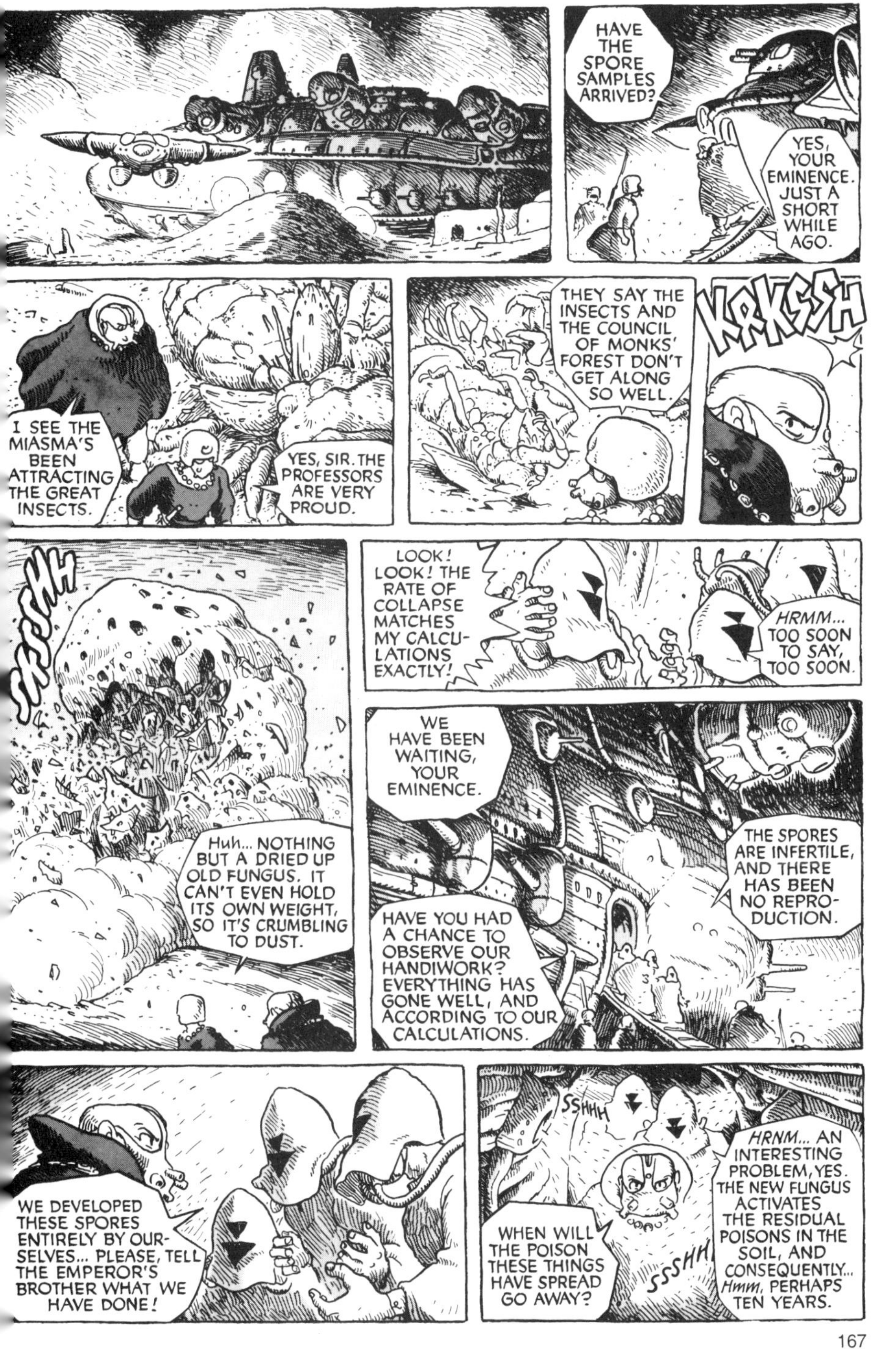

HAVE THE SPORE SAMPLES ARRIVED?
YES, YOUR EMINENCE. JUST A SHORT WHILE AGO.
I SEE THE MIASMA'S BEEN ATTRACTING THE GREAT INSECTS.
YES, SIR. THE PROFESSORS ARE VERY PROUD.
THEY SAY THE INSECTS AND THE COUNCIL OF MONKS' FOREST DON'T GET ALONG SO WELL.
KRKSSH
SHSSHH
LOOK! LOOK! THE RATE OF COLLAPSE MATCHES MY CALCULATIONS EXACTLY!
HRMM... TOO SOON TO SAY, TOO SOON.
Huh... NOTHING BUT A DRIED UP OLD FUNGUS. IT CAN'T EVEN HOLD ITS OWN WEIGHT, SO IT'S CRUMBLING TO DUST.
WE HAVE BEEN WAITING, YOUR EMINENCE.
THE SPORES ARE INFERTILE, AND THERE HAS BEEN NO REPRODUCTION.
HAVE YOU HAD A CHANCE TO OBSERVE OUR HANDIWORK? EVERYTHING HAS GONE WELL, AND ACCORDING TO OUR CALCULATIONS.
WE DEVELOPED THESE SPORES ENTIRELY BY OURSELVES... PLEASE, TELL THE EMPEROR'S BROTHER WHAT WE HAVE DONE!
SSHHH
WHEN WILL THE POISON THESE THINGS HAVE SPREAD GO AWAY?
HRNM... AN INTERESTING PROBLEM, YES. THE NEW FUNGUS ACTIVATES THE RESIDUAL POISONS IN THE SOIL, AND CONSEQUENTLY... Hmm, PERHAPS TEN YEARS.
SSSHH

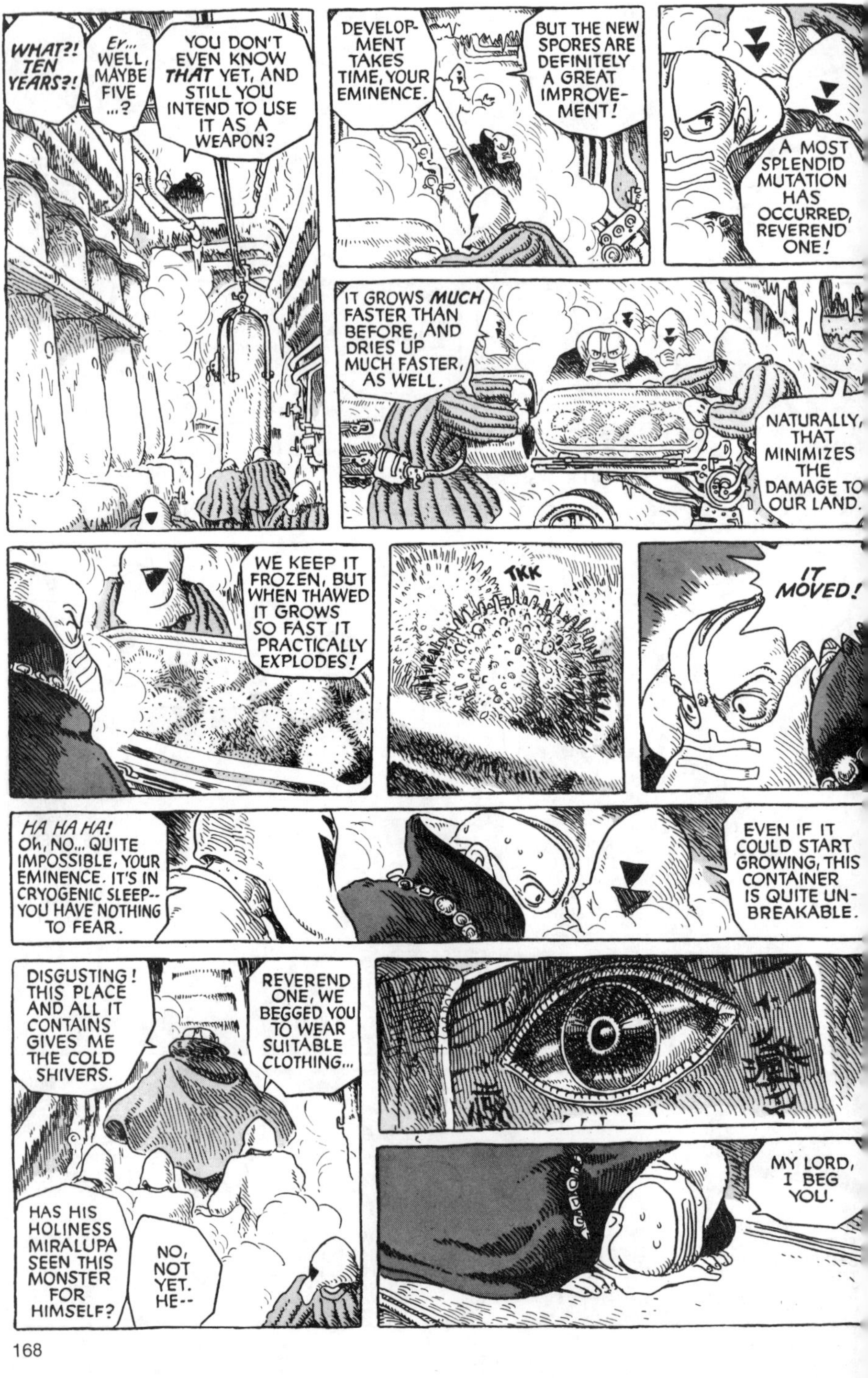

WHAT?! TEN YEARS?!
Er... WELL, MAYBE FIVE ...?
YOU DON'T EVEN KNOW THAT YET, AND STILL YOU INTEND TO USE IT AS A WEAPON?
DEVELOPMENT TAKES TIME, YOUR EMINENCE.
BUT THE NEW SPORES ARE DEFINITELY A GREAT IMPROVEMENT!
A MOST SPLENDID MUTATION HAS OCCURRED, REVEREND ONE!
IT GROWS MUCH FASTER THAN BEFORE, AND DRIES UP MUCH FASTER, AS WELL.
NATURALLY, THAT MINIMIZES THE DAMAGE TO OUR LAND.
WE KEEP IT FROZEN, BUT WHEN THAWED IT GROWS SO FAST IT PRACTICALLY EXPLODES!
TKK
IT MOVED!
HA HA HA! Oh, NO... QUITE IMPOSSIBLE, YOUR EMINENCE. IT'S IN CRYOGENIC SLEEP-- YOU HAVE NOTHING TO FEAR.
EVEN IF IT COULD START GROWING, THIS CONTAINER IS QUITE UNBREAKABLE.
DISGUSTING! THIS PLACE AND ALL IT CONTAINS GIVES ME THE COLD SHIVERS.
REVEREND ONE, WE BEGGED YOU TO WEAR SUITABLE CLOTHING...
HAS HIS HOLINESS MIRALUPA SEEN THIS MONSTER FOR HIMSELF?
NO, NOT YET. HE--
MY LORD, I BEG YOU.

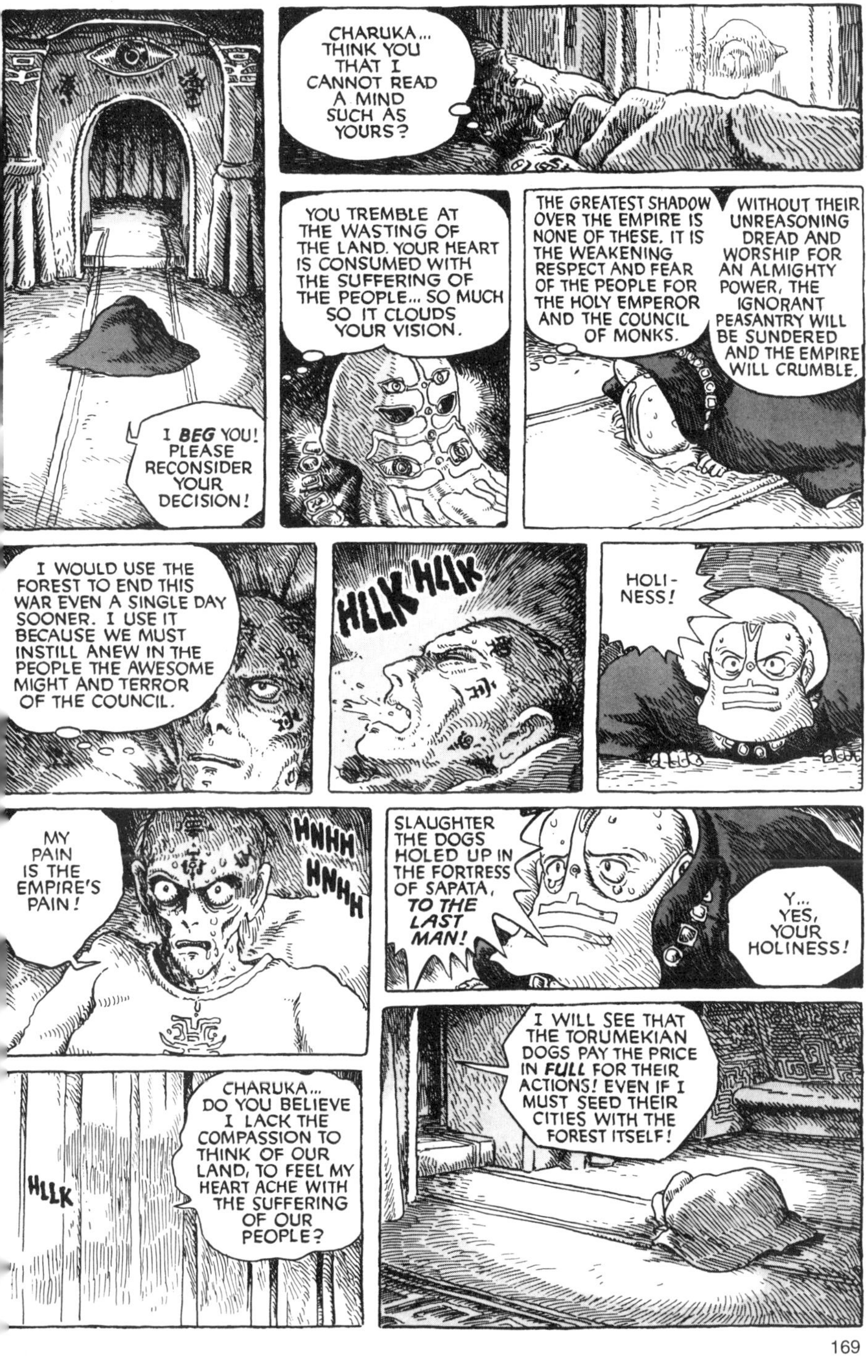
CHARUKA... THINK YOU THAT I CANNOT READ A MIND SUCH AS YOURS?
I BEG YOU! PLEASE RECONSIDER YOUR DECISION!
YOU TREMBLE AT THE WASTING OF THE LAND. YOUR HEART IS CONSUMED WITH THE SUFFERING OF THE PEOPLE... SO MUCH SO IT CLOUDS YOUR VISION.
THE GREATEST SHADOW OVER THE EMPIRE IS NONE OF THESE. IT IS THE WEAKENING RESPECT AND FEAR OF THE PEOPLE FOR THE HOLY EMPEROR AND THE COUNCIL OF MONKS.
WITHOUT THEIR UNREASONING DREAD AND WORSHIP FOR AN ALMIGHTY POWER, THE IGNORANT PEASANTRY WILL BE SUNDERED AND THE EMPIRE WILL CRUMBLE.
I WOULD USE THE FOREST TO END THIS WAR EVEN A SINGLE DAY SOONER. I USE IT BECAUSE WE MUST INSTILL ANEW IN THE PEOPLE THE AWESOME MIGHT AND TERROR OF THE COUNCIL.
HLLK HLLK
HOLI-NESS!
MY PAIN IS THE EMPIRE'S PAIN!
HNHH HNHH
SLAUGHTER THE DOGS HOLED UP IN THE FORTRESS OF SAPATA, TO THE LAST MAN!
Y... YES, YOUR HOLINESS!
CHARUKA... DO YOU BELIEVE I LACK THE COMPASSION TO THINK OF OUR LAND, TO FEEL MY HEART ACHE WITH THE SUFFERING OF OUR PEOPLE?
HLLK
I WILL SEE THAT THE TORUMEKIAN DOGS PAY THE PRICE IN FULL FOR THEIR ACTIONS! EVEN IF I MUST SEED THEIR CITIES WITH THE FOREST ITSELF!

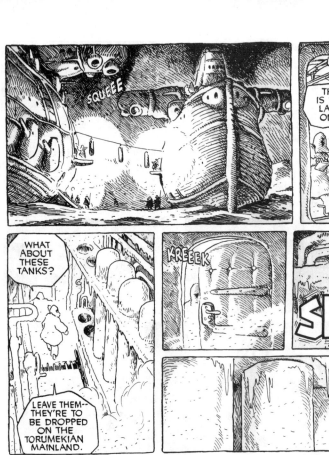

SQUEEE

THIS IS THE LAST ONE.

WHAT ABOUT THESE TANKS?

LEAVE THEM-- THEY'RE TO BE DROPPED ON THE TORUMEKIAN MAINLAND.

KREEEK

SLAM

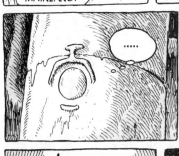

.....

SPRK

SKCHH

FMPP

FDD FDD

ET 'S URN ACK HE LOCK 1 HORT VHILE:

A SMALL CERAMIC MINING TOWN TWO HUNDRED LEAGUES EAST-NORTHEAST OF THE VALLEY OF WIND.

VNNNNNNNN

DON'T SPEND SO MUCH TIME GAWKING AROUND THAT YOU FORGET TO COME BACK!

YOU, TOO! DON'T SLEEP SO SOUNDLY THEY STEAL THE SHIP OUT FROM UNDER YOU!

"YUPA"...? NAW, THERE BE ALL KINDS OF SWORDSMEN AROUND THESE PARTS THESE DAYS.

THINK WE'RE WASTING OUR TIME?

NO. MASTER YUPA *HAD* TO COME TO THIS TOWN, I'M CERTAIN OF IT.

171

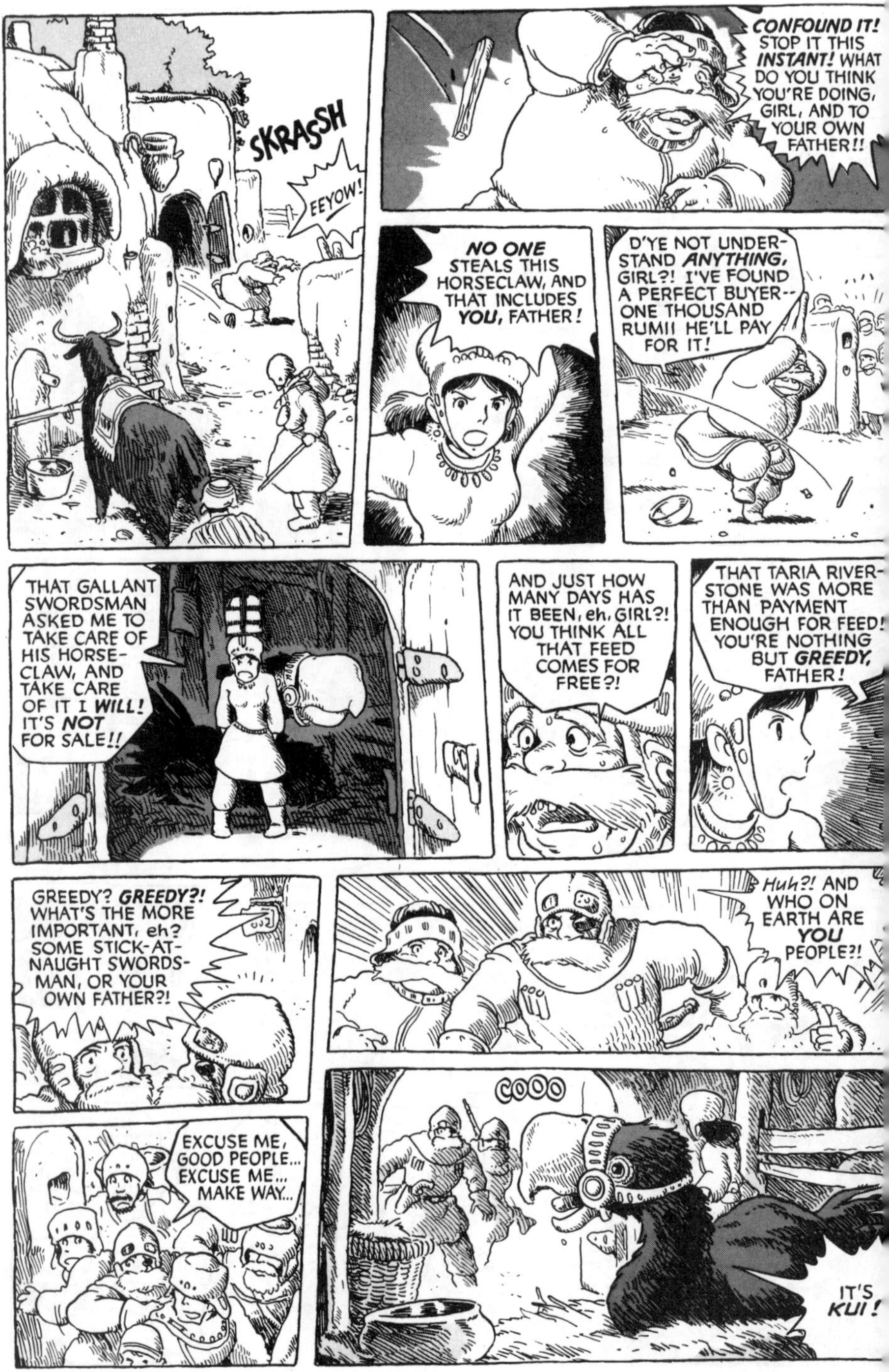
SKRASSH
EEYOW!
CONFOUND IT! STOP IT THIS INSTANT! WHAT DO YOU THINK YOU'RE DOING, GIRL, AND TO YOUR OWN FATHER!!
NO ONE STEALS THIS HORSECLAW, AND THAT INCLUDES YOU, FATHER!
D'YE NOT UNDERSTAND ANYTHING, GIRL?! I'VE FOUND A PERFECT BUYER-- ONE THOUSAND RUMI! HE'LL PAY FOR IT!
THAT GALLANT SWORDSMAN ASKED ME TO TAKE CARE OF HIS HORSECLAW, AND TAKE CARE OF IT I WILL! IT'S NOT FOR SALE!!
AND JUST HOW MANY DAYS HAS IT BEEN, eh, GIRL?! YOU THINK ALL THAT FEED COMES FOR FREE?!
THAT TARIA RIVERSTONE WAS MORE THAN PAYMENT ENOUGH FOR FEED! YOU'RE NOTHING BUT GREEDY, FATHER!
GREEDY? GREEDY?! WHAT'S THE MORE IMPORTANT, eh? SOME STICK-AT-NAUGHT SWORDSMAN, OR YOUR OWN FATHER?!
Huh?! AND WHO ON EARTH ARE YOU PEOPLE?!
EXCUSE ME, GOOD PEOPLE... EXCUSE ME... MAKE WAY...
COOO
IT'S KUI!

COO COO

COOO

KUI! WHAT THE DEVIL ARE *YOU* DOING HERE? WHERE'S MASTER YUPA?

LOOK...

COO

HONORED GUESTS, YOU'RE FRIENDS OF THAT SWORDSMAN, ARE YOU NOT? I'M SO GLAD-- I DIDN'T KNOW *WHAT* TO DO!

WHAT TH--?!

WHY SHOULD KUI LAY AN EGG *NOW?*

COOO

IT'S WONDERFUL, KUI... YOU *ARE* CALLED KUI, YES?

COULD SOMETHING HAVE HAPPENED TO KAI? THEY SAY THIS OFTEN HAPPENS WITH HORSECLAWS WHEN THEIR MATES DIE.

AYE... I'VE HEARD SO. AND HIM WITH THE PRINCESS, TOO...

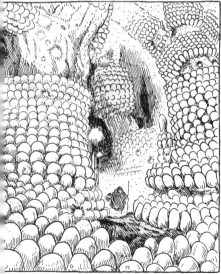

THESE ARE ALL EGGS OF THE *HEBIKFRA.*

I'VE NEVER BEFORE SEEN SUCH VAST EGG BEDS.

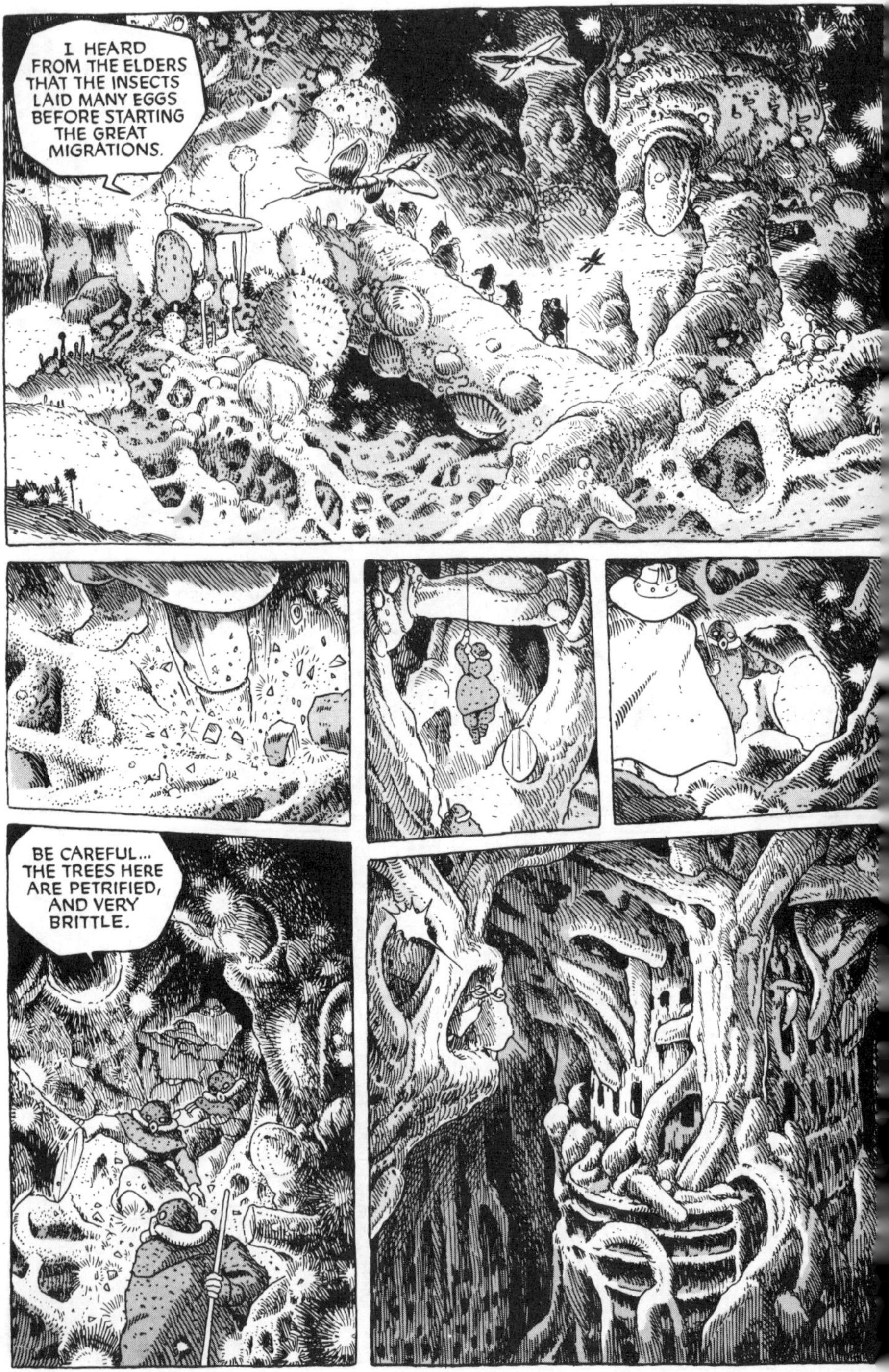
I HEARD FROM THE ELDERS THAT THE INSECTS LAID MANY EGGS BEFORE STARTING THE GREAT MIGRATIONS.
BE CAREFUL... THE TREES HERE ARE PETRIFIED, AND VERY BRITTLE.

THIS IS THE CAPITAL CITY OF THE KINGDOM OF EFTAL, SWALLOWED UP BY THE SEA OF CORRUPTION IN THE DAIKAISHO THREE HUNDRED YEARS PAST. IT'S BEEN COMPLETELY ENGULFED BY THE FOREST...

IT'S LITTLE MORE THAN SAND, NOW. DON'T GET TOO CLOSE--IT COULD CRUMBLE AT ANY MOMENT.

I THOUGHT WE'D BE ABLE TO TAKE OUR MASKS OFF WHEN WE REACHED THE BOTTOM.

ONLY A CENTURY HAS PASSED SINCE THIS CAVITY WAS FORMED... THE MIASMA LINGERS STILL.

BUT SOON IT WILL BE PURIFIED.

SOON?

YES... PERHAPS ANOTHER TWO HUNDRED YEARS.

YOU CALL TWO HUNDRED YEARS *SOON*?

SELM, YOU SAID THAT THE MIASMA IS CREATED BY WHAT THE TREES EXHALE WHEN THE FOREST ABSORBS THE POISONS IN THE SOIL.

YES. IT IS ONE STEP IN THE LONG PROCESS OF TURNING THE POISONS INTO HARMLESS, STABLE ELEMENTS. BEFORE LONG, THEY'LL BE REDUCED TO TINY CRYSTALS, TOO SMALL FOR THE EYE TO SEE.

THEN, WHEN ALL THE POISONS OF THE LAND HAVE BEEN FOSSILIZED, WILL THE FOREST PERISH?

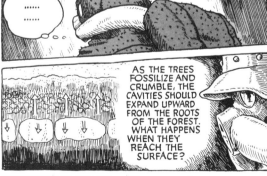

......
......

AS THE TREES FOSSILIZE AND CRUMBLE, THE CAVITIES SHOULD EXPAND UPWARD FROM THE ROOTS OF THE FOREST. WHAT HAPPENS WHEN THEY REACH THE SURFACE?

PLEASE... TELL US! IT'S BEEN A THOUSAND YEARS SINCE THE FOREST WAS FORMED--SOMEWHERE ON THIS PLANET MUST BE LANDS WHERE IT HAS ALREADY HAPPENED.

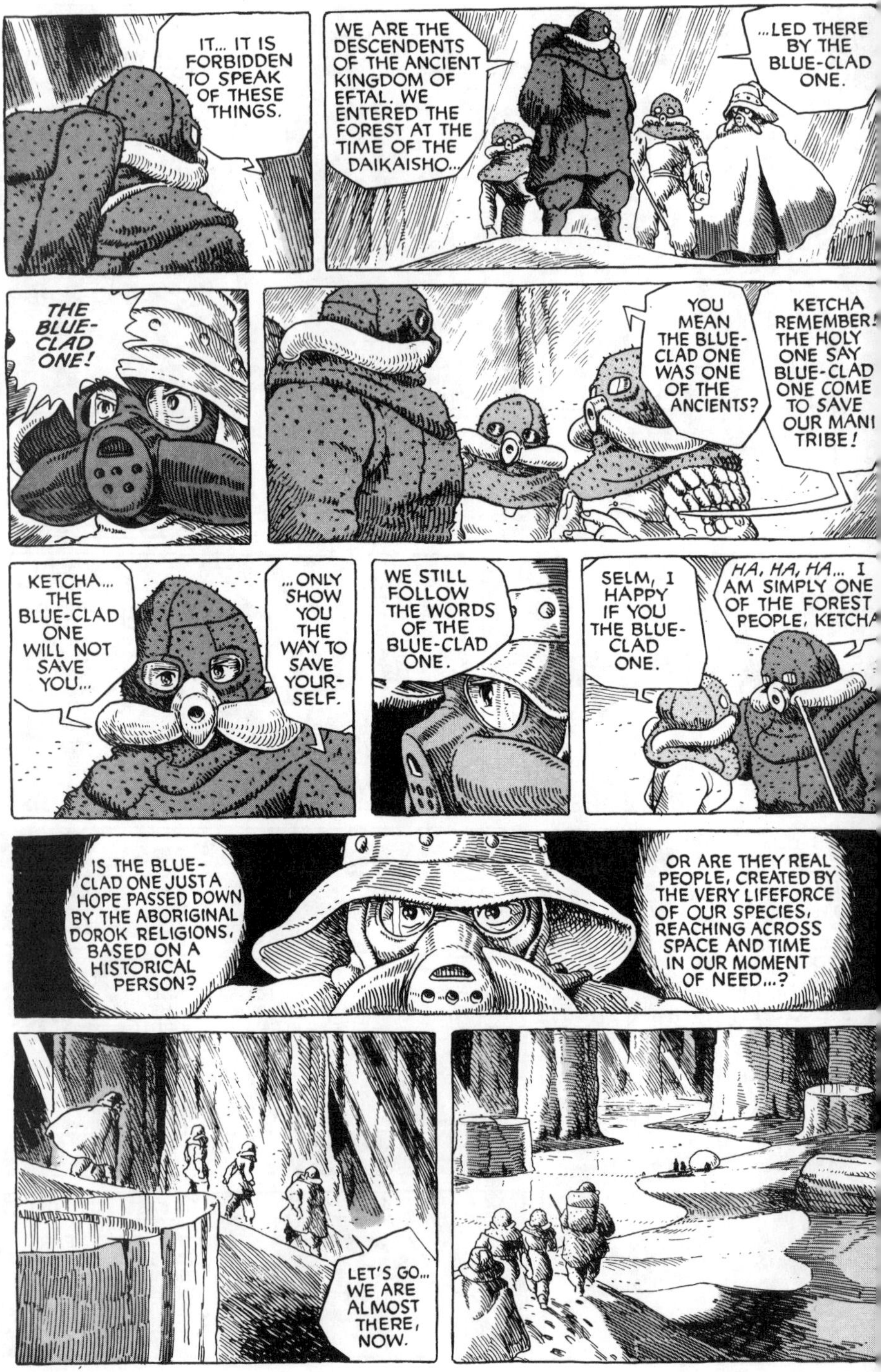
IT... IT IS FORBIDDEN TO SPEAK OF THESE THINGS.
WE ARE THE DESCENDENTS OF THE ANCIENT KINGDOM OF EFTAL. WE ENTERED THE FOREST AT THE TIME OF THE DAIKAISHO...
...LED THERE BY THE BLUE-CLAD ONE.
THE BLUE-CLAD ONE!
YOU MEAN THE BLUE-CLAD ONE WAS ONE OF THE ANCIENTS?
KETCHA REMEMBER! THE HOLY ONE SAY BLUE-CLAD ONE COME TO SAVE OUR MANI TRIBE!
KETCHA... THE BLUE-CLAD ONE WILL NOT SAVE YOU...
...ONLY SHOW YOU THE WAY TO SAVE YOURSELF.
WE STILL FOLLOW THE WORDS OF THE BLUE-CLAD ONE.
SELM, I HAPPY IF YOU THE BLUE-CLAD ONE.
HA, HA, HA... I AM SIMPLY ONE OF THE FOREST PEOPLE, KETCHA
IS THE BLUE-CLAD ONE JUST A HOPE PASSED DOWN BY THE ABORIGINAL DOROK RELIGIONS, BASED ON A HISTORICAL PERSON?
OR ARE THEY REAL PEOPLE, CREATED BY THE VERY LIFEFORCE OF OUR SPECIES, REACHING ACROSS SPACE AND TIME IN OUR MOMENT OF NEED...?
LET'S GO... WE ARE ALMOST THERE, NOW.

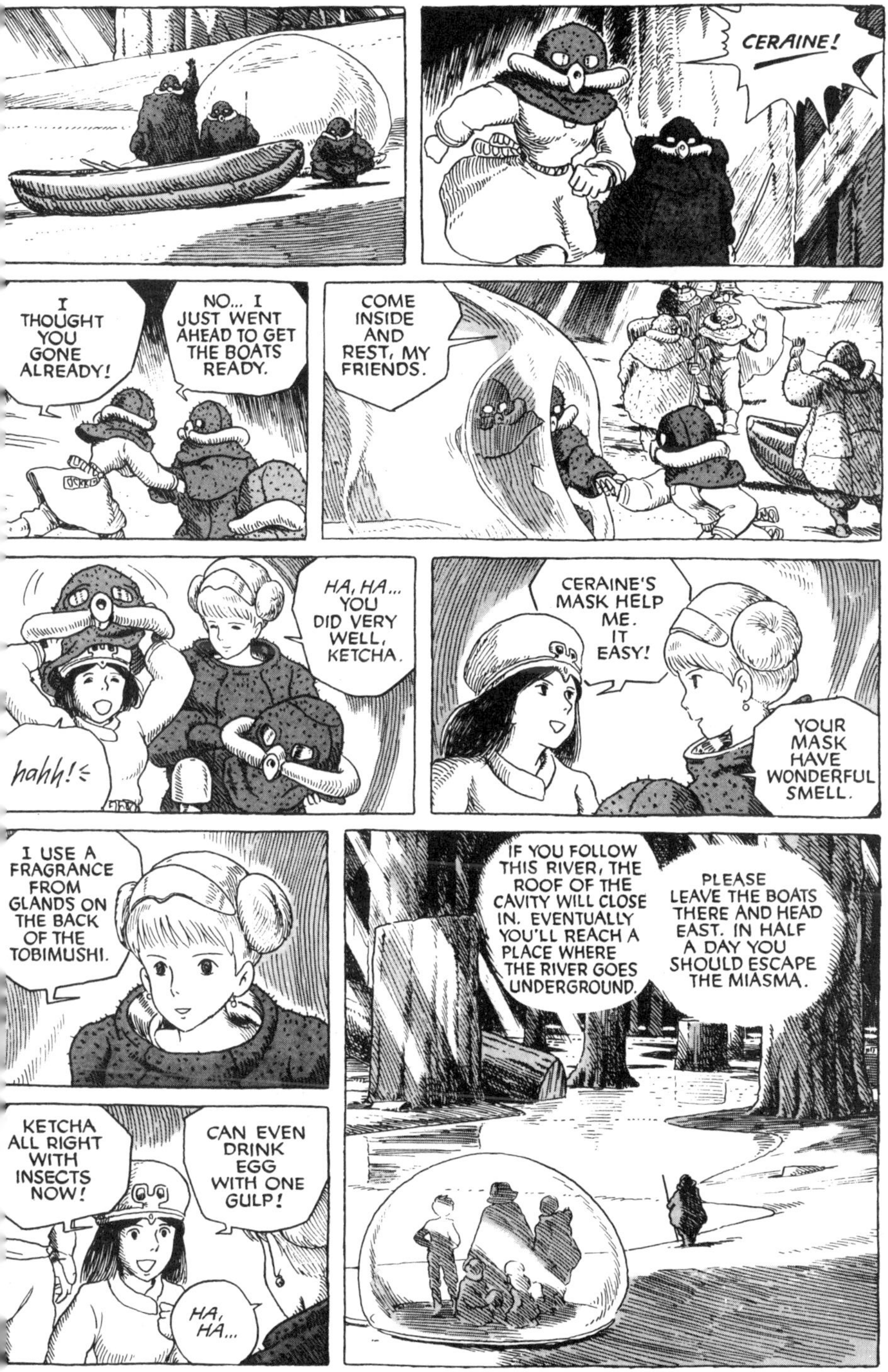
CERAINE!
I THOUGHT YOU GONE ALREADY!
NO... I JUST WENT AHEAD TO GET THE BOATS READY.
COME INSIDE AND REST, MY FRIENDS.
HA, HA... YOU DID VERY WELL, KETCHA.
hahh!
CERAINE'S MASK HELP ME. IT EASY!
YOUR MASK HAVE WONDERFUL SMELL.
I USE A FRAGRANCE FROM GLANDS ON THE BACK OF THE TOBIMUSHI.
KETCHA ALL RIGHT WITH INSECTS NOW!
CAN EVEN DRINK EGG WITH ONE GULP!
HA, HA...
IF YOU FOLLOW THIS RIVER, THE ROOF OF THE CAVITY WILL CLOSE IN. EVENTUALLY YOU'LL REACH A PLACE WHERE THE RIVER GOES UNDERGROUND.
PLEASE LEAVE THE BOATS THERE AND HEAD EAST. IN HALF A DAY YOU SHOULD ESCAPE THE MIASMA.

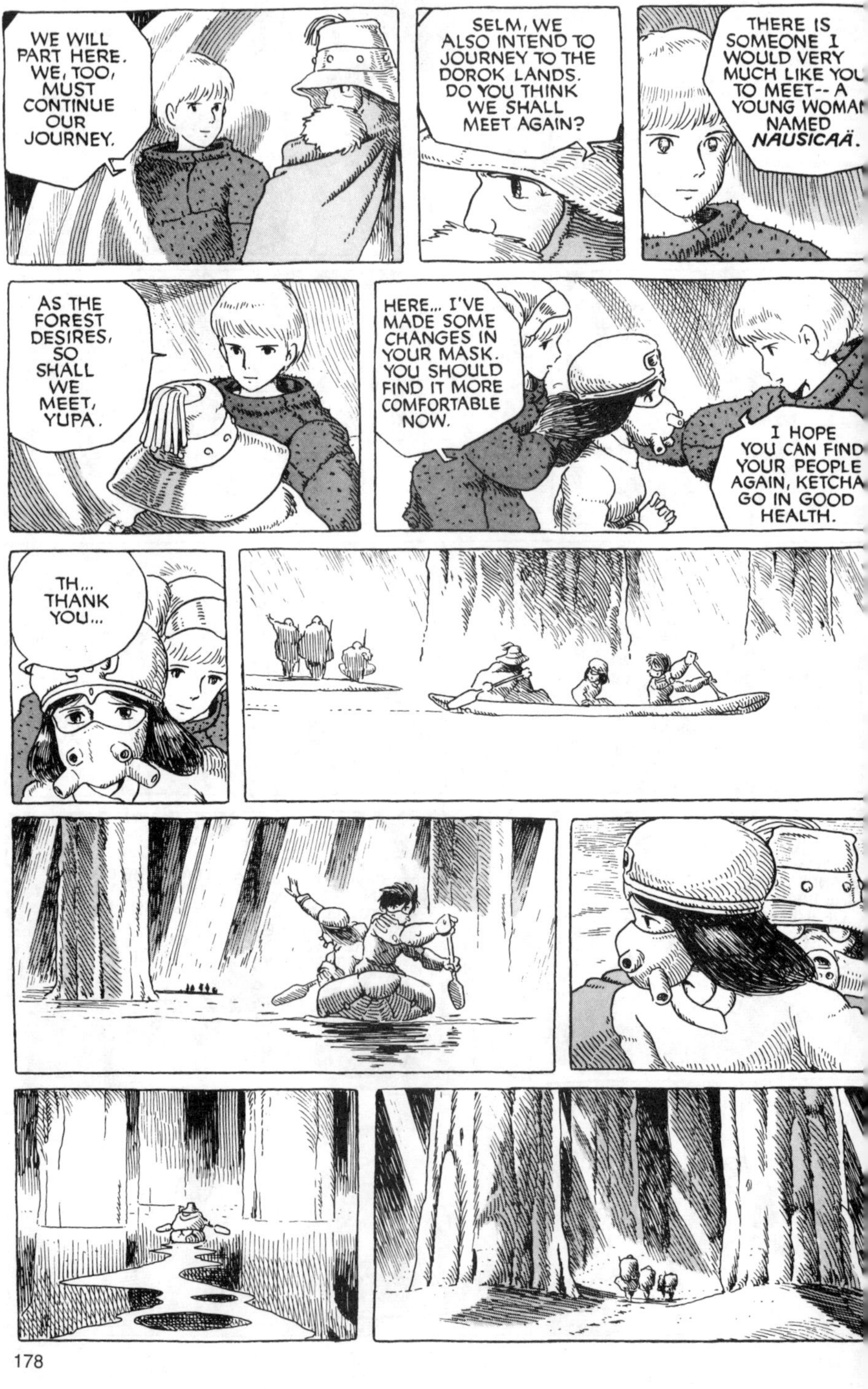
WE WILL PART HERE. WE, TOO, MUST CONTINUE OUR JOURNEY.
SELM, WE ALSO INTEND TO JOURNEY TO THE DOROK LANDS. DO YOU THINK WE SHALL MEET AGAIN?
THERE IS SOMEONE I WOULD VERY MUCH LIKE YOU TO MEET-- A YOUNG WOMAN NAMED NAUSICAÄ.
AS THE FOREST DESIRES, SO SHALL WE MEET, YUPA.
HERE... I'VE MADE SOME CHANGES IN YOUR MASK. YOU SHOULD FIND IT MORE COMFORTABLE NOW.
I HOPE YOU CAN FIND YOUR PEOPLE AGAIN, KETCHA. GO IN GOOD HEALTH.
TH... THANK YOU...

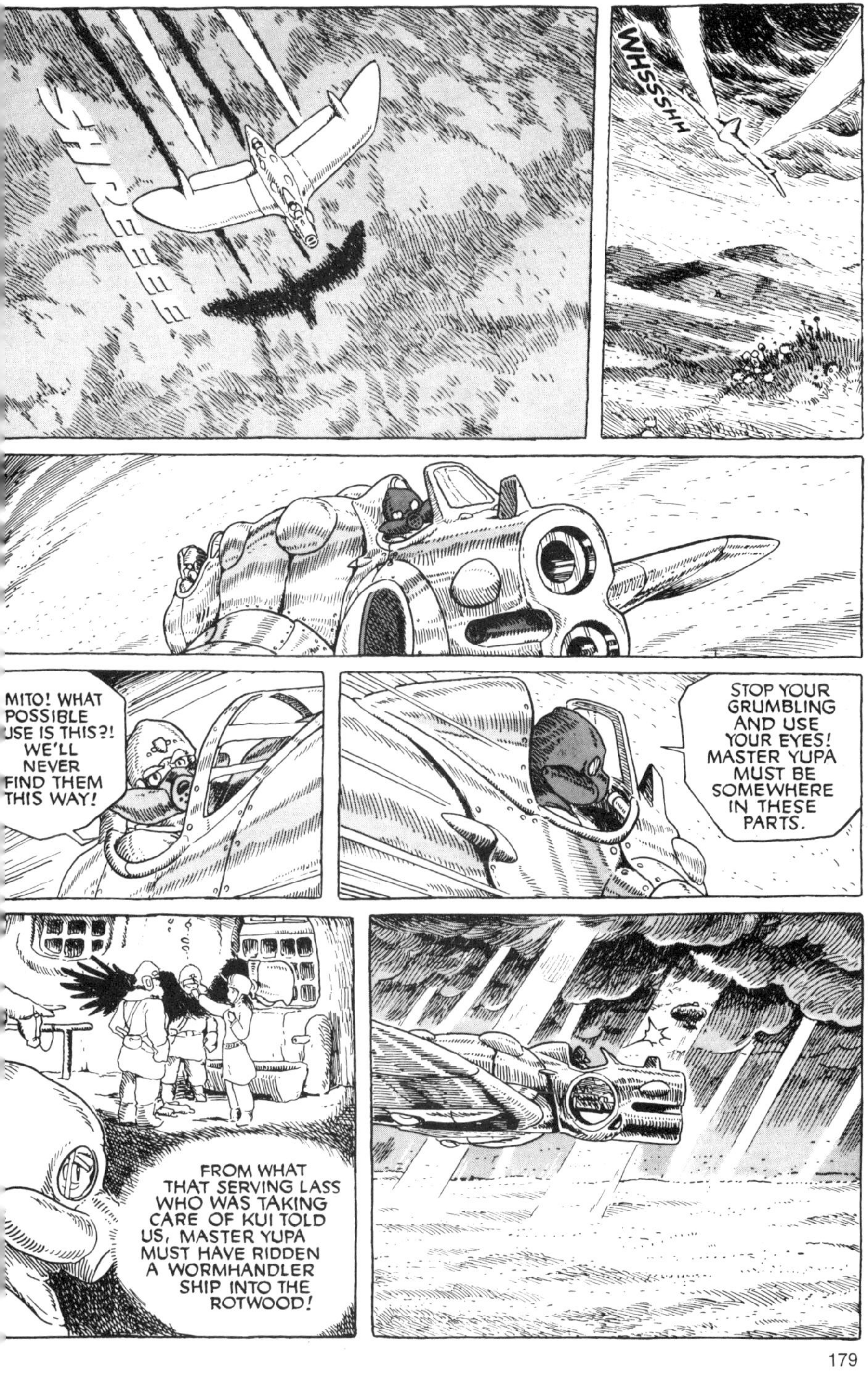
SHREEEEEEE
WHSSSSHH
MITO! WHAT POSSIBLE USE IS THIS?! WE'LL NEVER FIND THEM THIS WAY!
STOP YOUR GRUMBLING AND USE YOUR EYES! MASTER YUPA MUST BE SOMEWHERE IN THESE PARTS.
FROM WHAT THAT SERVING LASS WHO WAS TAKING CARE OF KUI TOLD US, MASTER YUPA MUST HAVE RIDDEN A WORMHANDLER SHIP INTO THE ROTWOOD!

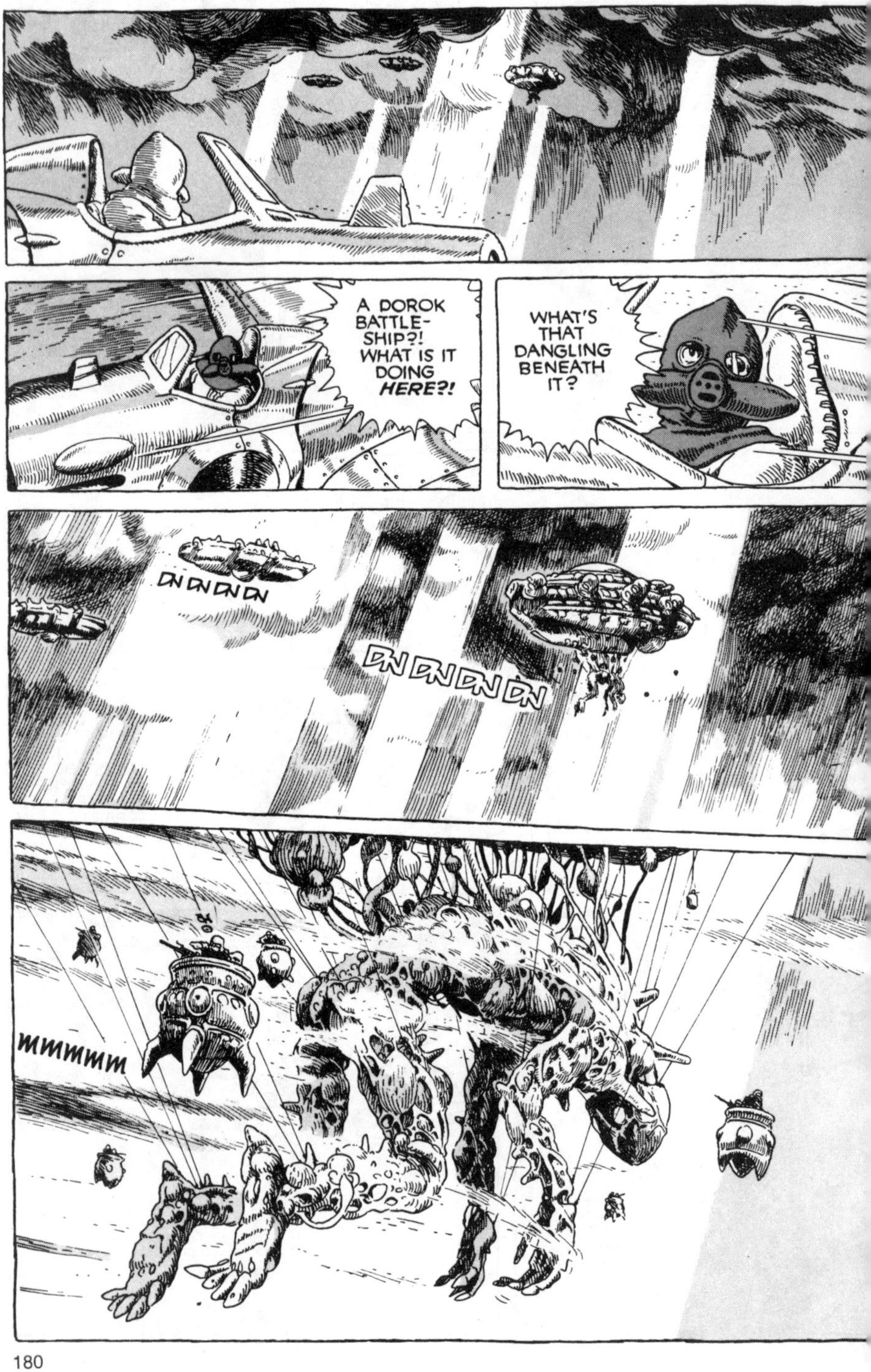
A DOROK BATTLE-SHIP?! WHAT IS IT DOING HERE?!
WHAT'S THAT DANGLING BENEATH IT?
DN DN DN DN
DN DN DN DN DN
MMMMMM

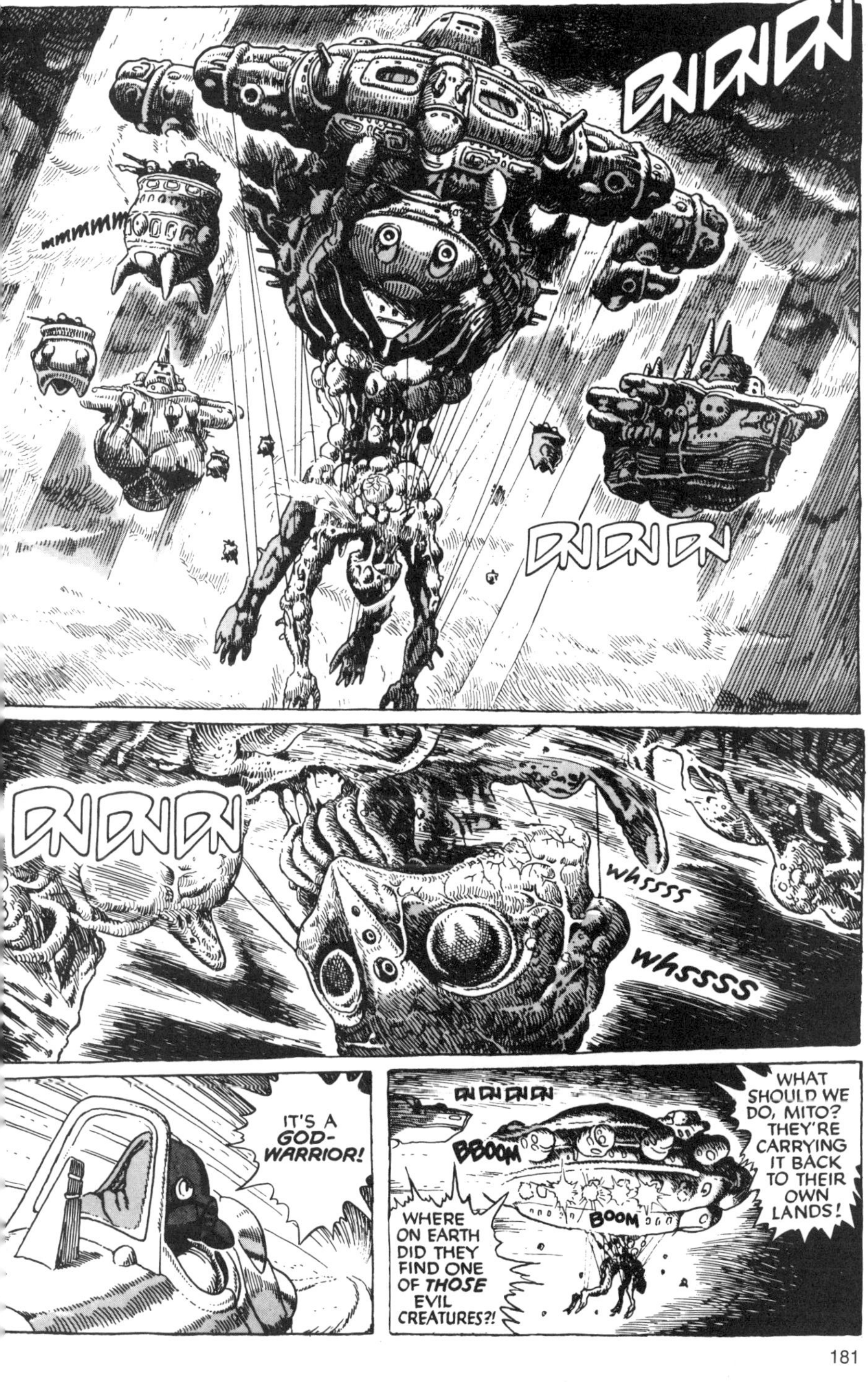
DN DN DN
mmmmmm
DN DN DN
DN DN DN
whssss
whsssss
IT'S A GOD-WARRIOR!
DN DN DN DN
BBOOM
BOOM
WHAT SHOULD WE DO, MITO? THEY'RE CARRYING IT BACK TO THEIR OWN LANDS!
WHERE ON EARTH DID THEY FIND ONE OF THOSE EVIL CREATURES?!

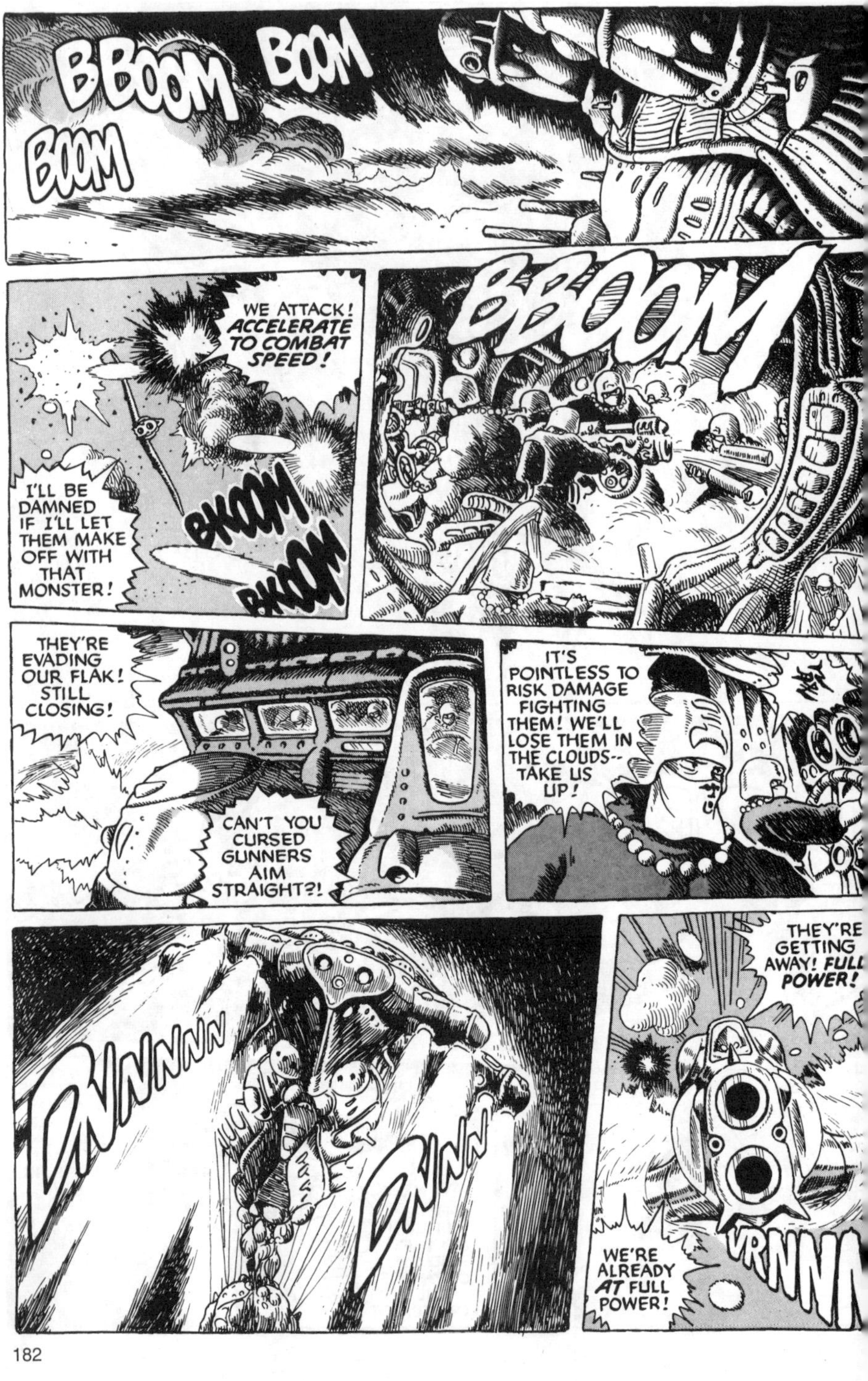
BBOOM BOOM
BOOM
WE ATTACK! ACCELERATE TO COMBAT SPEED!
I'LL BE DAMNED IF I'LL LET THEM MAKE OFF WITH THAT MONSTER!
BKOOM
BKOOM
BBOOM
THEY'RE EVADING OUR FLAK! STILL CLOSING!
CAN'T YOU CURSED GUNNERS AIM STRAIGHT?!
IT'S POINTLESS TO RISK DAMAGE FIGHTING THEM! WE'LL LOSE THEM IN THE CLOUDS-- TAKE US UP!
DNNNNNN
DNNN
THEY'RE GETTING AWAY! FULL POWER!
WE'RE ALREADY AT FULL POWER!
VRNNN

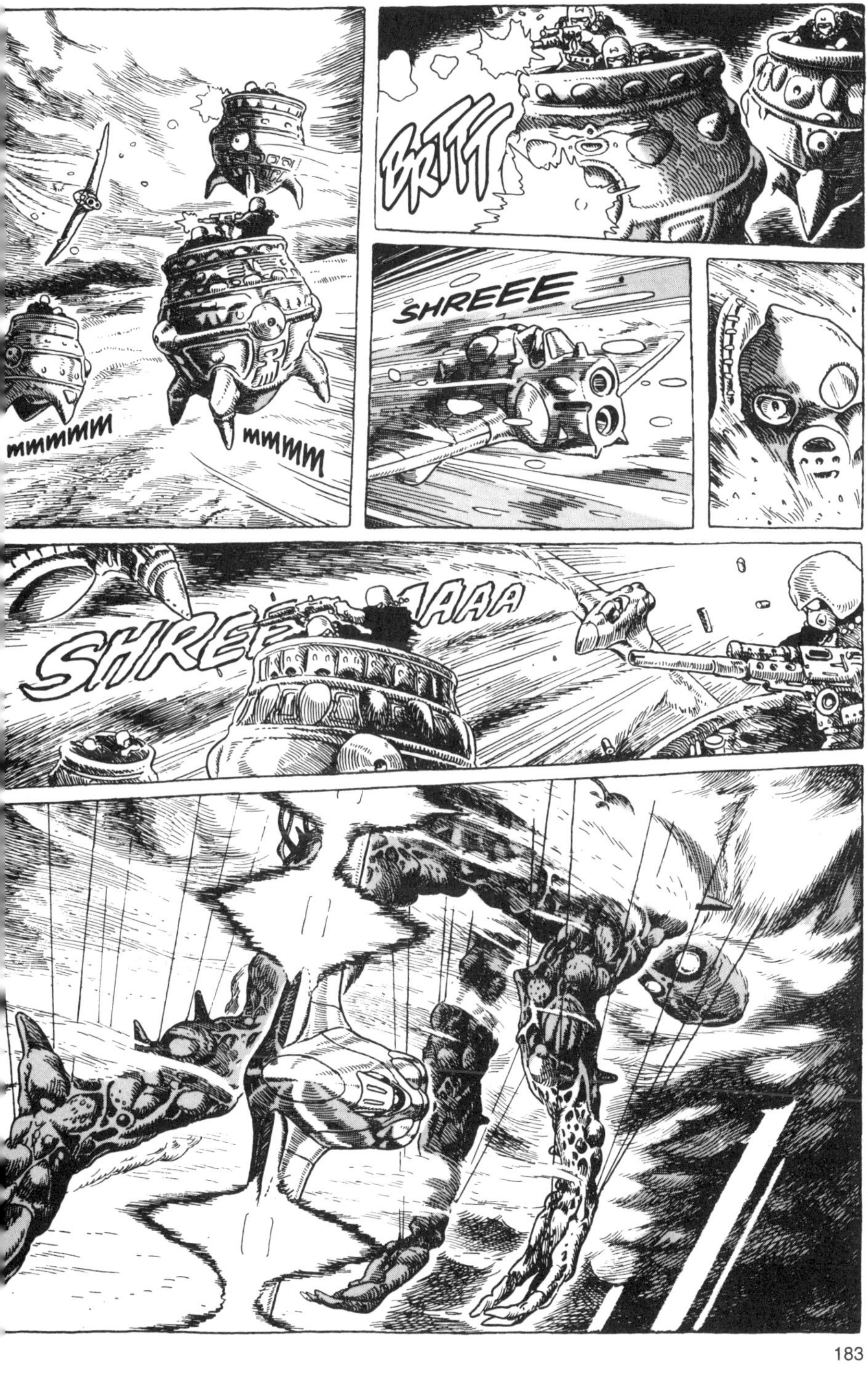
mmmmm
mmmm
BRTTT
SHREEE
SHREEAAAA

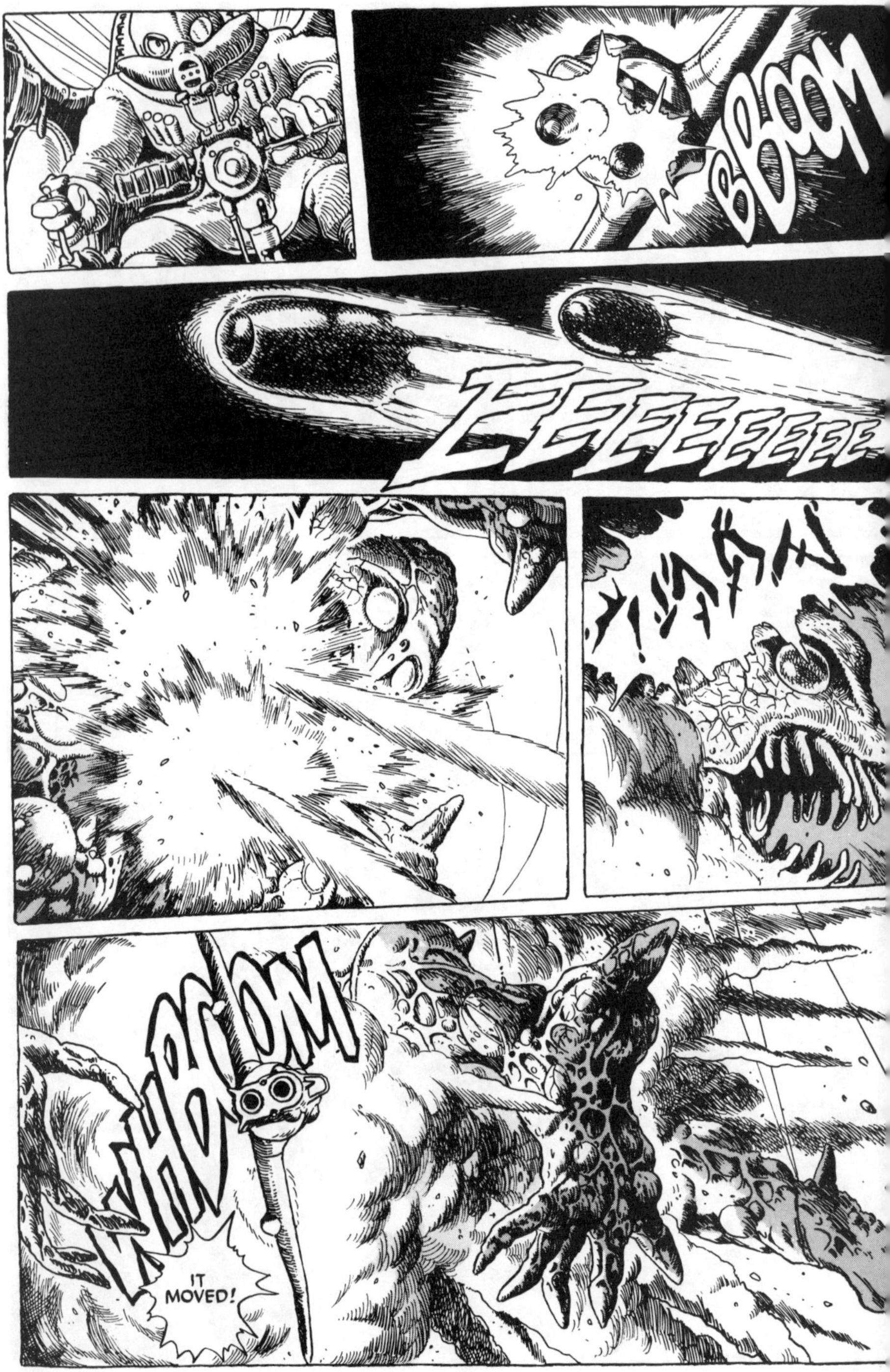
BOOOM
EEEEEEEEE
WHOOOM
IT MOVED!

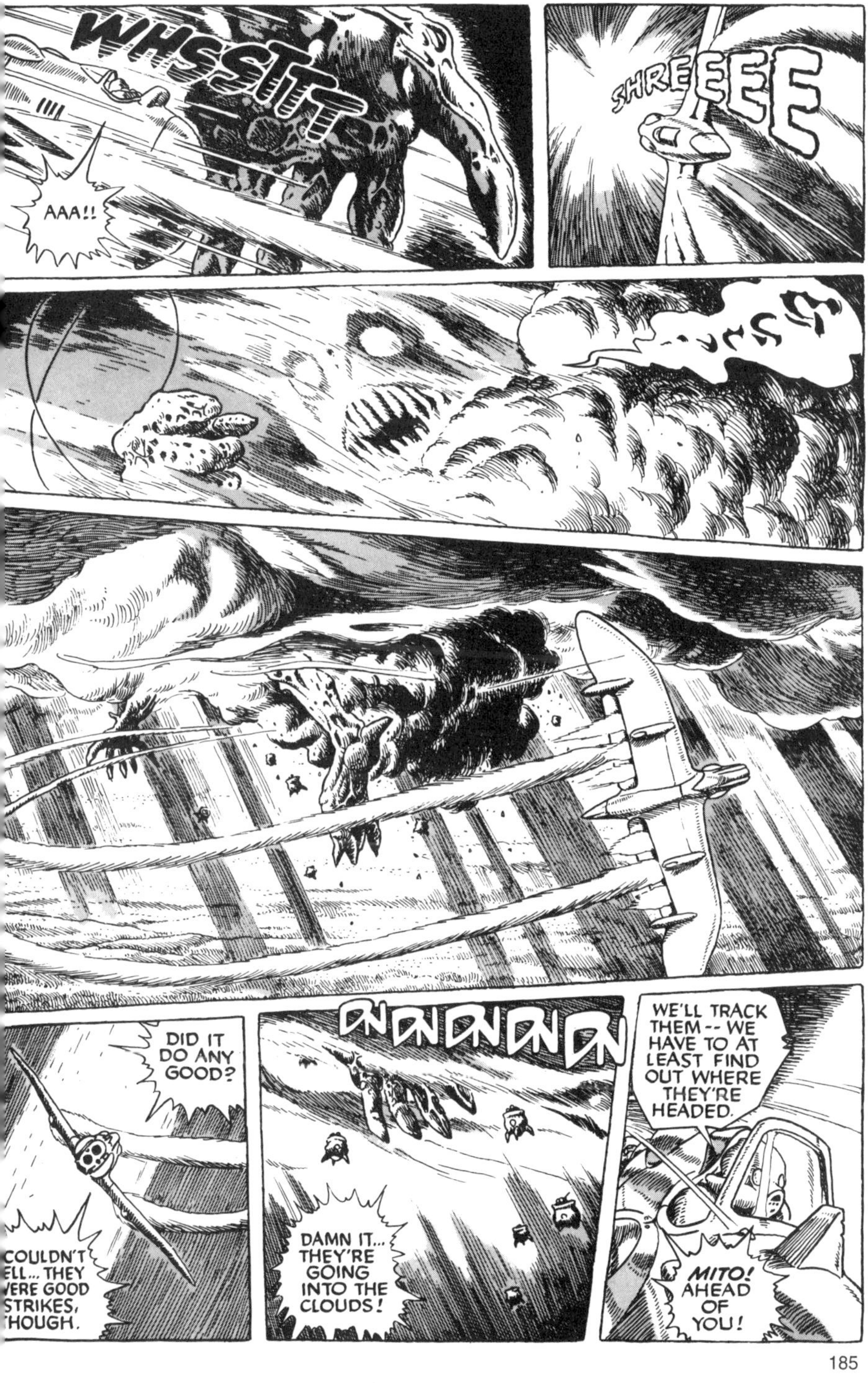
WHSSTT
AAA!!
SHREEEE
DNDNDNDNDN
DID IT DO ANY GOOD?
COULDN'T TELL... THEY WERE GOOD STRIKES, THOUGH.
DAMN IT... THEY'RE GOING INTO THE CLOUDS!
WE'LL TRACK THEM -- WE HAVE TO AT LEAST FIND OUT WHERE THEY'RE HEADED.
MITO! AHEAD OF YOU!

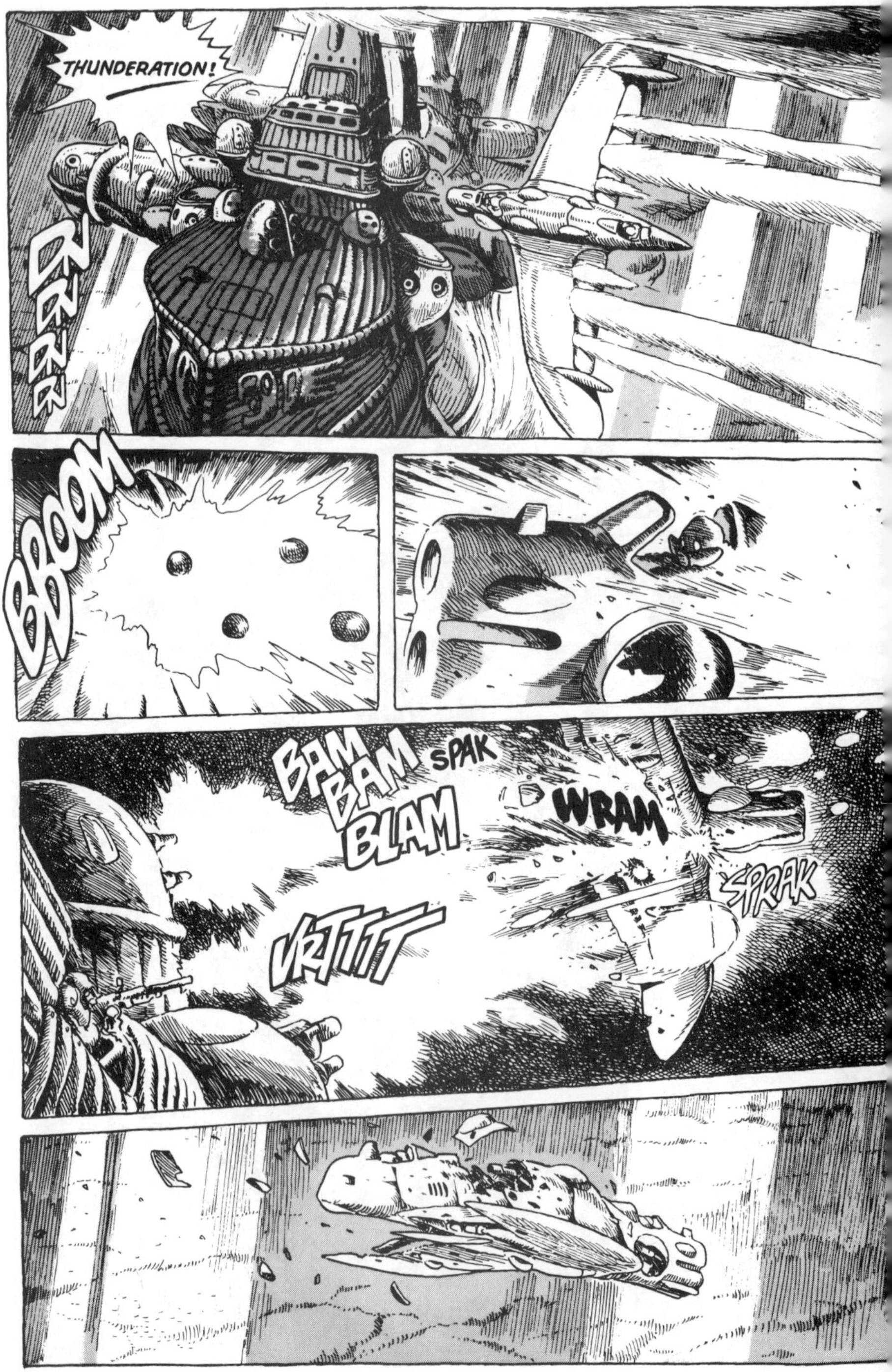
THUNDERATION!
DRRRR
BBOOM
BAM
BAM
SPAK
BLAM
WRAM
SPRAK
VRTTTT

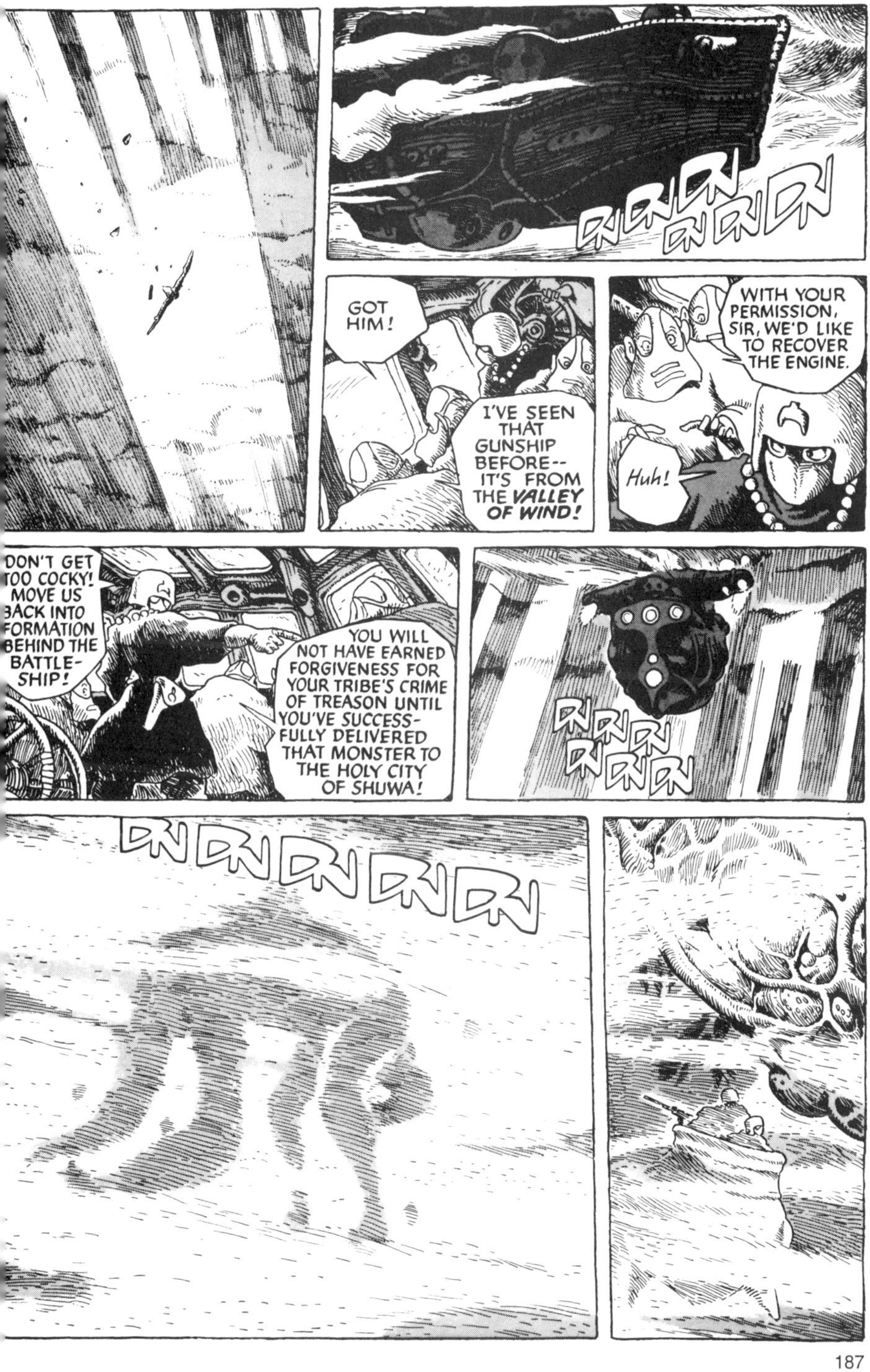
DRN DRN DRN DRN DRN DRN
GOT HIM!
I'VE SEEN THAT GUNSHIP BEFORE-- IT'S FROM THE *VALLEY OF WIND!*
WITH YOUR PERMISSION, SIR, WE'D LIKE TO RECOVER THE ENGINE.
Huh!
DON'T GET TOO COCKY! MOVE US BACK INTO FORMATION BEHIND THE BATTLE-SHIP!
YOU WILL NOT HAVE EARNED FORGIVENESS FOR YOUR TRIBE'S CRIME OF TREASON UNTIL YOU'VE SUCCESSFULLY DELIVERED THAT MONSTER TO THE HOLY CITY OF SHUWA!
DRN DRN DRN DRN DRN DRN
DRN DRN DRN DRN DRN DRN DRN DRN

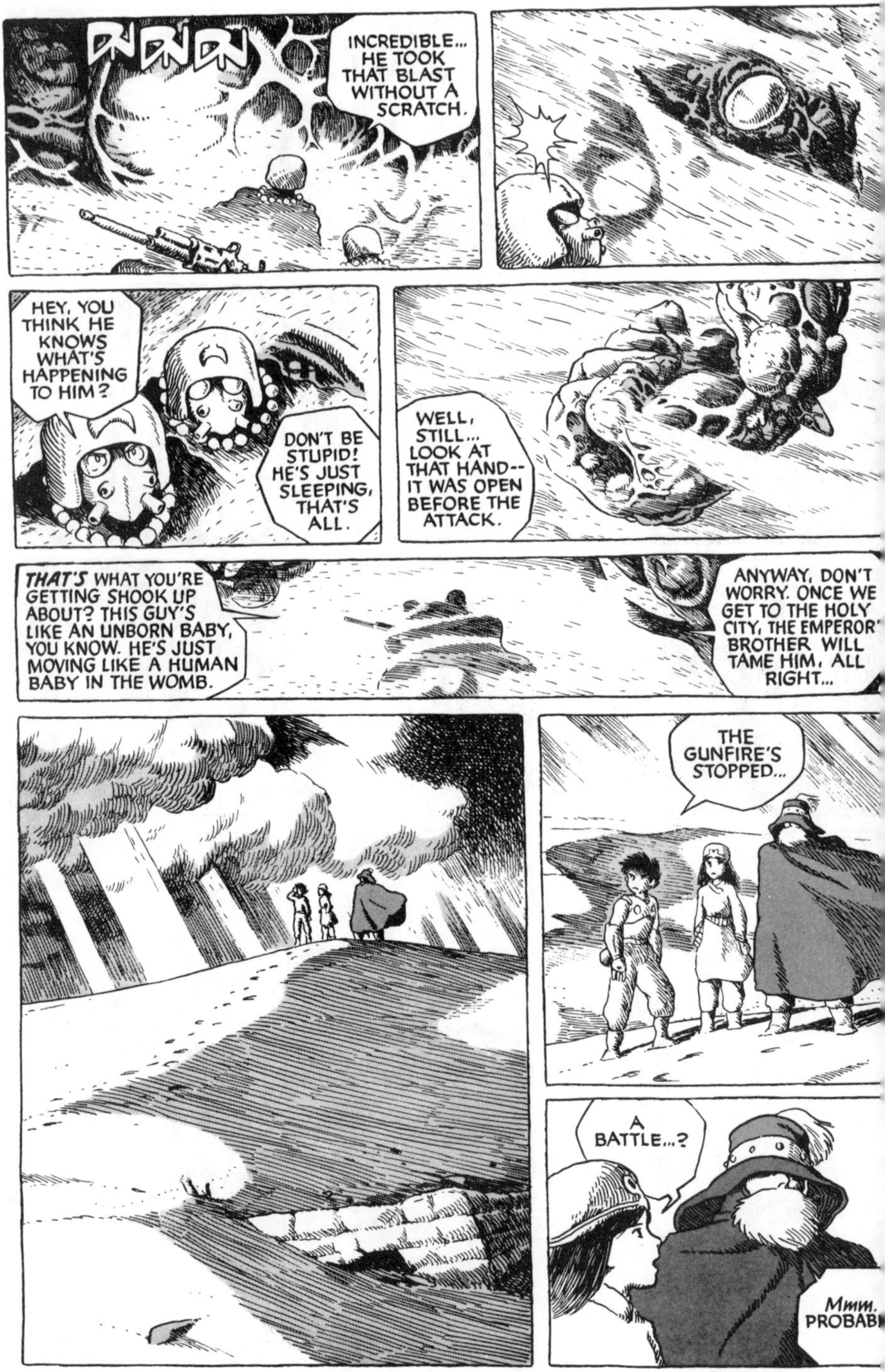

INCREDIBLE... HE TOOK THAT BLAST WITHOUT A SCRATCH.
HEY, YOU THINK HE KNOWS WHAT'S HAPPENING TO HIM?
DON'T BE STUPID! HE'S JUST SLEEPING, THAT'S ALL.
WELL, STILL... LOOK AT THAT HAND-- IT WAS OPEN BEFORE THE ATTACK.
THAT'S WHAT YOU'RE GETTING SHOOK UP ABOUT? THIS GUY'S LIKE AN UNBORN BABY, YOU KNOW. HE'S JUST MOVING LIKE A HUMAN BABY IN THE WOMB.
ANYWAY, DON'T WORRY. ONCE WE GET TO THE HOLY CITY, THE EMPEROR' BROTHER WILL TAME HIM, ALL RIGHT...
THE GUNFIRE'S STOPPED...
A BATTLE...?
Mmm. PROBAB

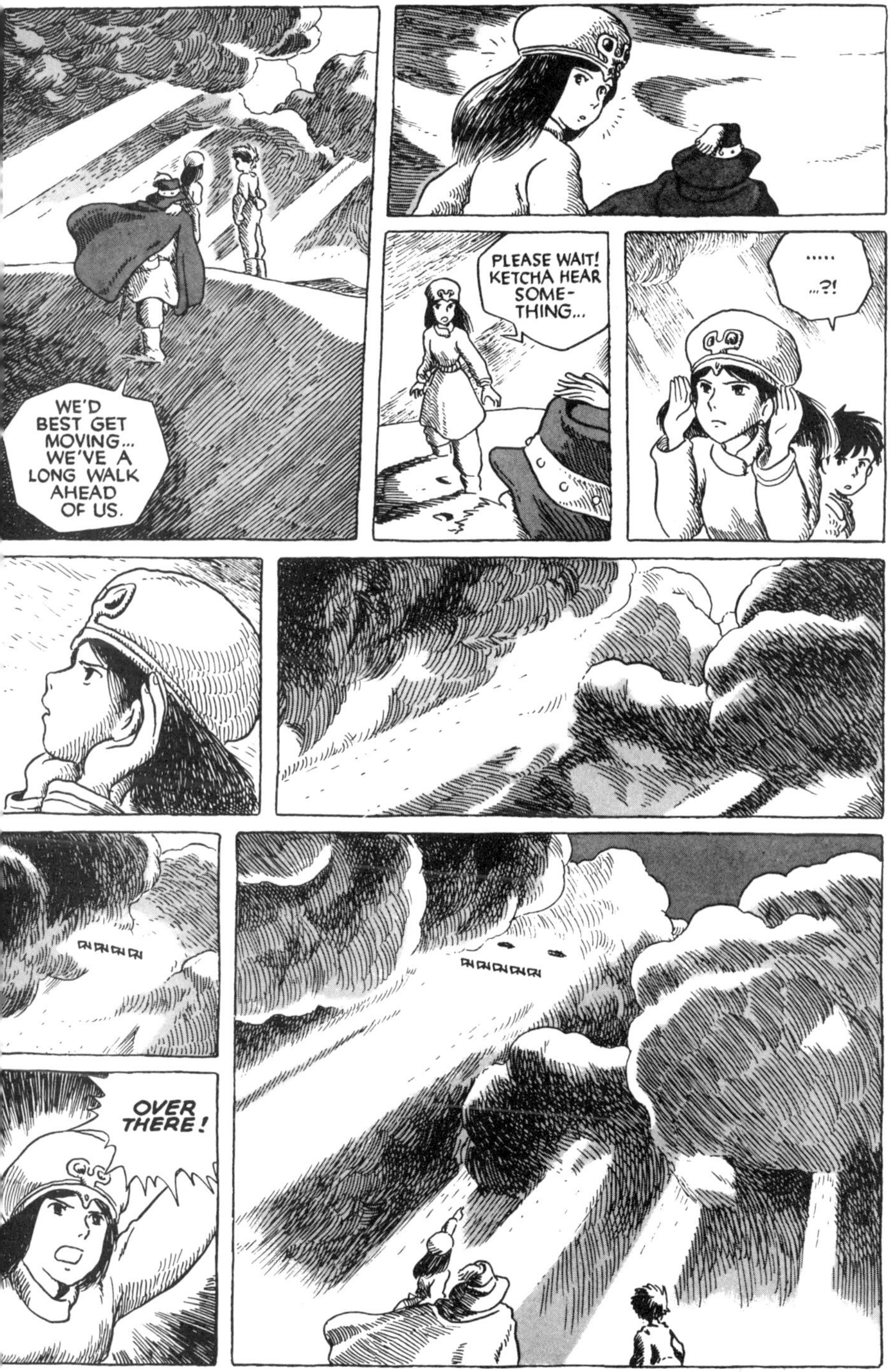
WE'D BEST GET MOVING... WE'VE A LONG WALK AHEAD OF US.
PLEASE WAIT! KETCHA HEAR SOME-THING...
.....
...?!
OVER THERE!

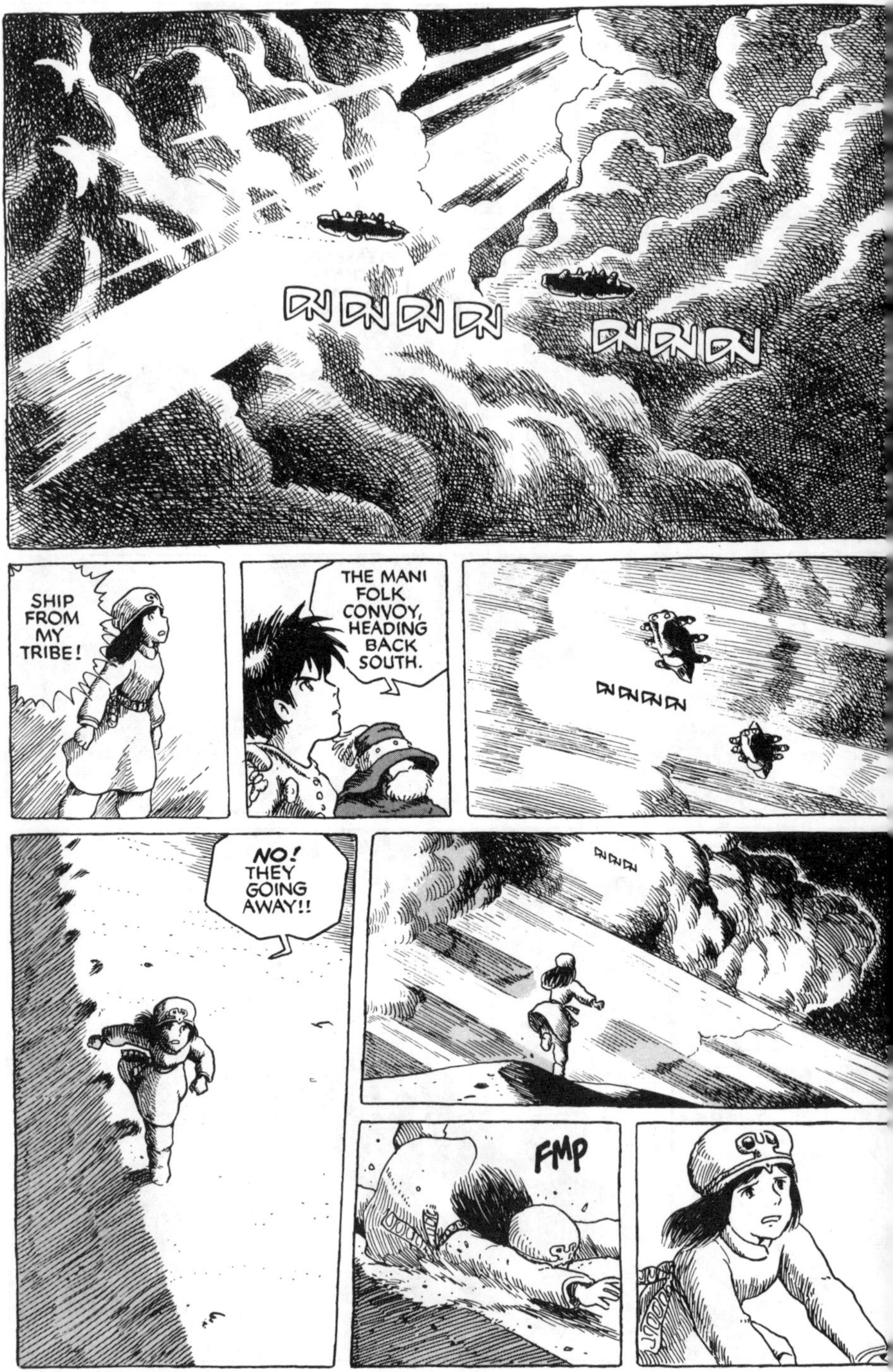
DN DN DN DN
DN DN DN
SHIP FROM MY TRIBE!
THE MANI FOLK CONVOY, HEADING BACK SOUTH.
DN DN DN DN
NO! THEY GOING AWAY!!
DN DN DN
FMP

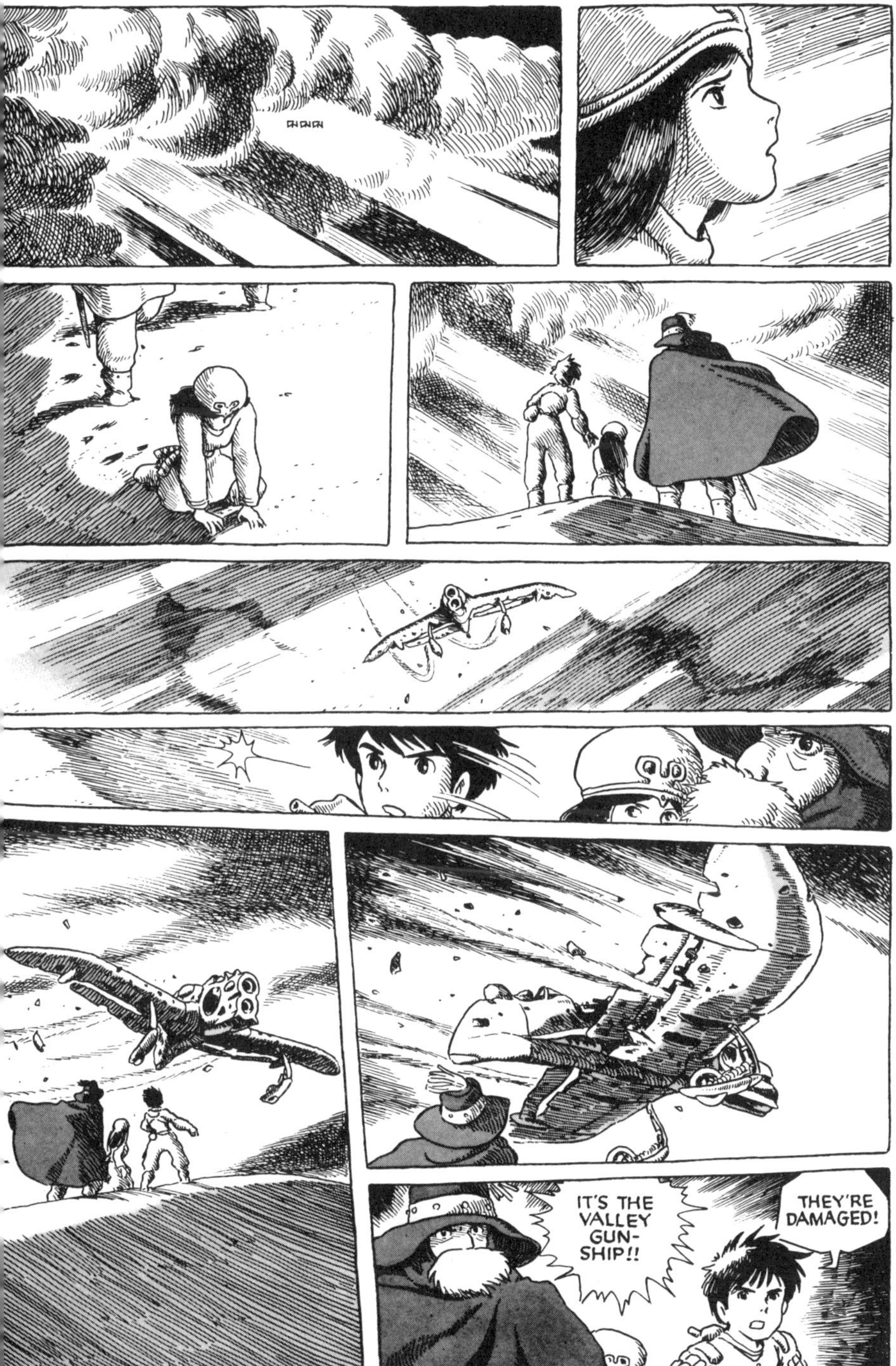
IT'S THE VALLEY GUN-SHIP!!
THEY'RE DAMAGED!

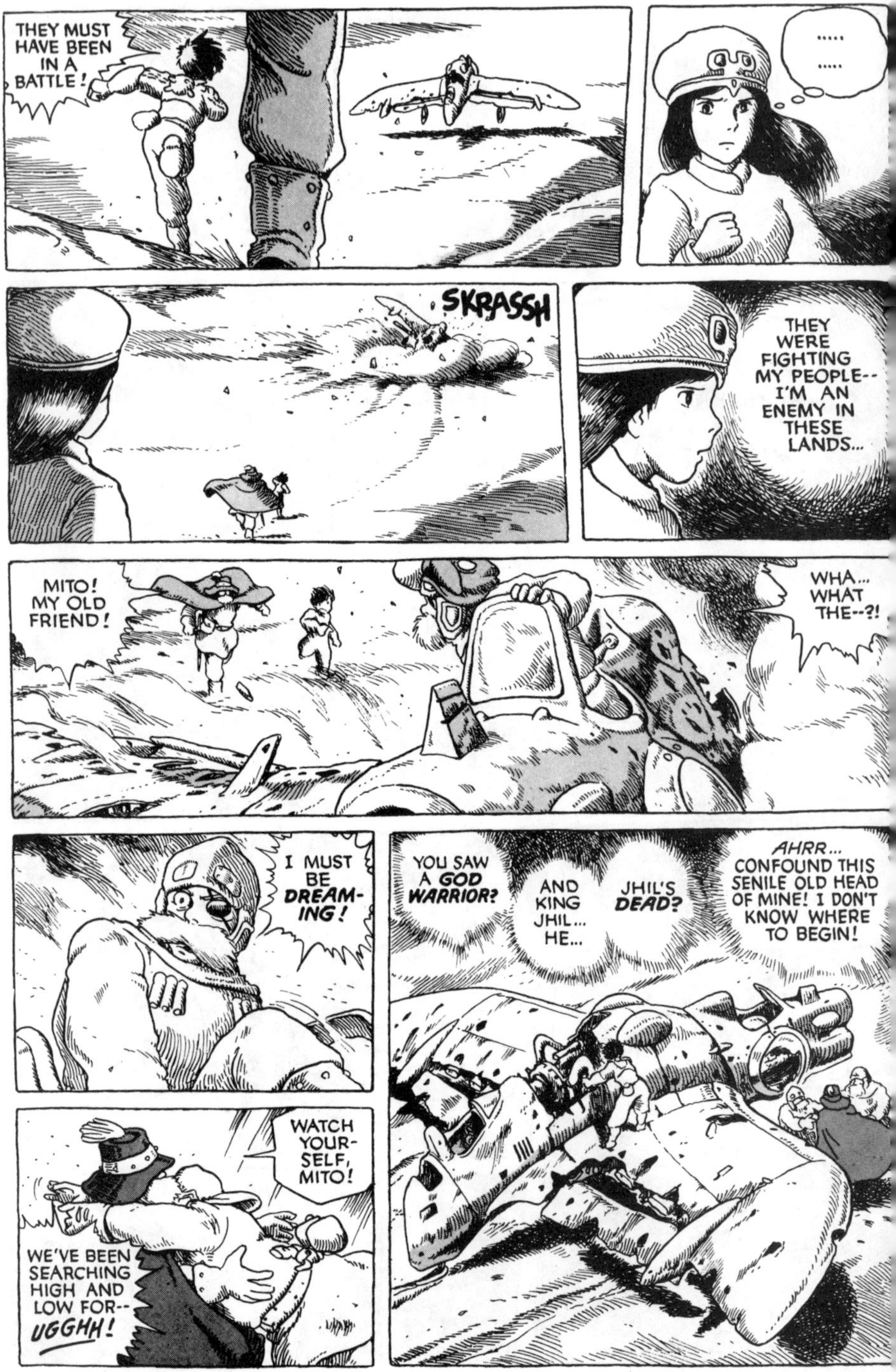

THEY MUST HAVE BEEN IN A BATTLE!
.....
.....
SKRASSH
THEY WERE FIGHTING MY PEOPLE-- I'M AN ENEMY IN THESE LANDS...
MITO! MY OLD FRIEND!
WHA... WHAT THE--?!
I MUST BE DREAMING!
YOU SAW A GOD WARRIOR?
AND KING JHIL... HE...
JHIL'S DEAD?
AHRR... CONFOUND THIS SENILE OLD HEAD OF MINE! I DON'T KNOW WHERE TO BEGIN!
WATCH YOURSELF, MITO!
WE'VE BEEN SEARCHING HIGH AND LOW FOR-- UGGHH!

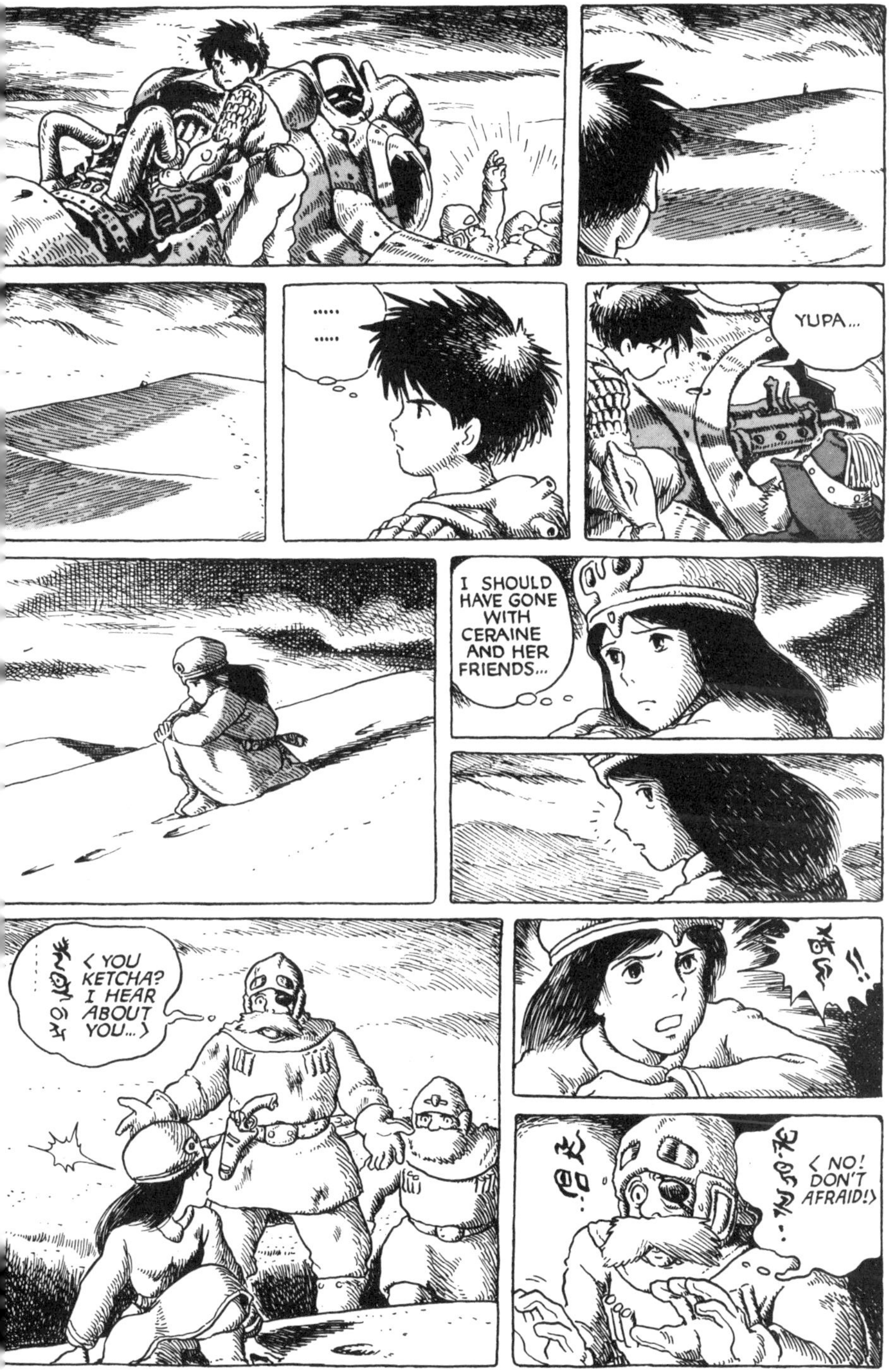

......
......
YUPA...
I SHOULD HAVE GONE WITH CERAINE AND HER FRIENDS...
< YOU KETCHA? I HEAR ABOUT YOU... >
!!
< NO! DON'T AFRAID! >

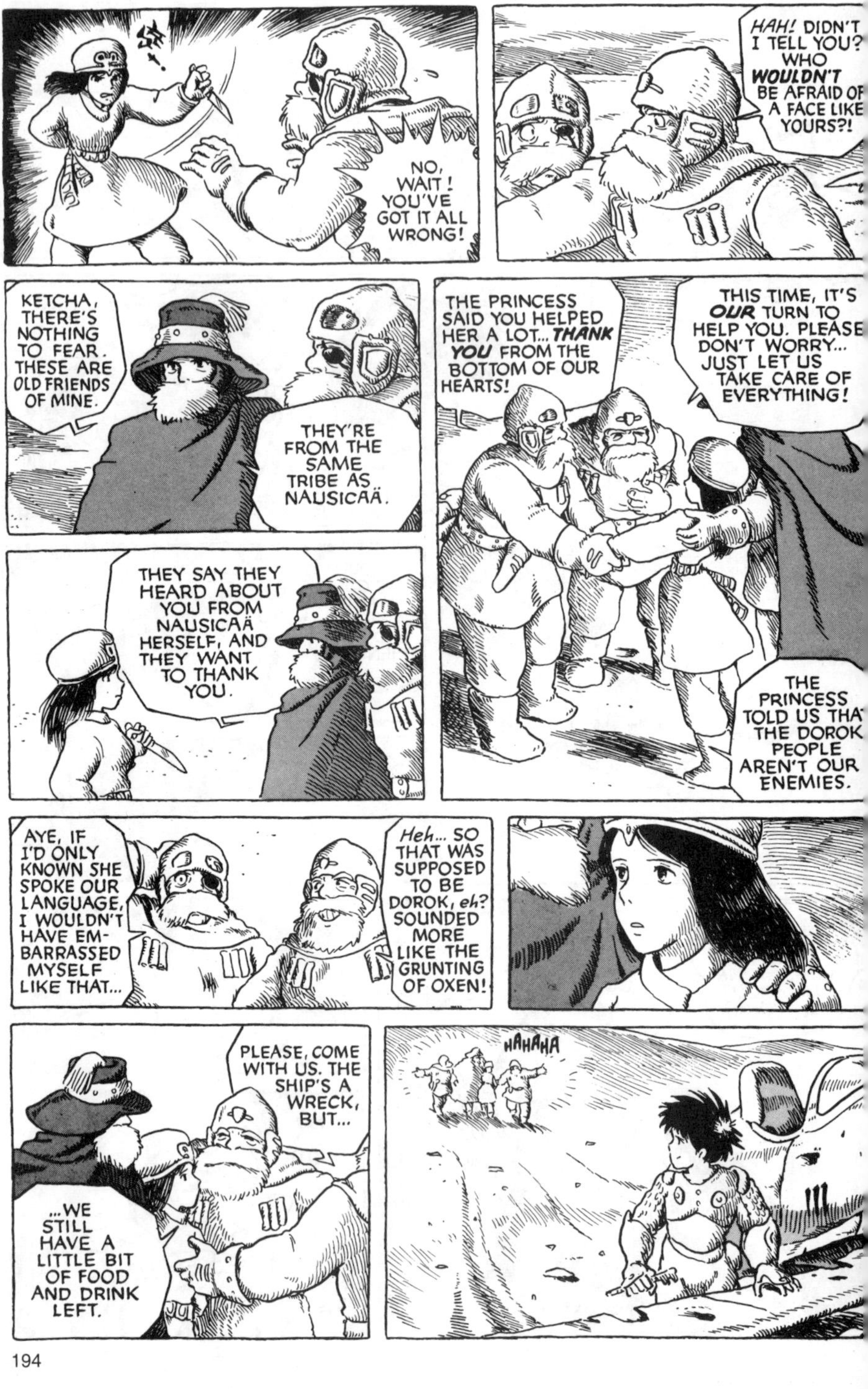
NO, WAIT! YOU'VE GOT IT ALL WRONG!
HAH! DIDN'T I TELL YOU? WHO WOULDN'T BE AFRAID OF A FACE LIKE YOURS?!
KETCHA, THERE'S NOTHING TO FEAR. THESE ARE OLD FRIENDS OF MINE.
THEY'RE FROM THE SAME TRIBE AS NAUSICAÄ.
THEY SAY THEY HEARD ABOUT YOU FROM NAUSICAÄ HERSELF, AND THEY WANT TO THANK YOU.
THE PRINCESS SAID YOU HELPED HER A LOT... THANK YOU FROM THE BOTTOM OF OUR HEARTS!
THIS TIME, IT'S OUR TURN TO HELP YOU. PLEASE DON'T WORRY... JUST LET US TAKE CARE OF EVERYTHING!
THE PRINCESS TOLD US THAT THE DOROK PEOPLE AREN'T OUR ENEMIES.
AYE, IF I'D ONLY KNOWN SHE SPOKE OUR LANGUAGE, I WOULDN'T HAVE EMBARRASSED MYSELF LIKE THAT...
Heh... SO THAT WAS SUPPOSED TO BE DOROK, eh? SOUNDED MORE LIKE THE GRUNTING OF OXEN!
PLEASE, COME WITH US. THE SHIP'S A WRECK, BUT...
...WE STILL HAVE A LITTLE BIT OF FOOD AND DRINK LEFT.
HAHAHA

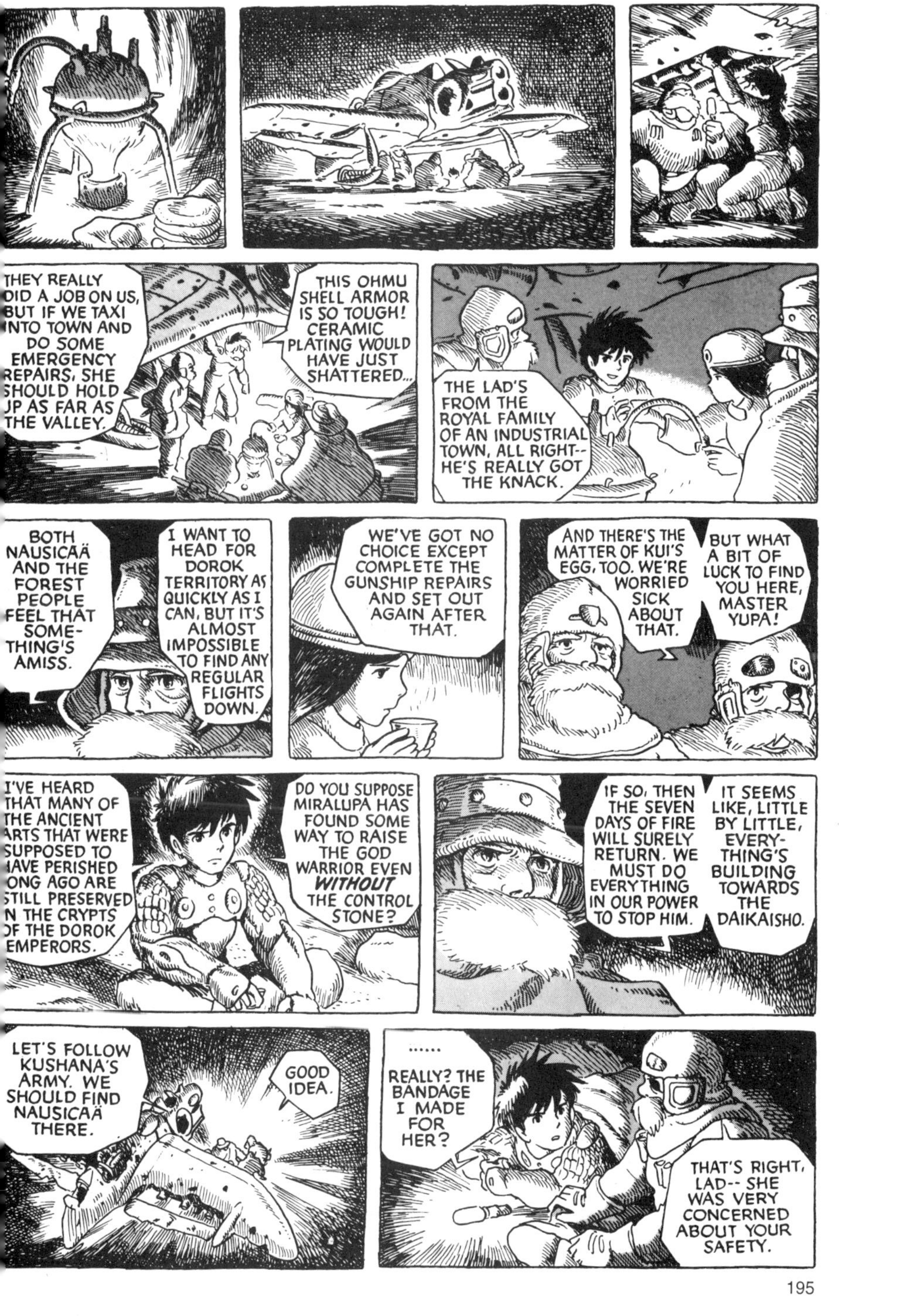
THEY REALLY DID A JOB ON US, BUT IF WE TAXI INTO TOWN AND DO SOME EMERGENCY REPAIRS, SHE SHOULD HOLD UP AS FAR AS THE VALLEY.
THIS OHMU SHELL ARMOR IS SO TOUGH! CERAMIC PLATING WOULD HAVE JUST SHATTERED...
THE LAD'S FROM THE ROYAL FAMILY OF AN INDUSTRIAL TOWN, ALL RIGHT-- HE'S REALLY GOT THE KNACK.
BOTH NAUSICAÄ AND THE FOREST PEOPLE FEEL THAT SOMETHING'S AMISS.
I WANT TO HEAD FOR DOROK TERRITORY AS QUICKLY AS I CAN, BUT IT'S ALMOST IMPOSSIBLE TO FIND ANY REGULAR FLIGHTS DOWN.
WE'VE GOT NO CHOICE EXCEPT COMPLETE THE GUNSHIP REPAIRS AND SET OUT AGAIN AFTER THAT.
AND THERE'S THE MATTER OF KUI'S EGG, TOO. WE'RE WORRIED SICK ABOUT THAT.
BUT WHAT A BIT OF LUCK TO FIND YOU HERE, MASTER YUPA!
I'VE HEARD THAT MANY OF THE ANCIENT ARTS THAT WERE SUPPOSED TO HAVE PERISHED LONG AGO ARE STILL PRESERVED IN THE CRYPTS OF THE DOROK EMPERORS.
DO YOU SUPPOSE MIRALUPA HAS FOUND SOME WAY TO RAISE THE GOD WARRIOR EVEN *WITHOUT* THE CONTROL STONE?
IF SO, THEN THE SEVEN DAYS OF FIRE WILL SURELY RETURN. WE MUST DO EVERYTHING IN OUR POWER TO STOP HIM.
IT SEEMS LIKE, LITTLE BY LITTLE, EVERYTHING'S BUILDING TOWARDS THE DAIKAISHO.
LET'S FOLLOW KUSHANA'S ARMY. WE SHOULD FIND NAUSICAÄ THERE.
GOOD IDEA.
......
REALLY? THE BANDAGE I MADE FOR HER?
THAT'S RIGHT, LAD-- SHE WAS VERY CONCERNED ABOUT YOUR SAFETY.

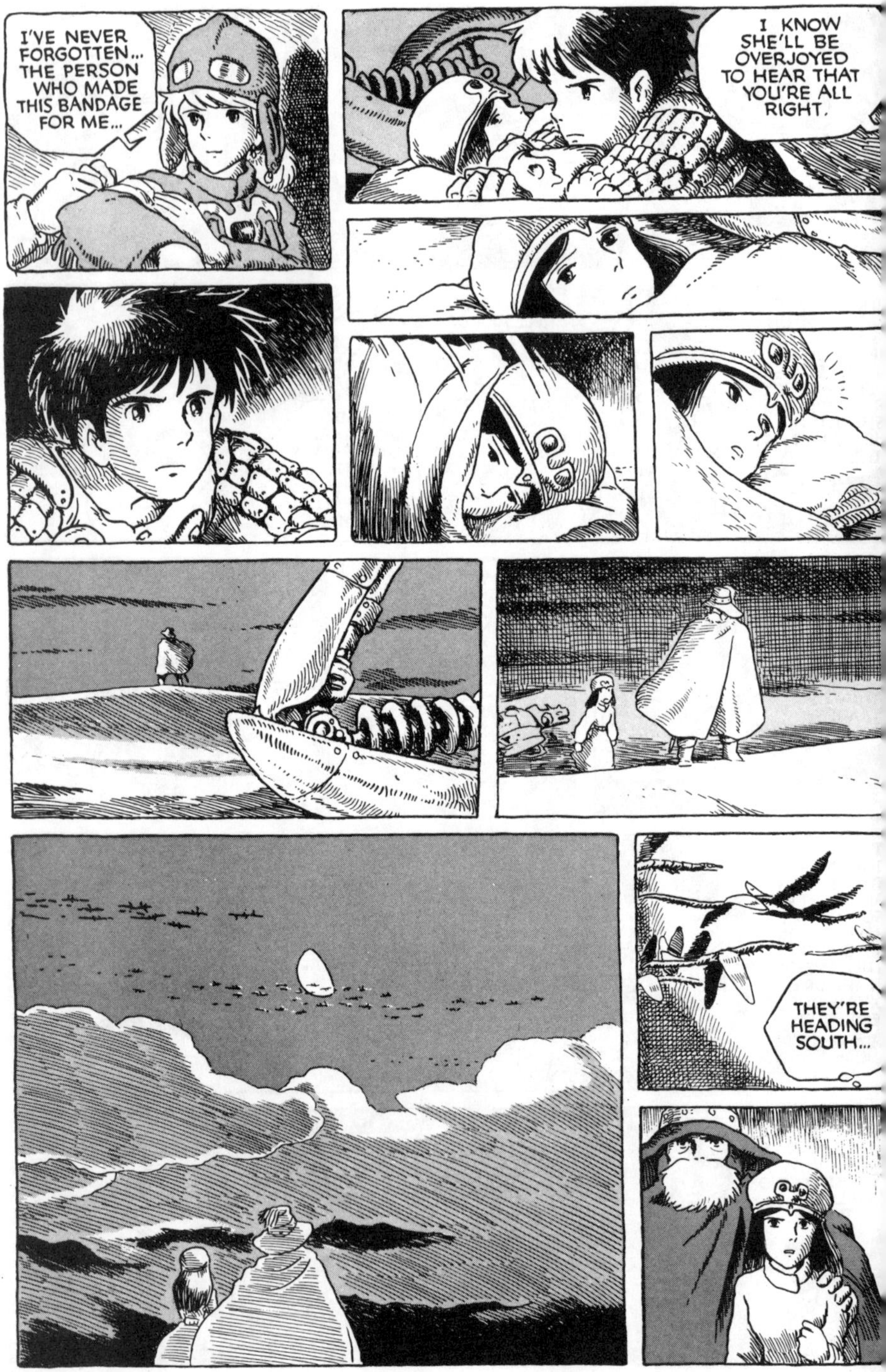
I'VE NEVER FORGOTTEN... THE PERSON WHO MADE THIS BANDAGE FOR ME...
I KNOW SHE'LL BE OVERJOYED TO HEAR THAT YOU'RE ALL RIGHT.
THEY'RE HEADING SOUTH...

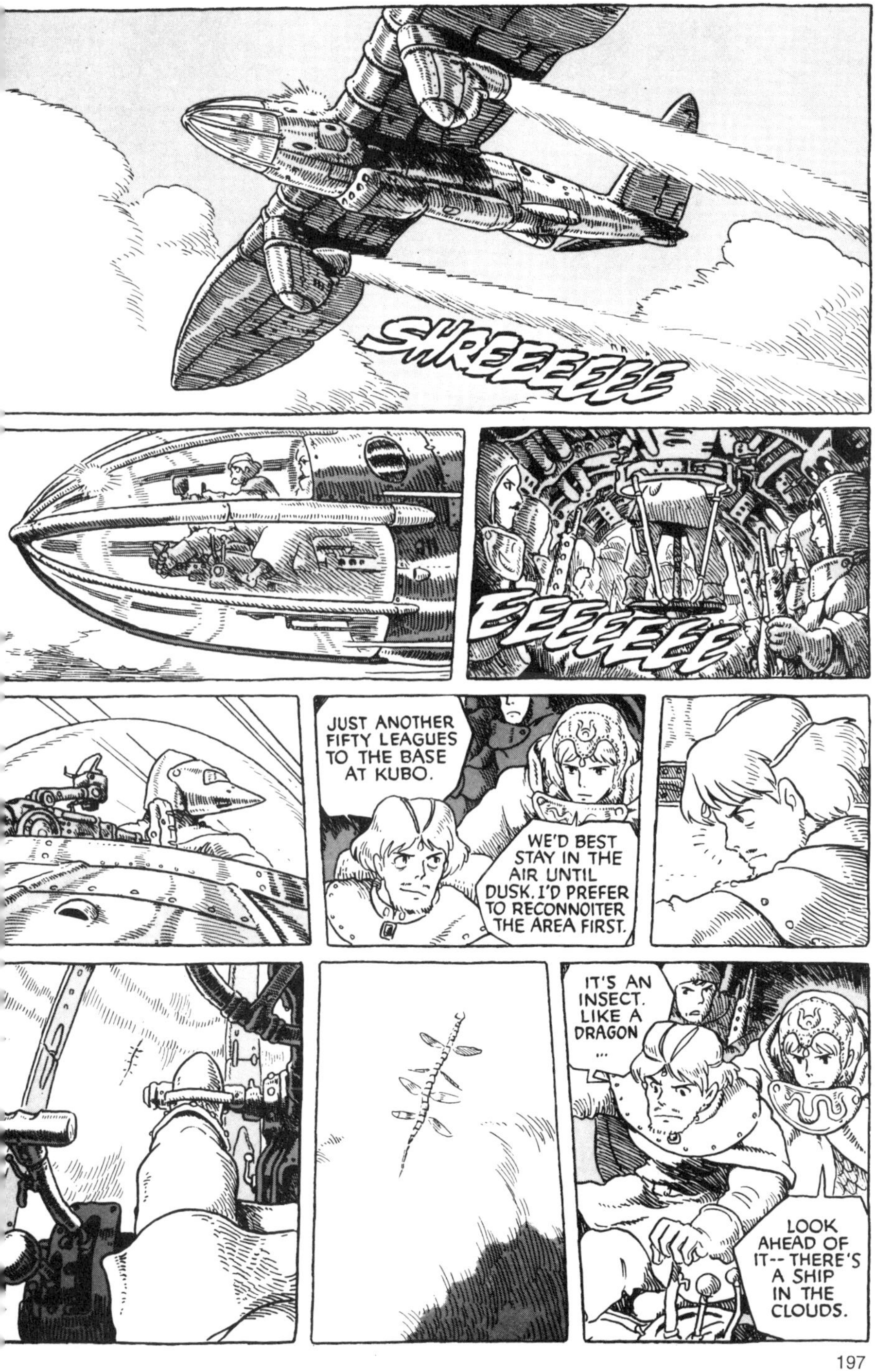
SHREEEEEEE
EEEEEEEE
JUST ANOTHER FIFTY LEAGUES TO THE BASE AT KUBO.
WE'D BEST STAY IN THE AIR UNTIL DUSK. I'D PREFER TO RECONNOITER THE AREA FIRST.
IT'S AN INSECT. LIKE A DRAGON ...
LOOK AHEAD OF IT-- THERE'S A SHIP IN THE CLOUDS.

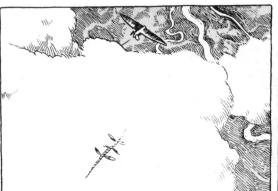

THE BUG'S GONE INTO THE CLOUDS, TOO. THOSE TWO ARE IN FOR A RENDEZVOUS...

THERE'S A FRIENDLY SHIP OVERHEAD! IT'S KEEPING STATION WITH US.

HEY! LOOK OVER THERE! IN THAT CLOUD!

IT'S A **WORM!** HE'S HUGE!

WHAT'S ONE OF THOSE INSECTS DOING AROUND HERE?!

ALL STATIONS, HOLD YOUR FIRE! DON'T ANTAGONIZE IT!

IT... IT'S COMING CLOSER!

GRNGRNGRN

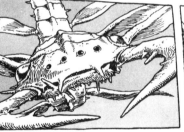

IT'S OVER-TAKING US! PUT ON MORE SPEED!

SHREEE

THAT DRAGON INSECT IS FASTER THAN A BUMBLE-CROW...!

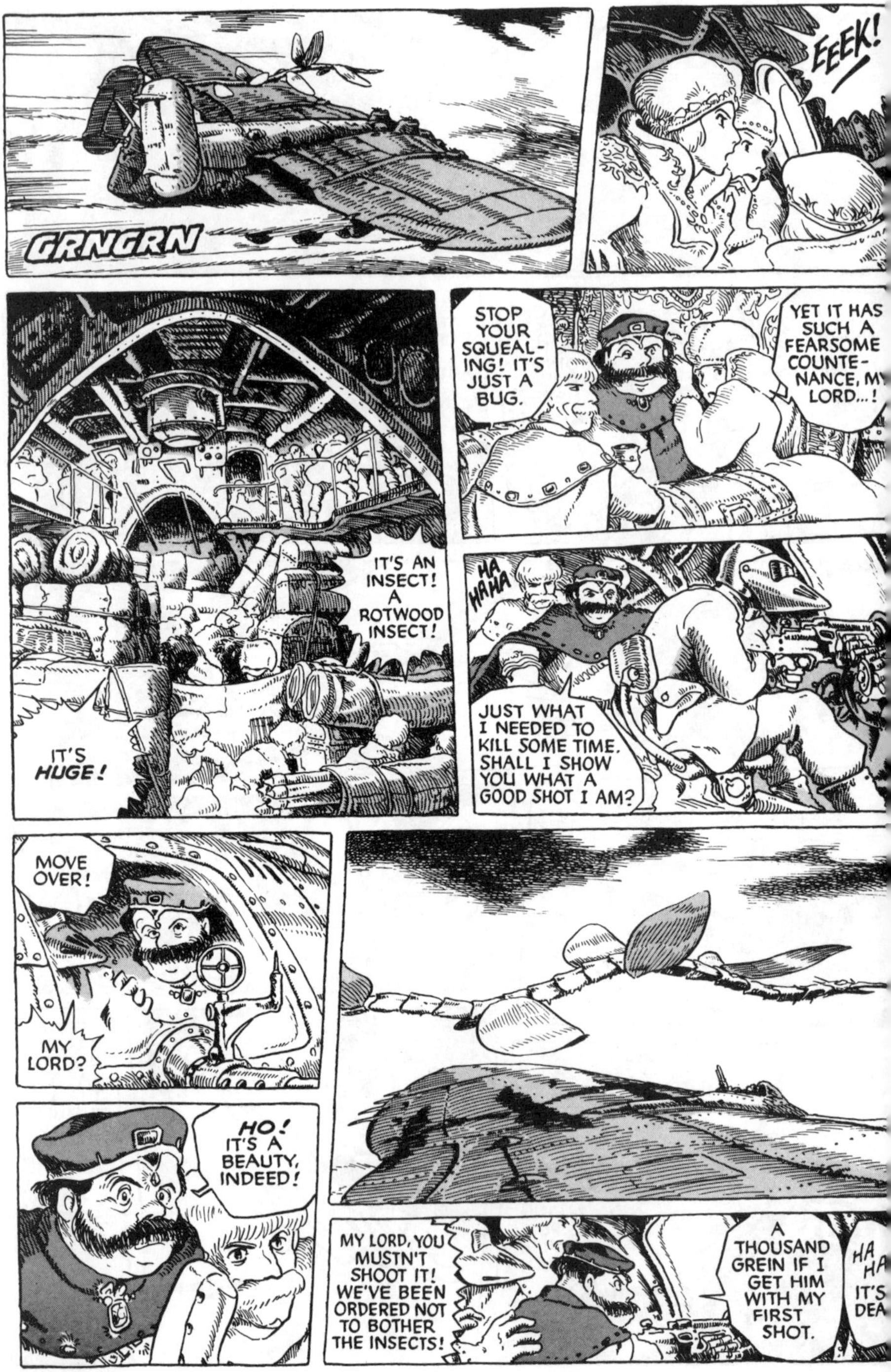
GRNGRN
EEEK!
STOP YOUR SQUEALING! IT'S JUST A BUG.
YET IT HAS SUCH A FEARSOME COUNTENANCE, MY LORD...!
IT'S AN INSECT! A ROTWOOD INSECT!
IT'S HUGE!
HA HAHA
JUST WHAT I NEEDED TO KILL SOME TIME. SHALL I SHOW YOU WHAT A GOOD SHOT I AM?
MOVE OVER!
MY LORD?
HO! IT'S A BEAUTY, INDEED!
MY LORD, YOU MUSTN'T SHOOT IT! WE'VE BEEN ORDERED NOT TO BOTHER THE INSECTS!
A THOUSAND GREIN IF I GET HIM WITH MY FIRST SHOT.

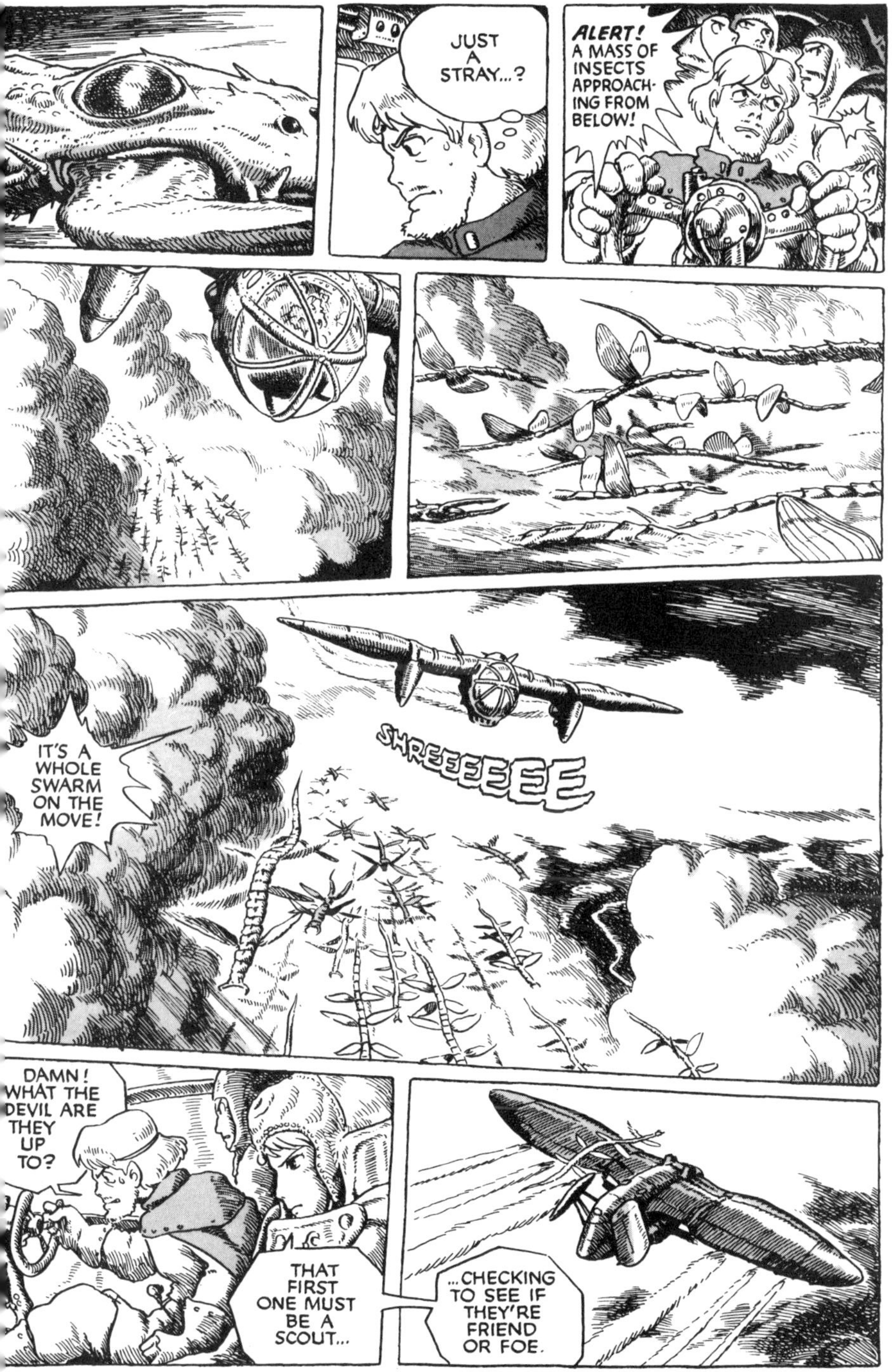
JUST A STRAY...?
ALERT! A MASS OF INSECTS APPROACHING FROM BELOW!
IT'S A WHOLE SWARM ON THE MOVE!
SHREEEEEEE
DAMN! WHAT THE DEVIL ARE THEY UP TO?
THAT FIRST ONE MUST BE A SCOUT...
...CHECKING TO SEE IF THEY'RE FRIEND OR FOE.

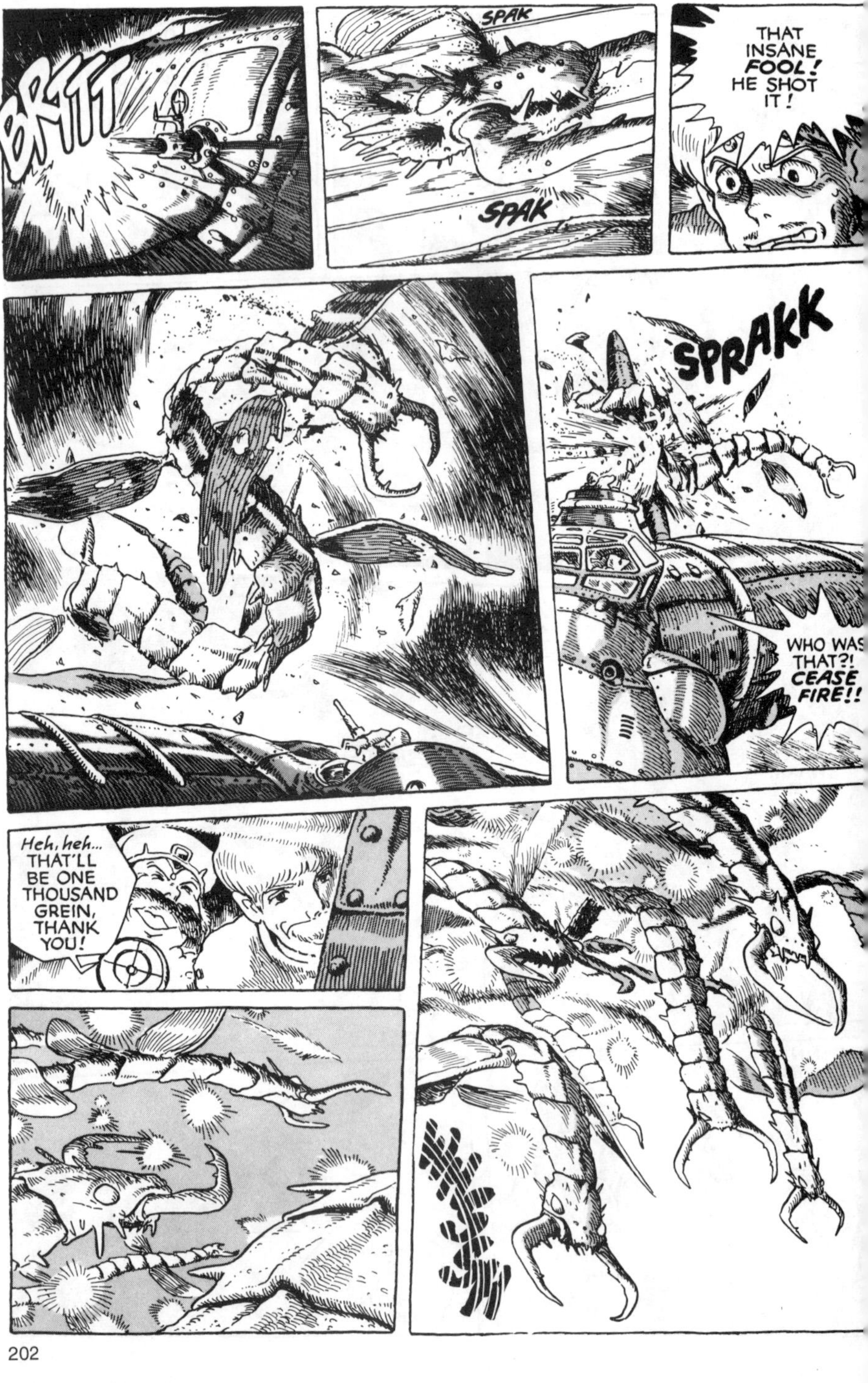
BRTTT
SPAK
SPAK
THAT INSANE FOOL! HE SHOT IT!
SPRAKK
WHO WAS THAT?! CEASE FIRE!!
Heh, heh... THAT'LL BE ONE THOUSAND GREIN, THANK YOU!

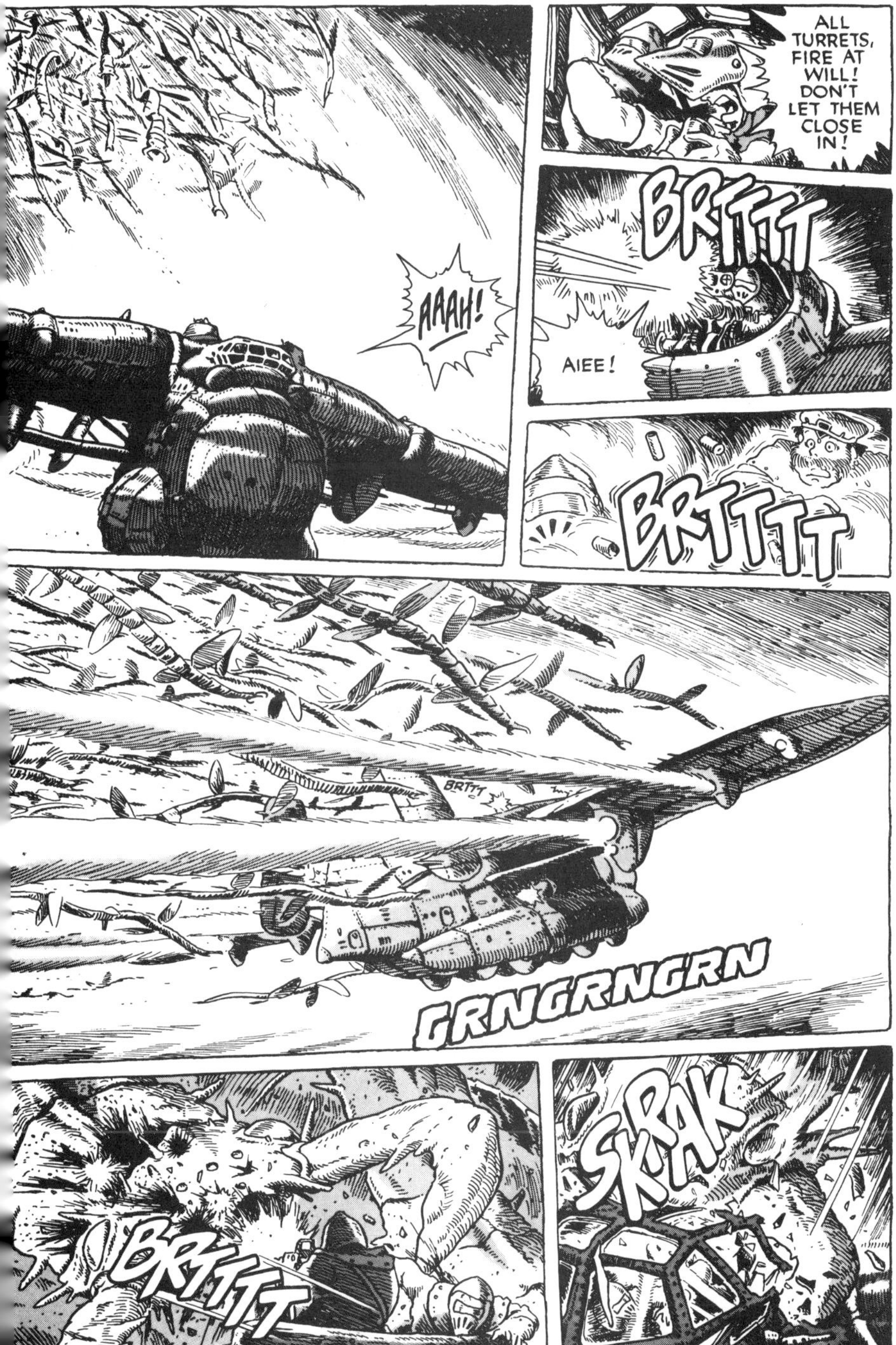
ALL TURRETS, FIRE AT WILL! DON'T LET THEM CLOSE IN!
AAAH!
BRTTTT
AIEE!
BRTTTTT
BRTTT
GRNGRNGRN
BRTTTTT
SKRAK

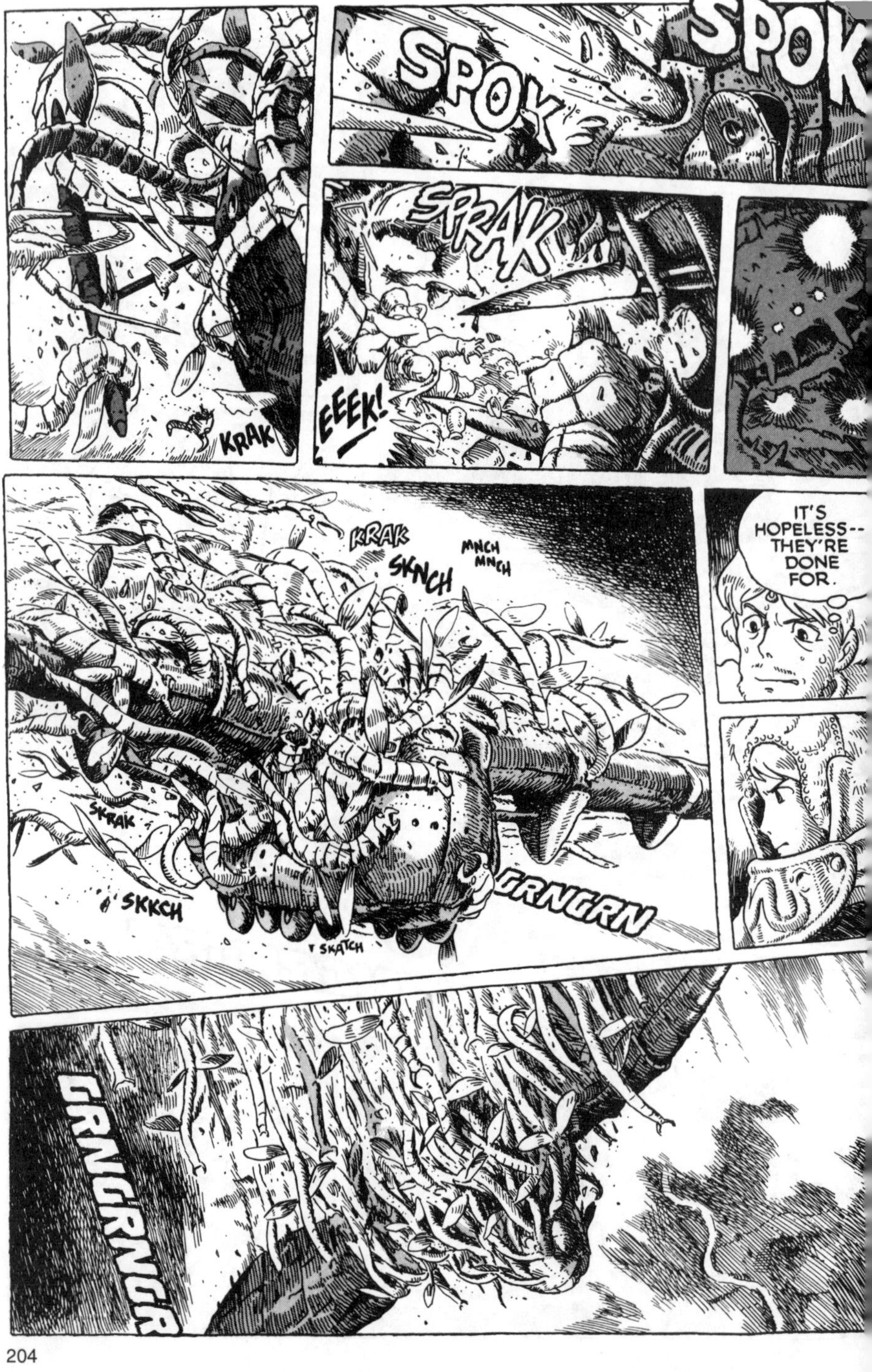
KRAK
SPOK
SPOK
SPRAK
EEEK!
KRAK
SKNCH
MNCH MNCH
SKRAK
SKKCH
SKATCH
GRNGRN
IT'S HOPELESS-- THEY'RE DONE FOR.
GRNGRNGR

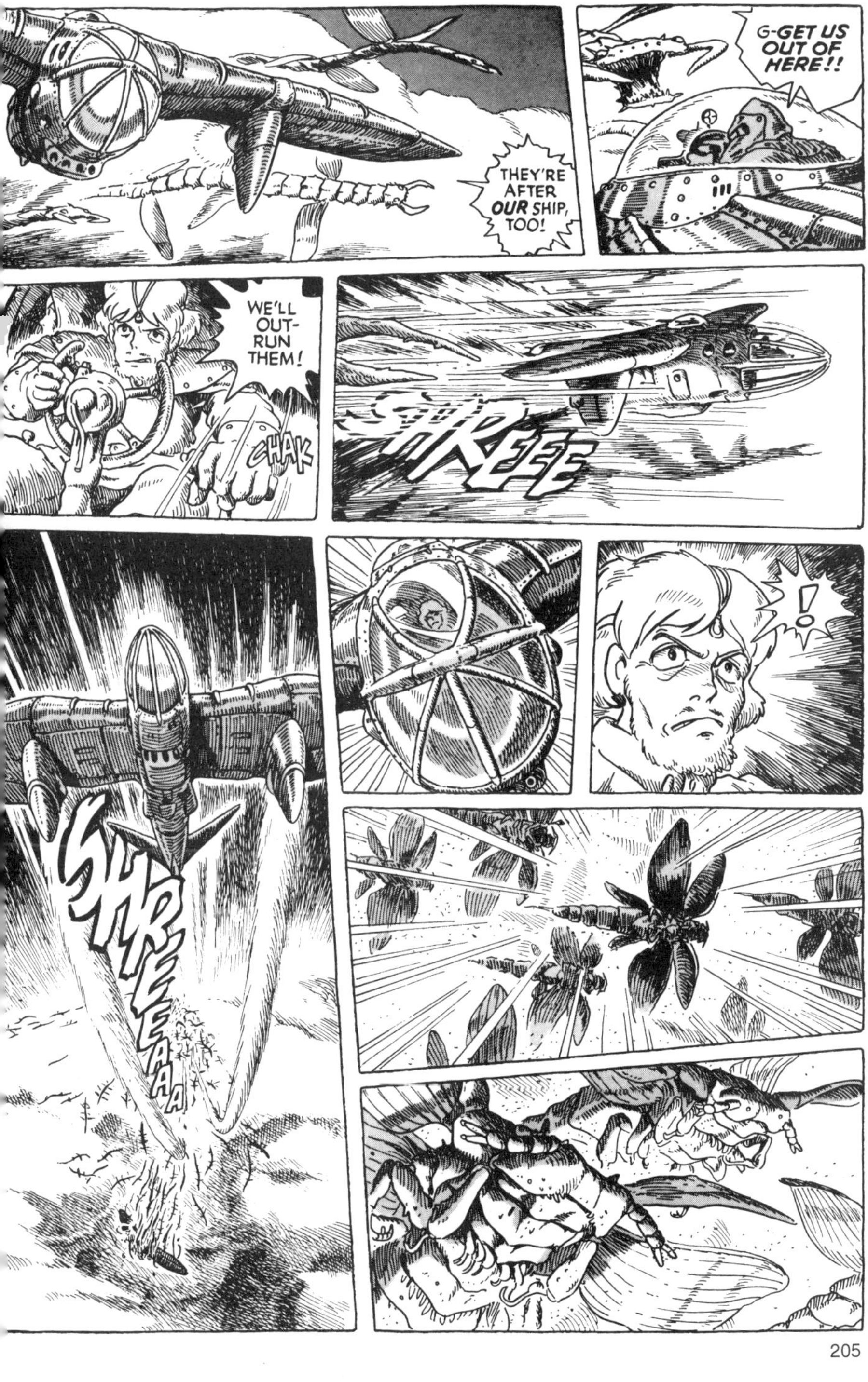
THEY'RE AFTER OUR SHIP, TOO!
G-GET US OUT OF HERE!!
WE'LL OUT-RUN THEM!
CHAK
SHREEEE
SHREEAAA
!

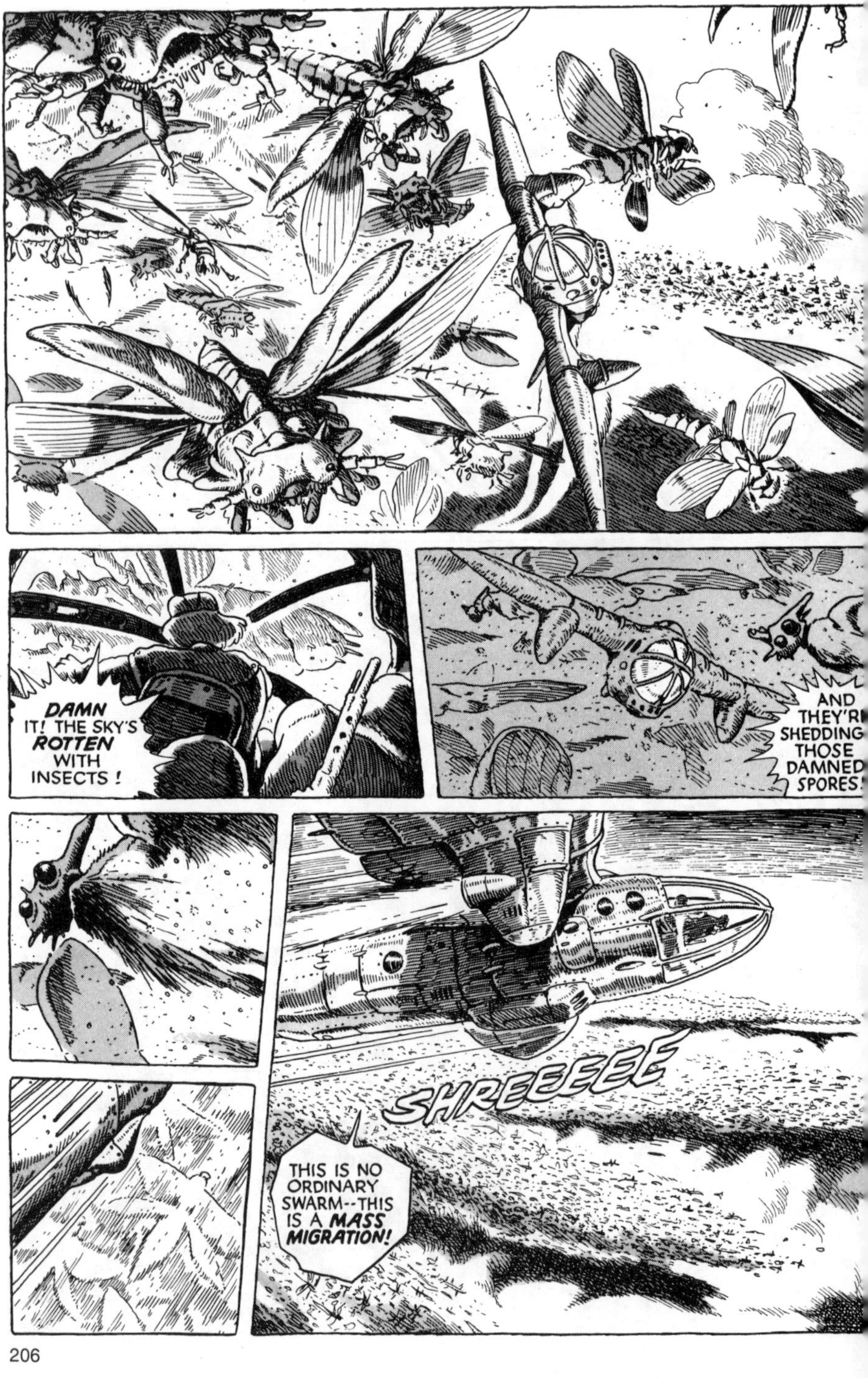

DAMN IT! THE SKY'S ROTTEN WITH INSECTS !
AND THEY'R SHEDDING THOSE DAMNED SPORES!
SHREEEEEE
THIS IS NO ORDINARY SWARM--THIS IS A MASS MIGRATION!

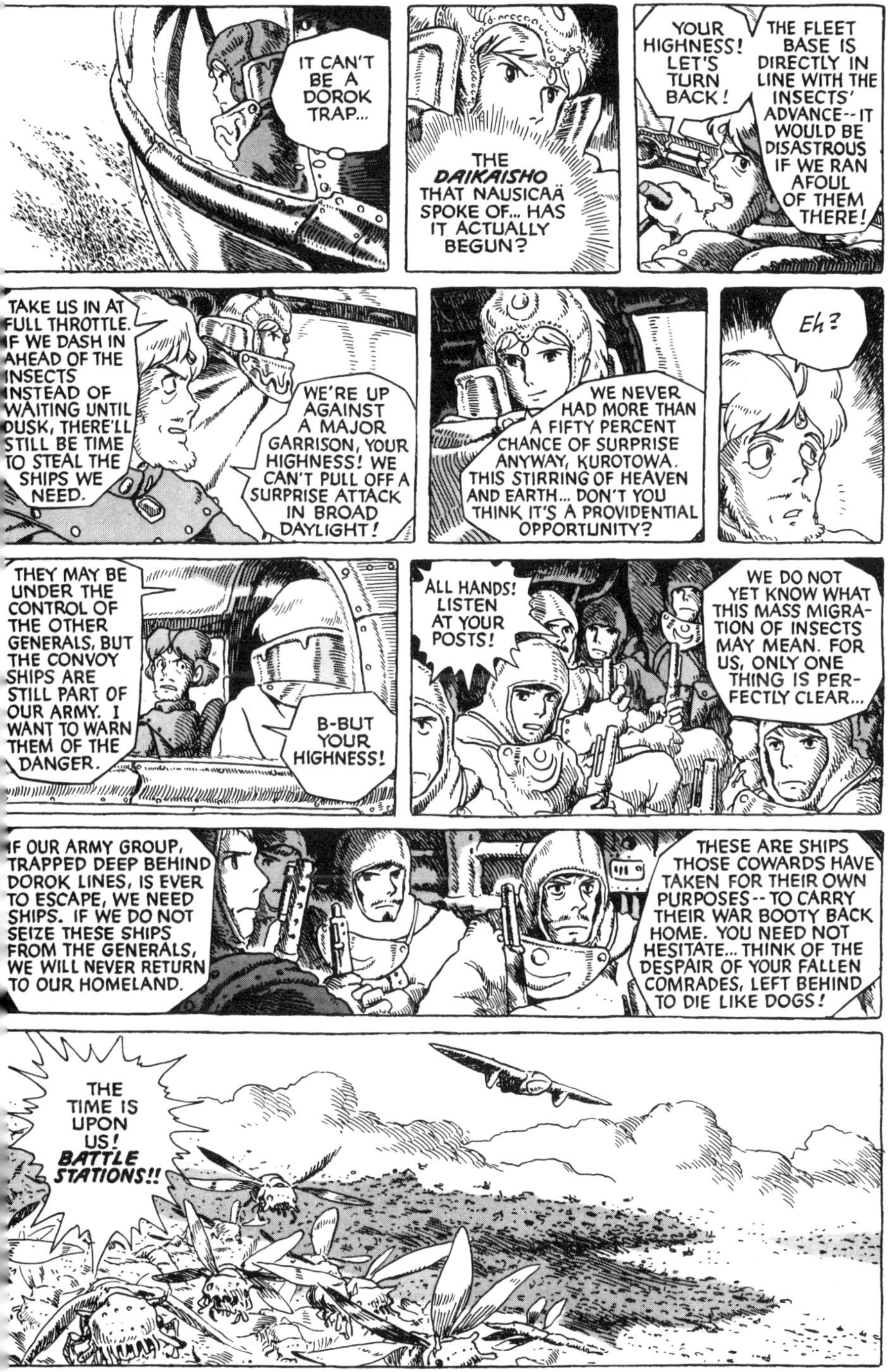
IT CAN'T BE A DOROK TRAP...
THE *DAIKAISHO* THAT NAUSICAÄ SPOKE OF... HAS IT ACTUALLY BEGUN?
YOUR HIGHNESS! LET'S TURN BACK!
THE FLEET BASE IS DIRECTLY IN LINE WITH THE INSECTS' ADVANCE--IT WOULD BE DISASTROUS IF WE RAN AFOUL OF THEM THERE!
TAKE US IN AT FULL THROTTLE. IF WE DASH IN AHEAD OF THE INSECTS INSTEAD OF WAITING UNTIL DUSK, THERE'LL STILL BE TIME TO STEAL THE SHIPS WE NEED.
WE'RE UP AGAINST A MAJOR GARRISON, YOUR HIGHNESS! WE CAN'T PULL OFF A SURPRISE ATTACK IN BROAD DAYLIGHT!
WE NEVER HAD MORE THAN A FIFTY PERCENT CHANCE OF SURPRISE ANYWAY, KUROTOWA. THIS STIRRING OF HEAVEN AND EARTH... DON'T YOU THINK IT'S A PROVIDENTIAL OPPORTUNITY?
Eh?
THEY MAY BE UNDER THE CONTROL OF THE OTHER GENERALS, BUT THE CONVOY SHIPS ARE STILL PART OF OUR ARMY. I WANT TO WARN THEM OF THE DANGER.
B-BUT YOUR HIGHNESS!
ALL HANDS! LISTEN AT YOUR POSTS!
WE DO NOT YET KNOW WHAT THIS MASS MIGRATION OF INSECTS MAY MEAN. FOR US, ONLY ONE THING IS PERFECTLY CLEAR...
IF OUR ARMY GROUP, TRAPPED DEEP BEHIND DOROK LINES, IS EVER TO ESCAPE, WE NEED SHIPS. IF WE DO NOT SEIZE THESE SHIPS FROM THE GENERALS, WE WILL NEVER RETURN TO OUR HOMELAND.
THESE ARE SHIPS THOSE COWARDS HAVE TAKEN FOR THEIR OWN PURPOSES--TO CARRY THEIR WAR BOOTY BACK HOME. YOU NEED NOT HESITATE... THINK OF THE DESPAIR OF YOUR FALLEN COMRADES, LEFT BEHIND TO DIE LIKE DOGS!
THE TIME IS UPON US! ***BATTLE STATIONS!!***

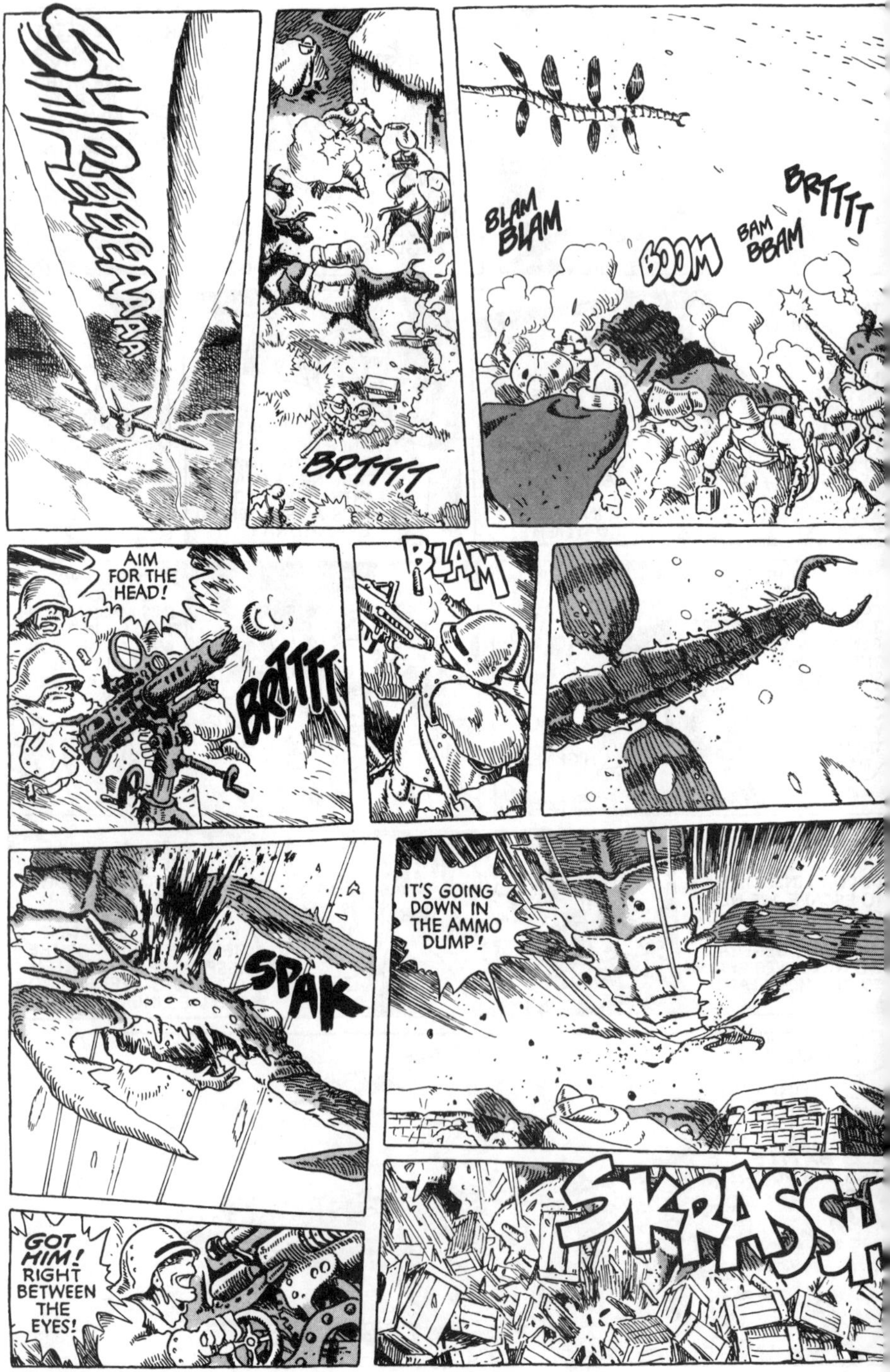
SHREEEAAAAA
BRTTTTT
BLAM BLAM
BOOM
BAM BBAM
BRTTTTT
AIM FOR THE HEAD!
BRTTTT
BLAM
SPAK
IT'S GOING DOWN IN THE AMMO DUMP!
GOT HIM! RIGHT BETWEEN THE EYES!
SKRASSH

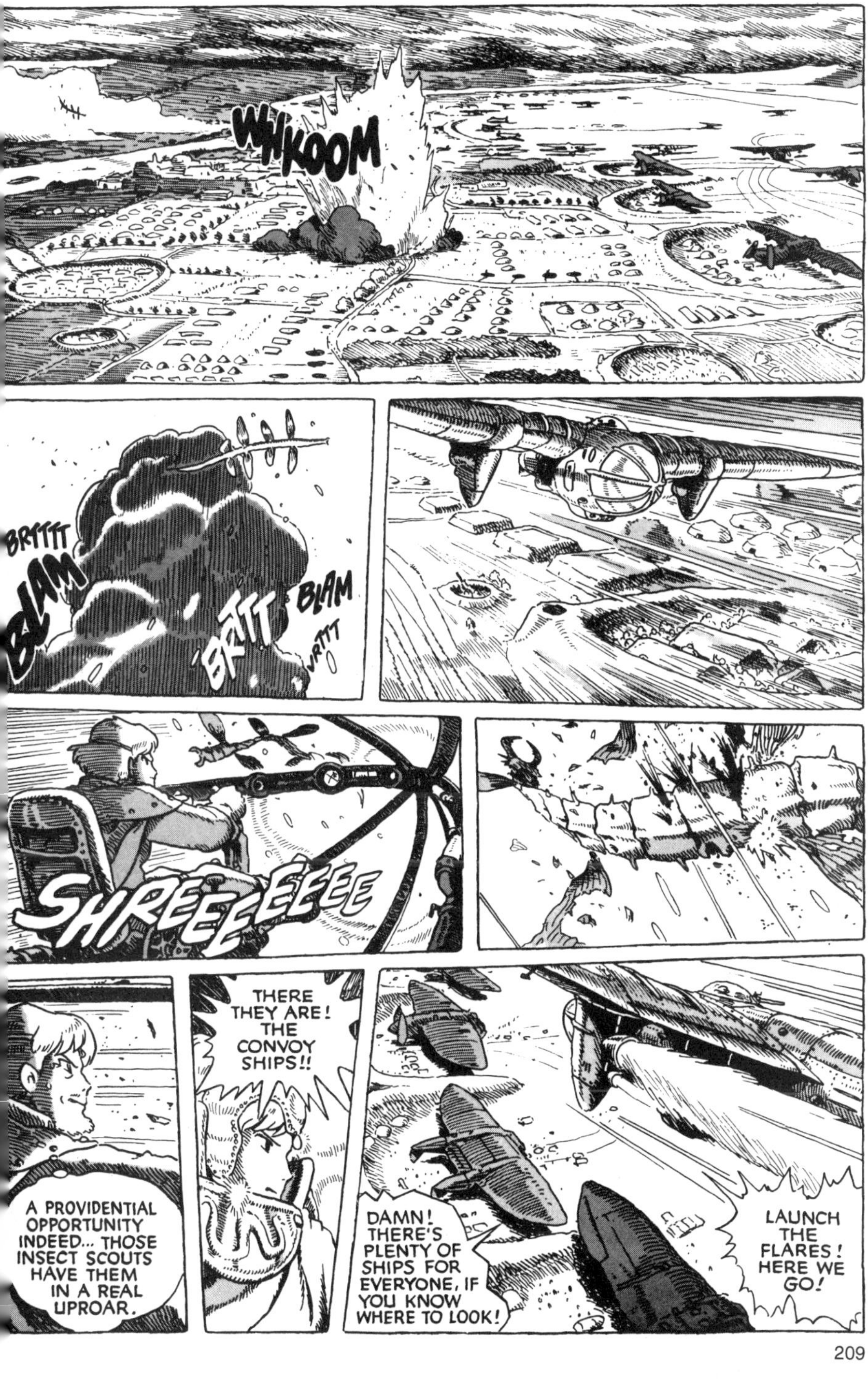
WHKOOM
BRTTTT
BLAM
BRTTT
BLAM
VRTTT
SHREEEEEEE
A PROVIDENTIAL OPPORTUNITY INDEED... THOSE INSECT SCOUTS HAVE THEM IN A REAL UPROAR.
THERE THEY ARE! THE CONVOY SHIPS!!
DAMN! THERE'S PLENTY OF SHIPS FOR EVERYONE, IF YOU KNOW WHERE TO LOOK!
LAUNCH THE FLARES! HERE WE GO!

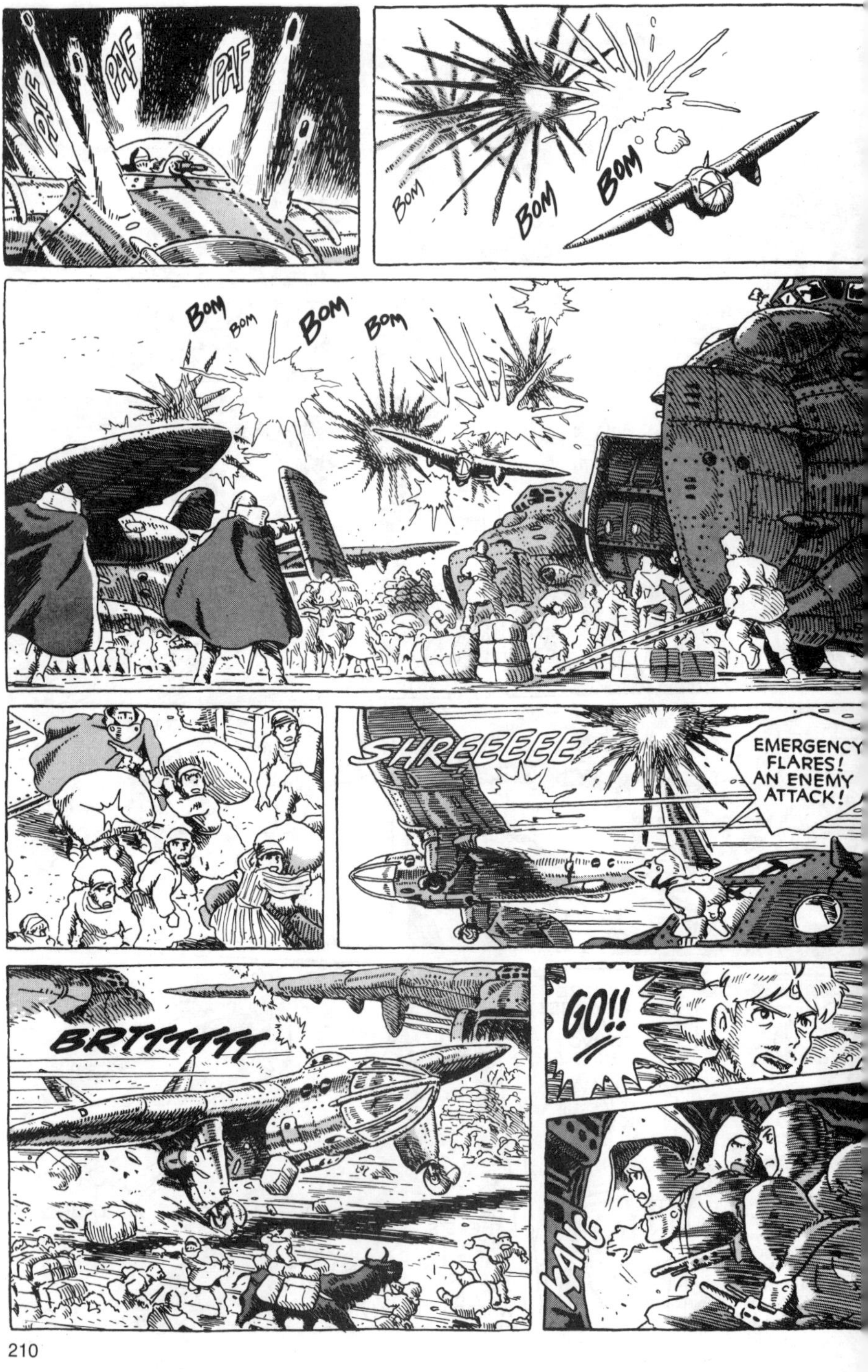
PAF
PAF
PAF
BOM
BOM
BOM
BOM
BOM
BOM
BOM
SHREEEEEE
EMERGENCY FLARES! AN ENEMY ATTACK!
BRTTTTTT
GO!!
KANG

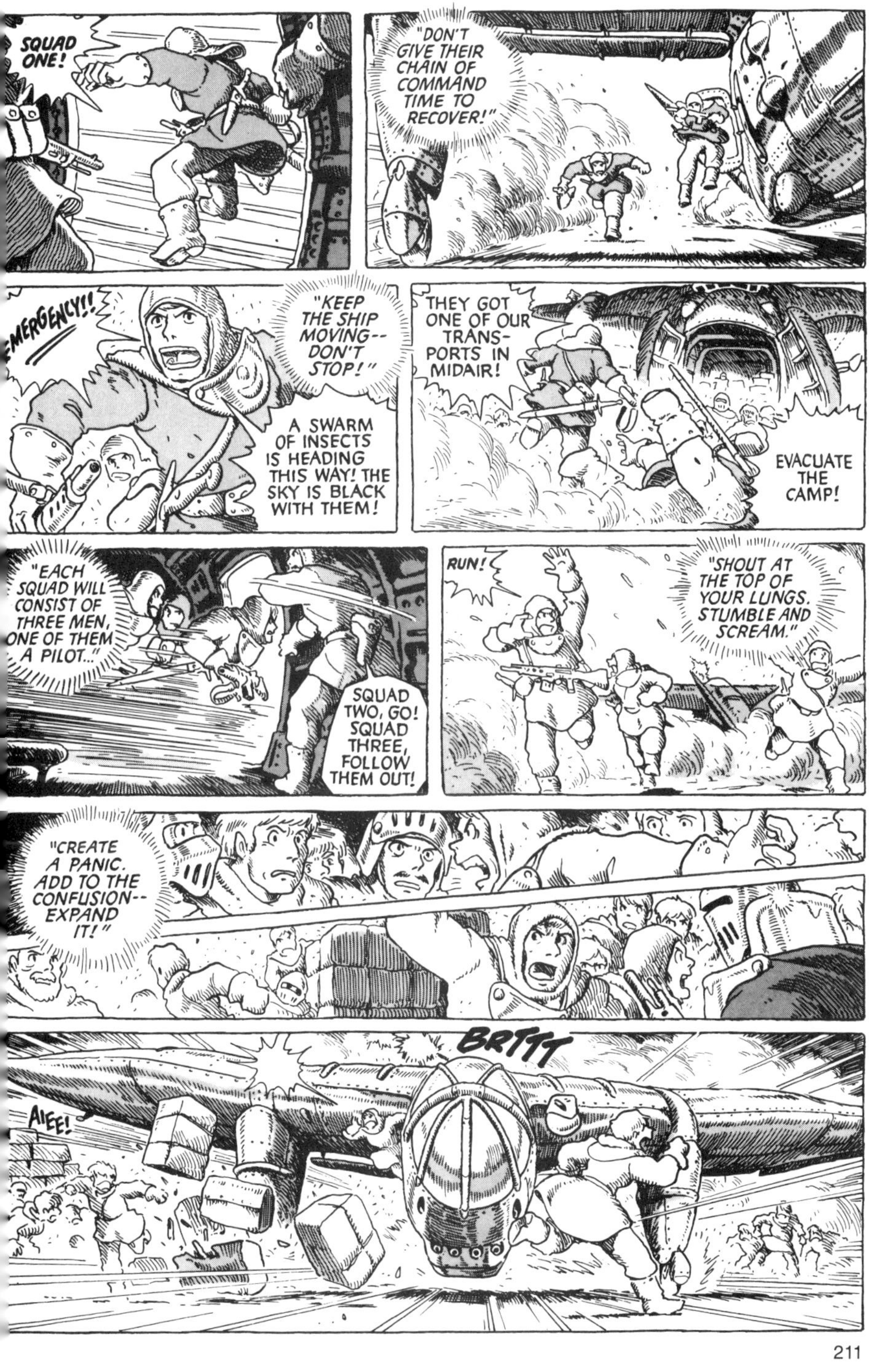
SQUAD ONE!
"DON'T GIVE THEIR CHAIN OF COMMAND TIME TO RECOVER!"
EMERGENCY!!
"KEEP THE SHIP MOVING-- DON'T STOP!"
A SWARM OF INSECTS IS HEADING THIS WAY! THE SKY IS BLACK WITH THEM!
THEY GOT ONE OF OUR TRANS-PORTS IN MIDAIR!
EVACUATE THE CAMP!
"EACH SQUAD WILL CONSIST OF THREE MEN, ONE OF THEM A PILOT..."
SQUAD TWO, GO! SQUAD THREE, FOLLOW THEM OUT!
RUN!
"SHOUT AT THE TOP OF YOUR LUNGS. STUMBLE AND SCREAM."
"CREATE A PANIC. ADD TO THE CONFUSION-- EXPAND IT!"
BRTTT
AIEE!

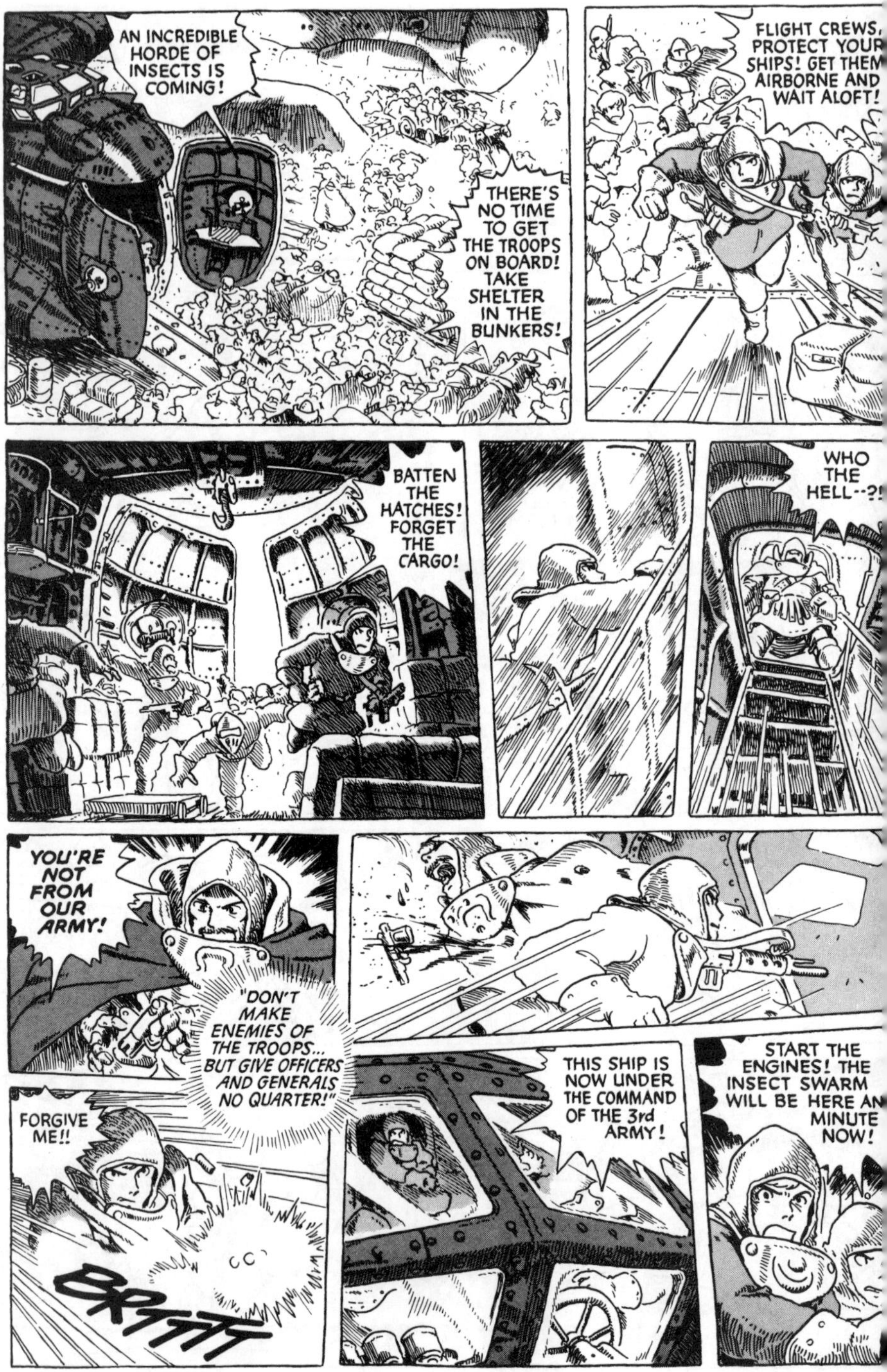
AN INCREDIBLE HORDE OF INSECTS IS COMING!
THERE'S NO TIME TO GET THE TROOPS ON BOARD! TAKE SHELTER IN THE BUNKERS!
FLIGHT CREWS, PROTECT YOUR SHIPS! GET THEM AIRBORNE AND WAIT ALOFT!
BATTEN THE HATCHES! FORGET THE CARGO!
WHO THE HELL--?!
YOU'RE NOT FROM OUR ARMY!
"DON'T MAKE ENEMIES OF THE TROOPS... BUT GIVE OFFICERS AND GENERALS NO QUARTER!"
FORGIVE ME!!
BRTTTT
THIS SHIP IS NOW UNDER THE COMMAND OF THE 3rd ARMY!
START THE ENGINES! THE INSECT SWARM WILL BE HERE AN MINUTE NOW!

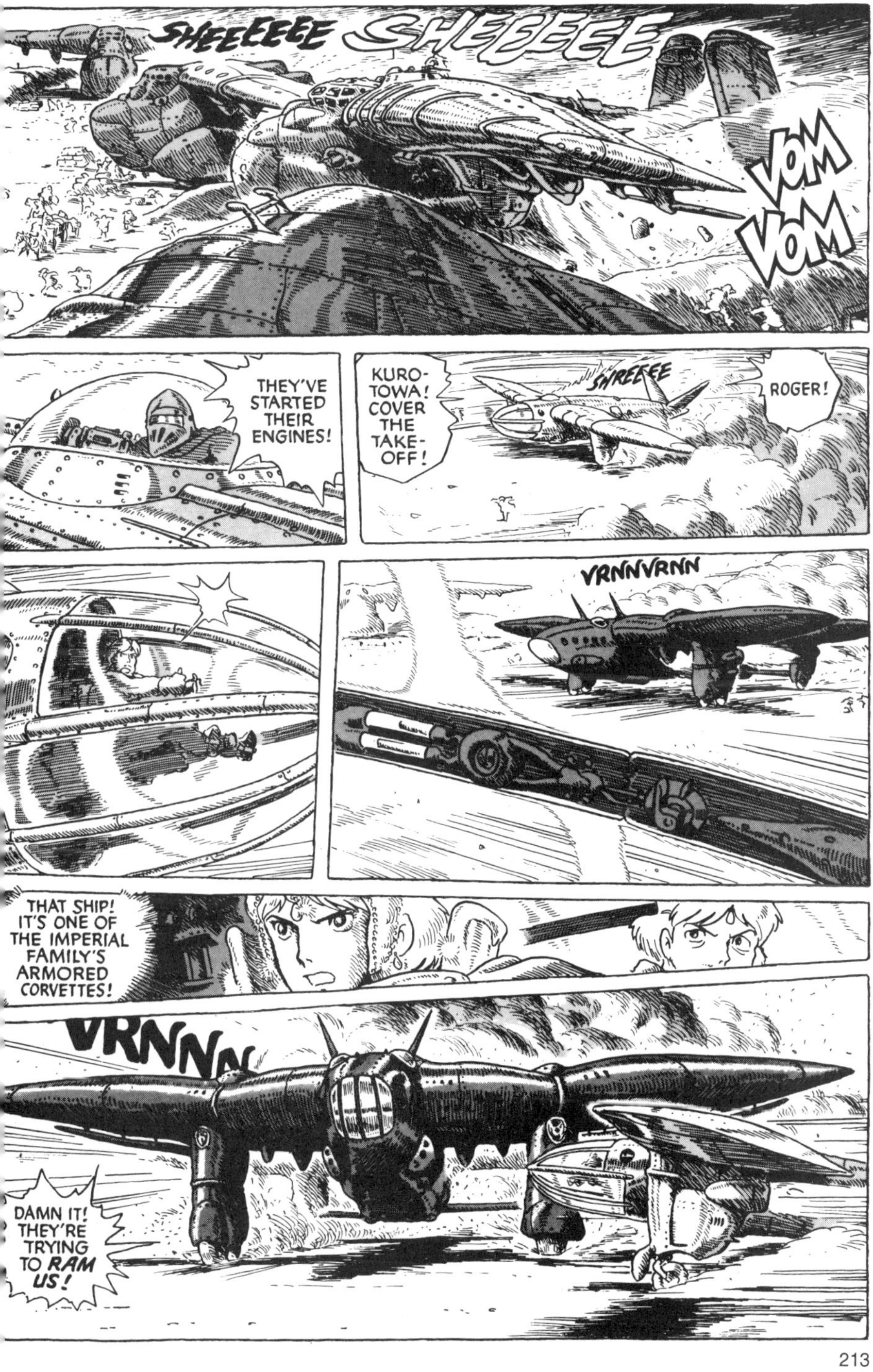
SHEEEEEE SHEEEEEE
VOM VOM
THEY'VE STARTED THEIR ENGINES!
KURO-TOWA! COVER THE TAKE-OFF!
SHREEEEE
ROGER!
VRNNVRNN
THAT SHIP! IT'S ONE OF THE IMPERIAL FAMILY'S ARMORED CORVETTES!
VRNNN
DAMN IT! THEY'RE TRYING TO *RAM US!*

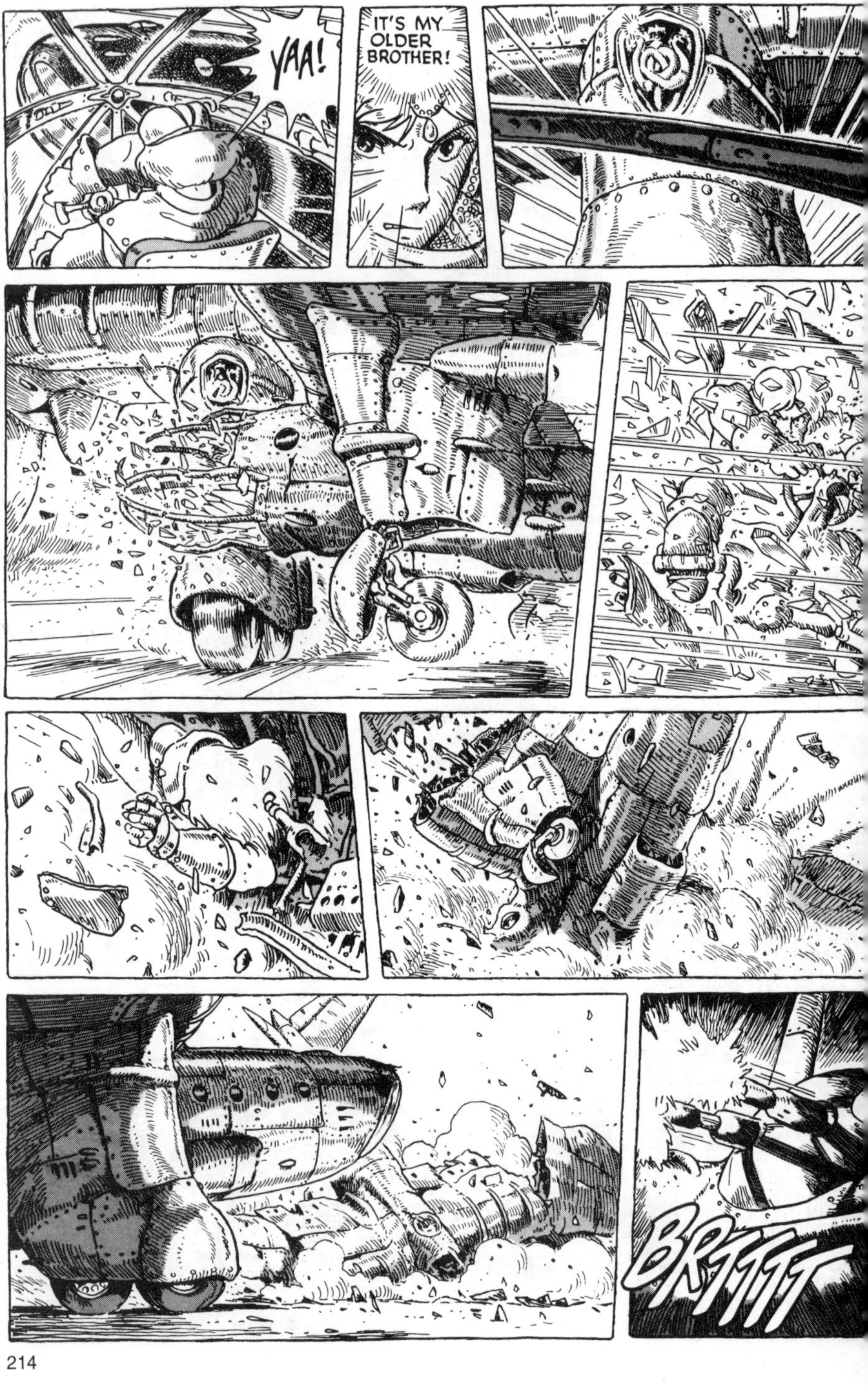
YAA!
IT'S MY OLDER BROTHER!
BRTTTT

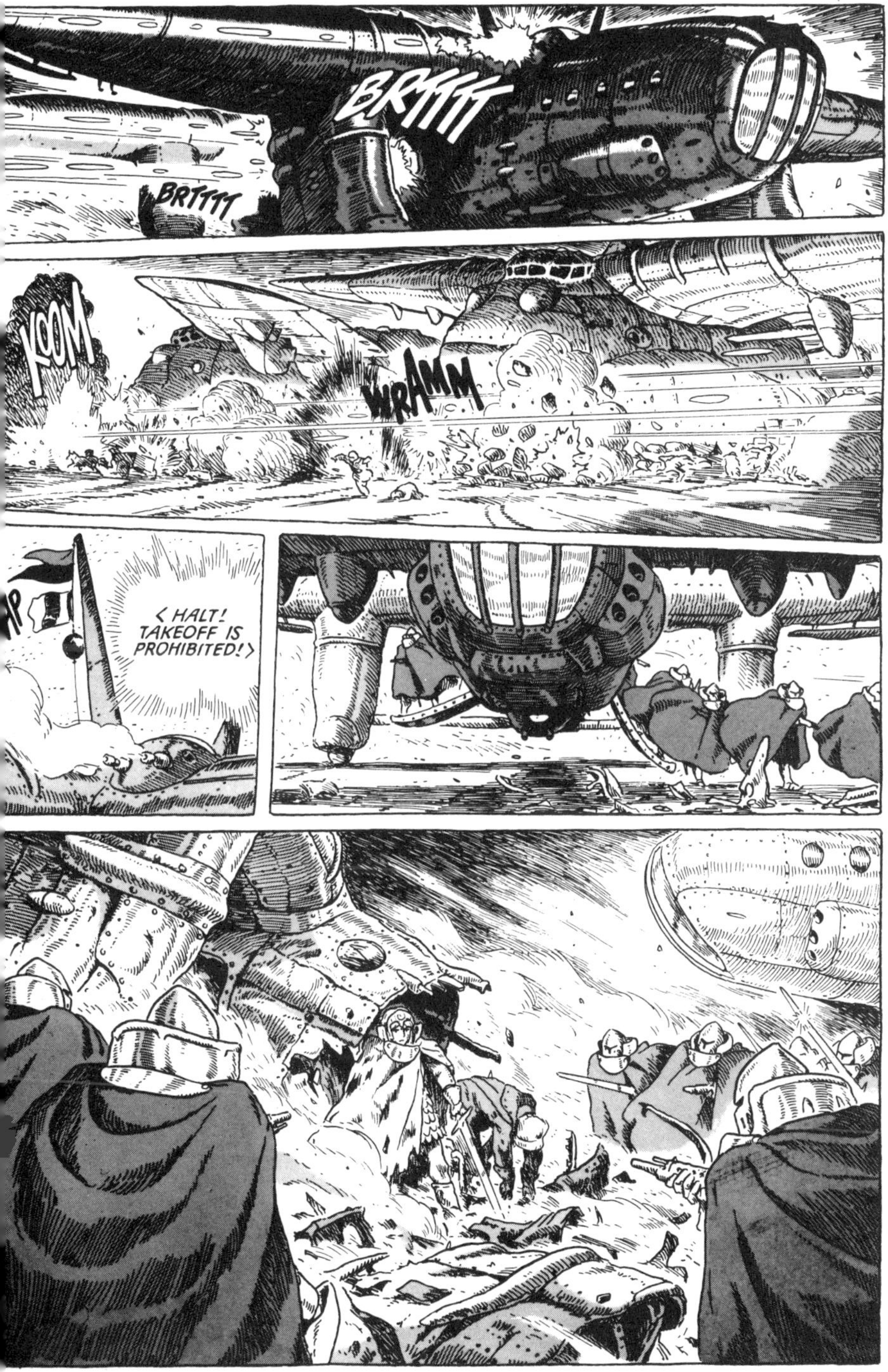
BRTTTT
BRTTTT
KOOM
WRAMM
< HALT! TAKEOFF IS PROHIBITED! >

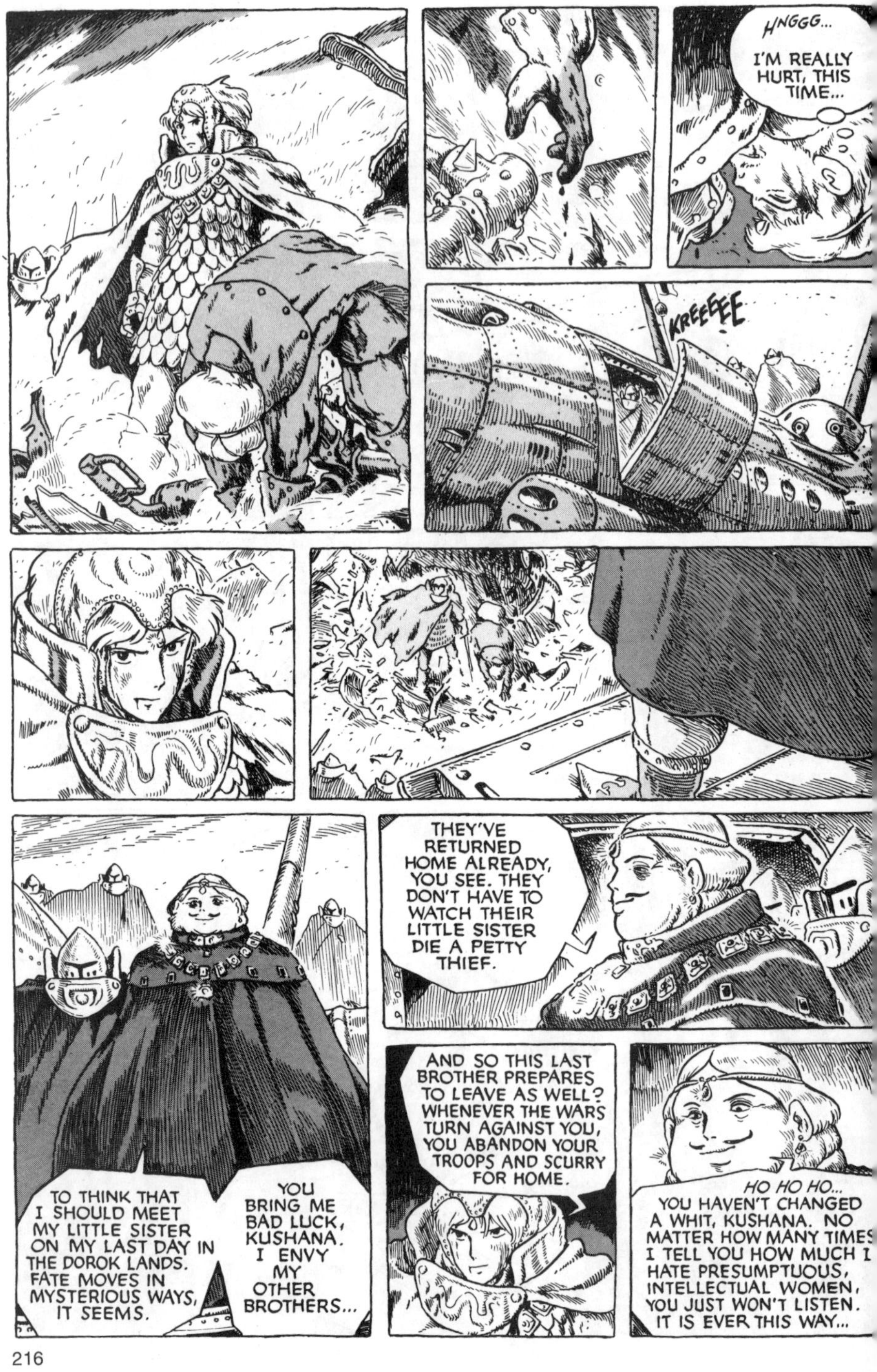
HNGGG...
I'M REALLY HURT, THIS TIME...
KREEEEEE
THEY'VE RETURNED HOME ALREADY, YOU SEE. THEY DON'T HAVE TO WATCH THEIR LITTLE SISTER DIE A PETTY THIEF.
TO THINK THAT I SHOULD MEET MY LITTLE SISTER ON MY LAST DAY IN THE DOROK LANDS. FATE MOVES IN MYSTERIOUS WAYS, IT SEEMS.
YOU BRING ME BAD LUCK, KUSHANA. I ENVY MY OTHER BROTHERS...
AND SO THIS LAST BROTHER PREPARES TO LEAVE AS WELL? WHENEVER THE WARS TURN AGAINST YOU, YOU ABANDON YOUR TROOPS AND SCURRY FOR HOME.
HO HO HO...
YOU HAVEN'T CHANGED A WHIT, KUSHANA. NO MATTER HOW MANY TIMES I TELL YOU HOW MUCH I HATE PRESUMPTUOUS, INTELLECTUAL WOMEN, YOU JUST WON'T LISTEN. IT IS EVER THIS WAY...

Ah, yes... NOW I REMEMBER. THERE WAS ANOTHER WOMAN LIKE THAT, ONCE--THE ONE WHO GAVE YOU BIRTH.

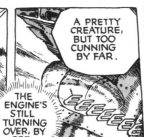

A PRETTY CREATURE, BUT TOO CUNNING BY FAR.

THE ENGINE'S STILL TURNING OVER, BY GOD...

EEEEEEE

I WENT AND SAW HER NOT LONG AGO.

I WAS RATHER SURPRISED. TO IMAGINE THAT SHE'D STILL BE ALIVE! THAT IS, IF YOU CALL THAT *LIVING...*

DON'T YOU DARE TOUCH MY MOTHER!

HAVE SOME DECENCY! LEAVE HER IN PEACE!

HO HO HO... WHO WOULD *WANT* TO TOUCH A DISGUSTING CREATURE LIKE THAT?

SHE DOES NOTHING BUT HUDDLE IN A CORNER OF HER ROOM, TREMBLING AND CLUTCHING A FILTHY DOLL.

IT WAS QUITE HORRIBLE...

HRRG!

THIS BODES ILL... KUSHANA THE ICE QUEEN IS LOSING HER TEMPER...

SILENCE! WHO WAS IT THAT MADE HER THAT WAY!?!

I WILL PERMIT *NO ONE* TO INSULT MY MOTHER! *NO ONE!!*

THIS IS GETTING WORSE... I'VE GOT TO BUY US SOME TIME...

HHHNN... ΛΛΛΛ....

OUCH... DAMNED RIBS ARE BROKEN...

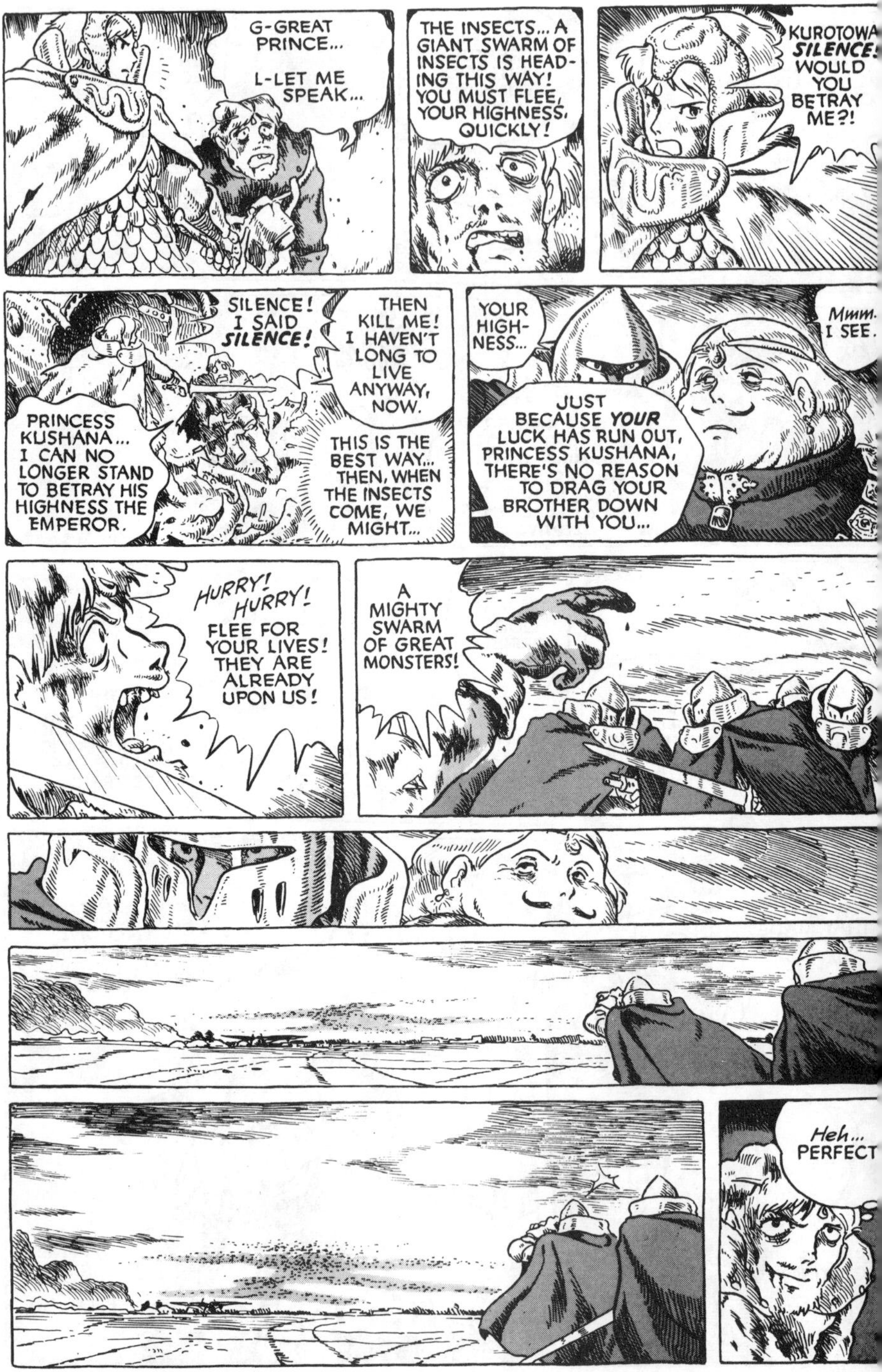
G-GREAT PRINCE... L-LET ME SPEAK...
THE INSECTS... A GIANT SWARM OF INSECTS IS HEADING THIS WAY! YOU MUST FLEE, YOUR HIGHNESS, QUICKLY!
KUROTOWA SILENCE! WOULD YOU BETRAY ME?!
SILENCE! I SAID SILENCE!
PRINCESS KUSHANA... I CAN NO LONGER STAND TO BETRAY HIS HIGHNESS THE EMPEROR.
THEN KILL ME! I HAVEN'T LONG TO LIVE ANYWAY, NOW.
THIS IS THE BEST WAY... THEN, WHEN THE INSECTS COME, WE MIGHT...
YOUR HIGHNESS...
JUST BECAUSE YOUR LUCK HAS RUN OUT, PRINCESS KUSHANA, THERE'S NO REASON TO DRAG YOUR BROTHER DOWN WITH YOU...
Mmm. I SEE.
HURRY! HURRY!
FLEE FOR YOUR LIVES! THEY ARE ALREADY UPON US!
A MIGHTY SWARM OF GREAT MONSTERS!
Heh... PERFECT

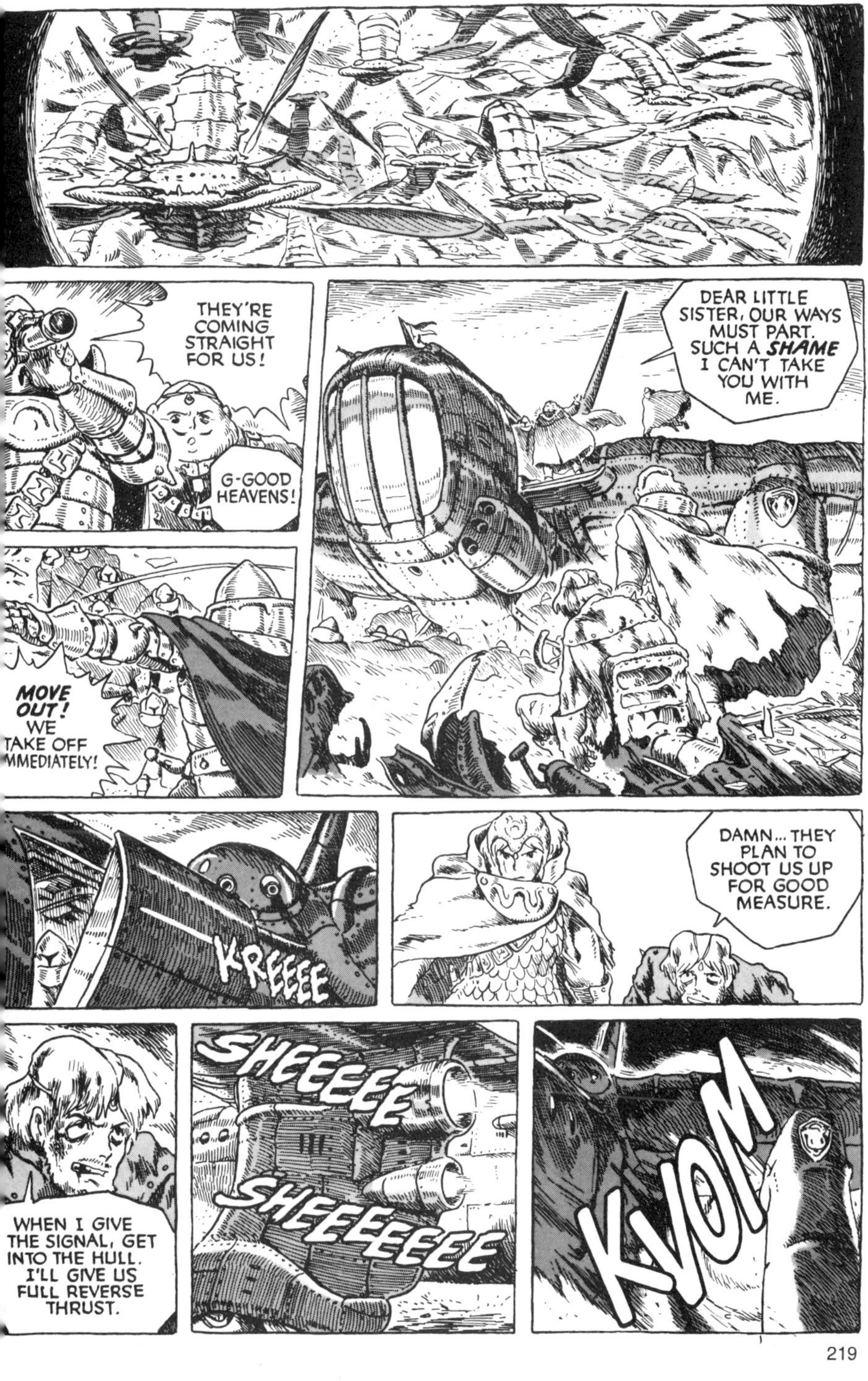
THEY'RE COMING STRAIGHT FOR US!
G-GOOD HEAVENS!
DEAR LITTLE SISTER, OUR WAYS MUST PART. SUCH A SHAME I CAN'T TAKE YOU WITH ME.
MOVE OUT! WE TAKE OFF IMMEDIATELY!
KREEEEE
DAMN... THEY PLAN TO SHOOT US UP FOR GOOD MEASURE.
WHEN I GIVE THE SIGNAL, GET INTO THE HULL. I'LL GIVE US FULL REVERSE THRUST.
SHEEEEEE
SHEEEEEEEEE
KVOM

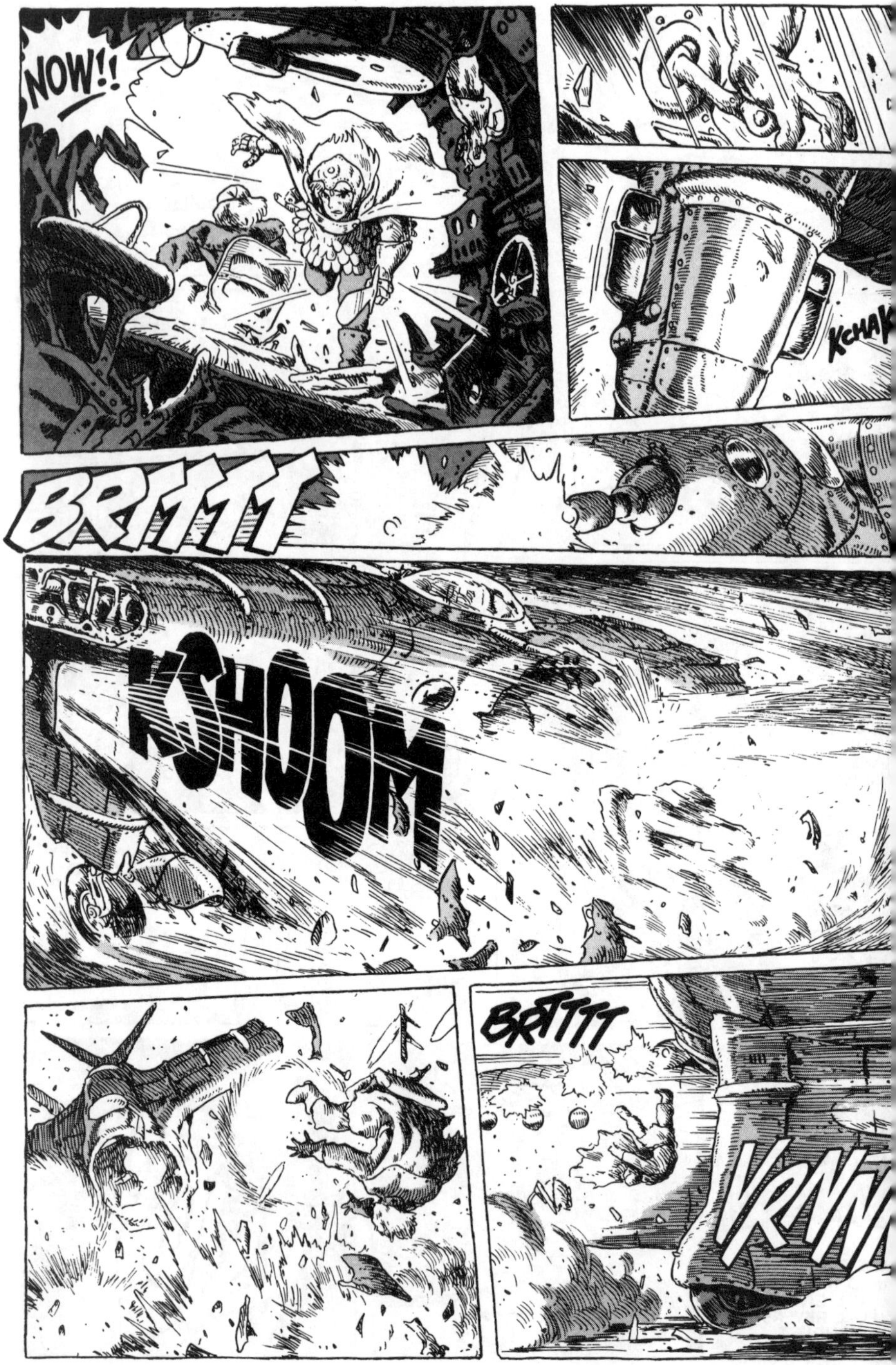
NOW!!
KCHAK
BRTTTT
KSHOOM
BRTTTT
VRNN

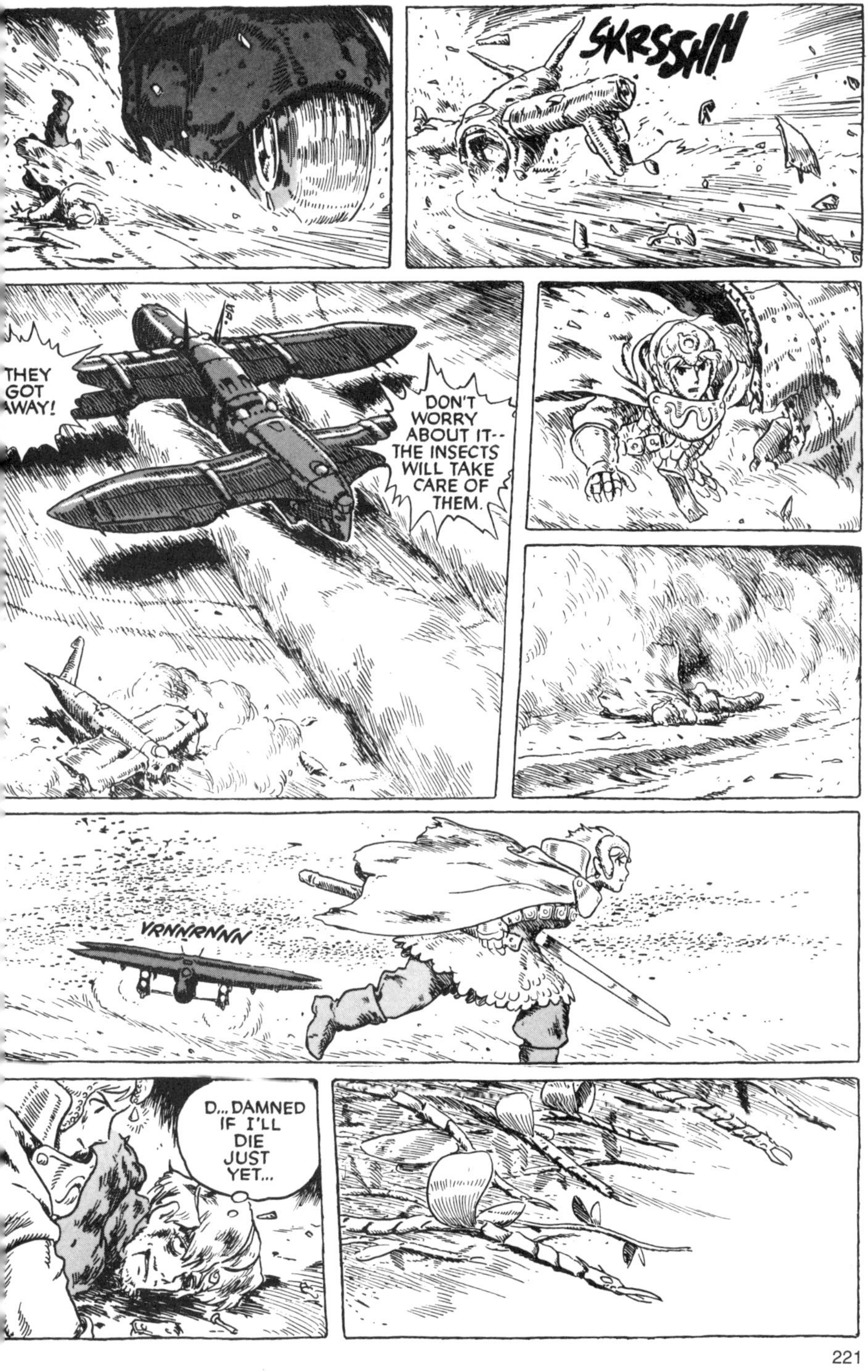
SKRSSHH
THEY GOT AWAY!
DON'T WORRY ABOUT IT-- THE INSECTS WILL TAKE CARE OF THEM.
VRNNRNNN
D...DAMNED IF I'LL DIE JUST YET...

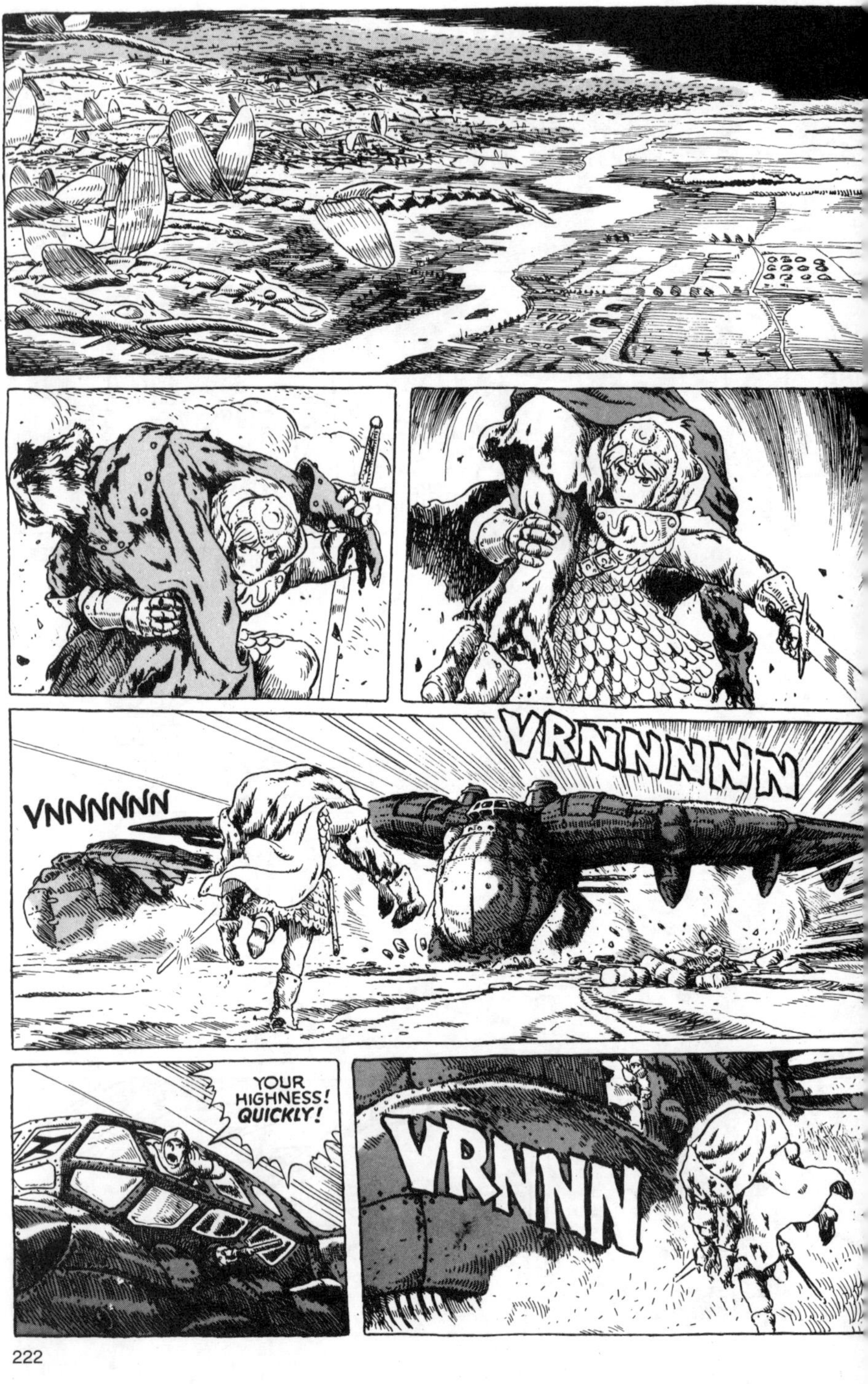
VRNNNNNN
VNNNNNN
YOUR HIGHNESS! QUICKLY!
VRNNN

VRNNRNN

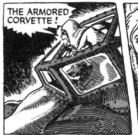

THE ARMORED
CORVETTE!

KRAK

SKNCH

SPRAKK

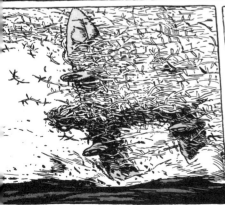

WHKOO OOM

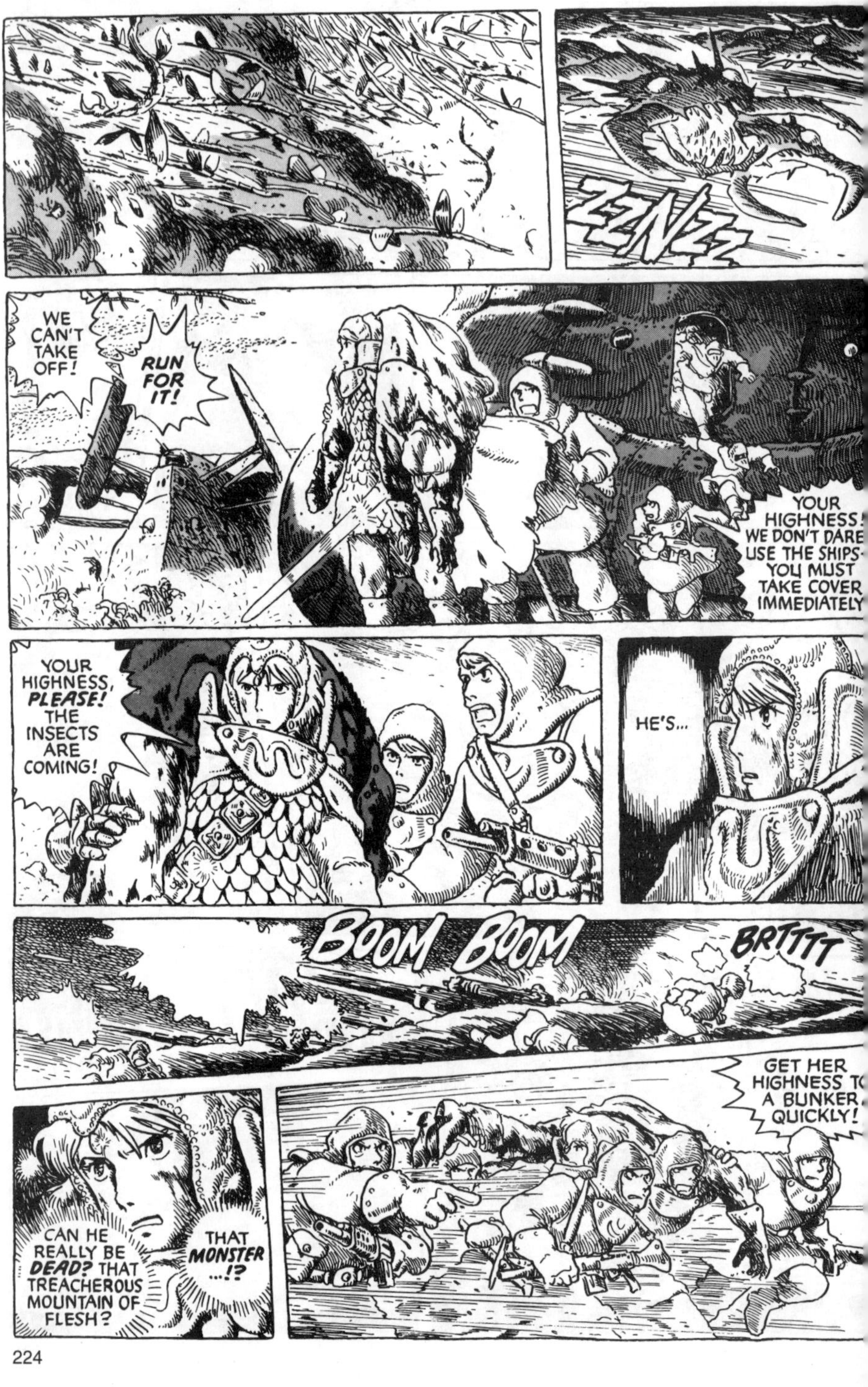
ZZNZZ
WE CAN'T TAKE OFF!
RUN FOR IT!
YOUR HIGHNESS! WE DON'T DARE USE THE SHIPS- YOU MUST TAKE COVER IMMEDIATELY
YOUR HIGHNESS, PLEASE! THE INSECTS ARE COMING!
HE'S...
BOOM BOOM
BRTTTT
GET HER HIGHNESS TO A BUNKER, QUICKLY!
CAN HE REALLY BE DEAD? THAT TREACHEROUS MOUNTAIN OF FLESH?
THAT MONSTER ...!?

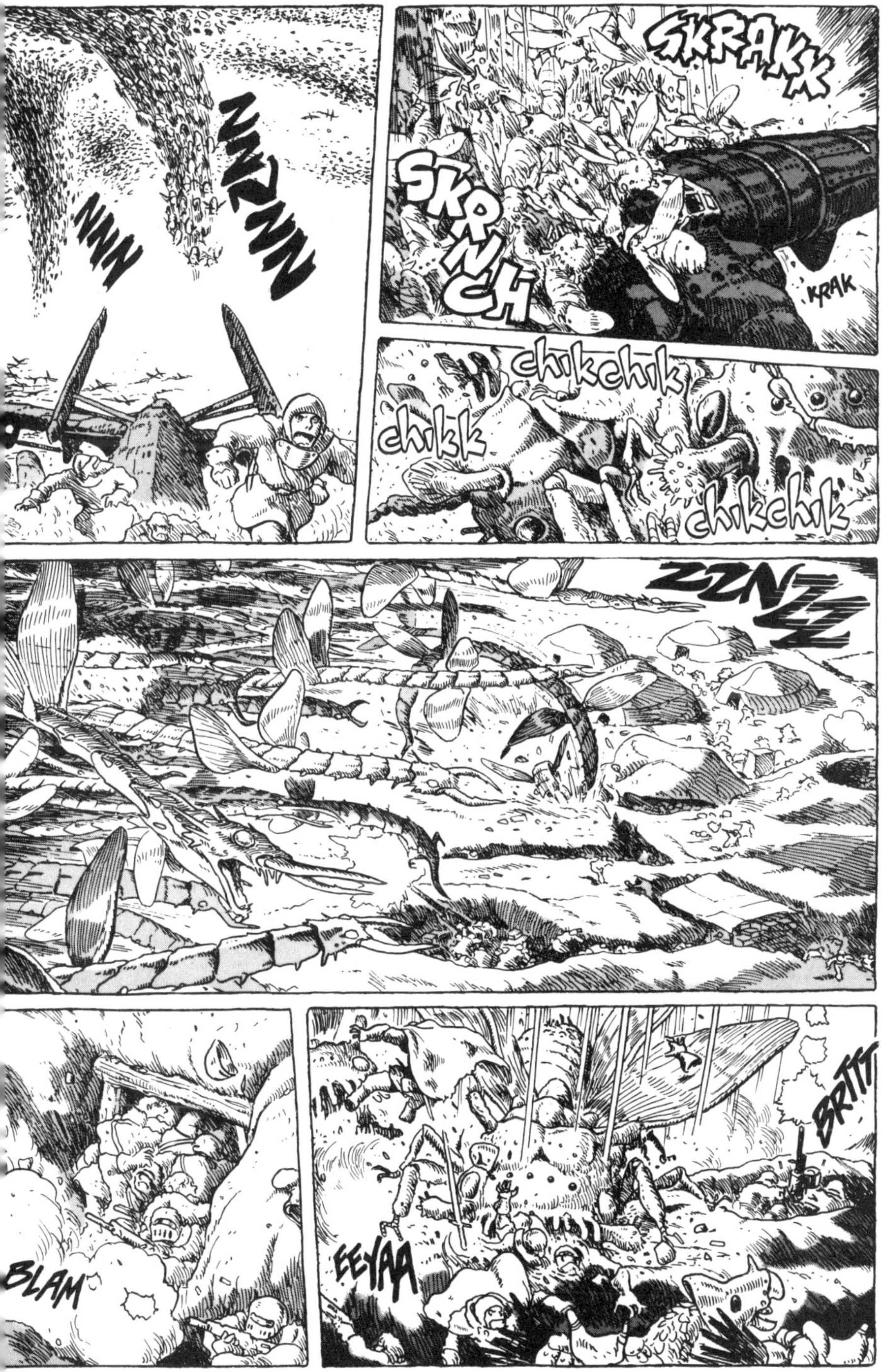
NNN
SKRAKK
SKRNCH
KRAK
chikchik
chikk
chikchik
ZZNZZ
BLAM
EEYAA
BRTTT

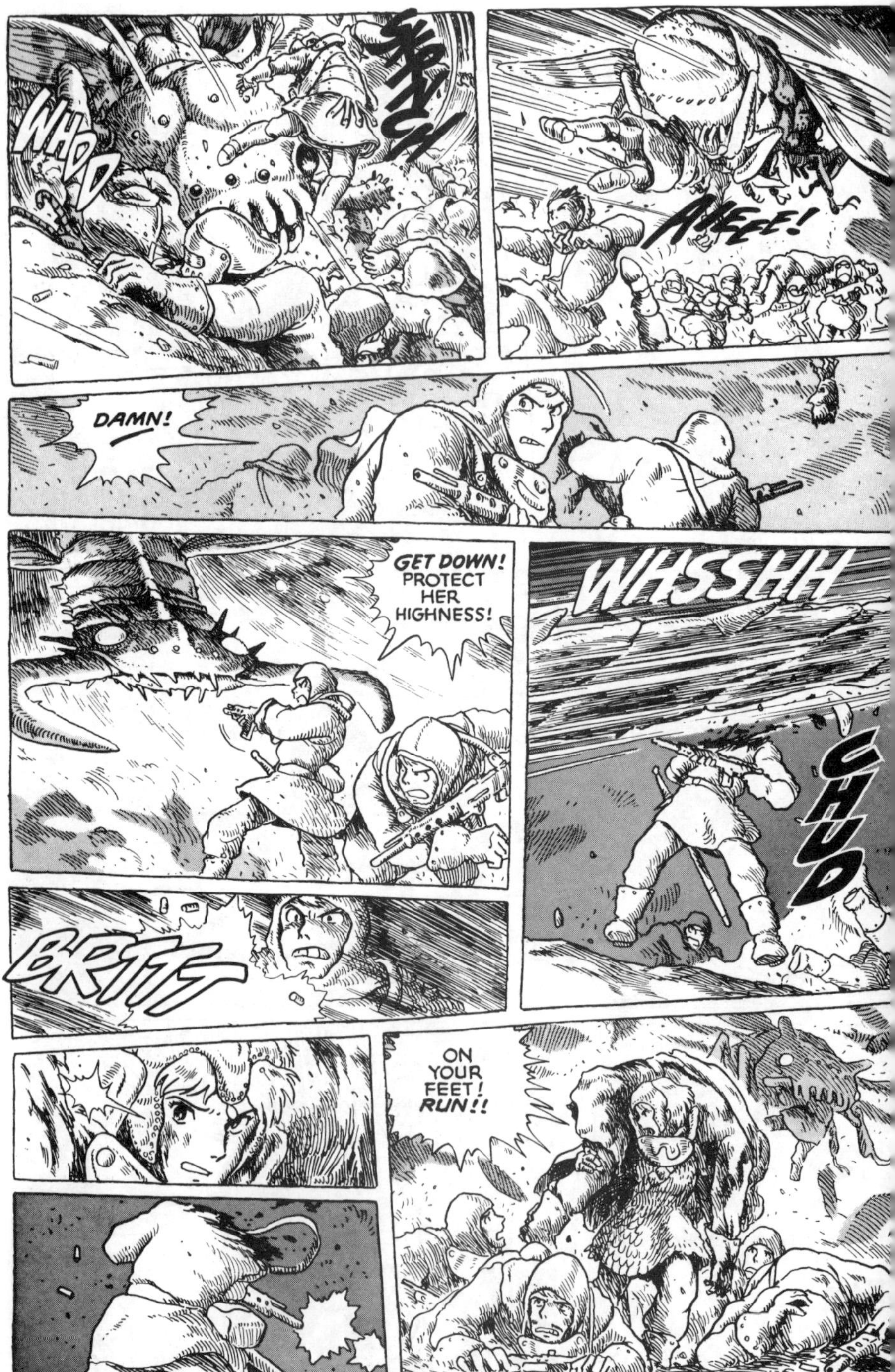
WHOOD
SKRUNCH
AIEEEE!
DAMN!
GET DOWN! PROTECT HER HIGHNESS!
WHSSHH
CHUD
BRTTT
ON YOUR FEET! RUN!!

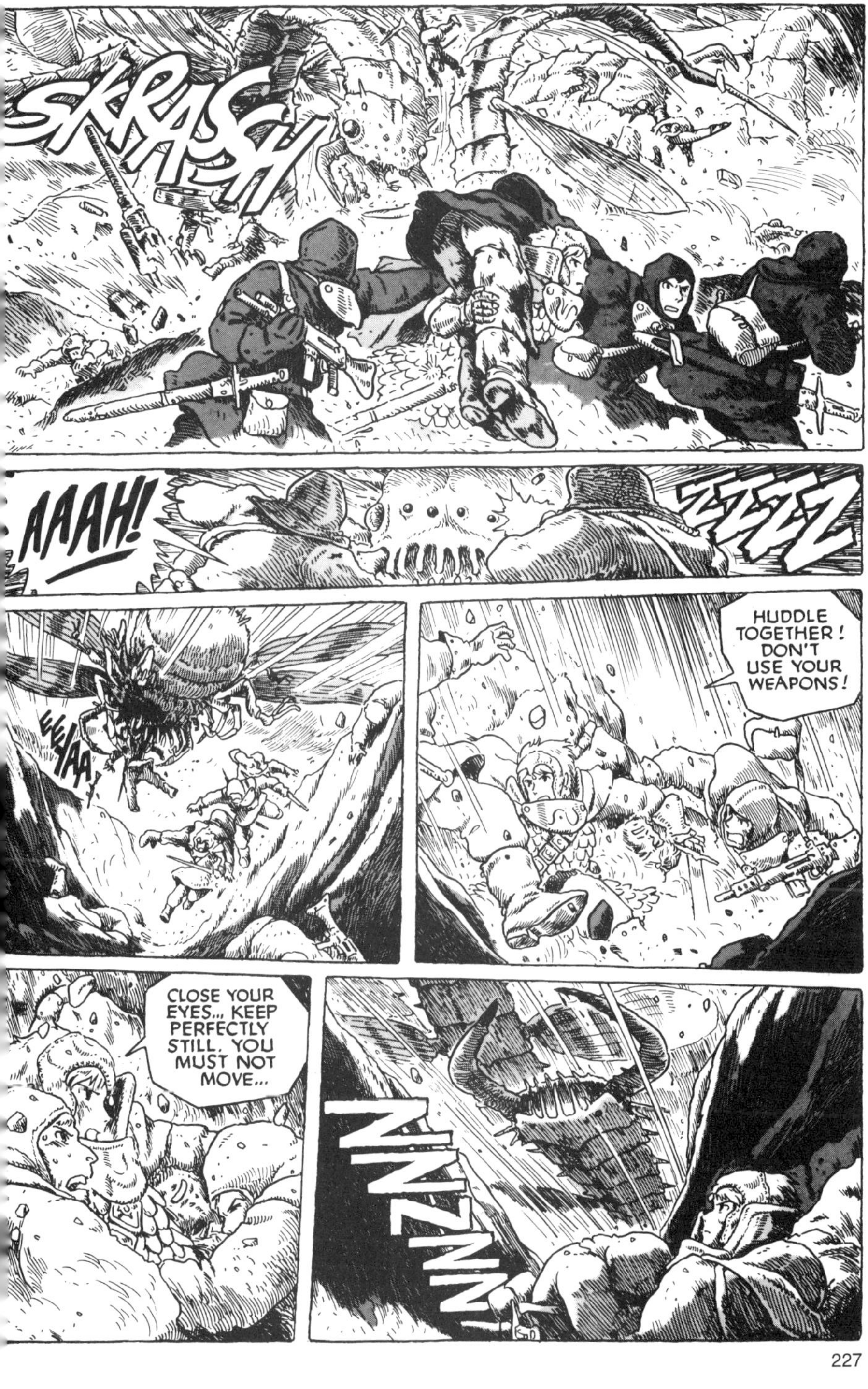
SKRASH
AAAH!
ZZZZZ
WEHAA
HUDDLE TOGETHER! DON'T USE YOUR WEAPONS!
CLOSE YOUR EYES... KEEP PERFECTLY STILL. YOU MUST NOT MOVE...
NNNNN

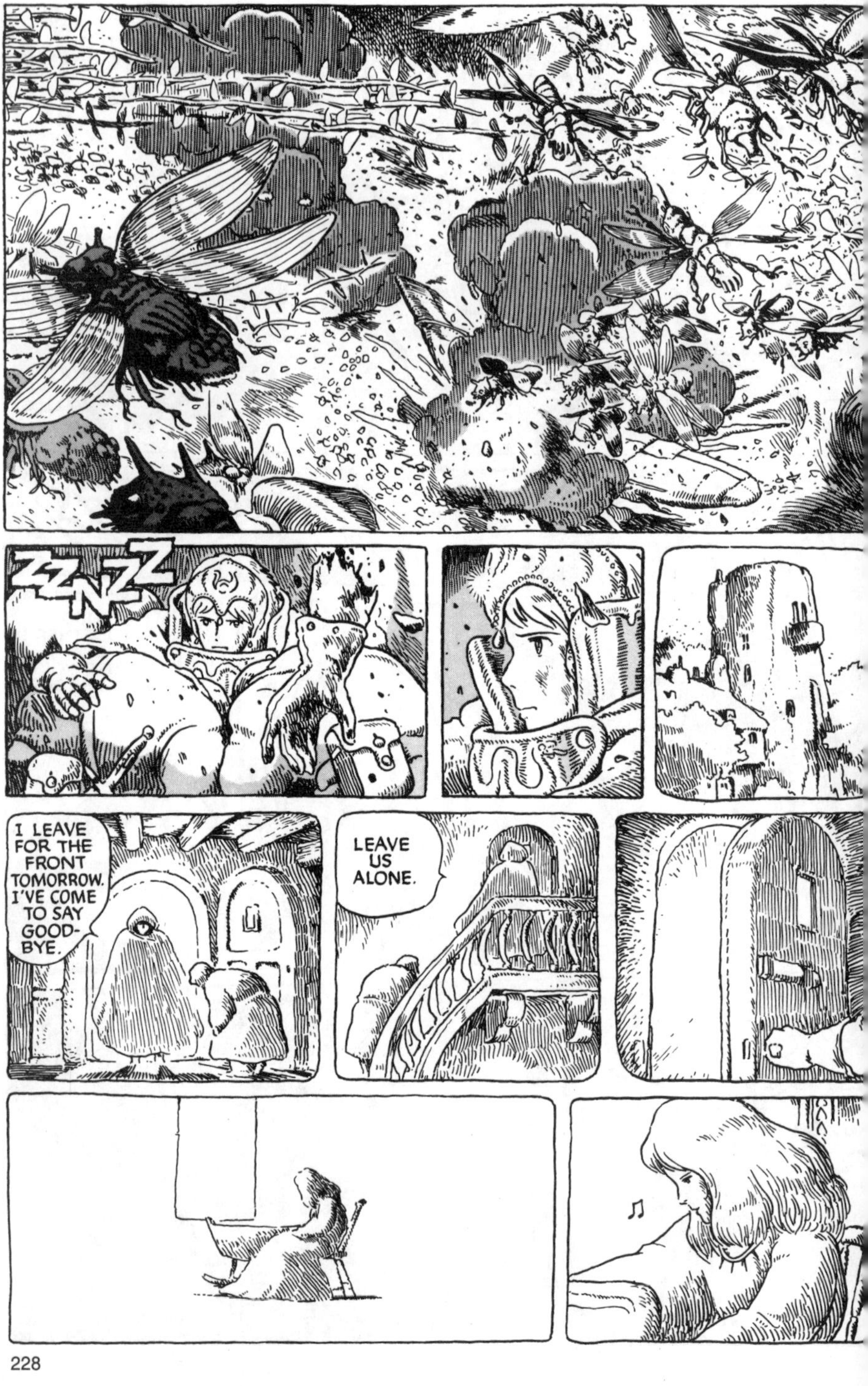
ZZNZZ
I LEAVE FOR THE FRONT TOMORROW. I'VE COME TO SAY GOOD-BYE.
LEAVE US ALONE.

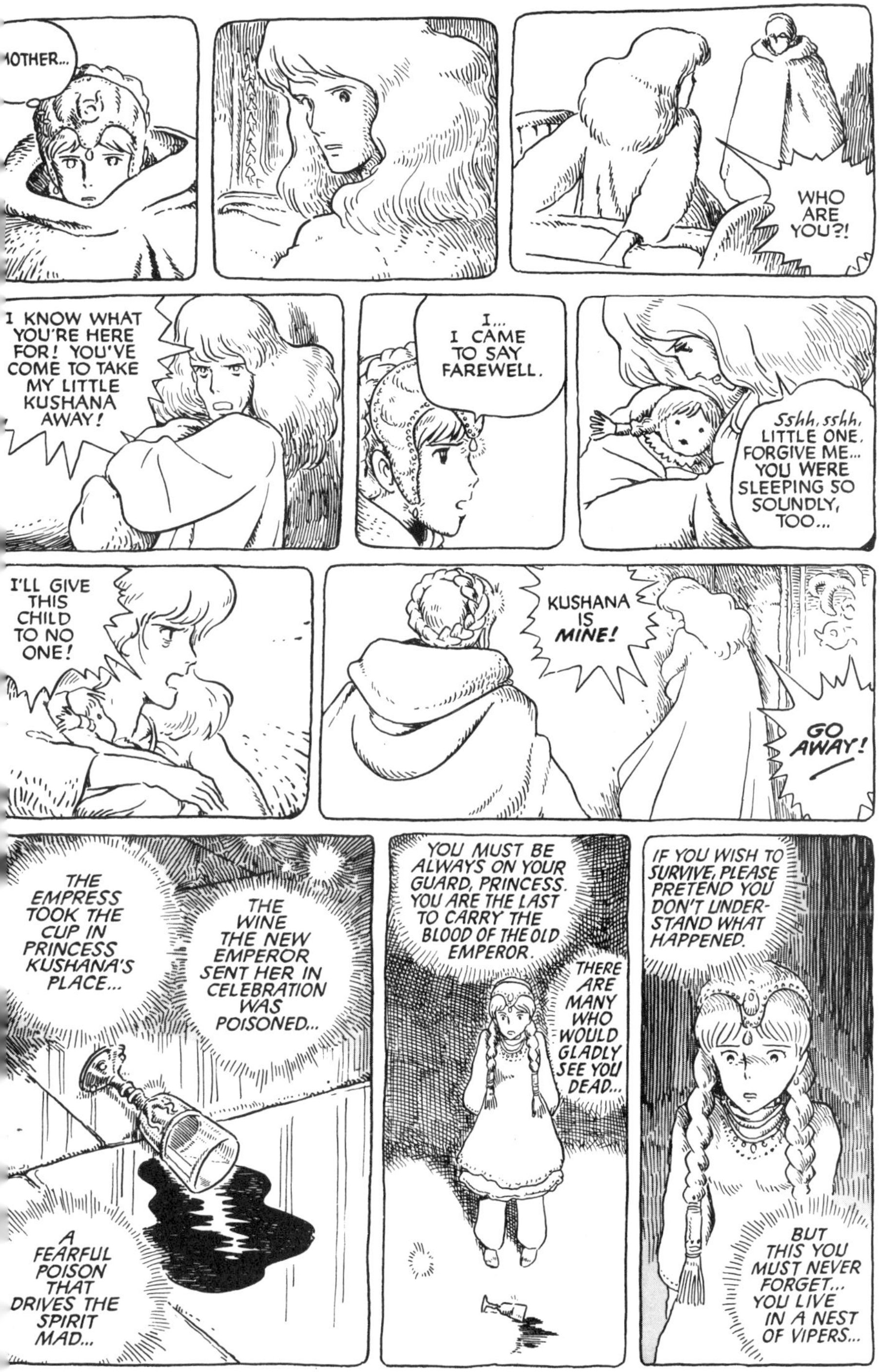
MOTHER...
WHO ARE YOU?!
I KNOW WHAT YOU'RE HERE FOR! YOU'VE COME TO TAKE MY LITTLE KUSHANA AWAY!
I... I CAME TO SAY FAREWELL.
Sshh, sshh, LITTLE ONE. FORGIVE ME... YOU WERE SLEEPING SO SOUNDLY, TOO...
I'LL GIVE THIS CHILD TO NO ONE!
KUSHANA IS MINE!
GO AWAY!
THE EMPRESS TOOK THE CUP IN PRINCESS KUSHANA'S PLACE...
THE WINE THE NEW EMPEROR SENT HER IN CELEBRATION WAS POISONED...
A FEARFUL POISON THAT DRIVES THE SPIRIT MAD...
YOU MUST BE ALWAYS ON YOUR GUARD, PRINCESS. YOU ARE THE LAST TO CARRY THE BLOOD OF THE OLD EMPEROR.
THERE ARE MANY WHO WOULD GLADLY SEE YOU DEAD...
IF YOU WISH TO SURVIVE, PLEASE PRETEND YOU DON'T UNDERSTAND WHAT HAPPENED.
BUT THIS YOU MUST NEVER FORGET... YOU LIVE IN A NEST OF VIPERS...

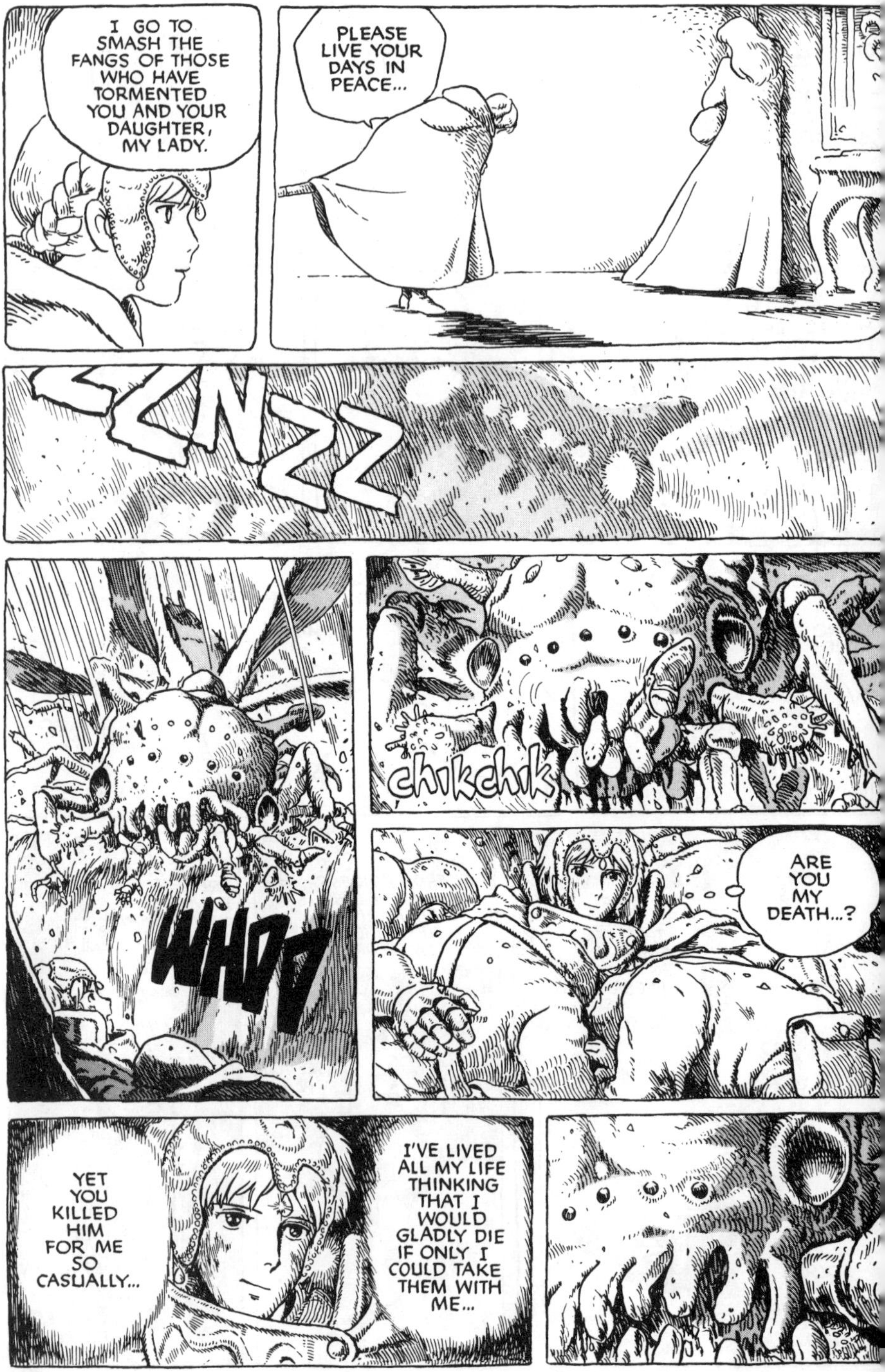
I GO TO SMASH THE FANGS OF THOSE WHO HAVE TORMENTED YOU AND YOUR DAUGHTER, MY LADY.
PLEASE LIVE YOUR DAYS IN PEACE...
ZZNZZ
WHOO
chikchik
ARE YOU MY DEATH...?
I'VE LIVED ALL MY LIFE THINKING THAT I WOULD GLADLY DIE IF ONLY I COULD TAKE THEM WITH ME...
YET YOU KILLED HIM FOR ME SO CASUALLY...

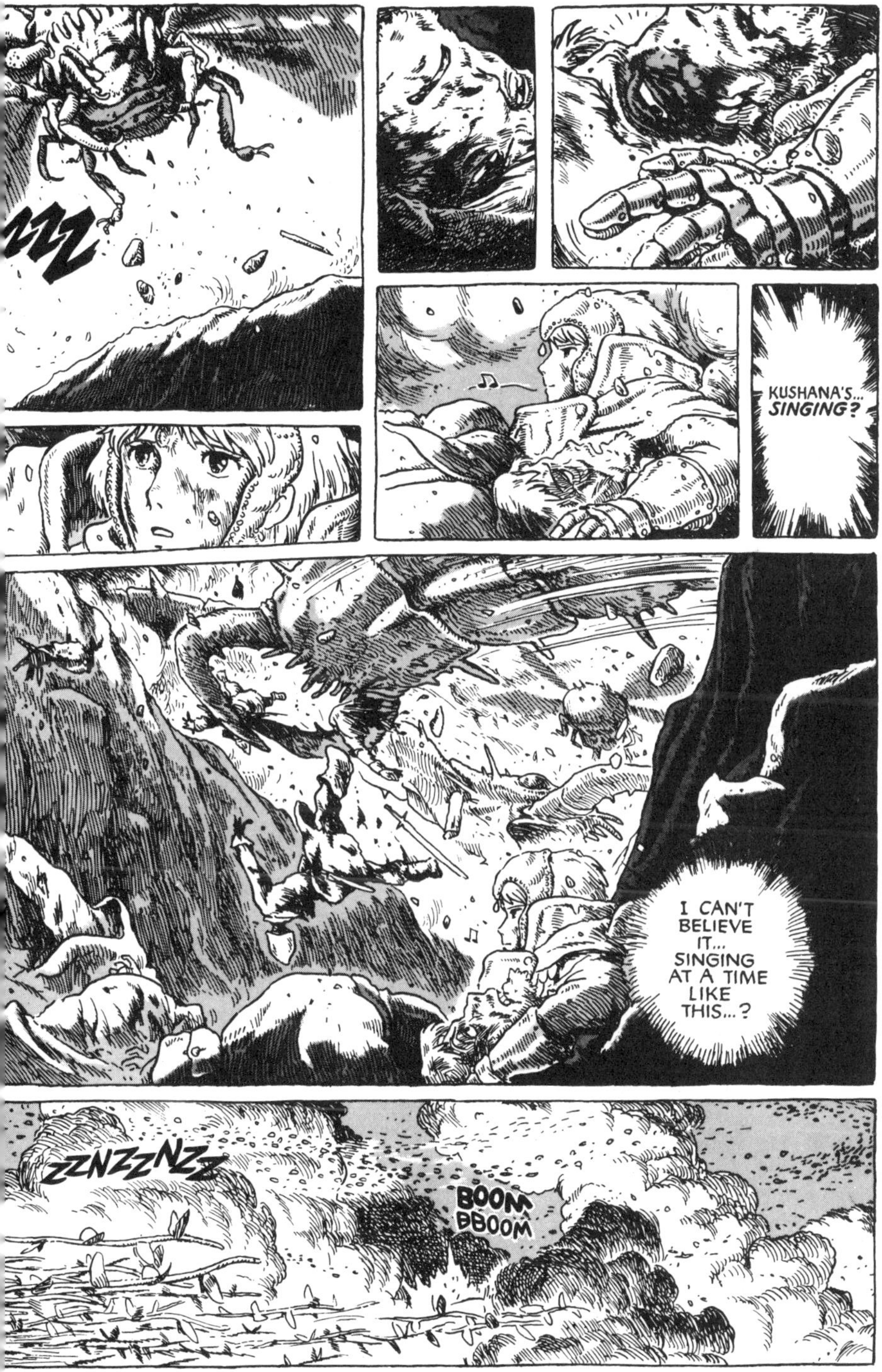
ZZZ
KUSHANA'S... SINGING?
I CAN'T BELIEVE IT... SINGING AT A TIME LIKE THIS...?
ZZNZZNZZ
BOOM BBOOM

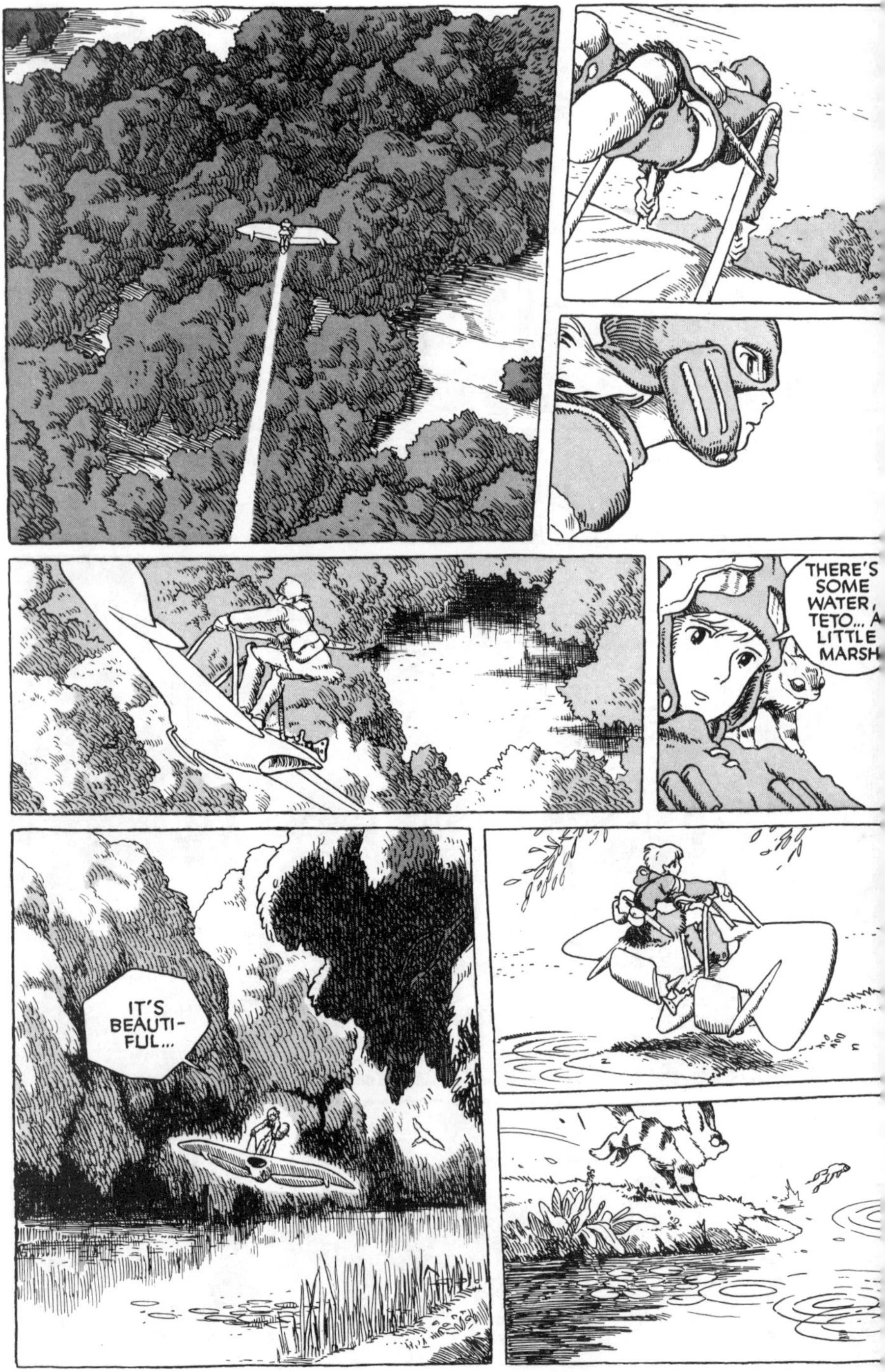
THERE'S SOME WATER, TETO... A LITTLE MARSH
IT'S BEAUTI-FUL...

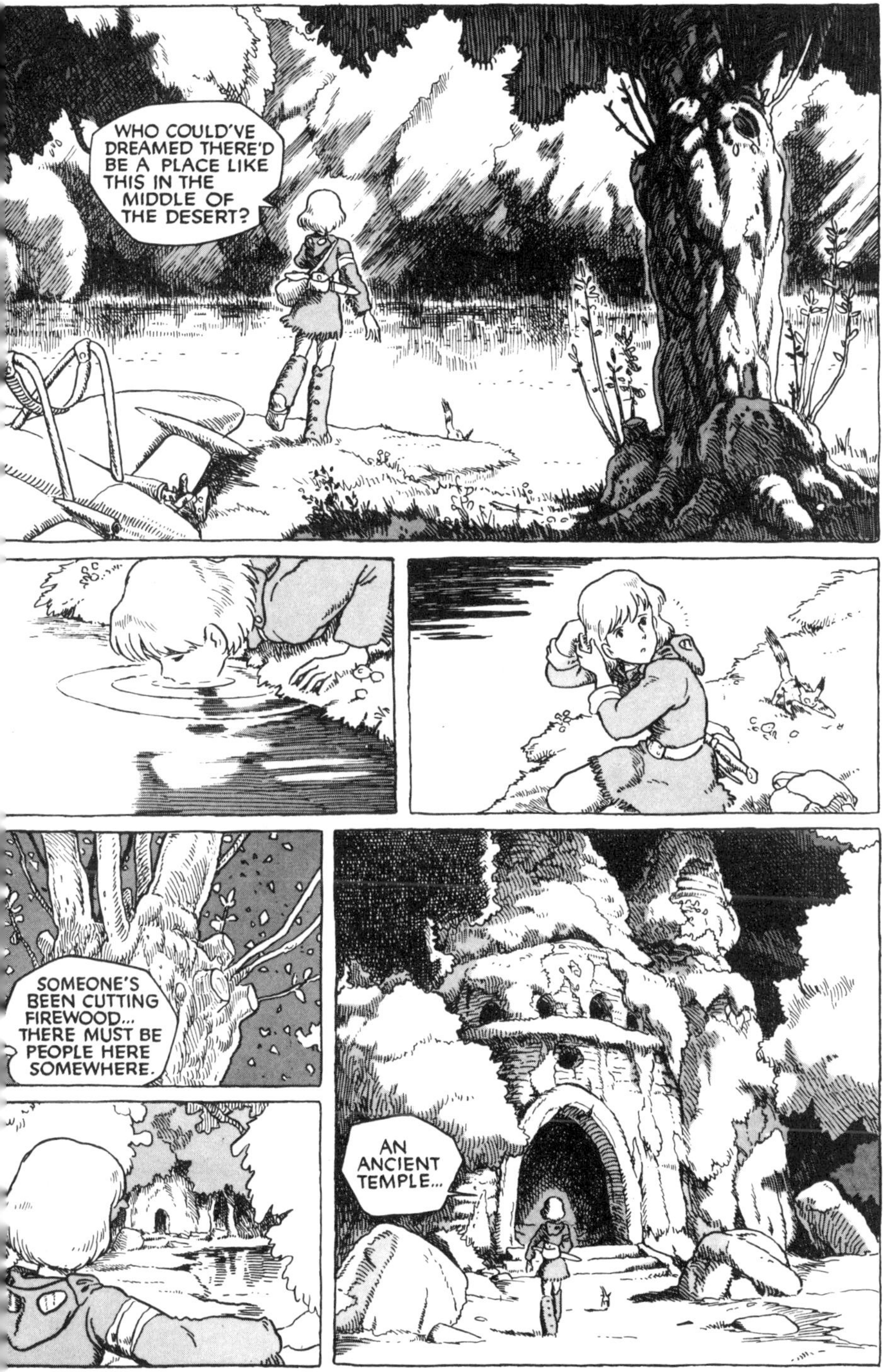
WHO COULD'VE DREAMED THERE'D BE A PLACE LIKE THIS IN THE MIDDLE OF THE DESERT?
SOMEONE'S BEEN CUTTING FIREWOOD... THERE MUST BE PEOPLE HERE SOMEWHERE.
AN ANCIENT TEMPLE...

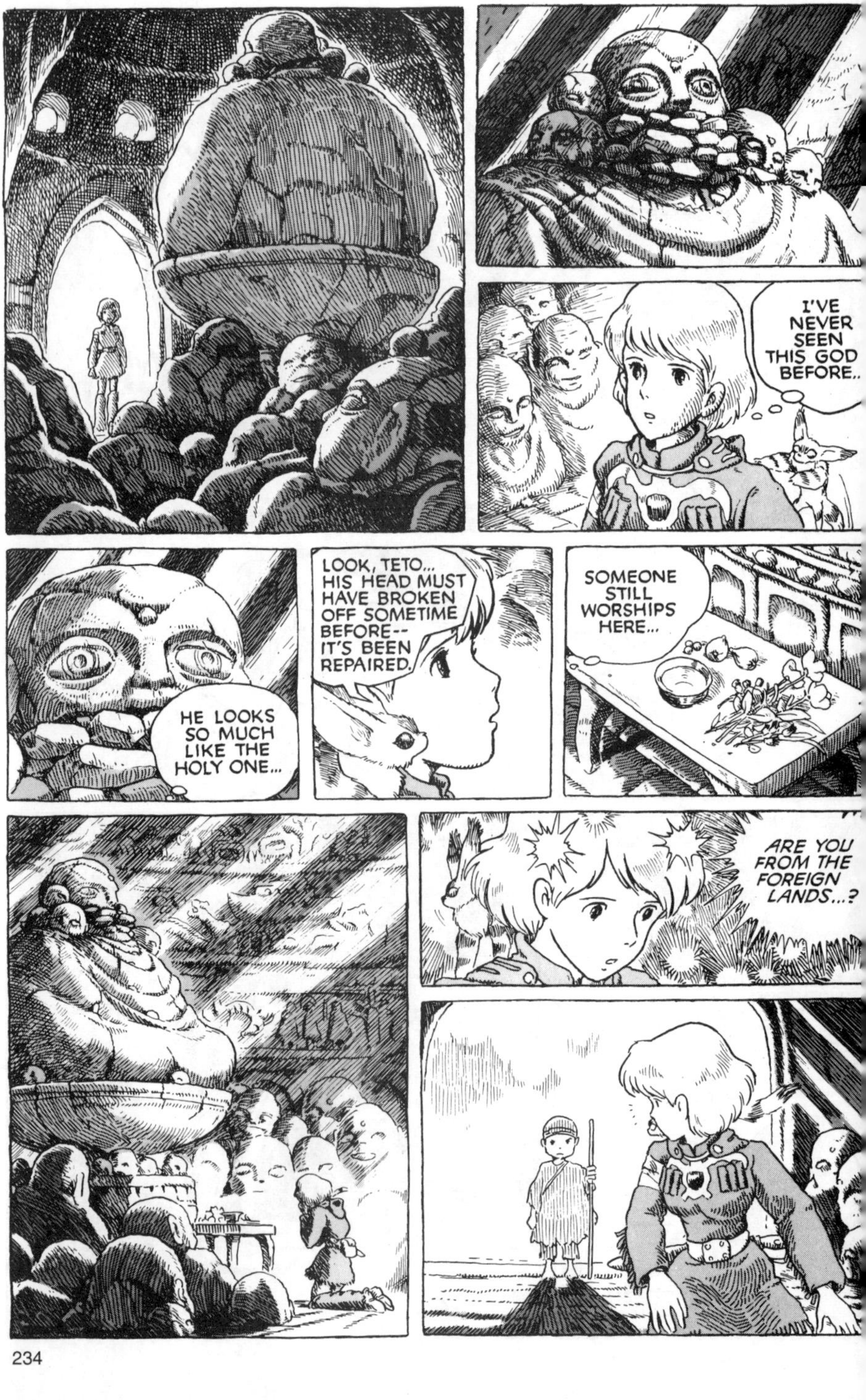
I'VE NEVER SEEN THIS GOD BEFORE..
HE LOOKS SO MUCH LIKE THE HOLY ONE...
LOOK, TETO... HIS HEAD MUST HAVE BROKEN OFF SOMETIME BEFORE-- IT'S BEEN REPAIRED.
SOMEONE STILL WORSHIPS HERE...
ARE YOU FROM THE FOREIGN LANDS...?

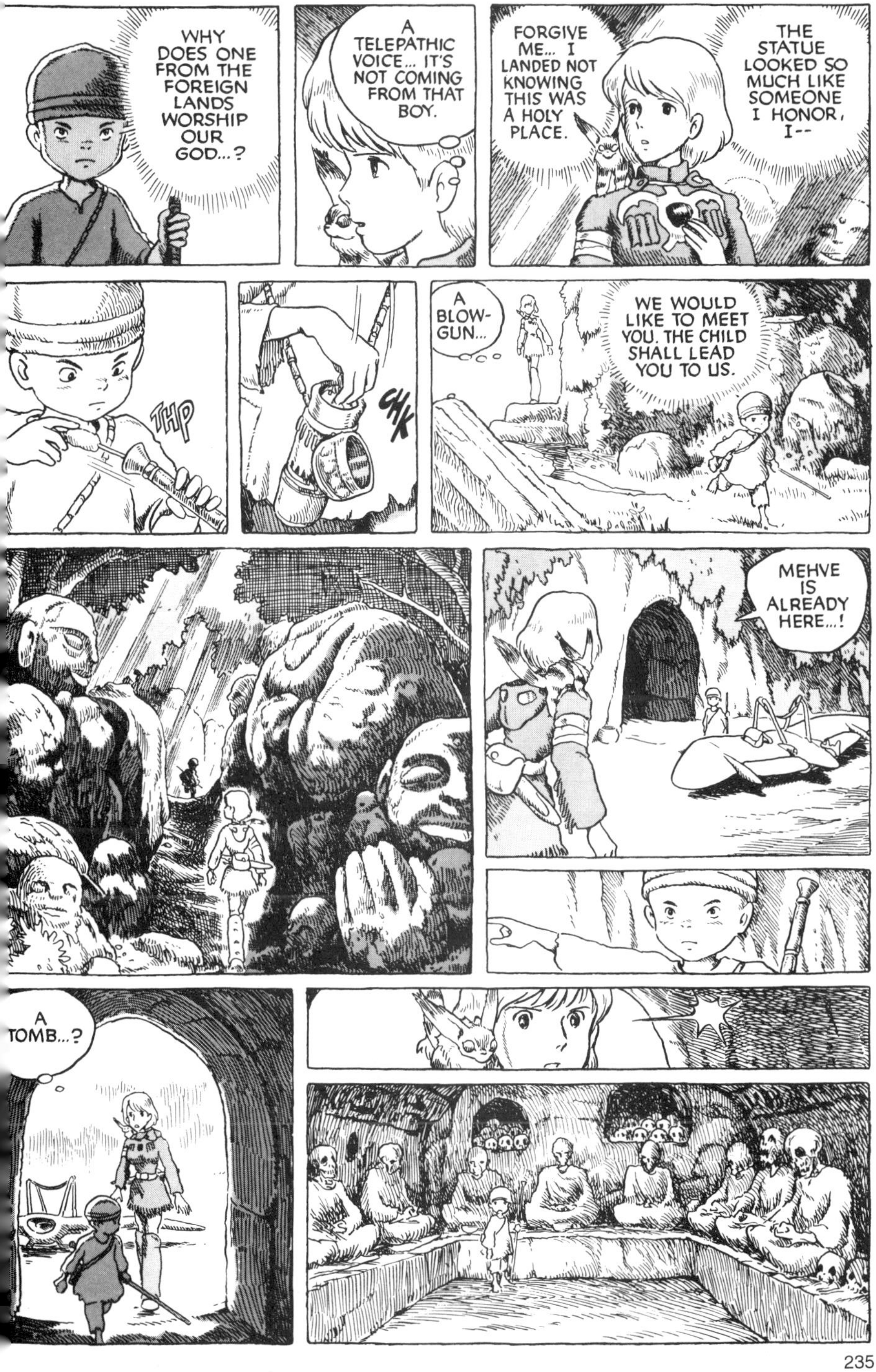
WHY DOES ONE FROM THE FOREIGN LANDS WORSHIP OUR GOD...?
A TELEPATHIC VOICE... IT'S NOT COMING FROM THAT BOY.
FORGIVE ME... I LANDED NOT KNOWING THIS WAS A HOLY PLACE.
THE STATUE LOOKED SO MUCH LIKE SOMEONE I HONOR, I--
THP
CHK
A BLOW-GUN...
WE WOULD LIKE TO MEET YOU. THE CHILD SHALL LEAD YOU TO US.
MEHVE IS ALREADY HERE...!
A TOMB...?

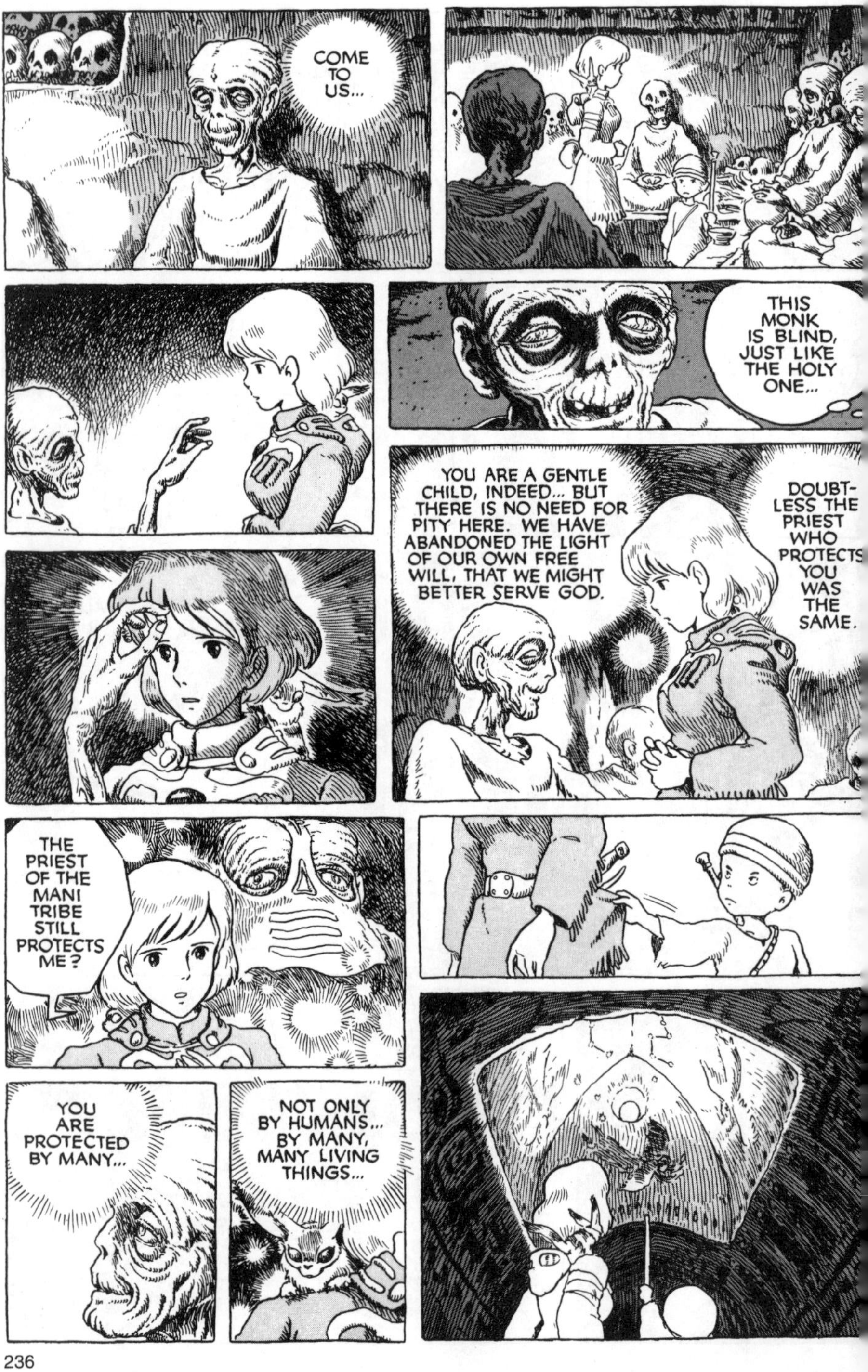
COME TO US...
THIS MONK IS BLIND, JUST LIKE THE HOLY ONE...
YOU ARE A GENTLE CHILD, INDEED... BUT THERE IS NO NEED FOR PITY HERE. WE HAVE ABANDONED THE LIGHT OF OUR OWN FREE WILL, THAT WE MIGHT BETTER SERVE GOD.
DOUBTLESS THE PRIEST WHO PROTECTS YOU WAS THE SAME.
THE PRIEST OF THE MANI TRIBE STILL PROTECTS ME?
YOU ARE PROTECTED BY MANY...
NOT ONLY BY HUMANS... BY MANY, MANY LIVING THINGS...

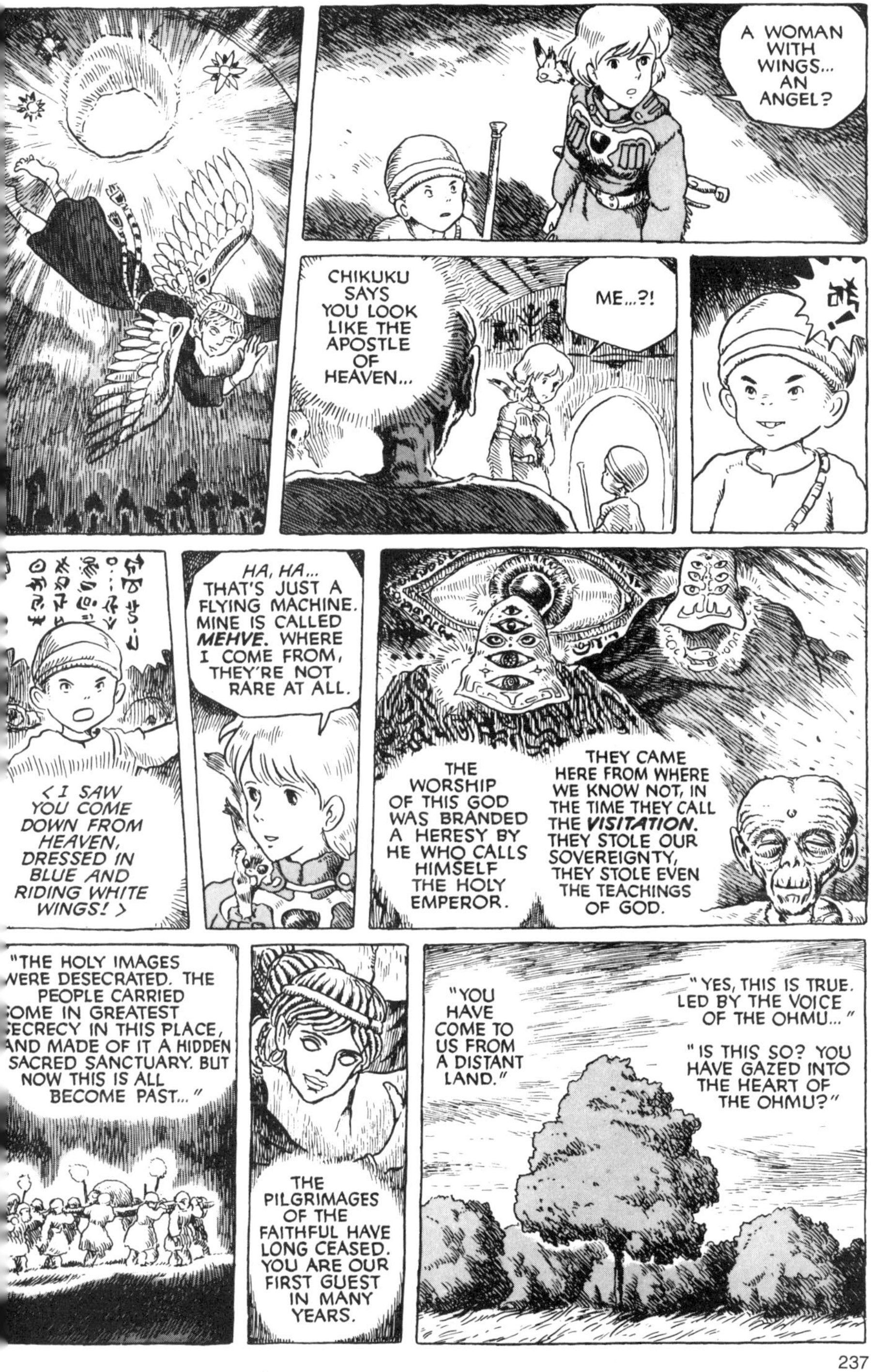

A WOMAN WITH WINGS... AN ANGEL?
CHIKUKU SAYS YOU LOOK LIKE THE APOSTLE OF HEAVEN...
ME...?!
<I SAW YOU COME DOWN FROM HEAVEN, DRESSED IN BLUE AND RIDING WHITE WINGS!>
HA, HA... THAT'S JUST A FLYING MACHINE. MINE IS CALLED MEHVE. WHERE I COME FROM, THEY'RE NOT RARE AT ALL.
THE WORSHIP OF THIS GOD WAS BRANDED A HERESY BY HE WHO CALLS HIMSELF THE HOLY EMPEROR.
THEY CAME HERE FROM WHERE WE KNOW NOT, IN THE TIME THEY CALL THE VISITATION. THEY STOLE OUR SOVEREIGNTY, THEY STOLE EVEN THE TEACHINGS OF GOD.
"THE HOLY IMAGES WERE DESECRATED. THE PEOPLE CARRIED SOME IN GREATEST SECRECY IN THIS PLACE, AND MADE OF IT A HIDDEN SACRED SANCTUARY. BUT NOW THIS IS ALL BECOME PAST..."
THE PILGRIMAGES OF THE FAITHFUL HAVE LONG CEASED. YOU ARE OUR FIRST GUEST IN MANY YEARS.
"YOU HAVE COME TO US FROM A DISTANT LAND."
"YES, THIS IS TRUE. LED BY THE VOICE OF THE OHMU..."
"IS THIS SO? YOU HAVE GAZED INTO THE HEART OF THE OHMU?"

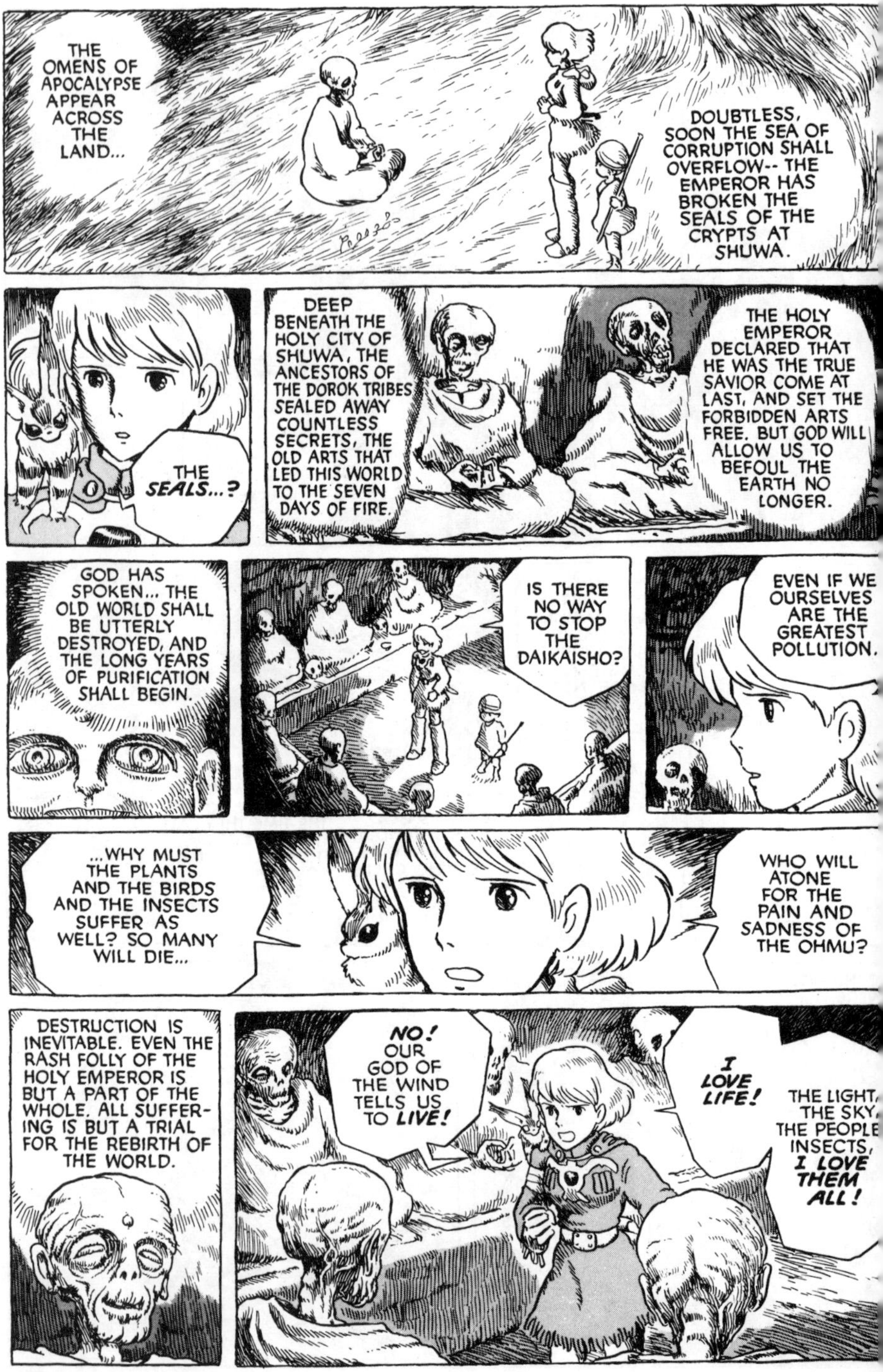
THE OMENS OF APOCALYPSE APPEAR ACROSS THE LAND...
DOUBTLESS, SOON THE SEA OF CORRUPTION SHALL OVERFLOW-- THE EMPEROR HAS BROKEN THE SEALS OF THE CRYPTS AT SHUWA.
THE SEALS...?
DEEP BENEATH THE HOLY CITY OF SHUWA, THE ANCESTORS OF THE DOROK TRIBES SEALED AWAY COUNTLESS SECRETS, THE OLD ARTS THAT LED THIS WORLD TO THE SEVEN DAYS OF FIRE.
THE HOLY EMPEROR DECLARED THAT HE WAS THE TRUE SAVIOR COME AT LAST, AND SET THE FORBIDDEN ARTS FREE. BUT GOD WILL ALLOW US TO BEFOUL THE EARTH NO LONGER.
GOD HAS SPOKEN... THE OLD WORLD SHALL BE UTTERLY DESTROYED, AND THE LONG YEARS OF PURIFICATION SHALL BEGIN.
IS THERE NO WAY TO STOP THE DAIKAISHO?
EVEN IF WE OURSELVES ARE THE GREATEST POLLUTION.
...WHY MUST THE PLANTS AND THE BIRDS AND THE INSECTS SUFFER AS WELL? SO MANY WILL DIE...
WHO WILL ATONE FOR THE PAIN AND SADNESS OF THE OHMU?
DESTRUCTION IS INEVITABLE. EVEN THE RASH FOLLY OF THE HOLY EMPEROR IS BUT A PART OF THE WHOLE. ALL SUFFERING IS BUT A TRIAL FOR THE REBIRTH OF THE WORLD.
NO! OUR GOD OF THE WIND TELLS US TO LIVE!
I LOVE LIFE!
THE LIGHT, THE SKY, THE PEOPLE INSECTS, I LOVE THEM ALL!

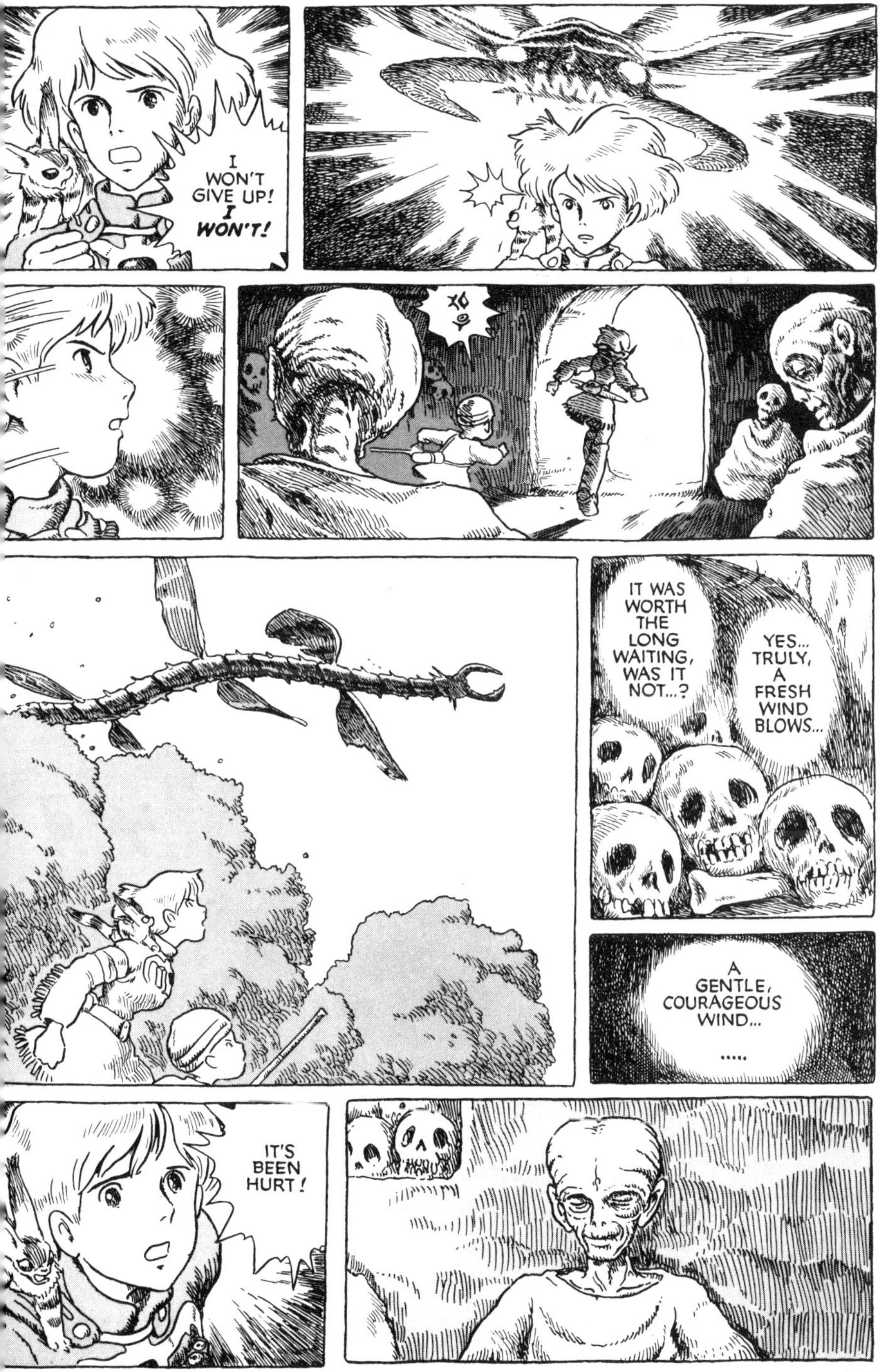
I WON'T GIVE UP! I WON'T!
IT WAS WORTH THE LONG WAITING, WAS IT NOT...?
YES... TRULY, A FRESH WIND BLOWS...
A GENTLE, COURAGEOUS WIND...
.....
IT'S BEEN HURT!

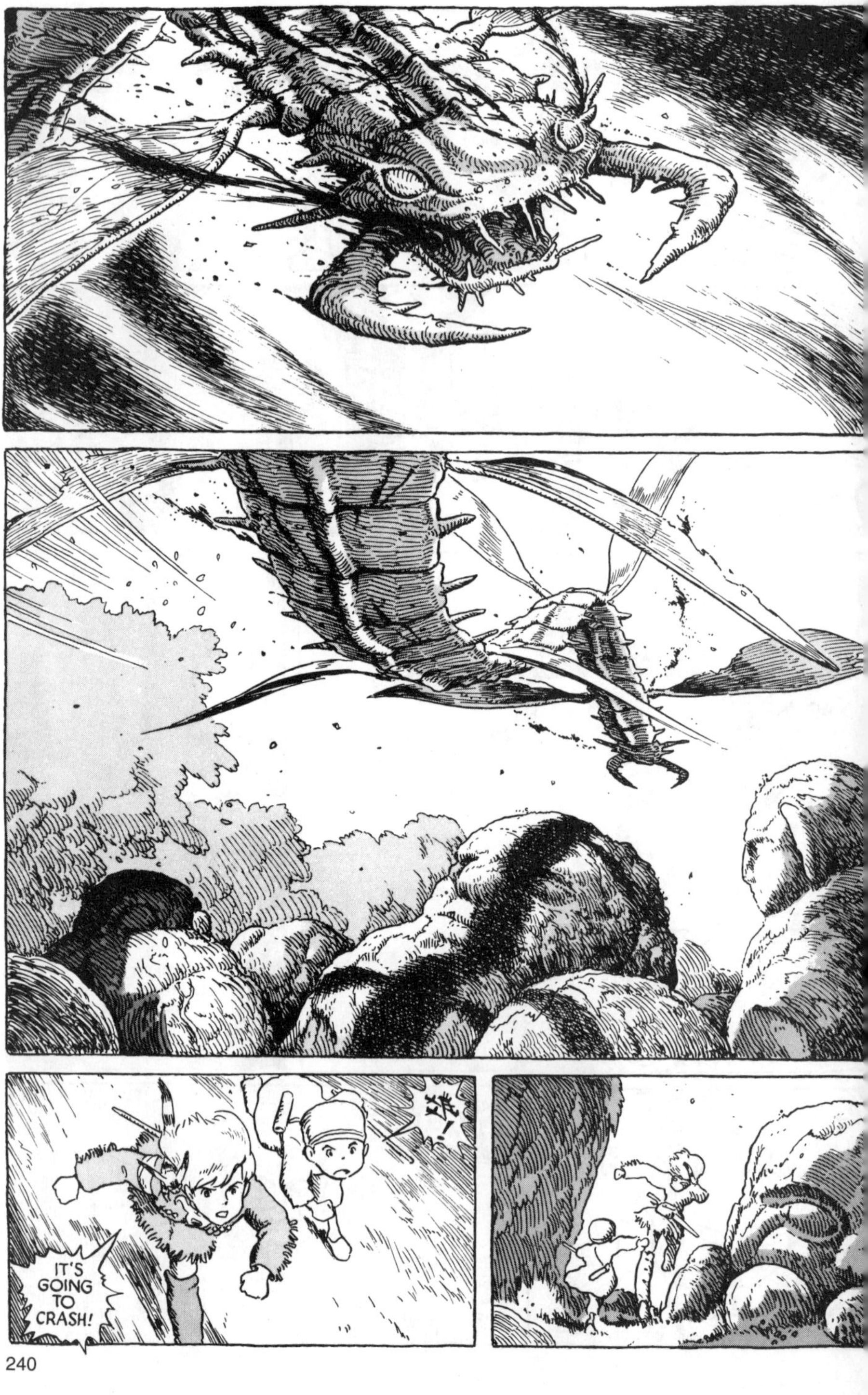
IT'S GOING TO CRASH!

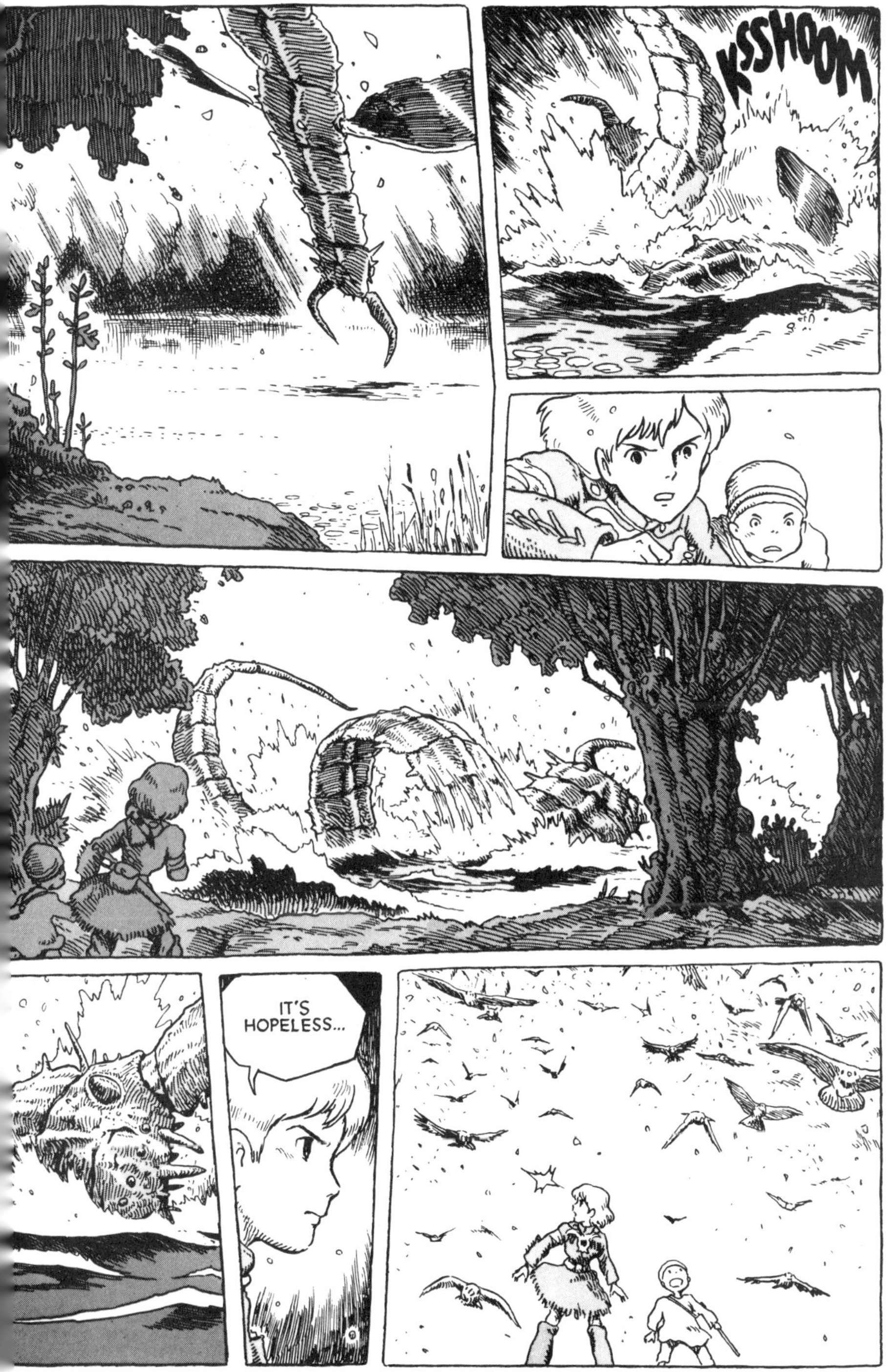
KSSHOOM
IT'S HOPELESS...

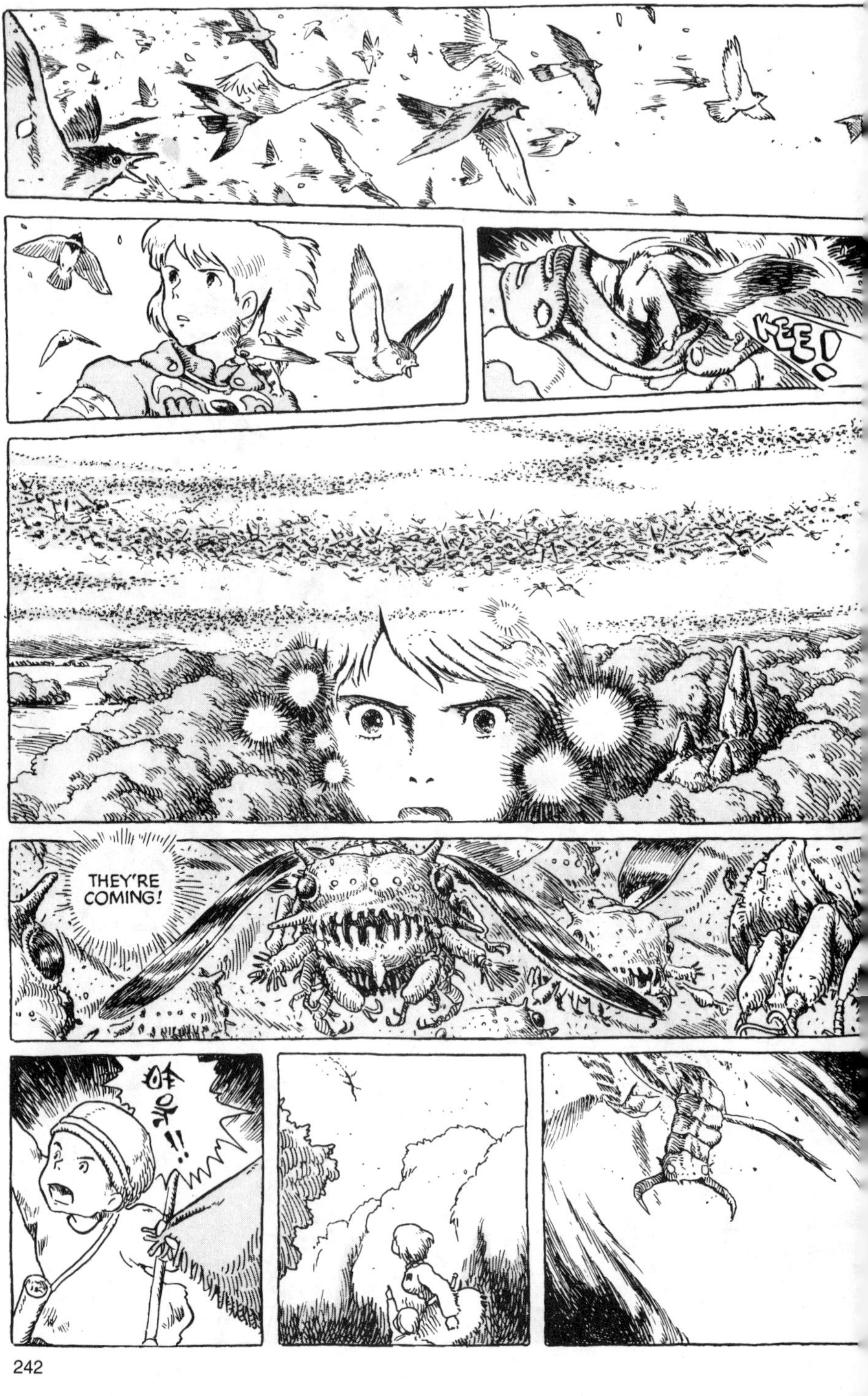
KEE!
THEY'RE COMING!

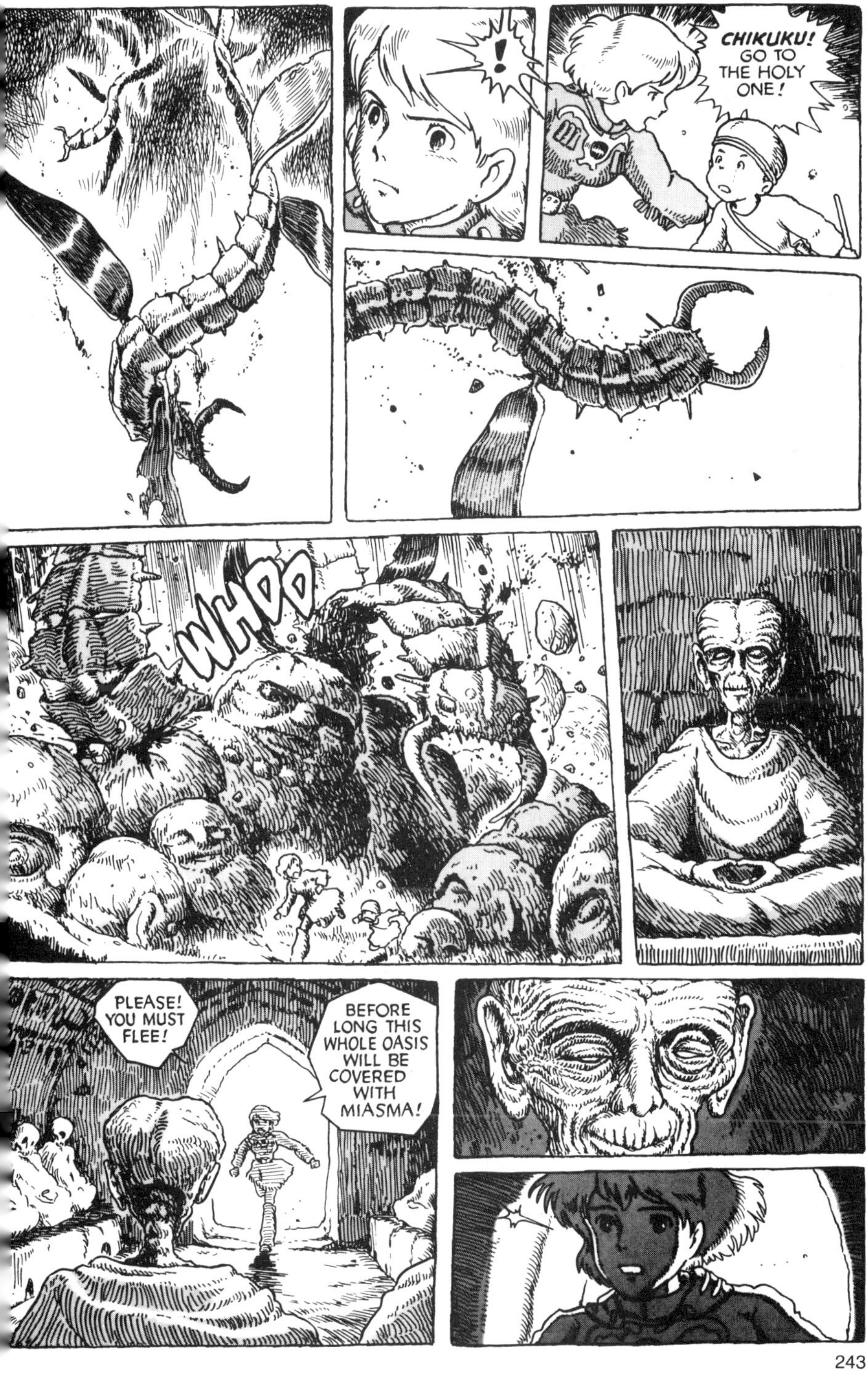
CHIKUKU! GO TO THE HOLY ONE!
WHOO
PLEASE! YOU MUST FLEE!
BEFORE LONG THIS WHOLE OASIS WILL BE COVERED WITH MIASMA!

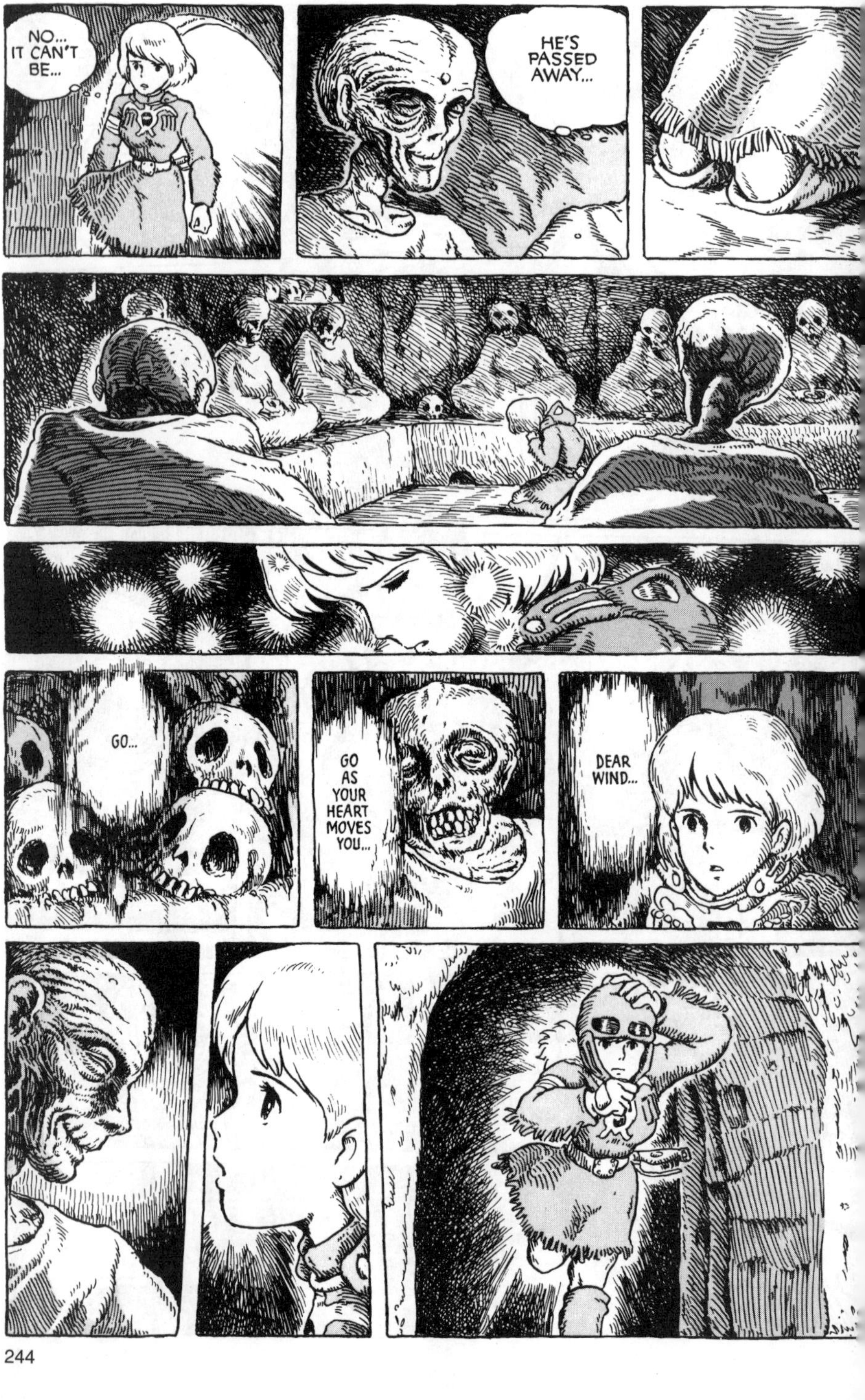

NO... IT CAN'T BE...
HE'S PASSED AWAY...
GO...
GO AS YOUR HEART MOVES YOU...
DEAR WIND...

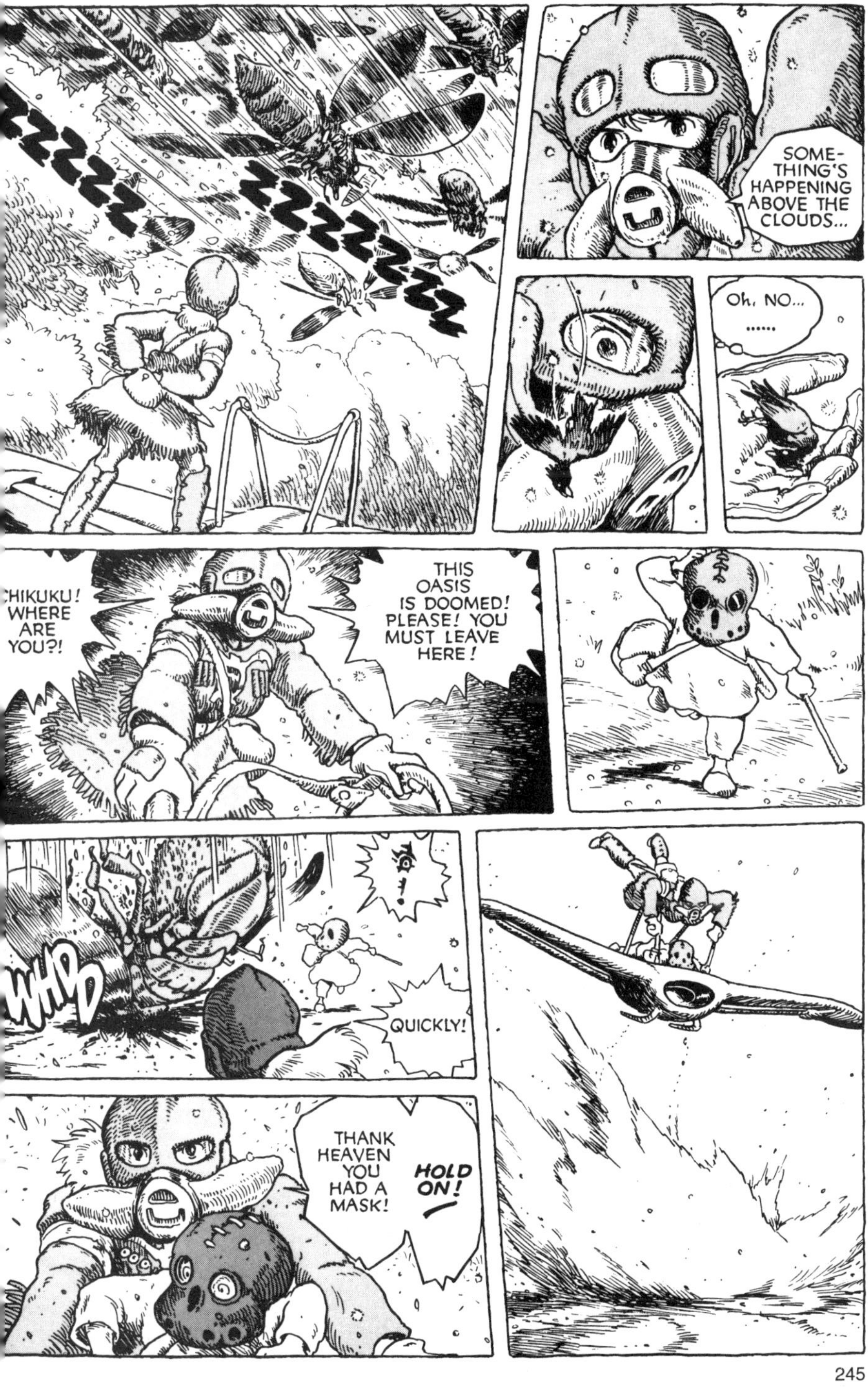

ZZZZZZ
ZZZZZZZZZ
SOME-THING'S HAPPENING ABOVE THE CLOUDS...
Oh, NO... ......
CHIKUKU! WHERE ARE YOU?!
THIS OASIS IS DOOMED! PLEASE! YOU MUST LEAVE HERE!
WHD
QUICKLY!
THANK HEAVEN YOU HAD A MASK!
HOLD ON!

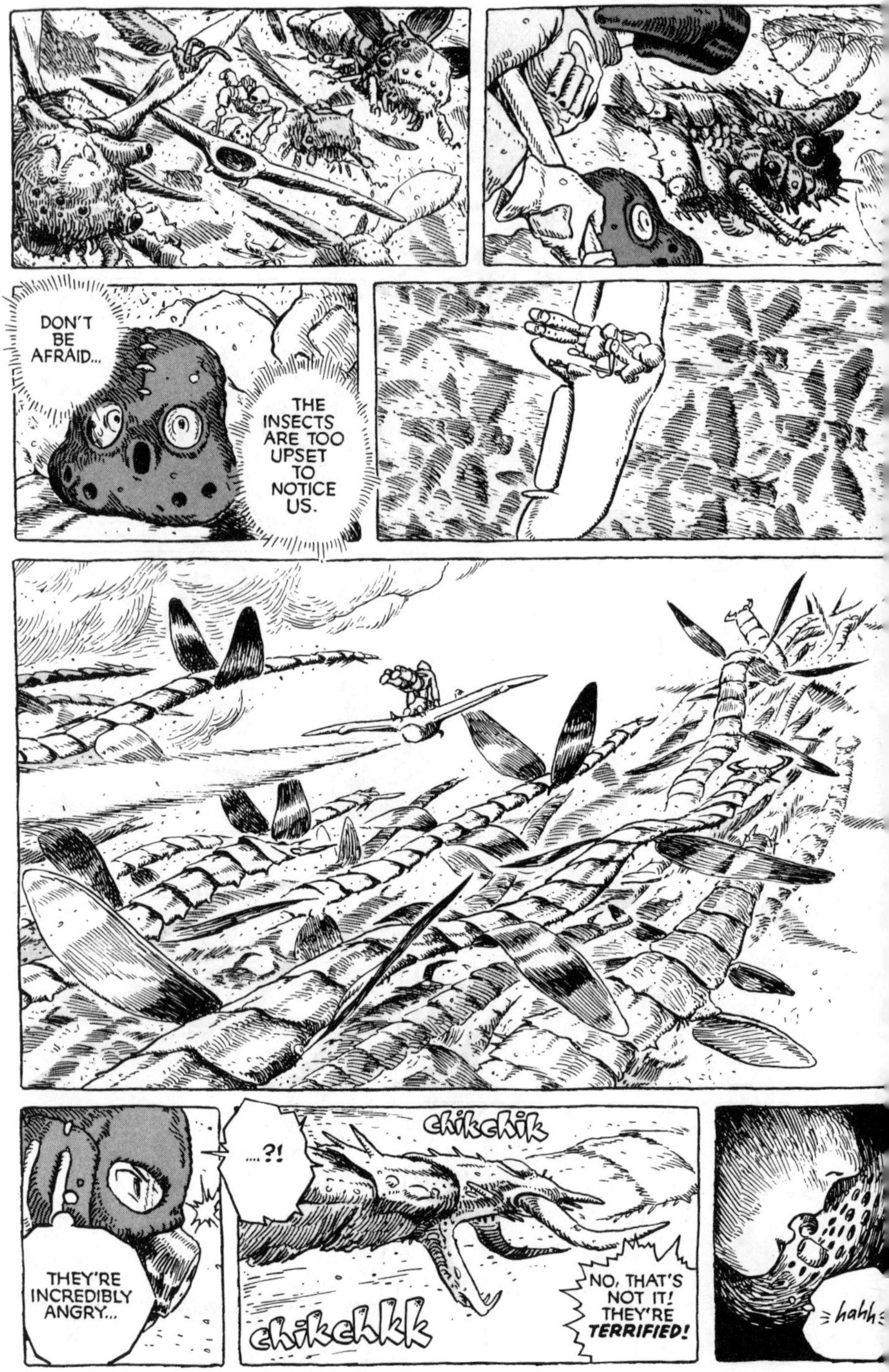
DON'T BE AFRAID...
THE INSECTS ARE TOO UPSET TO NOTICE US.
THEY'RE INCREDIBLY ANGRY...
....?!
chikchik
chikchkk
NO, THAT'S NOT IT! THEY'RE TERRIFIED!
hahh

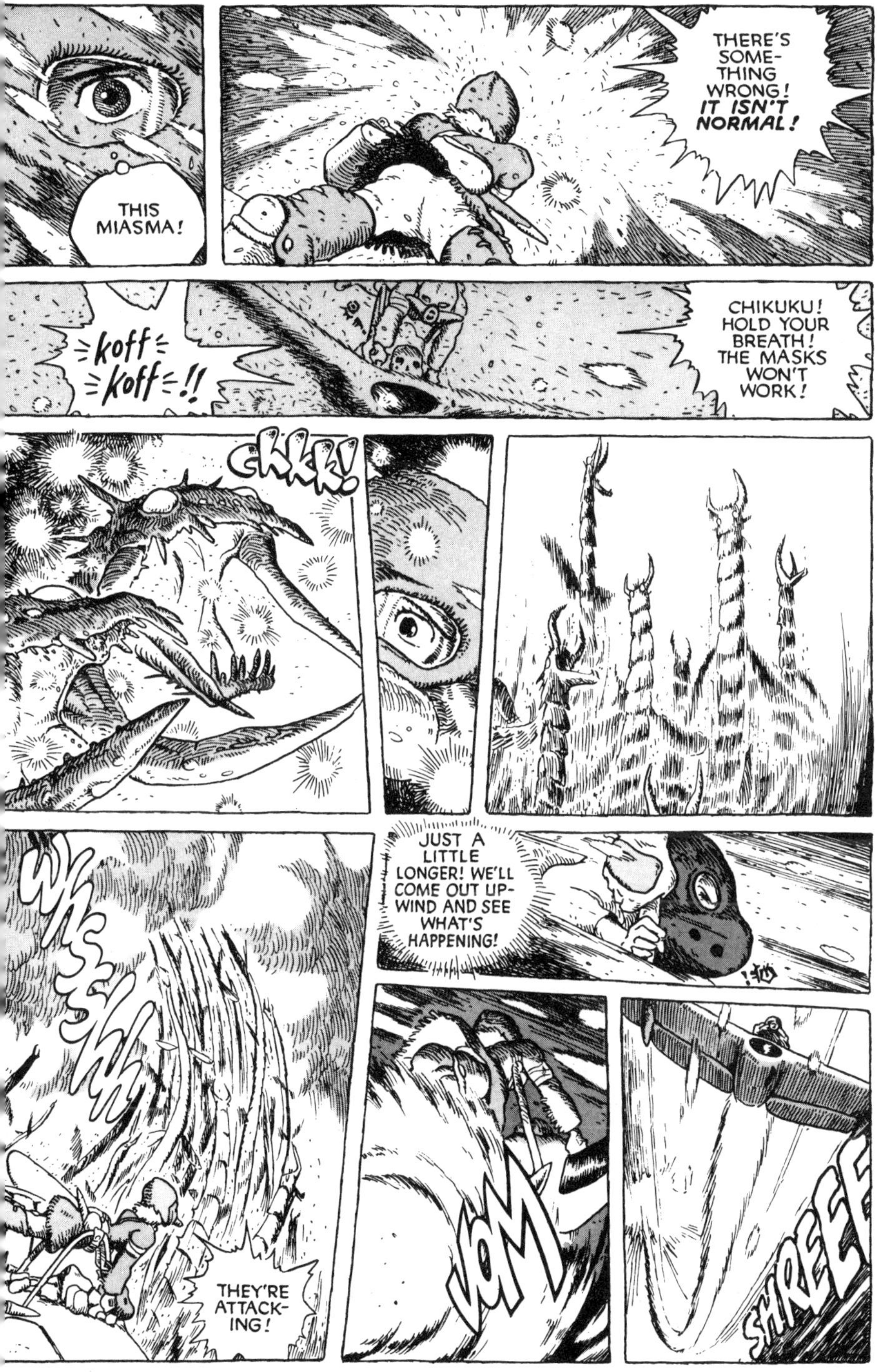
THIS MIASMA!
THERE'S SOMETHING WRONG! IT ISN'T NORMAL!
CHIKUKU! HOLD YOUR BREATH! THE MASKS WON'T WORK!
koff koff !!
chkk!
JUST A LITTLE LONGER! WE'LL COME OUT UPWIND AND SEE WHAT'S HAPPENING!
THEY'RE ATTACKING!
VOM
SHREEE

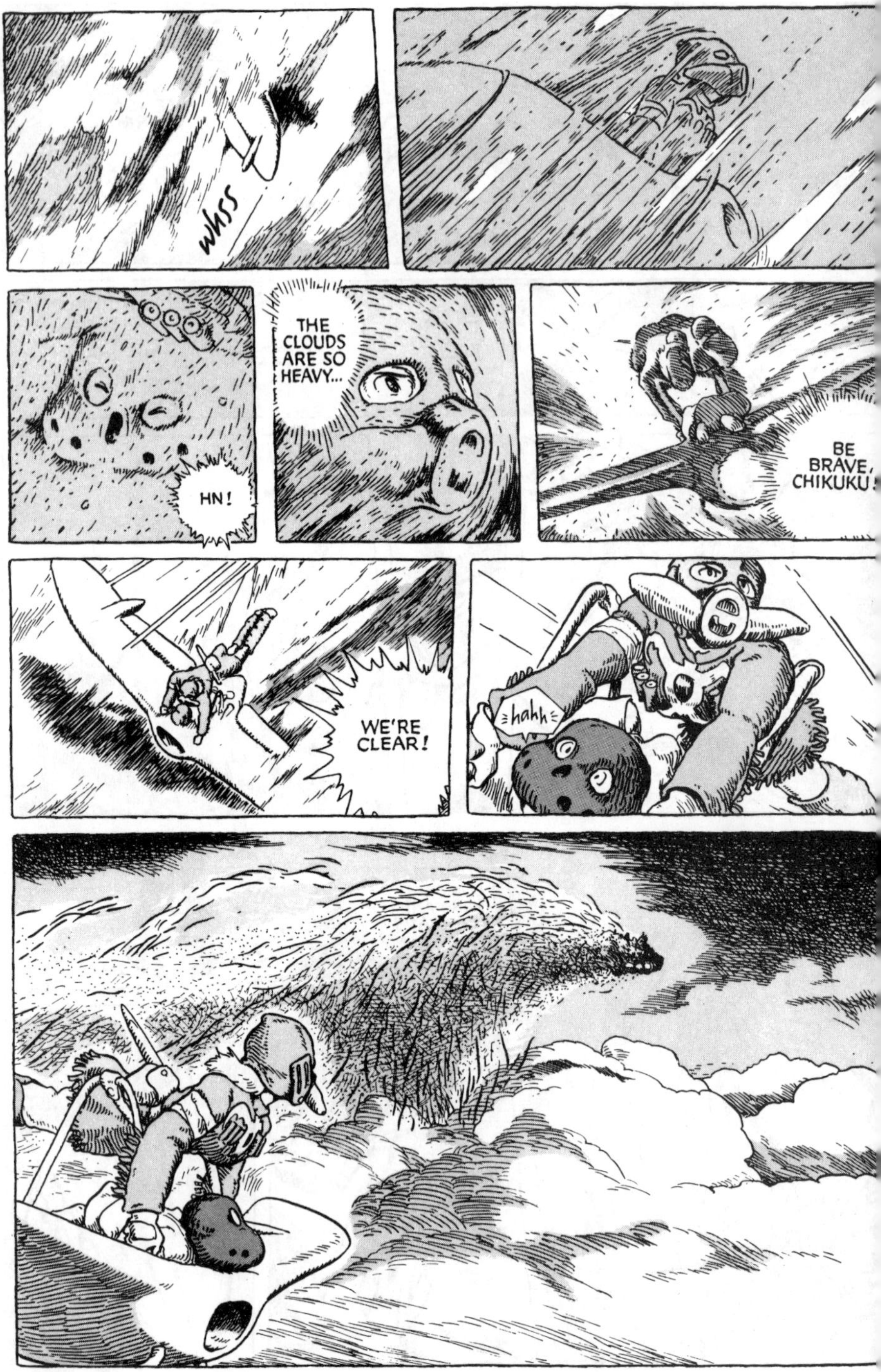
whss
HN!
THE CLOUDS ARE SO HEAVY...
BE BRAVE, CHIKUKU!
WE'RE CLEAR!
hahh

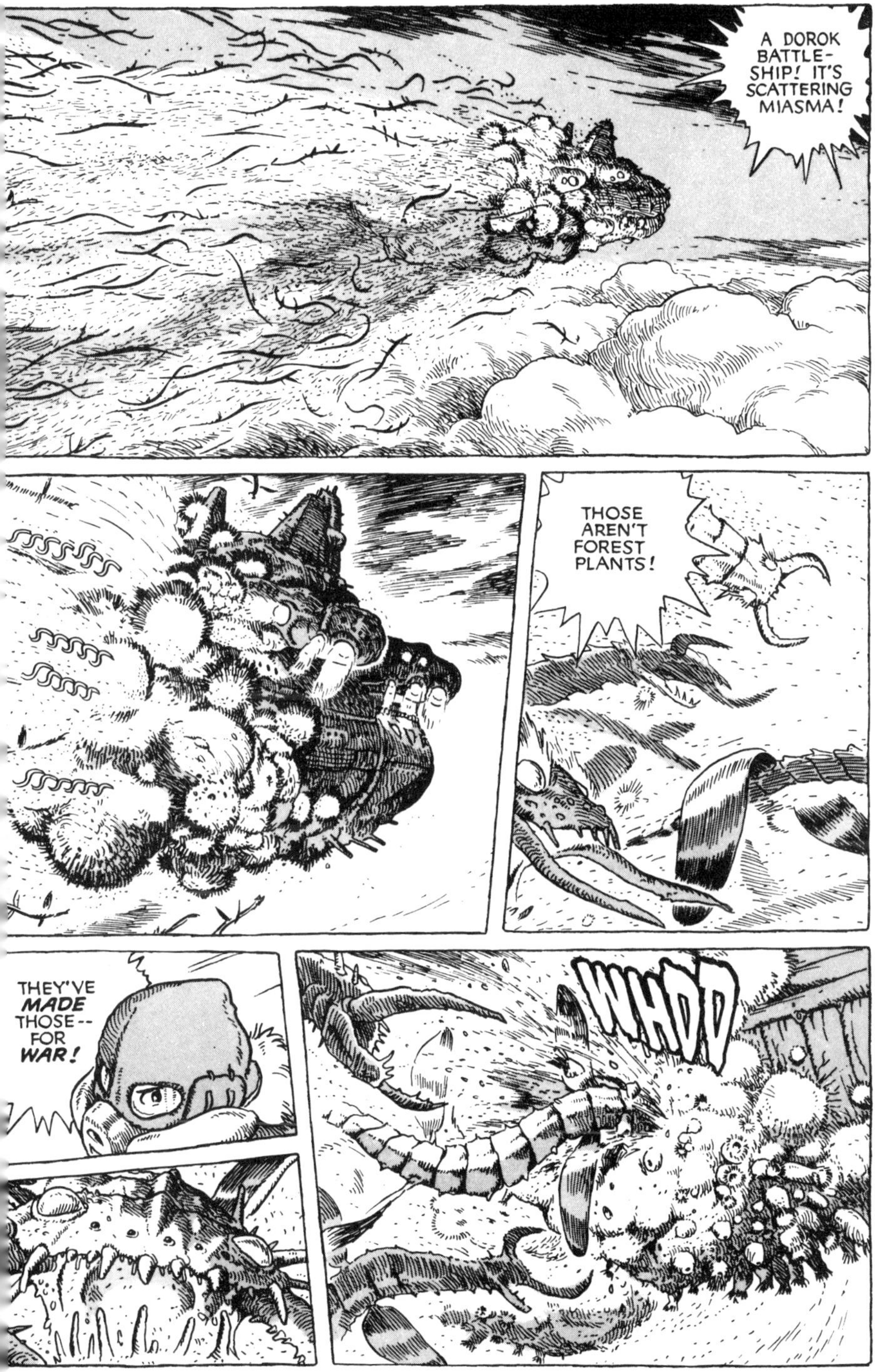
A DOROK BATTLE-SHIP! IT'S SCATTERING MIASMA!
THOSE AREN'T FOREST PLANTS!
THEY'VE MADE THOSE-- FOR WAR!
WHOO

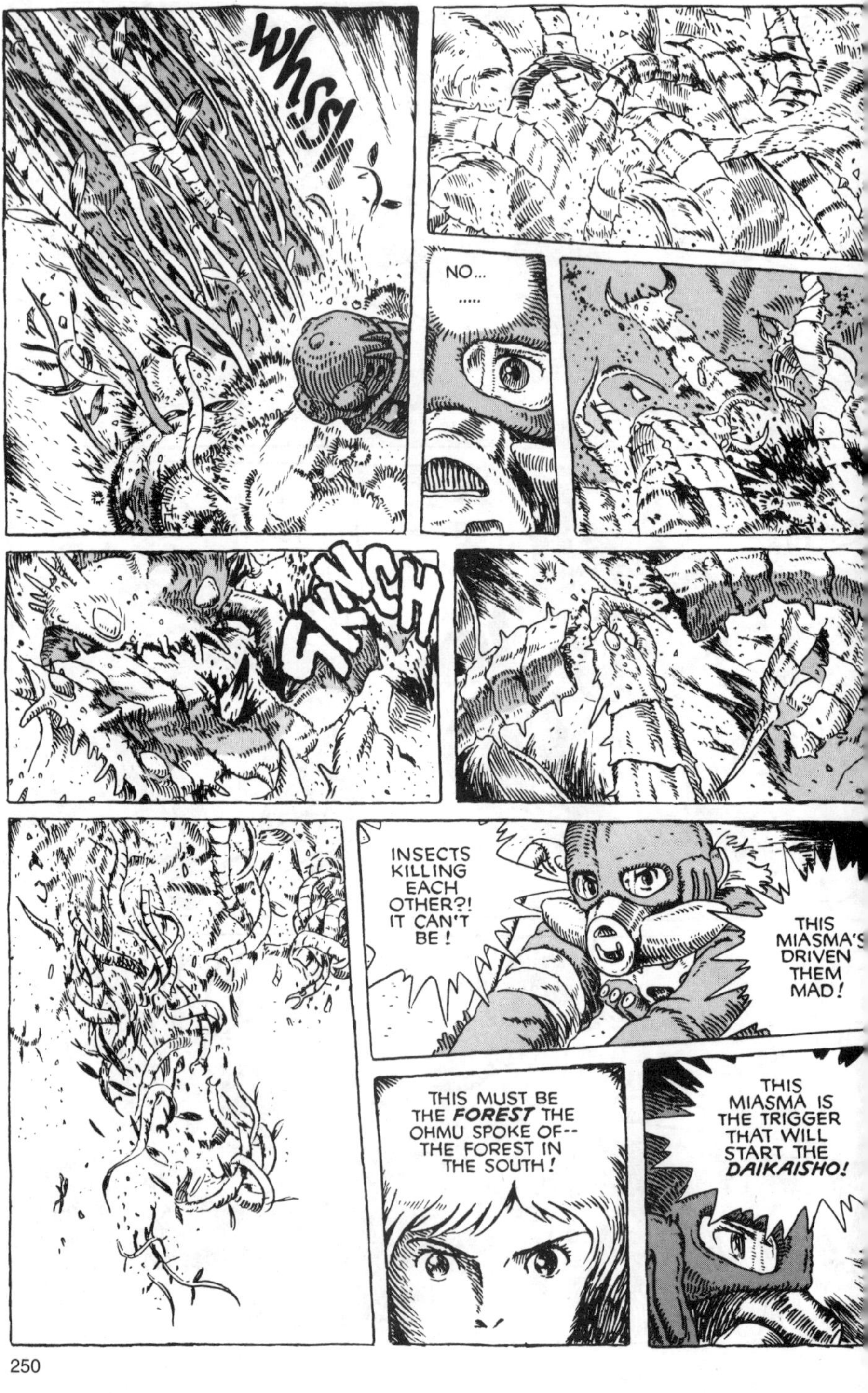
WHSSH
NO...
.....
SKNCH
INSECTS KILLING EACH OTHER?! IT CAN'T BE!
THIS MIASMA'S DRIVEN THEM MAD!
THIS MUST BE THE *FOREST* THE OHMU SPOKE OF-- THE FOREST IN THE SOUTH!
THIS MIASMA IS THE TRIGGER THAT WILL START THE *DAIKAISHO!*

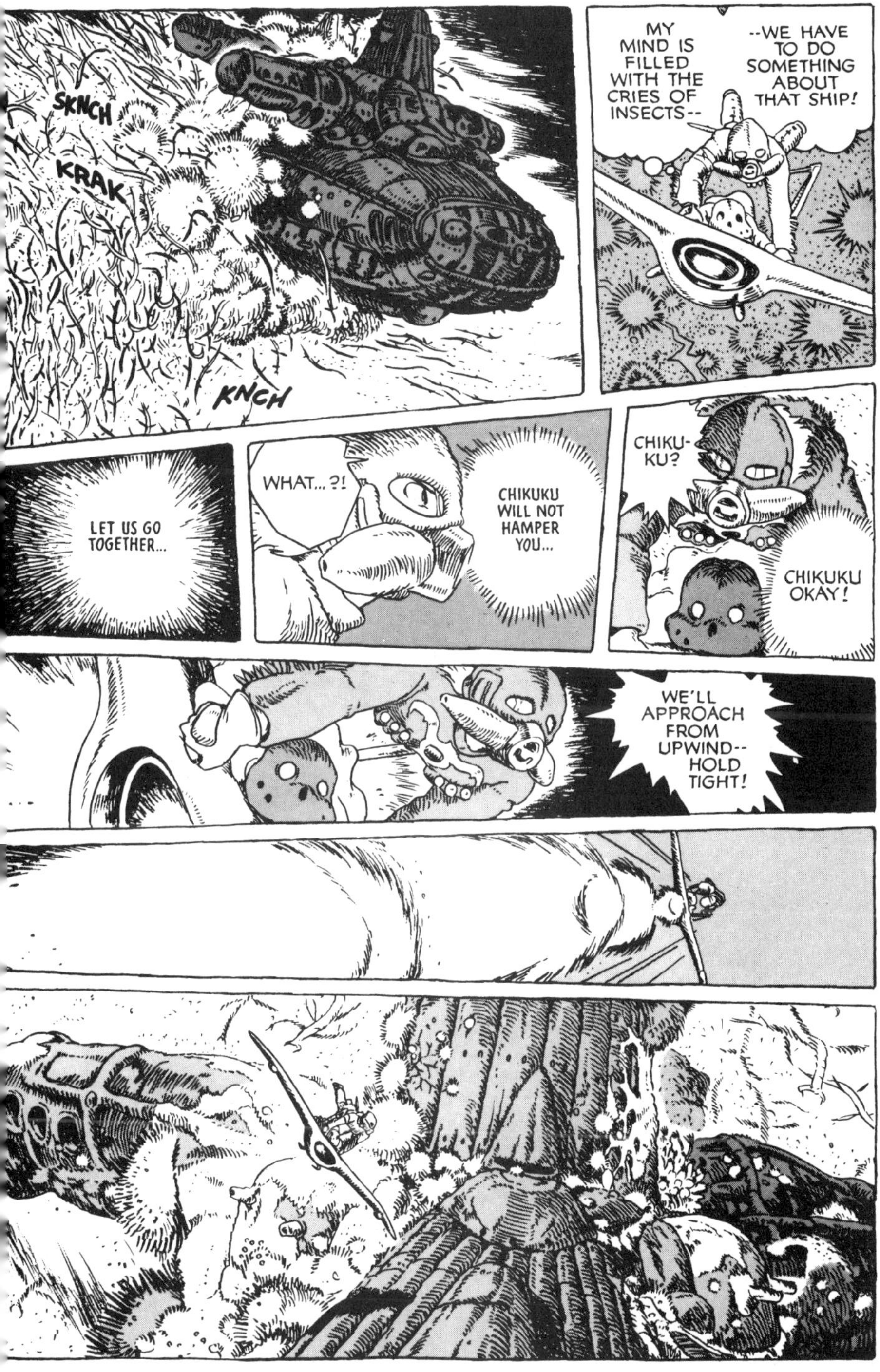
SKNCH
KRAK
KNCH
MY MIND IS FILLED WITH THE CRIES OF INSECTS--
--WE HAVE TO DO SOMETHING ABOUT THAT SHIP!
CHIKU-KU?
CHIKUKU OKAY!
WHAT...?!
CHIKUKU WILL NOT HAMPER YOU...
LET US GO TOGETHER...
WE'LL APPROACH FROM UPWIND--HOLD TIGHT!

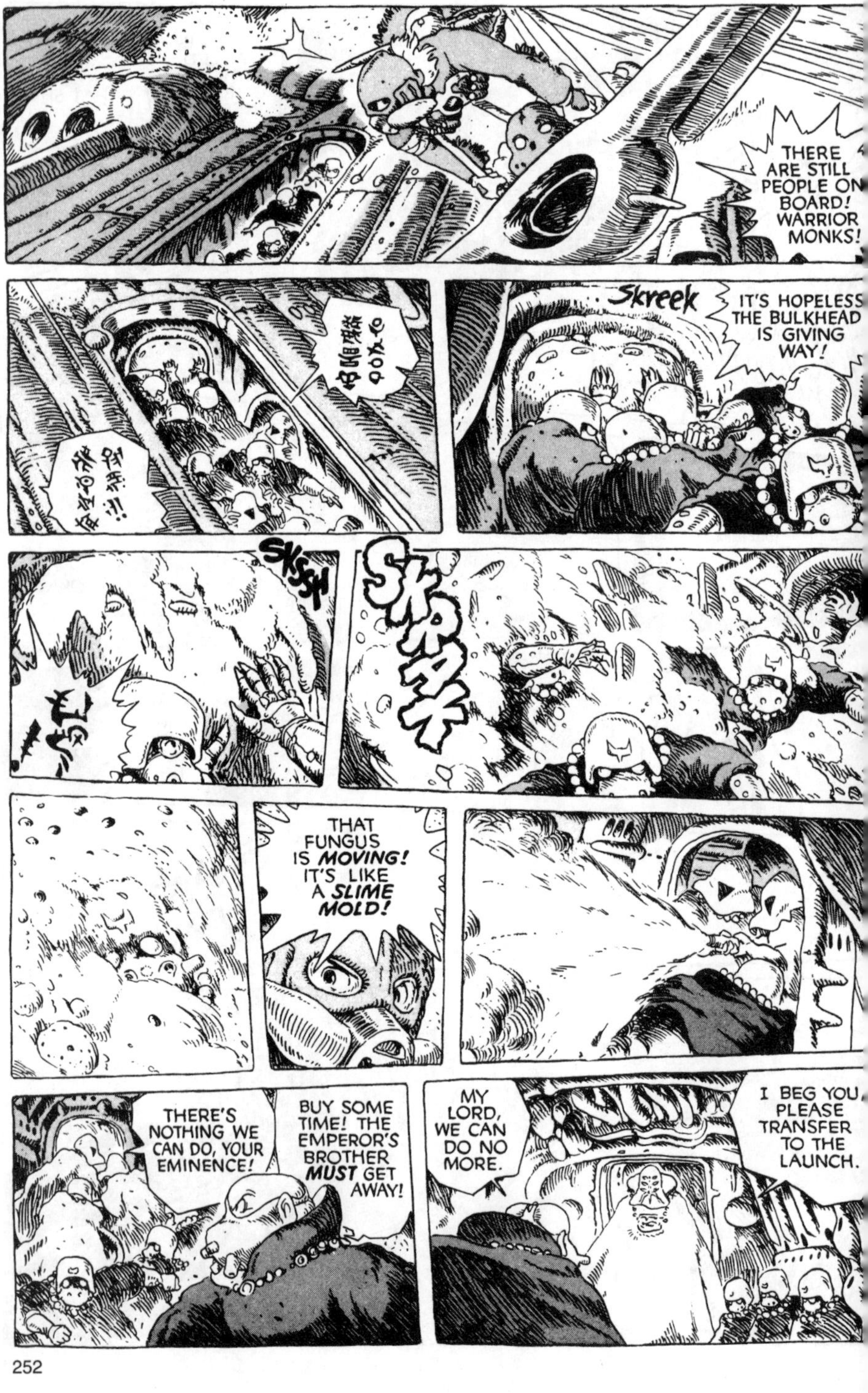
THERE ARE STILL PEOPLE ON BOARD! WARRIOR MONKS!
Skreek
IT'S HOPELESS THE BULKHEAD IS GIVING WAY!
SKSSH
SKRAK
THAT FUNGUS IS MOVING! IT'S LIKE A SLIME MOLD!
THERE'S NOTHING WE CAN DO, YOUR EMINENCE!
BUY SOME TIME! THE EMPEROR'S BROTHER MUST GET AWAY!
MY LORD, WE CAN DO NO MORE.
I BEG YOU, PLEASE TRANSFER TO THE LAUNCH.

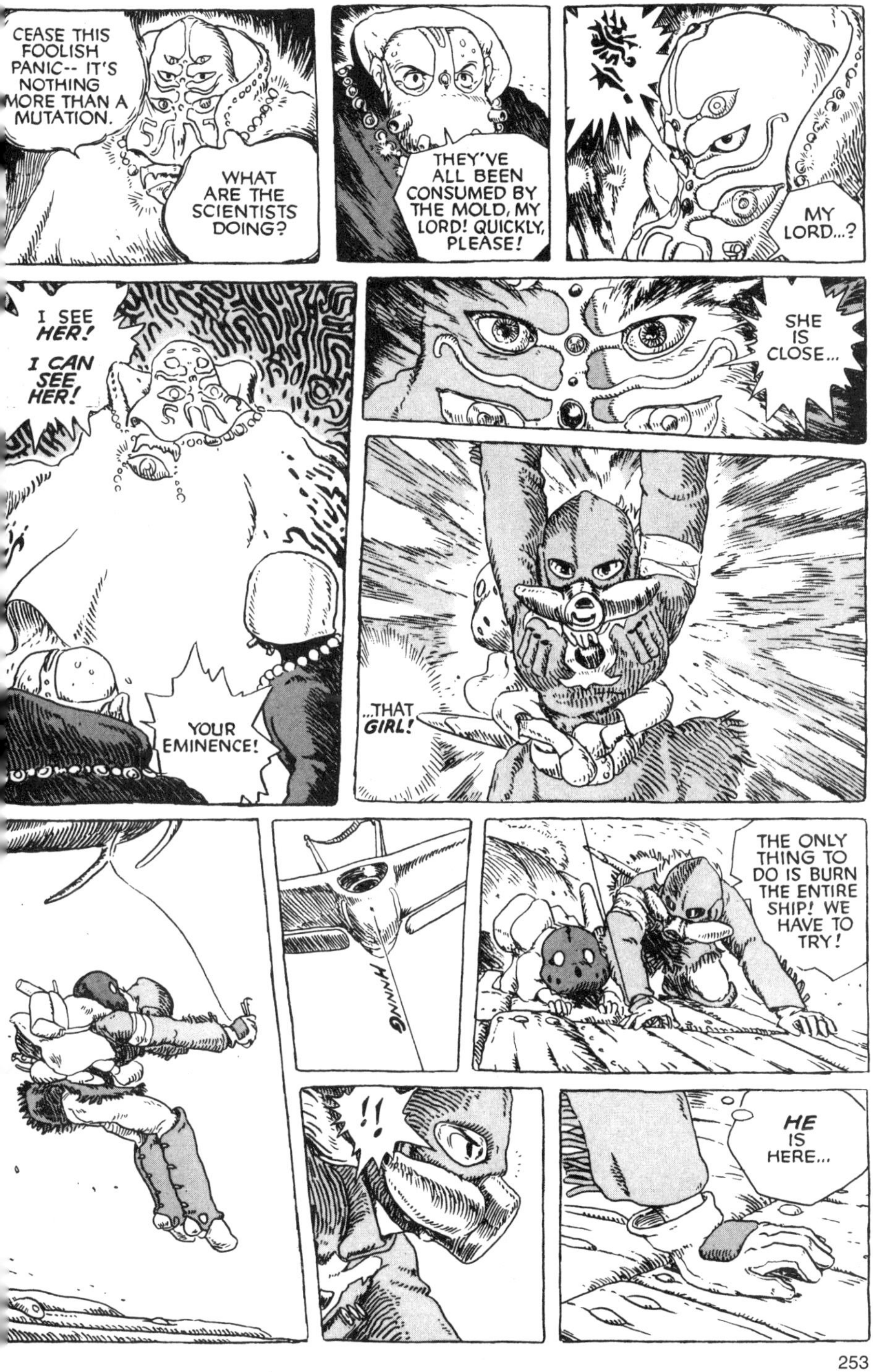
CEASE THIS FOOLISH PANIC-- IT'S NOTHING MORE THAN A MUTATION.
WHAT ARE THE SCIENTISTS DOING?
THEY'VE ALL BEEN CONSUMED BY THE MOLD, MY LORD! QUICKLY, PLEASE!
MY LORD...?
I SEE HER!
I CAN SEE HER!
SHE IS CLOSE...
YOUR EMINENCE!
...THAT GIRL!
HNNNG
THE ONLY THING TO DO IS BURN THE ENTIRE SHIP! WE HAVE TO TRY!
!!
HE IS HERE...

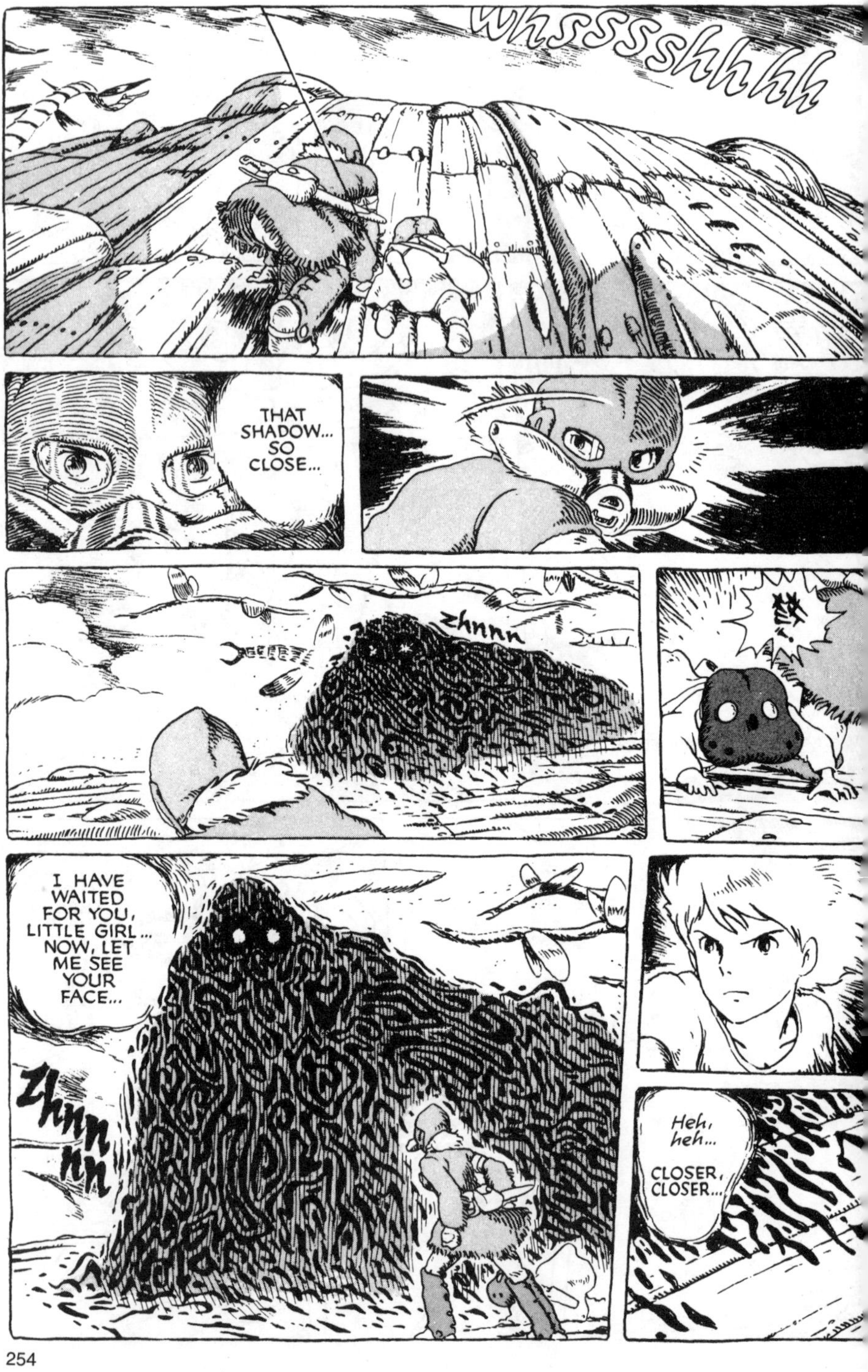
whsssshhhh
THAT SHADOW... SO CLOSE...
zhnnn
I HAVE WAITED FOR YOU, LITTLE GIRL... NOW, LET ME SEE YOUR FACE...
Zhnnnnn
Heh, heh...
CLOSER, CLOSER...

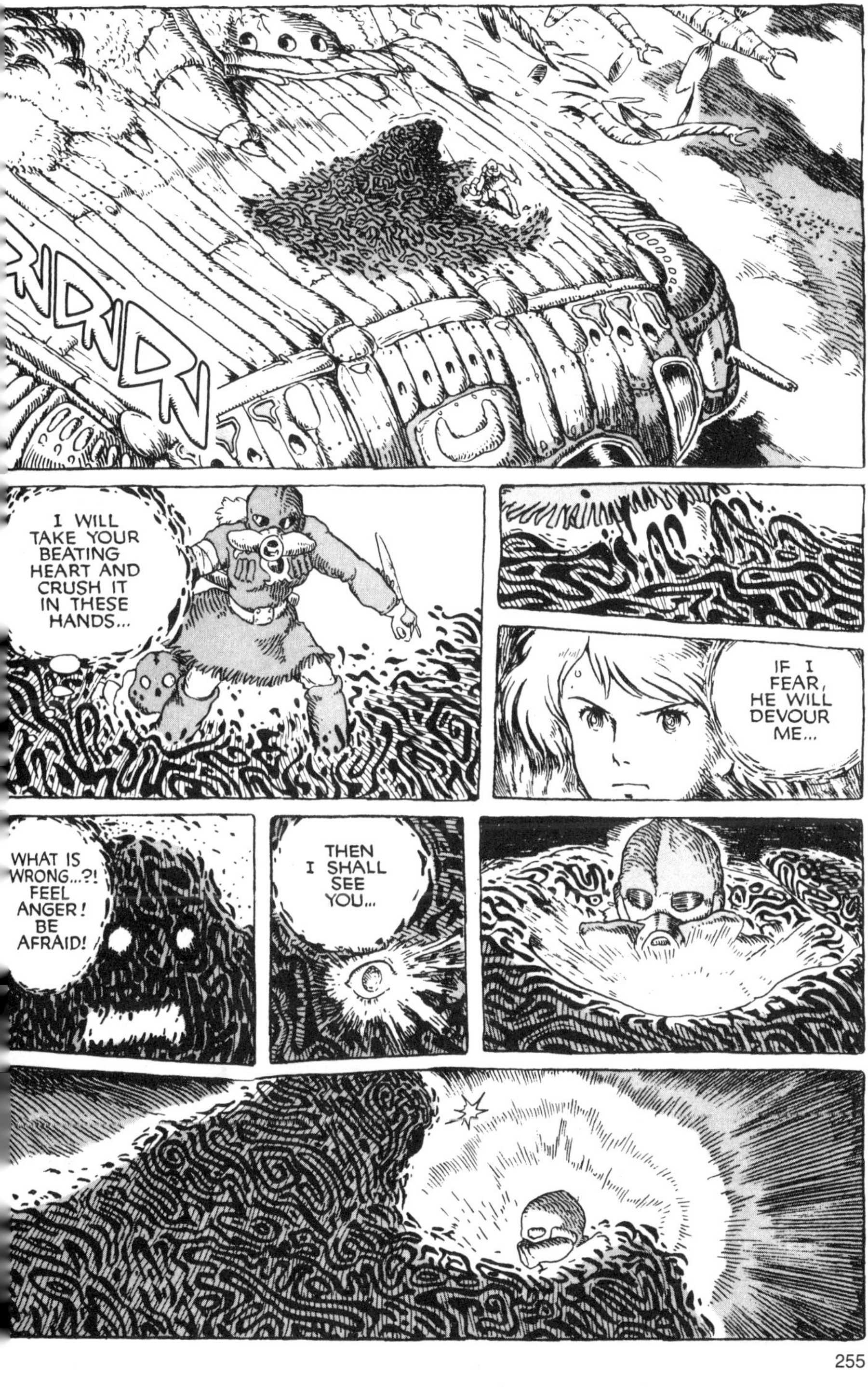

DRDRDR
I WILL TAKE YOUR BEATING HEART AND CRUSH IT IN THESE HANDS...
IF I FEAR, HE WILL DEVOUR ME...
WHAT IS WRONG...?! FEEL ANGER! BE AFRAID!
THEN I SHALL SEE YOU...

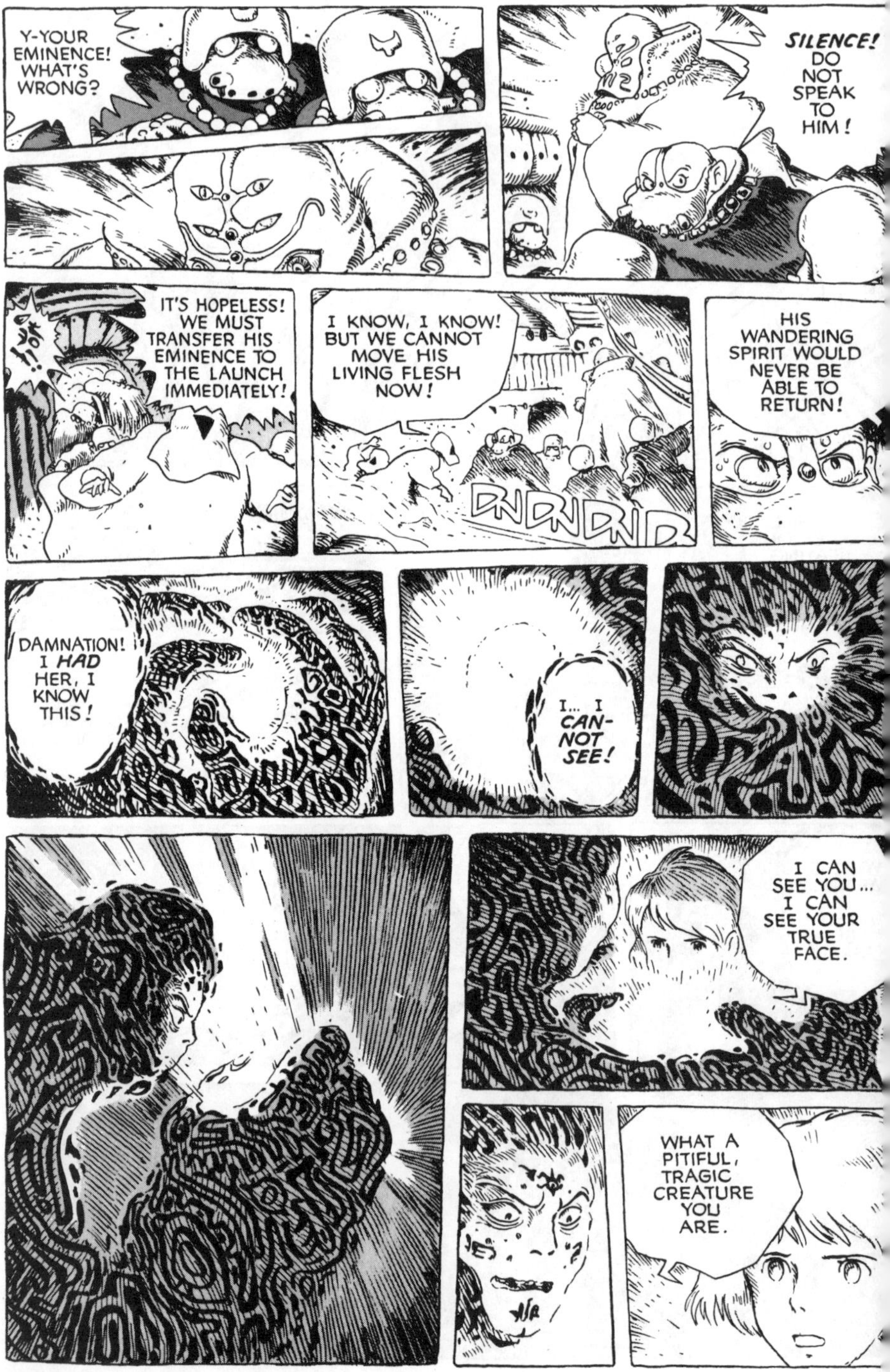
Y-YOUR EMINENCE! WHAT'S WRONG?
SILENCE! DO NOT SPEAK TO HIM!
IT'S HOPELESS! WE MUST TRANSFER HIS EMINENCE TO THE LAUNCH IMMEDIATELY!
I KNOW, I KNOW! BUT WE CANNOT MOVE HIS LIVING FLESH NOW!
HIS WANDERING SPIRIT WOULD NEVER BE ABLE TO RETURN!
DNDNDNDNDN
DAMNATION! I HAD HER, I KNOW THIS!
I... I CAN-NOT SEE!
I CAN SEE YOU... I CAN SEE YOUR TRUE FACE.
WHAT A PITIFUL, TRAGIC CREATURE YOU ARE.

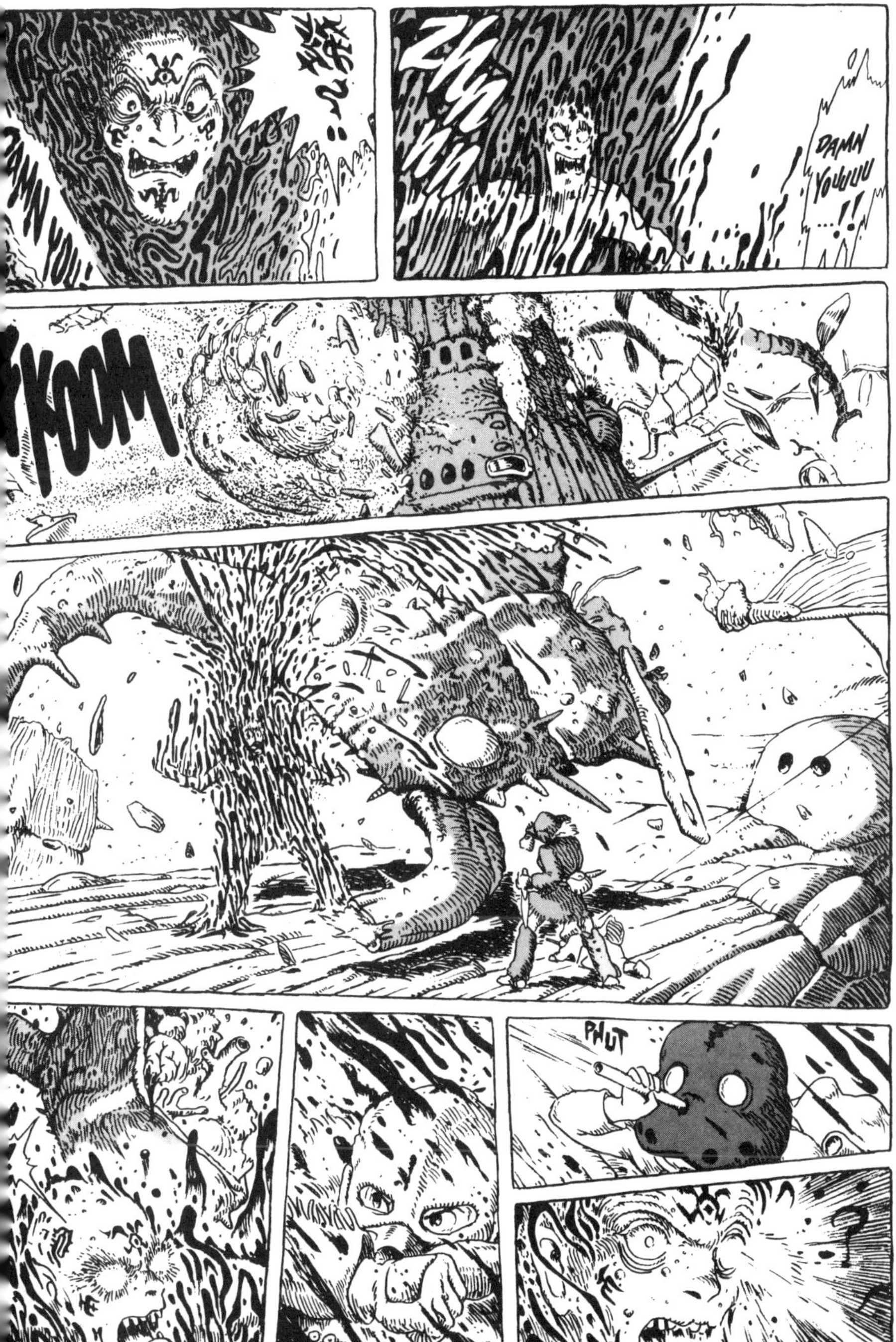

DAMN YOU!
ZMMM
DAMN YOUUUU ...!!
KOOM
PHUT
?

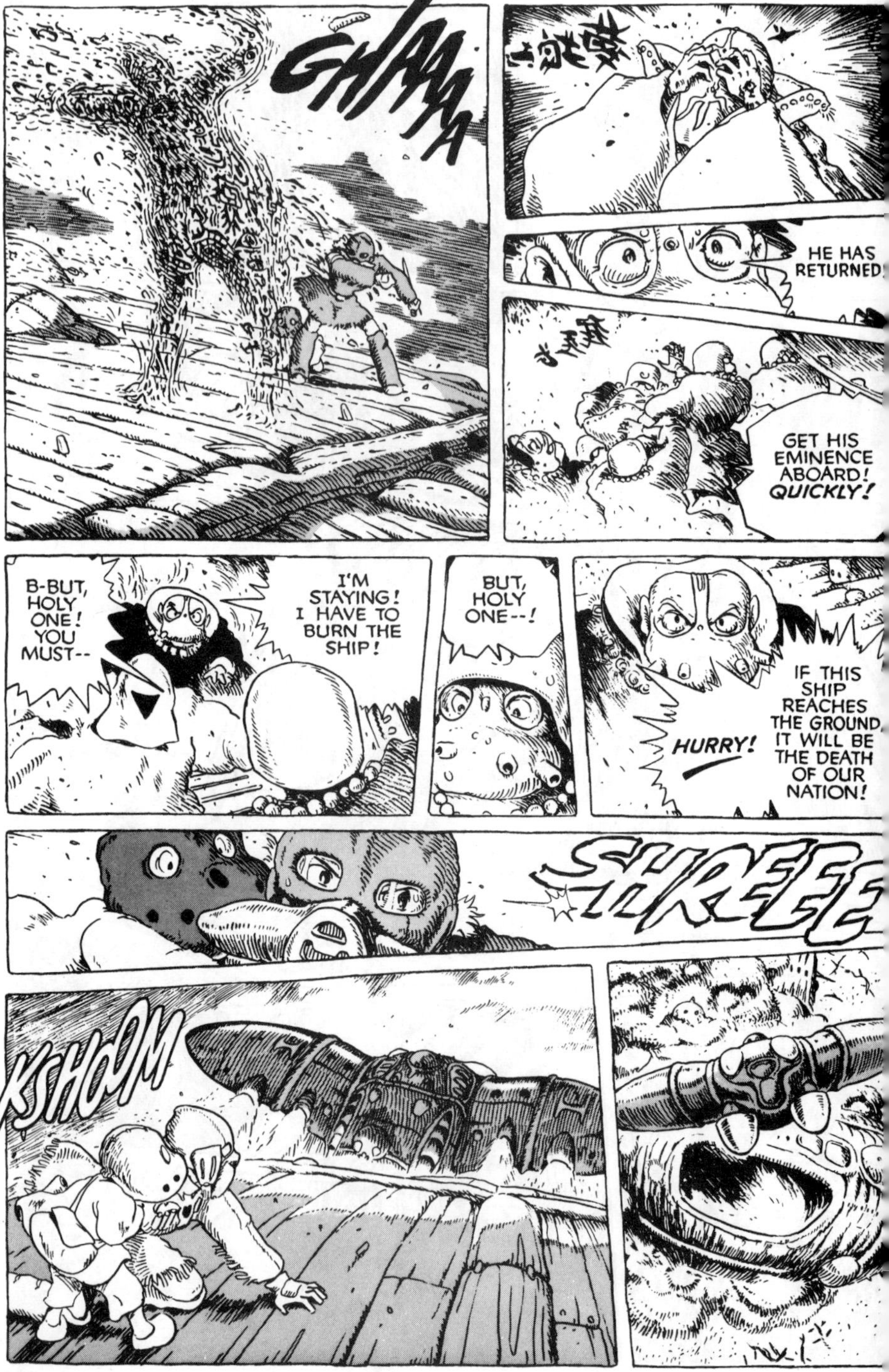

GHAAAAAA
HE HAS RETURNED!
GET HIS EMINENCE ABOARD! QUICKLY!
B-BUT, HOLY ONE! YOU MUST--
I'M STAYING! I HAVE TO BURN THE SHIP!
BUT, HOLY ONE--!
HURRY!
IF THIS SHIP REACHES THE GROUND, IT WILL BE THE DEATH OF OUR NATION!
SHREEE
KSHOOM

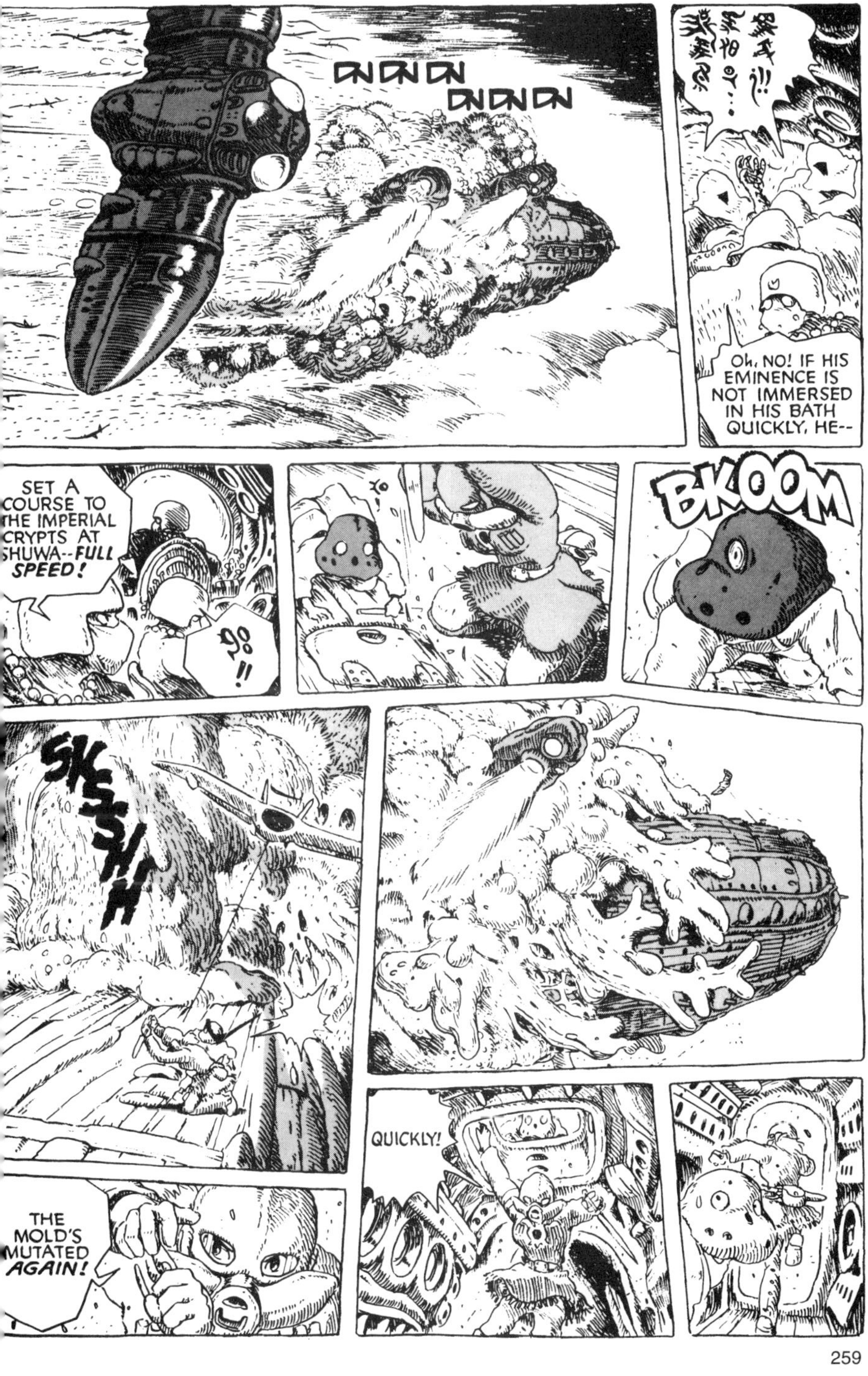
DN DN DN
DN DN DN
Oh, NO! IF HIS EMINENCE IS NOT IMMERSED IN HIS BATH QUICKLY, HE--
SET A COURSE TO THE IMPERIAL CRYPTS AT SHUWA--**FULL SPEED!**
BKOOM
SKSSHH
THE MOLD'S MUTATED ***AGAIN!***
QUICKLY!

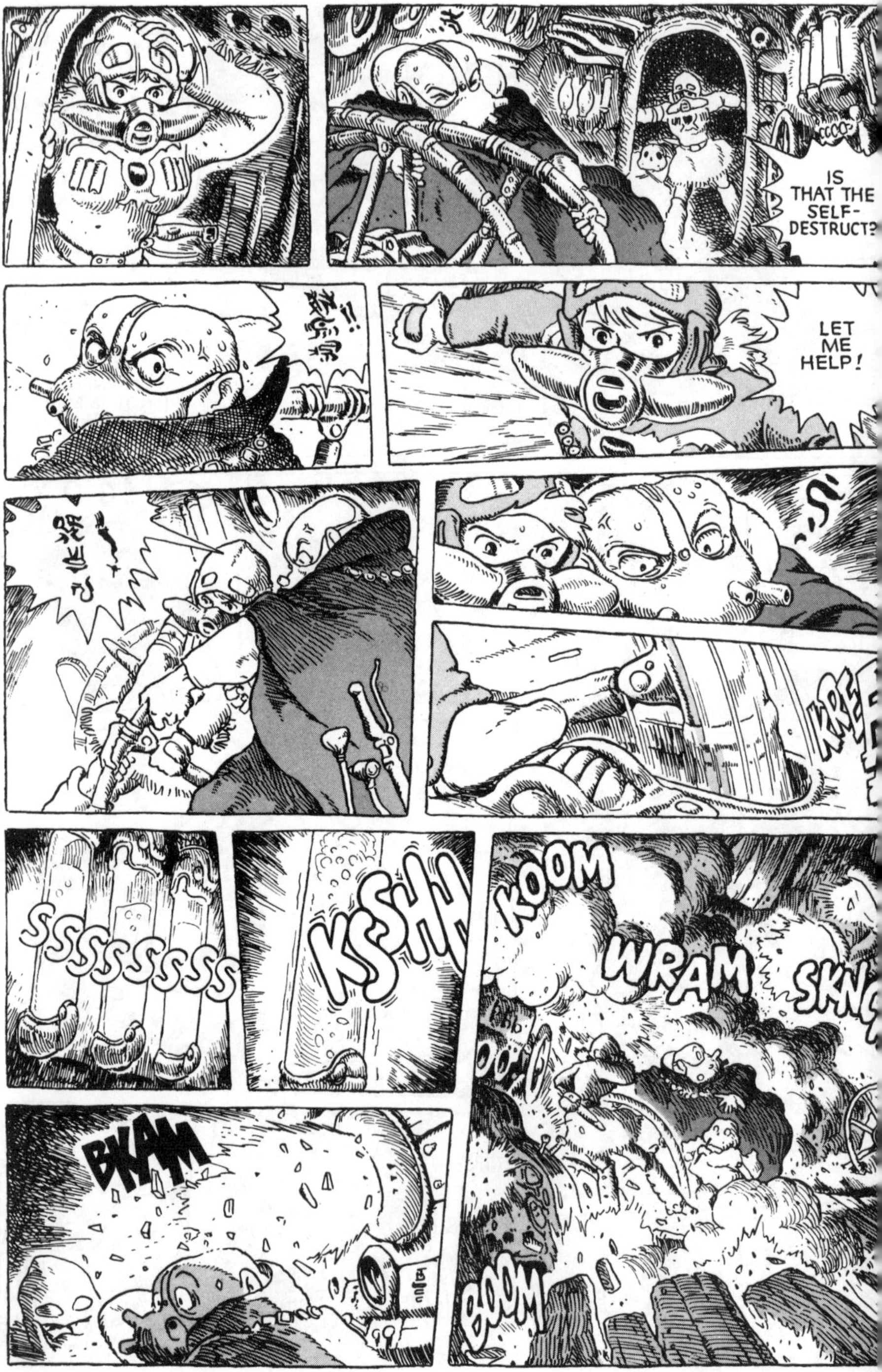
IS THAT THE SELF-DESTRUCT?
LET ME HELP!
SSSSSSSSS
KSHH
KOOM
WRAM
BKAM
BOOM

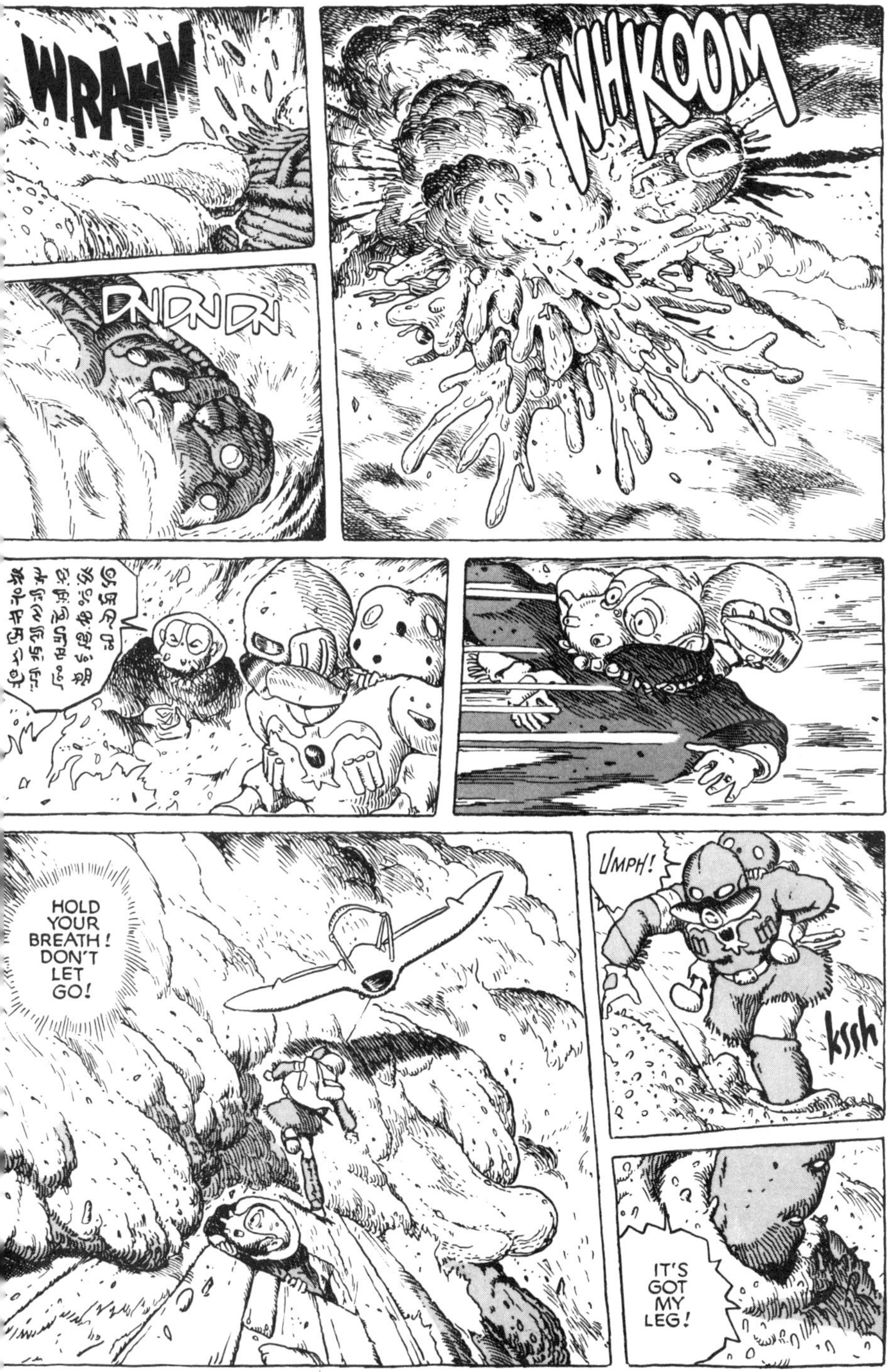
WRAMM
WHKOOM
DNDNDN
HOLD YOUR BREATH! DON'T LET GO!
UMPH!
kssh
IT'S GOT MY LEG!

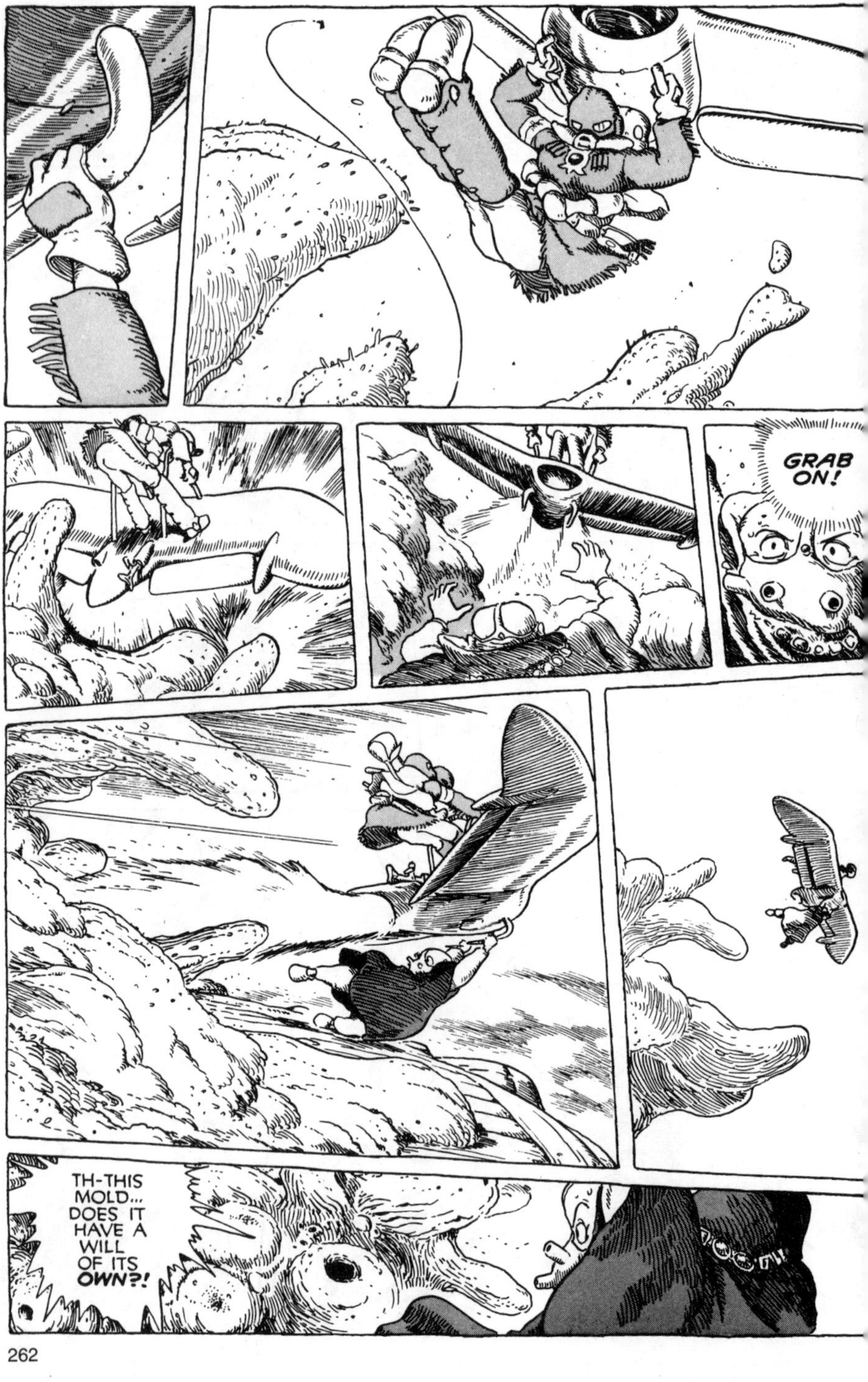
GRAB ON!
TH-THIS MOLD... DOES IT HAVE A WILL OF ITS OWN?!

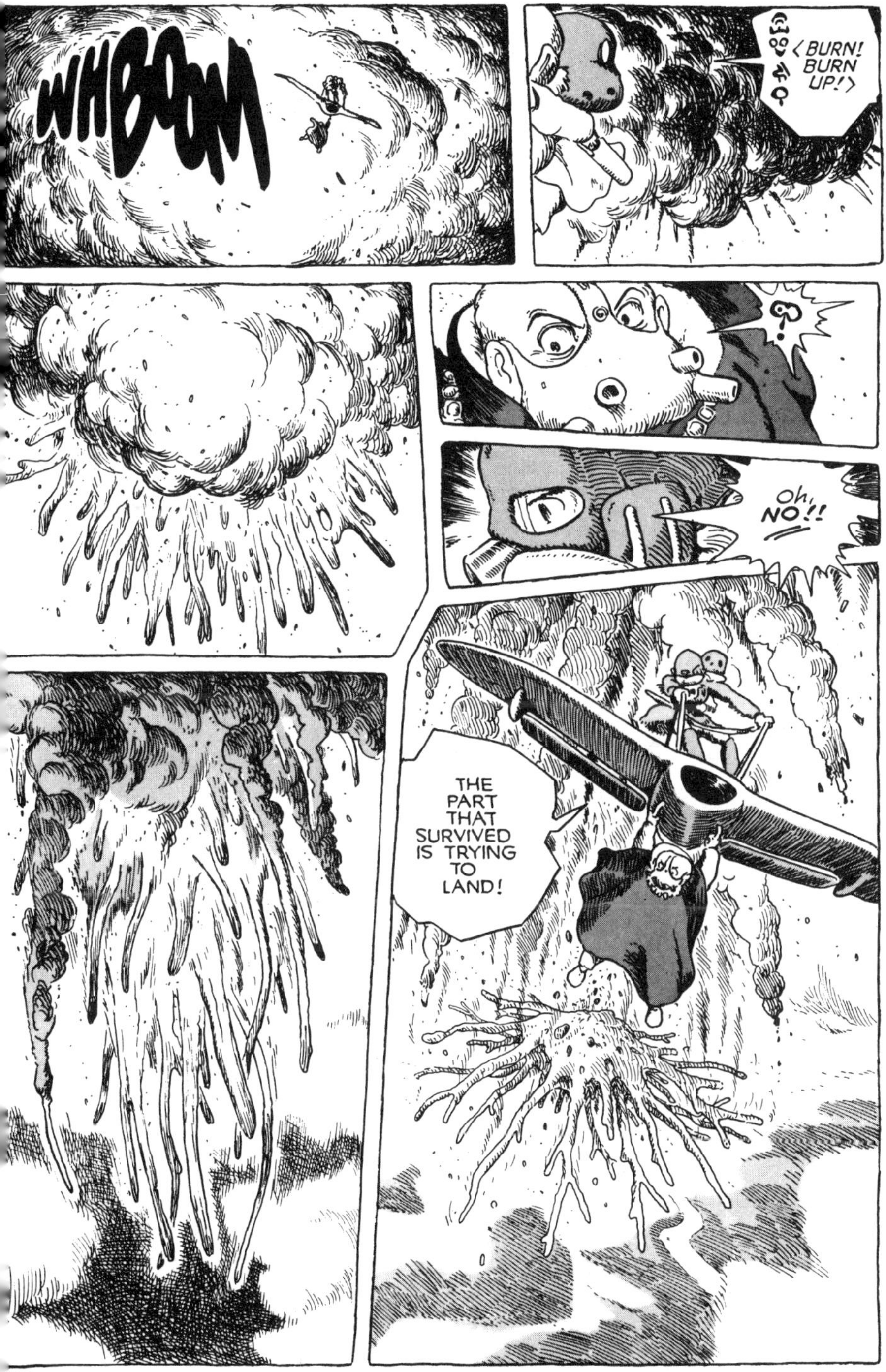
WHBOOM
<BURN! BURN UP!>
Oh, NO!!
THE PART THAT SURVIVED IS TRYING TO LAND!

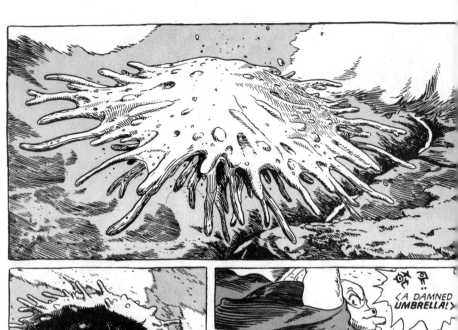

FWUP

‹A DAMNED UMBRELLA!›

YOU MUST LET GO! QUICKLY!

WE'LL STALL OUT! *LET GO!*

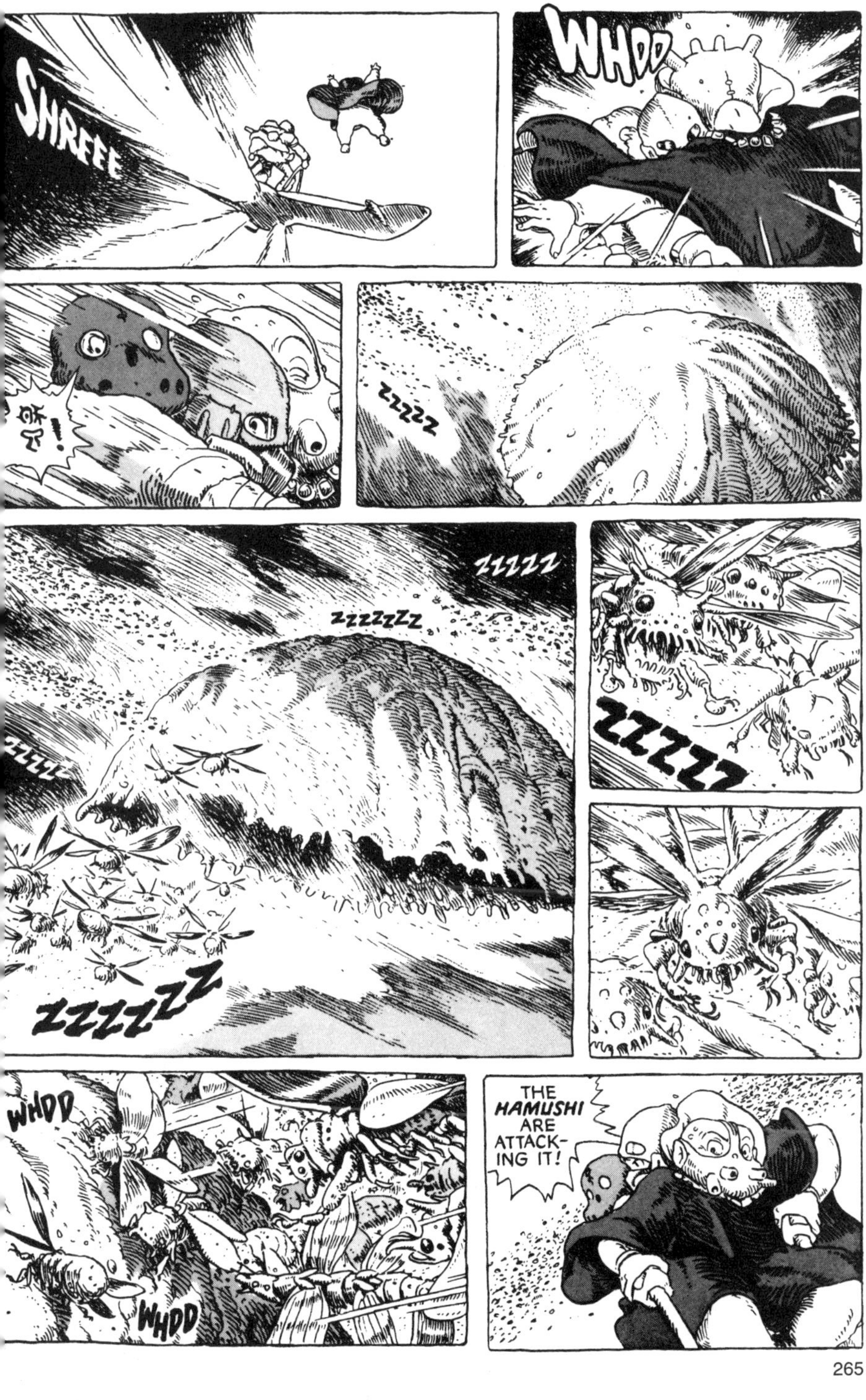
SHREEE
WHDD
ZZZZZ
ZZZZZ
ZZZZZZZ
ZZZZZZZ
ZZZZZZ
WHDD
WHDD
THE *HAMUSHI* ARE ATTACKING IT!

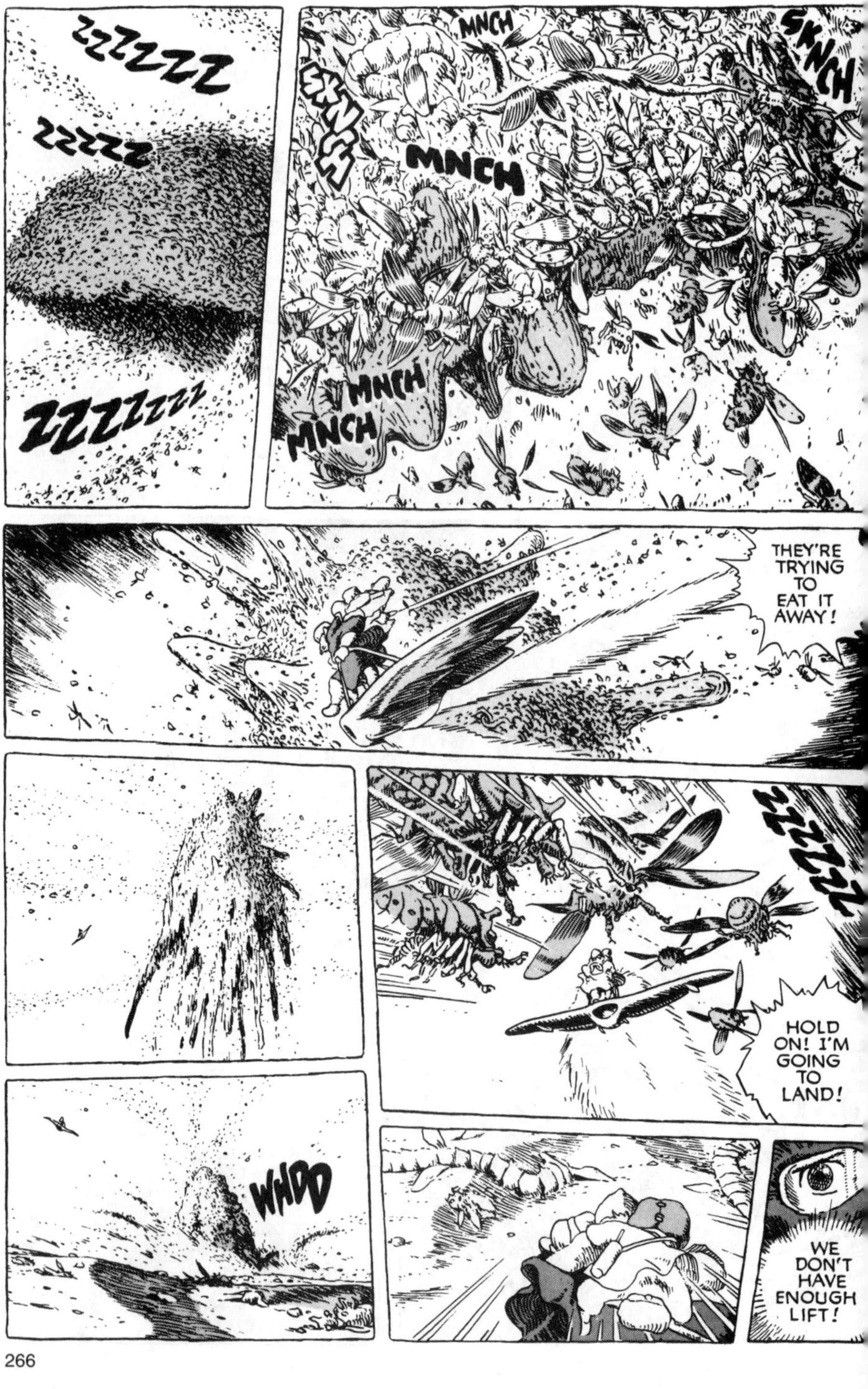
ZZZZZZZ
ZZZZZ
ZZZZZzzz
MNCH
SKNCH
SKNCH
MNCH
MNCH
MNCH
THEY'RE TRYING TO EAT IT AWAY!
ZZZZZZ
HOLD ON! I'M GOING TO LAND!
WHDD
WE DON'T HAVE ENOUGH LIFT!

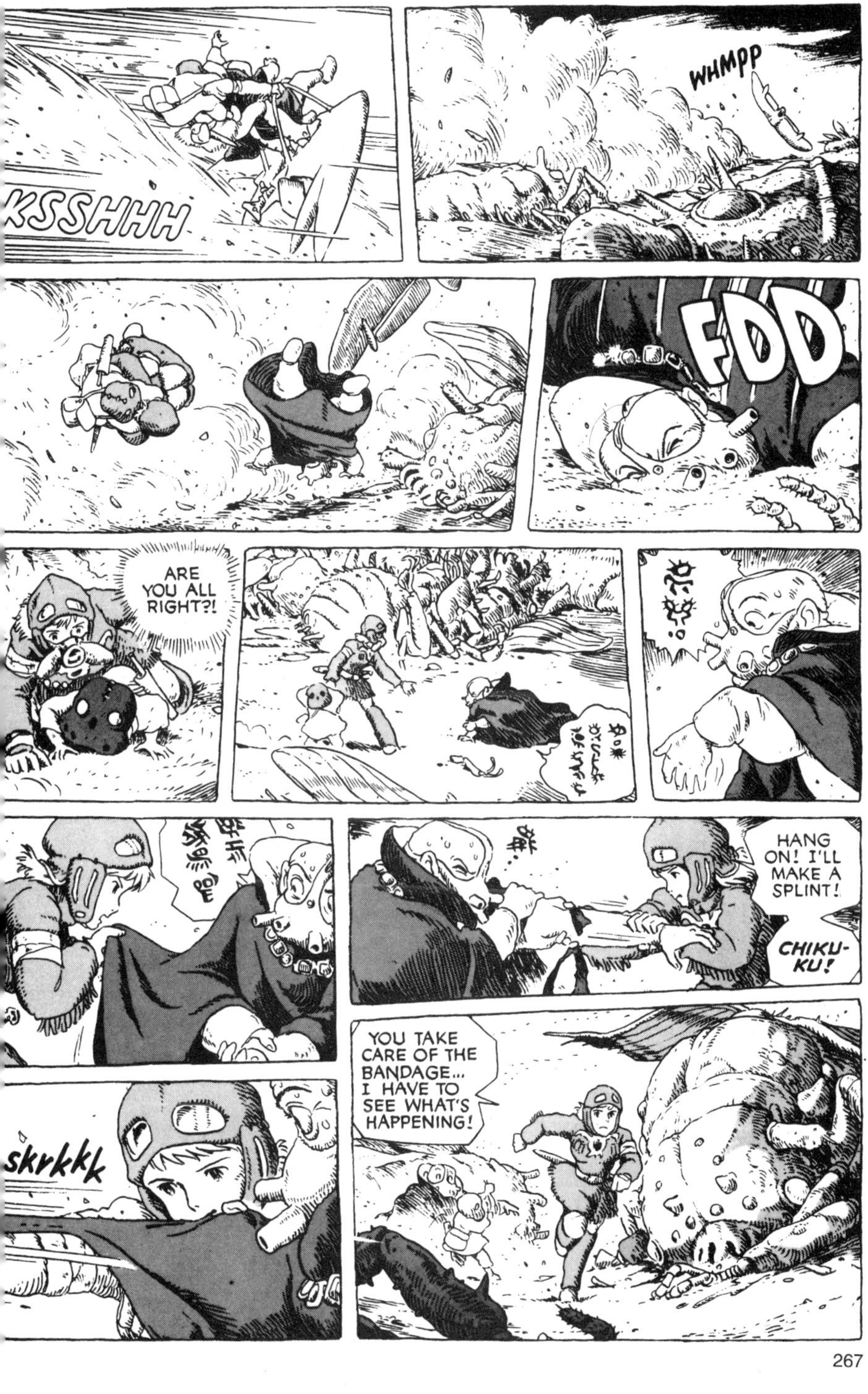
KSSHHH
WHMPP
FDD
ARE YOU ALL RIGHT?!
HANG ON! I'LL MAKE A SPLINT!
CHIKU-KU!
skrkkk
YOU TAKE CARE OF THE BANDAGE... I HAVE TO SEE WHAT'S HAPPENING!

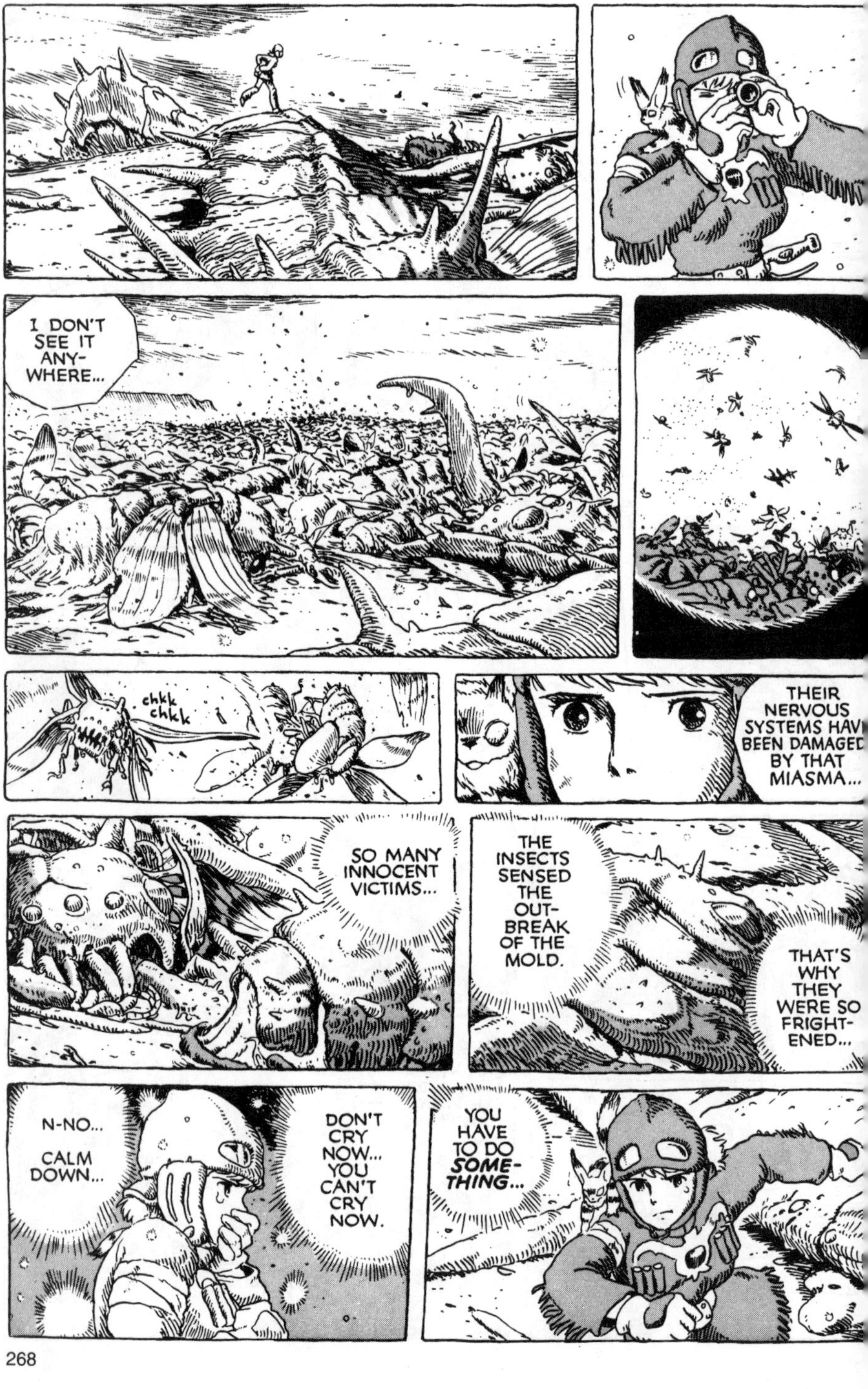
I DON'T SEE IT ANYWHERE...
chkk chkk
THEIR NERVOUS SYSTEMS HAVE BEEN DAMAGED BY THAT MIASMA...
SO MANY INNOCENT VICTIMS...
THE INSECTS SENSED THE OUTBREAK OF THE MOLD.
THAT'S WHY THEY WERE SO FRIGHTENED...
N-NO...
CALM DOWN...
DON'T CRY NOW... YOU CAN'T CRY NOW.
YOU HAVE TO DO *SOMETHING*...

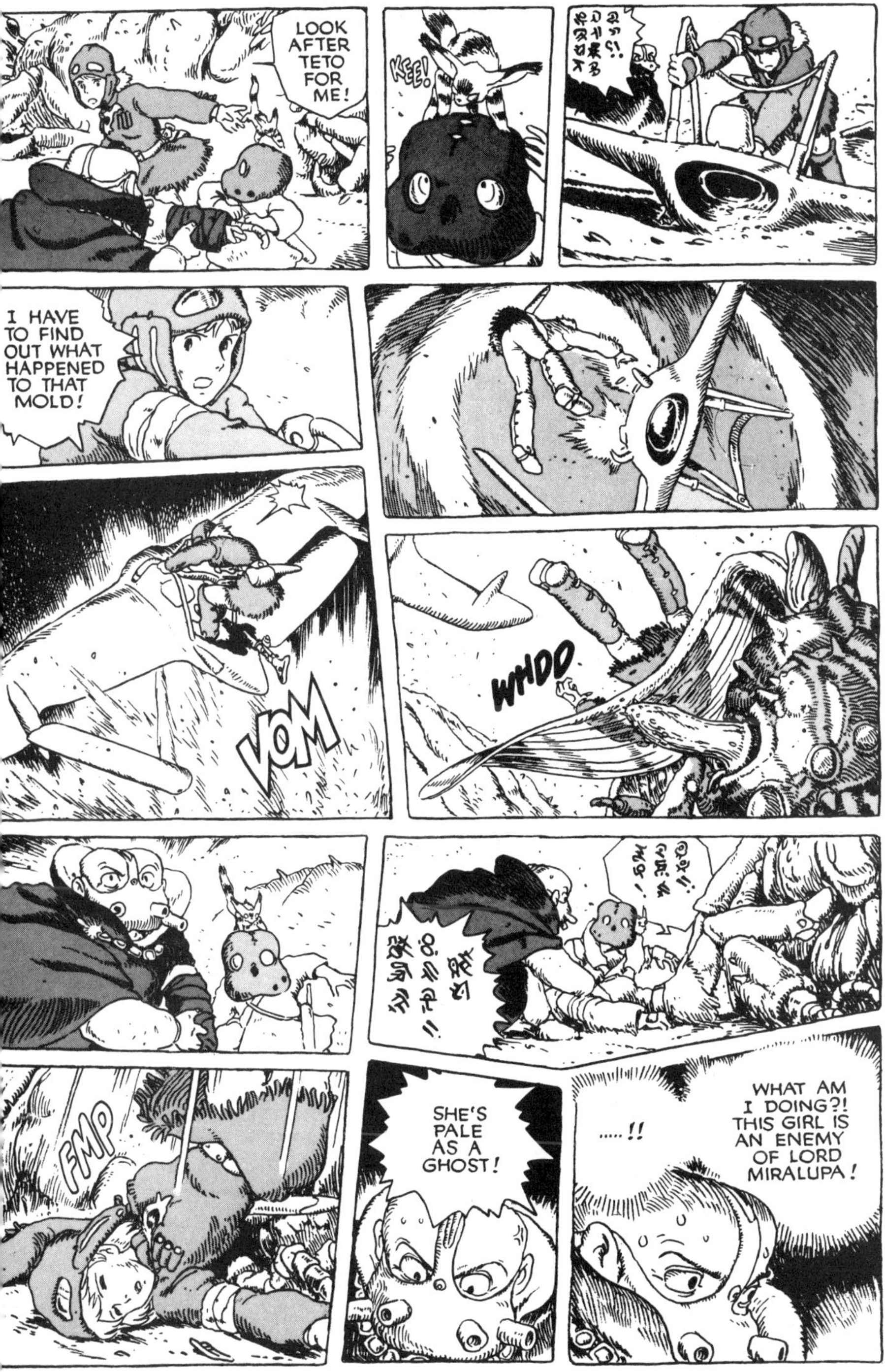
LOOK AFTER TETO FOR ME!
KEE!
I HAVE TO FIND OUT WHAT HAPPENED TO THAT MOLD!
VOM
WHDD
FMP
SHE'S PALE AS A GHOST!
.....!!
WHAT AM I DOING?! THIS GIRL IS AN ENEMY OF LORD MIRALUPA!

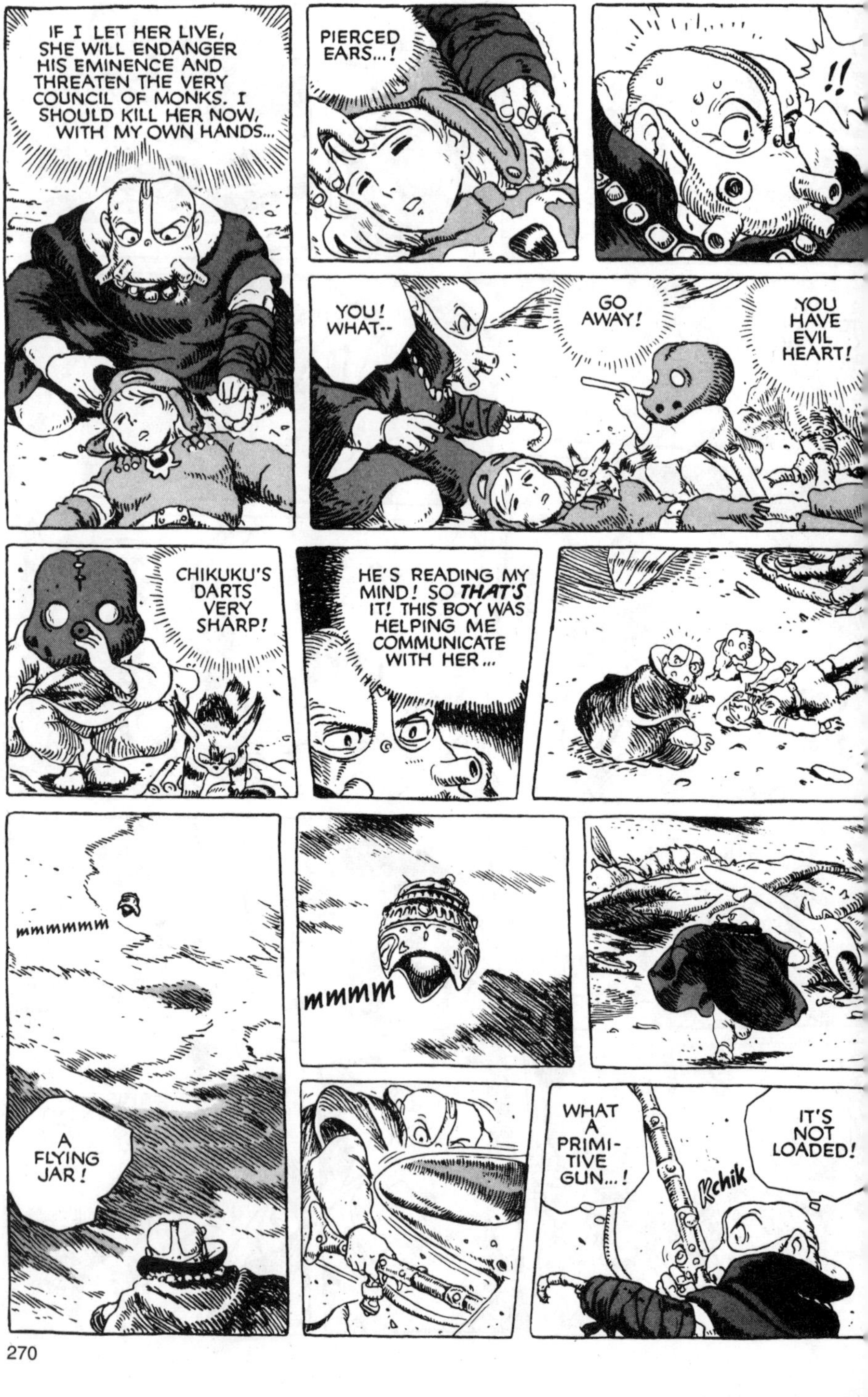
IF I LET HER LIVE, SHE WILL ENDANGER HIS EMINENCE AND THREATEN THE VERY COUNCIL OF MONKS. I SHOULD KILL HER NOW, WITH MY OWN HANDS...
PIERCED EARS...!
!!
YOU! WHAT--
GO AWAY!
YOU HAVE EVIL HEART!
CHIKUKU'S DARTS VERY SHARP!
HE'S READING MY MIND! SO THAT'S IT! THIS BOY WAS HELPING ME COMMUNICATE WITH HER...
mmmmmm
mmmm
A FLYING JAR!
WHAT A PRIMITIVE GUN...!
Kchik
IT'S NOT LOADED!

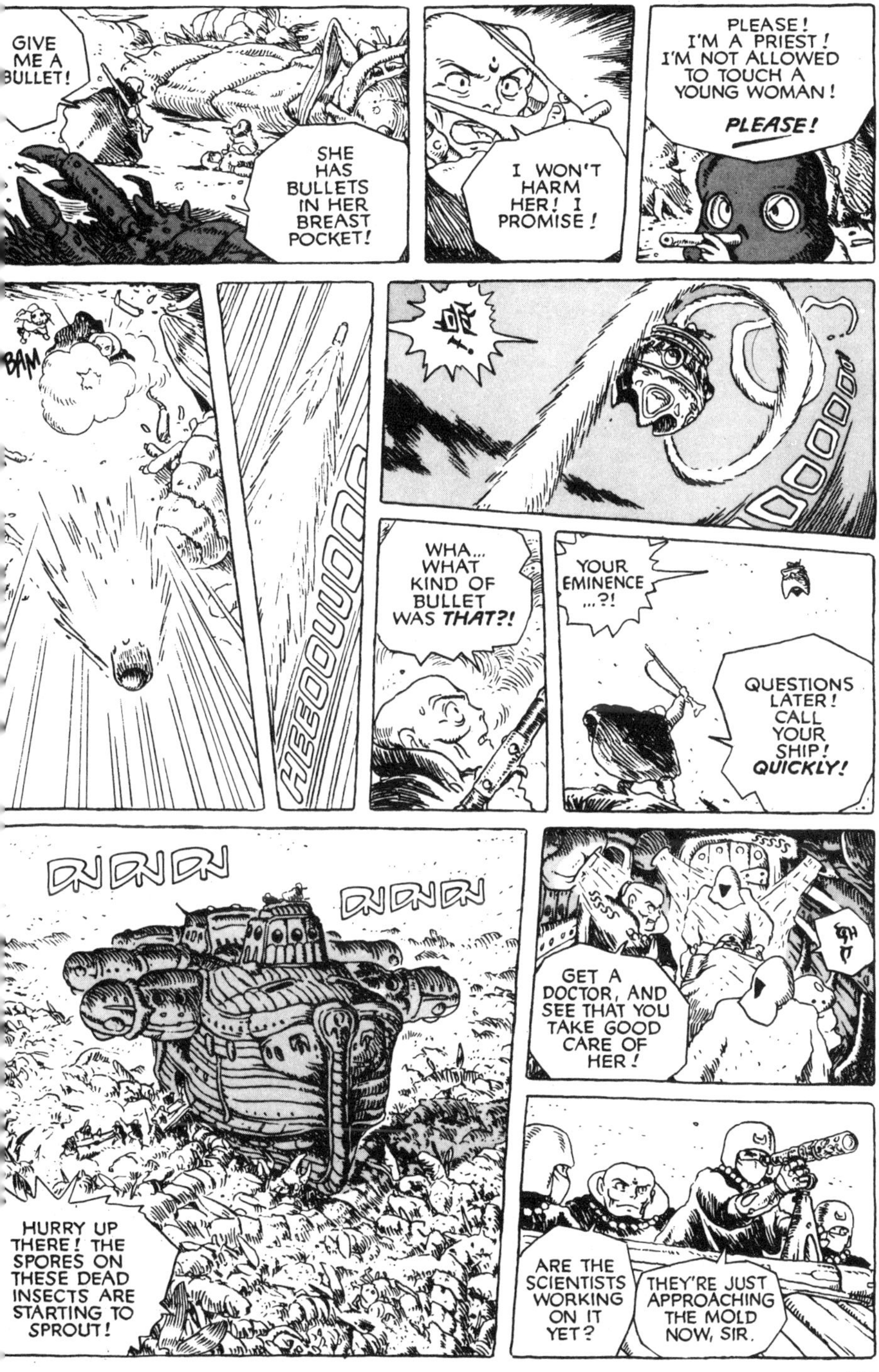

GIVE ME A BULLET!
SHE HAS BULLETS IN HER BREAST POCKET!
I WON'T HARM HER! I PROMISE!
PLEASE! I'M A PRIEST! I'M NOT ALLOWED TO TOUCH A YOUNG WOMAN!
PLEASE!
BAM
HEEOUUOOO
WHA... WHAT KIND OF BULLET WAS THAT?!
YOUR EMINENCE ...?!
QUESTIONS LATER! CALL YOUR SHIP! QUICKLY!
DN DN DN DN
DN DN DN DN
HURRY UP THERE! THE SPORES ON THESE DEAD INSECTS ARE STARTING TO SPROUT!
SSSSS
SSSSS
GET A DOCTOR, AND SEE THAT YOU TAKE GOOD CARE OF HER!
ARE THE SCIENTISTS WORKING ON IT YET?
THEY'RE JUST APPROACHING THE MOLD NOW, SIR.

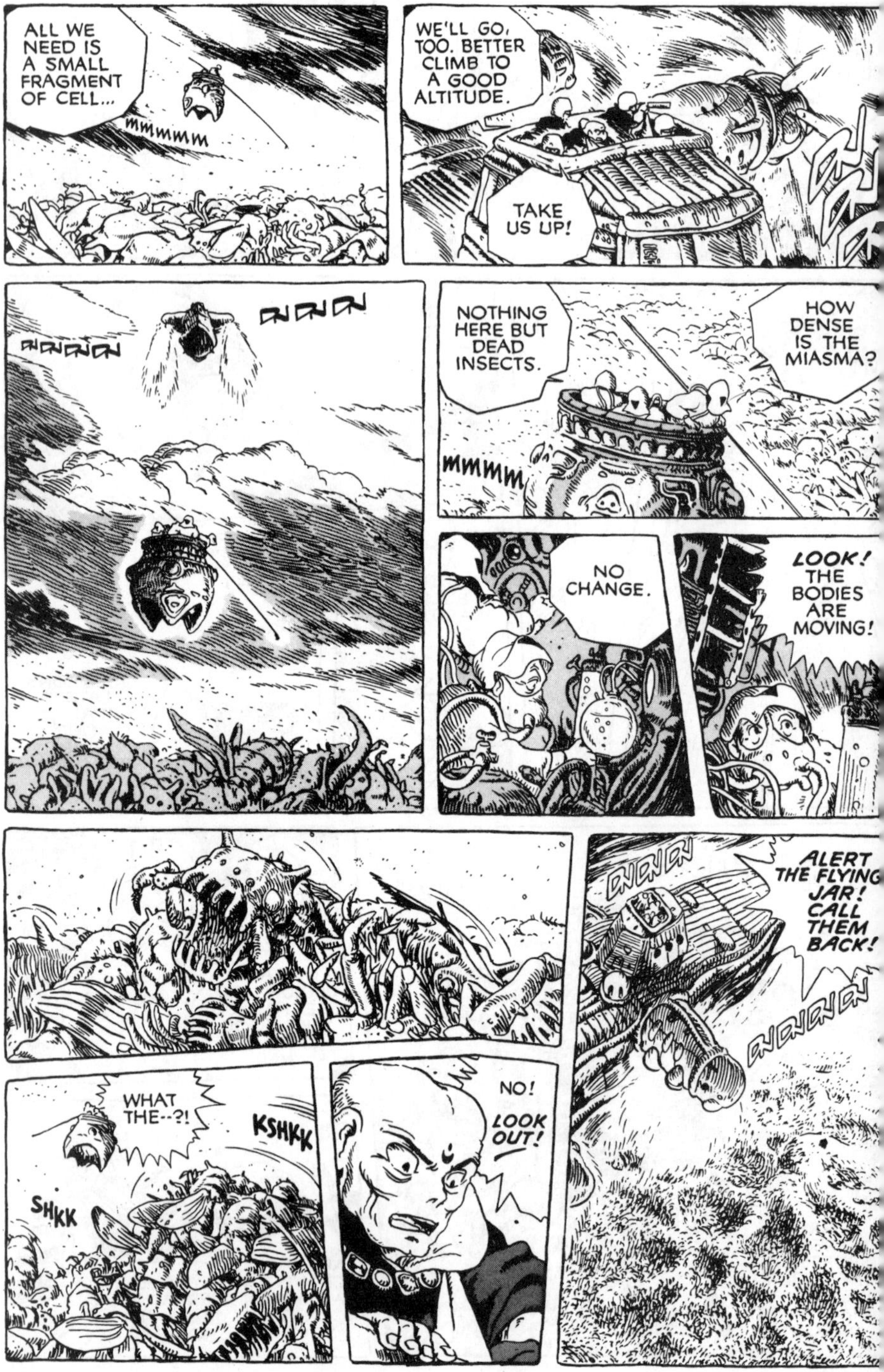

ALL WE NEED IS A SMALL FRAGMENT OF CELL...
MMMMMM
WE'LL GO, TOO. BETTER CLIMB TO A GOOD ALTITUDE.
TAKE US UP!
NOTHING HERE BUT DEAD INSECTS.
HOW DENSE IS THE MIASMA?
MMMMM
NO CHANGE.
LOOK! THE BODIES ARE MOVING!
ALERT THE FLYING JAR! CALL THEM BACK!
WHAT THE--?!
KSHKK
SHKK
NO! LOOK OUT!

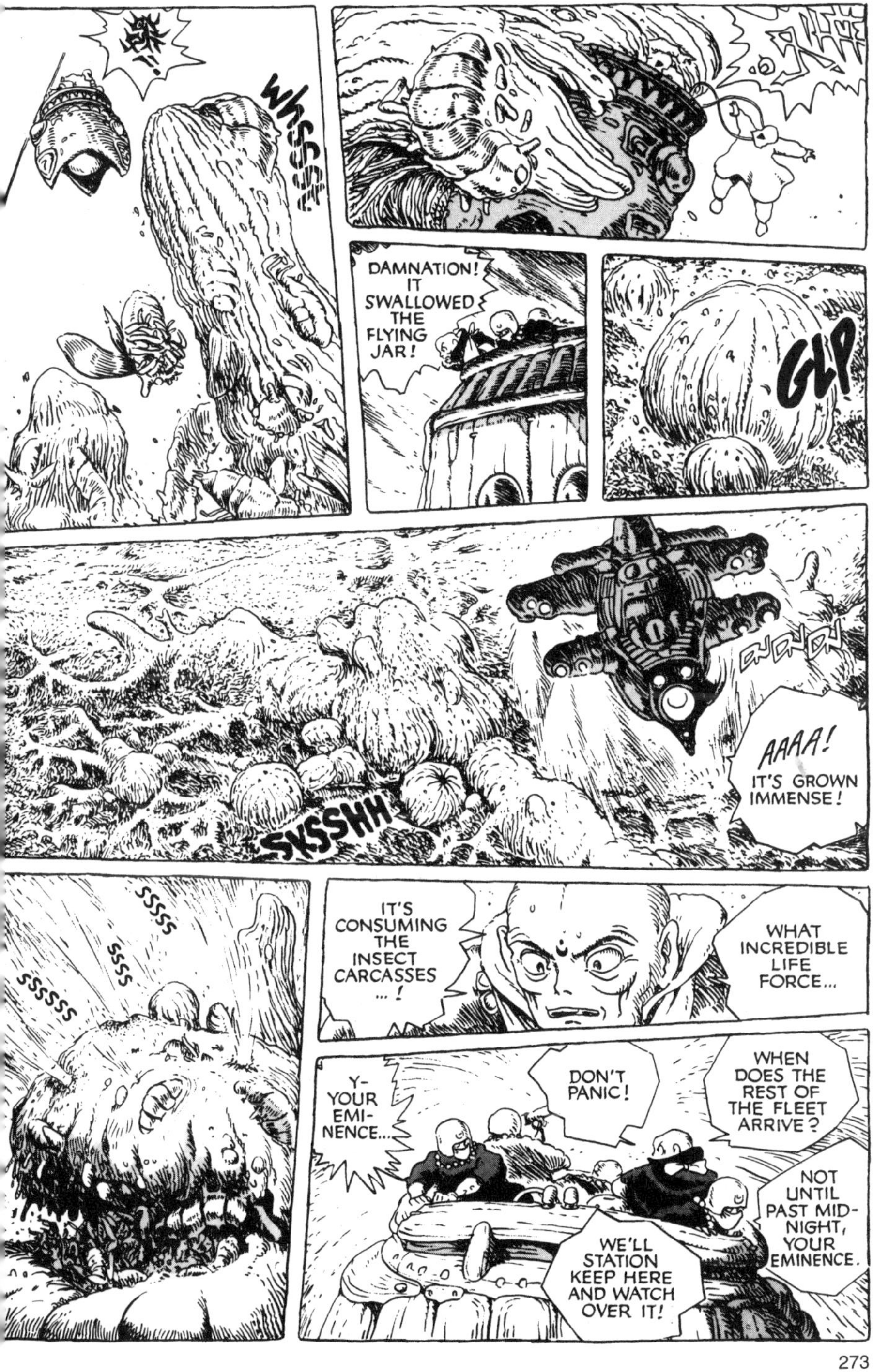
WHSSSSH
DAMNATION! IT SWALLOWED THE FLYING JAR!
GLP
AAAA! IT'S GROWN IMMENSE!
SKSSHH
SSSSS
SSSS
SSSSSS
IT'S CONSUMING THE INSECT CARCASSES ...!
WHAT INCREDIBLE LIFE FORCE...
Y- YOUR EMI-NENCE...
DON'T PANIC!
WHEN DOES THE REST OF THE FLEET ARRIVE?
NOT UNTIL PAST MID-NIGHT, YOUR EMINENCE.
WE'LL STATION KEEP HERE AND WATCH OVER IT!

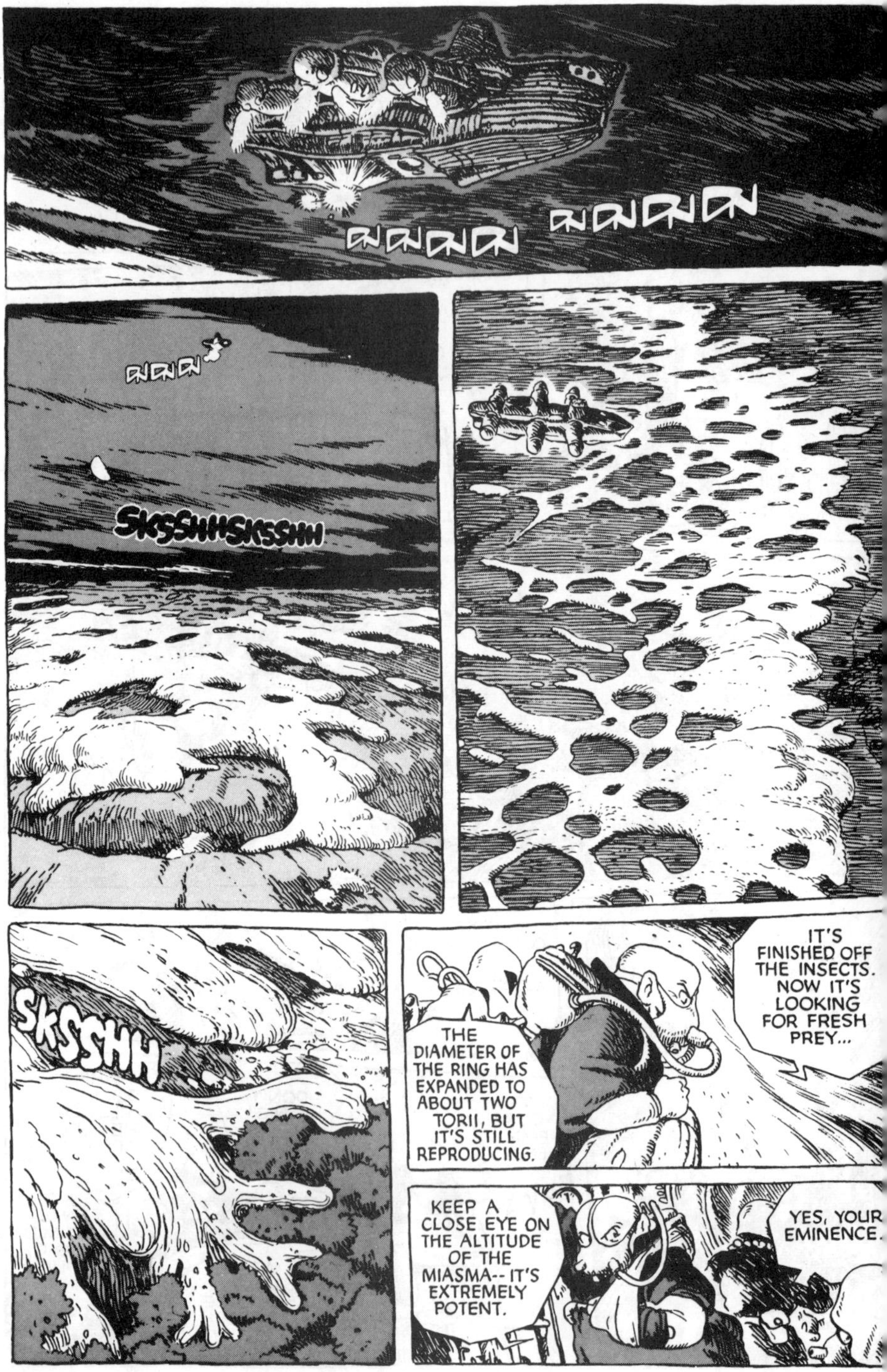
DN DN DN DN
DN DN DN DN
DN DN DN
SKSSHHSKSSHH
SKSSHH
THE DIAMETER OF THE RING HAS EXPANDED TO ABOUT TWO TORII, BUT IT'S STILL REPRODUCING.
IT'S FINISHED OFF THE INSECTS. NOW IT'S LOOKING FOR FRESH PREY...
KEEP A CLOSE EYE ON THE ALTITUDE OF THE MIASMA-- IT'S EXTREMELY POTENT.
YES, YOUR EMINENCE.

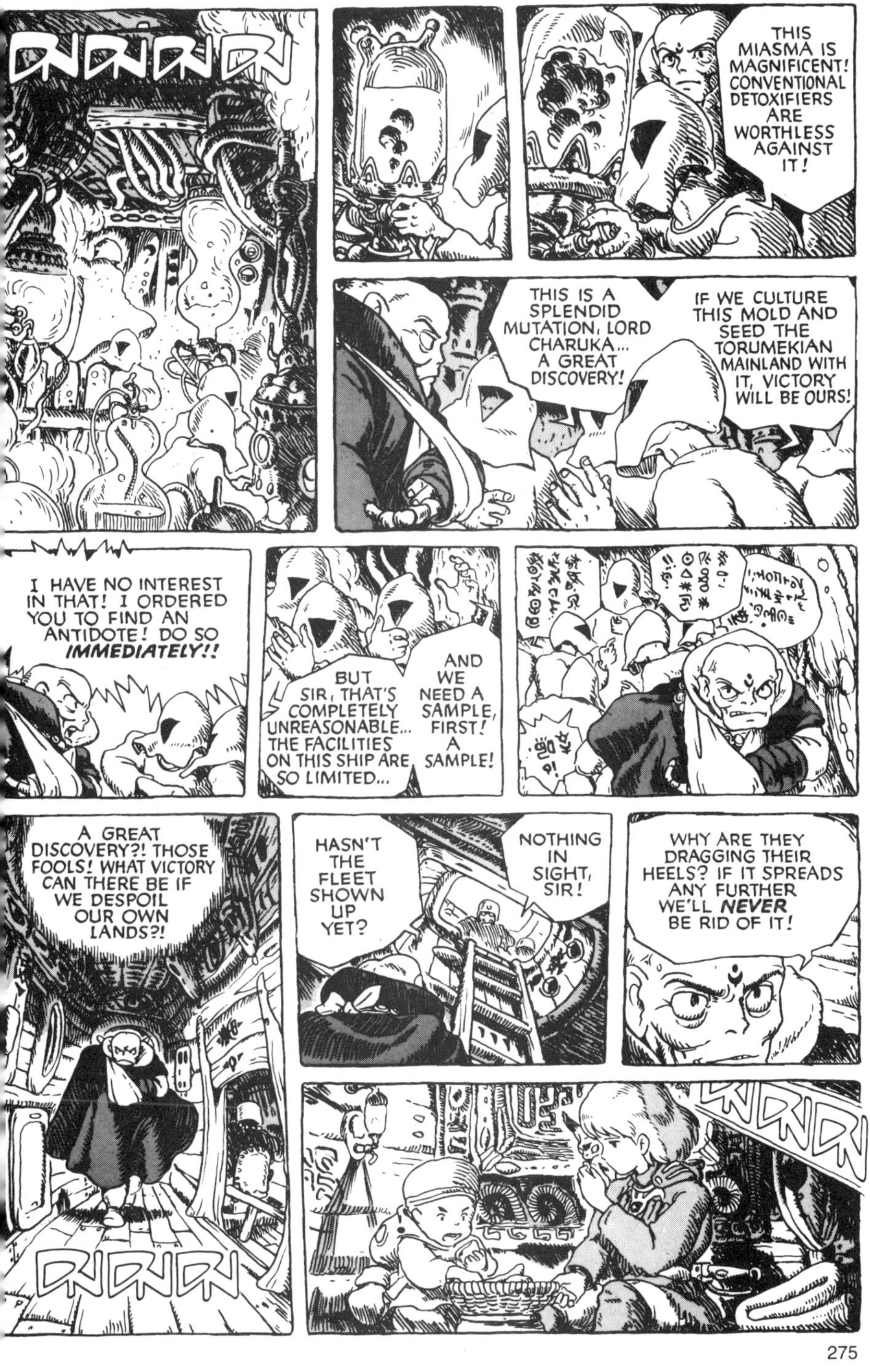
DRDRDRDRDR
THIS MIASMA IS MAGNIFICENT! CONVENTIONAL DETOXIFIERS ARE WORTHLESS AGAINST IT!
THIS IS A SPLENDID MUTATION, LORD CHARUKA... A GREAT DISCOVERY!
IF WE CULTURE THIS MOLD AND SEED THE TORUMEKIAN MAINLAND WITH IT, VICTORY WILL BE OURS!
I HAVE NO INTEREST IN THAT! I ORDERED YOU TO FIND AN ANTIDOTE! DO SO IMMEDIATELY!!
BUT SIR, THAT'S COMPLETELY UNREASONABLE... THE FACILITIES ON THIS SHIP ARE SO LIMITED...
AND WE NEED A SAMPLE, FIRST! A SAMPLE!
A GREAT DISCOVERY?! THOSE FOOLS! WHAT VICTORY CAN THERE BE IF WE DESPOIL OUR OWN LANDS?!
HASN'T THE FLEET SHOWN UP YET?
NOTHING IN SIGHT, SIR!
WHY ARE THEY DRAGGING THEIR HEELS? IF IT SPREADS ANY FURTHER WE'LL NEVER BE RID OF IT!
DRDRDRDR
DRDRDRDR

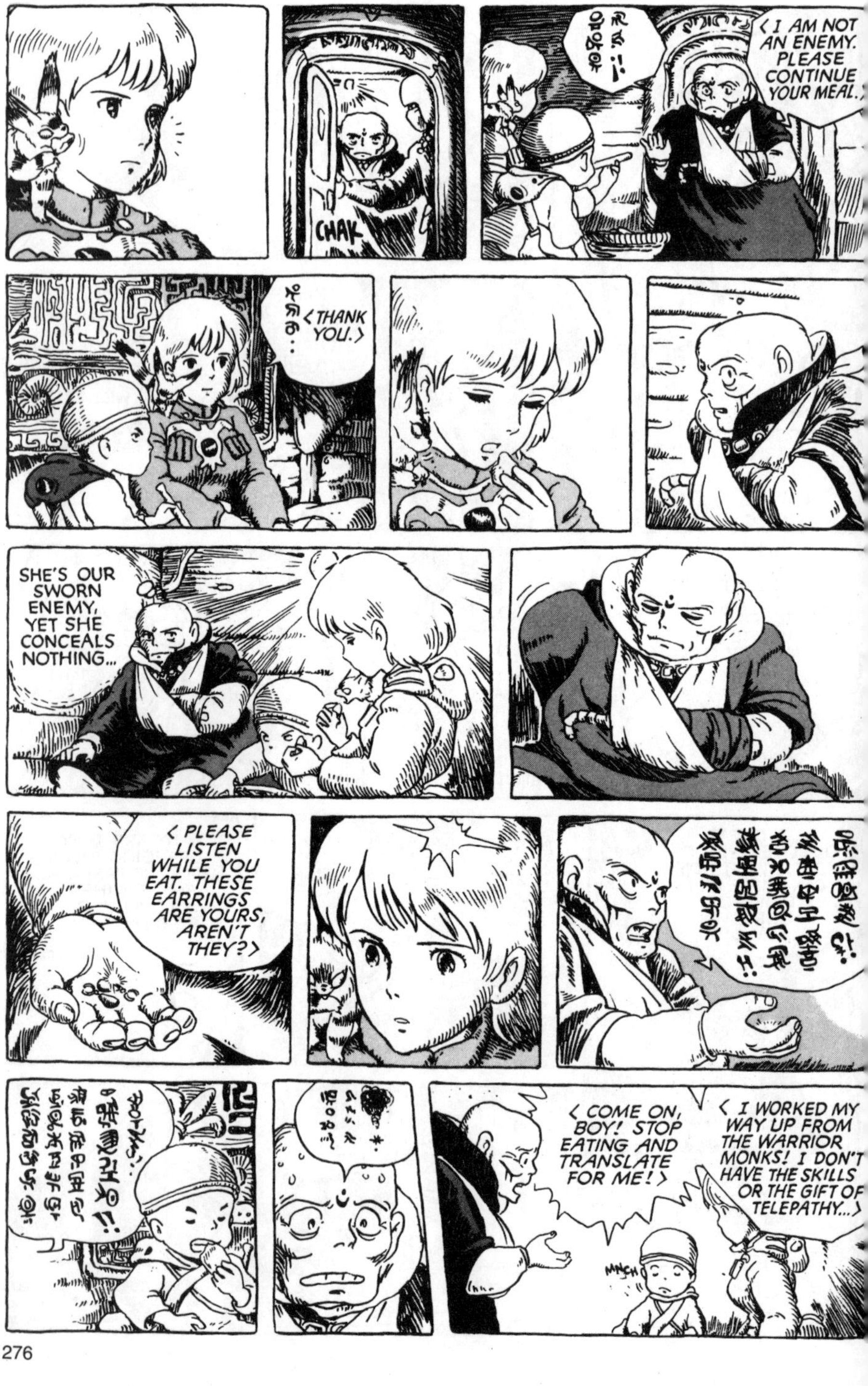
CHAK
< I AM NOT AN ENEMY. PLEASE CONTINUE YOUR MEAL. >
< THANK YOU. >
SHE'S OUR SWORN ENEMY, YET SHE CONCEALS NOTHING...
< PLEASE LISTEN WHILE YOU EAT. THESE EARRINGS ARE YOURS, AREN'T THEY? >
< COME ON, BOY! STOP EATING AND TRANSLATE FOR ME! >
< I WORKED MY WAY UP FROM THE WARRIOR MONKS! I DON'T HAVE THE SKILLS OR THE GIFT OF TELEPATHY... >
MNCH

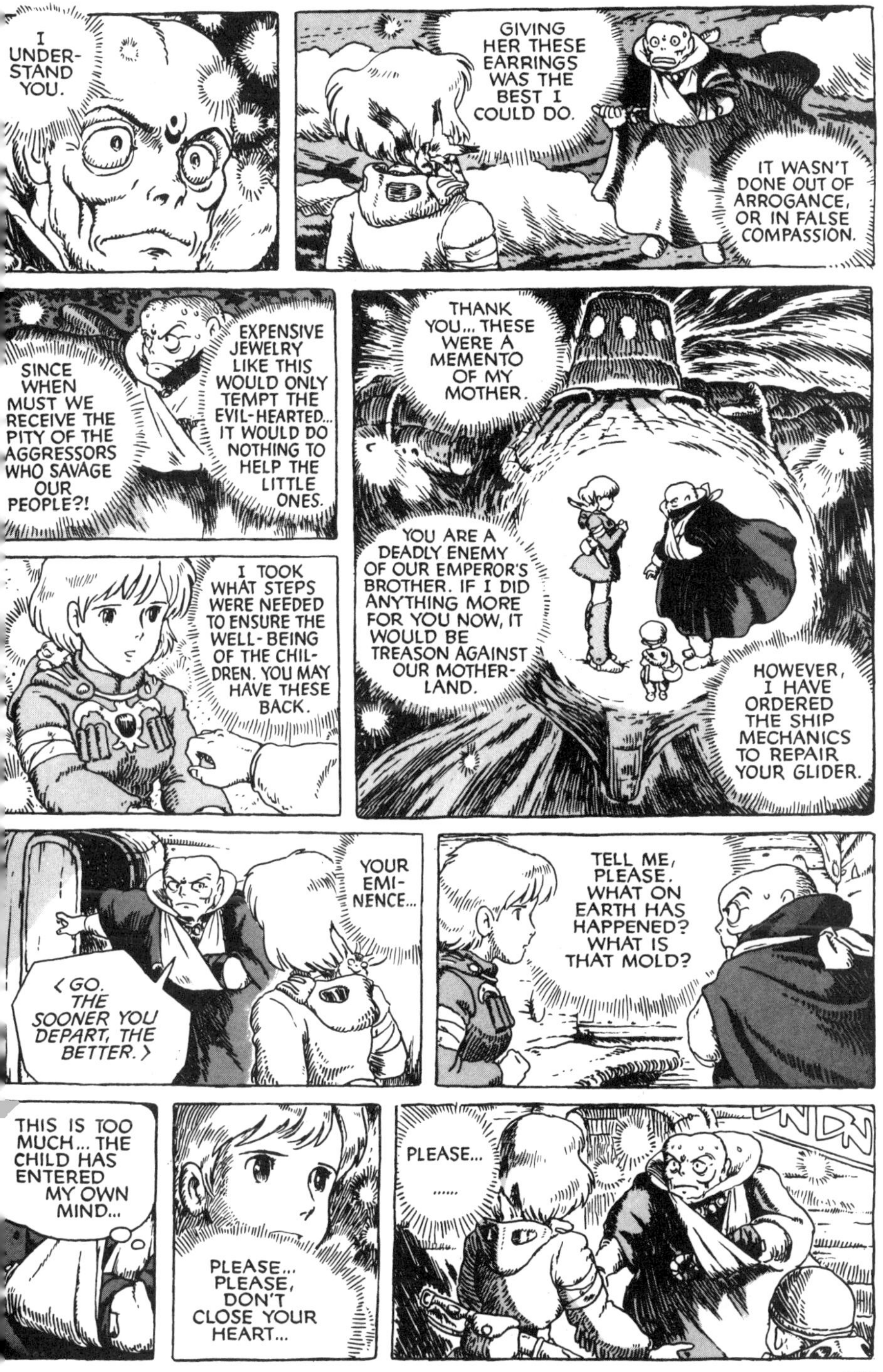
I UNDERSTAND YOU.
GIVING HER THESE EARRINGS WAS THE BEST I COULD DO.
IT WASN'T DONE OUT OF ARROGANCE, OR IN FALSE COMPASSION.
SINCE WHEN MUST WE RECEIVE THE PITY OF THE AGGRESSORS WHO SAVAGE OUR PEOPLE?!
EXPENSIVE JEWELRY LIKE THIS WOULD ONLY TEMPT THE EVIL-HEARTED... IT WOULD DO NOTHING TO HELP THE LITTLE ONES.
THANK YOU... THESE WERE A MEMENTO OF MY MOTHER.
YOU ARE A DEADLY ENEMY OF OUR EMPEROR'S BROTHER. IF I DID ANYTHING MORE FOR YOU NOW, IT WOULD BE TREASON AGAINST OUR MOTHERLAND.
HOWEVER, I HAVE ORDERED THE SHIP MECHANICS TO REPAIR YOUR GLIDER.
I TOOK WHAT STEPS WERE NEEDED TO ENSURE THE WELL-BEING OF THE CHILDREN. YOU MAY HAVE THESE BACK.
YOUR EMINENCE...
< GO. THE SOONER YOU DEPART, THE BETTER. >
TELL ME, PLEASE. WHAT ON EARTH HAS HAPPENED? WHAT IS THAT MOLD?
THIS IS TOO MUCH... THE CHILD HAS ENTERED MY OWN MIND...
PLEASE... PLEASE, DON'T CLOSE YOUR HEART...
PLEASE...
......

WHAT ?!

IT'S TRUE.

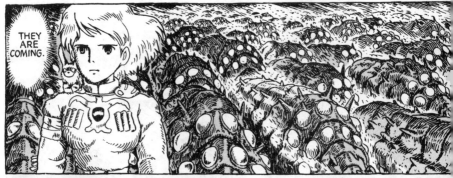

THEY ARE COMING.

WHAT OF IT? IT'S BUT A COINCIDENCE-- NOTHING MORE THAN AN INSECT MIGRATION!

THE DAIKAISHO IS A FOOLISH HERESY, BORN OF AN INFIDEL RELIGION!

YOUR EMINENCE, THE MESSENGERS HAVE RETURNED.

EXCELLENT-- I'LL BE THERE IMMEDIATELY.

WHERE IS THE FLEET?

mmmmm

WE'LL LAUNCH A MASS INCENDIARY ATTACK BY THE ENTIRE FLEET AND BURN THAT MONSTROSITY TO ASHES!

MUTATIONS HAVE BROKEN OUT ALL ALONG THE FRONT-- THE FLEET CAN'T COME!

WHA ?!

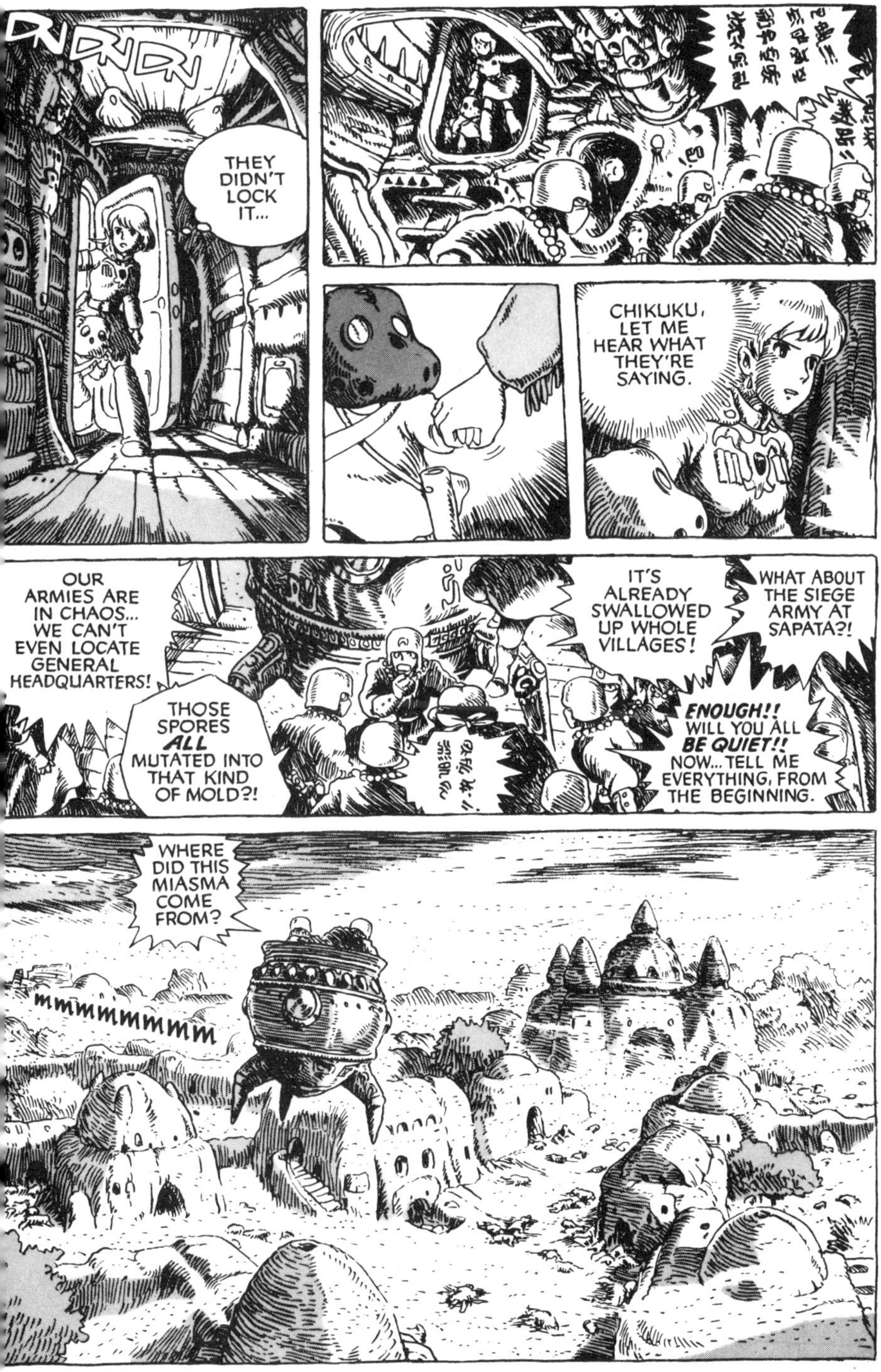
DNDNDN
THEY DIDN'T LOCK IT...
CHIKUKU, LET ME HEAR WHAT THEY'RE SAYING.
OUR ARMIES ARE IN CHAOS... WE CAN'T EVEN LOCATE GENERAL HEADQUARTERS!
THOSE SPORES **ALL** MUTATED INTO THAT KIND OF MOLD?!
IT'S ALREADY SWALLOWED UP WHOLE VILLAGES!
WHAT ABOUT THE SIEGE ARMY AT SAPATA?!
ENOUGH!! WILL YOU ALL **BE QUIET!!** NOW... TELL ME EVERYTHING, FROM THE BEGINNING.
WHERE DID THIS MIASMA COME FROM?
MMMMMMMMMM

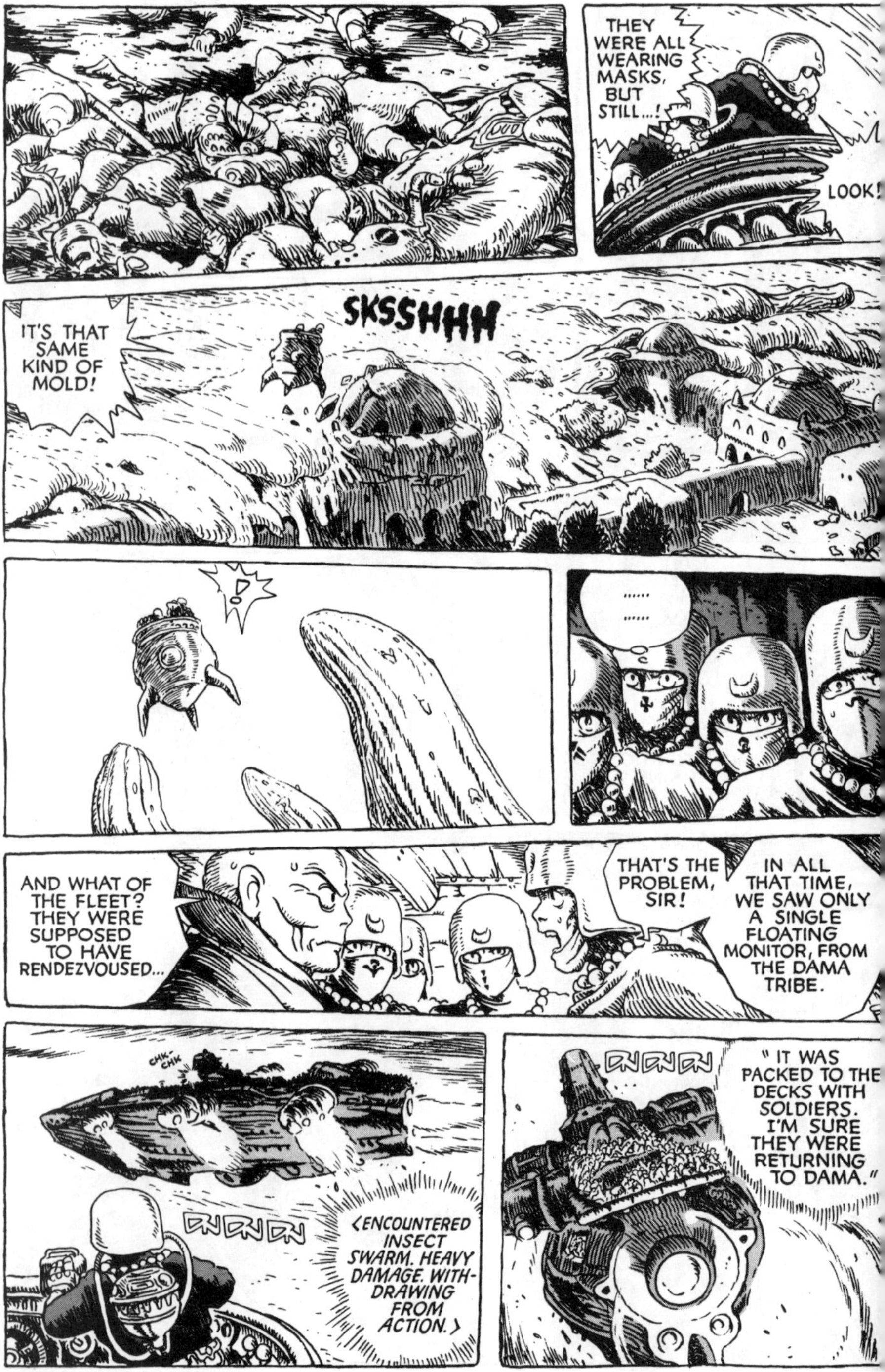
THEY WERE ALL WEARING MASKS, BUT STILL...!
LOOK!
SKSSHHH
IT'S THAT SAME KIND OF MOLD!
!
......
......
AND WHAT OF THE FLEET? THEY WERE SUPPOSED TO HAVE RENDEZVOUSED...
THAT'S THE PROBLEM, SIR!
IN ALL THAT TIME, WE SAW ONLY A SINGLE FLOATING MONITOR, FROM THE DAMA TRIBE.
CHK-CHK
DN DN DN
<ENCOUNTERED INSECT SWARM. HEAVY DAMAGE. WITH-DRAWING FROM ACTION.>
DN DN DN
" IT WAS PACKED TO THE DECKS WITH SOLDIERS. I'M SURE THEY WERE RETURNING TO DAMA."

AT THIS RATE, THE ENTIRE FRONT WILL COLLAPSE!

YOUR EMINENCE...

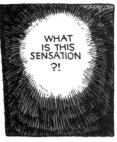

WHAT IS THIS SENSATION ?!

I'VE NEVER FELT ANYTHING LIKE IT BEFORE.

SOMEONE'S WATCHING US...

TRYING TO... PULL US TO IT...

KEE

‹WHAT DO YOU THINK YOU'RE DOING, GIRL?!›

WE'RE IN DANGER! *CLIMB!*

QUICKLY!!

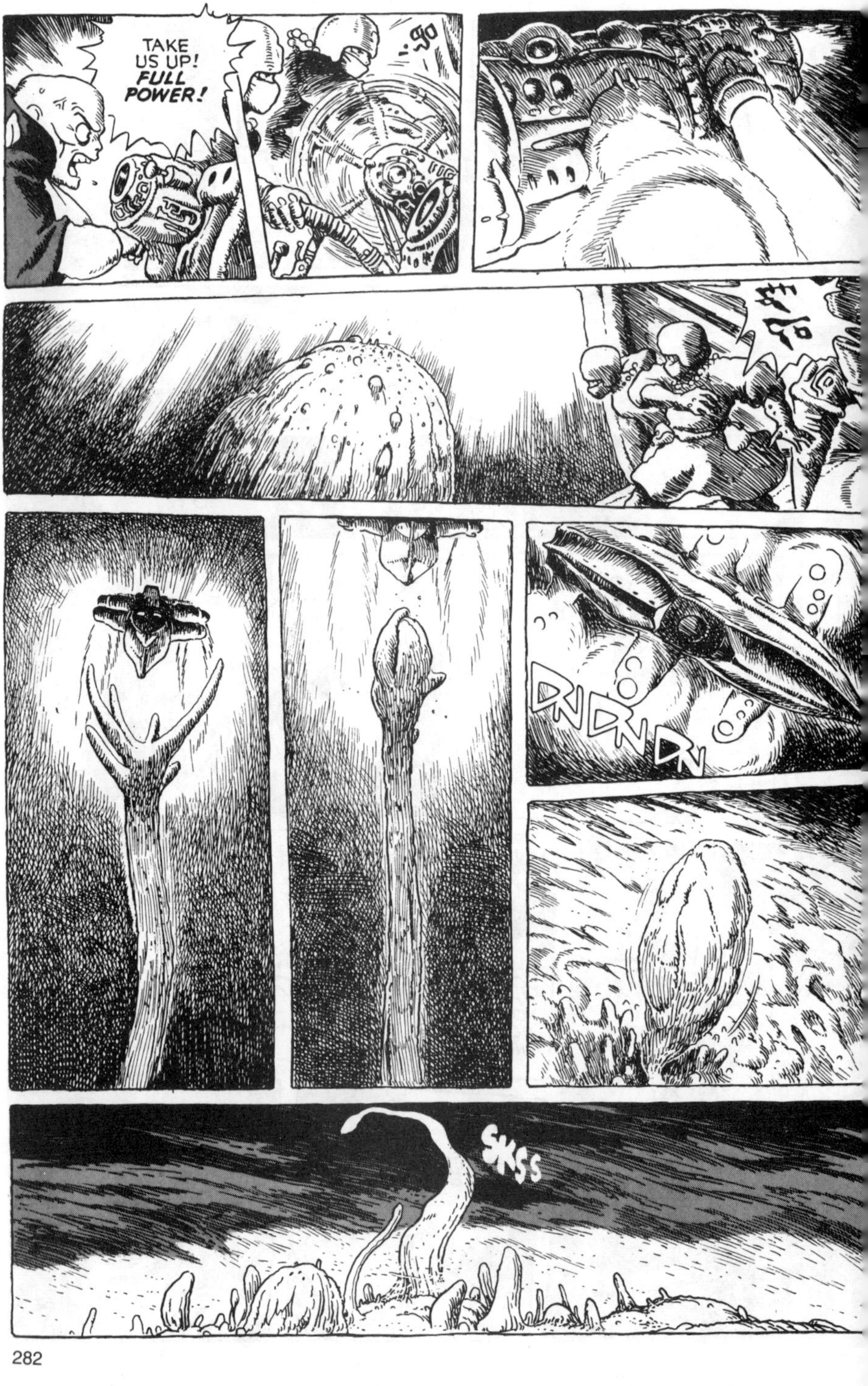
TAKE US UP! FULL POWER!
DN DN DN DN
SKSS

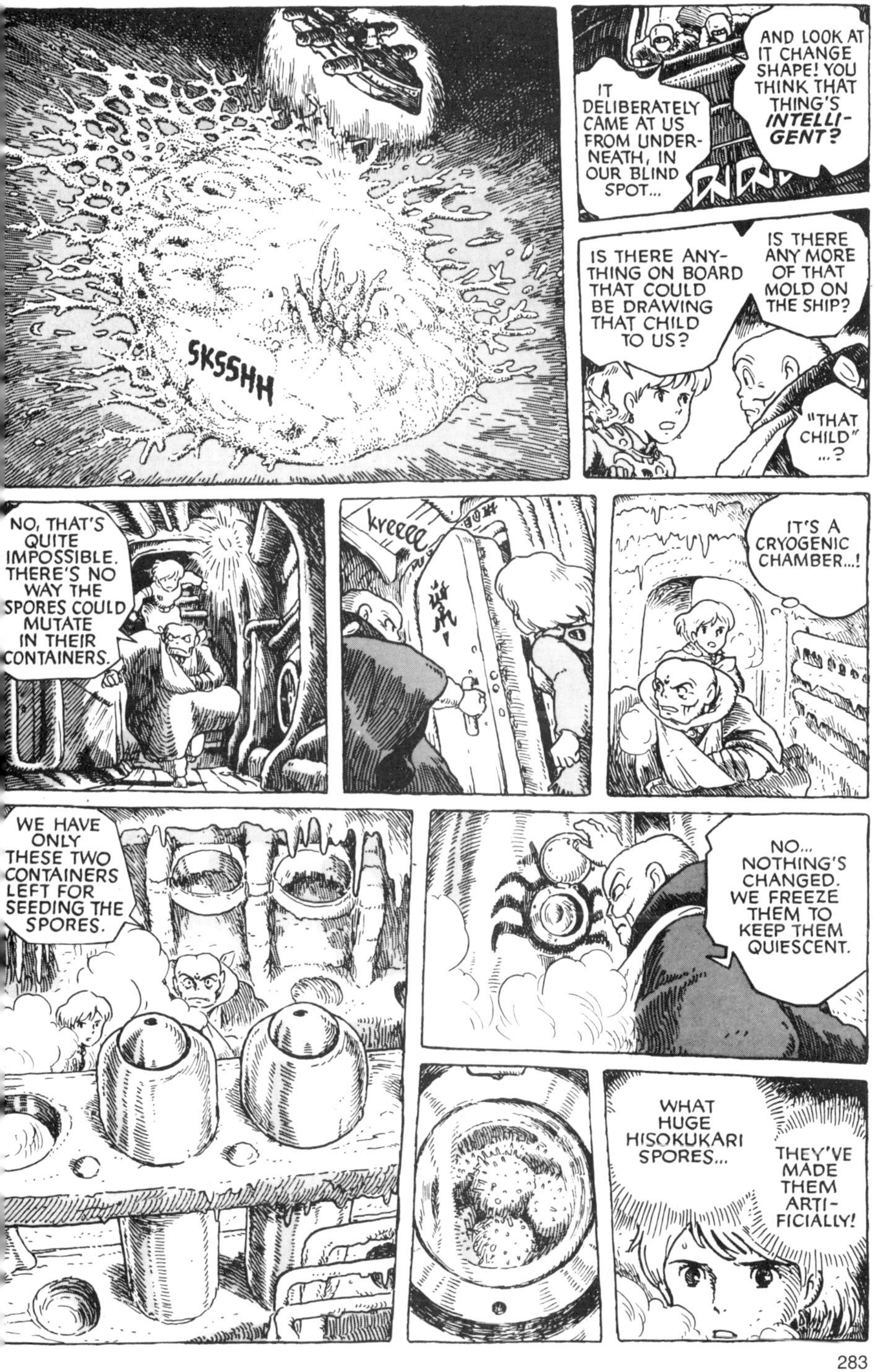
SKSSHH
IT DELIBERATELY CAME AT US FROM UNDERNEATH, IN OUR BLIND SPOT...
AND LOOK AT IT CHANGE SHAPE! YOU THINK THAT THING'S ***INTELLIGENT?***
IS THERE ANY MORE OF THAT MOLD ON THE SHIP?
IS THERE ANYTHING ON BOARD THAT COULD BE DRAWING THAT CHILD TO US?
"THAT CHILD" ...?
NO, THAT'S QUITE IMPOSSIBLE. THERE'S NO WAY THE SPORES COULD MUTATE IN THEIR CONTAINERS.
kreeee
IT'S A CRYOGENIC CHAMBER...!
WE HAVE ONLY THESE TWO CONTAINERS LEFT FOR SEEDING THE SPORES.
NO... NOTHING'S CHANGED. WE FREEZE THEM TO KEEP THEM QUIESCENT.
WHAT HUGE HISOKUKARI SPORES...
THEY'VE MADE THEM ARTIFICIALLY!

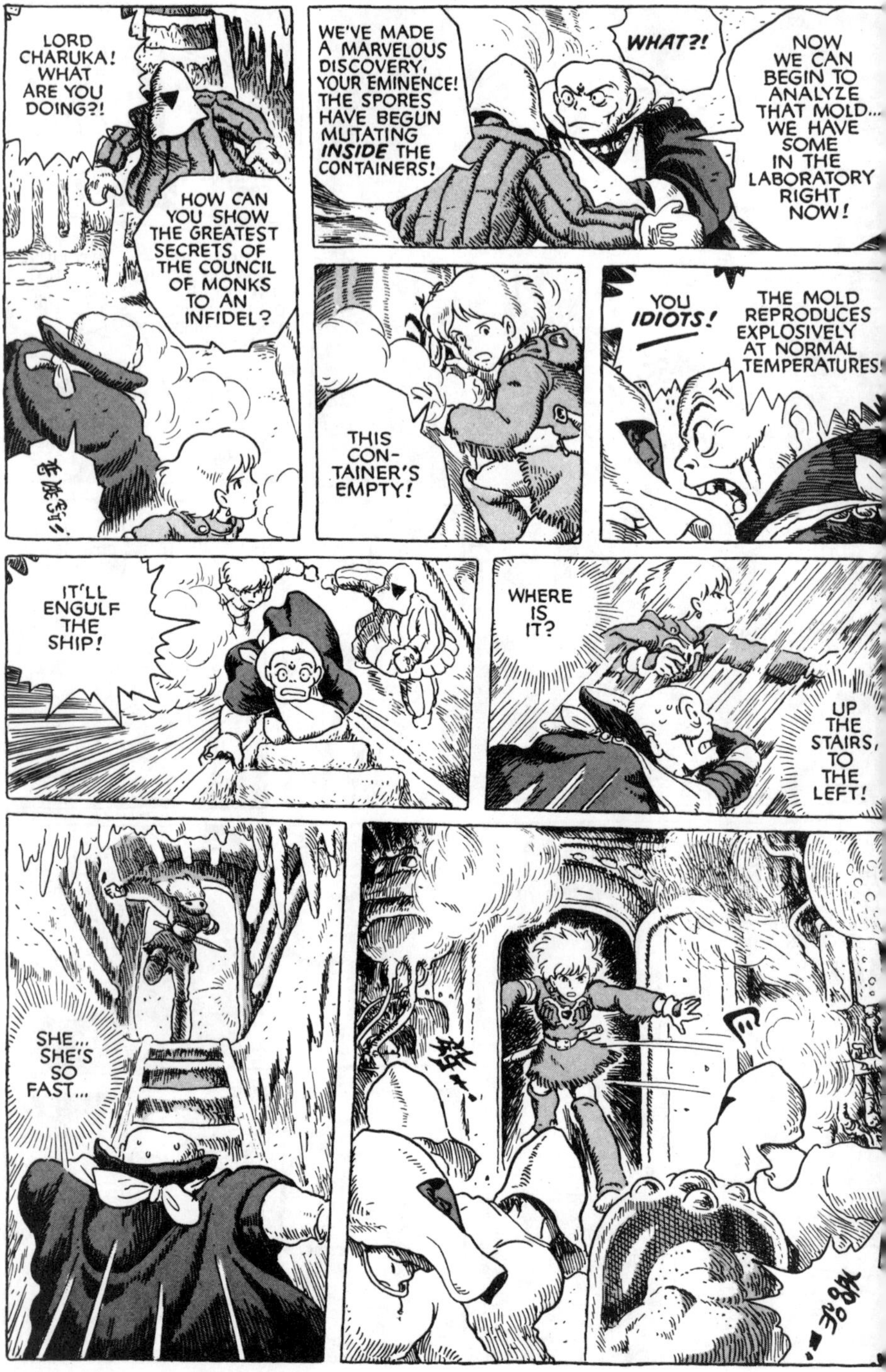
LORD CHARUKA! WHAT ARE YOU DOING?!
HOW CAN YOU SHOW THE GREATEST SECRETS OF THE COUNCIL OF MONKS TO AN INFIDEL?
WE'VE MADE A MARVELOUS DISCOVERY, YOUR EMINENCE! THE SPORES HAVE BEGUN MUTATING INSIDE THE CONTAINERS!
WHAT?!
NOW WE CAN BEGIN TO ANALYZE THAT MOLD... WE HAVE SOME IN THE LABORATORY RIGHT NOW!
THIS CONTAINER'S EMPTY!
YOU IDIOTS!
THE MOLD REPRODUCES EXPLOSIVELY AT NORMAL TEMPERATURES!
IT'LL ENGULF THE SHIP!
WHERE IS IT?
UP THE STAIRS, TO THE LEFT!
SHE... SHE'S SO FAST...

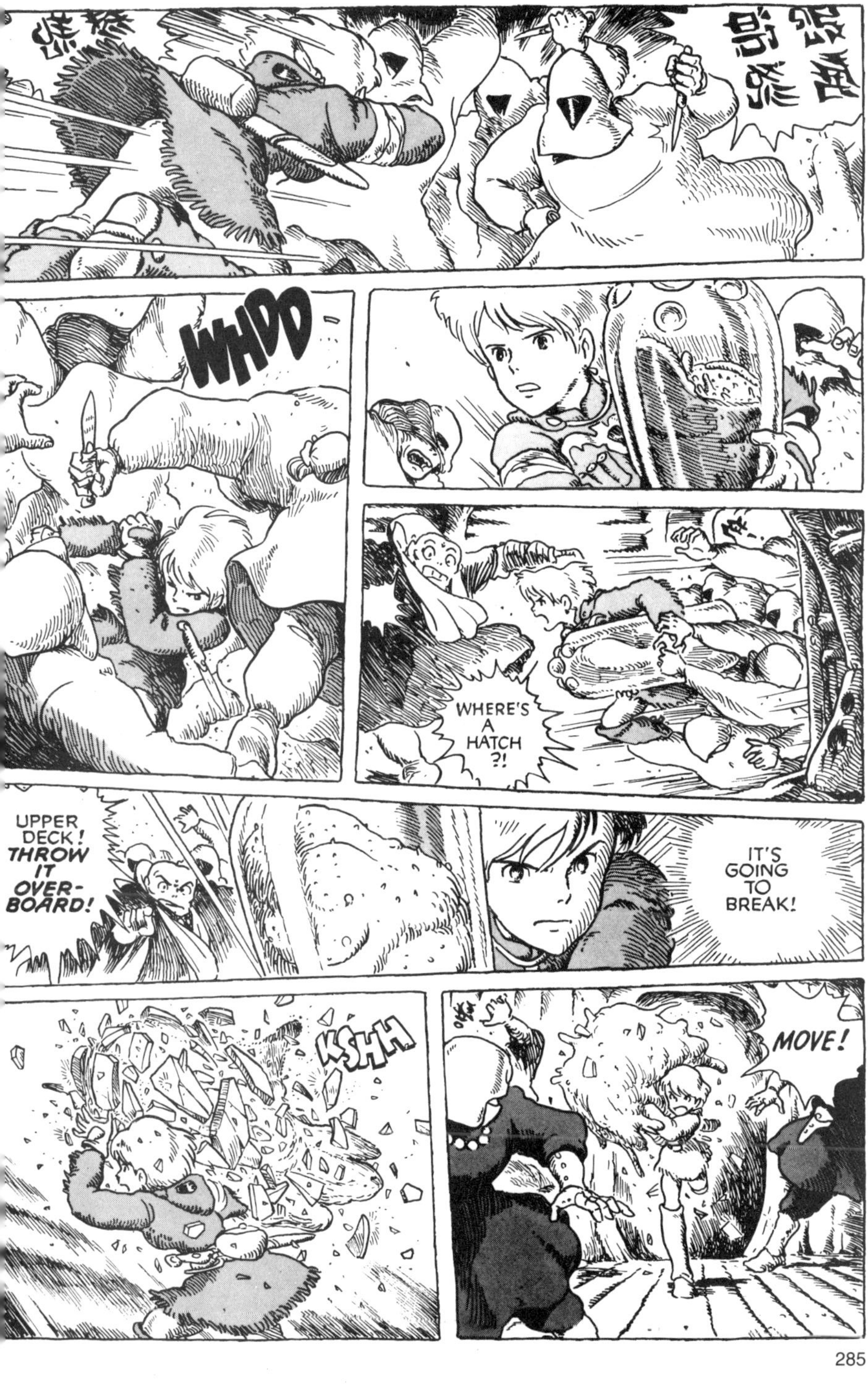
WHDD
WHERE'S A HATCH ?!
IT'S GOING TO BREAK!
UPPER DECK! THROW IT OVER-BOARD!
KSHH
MOVE!

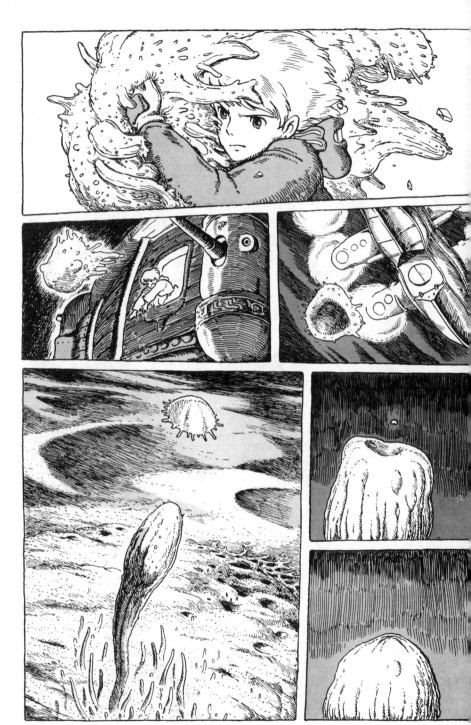

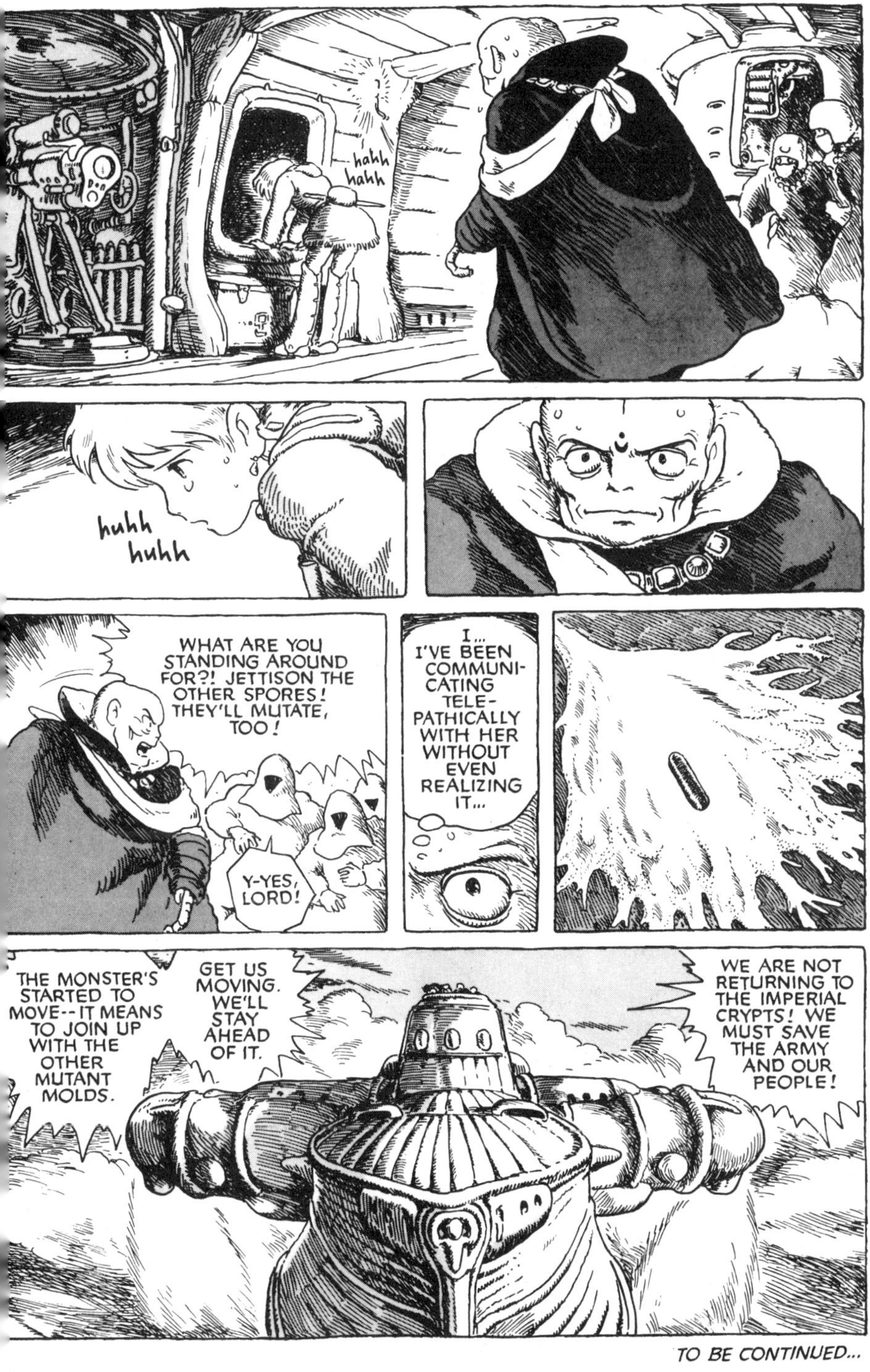
hahh hahh
huhh huhh
WHAT ARE YOU STANDING AROUND FOR?! JETTISON THE OTHER SPORES! THEY'LL MUTATE, TOO!
Y-YES, LORD!
I... I'VE BEEN COMMUNICATING TELEPATHICALLY WITH HER WITHOUT EVEN REALIZING IT...
THE MONSTER'S STARTED TO MOVE--IT MEANS TO JOIN UP WITH THE OTHER MUTANT MOLDS.
GET US MOVING. WE'LL STAY AHEAD OF IT.
WE ARE NOT RETURNING TO THE IMPERIAL CRYPTS! WE MUST SAVE THE ARMY AND OUR PEOPLE!

TO BE CONTINUED...

ARMAGEDDON FILLS THE CRUMBLING SKY

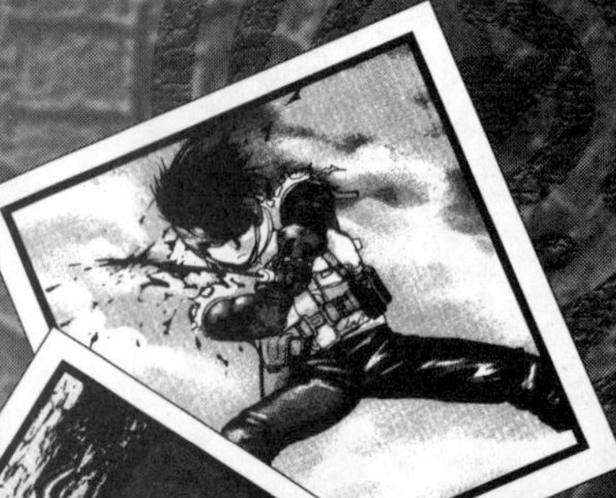

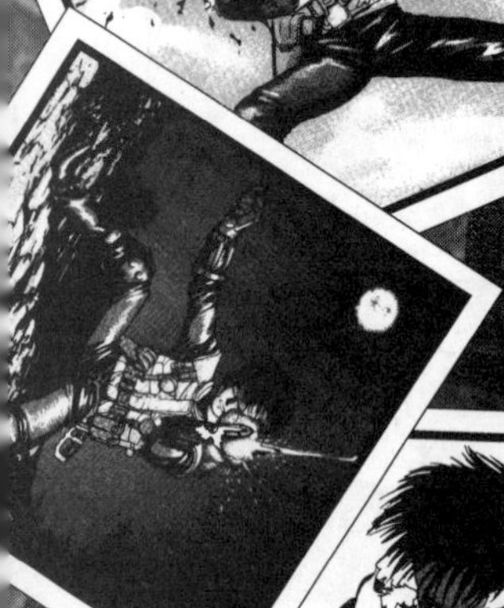

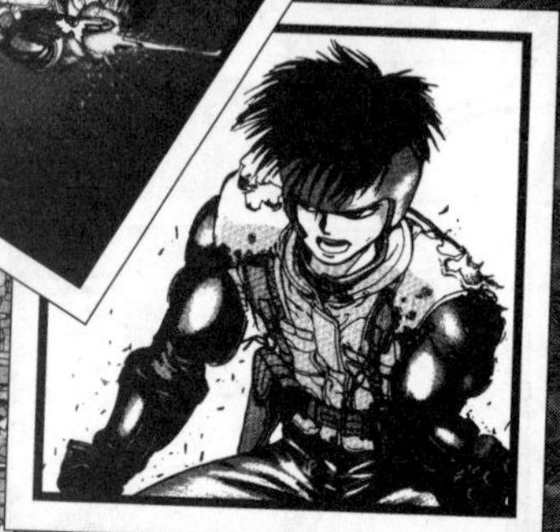

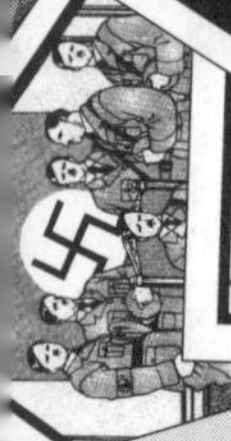

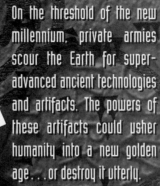

On the threshold of the new millennium, private armies scour the Earth for super-advanced ancient technologies and artifacts. The powers of these artifacts could usher humanity into a new golden age. . . or destroy it utterly.

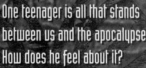

One teenager is all that stands between us and the apocalypse. How does he feel about it?

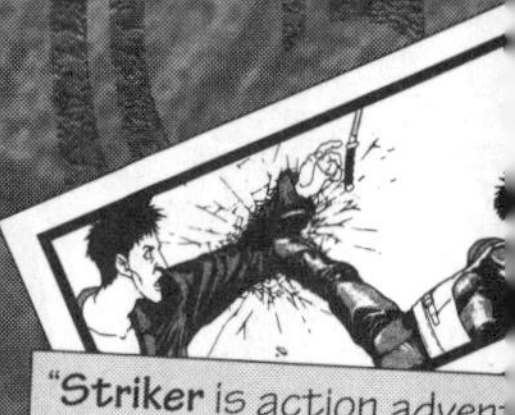

"**Striker** is action adven at its finest. . . an interes ing, way-out slugfest ful cool tricks, wild characte and intense action."
—*Comic Buyer's Gu*

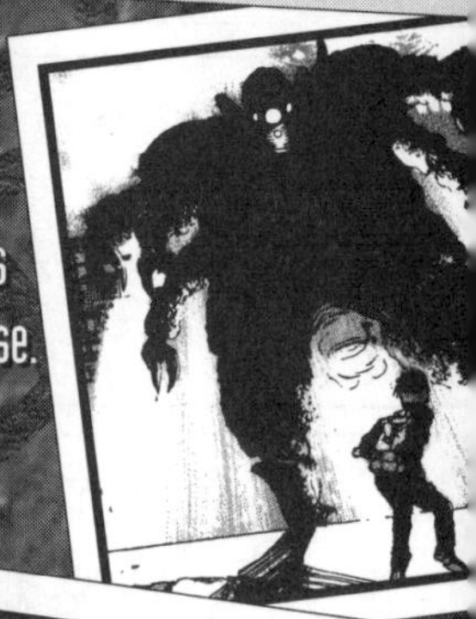

PERSONNEL FILE
NAME: Yu Ominae
CODE NAME: Striker
EMPLOYER: Arcam Foundation
SPECIAL ABILITIES: Outfitted with Arcam's Omihalcon armored muscle suit, this high school student's strength is multiplied thirty-fold. Arcam's top operative, Striker has proved his mettle in battle repeatedly.
ARCAM'S MISSION STATEMENT: To find and destroy or seal away extremely dangerous ancient technology and artifacts to keep them out of the wrong hands.
MISSION REPORTS:
Striker: The Armored Warrior
Striker: The Forest Of No Return
Striker vs. The Third Reich

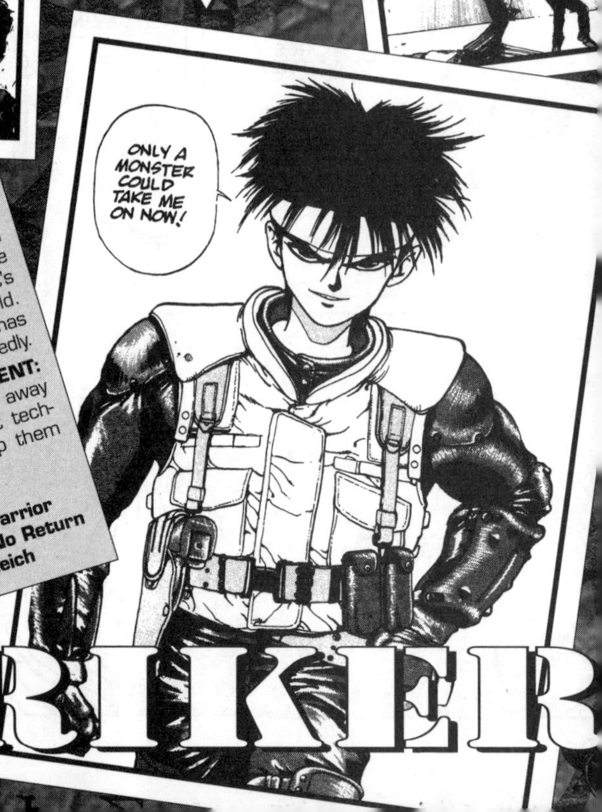
ONLY A MONSTER COULD TAKE ME ON NOW!

STRIKER

VIZ GRAPHIC NOVELS.